HOPE RENEWED

❦ The General Series ❦

HOPE RENEWED

◉ The General Series ◉

S.M. Stirling
David Drake

HOPE RENEWED

The Sword copyright © 1995 by S.M. Stirling and David Drake.
The Chosen copyright © 1996 by S.M. Stirling and David Drake.

A Baen Books Original

Baen Publishing Enterprises
P.O. Box 1403
Riverdale, NY 10471
www.baen.com

ISBN: 978-1-4767-3658-7

Cover art by Kurt Miller

First Baen paperback printing, July 2014

Distributed by Simon & Schuster
1230 Avenue of the Americas
New York, NY 10020

Library of Congress Cataloging-in-Publication Data

Drake, David, 1945-
[Novels. Selections]
  Hope renewed / David Drake and S.M. Stirling.
     pages cm
Includes bibliographical references and index.
  ISBN 978-1-4767-3658-7 (paperback)
  1. Whitehall, Raj (Fictitious character)--Fiction. 2. Imaginary wars and bat-
tles--Fiction. 3. Space warfare--Fiction. 4. Science fiction, American. I.
Stirling, S. M. II. Stirling, S. M. Sword. III. Stirling, S. M. Chosen. IV. Title.
  PS3569.T543H68 2014
  813'.54--dc23
                                        2014014391

Printed in the United States of America

10 9 8 7 6 5 4 3 2 1

CONTENTS

V

THE SWORD

❀ ❀ ❀
To Jan
❀ ❀ ❀

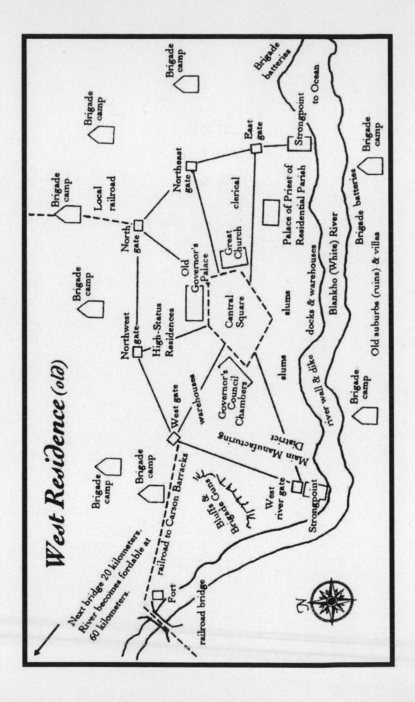

West Residence (old)

Next bridge 20 kilometers. River becomes fordable at 60 kilometers.

Fort

railroad bridge

railroad to Carson Barracks

Bluffs Guns & Brigade

West river gate

Strongpoint

Main Manufacturing District

Governor's Council Chambers

warehouses

West gate

Brigade camp

Northwest gate

High-Status Residences

Old Governor's Palace

Central Square

slums

slums

Brigade camp

North gate

Local railroad

Brigade camp

Northeast gate

Great Church

clerical

East gate

Strongpoint

to Ocean

Brigade batteries

Palace of Priest of Residential Parish

docks & warehouses

river wall & dike

Blankho (White) River

Brigade camp

Brigade batteries

Brigade camp

Old suburbs (ruins) & villas

Brigade camp

Brigade camp

N

CHAPTER ONE

"Raj?" Thom Poplanich muttered.

Then, slowly: "Raj, how old are you?"

Raj Whitehall managed a smile. "Thirty," he said.

The perfect mirrored sphere of Sector Command and Control Unit AZ12-b14-c000 Mk. XIV's central . . . being . . . showed an image which seemed to give the lie to that. It wasn't the gray hairs or the scars on the backs of his hands that made him seem at least forty, or ageless.

It was the eyes.

Thom looked at his own image. Nothing at all had changed since that moment when he'd frozen into immobility, five years ago. Not the unhealed shaving nick on his thin olive cheek, or the tear in his floppy tweed trousers from a revolver bullet.

life is change, Center said. The voice of the ancient computer was like their own thoughts, but with a vibrato overtone that somehow carried a sense of immense weight like a pressure against the film of consciousness. **even i change.**

Raj and Thom looked up, startled. "Center? You're alive?" Thom asked.

No words whispered in their skull. Thom looked at his friend. *Raj looks like an old man.*

I haven't changed a hair, outwardly . . . but that's the least of it.
Five years of mental communion with the machine that held all
Mankind's accumulated knowledge. Five years, or eternity. He
thought of his life before that day, and it was . . . unimaginable. Less
real than the scenarios Center could spin from webs of data and
stochastic analysis.

The two men gripped forearms, then exchanged the *embrahzo*
of close friends. Thom could smell coal-smoke and gun-oil on the
wool of his friend's uniform jacket, that and riding dogs and Suzette
Whitehall's sambuca jasmine perfume.

The scents cut through the icy certainties Center's teaching had
implanted in his mind. Unshed tears prickled at his eyes as he held
the bigger man at arm's length.

"It's good to see you again, my friend," he said quietly.

"Yes, that's . . . well, I came to say goodbye."

"Goodbye?" Thom asked sharply.

"That's right," Raj said, turning slightly away. His eyes moved
across the perfect mirrored surface of the sphere, that impossibly
reflected without distorting. "Things . . . well, Cabot Clerett, the
Governor's nephew" —and heir, they both knew— "was along on the
campaign. There were a number of difficulties, and he, ah, was killed."

"Spirit of Man of the *Stars*," Thom blurted. "You came back to
East Residence after *that*? Barholm was suspicious of you anyway."

Raj gave a small crooked smile and shrugged. "I didn't reconquer
the Southern and Western Territories for the Civil Government just
to set myself up as a warlord," he said. "Center said that would be
worse for civilization than if I'd never lived at all."

an oversimplification but accurate to within 93%, ±2, Center
added remorselessly. Over the years their minds had learned subtlety
in interpreting that voice; there was a tinge of . . . not pity, but perhaps
compassion to it now. **the long-term prospects for restoration of
the federation, here on bellevue and eventually elsewhere in the
human-settled galaxy, required raj whitehall's submission to the
civil authorities. too many generals have seized the chair by force.**

Thom nodded. The process had started long before Bellevue was
isolated by the destruction of its Tanaki Spatial Displacement net.

The Federation had been slagging down in civil wars for a generation before that, biting out its own guts like a brain-shot sauroid. The process had continued here in the thousand-odd years since, and according to Center everywhere else in the human-settled galaxy as well.

"Couldn't Lady Anne do something?" he asked. Barholm's consort was a close friend of Raj's wife Suzette, had been since Anne was merely the . . . entertainer was the polite phrase . . . that young Barholm had unaccountably married despite being the Governor's nephew. The other court ladies had turned a cold shoulder back before Barholm assumed the Chair; Suzette hadn't.

"She died four months ago," Raj said. "Cancer."

A brief flash of vision: a canopied bed, with the incense of the Star priests around it and the drone of their prayers. A woman lying motionless, flesh fallen in on the strong handsome bones of her face, hair a white cloud on the pillow with only a few streaks of its mahogany red left. Suzette Whitehall sat at the bedside, one hand gripping the ivory colored claw-hand of her dying friend. Her face was an expressionless mask, but slow tears ran from the slanted green eyes and dripped down on the priceless snowy torofib of the sheets.

"Damn," Thom said. "I know she wanted every Poplanich dead, but . . . well, Anne had twice Barholm's guts, and she was loyal to her friends, at least."

Raj nodded. "It was right after that that I was suspended from my last posting—Inspector-General—and my properties confiscated. Chancellor Tzetzas handled it personally."

"That . . . that . . . he gives graft a bad name," Thom spat.

Raj smiled wanly. "Yes, if the Chancellor didn't hate me, I'd wonder what I was doing wrong."

A flash from Center; a tall thin man in a bureaucrat's court robe sitting at a desk. The room was quietly elegant, dark, silent; a cigarette in a holder of carved sauroid ivory rested in one slim-fingered hand. He signed a heavy parchment, dusted the ink with fine sand, and smiled. A secretary sprang forward to melt wax for the seal . . .

Raj nodded. "I expect to be arrested at the levee this afternoon. Barholm's worried—"

Thom laid a hand on Raj's shoulder. The muscle under the wool jacket was like india rubber. It quivered with tension.

"You *should* make yourself Governor, Raj," he said quietly. "Spirit knows, you couldn't be *worse* than Barholm and his cronies."

Raj smiled, but he shook his head. "Thanks, Thom—but if I have a gift for command, it's *only* for soldiers. Civilians . . . I couldn't get three of them to follow me into a whorehouse with an offer of free drinks and pussy. Not unless I had a squad behind them with bayonets; and you *can't* govern that way, not for long. I'd smash the machinery trying to make it work. Barholm is a son-of-a-bitch, but he's a *smart* one. He knows how to stroke the bureaucracy and keep the nobility satisfied, and he really is binding the Civil Government together with his railroads and law reforms . . . granted a lot of his hangers-on are getting rich in the process, but it's working. I couldn't do it. Not so's it'd last past my lifetime."

observe:

—and they saw Raj Whitehall on a throne of gold and diamond, and men of races they'd never heard of knelt before him with tribute and gifts . . .

. . . and he lay ancient and white-haired in a vast silken bed. Muffled chanting came from outside the window, and a priest prayed quietly. A few elderly officers wept, but the younger ones eyed each other with undisguised hunger, waiting for the old king to die.

One bent and spoke in his ear. "Who?" he said. "Who do you leave the keyboard and the power to?"

The ancient Raj's lips moved. The officer turned and spoke loudly, drowning out the whisper: "He says, *to the strongest.*"

Armies clashed, in identical green uniforms and carrying Raj Whitehall's banner. Cities burned. At last there was a peaceful green mound that only the outline of the land showed had once been the Gubernatorial Palace in East Residence. Two men worked in companionable silence by a campfire, clad only in loincloths of tanned hide. One was chipping a spearpoint from a piece of an ancient window, the shaft and binding thongs ready to hand. His fingers moved with sure skill, using a bone anvil and striker to spall long flakes from the green glass. His comrade worked with equal artistry, butchering a carcass with a heavy hammerstone and slivers of flint. It took a moment to realize that the body had once been human.

Raj shivered. *That* was the logical endpoint of the cycle of collapse here on Bellevue, and throughout what had once been the Federation; if it wasn't prevented, there would be savagery for fifteen thousand years before a new civilization arose. The image had haunted him since Center first showed it. It felt *true*.

"Spirit knows, I don't *want* Barholm's job," he went on. "I like to do what I do well, and that isn't my area of expertise. The problem is getting Barholm to understand that."

barholm's data gives him substantial reason for apprehension, Center pointed out. **not only does raj whitehall have the prestige of constant victory, but more than sixteen battalions of the civil government's cavalry are now comprised of ex-prisoners from the former military governments.**

Squadrones and Brigaderos; Namerique-speaking barbarians, descendants of Federation troops gone savage up in the desolate Base Area of the far northwest. They'd swept down and taken over huge chunks of the Civil Government, imposing their rule and their heretical Spirit of Man of This Earth cult on the population. Nobody had been able to do anything about it . . . until Barholm sent Raj Whitehall to reconquer the barbarian realms of the Military Governments.

Governor Barholm had officially proclaimed Raj the Sword of the Spirit of Man. The prisoners who'd volunteered to serve the Civil Government had seen him in operation from both sides. They *believed* that title.

"Then stay here!" Thom said. "Center can hold you in stasis, like me—hold you until Barholm's dust and bones. You've done all you can, you've done your duty, now you *deserve* something for yourself. It won't further the reunification of Bellevue for you to commit suicide!"

probability of furthering the restoration of the federation is slightly increased if raj whitehall attends the levee, Center said.

"I must go. I *must*. I—"

Raj turned back, and Thom recoiled a half step. The other man's teeth were showing, and a muscle twitched on one cheek. "I . . . there's been so much dying . . . I *can't* . . . so many dead, so many, how can I save myself?"

"They were enemies," Thom said softly.

"No! Not *them*. My own men! I used men like bullets! There aren't one in three of the 5th Descott Guards remaining, of the ones who rode out with me against the Colony five years ago. Poplanich's Own—raised from your family estates, Thom—had a hundred and fifty casualties in one battle, and *I* was leading them."

Thom opened his mouth, then closed it again. Center cut in on them, an iron impatience in its non-voice:

leading is the operative word, raj whitehall. you were leading them. observe:

"Back one step and volley!" Raj shouted, hoarse with smoke and dust.

Around him the shattered ranks firmed. Colonial dragoons in crimson djellabas rode forward, reins in their teeth as they worked the levers of their repeating carbines. The muzzles of their dogs snaked forward, then recoiled from the line of bayonets.

BAM. Ragged, but the men were firing in unison.

"Back one step and volley!" Raj shouted again.

He fired his revolver between two of the troopers, into the face of a Colonial officer who yipped and waved his yataghan behind the line of dragoons. The carbines snapped, and the man beside Raj stumbled back, moaning and pawing at the shattered jaw that dangled on his breast.

"Hold hard, 5th Descott! *Back one step and volley*."

Raj blinked back to an awareness of the polished sphere that was Center's physical being. That had been too vivid: not just the holographic image that the ancient computer projected on his retina; he could still *smell* the gunpowder and blood.

if you had not struck swiftly and hard, the wars would have

dragged on for years. deaths would have been a whole order of magnitude greater, among soldiers of both sides and among the civilians. as well, entire provinces would be so devastated as to be unable to sustain civilized life.

Images flitted through their minds: bones resting in a ditch, hair still fluttering from the skulls of a mother and child; skeletal corpses slithering over each other as men threw them on a plague-cart and dragged it away down the empty streets of a besieged city; a room of hollow-eyed soldiers resting on straw pallets slimed with the liquid feces of cholera.

"That's true enough for a computer," Raj said.

Even then, Thom noted the irony. He was East Residence born, a city patrician, and back when they both believed *computer* meant *angel* he'd doubted their very existence. That had shocked Raj's pious country-squire soul; Raj never doubted the Personal Computer that watched over every faithful soul, and the great Mainframes that sat in glory around the Spirit of Man of the Stars. Now they were both agents of such a being.

Raj's voice grew loud for a moment. "That's true enough for the Spirit of Man of the Stars made manifest, true enough for *God.* I'm not God, I'm just a man—and I've done the Spirit's work without flinching. But I'd be *less* than a man if I didn't think I deserve death for it." Silence fell.

"They ought to hate me," he whispered, his eyes still seeing visions without need of Center's holographs. "I've left the bones of my men all the way from the Drangosh to Carson Barracks, across half a world . . . they ought to hate my *guts.*"

they do not, Center said. **instead—**

A group of men swaggered into an East Residence bar, down the stairs from the street and under the iron brackets of the lights, into air thick with tobacco and sweat and the fumes of cheap wine and *tekkila.* Like most of those inside, they wore cavalry-trooper uniforms—it was not a dive where a civilian would have had a long life expectancy—but most of theirs carried the shoulder-flashes of the 5th Descott Guards, and they wore the red-and-white checked neckerchiefs that were an unofficial blazon in that unit. They were dark close-coupled stocky-muscular men, like most Descotters; with them were troopers from half a dozen other units, some of them blond giants with long hair knotted on the sides of their heads.

There was a general slither of chairs on floors as the newcomers took over the best seats. One Life Guard trooper who was slow about vacating his chair was dumped unceremoniously on the sanded floor; half a dozen sets of eyes tracked him like gun turrets turning as he came up cursing and reaching for the knife in his boot. The Life Guardsman looked over his shoulder, calculated odds, and pushed out of the room. The hard-eyed girl who'd been with him hung over the shoulder of the chair's new occupant. The men hung their sword belts on the backs of their chairs and called for service.

"T'Messer Raj," one said, raising a glass. "While 'e's been a-leadin' us, nivver a one's been shot runnin' away!"

— they do not hate you. they *fear* you, for they know you will expend them without hesitation if necessary. but they know raj whitehall will lead from the front, and that with him they have conquered the world.

"Then they're fools," Raj said flatly.

"They're men," Thom said. "All men die, whether they go for soldiers or not. But maybe you've given them something that makes the life worth it, just as you have Center's Plan to rebuild civilization throughout the universe."

They exchanged the *embrahzo* again. Thom stepped back and froze, his body once again in Center's timeless stasis.

Raj turned and took a deep breath. "Can't die deader than dead," he murmured to himself.

CHAPTER TWO

The great corridor outside the Audience Hall shone with the delicate colored marble and semiprecious stone that made up the intaglio work of the floor. The walls were arched windows on the outer side, and religious murals on the inner—icons of the Saints, lives of the martyrs, stars, starships, Computers calling forth Order from Primeval Chaos. Though the day was overcast, hidden gaslights threw a bright radiance through mirrors.

Soldiers in the black uniforms and black breastplates of the Life Guards stood along the walls every few paces, rifles at port; officers had their swords drawn and the points resting at their boots. The uniforms were Capital-crisp, but the faces under the plumed helmets were closed and watchful—square beak-nosed faces, dark and hard, on men slightly bowlegged from riding as soon as they could walk. The Life Guards were recruited from the Barholm family estates back in Descott county, from vakaros and yeoman-tenant *rancheros*. When Descotters ate a man's salt they took the responsibilities seriously, in the main.

Suzette adjusted Raj's cravat, beneath the high wing collar of the dress-uniform jacket. There was a fixed, intent look on her face. Raj recognized it; it was the look you got when the overall situation was completely out of control, so you focused on the immediate skill you *could* master. Suzette had been brought up in East Residence, and her family had been patrician for fourteen generations. Court etiquette—and the intricate currents of court intrigue—were as much her heritage as the saddle of a war-dog or the hilt of a saber were to him.

He'd seen the same look on a Brigade trooper's face, adjusting the grip on his sword and the angle of the blade—as he rode into the muzzle of a cannon loaded with grapeshot.

Three of his Companions were standing around, with similar expressions. *They* were looking at the Life Guards, and figuring the odds on a firefight if an order came through to arrest Raj on the spot. *Not good*, he thought.

"Relax," he said quietly. "There isn't going to be any trouble here today."

The party around Raj Whitehall stood in a bubble of social space, lower-ranking courtiers and messengers either avoiding their eyes or staring fascinated at the famous General Whitehall; for the last time, if rumor was correct. Many of them were probably thinking how lucky they were never to have risen so high. The stalk that stood out above the others was the first to be lopped off.

Which is why the Civil Government doesn't rule the whole Earth, as it should, Raj thought with an old, cold anger.

correct, Center replied. Then it added pedantically: **bellevue. earth will come later.**

The crowd parted as a man came through. He wasn't particularly imposing; no more than twenty-one or so, and slimly handsome. His left arm ended at a leather cup and steel hook where the hand should have been. His uniform was standard issue for Civil Government cavalry, blue swallowtail coat and loose maroon breeches, crimson sash under the Sam Browne belt; all tailored with foppish care, but travel-worn and stained with sea salt in places. He carried his round bowl helmet with the chainmail neck-guard and twin captain's stars tucked under his left arm. The right fist snapped to his chest as he saluted, then bowed to Suzette.

"Messer Raj," he said. "My lady Whitehall." A smile as he glanced past them to the other Companions. "Dog-brothers."

"Spirit," Raj said mildly, shaken out of his strait preoccupation with what would probably happen in the next half-hour. "I thought you were back in the Western Territories with the 5th, Bartin."

Not to mention with Colonel Gerrin Staenbridge; Bartin Foley had gotten into the 5th as Gerrin's protégé-cum-boyfriend. He was far more than that now, of course.

"Administrator Historiomo decided," the young officer said, voice carefully neutral, "that since the Brigade survivors in the Western Territories were cooperating fully, a number of units were surplus to garrison needs."

"Which units?" Raj said.

Bartin cleared his throat. "The 5th Descott Guards," he said. *Raj's Own, as they liked to call themselves.*

"The 7th Descott Rangers, 1st Rogor Slashers, Poplanich's Own, and the 18th Komar Borderers," he went on.

The cavalry units most closely associated with Raj, and the ones commanded by the men who'd become his Companions, the elite group of close comrades he relied on most.

"In addition, the 17th Kenden County Foot, and the 24th Valencia," he continued.

Jorg Menyez commanded the 17th: a Companion, and the Civil Government's best infantry specialist, able to turn the despised foot soldiers into fighting men of sorts. The 24th . . . *Ferdihando Felasquez.* Good man . . .

"And last but not least, the 1st and 2nd Mounted Cruisers."

Recruited from the defeated barbarians of the Squadron, after Raj crushed them in a single month's campaign back in the Southern Territories, three years ago. They'd always been warriors; under civilized instruction, they'd also become quite capable soldiers. The commander of the 1st Cruisers, Ludwig Bellamy, had made the same transition; but as a Squadrone nobleman he also regarded himself as Raj's personal liegeman. Tejan M'Brust, the Descotter Companion who'd taken over the 2nd Cruisers, probably thought the same way— although he wasn't supposed to, being a civilized man.

"They're all," Bartin went on, with a slight smile, bowing over Suzette's hand, "on their way back. Together with the field artillery.

I came ahead on one of the steam rams, but everyone should be here in a day or three, if the weather stays fine."

Beside Raj, Colonel Dinnalsyn pricked up his ears. The artillery specialist had hated being separated from his beloved weapons. He'd trained those crews himself.

Joy, Raj thought. It just *happened* to look like Raj's own personal army was heading back to the East Residence at flank speed.

Antin M'lewis cracked his fingers. "What happen t'Chivrez?"

The Honorable Fedherko Chivrez had been sent out to take command of the Western Territories after Raj conquered them—and had arrived to find the Governor's promising young heir Cabot Clerett dead at Raj's feet, with a smoking carbine in Raj's hand.

Suzette gave him a single cool violet look from her slanted eyes and then turned them away, her face the unreadable mask of an East Residence aristocrat.

Raj remembered Cabot's eyes bulging, as Suzette shot him neatly behind the ear, in the instant before his trigger finger would have punched an 11mm pistol round through Raj's body. Chivrez had seen; Chivrez had been Director of Supply in Komar back five years ago, and had tried to withhold supplies from Raj's men. Two Companions named Evrard and Kaltin Gruder had run him out a closed window headfirst, then held him while Antin M'lewis started to flay him from the feet up. Raj had gotten the supplies and won the campaign.

The trouble with that sort of method was the long-term problems. On the other hand, if Raj *hadn't* gotten those supplies, his troops would have been wiped out by the Colonials in the desert fighting. You paced yourself to the task, and if the task got done you worried about secondary consequences later.

"Ah." Bartin Foley considered the tip of his hook. "Well, Messer Chivrez seems to have betrayed the Governor's trust and absconded with some of the Brigade's treasures."

observe, Center said.

A bedroom in the palace of the Generals of the Brigade, in the Western Territories. Chivrez thrashing, his arms and legs held down by four strong men, another pressing a pillow over his face. The stubby limbs thrashed against the bedclothes. After a few minutes they grew still; Ludwig Bellamy wrapped the body in the sheets and hoisted it. Even masked, Raj recognized Gerrin Staenbridge as the one holding open the door.

The scene shifted, to the swamps outside Carson Barracks. The same men tipped a burlap-wrapped bundle off the deck of a small boat. It vanished with scarcely a splash, weighed down with lengths of chain and a cast-iron roundshot weighing forty kilos. Gerrin raised a meter-diameter blazon of the Brigade's sunburst banner, crafted in silver and gold with the double lightning flash across it picked out in diamond.

"Pity," he murmured. "Not bad work in a garish sort of barbarian way, and it would buy a good many opera tickets and dinners at the Centoyard back home. Ah, well—authenticity."

He tossed the disk after the bureaucrat's body. It sank with a popping bubble of marsh gas. Somewhere off in the swamps a hadrosauroid bellowed.

Antin M'lewis grinned uneasily as the Companions exchanged glances. They knew, of course . . . but he wasn't quite sure if Messer Raj knew. They were all of the Messer class by birth themselves; he'd levered himself up into it by hitching his star to Messer Raj's wagon. *Ye takes t'risk a' fallin', too,* he thought.

M'lewis had started off as a Bufford Parish bandit, a sheep stealer by hereditary profession, and made even that most lawless part of not-very-lawful Descott County too hot for him. Enlistment had been the alternative to a rope—or a less formal appointment with a knife. He'd met Raj over a little matter of a peasant's pig gone missing despite a no-foraging order. One look had told him this was a man who had to be either served or killed, and he'd made *his* decision. It had led him near enough to death more times than he could count, and also to advancement beyond his dreams.

On the other hand, one of the things that surprised him about gentlemen born was how bad they were at making use of their advantages. There were good points to a rough upbringing. One of them was being able to say the unsayable.

"Ah, ser," he suggested, leaning forward and whispering, "what wit' t' lads comin' in s'soon, mebbe we'uns ud better dip out loik—come back wit' better company inna day er two?"

Raj spoke in a clear, conversational tone, without looking around: "I'm attending this levee as ordered by the Sovereign Mighty Lord, Captain M'lewis. You may do as you please."

M'lewis spat on the intaglio floor. Spirit. Mebbe I should a' stayed in sheep-stealin'.

He followed nonetheless; he might have been born a thief, but he'd eaten this man's bread and salt.

A metal-shod staff thumped the floor, and the tall bronze panels of the Audience Hall swung open. The gorgeously robed figure of the Janitor—the Court Usher—bowed and held out his staff, topped by the Star symbol of the Civil Government.

Suzette took Raj's arm. The Companions fell in behind him, unconsciously forming a column of twos. A Life Guard officer stepped forward.

"Your weapons, Messers," he said, his face expressionless.

Raj made a chopping gesture with his free hand, and the forward rustle of the Companions died. He handed over ceremonial revolver and court sword. This time it was Bartin Foley who whispered in his ear:

"A company of the 5th arrived *with* me, sir. If you're arrested . . ."

"Captain Foley, the Sovereign Mighty Lord's orders will be *obeyed* by all troops under my command—is that clear?"

observe, Center whispered in his mind. Raj, in a cell, darkness and the flickering light of lanterns. Rifle-fire from the halls outside, flat slapping echoes off the stone, and the turnkey's shotgun pointed through the bars at Raj's face, the hammer falling as he jerked the trigger . . .

"I've served my Governor and the Spirit of Man to the best of my ability," Raj added. "I chose to assume that the Governor, upon whom be the blessings of the Spirit always, will see it the same way."

The functionary's voice boomed out with trained precision through the gold-and-niello speaking trumpet:

"General the Honorable Messer Raj Ammenda Halgern da Luis

Whitehall, Whitehall of Hillchapel, Hereditary Supervisor of Smythe Parish, Descott County! His Lady, Suzette Emmaenelle—" *None of his other titles,* Raj noted. He'd been officially hailed *Sword of the Spirit of Man* and *Savior of the State* in this room.

He ignored the noise, ignored the brilliantly decked crowds who waited on either side of the carpeted central aisle, the smells of polished metal, sweet incense, and sweat. The Audience Hall was two hundred meters long and fifty high, its arched ceiling a mosaic showing the wheeling galaxy with the Spirit of Man rising head and shoulders behind it. The huge dark eyes were full of stars themselves, staring down into your soul.

Along the walls were automatons, dressed in the tight uniforms worn by Terran Federation soldiers twelve hundred years before. They whirred and clanked to attention, powered by hidden compressed-air conduits, bringing their archaic and quite non-functional battle lasers to salute. The Guard troopers along the aisle brought their entirely functional rifles up in the same gesture.

The far end of the audience chamber was a hemisphere plated with burnished gold, lit via mirrors from hidden arcs. It glowed with a blinding aura, strobing slightly. The Chair itself stood four meters in the air on a pillar of fretted silver, the focus of light and mirrors and every eye in the giant room. The man enChaired upon it sat with hieratic stiffness, light breaking in metallized splendor from his robes, the bejeweled Keyboard and Stylus in his hands. A tribal delegation was milling about before it, still speaking through its hired interpreter.

The linguist's face was professionally bland, but occasionally a look of horror would cross his features as he moved his lips, working out Sponglish equivalents of the mountaineers' singsong native tongue:

"Hjburni-burni-burni—"

"Humbly we beseech you, O Sovereign Mighty One, Sole Autocrat, our poverty prevents other than our traditional border auxiliary duties—"

Center broke in: **more accurately rendered: back off, stonehouse-chief, or we'll see what terms the colony offers its**

border auxiliaries—we're closer to al kebir than east residence.

"Hjurni-burni-burni, burjimi murjimi urgimi—"

"In our humble huts in the mountains, we seek only to till our poor fields in peace—"

we're your allies and *you* **pay** *us* **for guarding the passes;**

"—kuljurni ablurni hjurni-burni Halvaardi burri murri—"

"—and surely there are closer, richer lands which need the attention of your talented administrators—"

—so the next tax collector who asks for "earth and water" from the halvaardi gets thrown down a well to find plenty of both.

Barholm made a slight gesture with one hand, and the tribesfolk were ushered out, protesting, amid a ripe stink from the butter they used to grease their braids. One of the wooden clocks they carried on their belts gave its mechanical *kuku, kuku* as the pillar that supported the Chair sank toward the white marble steps; at the rear of the enclosure two full-scale statues of gorgosauroids rose to their three-meter height and roared as the seat of the Governor of the Civil Government sank home with a slight sigh of hydraulics. A faint whine sounded, and the arc lights blazed brighter. At the center of the mirrors' focus Barholm blazed like a shape of white fire.

Raj took three paces forward and went down in the ceremonial prostration—the full prostration, since his former titles were stripped from him. He rose and knelt the prescribed three times; by his side there was a quiet rustle of silks and lace as Suzette sank down with an infinite gracefulness.

"What punishment," Barholm boomed, his voice amplified by the superb acoustics of the Audience Hall, "is fit for him who was foremost in Our trust? Yea, what baseness is more base, what vileness more vile, than one into whose hand the Sword of the State has been entrusted—when that most wretched of men turns the Sword against the very root and foundation, the Coax Cable of the Spirit—"

In East Residence, rhetoric was the most admired of the arts—far ahead of, for instance, military or administrative skill; infinitely more so than engineering. A speech like this could go on for hours, when the entire content could be boiled down to "kill him."

The semicircle of high ministers stirred behind their desks. The tall slender form of Chancellor Tzetzas turned sharply to hiss General Gharzia, Commander of Eastern Forces, into silence; the elderly soldier was listening to a messenger—a courier in tight leathers, not a court usher or an aide. From the floor, Raj watched Gharzia's face congeal like cooling lard. He didn't have to pay attention to what Barholm said, he knew how that would end . . .

Gharzia rose and circled to Tzetzas' side. The Chancellor tried to shake off the hand that plucked at his sleeve, then turned to listen with a tight, controlled fury that would have frightened Raj if he'd been in Gharzia's shoes. People who seriously annoyed the Chancellor tended to have accidents, or develop severe stomach problems, or be killed in duels.

Raj had never seen Tzetzas frightened before. It was a far less pleasant experience than he would have thought; whatever his other vices, nobody had ever even accused the Chancellor of cowardice. To make him interrupt the ceremony of triumph over his most hated rival, it had to be something massive.

"And—" Barholm noticed the movement to his right and broke off, flipping up the smoked-glass eyeshield. "Tzetzas! *What* do you think you're doing?"

The raw fury in his voice made Tzetzas check half a step. The Governor was the Spirit's Viceregent on Earth; if he ordered the Guards to cut the Chancellor to pieces on the steps of the Chair, they would obey without hesitation. That had happened in past reigns, more than once. Wise Governors remembered that those reigns had been short . . . but Barholm Clerett had been growing more and more unstable since his wife died.

"Sovereign Mighty Lord," Tzetzas said, his voice a cool precision instrument, handled with faultless skill. "I deserve your anger for my boorishness. Yet concern drives your servant. The Colony has invaded our territories; news has arrived by heliograph."

There was a chain of stations between the frontiers and East Residence; high-priority messages could be relayed in hours, where couriers would take days or weeks. Only the Colony and the Civil Government possessed such means, on Bellevue.

"You interrupt me for a *raid*?"

The Bedouin and the Civil Government's Borderers had been stealing girls and sheep and cutting each other up over waterholes since time immemorial. It was a peaceful week that passed without a minor skirmish, and there were several *razziah* a year from either side. It usually didn't even cause a ripple in the profitable trade carried on between the more civilized urban element on both sides of the frontier.

Tzetzas threw himself down on his knees. "Not a raid, Sovereign Mighty Lord. Invasion. The Settler of the Colony himself, Ali—and his one-eyed brother and general, Tewfik. They have taken Gurnyca."

A low moan swept through the Audience Hall. That was the largest city on the lower Drangosh river and the closest major settlement to the eastern frontier.

The mad anger disappeared from Barholm's face, as cleanly as if cut with a knife. A minute later, so did the eye-hurting brilliance of the arc lights. By contrast, the Audience Hall seemed black.

"The levee is closed," Barholm said, in a flat carrying voice.

There were yelps of protest from petitioners. The officer of the Life Guards barked an order, and hands rattled on stocks as the rifles came to present-arms.

"An immediate meeting of the State Council will be held in the Negrin Room," Barholm said into the sudden stillness. "All others are dismissed."

Raj rose to one knee. "Sovereign Mighty Lord," he said calmly. "Does the Sole Autocrat wish my presence?"

Barholm paused, looking over his shoulder. "Of course," he said. A snarl broke through the mask of his face. "Of course!"

"*Sayyida,*" the man said, bowing with hand to brows, lips and heart; his dress was the knee breeches and jacket of an East Residence bourgeois, but his tongue was the pure Syrian Arabic of Al Kebir, capital of the Colony. "Peace be with you."

"And upon you peace, Abdullah al'Aziz," Suzette Whitehall replied in the same language, the rolling gutturals falling easily from her tongue.

Her maids had replaced the split skirt, leggings, and blond wig of court formality with a noblewoman's day-robe; she wrote as she spoke, glancing up only occasionally. The steel nib of the pen skritched steadily on the paper.

"Are you ready?" she said.

"For the Great Game?" the Arab replied, smiling whitely in his neatly trimmed black beard. "Always, my lady."

"Good. Here are papers, and a sight-draft on Muzzaf Kerpatik."

The Whitehalls' chief steward, among other things. A Borderer from the southern city of Komar, and no friend of any Arab, but also not likely to let personal feelings interfere with his work.

"My instructions, *sayyida*?"

"Proceed at once to Sandoral on the Drangosh. Military intelligence for my lord, if it presents itself; for myself I wish full information on the higher officers of the garrison and the local nobles: loves, hates, histories, feuds, alliances. Also any information from the Colony."

He took the papers and repeated the bow, using the documents for added flourish. "I obey like those multiplex of wing and eye who served Sulieman bin'-Daud, my lady," he said cheerfully. "That city I know of old." He'd done similar work for her the last time Raj commanded in the East, four years before.

"See that nobody stuffs you into a bottle," she added dryly, dropping back into Sponglish.

"I shall be most careful," he replied in the Civil Government's tongue, faultless down to the capital-city middle-class crispness of his vowels. "There is yet much to be done to repay my debt to you, my lady. And," he added with a cold glint in his dark eyes, "to those Sunni sons of pigs in Al Kebir, also."

Druze were few on Bellevue; less, since the Settlers had decided to purify the House of Islam a generation ago. Those sniffed out by the mullahs could count themselves lucky to be sold as slaves to the sulfur mines of Gederosia. The path from there to Suzette Whitehall's household and manumission had been long and complex . . .

"Your family are provided for?" Abdullah nodded. "Go, then, thou Slave of God," Suzette said, once more in Arabic, playing on the literal meaning of the man's name. "Thy God and mine be with thee."

"And the Merciful, the Lovingkind with thee and thy lord, *sayyida*," he replied, and left.

"Fatima," Suzette went on.

"Messa?"

"Take this to the Renunciate Sister Conzwela Dihego; she's second administrative assistant for medical affairs to the Arch-Sysup of East Residence. It's an authorization to mobilize priest-doctors and medical nuns, with the necessary supplies and transport for immediate dispatch to Sandoral."

"Wasn't she with us in the Western Territories?" the Arab girl asked.

"Yes; and Anne got her that job on my say-so when we got back." Suzette sighed; she missed Anne. "Quickly. And send in Muzzaf."

The Companion sidled through the door as Fatima left; the opening showed a controlled chaos of packing. He was a short slight man, with the dark complexion of a Borderer and a singsong Komarite accent. He was dressed in jacket and breeches of white linen, the little peaked fore-and-aft cap of his region, and a sash which nearly concealed the pepperpot pistol and pearl-handled gravity knife he preferred. He bowed deeply, a gesture much like Abdullah's.

Nearly a thousand years of conflict had left the Borderers much resembling their enemies of the Colony, though it was a killing matter to suggest it aloud.

"Messa Whitehall," he said, showing white teeth against his spiked black chin-beard. Like everyone else in the household, he was reacting to the news of Raj's reinstatement with almost giddy relief. "We campaign again?"

"Yes," Suzette said.

She pushed a document across the table with a finger. "One of your relatives is contractor for the East Residence municipal coal yards, isn't he?"

Muzzaf nodded; men from Komar and the other Border cities were prominent in trade all over the Civil Government, and in the new joint-risk companies.

"Subcontractor, Messa. The primary contract is farmed to an . . . associate of Chancellor Tzetzas." He took up the paper and whistled silently. "That is a great *deal* of coal."

"Subcontractor is good enough. Have him release that amount to the Central Rail; and drop a suggestion with their dispatching agent that they begin to accumulate rolling stock *immediately*. Sweeten the suggestion if you have to."

"Immediately."

They exchanged a smile; Chancellor Tzetzas had confiscated all Raj's wealth . . . all that he had been able to find, at any rate. Neither the Chancellor nor Raj knew exactly how much the Whitehalls had had; Raj left such things to Muzzaf and Suzette . . . and they had anticipated the evil day long before. Raj knew how to handle guns and men, and even politics after a fashion, but money could also be a useful tool.

Silence fell as the steward left, broken only by the scritching of the pen and the faint thumps and scraping of the packing in the outer chambers. On the bed behind her were Raj's campaigning gear: plain issue swallowtail jacket of blue serge, maroon pants, boots, helmet, saber, pistol, map case, binoculars. Beside it was her linen riding costume and a captured Colonial repeating carbine, her own personal weapon . . . and the one, she reflected, that had disposed of the Clerett's heir.

A pity, she thought absently, tapping her lips with the tip of the pen before dipping the nib in the inkwell again. *A very pleasant young man.*

And easy to manipulate. Which had been crucial; like his uncle, he'd been mad with suspicion against Raj. With envy, too, in young Cabot's case: of Raj's reputation, his victories, his hold over his soldiers, and his wife.

A pity she'd had to kill him. Particularly just then. Shooting people was a crude emergency measure . . .

Which reminded her. She crossed to her jewel table and reached beneath for a small rosewood box. A tiny combination lock closed it, and she probed at that with a pin from a brooch.

Yes, the crystal vials of various liquids and powders within were all full and fresh—there was a slip of paper with a recent date inside to remind her, one of Abdullah's many talents.

You never knew what sort of help Raj would need . . . whether he knew it or not.

"You *will* triumph, my knight," she whispered to herself, closing the box with a click. "If I have anything to do with the matter."

CHAPTER THREE

Governor Barholm stood while the servants stripped off the heavy robes; apart from Raj, they were the only people in the chamber who didn't look terrified . . . and they didn't have to watch the Governor's face. A sicklefoot had that sort of expression, just before it pivoted and slashed open its prey's belly with the four-inch dewclaw on one hind foot.

The Negrin Room was three centuries old. Walls were pale stone, traced over with delicate murals of reeds and flying dactosauroids and waterfowl; there was only one small Star, a token obeisance to religion as had been common in that impious age. The heads of the Ministries were there: Chancellor Tzetzas, of course; General Fiydel Klostermann, Master of Soldiers; Bernardinho Rivadavia, the Minister of Barbarians; Mihwel Berg of the Administrative Service; Gharzia, Commander of Eastern Forces. The courier from the east as well.

It was strange not to see Lady Anne Clerett, the Governor's wife. Barholm didn't have anyone he really trusted now that she was dead, and it was affecting his judgment.

"Heldeyz," Barholm snapped. "*Give* us the report, man."

Ministerial couriers were men of some rank themselves, but it was still strange how unintimidated Heldeyz looked, even facing the stark fury in Barholm Clerett's eyes. His own were fixed and distant, in a face still seamed by trail dust.

Barholm went on fretfully: "I *don't* know why Ali has done this. The treaty after the last war was generous to a fault—particularly since we *won* the war. The gifts of friendship . . ."

observe:

Sweating slaves heaved at bundles of iron bars, heaping them on the flatbed rail-cars and lashing them down. One slipped and fell to the paving stones of East Residence's main station. A bar snapped across; as a clerk bustled over a guard rolled the broken end beneath his boot.

"Spirit," he said in a tone of mild curiosity. The interior of the fracture showed a gray texture. "That's not wrought iron, it's *cast*."

Cast iron came straight from the smelting furnace; it was hard, brittle and full of impurities. Only after treatment in a puddling mill did it become the ductile, easily worked material so valuable for machinery and tools.

The clerk cleared his throat. "I think you'll find," he said significantly, "that the Chancellor has inspected the manifests quite carefully."

The guard grinned; he was a thin man with a long nose and a pockmarked face, an East Residencer by birth with all the ingrained respect for a good swindle that marked that breed. He brushed his thumb over the first three fingers of his right hand. The clerk smiled back.

"Sovereign Mighty Lord," Raj said. "I think you'll find that quality, quantity, and delivery dates on our tribute—pardon, our gifts of friendship—to the Colony have been below the Treaty terms."

Figures scrolled before his eyes, and he read them in an emotionless monotone worthy of Center.

Barholm blinked. He turned his eyes on Tzetzas, and a fine beading of sweat broke out on the Chancellor's olive face. "Sole Autocrat," the minister said, spreading his hands. "When contracts are handed out, something always sticks—so many layers of oversight, so many hands—you know—"

The Governor's fist struck the table. Gold-rimmed *kave* cups bounced and clattered in their saucers.

"I know who's responsible for seeing that the payments were met!" he roared; suddenly there was the slightest trace of Descott County rasp in his Sponglish. "You *fool*, I don't expect you to work for your salary alone, but I *did* expect you to know enough not to piss in our own well! D'you have any idea what this war is going to cost in lost taxes and off-budget funding?"

He paused, and when he continued his voice was calm. "You'd better have some idea, because you're going to pay the overage—personally."

"Sovereign Mighty Lord," Raj said. "Right now, I think we'd better concern ourselves with the state of the garrisons on the Drangosh frontier."

Barholm snapped his fingers. "Gurnyca had a garrison of—"

"Ten thousand men, Sole Autocrat," Mihwel Berg said helpfully. "At least, ten thousand on the paybooks."

Chancellor Tzetzas busied himself with his papers. When Barholm spoke, it was to General Gharzia.

"General," he said, his voice soft and even, "tell me—and if you lie, it would be better for you if you had never been born—how many troops were *actually* on the strength of the Gurnyca garrison? In what condition?"

Gharzia licked his lips, going gray under the tanned olive of his skin. "Two thousand, Sovereign Mighty Lord. In . . . ah, poor condition."

Somebody had been collecting the pay of the missing eight thousand. All eyes turned to the Chancellor.

The ruler turned back to the courier from the east. "Now, Messer Heldeyz," he said evenly. "Your report, please."

"Yes, Sole Autocrat."

Heldeyz stared at his hands. "I met the Colonials fifty klicks south of Gurnyca," he began. "They—"

observe, Center said:

Terrible as an army with banners. Bartin Foley had quoted that to Raj, once; it was a fragment of Old Namerique, from the codices that survived the Fall.

There were plenty of banners in the forefront of the Colonial host that crossed the Drangosh. The green flag of Islam, marked with the crescent, or with the house blazons of regiments and noble *amirs*. The peacock-tail of the Settlers; that meant Ali was present in person. And a black pennant marked with the Seal of Solomon in red. *Tewfik.* Ali's brother, disqualified from the Settler's throne because of the eye he'd lost in the Zanj Wars, but the Colony's right arm nonetheless.

Raj recognized the terrain instantly; he'd campaigned out east himself, five years ago. Generations of the Civil Government's soldiers had taken their blooding in that ghastly lunar landscape of eroded silt, and all too many left their bones there. Just north of the border and the river forts, by the look of it, in one of the locations where the right—the western—bank was too high for irrigation. In consequence nothing grew there, except for a few bluish-green native shrubs.

The oily-looking greenish-gray waters of the Drangosh were a kilometer and a half across. A bridge of boats had been built across it, big river-barges of the type used for trade up and down the river from Sandoral to Al Kebir and the far-off Colonial Gulf. *Good engineering,* Raj thought; as good as the Civil Government's army, or a little better. The barges were lashed together with huge sisal cables as thick as a man's waist; then timbers and planks were laid across to make a deck, and pounded clay half a meter thick on top of that to give the men and animals a firm surface. There were even straw balustrades on either side, chest high, to keep the beasts from spooking at the water curling up around the blunt prows of the barges.

Men flowed across in a steady stream: Colonial dragoon *tabors*, battalions, riding in column of fours, mainly. Mounted on slender Bazenjis and greyhounds, lever-action repeating carbines in scabbards by their right knees, scimitars or yataghans at their belts, bandoliers over the chests of their faded scarlet djellabas. The sun glittered on the polished spikes of their conical helmets, and the pugarees wound about them fluttered in the breeze. Between the blocks of cavalry came guns: light pompoms, quick-firers throwing a two-kilo shell from a clip magazine; field guns, much like the Civil Government's 75mms; and heavier pieces drawn by oxen. Those were cast-steel muzzle-loading rifles, heavy pieces up to 150mm, siege guns. And there was transport, light dog-drawn two-wheel carts, heavy wagons pulled by sixteen pair of oxen.

Officers directed the traffic with flourishes of their nine-tailed ceremonial whips, each thong tipped with a piece of jagged steel.

Where— Raj thought. Center's viewpoint shifted to the western bank.

In the Colony's army, as in the Civil Government's, infantry were usually second-line troops, good enough to hold forts and lines of communication. Ali—Tewfik, probably—had sent his over first, and they were hard at work. Swarms of men stripped to their loincloths or pantaloons, burned from their natural light brown to an almost black color, swinging picks and shoveling dirt into the baskets others hauled. They moved over the land like disciplined ants, and a pentagonal earthwork fortress was rising around the western end of the pontoon bridge. A fairly formidable one, too; deep ditch, ten-meter walls, ravelins and bastions at the corners with deep V-notches for the muzzles of the guns. The Colony's green flag and the Settler's peacock already flapped around a huge pavilion-tent in its center. Within, ditched roadways had been laid out, and neat rows of pup tents, heaps of stores, and picket-lines for the dogs were rising.

Enough for—

"Sixty thousand men," Raj said. "Fifty thousand cavalry, ten thousand infantry or a little more to hold the bridgehead."

Heldeyz stopped, flustered. "Yes, *heneralissimo*," he said; evidently the news of Raj's demotion hadn't reached the eastern marches yet. "That's my estimate. How did you know?"

"Logistics. If Ali's planning on moving as far north as Sandoral, that's the maximum number he can supply overland from the bridgehead. Our forts at the border can hold out for six months or more, even if the Colony put in a full attack—which they won't or they couldn't put that large a field army into action. They'll have blockforces around the frontier strongpoints, but they can't use river transport to supply Ali. So they moved north and crossed upstream of the forts."

Both the Colony and the Civil Government had put generations of effort into those defenses. The giant cast-steel rifles in the forts would smash anything that tried to steam past them on the river. That ruled out supply by riverboat.

"Ali—Tewfik—must have built a railroad line to the east bank," Raj said. "But on the western shore, it'll be animal transport. Even with what they can forage, no more than fifty thousand men and riding dogs. They wouldn't bring less, not for a full-scale invasion, and they couldn't feed more."

Barholm shot Raj a considering look. "Go on," he said to Heldeyz. The courier nodded. "I met—"

observe, Center whispered in Raj's mind:

Heldeyz knelt before a throne. It was lightly built, of cast bronze fretwork, but inlaid with gold and gems in a pattern that flared out behind the seat like a peacock's tail. A man in shimmering cloth-of-gold sat on it. Throne and man glittered when stray beams of light penetrated the lacework canopy that slaves held above it; a spray of peacock feathers sprang from the great ruby in the clasp at the front of his turban. Around the Settler stood generals and noblemen, a few Bedouin chiefs in goathair robes and ha'ik, mullahs in black, servants with flasks of iced sherbert, crouching clerks and accountants with paper and pen and abacus. None of them came within the ring of guardsmen, black slave-mamluks with great curved swords naked in their hands, or bell-mouthed riot guns at the ready.

"Your master, the *kaphar* king, has offended me grievously," Ali said, speaking fair Sponglish. "He has violated the terms of our treaty . . . and my father's blood cries out for vengeance. No duty is more sacred. Yet Allah, the Merciful, the Lovingkind, enjoins us to peaceful deeds."

Ali's face was heavy-featured but regular, the curved beak of the nose dominating, offset by full red lips and a forked beard. His eyes were large and brown, luminous and somehow disturbing. Apart from an occasional twitching tic of his right cheek, the expression was one of mild reason.

An officer approached, going down on both knees and bowing until the point of his helmet-spike touched the glowing Al Kebir carpets that covered the ground before the Settler's pavilion and campaign-throne.

"*Amir el Mumineen*, Commander of the Faithful, the infidel emissaries from the city of Gurnyca crave the honor of your presence."

Ali's eyebrows rose slightly. He leaned back in the portable throne, and servants stepped forward to spray rosewater from crystal ewers through rubber bulbs. He sipped sherbert from a glass globe through a silver straw and waited.

"By all means, let them enter," he said gently.

The delegates ignored Heldeyz, prone on the carpet before the Settler. There were half a dozen of them, mostly in the dress of wealthy merchants, one in Civil Government uniform. They threw themselves prostrate; a gesture that only the ruler of the *Gubernio Civil* was legally due. In fact, it was forbidden to any other on penalty of death, but the Governor was in East Residence, and Ali was very much present before their gates with fifty thousand men.

"Sovereign lord," the head of the delegation mumbled into the carpet; he was an elderly man, sweating in the heat, the wattles under his chin sliding down into the expensive but dust-stained silver lace of his cravat. "Spare us."

Well, thought Raj. That's straightforward enough.

"Surely," the *alcalle* of Gurnyca said, "we may make amends to Your Supremacy for any offense we have unwittingly given. We are but poor merchants, not the lords of State. We have no knowledge of high matters. Yet if wrong has been done you, we are willing to pay. Surely there can be peace—who would benefit from war?"

Ali smiled. "There may be peace, if God wills. There is but one God, and all things are accomplished according to the will of God." He nodded, and added in his own tongue: "*Salaam, insh'allah.*"

One ringed hand stroked his beard, and he flicked a finger at a clerk. "You spoke of payment. The tribute from you *kaphar* ingrates is in arrears to the extent of—"

"—twenty-one hundred thousand gold *dinars*, O Lion of Islam," the clerk said. "That is not counting interest on late payments at—"

"Silence," Ali purred, a lethal amusement in his voice. "Am I a merchant, to haggle? By all means, if this is made good, let there be peace."

Even under the Colonial guns, that brought a wail of protest. "Lord, Lord," the alcalle said. "We are but one city! There is not that much gold in all Gurnyca, not if we stripped the dome of the cathedron and the fillings from our teeth."

"Both of which," Ali pointed out genially, "will be done if the city is put to the sack." He raised a hand. "It is the time of prayer. Surely, we may speak again of this later; and you shall return to your city with an escort and safe passage. In the morning, I shall give my final decision."

The scene shifted, the sun dropping toward the horizon and both moons high, looking like translucent glass against the bright stars. Date palms and orange groves stood in darkening shadow as the Gurnyca elders and Heldeyz rode their dogs through the belt of irrigated land surrounding the city. Water chuckled in the canals that bordered the fields, oxen lowed, but there was no sight or sound of human beings, no smoke from the whitewashed huts of the peasantry. Fields lay empty, scattered with tossed-aside hoes and pruning hooks; a manor stood ghostly among its gardens, with only the raucous sound of a peacock strutting along the tiled portico.

Frontier reflexes, Raj thought grimly. They know when to make a bolt for the walls.

There were no buildings or trees within a half-kilometer of the fortifications, only pasture and field crops; and the city defenses were first-rate. Raj remembered them well from the archives, which he'd memorized long before Center entered his life. Modernized a century ago, and then again in his father's time. A clear field of fire, good moat, new-style walls sunk behind it, low and massive. Ravelins and bastions at frequent intervals, giving murderous enfilade fire all along the circuit, with a strong central citadel near the water. The guns were cast-iron muzzle-loaders like most fortress artillery, but formidable and numerous; there were some very up-to-date rifled pieces among them.

Resolutely held by a strong garrison, the city could have held for months against the Colonial army—and it would be impossible to bypass. Taking it by siege would require full-scale entrenchments, pushing artillery positions forward inch by bloody inch, escalade trenches, until enough heavy howitzers were close to the wall and you could pound it flat. Even then, storming it would be brutally expensive. By that time, the Civil Government would have had time to mobilize its field armies in the East and march to the city's relief. It was a strategy that had worked a dozen times in the endless eastern wars.

If the garrison was up to strength and competently led.

Center's viewpoint switched to the escort, a full half-battalion of them, two hundred and fifty men. They didn't look particularly impressive at first sight, dark bearded men, many with the tails of their pugarees drawn across their faces like veils. Raj looked for telltale signs: their hands, the wear on the hilts of scimitars and carbines, the way they sat their dogs, how often they had to check or spur to keep their dressing.

These lads have been to school. Their commander was a stocky man, one of the ones with the tail-end of his turban drawn across his face. Scars seamed the backs of his hands, and another gouged down from forehead to nose . . .

. . . and his eye was unmoving on that side. *Tewfik.* Raj cursed to himself. With a glass eye for once, rather than his trademark patch. He'd met the Colonial commander once, in a parley before the Battle of Sandoral, four years ago. *What's he doing there?* It was a job for a minor emir, not the commander-in-chief.

An image flickered through Raj's consciousness, tinged somehow with irony: himself, leading the 2nd Cruisers through the tunnel under Lion City's walls.

Point taken, Raj noted dryly.

The white dust of the road shone ruddy with the setting sun, streaked with the long shadow of the tall cypresses planted by its side. They came to the outer gatehouse of the city's defenses, where the highway crossed the moat on stone arches. Civil Government troops opened the iron portals: infantrymen, slovenly-looking even for footsoldiers. Raj ground his teeth at the rust on one man's rifle barrel. They eyed the Colonial troops with the prickly nervousness of a cat watching a pack of large dogs through a window. Heldeyz saluted their officer and opened his mouth to speak.

Tewfik drew his revolver and shot the man in the face.

A red spearhead seemed to connect the Arab's hand and the guard officer's nose for an instant, and then the footsoldier jerked backward as if kicked in the face by an ox. His helmet rang against the stone of the gatehouse, the last fraction of the *clank* lost in the snapping bark of carbines as the Colonials cut loose with their repeaters. They boiled forward, screaming in a wild falsetto screech. One of the Civil Government soldiers managed to get a round off, the deeper boom of his single-shot rifle painful in the confined space. Then he went down under a Colonial officer's yataghan, still stabbing upward with his bayonet.

The fight in the gateway lasted bare seconds, leaving Heldeyz and the city fathers sitting their dogs and gaping at the litter of bodies. Puffs of off-white smoke drifted by; the Colonials were wasting no time. Dozens of them stuck their carbines through gunslits in the doors and fired blind, as fast as they could work the levers, sending a lethal hail of the light bullets to ricochet off the stone walls within. Hand-bombs and axes pounded the doors open. The rest of the Colonial force formed a dense four-deep firing line at the inner gate, thumbing reloads from their bandoliers into the loading gates of their weapons. Heldeyz's head whipped around at the high shrill scream of a Colonial bugle.

Mounted men were pouring out of the orchards that ringed the city, spurring their dogs. The animals bounded forward at a dead run, covering the ground in huge soaring leaps as they galloped with heads down and hind legs coming up nearly to their ears on every jump. Rough hands threw the courier aside as the column poured into the strait confines of the gatehouse and broke out into the cleared ground beyond; a battery of pompoms followed, their long barrels jerking wildly as the gunners lashed their dogs. Iron wheels sparked on the paving stones, and behind them the roadway was red with crimson djellabas . . .

Barholm's fist hit the table as the courier's words stumbled into silence. He didn't have Center's holographic visions to flesh them out, but there was nothing wrong with his wits.

"They *knew* the wogs were there in force and they didn't keep a better guard than that?" he said.

"Sole Autocrat, the garrison was under-strength and badly trained," Raj said quietly. "In any case, they paid for their folly."

"Yes," Heldeyz said, his eyes remote. "They paid."

observe, Center said.

The scimitar flashed in the sun. A heavy *thack* sounded, with the harsher wet popping of fresh bone underneath. The *alcalle*'s head rolled free; his body collapsed from its kneeling position, heavy jets of arterial blood splashing into the reddish mud that stained the ground. Clouds of flies lifted, then settled again. The executioner flourished his heavy two-handed curved sword ritually.

The smoke from the burning buildings covered the smell, even from the pyramid of heads the Settler's mamluks were building beside the outer gate. Few of the chained coffles of Gurnycians marching out paid much attention to it; their faces were mostly blank, eyes to the ground. Mounted Colonial guards urged them on with snaps of the *kourbash*, the long sauroid-hide whip. They were the lucky ones: pretty women, strong young men, craftsmen, and children old enough to survive the trip south to the markets of Al Kebir.

Ali pointed. "No, cut that one's throat," he said, indicating a Star priest with a thin white beard. The executioner lowered his sword.

The old man's eyes were closed; he was praying quietly as the black-robed mamluk stepped up behind him and drew the curved dagger. Ali giggled when the body toppled thrashing to the ground.

"The *halall*," he said, sputtering laughter. The ritual throat-cutting that made meat clean for Muslims to eat. "Is it not fitting, for these beasts?"

Raj noted a mullah's lips tightening at the blasphemy. Nobody spoke.

The good humor on Ali's face turned gelid as he gripped Heldeyz's face in his hand and turned it to the heaps of severed heads.

"Do you *see*, infidel?" he screamed. "Do you *see*?"

A portly man in a green turban shoved his way through the crowd. A string of prisoners followed him, mostly girls in their early teens, with a few younger boys. He prostrated himself.

"Oh guardian of the sacred ka'ba, you wished—" he began in a falsetto voice.

Ali released the Civil Government courier. "Yes, yes," he said impatiently. His hand flicked to a girl and a boy. "Those two, and don't bother me again before the evening meal." He jerked his head at his guards. "Come. Bring the pig-eating *kaphar*."

Wagons took up most of the roadway, oxen lowing under the load. Inside, in the cleared space within the walls that Civil Government law commanded, were huge heaps of spoils; officers were directing the troopers as they piled it in neatly classified heaps. Cloth, metalware, tools, coin, precious vessels from the Star churches and temples . . . Beyond, only a few buildings still stood. As Heldeyz watched, a merchant's townhouse collapsed inward about the burning rafters, the thick adobe walls crumbling like mud. A ground-shaking thump, and the great dome of the Star temple followed; Raj recognized the sound of blasting charges.

"See, unbeliever," Ali went on. "The pig and son of pigs Barholm—it was not enough that he cheated me of the blood-price of my father's death, he expected me—*me*—Ali ibn'Jamal, to sit among the women and do nothing while he conquered all the world. Conquered all the world, then turned on me! Turned on the Faithful! No, *kaphar*, Ali ibn'Jamal, Guardian of Sinar, Settler of the House of Islam, is not such a fool as that.

"Tell Barholm I am coming for him." Ali's mouth was jerking, and his voice rose to a shrill scream. "Tell him I have something for him!"

Colonial soldiers were setting a sharpened stake in the ground. They dragged out the Arch-Sysup Hierarch of the Diocese of Gurnyca. He was a portly man, flabby in middle age, stripped to his silk underdrawers. The black giants holding his arms scarcely lost a step when he collapsed at the sight of the waiting impaling stake . . .

Silence fell around the table. At last, General Klosterman cleared his throat.

"Well, I don't think there's much doubt as to Ali's intentions," he said.

Barholm nodded abstractedly. "General Klosterman, how long would it take to mobilize all available field forces and meet the Colonists in strength?"

Klosterman paled. Master of Soldiers was an administrative post, but it did give the elderly officeholder a good grasp of the state of the Civil Government's defenses.

"Lord, Ali has fifty thousand of his first-line troops with him. If we summoned *all* available cavalry, we couldn't field half that in time to meet him south of Sandoral, or even south of the Oxhead Mountains . . . and forgive me, Sovereign Mighty Lord, but the troops we could summon would not be in good heart."

observe, said Center.

This time Center's projections started with a map. Raj recognized it, a terrain rendering of the Civil Government's eastern provinces. The Oxhead Mountains ran east-west, then hooked up northward; north of it was the sparsely settled central plateau, and to the south and east was the upper valley of the Drangosh and its tributary. That was densely settled in part, where irrigation was possible; elsewhere arid grazing country, with scattered villages around springs in the foothills.

Colored blocks moved, arrows showing their lines of advance. He nodded to himself; so and so many days to muster, supplies, roadways, the few railroad lines. Twenty thousand men maximum, perhaps thirty thousand if you counted the ordinary infantry garrisons called up from their land grants. And . . .

Men in blue and maroon uniforms fled, beating at their dogs with the flats of their sabers or with riding whips. A ragged square stood on a hill, with the Star banner at its center. Black puffballs of smoke burst over the tattered ranks, shellbursts, and Colonial field guns hammered giant shotgun blasts of canister in at point-blank range. Men *splashed* away from the shot in wedges. A line of mounted dragoons drew their scimitars in unison, flashing in the bright southern sun. *Five battalions*, Raj estimated with an expert eye. *Twenty-five hundred men*. Trumpets shrilled, and the scimitars rested on the riders' shoulders. Walk-march. Trot. The blades came down. Gallop. Charge. A single long volley blew gaps in their line, and they were over the thin Civil Government square. The Star banner went down. . . .

"Lord," Klosterman went on, "with humility, my advice is that we throw as many men into Sandoral and the eastern cities as we can. Ali cannot take them quickly."

Tzetzas spoke for the first time. "But he *could* bypass them," he said.

Raj nodded silently, conscious of eyes glancing at him sidelong. **observe,** said Center.

From horizon to horizon, the land burned; ripe wheat flared like tinder under the summer sun, sending clouds of red-shot black into the sky. Denser columns marked the sites of villages and manor-houses. In an orchard, peasants worked under Colonial guns, ringbarking the trees and piling burning bundles of straw against their roots.

A flicker, and he was outside a city: Melaga, from the look of the olive-covered hills around it. Raw red earth marked the siegeworks about it, a circumvallation with a high wall topped by a palisade. Zigzag works wormed inward from there, each ending in a redoubt protected by earth-filled wicker baskets. Swarms of men hauled cannon forward and dug at the earth. Guns boomed from the city walls, and men died in the siegeworks, but more took their places. Howitzers lobbed their shells into the sky, the fuses drawing trails of smoke and fire until they burst within the walls . . .

((•)) ((•)) ((•))

"No, that would be far too uncertain," Tzetzas went on. "Instead, well, the treasury is unusually full. We could offer Ali twice, three *times* the previous tribute."

Barholm snorted. "After we shorted him on the last agreement? I can just *see* him quietly going back to Al Kebir, demobilizing his army and waiting for the gold to arrive."

"Sovereign Mighty Lord," Heldeyz said, "he's not here for gold. He's here for blood. He's . . . he's not going to be bought off. You have to see him—"

ali would agree to the increased tribute, but remain on civil government soil, probability 97%, ±2. observe, said Center.

"Filth!" Ali screamed. He strode through the pavilions, kicking over platters filled with whole roast lambs, rice pillaus, fruits, and ices. "You call this a feast of welcome! Filth!"

The syndics of the town shrank backward, looking around with the instinctive gesture of men in a trap with no exit.

"That pig Barholm, that two-dinar Descotter hill chief who calls himself a conqueror, it isn't enough he makes me wait for my tribute, but he insults me too."

Ali stopped, smiled, relaxed. The expression was far more frightening than the bloodthirsty madness of a minute before.

"Well then, we'll have to show the *kaphar* what it means to insult the Commander of the Faithful, won't we?" he went on.

He eyed the assembled syndics with much the same expression that a farmwife would have, standing in the yard and fingering her knife as she selected a stewing pullet.

observe:

A younger Ali knelt behind a girl. Gardens bloomed around them, thick with flowers and softly murmurous with bees; the stars shone above, the only light on the rippling water of the fountain save for a few discreet lanterns. Ali had a hand on the girl's neck, pushing her face below the surface of the water as he thrust into her. He let her rise for an instant, long enough to take one breath and scream.

It bubbled out as he pushed her down again. Her hands beat

against the marble of the pool's rim, leaving bloody streaks on the carved stone.

observe:

Ali sat at a chessboard, across from a grave white-bearded man. The pieces were carved from sauroid ivory and black jadeite; they played seated on cushions of cloth-of-gold, beneath a fretted bronze pergola that served as support for a huge vine of sambuca jasmine. A slender girl naked except for the filmy veil that hid half her face poured cut-crystal goblets full of iced sherbert. Droplets of condensation stood out on the silver ewer.

"Checkmate, Prince of the Faithful," the older man said. "Congratulations. This is your best game yet."

Ali looked down at the chessboard, his lips moving as he traced out the possible movements. When he moved, it was so swiftly that the serving girl had time for only the beginning of a scream.

His hand grasped the *cadi*'s white beard, and the dagger slashed it across. He threw the tuft of hair in the older man's face.

"Sauroid-lover," he screamed. "You dare to insult me?"

The old man drew himself up. "You forget yourself, Ali," he said. "I am appointed by the Settler to guide your footsteps. You must learn restraint—"

Ali moved again, very quickly. The curved dagger in his hand was hilted with silver and pearls, but the blade was layer-forged Sinnar steel, sharp enough to part a drifting silk thread. It sliced more than halfway through the *cadi*'s throat. The old man turned, his blood arching out in a spraying stream of red across the priceless silk of the cushions and the white body of the girl. Ali stood silent, panting, watching the body tumble down the alabaster steps of the gazebo. Then he turned toward the servant, smiling. Blood ran down his mustaches, and speckled his lips.

observe:

Ali sat on the Peacock Throne of the Settlers, in a vaulted room whose ceiling was an intertwining mass of calligraphy picked out in gold, the thousand and one names of Allah, the Merciful, the Lovingkind. From a glass bull's-eye at the apex, light streamed down, mellow and gold, to the tessellated marble floor. Guards stood motionless around the walls of the great circular chamber. Others dragged a man forward; he was stripped to his baggy pantaloons, a hard-muscled man in his thirties with a close-cropped beard and a great beak of a nose.

"Greetings, Akbar my brother," Ali called jovially. "How good, how very good to see your face again!"

The Settler's brother drew himself up and spat on the marbled floor. "You have won, Ali," he said disdainfully. "Yours is the Peacock Throne. Bring out the irons and have done."

"Irons?" Ali said.

That was the traditional punishment for the losers, when a dead Settler's brothers fought for the throne. Only a man complete in his limbs and organs could be Commander of the Faithful; Tewfik was disqualified because he had lost an eye in battle. A red-hot iron fulfilled the same purpose.

"Irons?" Ali said again. "Oh, may Allah requite me if I should put out the eyes of one born of the same seed, of Jamal our father."

Eunuchs brought out a stout iron framework, like a high bedstead with manacles at each corner. Akbar began to bellow and thrash; the guards held him down with remorseless strength while the plump, smooth-faced eunuchs snapped the steel cuffs around wrist and ankle.

"Shaitan will gnaw your soul in hell if you shed a brother's blood!" Akbar yelled.

Ali stood and made a gesture. The guards saluted with fist to brow, and marched out of the great chamber.

"I? Shed your blood? Never, my brother."

Ali stood by the iron rack, stroking his beard. He pulled a handkerchief from one sleeve of his pearl-sewn robe and made as if to wipe his brother's face; when the other man opened his mouth to shout a curse Ali deftly stuffed the length of silk into it.

"There. It is unmannerly to interrupt the Settler. Do you not remember, brother, how you boasted to your captains during our brief, unfortunate civil strife—how you boasted to them that I should be sent into exile on an island in the Zanj Sea with only a mute crone to attend me? That a . . . how did you phrase it? A perverted bastard son of a diseased sheep like me did not deserve the delights of the hareem, and that the pearl-breasted beauties who served me would be shared among your *amirs*."

He clapped his hands. A line of women filed into the throne room, the long robes of their *chadors* brushing the floor and the sleeves hiding their hands.

Ali turned. "Zufika, Aisha," he said. "All of you—hide not the light of your faces."

Obediently, they dropped the filmy black cloaks to the floor. Several of them were carrying long slim knives; two bore a charcoal brazier between them, holding the metal frame with iron tongs. Others set a stool by the iron frame. Ali sank down with a satisfied sigh.

"No, I shall not shed a drop of your blood," he said. "But you surprise me, with this unseemly conduct. Don't you know it is unfitting for an entire male to look on the faces of the Settler's women?"

Zufika came forward, the knife in her hand. "Attend to it, my sweet one."

Through the gag, Akbar began to scream.

"Sovereign Mighty Lord," Raj said quietly.

Silence fell; even Barholm checked himself, dropping the finger he'd been wagging under Chancellor Tzetzas' nose.

"With your permission, lord, I'll take command in the East. Superseding the Commander of Eastern Forces and the garrison commandants."

There were nods all around the table, even from Gharzia. Right now the high command in the east was the sort of honor you took with you to an unmarked grave.

"And I'll take seven thousand cavalry *to* the border."

"Ridiculous—"

"That'll strip the garrisons of—"

"D'you want Ali to march right into East Residence "

Raj raised his hand. "Sovereign Mighty Lord, the troops are on their way to East Residence as we speak. Most of the garrison of the

Western Territories. Veteran fighters, the cream of our armies."

Barholm looked at him narrow-eyed. *And the soldiers most loyal to you.* The thought needed no words.

"That's forty-five hundred men, perhaps a little more. I'll take another two thousand of the Brigaderos prisoners who've been reequipped and organized along Civil Government lines, and some of the battalions who were with me in the Southern Territories campaign and are now attached to the Residence Area command."

Gharzia was scribbling on his pad. *"Heneralissimo—"* he began, giving Raj the title he'd been formally stripped of "—that'll still leave you well below Ali's numbers, discounting his infantry and line-of-communications troops. Shouldn't we pull back more of the Southern and Western Territories garrisons?"

Raj spread his hands. They were brown with sun, battered and nicked and callused from swords and reins, as out of place in this quiet elegant room as the man himself.

"That would take too long. Messers, Sole Autocrat, we don't have the *time.* Please understand, no matter what I do, the border area is going to get the worst working-over it's had in a century or more."

observe, Center said.

—and Colonial dragoons rode through a Borderer hamlet, tossing torches through the windows. Fire belched back, red flames and sooty smoke turning the whitewash black above the openings. Here and there a limestone lintel burned with white-hot fire as it sublimed.

—the last of a line of Arabs picked himself up off a woman and adjusted his robe. She lay motionless in the dust of the street, eyes empty, spittle running down from the corner of her mouth. The Colonial kicked her in the ribs, then called an order to the others. He had the crossed lines of a *naik*, a corporal, on the sleeve of his djellaba. Two of the troopers picked the woman up by the ankles and wrists, grunting at the limp dead weight. The naik jerked a thumb, and they dumped their semi-conscious victim head-first down the well.

—bursting charges spouted plumes of smoke and rock and pulverized dirt across the massive sloping front of the dam. It stretched two hundred meters across a U-shaped valley amid dry rocky hills, a stone-paved road on its top and stone and iron gates at one side where the tumbling water of the flume was channeled into a canal. For long moments nothing seemed to happen, and then water sprouted from the surface where the explosives had been laid. It gouted like erupting geysers, turning to rainbow splendor at the edges under the bright noon light. The sappers whooped and danced as the rushing torrent eroded the earthwork of the dam like a lump of sugar under a spout of hot tea. Then the earth shuddered as the dam collapsed in earnest, and the lake headed downstream in a roaring wall of brown silt and tumbling rocks.

"Yes, yes," Barholm said. The other advisors were silent as the two Descotters met each other's eyes.

"I think I can retrieve the situation," Raj said calmly. "Provided, of course, I have my Governor's full confidence. *Do* I have your confidence, my lord?"

Barholm's lips tightened. "Yes, yes," he said again. He snapped his fingers for a parchment, wrote, signed, extended his hand for the Gubernatorial seal. It thwacked into the purple wax with an angry sound.

He pushed it across the polished flamegrain wood of the table. Raj picked it up. It was a delegation of viceregal power, requiring all officers and officials of the Civil Government to tender him full cooperation—rare for a commander sent out into the *barbaricum*, unheard-of within the borders.

If I smash the Colonials, Raj thought—unlikely as that seemed right now—*that'll be the last strong opponent the Civil Government faces.* He'd reconquered the Southern and Western Territories; the Base Area was far away, and the Zanj states of the Southern Continent even farther. Once the Colony had been beaten back, Barholm Clerett's position would be safer than any Governor's in the past five hundred years. Safe enough that he would certainly no longer need a *heneralissimo supremo.*

"Yes," Barholm repeated. "Who could doubt that you have my *full* confidence?"

Raj stood, bowing and tucking the Gubernatorial Rescript into the sleeve-pocket of his uniform jacket.

"Then if you'll forgive me, Sovereign Mighty Lord, Messers."

His face held an abstracted frown as he left the room, ignoring the murmur behind him. Landing five thousand men and thirty guns, with all their dogs and stores, wasn't easy at the best of times. Getting them straight off the ships and headed east fast without a monumental foul-up would be real work.

disembarkation would be most efficiently achieved as follows, Center began.

CHAPTER FOUR

Corporal Minatelli clattered down the steep wooden steps into the hold of the freighter, his hobnail boots biting into the pinewood. The ship was pitching less now that the sails were furled and the steam tug was bringing it into port.

Minatelli shook his head, still a little bewildered at the sight. He'd grown up in Old Residence, in the Western Territories, and he was familiar enough with fine building. But Old Residence had shrunk steadily since the Brigade conquered it, with forest and groves and nobles' country-seats spreading over the old suburbs. These days it was just a big city.

East Residence was a *world*. It sprawled over the seven hills on all sides of its deep U-shaped harbor: houses and factories, up to the heights where gardens and marble marked the patricians' quarter and the Gubernatorial palaces. A haze of coal-smoke hung over it, a forest of masts and smokestacks darkened the water; squadrons of low-slung steam rams with their paddles churning the water, big-bellied merchantmen with grain from the Diva country of the far north, or ornamental stone and wine from Kelden, whole fleets of barges down from the Hemmar River. And all over the hills, the tracery of gaslight like fairy lights, still bright in the predawn hours.

He hoped he'd have time to see the great Star Temple that

Governor Barholm had built. It was supposed to make the one in Old Residence look like a hut—and now, that seemed possible.

Minatelli's feet and body took him through the crowded hold of the troopship without more than an occasional jostle; after the cleaner air on deck, the stink of it hit him again. His eight-man section was waiting by their gear.

"What's t'word, corp?"

"We're heading east," Minatelli said.

His own Sponglish was fluent now, but it still carried the accent of the Spanjol more common in the Western Territories. He'd been recruited into the 24th Valencia when Messer Raj came to make war against the Brigade; before that his local priest in Old Residence had taught him his letters and numbers, which was one reason he'd made watch-stander and then corporal so fast. Most of the Civil Government's infantry were of peon stock, and almost all illiterate.

He made a quick check of the gear laid out on each of the straw pallets. Waterproof blanket, blanket, long sword-bayonet, cartridge pouches with seventy-five rounds, another fifty in a cardboard box, entrenching spade or short pick, mess tin, canteen, haversack, spare clothing if any, bandage packet, blessed chlorine powder for purifying water, three days' hardtack . . .

The corporal picked up one of the Armory rifles and stuck his thumb into the loop of the lever before the handgrip. A push and the block went *snick*, snapping down at the front so the grooved ramp on top led to the chamber. He peered down the barrel, raising it to the light. *No rust, not too much oil.* He snapped the lever back: *clack*. A pull on the trigger brought a sharp *click* as the pin fell on the empty space where a cartridge would lie in combat.

"Not too bad, Saynchez," Minatelli said. "Awright, git the kit on."

A chorus of grumbles. "Yor all gone soft," he said relentlessly. "Be off yor backsides soon."

He swung his own on. Webbing belt, pouches, shoulder-straps, haversack and bayonet went on like a coat; all you had to do was snap the buckle on the belt. Everything else went into the blanket roll; you rolled that up into a sausage, strapped the roll shut with leather thongs, then bent it into a U-shape and slung it over your left shoulder with the tied-together ends at your right hip. He grunted a little as it settled down, shrugging until it rode properly; you could wear blisters the size of a cup if you didn't adjust it just right.

An officer and bugler came down the main hatchway. The brassy notes of *Full Kit* and *Ready to Move Out* sounded, loud through the dim crowded spaces. The troops erupted in cursing, crowding movement, all but the most experienced veterans—*they'd* gotten ready beforehand. Minatelli grinned at his squad.

"Happy now?"

It was a lot easier to put your gear on when a couple of hundred others weren't trying to do the same, and that in a hold packed with temporary pinewood bunks.

Saynchez snorted. He was a grizzled man in his thirties, one of two in the squad who'd been out east with the 24th the last time. He'd also been up and down the ladder of rank to sergeant and back to private at least twice; it was drink, mostly.

"We goin' east fer garrison, er t'fight?" he asked.

"Messer Raj didn't tell me, t'last time he had me over fer afternoon *kave* n' cakes," Minatelli said dryly.

He wouldn't be looking forward to garrison duty, himself. Some preferred it; in between active campaigns Civil Government infantry were assigned farms from the State's domains, with tenant families to work them. You had to find your own keep from the proceeds, minus stoppages for equipment. Provided your officers were honest—which Major Felasquez was, thank the Spirit—the total came to about the same as active-service cash pay. About what a laborer made, with more security and less work. But it sounded *dull*, especially to a city boy like him, and he hadn't joined up to be bored.

Mind you, some of the fighting in the Western Territories had been more interesting than he really liked. He remembered the long teeth of the Brigade curaissiers' dogs, the lanceheads rippling down, sweat stinging his eyes, and the sun-hot metal of the rifle as he brought it up to aim.

"Word is," he went on, relenting, "that t'wogboys is over the frontier. Messer Raj's bein' set out to put 'em back."

Saynchez shaped a silent whistle. Minatelli looked at him

hopefully; the far eastern frontier with the Colony was only a rumor to him. Saynchez had been with the 24th when Messer Raj whipped the ragheads and killed their king.

"Them's serious business," the older private said. "Them wogs is na no joke."

"Messer Raj done whup 'em before," one of the other soldiers said.

"Serious," Saynchez said softly. "Real serious."

Minatelli slung his rifle. The bugle sounded again: *Fall in.*

A locomotive let out a high shrill scream from its steam whistle. Its two man-high driving wheels spun, throwing twin streams of sparks from the strap-iron rails beneath. The long funnel with its bulbous crown belched steam and black smoke, thick and smelling of burnt tar. Behind it eight iron-and-wood cars lurched against the chain fastenings that bound them together. They were heaped with coal, and heavy. It took more wheel-spinning and lurching halts before the train finally gathered way and rocked southward through the city towards the Hemmar Valley and the long journey east.

Raj's hound Horace snarled slightly at the train. He ran a soothing hand down the beast's neck, clamping his legs slightly around its barrel. Other riders were having more trouble with their animals. Hounds tended to have good nerves; it was one of their strong points. They also tended to do exactly as they pleased whenever they felt like it, but everything was tradeoffs. Horace moved forward at a swinging walk, stepping high over the rails, his plate-sized paws crunching on the cinder and crushed rock of the roadbeds.

More coal trains pulled out, building up the reserves at the stations farther east along the Central Rail; barges lay beside the dock, heaped with the dusty black product of the Coast Range mines. Other trains were making up, of slat-sided boxcars with *40 hombes/8 dawg* freshly stenciled on their sides; forty men, or eight riding dogs. The railyards sprawled along a good part of East Residence's harbor. Barholm Clerett had built more kilometers of line than the previous ten Governors combined; whatever you said of him, he was a builder. Temples, forts, railways—the great Central Line from the capital to

Sandoral completed at last—dams, canals. Much of it financed with the plunder from Raj's campaigns, and dug by captives from them.

It was a mild early-summer day, the sky blue except for a few puffs of high cloud, both moons up—Maxiluna was three-quarters full, Miniluna a narrow crescent. Like the one on the Colony's green banner, the crescent of Islam.

Raj shook his head at the thought. Beyond the moons were the Stars, and the Spirit of Man of the Stars.

Today there were more soldiers than railway men in the marshaling yard. Men heaved rectangular crates onto the bed of a railcar. Each had the Star of the Civil Government stenciled on its side, and *11mm 1000 rnds*. A group of artillerymen—they were stripped to their baggy maroon pants, but those had a crimson stripe down the outside of the leg—was manhandling a field gun onto the flatcar behind, heaving it up a ramp of planks and lashing the tall iron-shod wheels down to eyebolts on the deck. Oilcloth covers were strapped over the muzzle and breech, to keep dust and moisture out of the mechanism. Near-naked slaves with iron collars embossed with *Central Rail* were pulling in handcarts loaded with rations: hardtack, raisins, blocks of goat cheese, sacks of dried meat, barrels of salt fish. A farrier-sergeant of the 5th Descott came by leading a string of riding dogs on a chain lead snapped to their bridles; they surged away in wuffling alarm as a locomotive hooted, and the man clung until his feet were nearly off the ground.

"Pochita! Fequez! Ye bitches brood, quiet a'down, er I'll—*sorry, Messer Raj*—"

"Carry on, sergeant."

"—I'll skin yer lousy hides, *quiet* there."

The giant carnivores calmed, but their ears stayed back, and lips curled away from teeth as long as a man's finger. Few of the beasts had ever seen a steam engine before, much less ridden in a train. For that matter, few of the troopers had either, even the natives of the *Gubernio Civil*; most of them were countrymen, the cavalry from border areas or backwaters like Descott County. What the half-savage westerners he'd brought into the service thought of it, the Spirit only knew.

A platoon of infantry passed him, rifles at their right shoulders and blanket rolls over the left. He read their shoulder-flashes, and gave the officer a salute.

"Glad to have you with me again, 24th Valencia," he said. "That was good work you did at the siege of East Residence, and the pursuit."

The lieutenant at their head snapped out his sword and returned the salute with a flourish. The men raised a deep shout of *Raj! Raj!* Some others picked it up, until he waved them to silence. In the relative quiet that followed, he heard a noncom cursing at a fatigue-party:

"Didn't hear t' General tell ye t'stop workin', did ye? Move yer butts! Put yer *backs* inta it."

What with one thing and another, it's probably for the best there's no time to address the men, he thought mordantly.

A speech from the commander was customary before taking the field, but the last thing he needed right now was the inevitable spies—in East Residence they were even thicker than fleas and almost as common as bureaucrats—giving a lurid description of his troops crying him hail. Far too many Governors had started out as popular generals; bought popularity more often than not, but winning battles would do as well. It made any occupant of the Chair suspicious, and usually more comfortable with mediocrities holding the high military ranks.

He looked around at the bustling yard: chaotic, but things were getting done.

"Good work, Muzzaf," he said to the man riding at his side.

The little Komarite looked up from his clipboard; there were dark circles under his eyes. "A matter of times and distances, *solamnti*," he said. "No different from calculating tonnages or profit margins." He grinned. "A pleasure working for a man who understands numbers, at that, my lord. Too few military nobles do."

Few nobles have Center advising them, Raj thought. Aloud: "I say again, good work."

It was that: a formidable bit of organization. Railways had been around for a long time now, but there had never been enough of them, or enough uninterrupted kilometers of line, to move large forces. He'd had enough to do managing the men; Muzzaf had been invaluable once Raj explained the basic idea. This was going to change warfare forever. Not that the railways were that much faster than dogback yet, but they were untiring—and more importantly, they could carry heavy supplies long distances at the same speed as light cavalry, without draft beasts eating up their loads or dying.

And it never hurt to acknowledge when a man did something right, either. Another thing too many nobles did was simply snap their fingers and expect things to fall into place. It was the engineers and administrators that made the Civil Government more than another feudal pigsty.

Muzzaf grinned. "Half of it was your lady's labors," he said. "Without her keeping the patricians off my back . . ." He shrugged meaningfully.

Raj nodded. Suzette Whitehall had been born in East Residence, to fifteen generations of city nobility. Nobody knew how to work the system better. It was one of her manifold talents. *The wonder is she picked a hill-squireen like me,* he thought with a smile. He'd been nothing in particular then, just another land-poor Descotter nobleman making his way in the professionals like his fathers before him.

And where—

"My lady," he said.

She stood with the command group, but she turned quickly at the sound of his voice. Her smile was slight, but it warmed the slanted gray eyes; Horace crouched, and Raj stepped free of the stirrups and bent over her hand. She was in Court walking-out dress, lace skirt split at the front and pinned back to show embroidered leggings, mantilla, the works. It surprised him; he'd expected her traveling gear. Fatima was beside her, carrying a tray with a bottle of Kelden Sparkler and several long-stemmed glasses, each with half a strawberry on its ice-cooled rim.

He reached out a hand—not for the wine, it was too early for him—but for the fruit. She touched his fingers with her folded fan.

"That's ammunition, my knight," she said.

A party of officials was picking their way through the shouting chaos of soldiers and guns and dogs, heading his way. He recognized the Municipal Prefect of East Residence—the Governors didn't allow the city an *alcalle* of its own, knowing the fickleness of an East Residence mob—and he looked deeply unhappy. Raj braced himself.

"*More* time lost," he growled deep in his throat.

Suzette touched him on the arm. "A minute, darling," she said. "I expected this. That's Rahol Himentez, and he had a mob stone his townhouse when the coal ran out one winter. He's had a bee in his breeches about it ever since."

She swept off towards the dignitaries.

"—winter reserves," Raj could hear the Prefect bleating. "And the enemy's on the *Lower* Drangosh, not the Upper—"

But he stopped, and his flunkies with him, milling around as Suzette's soothing voice cut through the plaintive whine.

Beside him, Gerrin Staenbridge chuckled with admiration. "Cut off by the flying squadron, by the Spirit," he said. "Commandeered my mistress to do it, too."

One of the other officers laughed. "Small loss to you," he said. Staenbridge had an eye for handsome youths.

"Well, she *is* the mother of my heir," he pointed out, and cocked an eye toward the civil servants Suzette had intercepted. They were beginning to move back towards the headquarters building, in a sort of Brownian motion gently shepherded by the women.

Raj nodded curtly. "Right, gentlemen," he said to the circle of battalion commanders; most of them his Companions, all of them veterans. "Now, you've all got your maps?"

They did, although some of the ex-barbarians, Squadrones and Brigaderos, were looking at them a little dubiously. The Civil Government's cartographic service was one of a number of advantages it had had over the Military Governments. Unfortunately, the Colony's mapmakers were just as skillful.

"This campaign," he went on, meeting their eyes, "is what we've been training for these past five years."

"Conquering half the world was a *training exercise*?" Ludwig Bellamy blurted.

Raj nodded, with an expression a stranger might have mistaken for a smile. "No offense, Messers, but we're not fighting barbarians this time. If we hold out a sausage grinder, they're not going to scratch their heads, mutter and then obligingly ram their dicks into it while we turn the crank.

"These are disciplined troops with first-rate equipment, operating closer to their base of supplies than we will be. And they have a first-rate commander; Tewfik ibn'Jamal is nobody's fool. I've fought him twice; lost one, won one—and the time I won, Tewfik had his father Jamal looking over his shoulder and jogging his elbow. Jamal was no commander."

Gerrin nodded. "This time he's got Ali along," he pointed out. His square, handsome face was dark olive, more typical of Descott than Raj's, who had a grandmother from Kelden County in the northwest. "Ali's not only no commander, by all accounts he's a raving bloody lunatic."

"That's our only advantage, and we'll need it. Messers, no mistakes this time. We move fast, and we hit like a hammer. Gerrin, detail two hundred of the 5th to me, and I'll take them ahead on the first train. You'll be rearguard here and come in on the last with the remainder of the battalion."

He held up a hand when the other man began to protest. "I need someone here I can trust to see the plan carried out, Colonel."

"We also serve who only stay and chivvy bureaucrats," Staenbridge said.

"Ludwig," Raj went on. "We're short of rolling stock. I'm giving you the 1st and 2nd Mounted Cruisers" —the former Squadron troops— "and the 3/591, 4/591 and 5/591" —all Brigadcros from the Western Territories— "and you'll follow on dogback. Entrain your baggage, commandeer what remounts you need from the Residence Area pens, and keep to the line of rail. You can pick up supplies at the railstops; nothing on the men but their weapons and personal gear. Understood?"

Ludwig Bellamy slapped one gauntleted fist into the other. "*Ci, mi heneral,*" he said, his Sponglish as pure as a native Civil Government officer; it even had a hint of a Descott Country rasp.

Nobody would mistake him for an Easterner, though. He stood a finger over Raj's 190 centimeters, and the hair cut in an Army bowl crop was yellow-blond. He'd been the son of a Squadron noble, one who surrendered to Raj to keep his lands. Ludwig had been part of the deal, a hostage for his father's good behavior. He was far more than that now. The man beside him was like enough to be his brother, and was his cousin-in-law; Teodore Welf, former second-in-command of the Brigade.

He tapped his fingers on his sword-hilt; unlike his kinsman by marriage, he kept the shoulder-length hair of a Military Government officer, and wore the basket-hilted longsword of the Brigade rather than an Easterner's saber.

"Good thinking, *mi heneral*," he said. "Some of the men . . ." He shrugged at the shrieking locomotives around them. "Well, they're not used to these modern refinements."

"True, Major Welf," Raj said. *Meaning,* he thought, *that steam engines scare them spitless.* They probably thought they were captive demons. "It'll toughen them up, too. See that they get in some drill with their Armory rifles, Ludwig."

Bellamy tossed his chin upward slightly in affirmation; with a slight start, Raj recognized the gesture as one of his own. *How times change.*

"The Brigaderos can use some hard marching," Ludwig Bellamy said judiciously. Welf shrugged unwilling agreement. "They're good shots and good riders, but a bit soft in the arse."

For that matter, there were plenty of officers in the Civil Government's armies who wouldn't dream of campaigning without half a dozen servants and a wagonload of luxuries.

Not the ones who went to war with Raj Whitehall, though.

"So." Raj turned to the other commanders. "Jorg, you and Ferdihando will bring the 17th Kelden Foot and the 24th Valencia on the next series of trains, right after me and my detachment of the 5th."

Jorg Menyez was a slender balding man, with receding brownish hair and mild blue eyes, red-rimmed as usual. He was violently allergic to dogs, the reason he'd gone into the low-prestige infantry service.

"Infantry first?" he said in mild surprise. He'd shown what foot soldiers could do if properly trained and led, but it was still odd.

"I need reliable men in Sandoral right away," Raj said. "Osterville's in charge there. Dogs aren't the most urgent priority, where dealing with Osterville's the problem."

There were a few snickers. Osterville had been sent to take over in the Southern Territories after the reconquest, when Raj was recalled in not-quite-disgrace. The command of the Fortress and District of Sandoral was quite a comedown. None of the officers who'd been with Raj had supported Osterville, for all that he was one of Barholm's Guards; that was one reason he'd lost the political struggle with Mihwel Berg of the Administrative Service. None of it was likely to make him kindly-disposed toward the *Heneralissimo Supremo*.

Menyez sneezed thoughtfully into a handkerchief. "He's supposed to have twenty thousand men there," he said. "I doubt there's half that fit for duty." Osterville would be drawing the pay of the vacant ranks; it was a common enough scam, if not on quite that scale.

"Five thousand if we're lucky, but that's more than enough to make trouble if Osterville's a mind to," Raj said. *Insane to make trouble with the Colonials over the border*, he thought absently—but he'd seen what jealousy could do to a man's mind. "Which is why I want your riflemen in place."

"*Si, mi heneral.*" Menyez frowned. "How *did* Berg manage to get Osterville canned from that post? Berg's not a bad sort, for a pen-pusher, but Osterville was one of Barholm's Guards, after all."

Raj shrugged. "He's pretty sure I did it," he said. "Spirit knows why. In any case, we'll cross Messer Osterville when we come to him. Movement: after Colonel Menyez, the remainder of the cavalry," he went on, listing the battalions. "Any questions?"

Kaltin Gruder, the commander of the 7th Descott Rangers, shrugged his heavy shoulders. Pale scars stood out against the olive tan of his face.

"*No problemo, mi heneral,*" he said. "Thrashing the wogboys has its attractions; the looting's good and I like the smell of harem girls."

Raj clenched his teeth for a moment. There were times when the task of restoring civilization on Bellevue was like pushing a boulder up a greased slope. Gruder was a professional; he wasn't supposed to be thinking like a MilGov barbarian noble or an enlisted man . . . then he caught the grin and answered it.

I talk to Center too much, he thought. *Angels have no sense of humor, it seems.*

The cool irony that touched the back of his mind was wordless, but it communicated none the less.

"Colonel Dinnalsyn, you'll space the guns out between the battalions. One last thing: we've a new issue of splatguns." There were exclamations of delight; the rapid-fire multibarreled guns were the first new weapon the Civil Government had adopted in a hundred twenty years. Raj had had them run up in the Kolobassian armories on his own authority—to Center's designs.

"Four per battalion. Remember they're infantry weapons, not guns; push them forward, and we'll give the Colonials some of the grief their repeaters and pom-poms do to us. If that's all, then, we'll get under way."

The Companions slapped fists in a pyramid of arms. "Hell or plunder, dog-brothers."

Gerrin Staenbridge watched the tall figure of the General ride away. "As I remember it, wasn't Lady Anne Clerett the one who dropped a word about Osterville in our Sovereign Mighty Lord's ear? I wonder who talked to *her*?"

They all looked in Suzette's direction. Staenbridge grinned. "Behind every great man . . ." he quoted.

"You know, Messers," he went on, drawing on his gauntlets, "I was with Messer Raj back when he took command of the 5th in the El Djem business, south of Komar. Only five years . . . and that one man has changed the world—and changed himself."

"Haven't we all," Kaltin Gruder said, touching the long scars on his face. The Colonist shrapnel that had carved those furrows had killed his younger brother, on Raj Whitehall's first independent campaign. "Haven't we all."

CHAPTER FIVE

"Damned hot," Tejan M'Brust said, using an end of his neckerchief to wipe his face.

"No shit," Ludwig Bellamy replied.

He reined aside to the verge of the road, his dog stepping wearily over the ditch and hanging its head, panting, under the shade of a plane tree.

The troopers' dogs were panting too, a massed sound like hundreds of wheezing bellows as they rode by in column of fours. A knee-high fog of dust rose from the crushed rock surface of the road; he sneezed and hawked and spat to one side. The Descotter followed suit and offered him a canteen, water with vinegar. It cut the gummy saliva and dust nicely. Bellamy drank and watched the 1st and 2nd Mounted Cruisers go by, the dogs at a fast ambling walk. Both units were under strength—they'd paid a substantial butcher's bill in the Western Territories and hadn't had time to recruit back to full roster yet—but they shaped well, to his critical eye. A few were even talking or joking as they rode, though most slumped a little, reins in one hand and eyes fixed on the rump of the dog ahead. The unit dressing was crisp, though.

"They're shaping better than the Brigaderos," M'Brust said, echoing his thought. "I don't think there's a regular cavalry unit better, my oath I don't. Not even the 5th Descott."

Ludwig nodded, grinning tiredly. His people, the Squadron, were accounted wilder than the Brigade; they'd come down from the Base Area later, and the Southern Territories they'd conquered had been a backwater. But these battalions had been longer under Messer Raj's discipline and were first-rate material to begin with, once they had childish notions about charging with cold steel knocked out of them.

For a moment the skin between his shoulders crawled, as he remembered the Squadron host advancing into volley-fire and massed artillery. The chanting, the waving banners, the sun bright on a hundred thousand swords . . . and Raj Whitehall waiting, his men a thin blue line looking as fragile and ordered as a snowflake by comparison. Waiting, then raising his sword and chopping it downward. . . .

He shook it off, removed his helmet and let the air dry his sweat-damp hair. To their left the land rose in rocky hills, dry and shimmering with heat in the summer sun. To the right were gentle slopes, citrus orchards, and then open grain-fields with peons bending over their sickles as they reaped. The dusty yellow of the wheat was like flashes of gold through the glossy green leaves of the fruit trees. More to the point, between road and orchards passed a rock-lined irrigation channel, and a slow current of water. It was dry and intensely hot here in the southern foothills of the Oxheads—the land was sloping down toward the sand deserts of the borderlands— and the sight and sound of the water was intoxicating. He squinted at the sun, then remembered to take out his watch and click open the cover; in the Southern Territories, even wealthy nobles hadn't carried them. There was no point; nobody needed to know the time that precisely, and they were impossible to keep repaired, anyway.

Civilization. "Benter," he said to the younger brother who was his aide. "Twenty minutes. Water the dogs."

He turned and heeled his dog westwards down the line of march; behind him the cool brassy notes of the trumpet sounded, and the signalers of each company passed it back. When it reached the rear of the column the last unit halted first—you had to do it that way, or the whole mass would collide with each other, like a drunken centipede. His lips quirked at the memory of his father trying to halt a mass of Squadron warriors on the move, back when he was a boy. *That* had taken the better part of an hour, even with the paid, full-time fighters of the household guard.

The three Cruiser battalions of ex-Brigaderos were full strength . . . except for their stragglers. Teodore Welf rode up, red in the face from the heat and from embarrassment.

"Major Bellamy," he said, saluting.

"Major Welf," Ludwig replied, glancing past him.

They spoke Sponglish, although the Squadron and Brigade dialects of Namerique were fairly close: regulations, and it was best to stay in the habit, since more than half the officers in their units were seconded Civil Government natives like M'Brust.

Men and dogs had collapsed in the road. Others were leading their animals from the wayside to the ditch, walking slowly with their legs straddled. A few had trotted over despite their saddle sores and lay with their heads and shoulders buried in the life-giving coolness. Ludwig frowned and jerked his head toward them.

Teodore cursed and drew his sword, spurring to the ditch. "Up and out of there, you slugs!" he shouted. The flat of the weapon whacked down on shoulders. "Purify it first, damn your arse! You can't fight with the runs!"

The soldiers stood, dripping. Officers rode up, as dust-caked as their men, and the troopers formed lines. Some led the dogs downstream; others scooped their canteens full and added the blessed purifying chlorine powder; it was a rite shared by the Spirit of Man of This Earth cult they followed and the Star Church of the Civil Government, but not all commanders were equally pious. Messer Raj insisted on the full canonical treatment—water for human drinking to be purified by powder or by ten minutes at a hard rolling boil, with no exceptions.

The Spirit favored him for it, too. It wasn't uncommon for armies in the field to lose five men to dysentery for every one killed in combat. That didn't happen to troops under Raj's command.

Welf trotted back. "Sorry, Ludwig," he said. "The Western Territories aren't this hot."

Ludwig nodded. The Western Territories were damned cold and

rainy, to his way of thinking—his own ancestors had plowed through them on their way to the southern side of the Midworld Sea, and he was glad of it. Of course, even the Western Territories were warm and dry compared to the Base Area, which explained why the Brigade had stopped there; they'd been the first of the Military Governments to pull up stakes and move south.

"And your fine gentlemen aren't used to sweating this hard," he replied, smiling to take the sting out of it.

"True enough," Welf said. He flexed the arm that had been broken by a Civil Government bullet outside Old Residence, nearly two years ago. "I'd never have dared drive them this hard, back . . . well, back then."

Ludwig nodded. Even the troopers had been nobles of a sort back home, with a few hundred hectares and peons to do the work. Of course, that had its compensations: plenty of leisure to practice and hunt. So they were fine riders, and mostly good shots. The Brigade had armed its men with muzzle loaders, but rifled percussion muskets, not the flintlock smoothbores that had been the best his people could make or maintain.

"How's my fair cousin?" Teodore went on.

"Marie? Still pregnant, according to the last letter," Ludwig said. "Thank the Spirit. Otherwise she'd be trying to outdo Messa Whitehall and riding with us."

Teodore shuddered elaborately. He turned to watch a dog-cart creak up, loaded with sunstruck Cruisers, their dogs on leading-ropes behind. "Throw some water on those!" he ordered.

Ludwig put his helmet back on. The leather-backed chainmail of the pentail thumped on his neck, and sweat from the sponge-and-cork lining ran into his hair and down his cheeks, greasy and stale.

"I'm beginning to wish we'd taken the train," he said.

"Getting there's half the fun," Teodore replied, blinking red-rimmed blue eyes.

A trainload of artillery began to pull out of the East Residence station, guns and men riding on flatcars, the draft dogs in boxcars farther back from the engine. As soon as it cleared the switchpoint, the remainder of the 5th Descott jogged forward, breaking into platoons as they swarmed into the last two trains.

"Alo sinstra, waymanos!" *By the left, forward march.* Ten minutes, and the final platoon was loaded into its boxcar.

Gerrin Staenbridge looked around. "The last?" he said.

Muzzaf Kerpatik looked just as exhausted as he did. "The very last, *mi colonel*," he said.

Staenbridge ran a hand over his chin, the sword-calluses rasping against the blueblack stubble. "Hard to believe." *Sleep. Razors. Food.* He didn't believe in those anymore, either.

Some sort of Palace flunky-in-uniform was wading toward him over the tracks and the litter of the three-day emergency. They'd been operating in battle mode: throw anything that breaks or isn't needed out of the way and think about cleaning up later. That included a fair bit of broken-down rolling stock, as well as dead dogs, dead draft oxen, about fifty tons of coal that had spilled in odd spots and wasn't worth the time and effort of collecting, and spare gear. Central Rail stevedore-slaves, dockworkers, and press-ganged clerks lay about in various stages of collapse.

But no soldiers. Every man, dog, gun, and round of ammunition was on its way east. *Spirit of man, I could sleep for a week.*

If that flunky meant what he thought it did—another message from some hysterical fool in the Palace who wanted his hand held—he'd be *talking* for a week. The people up on the First Hill hadn't grown any less terrified of Ali over the last couple of days, and they were still given to brainstorms, most of which started and ended with keeping more troops around to protect their own precious personal fundaments. If he'd wanted to listen to bleating, he would have stayed at home on the family estate and herded sheep.

"See you in Sandoral," he said to the little Komarite, and ran for the second train.

It was moving as he clamped his saber hand on an iron bracket and swung up onto the rear platform. This car had been tacked on at the last minute; it was the type used to carry railroad company guards through bandit country, with bunks and a cookstove inside. He'd found it parked on a siding, and be damned if he wasn't going to keep it all to himself; that way he'd stand some chance of getting a little sleep in the fifty hours or so it would take to get to Sandoral. There was some hardtack and dried sausage in his duffel—

The smell of curry startled him as he opened the rear door of the guardcar; his stomach growled a reminder of how long it had been since he ate. Fatima cor Staenbridge—the *cor* meant freedwoman—glanced around from the little stove.

"Ready in a minute, Gerrin," she said.

He opened his mouth to roar, thought better of it, and sat down, sighing and unbuckling his sword belt. *My own damned fault.* He'd rescued the girl during the sack of El Djem more or less on impulse; rather, she'd picked Bartin Foley to rescue her from a gang of Descotter troopers bent on gang rape, and he'd helped out. He'd *kept* her on impulse, too; Bartin had needed some experience with women—a nobleman had to marry and carry on his line eventually, whatever his personal tastes. She'd managed to keep up in the nightmare retreat through the desert, after Tewfik mousetrapped them, which demanded some respect; she'd also gotten pregnant—whether by him or Bartin was a moot point and no matter—which was more than the wife he visited once a year for duty's sake had managed to do.

"Imp," he said.

She stuck out her tongue at him and handed him the plate. *Spirit, she's still only twenty.* He'd freed her, of course, and acknowledged the child—two, now—his wife hadn't objected at all, since by Civil Government law he could divorce her for not giving him an heir. The children had to stay with her back on the estate most of the time after they were weaned, of course, as was fitting.

He began shoveling down the fiery curry, washing it down with water and a surprisingly drinkable red. Drinkable compared to ration issue, that was. *And to think I was accounted a gourmet once,* he thought. Polo, hunting, balls, theater, fine uniforms and parades and good restaurants, handsome youths, witty conversation . . . surprising how little he'd missed them, in the five years since Raj Whitehall had been given command of the 5th Descott and sent out to teach the wogs not to raid the Civil Government borders.

I resented him then, he mused. Gerrin had been senior . . . but he'd needed a commander to bring out his best. A furious perfection of willpower possessed Raj; Gerrin could recognize it without in the least desiring to have it himself. *And it's never been boring.* Back then, he'd been so bored he'd fiddled the battalion accounts out of sheer ennui.

He finished the plate. Fatima was sitting on the edge of the bunk, eyes demurely cast down; a good imitation of humility. *What an actress. The stage lost something when she was born Colonial.* Natural talent, he supposed, plus being hand-in-glove with Suzette Whitehall in her impressionable years.

Gerrin sighed again. As far as he was concerned, sex with women was like eating plain boiled rice without butter or salt—possible, but . . . *On the other hand.* A soldier learned to make do with what was at hand; when all you had was boiled rice, that was what you ate.

The mournful sound of the locomotive whistle echoed through the night. It was evening, and twilight was falling over the rolling hills of the Upper Hemmar River. To their right the last sunlight glittered on the surface of the river below, like a ribbon of hammered silver tracing its way through the darkening fields. The same light caught the three-meter wings of a pterosauroid as it soared over the water, gilding the naked skin and the short plush white fur of its body. Higher, the hills were dusty-green with olive trees, or carpeted with vines in their summer lushness. Terraced fields of barley were brown-gold on the lower slopes; cypresses and eucalyptus lined the dusty white streaks of roadway and surrounded the whitewashed adobe of villas.

Raj looked up from the maps. Center could provide better, holographic projections with all the information you needed, but he'd been raised with paper and it still had something the visions lacked. His father had taught him to read maps, going around Hillchapel— the Whitehall family estate, back in Smythe Parish, Descott County—with compass and the Ordinance Survey, until he learned to see the ground and the markings as one.

"*Sentahvo* for your thoughts, my heart," Suzette said.

She had her *gittar* in her lap, gently plucking at the strings.

"Thinking about Descott, and Hillchapel," Raj said. "Damn, but it's been a long time since we've seen it."

Suzette nodded. She'd fitted in surprisingly well; if she considered it a bleak stone barn in the middle of a wilderness, she'd never said so. Well, compared to East Residence, that was what it was; a kerosene lamp was a luxury, in Descott. Most of the County was upland volcanic wilderness, thin forest and thinner stony pasture where you needed ten hectares to feed a sheep. Bandit country too, and bad for killer sauroids.

He missed it.

"This is as domestic as we get, I'm afraid," Suzette said lightly.

Raj glanced around the railroad car. It had been fitted with table and chairs; there was a commode behind a blanket screen, a couple of skins of wine-and-water hanging from the wall, a lantern overhead, and a box of field rations—Suzette's version, and a vast improvement on Army issue. One of his aides was snoring on the floor.

In a car behind, the troopers were singing—they probably thought of it as singing, at least—in a roaring chorus:

> *"We're marchin' on relief over burnin' desert sands*
> *Six hundred fightin' Descotters, t' Colonel, an' t'band*
> *Ho! Git awa', ye bullock-man—ye've heard t'bugle blowed*
> *The Fightin' Fifth is comin', down the Drangosh Road—"*

"We're luckier than they are," Suzette said, lifting her head and looking off into the gathering night. "We're together, at least. . . . Their women have to sit and wonder. And every time someone rides up to the farmhouse door it might be a messenger with a bundled rifle and saber that's all they'll see of a lost husband, or a son."

"It's not much of a married life I've given you," Raj said.

Suzette smiled at him. "I wouldn't exchange it for any other," she replied. "I don't think you're one of those who're allowed to have a normal life, anyway."

"Not yet, at least," Raj said. *Never,* went unspoken between them.

It wasn't as if Barholm would give Raj an honored retirement, even, as a reward for victory.

i have found it unwise to use the term never, Center said.

Suzette's fingers strummed the *gittar* again. Raj pulled the greatcoat around his shoulders and let his head fall back. *Just a moment,* he thought. *A moment's rest.*

"*Git* yer arses out offen t'floor," the sergeant barked. "We'll be there anytimes."

Corporal Robbi M'Telgez blinked awake.

"Jist when I waz gittin' t'hang a sleepin' on these things," he said mournfully, picking straw out of his hair and yawning in the hot close darkness of the boxcar, thick with the smell of sweat.

The train was slowing, swaying more from side to side. All around was the flat irrigated plain of the Upper Drangosh. M'Telgez put his eye to the slats in the boxcar; it was good-looking country, dry but fit to sprout shoelaces where there was water. The wheat and barley were in, the fields being plowed for a summer crop of corn or millet; cotton and sugarcane and indigo were all well up, and there were orchards in plenty as well, mostly dates and citrus.

Good land fer the gentry, hell on farmers, he thought idly. Rich land meant poor men to work it; they'd all be peons around here. *Hotter n' blazes, too.*

They passed through a belt of country places, retreats for rich cityfolk built in an open, airy style that looked indecent somehow compared with the foursquare solidity of the houses he was accustomed to—but then, Descott was a long way north of this, and highland country too. He didn't suppose it got cold here even in winter. Then there were shanties on both sides of the rail line, crude booths of straw and reeds. He swore softly when he saw who was in them, besides refugee peasants from the countryside. Among them were men in Civil Government uniforms, only infantry, but still . . . they looked *hungry.*

"Ain't they supposed to pay 'em when they calls 'em in from t'farms?" he said.

The troop sergeant laughed sourly. "Wuz ye born yesstiday, M'Telgez?"

Trooper Smeet put his eye to a crack. "Good's a place t' croak as any," he said mournfully. "We'll a' git kilt, ye know. I hadda dream—"

The rest of the platoon threw bits of hardtack and cold bacon-rind and anything else handy.

"Ye keep sayin' thayt long 'nuff, it'll happen, yer bastid," M'Telgez said disgustedly.

Smeet grinned; he was missing his two front teeth, and his face was a brown wrinkled map of twenty years' service. "Ye knows a way 't live ferever, loik?"

Just inside the city walls the train screeched to a stop; he braced himself against the planking and shaded his eyes as the doors were thrown open.

"*Come* on," the sergeant yelled again.

The boxcars emptied rapidly, the men stretching, the dogs barking with hysterical relief. It was just as hot outside, with the dry baking heat that he remembered from the first campaign down here five years ago, but at least you could breathe in the open. M'Telgez unsnapped the lead-chain of his mount and spent a moment soothing her.

"Sooo, quiet now, Pochita, ye bitch," he said. A tongue the size of a washcloth and rough as industrial abrasive lapped at his face. "Quiet—down, girl."

Out of the corner of his eye he could see Messer Raj and the company commander and the captain in charge of the Scouts—M'lewis and his Forty Thieves were along, best to double-strap your pouch—talking earnestly. He worked faster, sliding his rifle into the scabbard at the right front of his saddle, tightening the girth and breast-straps, checking the neck-bandolier and the fastening on the saber hanging from the other side. He slid the blade free a handspan and tested the edge, then checked the loads on the revolver he had tucked into one boot-top.

Messer Raj would have a job of work for them to do, and no mistake. He'd been in the 5th Descott for five years now, and that was one thing you could rely on.

"Nice to be loved," Bartin Foley said.

"Not when they get in the way," Raj replied.

They rode at the head of the column, slowly. Cheering civilians packed the sidewalks, hysteria in their voices. Rose petals and rice showered down on the troops, as if they were a party of groomsmen bringing a bride home from her father's house. Individuals darted out to offer bottles of wine to the soldiers or, even more dangerous, food to the dogs. *What do they think's going to happen when they stick a roast in a war-dog's face?* Raj thought, turning in the saddle to see one of the crowd reeling back and clutching a gashed-open forearm. The crowd-stink was as palpable as the blurring waves of heat that radiated back from the whitewashed adobe of the buildings and soaked the uniform coat beneath his armpits.

The noise was spooking *all* the dogs, a solid roar between the whitewashed, blank-walled, flat-roofed houses.

"Trumpeter!" Raj snarled. "Sound *Draw*."

The sharp notes cut through the white-noise background of the crowd, as they were designed to cut through the clamor of battle. Two hundred hands slapped down on the saber hilts slung to the offside of their saddles; two hundred blades came free in a single slithering rasp, then flashed as they were brought back to rest over the shoulder. The dogs knew the calls as well as the men, and they snarled in unison, a chilling bass rumble. Long wet fangs glistened, each backed by half a ton of carnivore. War-dogs were bred for aggressiveness and trained to kill, and the bristling snake-headed posture of these indicated they were perfectly ready to do just that.

The crowd screamed and surged away; there would be deaths in the trampling . . . but not nearly as many as there would be if Ali sacked the city, which was what was going to happen if they kept getting in his way. Overhead, doors slammed shut as the wrought-iron balconies emptied. Raj heeled Horace into a trot; the bugler signaled again, and the whole column rocked into motion behind him. The iron wheels of the splatgun battery clattered behind them.

"Well, that'll make us less popular, *mi heneral*," Bartin said.

"Popularity be damned," Raj replied, feeling some of the tension drain out of his shoulders.

They broke into the *Plaza Real*, the square that formed the center of all Civil Government cities. The usual buildings fronted it: the Star Temple with its gilded dome, the arcaded Government House, the townhouses of wealthy landowners and merchants . . . and the cavalry barracks, conveniently to hand in case of trouble. Highly unusual were the tents and shanties that had gone up all over the square, crowding right up to the ornamental fountain and gardens in its center; the sour smoke of their cooking fires lingered, and the stink of an overloaded sewer system.

"Refugees," Raj said grimly. "Must be fifty or sixty thousand of them inside the walls."

"Sandoral has fifty thousand people in normal times," Suzette said. "With that many more . . ."

Raj nodded. "We'll definitely have to do something about that."

They drew rein before the barracks, a series of two-story buildings connected by walls and iron-grille gates, enclosing a central parade ground. They smelled even worse than the rest of the city, not just the inevitable aroma of dogshit that was inescapable where cavalry were stationed, but the fetid stink of overcrowding and neglect. They *looked* neglected—gates awry, stucco flaking in damp patches from the walls. But with the units as under strength as his intelligence had it, they shouldn't be crowded—and washing was hanging from the windows, women and children too numerous for camp followers leaning out and pointing, or lounging in the doorways.

"Captain Foley," Raj said. "Dismount the men, rifles, and a watchstander and troop here. Then accompany me, if you please."

The bugle sang. The men sheathed their sabers and pulled the Armory rifles out of the scabbards. Another call, and the dogs sank to a crouch; the men stepped free of the stirrups and bent to loop their reins over the hitching rail and watering trough that lined the plaza side of the garrison buildings. A long clicking sounded as they loaded their weapons; the 5th Descott didn't carry guns for show, and when they made a threat they meant it.

An officer came out of the main gate, fastening his sword belt. Raj ran an eye over him: thirty or so, but with an older man's belly straining against the sash and belt, unshaven, the blue uniform coat stained under the armpits. He didn't expect soldiers to waste time trying to look strack in the field, but in garrison keeping neat reminded them that they *were* soldiers; it was a sign of self-respect. They had running water here, for the Spirit's sake! And every eight-man section of cavalry troopers was allowed one soldier's servant to handle routine fatigues.

Also an officer should set an example.

Just about what I expected, in short, Raj thought, a cold anger tightening its hand under his breastbone. He returned the stranger's salute.

"Captain Hamelio Pinochet, 47th Santanner Dragoons," the man said.

"*Heneralissimo* Raj Whitehall," Raj replied. "I'm here to take command, Captain."

The unfortunate officer swallowed, attempting to brace to attention. "Ah, *mi heneral,* you'll understand, with the emergency and the refugees—"

"I understand perfectly, Captain." With housing at a premium, somebody had seen the profit potential in renting out the military's spare space. "Lead on."

Milling civilians looked at them curiously as they walked through the long barracks halls; each had space for a hundred men's cots, with rooms for the lieutenants and a suite for the company commander, plus a ready room and mess. Right now they were crowded with twice that number or more of refugees; from their clothes, well enough off to be making a fortune for whoever was running this scam. A swelling murmur ran through them as Raj passed. By the time they reached the buildings still in military use, it had preceded them a little; enough for protesting feminine squeals to be fading as women were hustled out of the barracks, and for the soldiers to have made emergency repairs. Not *much* in the way of repairs. Gear was piled in heaps all over the floors, few of the men were in full uniform, and there were still cards and dice lying in some corners. The troopers stood braced at the foot of their cots, visibly willing their vital functions to cease.

Raj ignored them for a moment. Instead he stripped a rifle out of the rack by the locker at the head of a cot and worked the action. "No rust here, at least," he said mildly. Then:

"Captain Pinochet, how many men are on muster here? You're rated at four battalions." Twenty-four hundred men or so, in theory.

"Ah . . . about one thousand, sir. Most of the officers aren't, ah . . ."

"Present at the moment, yes," Raj said. "Fall the men in, if you please, Captain."

Raj crossed his arms and waited while the bugles rang. It took a very long time for the garrison troops to sort out their equipment. *Starless Dark knows what shape the infantry's in,* he thought with a mental wince. This was the elite cavalry.

"Ten'*hut.*"

The noncom's bark brought the men to a ragged attention as Raj strode out; the banner of the 5th Descott was at his back, and his personal blazon. The two companies of the 5th tramped out at the double, and fell in at his back with the smooth economy of endless practice, the uniform crash of their hobnails sounding across the drillground and echoing back from the barracks and stables that ringed it.

Raj waited for a minute. "Men," he said at last, "I'm going to keep this short and sweet."

He pointed over his shoulder. "There's a bloody great wog army coming up the Drangosh; they're about five days' march that way. I've got troops coming in from the west, but we're going to need every man who can ride and shoot. That means *you.* Every soldier, that is. I'll be back in a few hours, and I expect to see you looking and acting like soldiers by then." He paused again.

"Captain Pinochet, please send runners to the remaining battalion officers of this command. You may inform them that any man holding the Governor's commission not present when I return may consider himself dismissed from the service." He turned his head to the bugler. "Sound *dismissed to quarters.*"

The garrison left much more quickly than they'd assembled. Raj nodded once, tapping a thumb against his chin. "I think they're getting the message," he said. "Now for Osterville."

Antin M'lewis was muttering under his breath. Raj knew the

song without needing to hear words or tunes: it was an old Army ditty whose chorus went *Lovely loot/That's the thing makes the boys git up an' shoot!*

Commandant Osterville's house was a looter's dream. The outer gates were gilded wrought iron, the inner Zanj ebony studded with miniature silver sauroid heads. A chandelier of Kolobassian crystal hung overhead, to light the three-story atrium. Floor and sweeping staircases were of marble; the walls held gilt-framed mirrors and paintings; man-high alabaster urns held trailing bougainvillea . . . Punkahs swayed, moving air cooled by fountains playing over fretted stone and scented by orange-blossom.

The majordomo bowed himself out of the way—a plump eunuch with a Colonial accent. *Poor bastard can't help it,* Raj thought; but they always put his teeth on edge. Osterville had put on weight and lost a lot of hair since Raj had seen him last. He'd always been ambitious, and Capital-smooth; now he had a sour pinch to his mouth and lines between there and his nostrils. Which were turned up as if at a bad smell. There was a crowd of hangers-on by him, aides and flunkies and the battalion commanders of the garrison.

"Whitehall," Osterville said frigidly. "What the devil do you think you're doing, coming in here and giving orders outside the chain of command?"

There was a murmur of indignation from the flunkies; but the battalion commanders stayed stony-silent, with a slight unconscious withdrawal, as if Osterville had something contagious. Raj gave them a swift glance. None of them had been living on their pay here—not with Osterville's example before them, not if Abdullah's reports were true—but they didn't love the Commandant for it. Especially not now that their careers and lives were on the line.

Raj reached into his jacket. "Commandant Osterville. By Gubernatorial Rescript, I have been given command of all Civil Government troops in this area. I hereby notify you that I am assuming control."

Osterville read through the note. "I acknowledge your overall authority," he said after a moment.

Raj could see the wheels turning behind the narrow black eyes. *Whitehall's in disfavor. Even if he wins, he'll be removed.*

"But this document does *not* give you authority to interfere in the internal command structure of the units under my authority as district commandant. You may give your orders to me, and I will carry them out as I see fit."

Divided command . . . Behind Raj, the Scout Troop—the Forty Thieves—tensed; they hadn't followed the exchange, not really, but they could read the hostility in the air well enough.

M'lewis had recruited the Scouts himself. None of them were men likely to hesitate if ordered to arrest the Commandant . . . or to take him and the others out back and shoot them, if it came to that. Osterville looked past Raj and his complexion turned a muddy gray.

Disaster, Raj knew. A good chance of a firefight right here in the city, or at least wholesale passive resistance by the garrison troops. This mission balanced on a knife edge as it was . . .

. . . and Osterville wouldn't back down. Not openly; whatever else the man was, he wasn't that type of coward.

Suzette moved forward. "Hernan, Hernan," she said, tapping him on the arm with her fan. "Last time I was in Sandoral there were more interesting things than a lot of smelly soldiers." She wrinkled her nose. "Don't tell me you've become a *complete* provincial out here, my dear. And you were such a gay blade back in the City." When someone in the Civil Government put a capital on it that way, only one city could be meant.

Osterville bowed over her hand.

"*I've* been trapped on a troop train for three days. Couldn't you find a decent meal for a poor, benighted gentlewoman so far from home? And fill me in on what passes for society out here? *And* find me a decent bath and somewhere to change out of these *impossible* clothes?"

Osterville was giving a good impression of a man who had just been struck between the eyes with a bag full of wet sand, but he rallied; after all, he *had* been at Court for the better part of a decade.

"Enchanted, Messa," he said suavely. "Business, however . . ."

Suzette made a dismissive gesture. "Oh, Raj just wants some help unloading trains." She tucked her hand under his arm. "Please?"

Osterville snapped his fingers at an aide. "Luiz, draw that up; here, I'll sign it. Certainly, certainly, my dear Messa Suzette . . . trains, you say? Logistics, clerks' work."

Raj stood silently as they strolled away across the intaglio floor. His head moved back to the officers who'd been attending Osterville, with the smooth tracking motion of a track-mounted fortress gun.

"Messers," he said flatly. "I remind you that you'll be needed with your units later this afternoon in the main cavalry barracks. Good day to you. Captain M'lewis, if you please."

He turned on his heel. Faintly, he could hear:

". . . quite acceptable dessert wines, but far too sweet for table. But I've found a mountain vintage from this village in the Oxheads . . ."

CHAPTER SIX

The City Offices of Sandoral were nearly as crowded as the barracks, although they smelled of musty paper and lamp-soot and ink rather than sewage and dogshit. Clerks in knee breeches and dirty ruffled shirts were running in all directions, waving papers in the air; abacuses clicked; wheeled carts full of folders of documents rumbled over the tiled floors of the corridors. There were petitioners in plenty about, too. The clamor died as Raj shouldered through; the forty troopers of the 5th tramping behind him with their rifles at port, bayonets fixed, were a stark reminder of why Sandoral was in an emergency in the first place.

Raj strongly suspected that most of the bureaucrats would continue to think of it as a tiresome interruption of routine right up until the Settler's troops came over the wall.

Civilization, he thought sourly, watching one man blink at him through thick lenses, fingers pausing on the counting stones. *The sacred trust I defend. The reason I obey purblind idiots.*

They clattered up a broad stairway; the upper corridor was considerably less crowded, a condition enforced by several slope-browed men with cudgels. All of whom sensibly faded into doorways at the sight of the naked steel and harsh uniform clatter of hobnails.

"You can't go in there! That's Chief Commissioner Kirmedez's—"

"Siddown," M'lewis snarled at the functionary. The man sat.

Kirmedez looked up from his desk as Raj entered. He was a thin dark man with receding hair, dressed plainly with a simple cravat. His eyes widened slightly as he took in Raj and the soldiers behind him; he rose and bowed.

"*Heneralissimo,*" he said politely. "How may I serve you?"

Raj took the measure of the man. *Honest,* he thought, *for a wonder.*

oversimplification, Center said, **but a valid approximation.** A grid snapped onto the administrator's face, with mottled patterns showing heat and the dilation of his pupils. **proceed.**

It was impossible to lie to Raj Whitehall . . . with an angel looking out through his eyes. He didn't like it, but it was useful, and he'd use any tool to get the job done.

Anything at all.

"Messer Kirmedez," Raj said, "Sandoral will be under siege by the Colonials within two weeks maximum. Possibly less."

Kirmedez sat and tapped the piles of documents on his desk. "*Heneralissimo*, this city cannot stand siege. We're grossly over-crowded, and the grain reserves are low."

Raj nodded. By law, a fortified border town like this was supposed to keep a year's reserve of basic foodstuffs, in return for remission of some taxes. He didn't need to ask what had happened to it.

"Exactly, Messer. I'm therefore evacuating all civilians to East Residence."

Kirmedez's hard thin face went fluid with shock for an instant. "That's impossible."

Raj allowed himself a flat smile. "On the contrary. Anyone who leaves on their own feet—or on dogback or in a carriage or by ox wagon—can take whatever they wish to carry. But whenever a troop train gets in, and I expect them at four-hour intervals, the garrison is going to sweep up enough people to fill it for the return trip. There will be absolutely no exceptions. Messer Commissioner, you'd also better inform the citizens immediately, because the first twelve hundred will be leaving in about two hours on the train that brought me. Is that understood?"

Kirmedez closed his mouth. He stared at Raj for a full thirty seconds, then looked at the feral faces of the Descotter gunmen behind him.

"You mean it," he said softly.

"I'm not in the habit of making empty threats, Messer," Raj said, equally quiet.

Kirmedez nodded.

The door was open, and the word had spread swiftly. A roar sounded through the offices, shading up into a hysterical wail. Kirmedez rose and reached for a brass bell on his desk, but Raj put out one hand.

"Captain," he said to M'lewis.

The Scout commander turned and barked an order. The column in the corridor outside turned and brought their rifles up in a single smooth jerk.

"*Fwego!*"

BAM. The volley slammed into the lath and plaster of the ceiling. Chunks and dust rained down on the faces of those who'd come out of their offices, and down the open stairwell onto the crowd below.

"Reload!"

Silence fell amid the *ping* of spent brass landing on the tiles and the metallic clatter of rounds being thumbed home and levers worked. Gray-white gunsmoke drifted down the hall and carried the stink of burnt sulfur.

Silence fell. Kirmedez's bell sounded through it. "Back to work, if you please," he called. "Messer Hantonio, step in here. We have a great deal to do."

He nodded thanks to Raj. "And they'll take it seriously, too. Good day to you, *Heneralissimo*."

Raj raised an eyebrow; it wasn't often you met an administrator with that firm a grip on reality.

"*Bwenya Dai,*" he replied politely.

And the bureaucrat was right. There was a great deal to do, fortunately. You could forget a lot, when you had work on hand.

(o·o) (o·o) (o·o)

Chief Commissioner Kirmedez snapped his fingers impatiently. "Stop babbling, man!" His assistant fell silent.

"It doesn't *matter* if it's impossible; it has to be done anyway. Now, send out the criers. But first, send runners to all the following households."

He handed over a list. The assistant whistled. "My apologies, *patron*," he said. "I should have thought of that."

Kirmedez nodded. "Hantonio, when this war is over, I will still be Chief Commissioner of Sandoral and District, whoever is Commandant. Those men will still be wealthy and powerful. And they will remember who gave them advanced warning to gather their personal possessions and their households for evacuation."

The assistant smiled with genuine admiration.

Kirmedez smiled back. "Favors are the grease that let the civil service wheels turn, Hantonio. Never forget it."

And Heneralissimo Supremo Whitehall has done me a favor, he thought, pausing briefly. I wonder if he realizes it?

"Jorg!" Raj called, pleasure in his voice.

Jorg Menyez pulled up his riding steer. It lowed, then swung a long brass-tipped horn down in Horace's face. The hound whuffled and reconsidered the grab it had been thinking of making at the long-legged riding animal's shank.

"Just in," the infantry commander said.

Behind him a column of footsoldiers poured down the street, shouldering the milling civilians aside; this time they were trying their best to get out of the way, not blocking the road with their welcome. The furled colors of the 17th Kelden Foot went by, to the steady *thrip . . . thrip* of the drum.

"The heliograph says Gerrin just boarded the last train out of East Residence, and Bellamy and his trained barbs are making good time, should be here in three days maximum."

"Spirit," Raj said, mildly surprised. "It's actually working."

Both men spat to their left and made the sign of the horns with their sword-hands; Raj touched his amulet, a circuit board blessed by Saint Wu herself a century before.

"You've seen where the infantry are kenneled?" Jorg said, anger flushing his fair-skinned face.

Raj nodded. "Think they'll be fit for anything?"

"Nothing complex, but we may be able to put some backbone into them," Jorg said. "They ought to enjoy the first part of the plan, anyway. Any trouble with Osterville?"

"No," Raj said.

Menyez hesitated, then let the bitten-off syllable stand.

The barracks-yard was far more crowded this time; all the cavalry, the ragged ill-kept lines of the infantry units, the two hundred of the 5th Descott beside Raj, and the neat formations of the 17th Kelden and 24th Valencia to either side. The sun was sinking behind the western edge of the barracks; Raj narrowed his eyes against it, seeing only the black silhouettes of the troops.

"Fellow soldiers," Raj said.

Of a sort. It wasn't these men's fault that they'd been badly commanded, but he didn't intend to let the consequences keep him from carrying out the mission. A lot of them were going to pay with their lives for their officers' slackness, before this was over.

"We've very little time. The 33rd Drangosh, the 12th Pardizia" — he listed the infantry battalions, about half the two thousand available— "will turn to and begin construction of the necessary boats and gear for a pontoon bridge to cross the Drangosh and carry our invasion force. This task will be performed under the direction of Colonel Dinnalsyn of the Artillery Corps."

A long murmur swept through the packed garrison formations. Raj stood like an iron idol, hands clasped behind his back, while the shouts of *Silence in the ranks!* controlled it. None of his veterans had moved; probably because none of them were surprised at what he intended.

"The cavalry formations based in Sandoral will immediately assume control of the gates. Only military personnel will be allowed to enter the city or approach on the main roads.

"The remainder of the infantry will begin clearing Sandoral and evacuating the civilian population to the railroad station, commencing immediately. No resistance is to be tolerated. All units will be accompanied by parties of the 5th Descott, the 17th Kelden, or the 24th Valencia.

"I'm aware that you men of the district infantry battalions have been seriously neglected. Effective immediately, all arrears of equipment, rations, and pay will be made up from the stocks in the city's treasury and arsenals. For the duration, you will be quartered inside the walls—to be precise, in the housing of the evacuated civilians."

Stunned silence sank over the parade ground. The formations rippled slightly as men turned to one another, then back to the figure standing on the stone dais. A helmet went up on a rifle among the infantry, and a voice cried out:

"Spirit bless Messer Raj!"

"Raj!"

"*Raj!*"

"*RAJ! RAJ!*"

He let it continue and build for a moment, judging, waiting until they were about to break ranks and crowd around him. A raised hand brought the sound back down from its white-noise roar, like receding surf on a beach.

"Cheer after we've beaten the wogs back to their kennels," he said. "Until then, we've a man's job of work to do. See to it."

"*RAJ! RAJ! RAJ! RAJ!*"

Corporal Minatelli turned back down the street. "*What's* the problem now?" he barked.

"Theynz warn't open up," the garrison soldier said timidly in a thick yokel burr. "They wouldn' give us no food either, when we wuz hongry. Turned us'n away frum d'doors."

Minatelli sighed. *Raggedy-ass excuse for a soldier*, he thought disgustedly. Literally; the man's buttocks were hanging out a great rent in his trousers, and the blue of his jacket was faded to sauroid's-egg color. He had a beard, too, like a barb or a wog.

"*Here's* how ye do it, dickhead. Y'ain't askin' 'em to dance, see?"

He stepped to one side and put the muzzle of his rifle against the lock. *Bam*, and bits of lead and metal pinged and whistled across the street. The ragged soldier yelped as one scored a line of red across the side of his face. Minatelli slammed the sole of his boot into the door beside the lock, and the wood boomed open against the hallway.

"What's the meaning of this?" shouted the man inside. "It's impossible—you peon scum, where's your officer? I'll have you flogged, *flogged*—"

Smack. The side of Minatelli's rifle-butt punched into the man's face. Blood spattered down the lace sabot of his shirt. The soldier chopped the butt up under the man's short ribs, and he folded over without a sound. Minatelli grabbed him by the collar and threw him out into the street.

"Anyone what ain't out in ten, gits shot!" he shouted to the crowd of family and servants. "Out, out, *out*. T'wogs is comin'!"

A torrent of civilians poured out of the townhouse door. Minatelli grinned to himself; a couple of them trampled on the head of the household before two with more presence of mind or family affection picked him up and carried him out into the crowded darkness of the street. The gas lamps were on, but the reddish light only made the milling crowd seem less human, a gleam of eyes and teeth and wailing voices in the hot night. Both sides of the street were lined with troopers, their fixed bayonets a bright line containing the shapeless movements of the crowd. Occasionally one would jab at someone who crowded too close, and a scream of pain would rise above the hubbub of confusion, fear and anger.

Minatelli's grin grew broader. Back in Old Residence, he'd been a stonecutter like his father and grandfather before him. They'd have sent him around to the servants' entrance if he so much as called on a house like this. Now he got to buttstroke one of the breed of stuck-up *riche hombes* bastards. Military service definitely had its good points.

The garrison soldier gaped at him for a slow twenty seconds. Then his crooked brown teeth showed in an answering smile. The glitter in his eyes was alarming.

"Sor!" he said, saluting smartly. Then, to his squadmates: "C'mon, boyos!"

Their boots and rifle-butts thundered on the next door down. Minatelli reloaded, slung his rifle and turned to Saynchez.

"How many, d'ye think?"

"Mebbe six, seven hundert," the older private said. "No different n'countin' sheep, a-back on me da's place. Me da ran sheep fer the squire."

"*Banged* the sheep, more like," one of their squad said, sotto voce.

"Wouldn't mind bangin' this one," another added. A feminine squeal came from the darkness.

"No fuckin' around!" Minatelli said sharply. "That's enough— move this bunch down to t'train station. *Hadelande!*"

"Tight! Get those boards *tight* before you nail them to the stringers!" Grammeck Dinnalsyn said, for the four hundredth time.

The infantryman gaped at him, then obligingly whacked at the edge of the board with his mallet. The dry wood splintered. Dinnalsyn winced, then skipped aside to let a dozen men go by with a beam. One of his officers followed, drawing lines on the timber with a piece of chalk and consulting a crumpled piece of paper in the other. A noncom stumbled after him, holding up a hurricane lantern. Both moons were up, luckily, and there were bonfires of scrap lumber scattered along the broad stretch of riverside as well. Wagons rumbled in with more wood; wheelbarrels went by loaded with mallets, nails, rope, and saws.

"Cut here, here and *here*," the young lieutenant said, giving a final slash with the chalk. Crews sprang to work with two-man drag saws.

The first pontoon was already ready to launch down by the river's edge, a simple breast-high wooden box of planks on rough-cut stringers, eight meters by twelve. The stink of hot asphalt surrounded it, as sweating near-naked soldiers slathered liquid black tar from pots onto the boards.

Dinnalsyn pulled out his slide rule. Si. Now, the river's nine hundred meters; make it eight meters per barge, allow a reserve of ten percent, and—

A dog pulled up beside him with a spurt of gravel. He looked up and pulled himself erect. *"Mi heneral,"* he said.

Raj nodded, his eyes light gray in the shadows under his helmet brim. "How's it coming, Grammeck?"

"On schedule, more or less."

"Will they float?"

"After a fashion, if we use enough tar and the wood swells tight. I'm going to float them as we finish them, that'll give the timber some time to soak."

"Good man," Raj said. "While you're at it, have your people run up steering oars and paddles. We'll put some of the garrison infantry to practicing maneuvering, that'll be important later. Here in the Drangosh valley, quite a few of them were probably riverboatmen before the press gang came through."

"Si, mi heneral. The Forty Thieves aren't with you?"

Raj was riding alone, save for his personal bannermen, buglers, and galloper-messengers. He nodded.

"Too much temptation in the city, under the circumstances. They're out living up to their *official* designation. M'lewis will get it done; he's a soldier, in his fashion." Raj turned in the saddle to watch the first pontoon boat being manhandled into the water. It splashed into the Drangosh and bobbed, riding unevenly. "They'll be enough?"

"Mi heneral, consider it done. I can finish the rest in time, if I get enough of the raw materials."

Raj's teeth showed slightly. "Oh, that ought not to be a problem. Poplanich's Own just detrained, they're out helping the 5th get the timber in, and we're moving quickly."

He paused. "One more thing; send out some of your people, use the garrison if you must, and confiscate every boat you can find; every fishing smack, barge, canoe, whatever. Not just here, in the suburbs and every section of the valley we can still reach."

"And *back*, ye bitches' brood."

The civilians still crowding the street wailed and stampeded; which was just fine as far as Robbi M'Telgez was concerned. Handling a lariat and a dog was second nature—his family were *rancheros*, yeoman tenants who herded on shares back in Descott—but this was tricky. One end of the braided leather rope was snubbed to the second-story end of a roof beam; the other was wrapped three times around the pommel of his saddle. Pochita sank down on her haunches and backed one tiny step at a time, and he could feel the thousand-pound body arching like a bow between his thighs. The rest of his platoon were doing likewise, one or two dogs to every rafter. The animals were used to working in unison, and they snarled beneath their panting as they hauled.

The adobe wall smoked dust for an instant and then collapsed towards them. Released from the pull, Pochita skipped back nimbly until her hindquarters touched the house on the other side of the irregular little plaza. M'Telgez coughed through the checked bandanna over his face; his dog sneezed massively and shook her head, the cheek-levers of the bridle rattling. *Got t'check 'em,* he thought. *They should be snug, not loose.*

Foot soldiers waded forward into the dust, rummaging for the planks and beams. They'd done the same thing here in Sandoral for material to build earthwork forts, in the last campaign against the wogs a few years ago; now they were tearing down rebuilt houses to make boats.

Always something new with Messer Raj.

Antin M'lewis sank closer to the earth, hugging it for shelter and trying to *think* dark like the moonless night. It was homelike, in an unpleasant sort of way; as a rustler by hereditary profession, he'd spent enough time like this back home working his way in past the *vakaros* pulling night guard on some unsuspecting squire's herds. Darkness, the dogs belly-down too in a gully a few hundred meters back, his face blacked with lamp soot or burnt cork. The wind moving into his face, so no scent went to the target or his dogs—infantry ahead here, but why take a chance, and there might be a mounted officer. Just like home.

Descott was rarely this hot, though. And most Descotter *vakaros* would be more alert than the wog ahead of him.

He eeled forward on his belly, moving every time the Colonial sentry's pacing turned him back toward this angle of approach. Useless sentry, the bugger was smoking a pipe and M'lewis could see the ember light with every draw, even smell the strong tobacco. Backlit by a watch-fire too, which must be playing hell with his night-vision.

Mother. The wog had stopped, and his spiked helmet was turning as he looked outward. He hesitated, almost taking the carbine from over his shoulder, then resumed his steady pacing. *Mother. Spirit.*

Forward another five meters. The dust was trying to make him sneeze, but Goodwife M'lewis hadn't raised any of her sons to be suicides. Now he was behind a head-high clump of alluvial clay, right where the towel-top would pass on his next circuit.

Come on, he thought. *Git yer wog arse over here. Come t'pappa.* His weight came up on his knees and one hand. The other went to the wooden toggle in his waist, callused fingers around satin-smooth pearwood. Ready. Ready. One knee bent under him, bare toes gripping the dirt.

The Colonial muttered something in Arabic and stopped. He bent, raising one foot and knocking the dottle out of his pipe on the heel of his curl-toed boot.

Thank you, Spirit, M'lewis thought, and moved very quickly. Straighten the knee, rising, right hand whipping forward and to the left in a hard sideways flick. Following the toggle and the wire it dragged, as if they were pulling him out of the dirt. Perfect soft weight on the hand, as the wire struck the left side of the wog's neck and whipped around, slapping the other toggle into his reaching left hand—practiced ten thousand times since he was a lad, and it *worked* when you had to. Wrists crossed, jam the knee into the wog's back, *heave.*

The sudden coppery smell of blood filled the night. M'lewis went down with the Colonial, abandoning the garrote that had sawn halfway through to his backbone and grabbing his equipment to muffle the clatter. Figures had started upright at the campfire; one of them seemed to be dancing a jig for an instant. The sounds were slight but definite. A meaty *thock*, the sound of a steel-shod rifle butt in the side of a head. The wetter, duller sound of steel in flesh. And once the unmistakable crackle of a breaking neck, like a thick green branch being popped. Then silence.

M'lewis jerked the garrote free and wiped it clean on the dead Arab's pugaree. The campfire was quiet when he came up, his men finishing rifling the pockets of the dead—he could have forbidden that, and he could tell a pig not to shit in the woods, too—and sitting calmly in the same positions with wog helmets on their heads. The Scout commander nodded to them as he passed, walking out into the dark and to the edge of the little cliff. There was a gully beyond it, then low eroded clay hills, and then flat farmland. Dim enough normally at two hours past midnight, except for the hundreds of neatly spaced campfires. More lights crossed the river, over to the western bank where the smoking ruins of Gurnyca lay.

He settled in with his sketchpad and pulled out his binoculars. Railroad to the riverbank; he checked, and saw fatigue parties still working on it. *Laid on t'dirt*, he noted on his pad as he sketched. No embankment or crushed-rock bedding for the ties. Emergency line, low capacity, but still enough to carry supplies. Mounds of supplies throughout the basecamp, within the normal earthworks and ditch. Ammunition boxes, shells, sacks with dogmash and dried fish and jerked meat, skins of vegetable oil, all the hundred-and-one items that an army on the march needed. Convoys were moving across the pontoon bridge even at night: wagons drawn by skinny long-legged oxen, and long guns with the distinctive soda-bottle shapes of built-up siege weapons, battering pieces. 130mm and 160mm, he decided. Rifled guns, good artillery, but bitches to move.

Rail to the river, but oxcarts over it. No grazing, except from the farms; if Ali was moving north, he'd be foraging to support his men, but once he stopped, the convoys would have to come in every day. About ten kay of troops holding the bridgehead and pontoons, sappers and line-of-communication infantry. It all looked very professional, as good as anything the Civil Government's army could do. Not at *all* like fighting the barbs out west. The MilGov barbs were full of fight, but dim as a yard up a hog's ass, most of the time. These wogs used their heads for something besides holding their turbans up.

M'lewis finished his estimate and duplicated the numbers and sketch-map. "Cut-nose, Talker," he whispered, as he eeled backward.

Cut-nose was a ratty little man, his cousin on his mother's side. They might have been brothers for looks—it was quite possible they *were* brothers, Old Man M'lewis had got around a fair bit before they hanged him—except for the missing organ. Then again, maybe they weren't close relations; no M'lewis would try to sell a dyed dog back to the man he'd stolen it from. Talker was a hulking brute from the mountains on the eastern fringe of Descott. They both had rawhide guards shrunk onto the forestocks of their rifles, and Talker had a couple of fresh severed ears on a loop of thong around his neck.

"Tak this t'Messer Raj," he said. "Swing east. Month's pay bonus iffn ye gits there afore me."

"Ser!" Cut-nose said, smiling yellow-brown with delight. Talker grunted.

M'lewis came to a crouch and headed back toward the gully and the dogs, the rest of the Scouts falling in behind him. He took the time to stamp his feet back into his boots before he straddled the crouching dog. He usually didn't bother with socks; a dollop of tallow in the boot served as well, if you didn't mind the smell.

"Ride," he said.

Messer Raj would have his news. It was bad news, as far as Antin M'lewis could see, but—thank the Spirit!—it wasn't his job to figure out what to do about it.

They swung into the saddle and followed the gully north, riding with muffled harness. Every kilometer or so he paused and headed for high ground; the eastern bank was generally a little above the level on the west, and there were few dwellers close to the main stream, if you avoided the raghead semaphore towers. Every stop showed Colonial watchfires on the other side; Ali's convoy guards, picketed all the way down his line of march northward towards Sandoral.

The third time showed something a little different. He closed his eyes for a minute before putting them to the glasses. There was a fair-sized Civil Government town on the other side of the river, and as he watched, the first of the buildings went up in a gout of flame. That gave enough light to watch the Settler's troops systematically stripping the warehouses and granaries before they put them to the torch; Ali'd be living off the land as much as he could, to spare the transport.

There was a migratory insect on Bellevue about the length of a man's thumb. Every century or so swarms of them would hatch north on the Skinner steppe and fly south, eating the land bare until they reached the empty deserts to spawn and die. Where they passed, famine followed.

Ali's men were more localized, but just about as thorough.

Barton Foley sat in the shade of the palm tree and tapped his lips thoughtfully with the end of his pencil. *Now, would* virile *go well with* while *in that stanza, or not?* he thought.

"Heads up!"

He sighed and tucked the volume back into the saddlebag. Someday he'd have the time to really write. *Someday I'll be dead*, he added sourly to himself—*although hopefully not soon*; twenty-one was a bit early even in this trade. *Maybe I'm not cut out to be a poet or a playwright.* History, now, that might be more interesting. He'd certainly got a close-up on some of it.

"More refugees?" a lieutenant asked.

"I don't think so," the young captain said thoughtfully, raising his glasses.

The picket of the 5th was two kilometers out from Sandoral: the roads were thick with refugees, heading into the city and then being routed out. It was better to intercept them a ways from the gates, to avoid crowding the roadways nearer the city. Two troops and a splatgun were enough to discourage even the most hysterical from bolting to the shelter of the walls. By now, most of them had gotten the message. There was a continuous traffic out of town too, hopeful magnates with their valuables in wagons, realistic ones with the hard cash on pack-dogs and the family in a fast well-sprung carriage.

It was easy duty, a way to rest the troops; a nice little date grove for shade, a good well for water. Some resourceful soul had a fire going and a couple of chickens roasting over it; the peons would never miss them. The smell was a pleasant overlay to the usual odors of dog and sweat-soaked wool uniforms and gun oil.

Foley wiped his face with his red-and-black checked neckcloth. *Ironic,* he thought. The 5th Descott had looted a warehouse full of them back in El Djem, the Colonial border town southwest of here. They'd just barely made it back alive from that one, after Tewfik mousetrapped them, but the scarves had become a unit trademark; it was as much as a soldier's life was worth to wear one, if he wasn't in the 5th.

The column of dust was heading in from the northwest, just now down into the flat irrigated land around Sandoral. Suspiciously regular dust, columns of it, with a thinner, wider film in front. Very much what a couple of battalions of Civil Government cavalry would make, riding hard in column with their scout-screens out ahead, all regulation and by the book. He waited until the first of the vedettes came into view, checked the silhouette and the breed of dog.

"Message to the *Heneralissimo*," he said. "The Cruisers and Welf's Brigaderos are here."

Very good time, too. No more than five days from the time they left East Residence just ahead of the first trains. Even with the railroad to supply them, it was a creditable performance, particularly if the dogs were still fit for action.

He was a little surprised. Those fair MilGov complexions were extremely pretty, but he'd doubted they could take the Eastern sun.

"Good timing," Raj said.

Ludwig Bellamy and Teodore Welf looked more like twins than ever, down to the thick coating of gray-white dust on their faces and the dark streaks of sweat through it.

"Rail convoys on schedule?" Bellamy asked.

They moved forward under the awning and collected bowls of soup and a bannock each; the line parted to let them through, but it was the same food as the troopers were waiting for. The medical staff—priest-doctors and nuns—was manning the pots, since there weren't any wounded to care for so far. Suzette dashed by, stopping long enough to thrust a cup of watered wine into Raj's hand. The others were dipping water out of a bucket; Ludwig waited politely until the others had drunk, then dumped the remainder over his head.

"I *needed* that," he said; the grin made you realize he wasn't yet thirty.

Neither am I, Raj remembered with slight surprise. He felt older, though.

Aloud, he went on: "I'll give Barholm Clerett that, he does get the trains running on time. We're expecting the last in at any moment. How are your men?"

"They'll be ready to fight after a night's sleep; and the dogs are mostly sound-footed. We took your advice and commandeered a big pack of remounts from the East Residence reserve before we left." Bellamy looked around. "You haven't been wasting time here."

There were few civilians left on the streets of Sandoral. Instead they swarmed with soldiers and dogs, wagons and carts, and an ordered chaos of movement under the harsh southern sun. The garrison infantry were doing most of the hauling and pushing, but they looked better fed, and far better dressed. A thud and plume of smoke and dust marked another house being demolished for building materials; off in the distance sounded the *heep . . . heep* of troops being drilled and a crackle of musketry practice. The artillery park filled most of the square, guns nose-to-trail with their limbers waiting behind, and Dinnalsyn's gunners giving them a last going-over.

"Speak of the devil," Bartin Foley said, smiling fondly.

A bugle sounded, and the color party of the 5th Descott came trotting into the square, the battalion banner floating beside the blue and silver Starburst of Holy Federation. Gerrin Staenbridge heeled his mount over to the clump of officers and saluted with an ironic flourish.

"*Mi heneral,* the remainder of your force, reporting as ordered." He looked around in his turn. "I see you've started the party without me."

"Just laying in the drinks and rehearsing the band, Gerrin," Raj said. "No problem getting under way?"

"No, but there might have been if I'd lingered. Our good

Chancellor Tzetzas isn't happy about having the field army so far from home, at all, at all. If I hadn't taken the last of the trains, I suspect the bureaucrats would have followed me all the way here to argue with you about it."

Raj laughed harshly. "Not with Ali so close," he said. "Although our good Commandant Osterville is almost as much of a pest, in his way. And he *is* here."

"Speak of the devil," Foley said again, his voice flat as gunmetal this time.

He took Staenbridge's arm and began whispering rapidly, gesturing with the hook on his left arm. Raj caught his own name and *Suzette* once or twice.

The Commandant of Sandoral and District was pushing his way through the thronging mass in the square; not looking very happy, and unhappier by the minute at the lack of deference, from Raj's veterans and from what were supposedly his own troops.

"Whitehall," he said. "General Whitehall," he amended; Raj's face was politely blank, but several of the Companions had dropped their hands to pistol-butts or the hilts of their sabers.

"Where the Starless Dark have you been?"

Raj straightened, finished the wine, and dipped his bannock into the stew. "Well, Commandant, I've been rather busy—getting ready for the war, you see."

Somebody chuckled, and Osterville turned a mottled color. "I'll thank you to accompany me to my headquarters," he said. "We've got several things to discuss."

"If you want to talk, *Colonel*, you'll talk here and now. Because as I mentioned, there is a war impending."

Words burst from the smaller man. "You're *destroying* my city!" he barked. "I've received petitions from every man of rank in the district—"

Raj raised an eyebrow. "I don't doubt you have," he said. "Let them petition Ali. That's the alternative, and I think they'd like his methods even less than mine. In any case, as you've made clear, you're the supreme civil authority in this area; relations with the local nobility are your responsibility."

The Commandant opened his mouth and closed it again. He snapped his fingers, and an aide put a sheaf of documents in his hand.

"Perhaps you've been too *busy*," he said, "to read these dispatches from the Capital? They've been coming over the semaphore by the dozens."

Raj mopped his bowl with the heel of the bannock and plucked the papers out of the smaller man's hand. He glanced through them, chewed, swallowed.

"Oh, I've been reading them," he said.

He ripped the thick sheaf through with casual strength, tossing the fragments into the dry hot wind. They fluttered off like gulls, and one of the newly arrived dogs of the 5th snapped inquiringly at a piece as it went by.

"I have the *Governor's* authority, signed by the Sovereign Mighty Lord himself. I received it in person, from his own hands. What are a few waggling flags to *that*?"

He tossed the last of the papers to the cobbles. "And now, Colonel Osterville, if you don't have any more problems . . ."

"But I do have *this*," Osterville said. The document he produced was thick parchment, impressively sealed with lead and ribbons.

Raj raised an eyebrow. "You have a decree from the Chair, a Vermilion Order, swaying the wide earth?" he asked, using the formal terminology.

"Not exactly," Osterville said. "But you will note it's from Chancellor Tzetzas, in the Governor's name, requiring you to cease and desist from interfering with private properties and instead attend to your assigned mission."

"From the Chancellor?" Raj said, examining the parchment. He crumpled it experimentally. It was first-quality sheepskin parchment, soft and supple. "By courier, I suppose?"

Osterville nodded toward a man in his entourage. Raj looked at him, and then around.

"M'lewis. Deal with this as it deserves," he said.

"Where are the jakes?" the Scout Captain said, putting down his bowl and unfastening his sword belt.

Like most Civil Government cities, Sandoral had public lavatories, simple brick boxes connected to storm-flushed sewers. M'lewis strode over to the nearest, and back a minute later. He was holding the now brown-streaked and stinking parchment by one corner between thumb and finger. Shocked silence gripped the Commandant's party as he walked over to the courier, unfastened the flap of his message pouch, and dropped the soiled parchment inside.

"Just so the Chancellor understands exactly what weight I attach to his attempts to interfere with my mission and the Governor's authority," Raj said.

"You're mad," Osterville said softly. "Mad. Nobody—Tzetzas will eat your *heart*."

Raj's smile sent Osterville back a step. "Perhaps I am mad, Colonel. Perhaps I'm the Sword of the Spirit of Man. In either case, I'm in charge here." He produced a document of his own. "And this is your own confirmation, directing your troops to cooperate in the transport of the civilians."

He held it up, and one of the Companions leaned over to read it with interest.

"That! That was that witch, she—" On the edge of ruin, Osterville pulled himself back. He'd been about to say something that would be a public provocation to a challenge. He ran a hand through his hair. "Where is *she*? I haven't seen her since . . ."

Raj laughed, an iron sound. "Colonel Osterville, I've answered your official inquiries. You can scarcely expect me to stretch business to the point of giving you an itinerary for my wife. Now, if you'll pardon me—"

He turned, and the officers followed him. Gerrin Staenbridge paused, holding his gauntlets in one hand and tapping them into the palm of the other. For a moment Osterville feared he would slap them across his face in challenge, but the hard dark features were relaxed in a smile. He held the order Osterville had signed—the order that Suzette Whitehall had somehow charmed out of him. He read it, pursing his lips, then looked up at Osterville with an expression of feline malice before he spoke one word.

"Sucker."

CHAPTER SEVEN

It was the hour before dawn, a little chilly even in summer in the clear dry southern air. The massed ranks of the army knelt as the Sysup-Suffragen of Sandoral paced by, with acolytes swinging censers that spread aromatic blue smoke across the men. He reached out his Star-headed staff in blessing as he passed the colors of each unit, and the men extended both hands out, palms down, in the gesture of reverence. Behind the hierarch came four priests bearing a litter on which rested a cube of something clearer than crystal and taller than a man. Light swirled in it, growing and flaring until the watchers bowed their heads and closed their eyes in awe. It shone through the closed lids, through hands flung up before faces, then died away amid a murmur of awe.

Raj touched his amulet as he rose. "The Spirit is with us," he said. *Or at least Center is. What a cynic I've become.*

realist, Center corrected.

Is there a difference?

He turned to the command group. Which included, from necessity, Colonel Osterville.

"Gentlemen, my congratulations. You've managed a very complex operation in record time and with surprisingly little confusion; my particular thanks to Colonels Menyez and Dinnalsyn.

Now it's time to show the wogs that two can play the invasion game. Colonel Osterville, I presume you'll wish to accompany the field force rather than remain in Sandoral?"

"I certainly will. Furthermore, I insist that the cavalry battalions of the Sandoral garrison be under my command."

Raj nodded. "By all means, Colonel. By all means."

Osterville shot him a suspicious glance, and found his face blandly unrevealing. He tugged at his mustachio thoughtfully.

colonel osterville is attempting to intuit the reason for your ready agreement, Center pointed out. **probability of success 12%±3.**

"Colonel Menyez, you will command the city garrison. I'm leaving you the 17th, the 24th, the garrison infantry, and three batteries of field guns. You'll also have the guns of the fixed defenses, of course."

Dinnalsyn looked up. "I've tested the militia artillery crews who volunteered to stay," he said. "Not bad at all, and the ammunition's plentiful."

Jorg Menyez nodded thoughtfully. "Any cavalry? The garrison units can stand behind a parapet and shoot, and the 17th and 24th can do anything cavalry can except ride and charge with the saber, but I could use a mobile reserve."

"I'll leave you three companies of the 5th Descott," Raj said. "That'll have to do. The field force will comprise three columns.

"The remainder of the 5th, the 1st and 2nd Mounted Cruisers, the 3/591, 4/591, and 5/591, and the main artillery reserve of thirty guns will go with me. Colonel Osterville, you'll command your garrison cavalry and two batteries. Major Gruder, you'll have the 7th Descott Rangers, the 1st Rogor Slashers, the Maximilliano Dragoons, and Poplanich's Own. Major Zahpata, you'll take your 18th Komar Borderers, the City of Delrio, and the Novy Haifa Dragoons. Plus two batteries of field guns each.

"We'll be advancing fast, close enough for mutual support; no wheeled transport except for the guns and the ammunition reserve. Spread out, live off the land; spare lives when you can, but burn and destroy everything else, so long as you can do it quickly. Let the semaphore posts stand long enough to get off messages. Portable plunder will be transferred to the central group, and from there back here to Sandoral for eventual division; do *not* allow the men to weigh themselves down with choice bits. When Tewfik comes looking for us, we're going to need every bit of mobility we can get.

"The purpose of this exercise is to create enough havoc that Ali will be forced to divert at least part of his army from the west bank of the Drangosh. We lay waste the nobles' estates; the nobles scream for protection. He can give any particular noble the chop, but he can't ignore too many of them—hopefully, he's not so much of a bloody lunatic as to forget that, at least not yet. We can't face the entire Colonial army in the field, but we may be able to give part of it a bloody nose. Move fast, and create the maximum amount of panic and alarm; that's more important than actual damage.

"Any questions?"

A few of the officers looked at each other, but none spoke. Raj slapped on his gloves. "Then to your men, Messers, and the work of the day."

Raj mounted Horace and turned the dog and his personal bannermen down the front of the assembled force. He halted before the ranks of the infantry.

"Fellow soldiers," he said, raising a hand. "I'm off to teach the wogs the price of invading the Civil Government of Holy Federation."

Silence reigned. "I can only do that if Sandoral is strongly held behind me." He pointed south. "Ali is coming, and more wogs than you can count are coming with him. If you hold these walls, we can win this war; otherwise, we all die. I'm riding out confident in the aid of the Spirit of Man of the Stars—and in your courage and discipline. Which is why, when the plunder is divided, all the infantry here will receive a full share, just as the cavalry troopers do. Are you lads ready to do a man's work today?"

The 17th began the cheering, and it spread down the line as Raj rode past, his personal flag dipping in salute as he passed each battalion's banner. The cavalry were massed on the other side of the square; you had to use a different manner with them.

He grinned as he reined in, facing the long rows of helmeted riders and the panting tongues of the dogs; they knew something was up as well, and their pricked-forward ears were mirrors of the men's excitement.

"To Hell or plunder, dog-brothers," Raj roared.

The men gave back a single exultant bark, and the dogs howled, thousands of them in antiphonal chorus, a sound that slammed back from the buildings around the plaza and made the hair crawl along the spine.

"Walk-march . . . trot."

"I might have known," Raj said, reining in on the little hillock beside the east-bank end of the bridge.

Suzette pulled up Harbie, her riding palfrey, beside Horace. The smaller dog wagged its tail and sniffed Horace's muzzle; after a moment Horace gave a snuffle in reply and turned his head away in lordly indifference.

"You do have a medical element along," Suzette said, her eyes bright with friendly mockery. She touched the first-aid kit slung from the saddlebow. "There's no reason I shouldn't join them."

The boards of the pontoon bridge rumbled as a splatgun battery crossed. Cavalry followed in columns of fours, the plate-sized paws thudding on the wooden pavement. Some of the dogs had their ears back at the unfamiliar slight swaying of the surface beneath their feet; others looked upstream or down. The men were singing, an old Descotter folktune:

> *"Goin' t'Black Mountain wit me saber an' me gun;*
> *Cut ye if yer stand, shoot ye if yer run—"*

"I can command thousands of armed men and not a single woman," Raj grumbled. *One armed woman*, he corrected himself. Suzette had her Colonial repeating carbine in a scabbard tucked under the saddle flaps before her left knee.

"Well, you did *marry* me, not *enlist* me, darling," Suzette said.

Raj snorted and returned his attention to the map. Below, the raiding force poured across the Drangosh, dogs and guns. *Twenty-*

five, thirty-five klicks a day, he thought, tracing it with his finger. South and east—there was nothing close to the river to raid, but the Ghor Canal ran a little farther east, and there was a thick belt of cultivation along it. *Three or four days should bring us to . . .* A city, called Ain el-Hilwa, about halfway between here and the Colonial bridgehead opposite Gurnyca.

By that time the wogs should be well and truly terrorized.

"*Scramento!*" Robbi M'Telgez swore.

The carbine bullet pecked dirt from the adobe wall into his eyes. He crouched and duckwalked along it, rising slightly to peer through the branches of a flowering bush a few meters farther on. There wasn't much shooting elsewhere in the hamlet, but this was the best house; therefore the one most likely to be defended.

"Ye, Smeet, Cunarlez, M'tennin," he said. "Cover us. Five rounds rapid. T'rest fix yer stickers. We'll tak Rosalie t'breakfast."

"We'll a' git kilt," Smeet muttered. "Hunnert meters, dog-brothers. I gits t'winda on 't lef." He blew on the round he loaded into the chamber.

M'Telgez drew the bayonet—nicknamed Rosalie from time immemorial—from the left side of his belt beneath the haversack and clipped it beneath the muzzle of his rifle. There was a multiple rattle and click as the other men of his squad followed suit.

The house ahead was bigger than most in the sprawling settlement along the irrigation ditch; probably the local headman's. It was about a hundred meters upstream from the burning wreckage of the *noria,* the water-powered millwheel that filled the distributory network of irrigation ditches. A small square house of two stories, blank whitewashed adobe below, a few narrow windows above, and most of it was courtyard enclosed by a wall. It hadn't been constructed as a fortress; it had been a long time since Civil Government troops came this far, and none of the local villages even had a defensive perimeter. From what he knew of raghead custom, the wogs built this way to keep neighbors from seeing their women. But it *functioned* perfectly well as a minor strongpoint.

"*Hadelande!*" he shouted, and vaulted the wall.

The three men he'd designated cut loose, firing as rapidly as they could work the levers and reload. The heavy bullets knocked dust-spouting holes in the mud brick around the windows, or went through—most of them went through, it was only fifty meters and everyone in the 5th ought to be able to hit a running man in the head at that range—beating down the enemy fire. A light bullet still pecked at the dust between his feet. He suppressed his impulse to leap and yell, concentrating on running.

The six Descotters flattened themselves by the doorway. No sense waiting there; it would just give someone upstairs time to think about dropping something unpleasant on them. He was suddenly conscious of his dry gummy mouth, the sweat trickling down from neck and armpits under his uniform jacket, the sound of a chicken clucking unconcerned out in the dusty yard. M'Telgez held out three fingers, two, one.

He and the next trooper stepped out and fired at the lock. They were lucky; nothing hit them when the crude wooden mechanism splintered. The other four fired a round each through the datewood planks while he and his partner stuck their bayonets through the gaps between and lifted the bar out of its brackets. The door burst inward, and they were through.

It was an open space of packed earth with a well in the center and rooms about it. An open staircase came down from the second story opposite him, and men were leaping down it. One pointed a long-barreled flintlock *jezail*.

It boomed, throwing a plume of smoke. Someone behind him yelled—yelled rather than screamed, so that couldn't be too serious. Armory rifles banged, and the other man with a firearm toppled from the stairs; he had a repeating carbine, which showed that this squad had a proper sense of target priorities. Then a wog was rushing at him, swinging a long scimitar.

Clang. M'Telgez caught the sword on his bayonet, and it skirled down the forearm-length of steel until it caught in the brass cross-guard. He let the inertia of the heavy sword push both weapons downward, and punched across with the butt of his rifle. It smacked into the Arab's bearded face with a crackle of breaking bone, a crunching he could feel through his hands. The Colonial pitched sideways, spinning and fouling the man behind who was trying to pull a double-barreled pistol out of the sash around his ample belly. His mouth opened in an "O" of surprise as M'Telgez spun his rifle around and lunged, driving his bayonet through the Arab's stomach and a handspan out his back.

There was a soft, heavy resistance, a feeling of things crunching and popping inside. He twisted sharply and withdrew, a few shards of white fat clinging to nicks in the blade of the bayonet. Blood spattered out; the wounded man's eyes rolled up in his head and he collapsed backward.

The men of the 5th waited an instant, taking cover behind the mudbrick columns that supported the second story of the house. M'Telgez reloaded his rifle and raised three fingers, then jerked them towards the stairs. Three men ran up them and through the open arched door at the top. A shadow moved at the corner of his eye. He whirled, just in time to see it was a veiled and robed woman with a big earthenware pot raised over her head in both hands. M'Telgez raised the muzzle of his rifle as his finger curled on the trigger, and the bullet smashed the vase into shards, leaving her standing with her hands spread and eyes wide.

He pivoted the rifle and jabbed the butt into her stomach. Air whooped out of her and she collapsed to the ground. The Descotter put a boot in the small of her back and pinned her to the dusty earth.

"Anythin' up thar?" he called sharply.

"Nothin'," a voice answered him. "Jist sommat wog kids."

"Bring 'em down," he called. "Rest a yer dog-brothers, search it. Look unner t'roof tiles, t'hearthstone, shove yer baynit inna any chink ye see. Nuthin' heavy, jist coin an' sich."

Which was a pity; cloth and tools and livestock would all fetch a good price back in the *Gubernio Civil* if they had time to send them back, not to mention the wogs themselves. A good stout wog would bring six or seven silver FedCreds sold to the slavers who usually followed the armies, a quarter the price of a riding dog. He'd picked up some coin that way in the Southern Territories. M'Telgez banked half his pay and most of his plunder with the battalion savings account; he had an eye on a little place back in the County when he'd done his twenty-five years. There were two schools of thought on that—some held that you had about one chance in four of living that long in the Army, so it made more sense to spend it on booze and whores as it came.

Robbi M'Telgez had noticed that troopers who thought that way tended to be careless, and to make up a large share of the discouraging statistics. Besides, his family could use the money too, if it came to that.

The three men he'd sent up came down again, one holding a small wooden box. "Found 'er in t'rafters, loik," he said, grinning broadly. "Coin, by t'Spirit."

Looking on the bright side, the wogs hadn't had time to really hide much.

Another herded a group of children, the oldest leading or carrying the younger. They set up a wail at the sight of the bodies in the courtyard, then surged back again when one of the troopers scowled and flourished his bayonet. Thumping and crashing sounds came from the ground floor, as the rest of the squad searched.

"Git t'kiddies out an' a-down by t'church, t'mosque, whatever." Orders were to spare noncombatants and the unresisting. "Yer!" He shouted through the ground-floor door. "Whin yer finished, set t'cookin' oil around."

That would start the fire nicely. He took a deep breath and exhaled, letting the tight belly-clamping tension of action fade a little. A pissant little skirmish, but he'd been in the Army seven years now, since he turned eighteen, and he knew you could die just as dead that way as in a major battle.

"And Smeet, plug that."

Trooper Smeet had a tear in the side of his jacket, and it was sodden and dripping. "'Tis nuttin'," he said. "We'll a' git kilt anyways—"

"Did I *asks* yer?" M'Telgez said, scowling. "Did I?"

"Co'pral half a year and already drunk wit' power," Smeet said, grinning with an expression that was half wince. He was coming down off the combat-high too; often you didn't really feel a minor wound until you had time to think about it. He leaned his rifle against a wall and shrugged out of his webbing gear and jacket. "I bin co'pral six, seven times—t' feelin' don't last nohows, dog-brother.'"

There was an ugly flesh wound along his ribs, only beginning to crust. One of his comrades washed it from his canteen, then applied the blessed powder and sealed, the priest-made bandage they all carried in a pouch on their belts. Smeet yelped and swore; the stuff stung badly, and many of the less pious men wouldn't use it on a cut unless you stood over them. M'Telgez wasn't much of a Church-going man, but Messer Raj insisted on following Church canons in such things, which was good enough for him.

The attending trooper used his bayonet to cut off one of the tails of Smeet's jacket, ripping it in half and using it to bind the padding over his ribs.

"An' git t'priest at it, soon as, or ye'll feel me boot up yer arse," M'Telgez warned. Smeet was a good enough fighting man, but he tended to be slack about kit and such.

M'Telgez looked down at the woman and smiled.

Pillars of black smoke stood out against the northern horizon. The smell drifted down with the wind, full of the unpleasant smells of things that should not burn. White-hot, the noon sun burned most color out of the land, turning the reaped grainfields to a pale yellow dust. Blocks of alfalfa and *berseem*-clover were almost eye-hurtingly vivid, and the odd patch of fruit trees or olives cast shade dense and black and sharp-edged. Where the 7th Descott Rangers waited beside their dogs, there was welcome shade from rows of eucalyptus on either side of the road, but the air was still and very hot. Insects shrilled in the dust, and a few tiny pterosauroids swooped after them, their long triangle-tipped tails flickering as they scooped cicadas into their needle-toothed little jaws.

The men squatted patiently beside their mounts, the gun teams lying down in their traces, satisfied after their drink in the roadside canal. The beasts looked glossy-coated and strong despite the heat and hard work; the all-meat diet of plundered Colonial stock agreed with them, after the usual mash of grain and beans eked out with bones and offal. Kaltin Gruder stood, eating grapes from the bunches in the helmet he held reversed in his left hand, waiting with the same stolidity as his troopers.

He ate more grapes and smiled. He'd soldiered against the Military Governments in the west without passion, and as much occasional mercy as advisable. He was a noble of the Civil Government, a Descotter, and a professional; war was his trade, the only trade unless he wanted the Church or to go home to the County and chase rustlers. The Colonials, though . . . his younger brother had died from a Colonial shellburst, in the El Djem campaign. He rubbed one thumb down the deep parallel scars that seamed the left side of his face.

This was personal.

The sound of paws came from the north, and the whistle of the pickets in their ambush positions passing them through. The scouts trotted up to him, sitting easily with their rifles across their thighs. The lieutenant who led them saluted.

"*Seyhor*," he said. "Sir. About two thousand of them; many carriages and dogs, and a substantial number of armed men."

"Regulars?"

"*Ferramenti, danad, seyhor,*" the young officer replied. "I'd swear, nothing, sir. Household guards, no twenty in the same livery."

That was the advantage of counter-attacking. Most of the military nobles, the *amirs*, and their *ghazis* would be over on the west bank, with Ali—all the ones who had any desire to fight and die for Islam, at least. Ali had gotten overconfident.

Still, it wouldn't do to emulate his mistake. Fighting for their homes and families could make even rabble desperate.

"Company commanders," he said.

Back along the road men shifted as the word passed down, fastening their webbing, here a man checking his rifle or tightening the girth on a dog. The mounts took their cues from their masters, keeping a well-drilled silence, but they bristled. The unit commanders gathered around Gruder's banner.

"The objective," he said, crouching and drawing in the dirt with a twig, "is a column of refugees about half a klick north. They're coming at fair speed for civilians, but we've gotten ahead of them. We'll debouch, deploy—*so*—and put in an attack. Captain Morinez, bring your guns along at the trot, if you please.

"The general order is to kill anyone who resists; let the rest run, as long as they do it on foot. We'll take provisions, spare dogs—I want to put the ammunition reserve in pack-saddles—and any high-value loot." He dumped the grapes out of his helmet and buckled it on. "Burn or smash whatever we don't take. Oh, and we're not taking any hundred-pound bundles of loot, either, so wooers be swift—or refrain."

There was a harsh chuckle, and nods. This was a military picnic so far; it wouldn't stay that way, but there was no reason not to make the most of it while they could.

"Hell or plunder, dog-brothers." He straddled his dog Fihdel and his feet found the stirrups as it rose. "Boots and saddles, gentlemen."

"Approximately one hundred seventy-seven thousand four hundred FedCreds. Gold," Muzzaf Kerpatik added. "That's allowing for the usual discounts on sales."

Raj grunted noncommittally, leaning one hand against the tentpole. It was a captured tent, from the baggage train Kaltin had overrun; they'd leave it behind in the morning. He looked out across the camp—not much of one, just the picket lines of staked-out dogs, the men cooking around their campfires. Odd to be in a camp where you heard more Namerique than Sponglish, but the central group was mostly MilGov troopers. *Fruits of conquest.* That was the true spoil of war; peace in the lands he'd retaken, and their fighting men here defending the Civil Government.

The MilGov soldiers, the ex-warriors of the Squadron and Brigade, were happy enough. An easy campaign so far, under leaders they trusted; they were warriors by birth and professional soldiers by the trade he'd given them, and indifferent to who they fought.

The sun was setting in the west, over toward the Drangosh thirty kilometers distant. It was hazed with burning, crops and buildings and towns; the raiding force had smashed a path of devastation a hundred kilometers southward. He could smell the smoke, faint under the cooking and dog odors of a war-camp.

"How much of that plunder is from Osterville's group?" Raj asked.

"Ah, unfortunately Colonel Osterville's battalions have had poor luck. Less than two thousand from them."

A chuckle ran around the table behind him. "I don't think," Raj said, "the men are going to find it amusing that Osterville's boys are holding out on them. Particularly given the recent service records, respectively."

"Raj, darling," Suzette said. "*Do* come and sit down. Or pace like a caged dog, but make up your mind."

He shrugged a little sheepishly and returned, sitting and taking up a drumstick. It was sauroid, but tasted pretty much like the chicken that was the alternative. As usual, Suzette had managed to find something better than you had any right to expect in the field; of course, the pickings were good. He stoked himself methodically.

"You don't like this, do you, darling?" Suzette said.

"No," Raj said. "I'm a thrifty man. The looting's good here because this area hasn't been fought over in a long time. It'll be generations recovering."

"Which will weaken the Colony," Gerrin Staenbridge pointed out.

He'd managed to shave and find a clean uniform, which was a minor miracle when they were all living out of saddlebags. *Every man pays the price he will for what he values,* Raj thought. Gerrin dressed for dinner the way he dressed line for a charge, with finicky care, as a mark of civilization.

"That's assuming the stalemate continues out here," Raj said. "The Civil Government of Holy Federation is the legitimate ruler of *all* humankind. The Colonials included."

Staenbridge raised an eyebrow: "Well, it hasn't had much luck enforcing that for millennia or so," he pointed out.

During which time the Colonials had besieged East Residence twice and the Civil Government had reached as far as Al Kebir once.

"I don't like it either," Bartin Foley said.

They looked at him, and the younger man dropped his eyes to the cut-down shotgun on the table before him, his single hand slowly reassembling the clean, oil-gleaming parts. They went together with smooth clicks and snaps, and he slid it into the harness he usually wore over his back.

"It's not real soldiers' work, harrying peasants like this," he went on doggedly.

Gerrin and Raj nodded in chorus, and smiled at the coincidence. "Not good for morale, really," Raj said. "Not too much of it."

"Gets the men thinking like bandits," Staenbridge agreed.

Suzette shook her head. "Such perfect knights," she said with gentle mockery. Then: "Ah, Abdullah."

The Druze entered with two suspicious troopers at his heel, their bayonets hovering not far from his kidneys, and Antin M'lewis to one side. He bowed: "*Sayyid. Sayyida.*"

Raj leaned back in the captured folding chair, some *amir*'s hunting equipment. *I'll be damned. I didn't expect to see* him *alive again, I really didn't.* Suzette had an eye for picking reliable servants, though.

"That's all, men," he said to the troopers. They hesitated, and his tone grew dry. "I can handle one Arab, thank you." They saluted, threw Abdullah a warning glance, and wheeled smartly out.

Damn, this living legend shit can get wearing. The men wouldn't leave him alone for a moment, watching, listening, guarding. Damn their dear loyal souls. What was he, an invalid?

you are their talisman, Center said. **without you they would feel themselves lost.**

I'm only one man, Raj thought/protested. And I've got competent officers.

belief is its own reality.

Abdullah pulled documents from his ha'aik. He also accepted a goblet of watered wine; his particular brand of exceedingly eccentric shi'a Islam had some liberal notions.

"Lord," he began. "Ain el-Hilwa is swollen to bursting with refugees. Perhaps a hundred and seventy, a hundred and eighty thousand in all. They crowd the city and the suburbs outside the wall."

Raj nodded. That was no surprise. The spy's long brown fingers moved dishes to tack down the map and papers against the warm breeze of evening.

"The garrison includes ten thousand men of the Settler's regulars and the *ghazis* of the local *amirs*, but of these no more than two hundred are of single *tabors*." *Banners*, the Colonial equivalent of the Civil Government's battalions, although usually a little smaller. "The rest have been sent on detachment to the Settler's army across the Drangosh.

"Likewise, their officers quarrel. The provincial *wali*, Muhmed bin Tarish, is a court favorite; he hides among his women and sends messages commanding the men to stand fast within the walls. Haffez al'Husseini, the most senior of the military officers, is a veteran of the Zanj wars, but slowed by his wounds. He—"

The report flowed on, full and concise; units, strengths, weapons, dispositions, guns, the state of the fortifications and the water supply (which was good, since the city straddled the Ghor Canal). Center drew holographic projections over the map.

Abdullah's voice ceased. The others waited, in a silence filled by the flutter of canvas in the wind and the muted sounds of the camp; a dog howling, the brass of a trumpet calling, a challenge and response at an outlying vedette. Ten minutes later Raj blinked.

"Yes," he said, softly, to himself. "That should do." He looked up. "Excellent work, Abdullah. You won't regret it."

Abdullah bowed. "My life is to serve, *sayyid*."

Raj waved a hand. "If your son still wants that cavalry ensign's commission—and I'm still around and in command when he turns sixteen—it's his."

A very rare honor for one not of the Star Church; although Abdullah's faith allowed its adherents to freely observe the ceremonies of other religions, where advisable. The Druze bowed again, more deeply.

"Gerrin," Raj went on. "We'll be concentrated by 0900 tomorrow?"

"All except for Osterville," Staenbridge said. "But he's—"

"—closer nor he said, ser," M'lewis put in. "Nobbut six klicks east."

Raj nodded. "Here's what we'll do. Bartin, write this up. At dawn—"

CHAPTER EIGHT

"Allahu Akbar! Gur! Gur!"

The band of Colonials swept out of a side street in the maze of alleys. The morning sun burned bright on their scimitars and spiked helmets; beneath their djellabas they had wound tight linen strips, the winding-sheets of men determined to seek Paradise in battle with the unbelievers.

The main street was narrow and crooked as well; only one file of troopers was between Raj and the attack. Horace spun beneath him with a roaring growl, and his hand swept out saber and pistol. A grid of green lines clamped down over his vision, and the outlines of the Colonial troopers glowed. One strobed; the one with his carbine in his hands. Still a hundred paces away: a long pistol-shot but not impossible for a skilled man on dogback to make with a shoulder-weapon. And the Arab looked good. . . .

Raj moved his wrist. A red dot settled on the Colonial's midriff. His finger squeezed the trigger. *Crack.* The carbineer flipped over the cantle of his saddle. *Crack.* Another down. Place the dot and the bullet went where Center indicated it would. *Crack—crack—crack.* The revolver was empty, and the Colonials were through.

A clang of steel on steel as a scimitar met his saber. He flexed his wrist to let the sharply curved blade hiss by, then cut backhand across the Arab's face. A second was barreling in with his blade upraised. Horace lunged with open mouth for the Bazenji's throat. Raj stabbed, and the point of his weapon went in below the breastbone. He ripped it free with desperate strength, wheeling. Suzette's carbine clanged and nearly dropped from her hands as she used it to deflect a cut. Raj rose in the stirrups and chopped downward; there was a jar like the blade hitting seasoned oak, and a splitting sound. It nearly wrenched from his hand, sunk to brow-level in the Colonial's skull, but the weight of the falling body pulled the metal free.

There had been no time for fear. Something contracted in a hard knot under his ribs when he saw his wife clutching at her upper arm.

"It's nothing, light cut," she said.

He checked; in the background rifles barked as the troopers put down the dogs of the dead Arabs where they stood snarling over their masters' bodies. She was right; she held a dressing over the superficial wound while he tied it off.

"Damn, that was too close," he said. "Anyone else wounded?"

His bannerman had gashed fingers where he'd used the staff to block a cut. Suzette heeled Harbie closer and went to work on that. The sergeant of the color-party was looking at him wide-eyed.

"Spirit, ser," he blurted. "Five dead wit' five shots!"

Raj felt a flush of embarrassment. He wasn't actually a first-rate pistol-shot; the sword was his personal weapon of choice, and with that he was very good. With Center's eerie trick, you didn't *have* to be good. He didn't much like the experience. It was too much like being a weapon yourself, in another's hand.

Whatever works, he thought.

precisely.

"Keep moving," he said sharply.

The suburbs of Ain el-Hilwa were burning already, as the Civil Government troops shot and hacked their way through the crowds who ran screaming towards the gates. Shells went by overhead in long ripping-canvas arcs, to crash on the massive stone-faced walls behind the moat. It was a wet moat, full of canal water, right now dark with the heads of refugees swimming across; and getting no help from the garrison. The gates were jammed tight with a press of humanity.

"Forward!" he said again. "Dammit, bugler, sound *Advance at speed!*"

The brazen scream cut through the white noise of the crowds, the gathering roar of the flames. Sheer press of numbers was slowing the advance despite complete surprise. The people ahead *wanted* to get out of the way of the sharp blades and snarling meter-long jaws and rifle fire; they *couldn't.*

Should have stayed in their houses, he thought—or in the sprawling city of reed shanties and tents outside the suburbs. There was no wisdom in panic.

A field gun bounced up behind him. The crew pulled the trail free of the limber and spun it around, running it forward with the long pole held up and the nose of the gun down. They pushed it through the front line of Civil Government troopers and let the trail fall.

"Stand clear!" the gun commander said. He skipped aside himself and pulled the lanyard.

Pomph. The shock of discharge slapped at him, bouncing back and forth from the narrow walls.

So did the hundreds of lead shot in the canister charge. Men—and women and children—splashed away from the spreading scythe of it.

"Waymanos!" Raj shouted again. "Forward!"

The buildings dropped away on either side as they came out into the broad cleared area around the moat. Cannon and pompoms were firing from the walls, but most of the shots went overhead, into the belt of houses, helping with the work of destruction. In the gates, the garrison were firing down into their own people, dropping handbombs and pouring burning naphtha from the murder-holes over the arched entrances to clear the press. The gates swung shut, and the bridges over the moats gaped as hinged sections were pulled up.

"Damn," Raj said aloud. "Runner, to battalion commanders. Get the fires going and pull back."

A shell burst twenty yards ahead. Raj stood in his stirrups and brought out his field glasses, sweeping along the walls. Chaos, but active chaos—groups in the crimson djellabas of Colonial regular troops, infantry from the looks of them, and the white-and-colored patchwork of city militia. More and more of the fortress guns were getting into operation, too.

He turned Horace to the rear. "Come on, let's get out before the fires spread."

He was conscious of a few odd looks. Technically, this was a defeat—they hadn't been able to rush the gates, despite the shambolic panic of the Colonial garrison's response. Raj grinned a little wider.

A reputation for having something up your sleeve could be quite helpful. Even when you *did* have something up your sleeve.

Suzette was flexing her arm, wincing only a little, as they turned and trotted back through the smoke and noise. Shells whirred by overhead; ash and bits of debris fell into the dirt streets about them.

I'm almost glad that happened, Raj thought. Something sounded an interrogative at the back of his mind. I was beginning to wonder whether I'd lost my capacity for strong emotion.

i am not contagious.

The hell you're not, Raj thought. For example, I wouldn't have dared to talk this way to an angel a few years ago. He looked down at the city. For another, I wouldn't do what I'm going to do to Osterville a few years ago. Even to Osterville.

ah. that is the effect known as "life," raj whitehall. and it is contagious; not only that, but fatal. for all of us.

"Should be ready in about three hours, *mi heneral,*" Dinnalsyn said.

The gunner and Raj stood together outside the earthworks, five kilometers from Ain el-Hilwa. Two thousand troopers and as many press-ganged Colonial refugees dug steadily, hauling the dirt from the growing ditch upslope in baskets, buckets, helmets, and cloth slings improvised from coats. The sun was high, and the men sweated as they worked; an hour on and an hour off, with the off spent standing guard or watering and feeding the dogs. The earthwork fort was two hundred meters on a side, a standard marching camp with a ditch as deep as a standing man, an earthwork rampart as high inside with a palisade on top, and bastions at the corners and gates with V-notches for the guns. The air was full of the smell of sweat and freshly turned earth.

He walked over to the edge. "Found that buried cask of beer yet, dog-brothers?" Raj called in Namerique.

The big fair men in the nearest section groaned laughter. "Don't worry, lord," one yelled back. "By the Spirit of Man of This Earth, we'll have a grave big enough for all the enemy we kill if it takes us all day."

Raj waved as he turned away. *Not bad,* he thought. Back home, these men scorned digging in the earth as fit for peons and women; real men fought, hunted, and drank. They'd learned something of soldiering, then—granted he'd had to kill about a third of the adult males in their nations to get their attention, but they were learning.

Within the enclosure medics were setting up, and tents being pitched in neat rows along the streets; everything necessary for a mobile military city of five thousand men. It could be made more elaborate the longer they stayed, but by midafternoon the camp would be ready to defend. It was said, not without truth, that watching a Civil Government army encamp was more discouraging for barbarians than fighting a battle with them. The Colonials wouldn't be intimidated, but they'd know exactly how hard it was to storm this sort of earthworks.

"Good, Grammeck," he said. "Keep pushing it. Gerrin, once we've got the wall up, let all these Colonials go—it won't hurt the troops to finish up by themselves. Kaltin, you've got overwatch—"

"Ser," his color-sergeant said.

Raj looked around. A party of Civil Government officers was riding up; not his own, Osterville's banner. Raj waited in silence.

"General," Osterville said.

"Colonel," Raj replied. Formally: "Colonel Osterville, I'm ordering you to bring your command within the walls of this encampment."

Osterville sneered, a rather theatrical expression. "I'll have to deprive you and Messa Whitehall of that pleasure. As Commandant of the Military District of Sandoral, our authority is concurrent. These commands remain separate, and *I'm* not afraid of that lot of wogs over there."

He pointed; his own four battalions were setting up camp on a hill no more than a kilometer from the walls. Beyond that was a dense pall of smoke, as the ruins of the suburbs beyond the wall smoldered. Not coincidentally, there was an orchard and pleasant little country villa on the hill.

"I warn you," Raj went on, stroking his chin, "that the Colonials may try to sally. Your position is more vulnerable than mine."

Osterville spat—toward the city, which made the gesture ambiguous. "They're scum, with incompetent officers. Obviously, or they'd be over the river with Ali, wouldn't they?" His voice took on a faint hectoring, lecturing note. "Look at the way they reacted when we attacked this morning. As I said, *I'm* not afraid of them, and neither are my men. We're staying where we are."

"By all means, Colonel Osterville," Raj said mildly. "Perhaps it's advisable, all things considered."

From the ranks of officers around Raj a loud whisper continued the thought: "Considering what our men would do to those garrison pussies who've been shorting the take."

Osterville's head whipped around, finding a wall of bland politeness. He saluted and pulled his dog around, with a violence that brought a protesting whimper as the cheek-levers of the bridle gouged.

"Ser." A messenger this time, from the heliograph detachment who'd been setting up a relay back to the bridgehead. "Message from Colonel Menyez."

The silence grew tense. Raj read. "Ali's arrived," he said. "And tried the usual. So far—"

observe, Center said.

"Noisy beggars," Major Ferdihando Felasquez said.

The Colonial army was parading past the walls of Sandoral, fifty thousand strong. *Tabor* after *tabor* of mounted men in crimson djellabas and pantaloons, in a perfect order that rippled with the rise and fall of the trotting dogs. Between the blocks of men came guns, light pompoms and 70mm field pieces, with heavier siege weapons behind. Beyond that, on a hillock just out of medium artillery range, an enormous tent-pavilion in brilliant stripes was already going up. From the tallest pole flew the green crescent banner and the peacock of the Settlers.

And over it all came an inhuman pulse of drums, like the beating heart of some great beast. Beneath that the clang of cymbals and the brazen scream of long curled trumpets.

Felasquez tapped his gauntlets against his thigh. "Should we send them a few love-notes?" he asked. "Some of the heavier pieces on the wall could reach that far."

"No," Jorg Menyez said, scanning down the line of units with the big tripod-mounted field glasses. "We're playing for time, so there's no sense in poking the sauroid through the bars. Ah, yes. Notice something?"

He stepped aside and Felasquez bent to the eyepieces. A forest of banners was going up before the Settler's pavilion. "Ali, Hussein the Wazir, the Grand Mufti of Sinnar, the Gederosian Dervishes . . . wait a minute."

Menyez nodded. "No Seal of Solomon. Tewfik's not here."

"Unless they want us to think that."

"No, that's not the way Colonials think."

Felasquez nodded. "I'd still feel easier if you weren't splitting up so much of the 24th Valencia," he went on.

"The garrison infantry need stiffening; we haven't had enough time to work them into first-class shape."

"You can't stiffen a bucket of spit with a handful of lead shot," Felasquez said.

Menyez clapped him on the shoulder. "It's not as bad as all that. They're trained men, sound at bottom; they've just been neglected recently. Standing behind a parapet and shooting is about the easiest type of combat for 'em. They just need some examples. How're the militia-gunner volunteers showing?"

"Pretty well; still have to see how they stand fire, of course. But the ones who stayed were the ones who *wanted* to fight. A lot of them were with us when we fought Jamal, five years ago."

Along the walls of Sandoral men stood to the parapet and looked out the merlons, but their numbers were sparse. Most of the garrison stood to in the cleared space within the walls, or waited in their billets. Apart from them the city was a ghostly place, where little moved but rats and cats almost as feral.

"It's all waiting now," Menyez went on, "and I want my supper. Runner; message to the *Heneralissimo*—"

This time the viewpoint shifted to a point on the rail line west. Raj recognized it: a long viaduct over a gully that was a torrent in the winter and spring. The burning remnants of the wooden trestle bridge lay scattered below.

A long file of Colonial dragoons rose from prayer and rolled up their issue rugs. Naiks and rissaldars screamed at them, and they returned to their work—hacking through the ties of the railway line. As each section of track came loose, they carried it at a run to one of the bonfires that blazed at intervals down the line and threw it on. The dry wood flared up like tinder, and in the heart of the furnace-heat he could see the thin strap iron turning cherry-red and then yellow, slumping and twisting into a mass of metallic spaghetti that would have to be carted to the forges and rolling-mills as scrap.

Raj nodded to himself, tight-lipped. No surprise; a railroad was the best military target there was. But it had taken generations to get the line from Sandoral to East Residence completed; until Barholm Clerett came to the throne and Raj reconquered the territories to the west, there always seemed to be a more urgent short-term priority.

The Colonials were doing a good professional job of the wrecking, and there were a lot of them.

Dust smoked up from the road. Sweat dripped off the twenty-hitch train of oxen as they strained at the trek-chain. The big tented wagon rolled forward, its axles groaning, man-high wheels turning at the steady, inexorable pace that would take it ten kilometers a day and neither more nor less. It was one of a line of two dozen, between them taking up several kilometers of road; all of them had the Crescent pyrographed on the wood of their sides, and the Peacock stenciled on their tilts.

The load was sacked grain, and bales of a repulsive-looking dried fish; even in the holographic vision he could imagine the mealy, oily smell of it. *Advocati*, the staple dog-fodder of the Drangosh valley, a sucker-mouthed parasitic bottom-feeder with no backbone. Dogs would eat it, just; even slaves would refuse it if they could. As he watched, the oxen halted as the drivers snapped their whips. Men with baskets of grain and dried alfalfa pellets went down the train, dumping loads by the draft cattle.

The escort sank down and unlimbered the goatskin water-bottles at their waists, stacking their light lever-action rifles. Infantry, with short curved falchions at their belts rather than the scimitars of the cavalry. Tewfik wouldn't be wasting his best men on duty like this, but here was about a platoon of them. The drovers were civilians, slight men in ragged clothes.

A voice called, and drovers and soldiers alike knelt in the dust, performing the ritual washing and unrolling their mats. A call, and they knelt to distant Sinnar, the holy city where the first humans on Bellevue had landed, bringing a fragment of the ka'ba from ruined Mecca.

A Colonial officer with gold-rimmed spectacles and a green-dyed beard stood beside a hole. It was outside the walls of Sandoral—he could see the city in the middle distance—but outside ordinary artillery range. There were several hundred Colonials working in the hole, mostly stripped to their loincloths, but they had the look of soldiers. Probably engineers; the Colony had whole units of them, rather than expecting line units to be able to double up at need, the way the Civil Government did. He'd never seen men work harder, or with more skill.

Picks were flying; plank ramps went down into the hole, and wheelbarrows came up at a trot, full of earth. The dirt was piled neatly in heaps not far away; other men were filling sandbags from the heaps. Still more shaped timber, raw beams from orchards around the city, or seasoned timber salvaged from houses. A knocked-down floor of planks waited to be assembled.

A bunker, Raj decided. Cursed large one, too. Probably for Ali.

(((•))) (((•))) (((•)))

Raj blinked, conscious of the eyes on him. They were all used to his . . . spells of inattention . . . by now.

He cleared his throat. "Ali's reached Sandoral and he's digging in around the city. So far he hasn't mounted an assault—bringing up his siege train, at a guess. He's got the full fifty thousand men with him; it must be straining his supply of wagons and fodder to keep them fed. Tewfik's banner isn't with the main army."

There was a stir at that. "What do we do, *mi heneral?*" Staenbridge asked.

"We dig, and we wait."

"Wait for what?"

"For the wogs" —he nodded toward Ain el-Hilwa— "to take the bait. In which case, we—"

The officers waited in silence, a few taking notes. "Is all that clear?" Raj finished.

"No reserve?" Staenbridge asked.

"Not this time; it's a calculated risk, but so's this whole expedition."

He turned and looked at the Arab city, surrounded by the smoldering wreck of its suburbs, crammed to the very wall with refugees.

"Either this will be easy, or it'll be impossible," he said.

probability of action proceeding according to current projections, 78%±7, Center said helpfully.

"I'd put it at about three to one on easy," he went on. "If not, we'll just have to react fast."

> *"When you go by the Camina Bellica*
> *As thousands have traveled before*
> *Remember the Luck of the Soldier*
> *Who never saw home anymore!*
> *Oh, dear was the lover who kissed him*
> *And dear was the mother that bore;*
> *But then they found his sword in the heather,*
> *And he never saw home anymore!"*

"Ser." Antin M'lewis was Officer of the Day; he slipped into the circle around the fire. "Major Hwadeloupe t'see yer."

Raj finished the mouthful of fig-bread and dusted his hands, leaning back on the cushions—someone had salvaged them from a nearby Colonial mansion, and they were all resting on them and the Al Kebir carpets from the same source. A roast sheep on rice had been demolished, and they were punishing the sweetmeats and pastries the Colonials were famous for. The wine was too sweet, even diluted, but nobody was drinking all that much of it anyway; they knew him better than that. The firelight played on the faces around it, bringing out scars on Kaltin Gruder's as he leaned forward to light a twig and puff a cheroot alight.

"By all means, Antin, bring him along," Raj said.

Hwadeloupe commanded the 44th Camarina Dragoons, one of Osterville's battalions.

"An' ser . . . he's got 'is men out there. Hunnerts of 'em, not too far."

"Keep an eye on them, Captain."

The strong male voices were roaring out the next verse, the one that had gotten the song officially banned centuries ago. It was a truth the Governors preferred that the Army not be too conscious of:

> *"When you go by the Camina Bellica*
> *From the City to Sandoral,*
> *Remember the Luck of the Soldier*
> *Who rose to be master of all!*
> *He carried the rifle and saber,*
> *He stood his watch and rode tall,*
> *Till the Army hailed him as Governor*
> *And he rose to be master of all!"*

"Glad you could join us," Raj said as Hwadeloupe strode up. "No, no, no salutes in the mess, Major. Have some wine."

The soldier-servant handed him a mug of half-and-half, watered wine. He gripped it distractedly, a middle-aged man with the marks of long service on the southern border on his leathery face.

"*Mi heneral*, if we could speak privately?"

"I have no secrets from my officers and Companions, Major." Not *quite* true, but it was a polite way of telling Hwadeloupe that he couldn't expect to hedge his bets.

"Ah . . . sir, I would like to transfer my battalion to your command—to this encampment, that is."

The rest of the command group had fallen silent; Suzette kept strumming her *gittar*, but softly. Without the song, the minor noises of the camp came through: dogs growling, a challenge from the walls, the iron clatter of a field gun's breechblock being opened for some reason.

"If I might ask why?" Raj went on implacably.

Hwadeloupe stood very straight. "Sir. Colonel Osterville thinks there's no risk from the garrison of Ain el-Hilwa. But I know you don't think so, and I see your men still have their boots on, and your guns are limbered up. Colonel Osterville may be right. On the whole, though, when he and you disagree, I'll bet on you. With respect, sir."

Raj shoulder-rolled and came erect. "I can always use good men," he said. "And I don't think you'll regret that decision. Captain M'lewis will show your men to their bivouac area within the earthworks."

"Ah, sir. There's one other matter." Hwadeloupe kept his eyes fixed over Raj's shoulder. "We have, ah, a considerable quantity of booty with us. Just picked up, you understand. We'd like to turn it in now to the common fund, as per your standing orders."

Raj raised an eyebrow; one of Gerrin's expressions, and very useful in situations like this. "That's odd, Major. We've had several smaller parties in from Colonel Osterville's camp, and they've all had some late-arriving booty to turn in too." He extended his hand. "No hard feelings. M'lewis will settle your people in."

"I'll see to that myself, if it's all the same to you, *mi heneral*," Hwadeloupe said, taking the extended hand in his own. "And thank you, sir."

Raj returned to his cushion beside Suzette. "That's about two hundred in all," he said.

"Separating the sheep from the goats," Staenbridge replied. "Or those too stupid to live from the remainder."

Foley frowned. "Some of them are staying over there to follow orders," he pointed out.

"My dear," Gerrin said, "what's that saying—from the Old Namerique codexes—"

Foley was something of a scholar. "'*Against Fate even the gods do not fight,*'" he quoted.

"Exactly."

Raj nodded and leaned back, his head not quite in Suzette's lap. Both moons were out and very bright, bright enough to interrupt the frosted arch of stars. Her fingers wandered over the strings.

> *"It's twenty-five marches to Payso*
> *It's forty-five more to Ayaire*
> *And the end may be death in the heather*
> *Or life on the Governor's Chair*
> *But whether the Army obeys us,*
> *Or we serve as some sauroid's fare*
> *I'd rather be Lola's lover*
> *Than sit on the Governor's Chair!"*

Cut-nose Marhtinez lay in the dark and breathed quietly. He was ten meters from the walls of Ain el-Hilwa, outside the north gate. An overturned two-wheel cart hid him; the bodies of the two dogs who'd been drawing it until they met a cannonball were fairly ripe after a day in the hot sun, and so was the driver: black, swollen, the skin split and dripping in places, like a windfallen plum. He'd had about seven FedCreds in assorted silver in his pouch, though.

The night was fairly dark, only one moon in the sky and that near the horizon. The starlight was enough for him to see men moving on the walls—and they were moving without torches. He could even hear some wog curse when he ran into something and barked his chin. A whistling and dull thudding followed, about the sound you'd expect one of those nine-barbed whips the wog officers used to make. The yelp of pain that followed was strangled, and the next slash brought no sound at all.

Quiet's a whorehouse on payday, he thought scornfully. It was a good thing there weren't any Bedouin scouts with the Ain el-Hilwa garrison. Those sand-humpers were too good for comfort.

Cut-nose moved his head slightly. The star he was using was still a fingerbreadth above the horizon. An hour and a bit short of dawn, call it an hour and twenty minutes.

He moved backward out of the wrecked cart, keeping it between him and the wall. Nothing on his body clinked or reflected light, and his hands and face were blacked; Mother Marhtinez might not have known exactly who his father was, but she hadn't raised any fools. Pause, move, pause, until he was behind a snag of ruined wall, still hot enough from the fire to feel on his skin. He picked up his rifle—nothing but a hindrance and a temptation in the blind where he'd spent the night—and eeled cautiously back to his dog.

Captain M'lewis was waiting there. Cut-nose grinned ingratiatingly. He didn't have much use for officers, and still less for a promoted ranker who might be a kinsman. He did have the liveliest respect for Antin M'lewis's wits, his wire garrote, and the skinning-knife he wore across the small of his back beneath the tails of his uniform jacket. All the Forty Thieves—the Scouts—had a standing invitation to go out behind the stables and settle things with knives if they felt they couldn't obey someone who wasn't Messer-born.

So far only one fool had taken M'lewis up on it; he was on the rolls as a deserter. Nobody had found the body. *Good riddance,* Cut-nose thought. The Scouts beat regular duty all to hell. Less boring, more plunder—a *lot* more in some cases—and no more dangerous. M'lewis wasn't the charge-the-barricade type.

"They're movin', ser. Gittin' ready, loike," he said in a soft whisper, directed at the ground—nothing to carry far.

M'lewis nodded. "Messer Raj was expectin' it, an' t'scouts at t'other gate says th' same," he observed. "Here, git this t'him fast."

"Sir."

Kaltin Gruder's voice. Raj rolled out of his blankets; Suzette was already reaching for her carbine. He fastened his weapons belt. His boots were already on; if the men had to sleep in them, so could he.

"Message from M'lewis just got in."

A Scout was behind the battalion commander. "Ser. Noise in t'wog town. I weren't more 'n ten meters off, an' heard it plain. North gates."

The ones nearest Colonel Osterville's camp. Raj took the message and read it. "Boots and saddles, please. Quietly. We'll deploy as arranged."

"Line of march?"

"Scout troop has pickets along it. They'll signal with shuttered lanterns."

Raj could hear the noise spreading; not very loud, no shouting, but a long-drawn out clatter as men rousted out of uneasy sleep and saw to their equipment. The Companions arrived, and the other battalion commanders. Shapes in the night, dimly lit by the embers of the fire, a feeling of controlled anxiety. He grinned into the dark. A night march. Difficult. An invitation to disaster, with any but very experienced troops. The handbooks were full of bungled night attacks, men firing on their comrades, whole battalions wandering off lost, irretrievable disaster.

"Barton," he said. "What's that toast again?"

"'He fears his fate too much, and his deserts are small, who will not put it to the touch—to win or lose it all.' "

"Exactly. Messers, to your units. *Waymanos!*"

An orderly brought up Horace; he put a foot in the stirrup and swung into the saddle. The headquarters party fell in around him, bannermen and buglers and gallopers. Men blinked and dogs yawned cavernously; the wet *clomp-clomp* sound of jaws snapping closed rippled through the dark streets. Iron-shod wheels rattled on dirt as the 75s and splatguns moved. He cantered down the east-west notional laneway of the camp, the *wia erente*, keeping to the side. Men and dogs were moving the same way, the lead element of the 5th, followed by the 1st and 2nd Cruisers. The other gates were all open as well, flanked by lantern-bearing pathfinders. Thousands of heavy paws thumped the earth, an endless rumbling sound.

Flat terrain, mostly. Nothing between him and Osterville's camp but four kilometers of fields, with the occasional orchard or shallow ditch. The objective was on the same side of the Ghor Canal, thank the Spirit, even *Osterville* wasn't stupid enough to put an obstacle that needed bridging between him and the only supports available. *Keep in column,* he decided. In column they could move down the laneways, at a fast walk. Once deployed into line their speed would drop by four-fifths.

The night was still quiet, almost chilly in the last moments of predawn; overhead the arch of stars was a frosted road leading to infinity. The command group rode silently, no need for talk unless something went very wrong. The palms that lined the roadway were black silhouettes against the sky. He looked over his shoulder to the west and caught the faintest rim of peach-pink there.

He reined Horace sideways into the fields, a hunching scramble through the ditch, then stood in the stirrups to look. Nothing but a few watchfires from Osterville's camp. The north gates of the city were hidden by the western wall. Flags rippled behind him, his personal banner and the Star. Over his shoulder he could see the other gates of the camp, now; the spiked-log barricades were pulled aside, and a steady stream of men and dogs and guns was pouring out. Not a single jam-up, not a voice raised . . . *damn, but these are good troops.*

Three columns, each about half a kilometer apart, each a little over two thousand strong. And—

" 'The gates flew back, and the din of onset sounded,' " Bartin murmured.

"More Old Namerique?" Raj said.

"From the Fall Codexes," the young man replied.

When the Fall began, books had died with the machines that recorded them—the Church called it the Great Simplification. In the first generation the survivors wrote down as much as they could, most of it in Old Namerique, the official language of the Federation. Bits and pieces survived, even a thousand years later.

The gates of Ain el-Hilwa had certainly flown back with a vengeance.

"One hell of a din, too," Raj said, even at more than three kilometers, it was louder than the noise his own men were making.

Then light winked from the parapet of the low-set city wall, and a deep whirring sound crossed the sky. A dull booming echoed, and under it the sharper sound of the exploding shells. The winking lights, scores of meters apart, rippled from east to west across the north face of the city. Heavy rifles, aimed at Osterville's camp. The shells seemed to be contact-fused rather than airburst, but it would still be an unpleasant way to wake up, and there were a lot of those guns.

The white dust of the road stretched out ahead of him. The dawn was just touching the western horizon behind him, but there was a sudden flare of white light stabbing north toward Osterville's position, arc-searchlights from the city wall. *My, all the modern refinements*, Raj thought. Intended to light up the Civil Government position for the attackers and blind any defenders looking toward the city.

Dun and off-white, men were running up the long gentle slope toward the smaller Civil Government camp. On foot, mostly, with gun teams among them, pulling the light five-shot pom-poms the Colonials favored for close support. They were shouting, too, high wailing shrieks. Raj unclipped his binoculars and brought them to his eyes, body adapting to the swing of his dog's trot with the unconscious skill of a lifetime.

Only half a kilometer from the walls. And they didn't dig in at all. Osterville had been very careless.

A stutter of gunfire broke out from Osterville's camp, building rapidly. Raj could imagine the chaos, men rushing half-dressed from their blanket rolls, grabbing up the rifles stacked by their campfires. Red light winked from the hilltop, muzzle flashes like fireflies in the dark; the sun was just edging over the horizon.

The Colonials were making some effort to deploy, spreading out in an irregular mass—more a thick skirmish order than a real firing line. The pom-poms wheeled about and opened up, firing uphill. The *CRACK-CRACK-CRACK-CRACK-CRACK* of the clip-loaded weapons sounded through the dawn, and their little one-kilo shells burst upslope in petals of fire. The return fire was building fast, panicked, with no ordered crash of volleys. Smoke began to shroud the hilltop, from the defensive fire and the incoming Colonial shells, and—

"Bugging out already," he said. In the long-shadowed light of dawn he could see a trickle of mounted men heading north from Osterville's encampment. "Ludwig, how many of the Colonials would you say?"

"Seven or eight thousand at least, *mi heneral.*"

Raj nodded thoughtfully. The whole garrison of Ain el-Hilwa, or near enough. Attacking Osterville's position was actually not a bad idea—he would have tried it, in their position—but sending everyone haring out of the gates like this? *No more sense than a bull carnosauroid in breeding season,* he decided.

"Captain Foley, the signal."

Barton swung down out of the saddle and stuck the launching-stick of a small rocket in the dirt.

Fissssssth. The little rocket soared into the paling sky and burst with an undramatic *pop*. Red and blue sparks shot out in a perfect round puffball. Behind Raj trumpets sang in harsh antiphonal chorus. The long column dissolved as units spurred out left and right, like a huge fan snapping open. It was lighter now, light enough to tell a dark thread from a white, the traditional dividing line between night and day. Light enough for the men to move across the fields without much trouble, at least.

The other columns were following suit. Ten minutes, and there was a continuous two-deep line moving northeastwards with his banner at the center. Not parade-ground neat—the line twisted and curled a little around obstacles, with fifty meters or so of gap between each battalion. The guns pulled through, heading east and a little south, setting up by groups of batteries on prechosen hillocks. The Colonials were fully occupied, their front ranks within two hundred meters of Osterville's position and moving in fast. Close enough to use their carbines, and a huge snapping crackle went up from their front ranks; not *only* from their front ranks, either—they were losing men to friendly fire, if he was any judge.

"Sound Prepare for Dismounted Action," he said.

The bugles sang again, taken up and relayed down the line. Men pulled the rifles from the scabbards before their right knees, resting the butts on their thighs.

"Are they bloody *blind*?" Staenbridge asked in amazement, looking at the Colonials.

"No, just very preoccupied, and extremely badly led," Raj said.

There were probably individual men in the Colonial force who could see what was happening, but it was a scratch put-together and whoever had done the putting hadn't arranged for signals and gallopers. A penalty of taking all your best troops along in a single expeditionary force; what was left to defend against a counterstroke wasn't up to much.

Six hundred meters, Raj thought.

five hundred eight-eight and decreasing to nearest enemy element. five hundred eighty. five seventy-six. Center provided a numbered scale on the whole Colonial formation; their right wing was just out of extreme rifle-shot.

More of Osterville's men were bugging out, but that wouldn't be visible to the wogs. A slamming close-range firefight ran in a C all around the front of the hill, as the larger Colonial force overlapped the Civil Government forces upslope. Most of the pom-pom shells were flying right over the hill, dangerous only to the deserters streaming northward—who deserved whatever they got. The Colonial rifle fire was uneven; their men were pumping out their seven-shell magazines and then pausing to reload. That had to be done by pushing one round at a time through the loading gate in the side of the weapon, which evened things out a little, but Osterville's fire was dropping off noticeably, as the Colonials beat down his men by sheer weight of numbers.

Five hundred meters. "Sound *Dismounted Advance.*"

The buglers sent the message down the lines: a four-note preparation, twice repeated, then a single sustained note taken up by the signalers in unit after unit. Six thousand dogs crouched. Not quite in unison, but nearly so within battalions. The men stepped free of the stirrups without pausing, and the dogs rose and walked behind, still in ranks as regular as the men's. A good cavalry battalion drilled six hours a day, six days a week for this moment, until the signals played directly on the nervous systems of men and mounts. Raj turned his binoculars to the far right of his line: Hwadeloupe's men were badly under strength, but they were carrying it off quite well.

A long clatter as the men loaded. Raj's head went back and forth; the troops were advancing at a steady walk, the splatguns trundling forward with the soldiers, two per battalion. They were light enough for the crews to manhandle them like that; they looked much like field guns, but each was actually thirty-five double-length rifle barrels clamped in a tube. He watched as one crew let the trail thump to the ground and loaded. One man swung the lever down, another inserted an iron plate with thirty-five rifle cartridges, the lever went back up with a thump. Waiting for the order—but they were artillerymen and very good at estimating ranges. He chopped out his palm. The buglers took it up. All up and down the line men checked a half-pace. And . . .

"Halto!"

Officers ducked ahead and spread arm and drawn saber to mark the firing line. Another bugle call and the front rank dropped to the ground and the men behind them went to one knee, right elbow resting on it. The platoon commanders and senior noncoms walked quickly between the two ranks for a moment, checking that the sights were adjusted for the range. The muzzles quivered as each trooper picked a target. The dogs crouched; only the mounted officers, Company-grade and above, marked the line. Company pennants and battalion banners too, of course; the men took their dressing from the flags.

Raj took a deep breath. It was a peculiar exultation, like handling a fine sword with perfect balance; the pleasure that came only from a difficult task performed exactly as it should be.

Some of the enemy were turning now, firing frantically. Far too late. The trumpets spoke again, preparing men for the order:

"Fwego!"

BAMMMbambambambabam . . . Six thousand rifles fired within a few seconds of each other. A discordant medley of battalion trumpeters sounded the *Fire by Platoon Volleys*. BAM. BAM. BAM. Rippling down the formation. Front line prone, second rank kneeling. Front rank fire-and-reload, second rank fire-and-reload, a steady pounding crackle. The dawn wind was from the east, blowing the new fogbank of powder smoke backward in tatters. The smell was overwhelming in the fresh morning air: a sharp unpleasant reek of burnt sulfur and stinging saltpeter. The smell of death.

The splatgun crew spun the crank at one side of the breechblock. *Brraaaap.* A long splat of sound as the thirty-five rounds snapped out. *K-chung* as the lever went back and the plate was lifted out by the loop on its top, a rattle as another was slapped home and the lever worked. *Brraaaap. Brraaaap.* Three hundred rounds a minute. An ancient design, ancient before the Fall, from man's first rise; primitive enough that men in these days could build it. The priests said that Man had been perfect, before the Fall. Raj had always been a believer; it was obscurely disturbing that part of that perfection was better and better mechanisms of slaughter.

He threw the thought aside, with a touch to the amulet blessed by Saint Wu; there was the work of the day to be done. Raj turned and cantered down the line. The Civil Government formation was at right angles to the Colonial formation, like the crossbar on a "T." The whole weight of its fire was crashing into the end of the Arab line. And most of the Civil Government cavalrymen could *hit* a man-sized target at three hundred meters, many of them at twice that range. Even if they missed, their 11mm bullets would run the entire length of the enemy line, with good odds of hitting *something*. The Colonials were melting away, men smashed to the ground by the heavy hollowpoint bullets with massive exit wounds that bled them out in seconds, or tore limbs from bodies.

He paused behind one of the ex-Brigadero units. A noncom was walking down the line, slapping men across the shoulders with the flat of his saber when they instinctively rose to fire standing. *Problem,* Raj though. They'd trained on muzzle-loading rifle muskets. You had to stand to reload those, tearing open the paper cartridge and pouring the powder down the barrel. They were excellent shots even by Descotter standards, but not used to getting under cover—and even at this range, some of the Colonial carbine-bullets would hit standing men. A few snapped by him.

Ludwig Bellamy rode up. "It's a slaughter, *heneralissimo*," he said enthusiastically. "Teodore—Major Welf—asks permission to remount his battalion and charge—"

"Denied," Raj said sharply.

Welf had been a very tricky opponent in the Western Territories, but he was still a Brigadero at heart and had a lingering fondness for cold steel. The Civil Government military style was economical of men where it could be, not having so many trained soldiers to expend.

"I'm not going to waste men on this lot." He raised the binoculars again. "Besides, about now—"

There was boiling confusion all down the front of the Arab army. A knot of mounted officers around a huge green banner was galloping toward the threatened flank, with more courage than sense. At their head was a portly gray-bearded man waving his ceremonial lash and shouting furiously, probably trying to pull units out of line and get them to face front left. Small chance of that, since Osterville's men were still firing from *their* front, besides which most of them probably hadn't realized what was happening, and facing about would put the morning sun directly in their eyes.

The enemy bannerman went down. Seconds later half a dozen of the officers around him did, and then the elderly man with the whip punched backward over the cantle of his saddle. His dog whipped about and sniffed him, then sank down on its haunches and howled.

"—they're going to bug out."

It started with the men in sight of the dead commander. They broke like a glass pitcher dropped on a stone floor, and fled back toward the city. Bullets kicked up dust around their feet like the first raindrops of a storm, and littered the ground with bodies. That unmasked the central part of the Colonial host, and for the first time they could see exactly what it was that had devoured the left wing of their army. And the steady, unhurried volleys punched out, from a Civil Government line marked by a growing tower of smoke that made their position clear even a kilometer away. The Arabs disintegrated like a rope unraveling from the left end, men throwing away their weapons to run screaming for the city gates. Droves piled up at ditches that a man could leap easily, as the first tripped and the men behind trampled on them.

"*Spirit*, sir—if we charge now—"

"Major Bellamy, all that charging now would do is give *them* an opportunity to hurt *us*." He looked around. "Messenger to Major Gruder: advance from the left in line, by battalions, pivoting on . . ." —he considered— "on the 3/591st." You had to start moving the outside of a line first, or the whiplash effect would leave the outermost man running.

"Are we going to let them back into the city, *mi heneral?*" Ludwig Bellamy asked, crestfallen.

Raj smiled unpleasantly. "By no means, Major. By no means."

"Range three thousand. Up three. And a bit. Contact fuse. Load."

Grammeck Dinnalsyn raised his eyes from the split-view rangefinder. Three batteries were deployed along the slight rise: twelve guns. Another three were a few hundred meters farther on, setting up amid the outer spray of the dead Colonials. Dismounted men were trotting by in waves as the left flank of the Civil Government force swung in to pin the retreating Colonials against the walls of Ain el-Hilwa, but that was no concern of the artillery today; they weren't tasked with supporting the dogboys. The riflemen were firing as they advanced, independent fire in a continuous crackle all up and down the line. The sun sparkled on the bright brass of the spent cartridge cases.

Breechblocks clattered as the big 75mm shells were passed from the limber and rammed home. The crew stood aside as the master gunner clipped his lanyard to the trigger and payed it out.

"Ranging gun, shoot," Dinnalsyn said.

Battery commander's work, really, but enjoyable, and he rarely got a chance to do it these days. The gunner jerked sharply.

POUMPH. A long jet of smoke shot out from Number One of A Battery. The gun threw itself backward in recoil, the trail gouging a trough in the clay. The crew jumped forward as soon as it came to rest, grabbing the trail and the tall wheels and running it back to the original position.

Dinnalsyn raised his binoculars. A tall plume of black dust sprouted from the roadway outside the northeast gate of the city, like an instant poplar that bent in the breeze and dispersed as the dirt scattered.

"Excellent," he said. "Batteries, range."

The thick tubes of the guns rose as the gunners spun the elevating screws under the breeches.

Excellent shooting on the first try, and it was excellent to serve under a commander who *understood* what artillery could and could not do.

The other two batteries were tasked with the northwestern gate, a bit farther—near maximum effective range. Their ranging gun fired seconds after his, and the gout of dirt flung skyward was a hundred meters short. Even that trial shot told, flinging parts of men and equipment skyward. Both roads into Ain el-Hilwa were black with running men, and more every second. They tried again, and the next round fell neatly before the open gates.

"Airburst, three-second fuse, shrapnel, load."

Blue-banded shells from the limbers, passed forward hand to hand three times; gun crews had redundant members to replace casualties in action. Not that there looked to be much counterfire this time. The master gunners pulled the ring-shaped blockers out of the noses of the shells, arming the fuses. Into the narrow hole went a two-pronged tool they carried chained to their wrists, to adjust the timers. A brass ring on the fuse turned, listing the time in seconds; within, drilled beechwood turned in a perforated brass tube, exposing a precisely calculated length of powder-train.

"Number one gun ready!"

"Number two gun ready!"

"Number three gun ready!"

"Number four gun ready!"

"Battery A ready!"

"Batteries will shoot, for effect. On the word of command."

He raised his free hand, the other holding his binoculars. *Use your judgment,* the general had said. Men were running through, but that was the first spray of them. He waited, gauntleted hand in the air. The gates were narrow, and so were the arched bridges that carried the roadways over the city moat. You *wanted* city gates to be a chokepoint, for defensive reasons, and Ain el-Hilwa had excellent fortifications. Routed, the Arab troops were not going to wait while they were marshaled through with maximum efficiency. Every man for himself meant a tie-up.

Sure enough, the roadways were black with men and great fans of them were spreading out along the edge of the moat. He chopped his hand downward.

"*Now!*"

POUMP. The first gun fired. A precise twenty seconds later the second followed. *POUMP. POUMP. POUMP.* By the time the last gun fired, the first had been pushed back into battery and was ready to fire again. A steady two rounds a minute, to conserve barrels and break armies. No problem, with the men fresh. Pushing the ton weights of metal around was hard work, but they were trained to a hair and the day was young.

Four *crack* sounds downrange, as the shells burst. Ragged black smokeballs in the air over the crowd at the gates; below them panic, as the shells' loads of musketballs scythed forward in an oval pattern of destruction.

POUMP. POUMP. POUMP. POUMP. This time one of the rounds hammered into the dirt before exploding, a faulty time-fuse. No great problem this time; the crater made the pileup greater. He shifted his glasses to the other gate. The spread of shell was wider there, some far enough from the gate to kick up dust, but you expected that at extreme range.

The general cantered up with his staff and messengers. He paused for a moment, leaning on the pommel with both hands and studying the artillery. *Strange man,* Dinnalsyn thought. He saw too much, knew too much. Knew as much about guns as he did himself, and was better at judging distance and trajectories; a cannon-cocker's skills, not a talent you expected in a hill-squireen out of Descott. And he never *forgot* anything, never missed a detail—as if angels were whispering in his ear. There were those strange little trances, too. Grammeck was city-born to a merchant family, and prided himself on his modernity, but there might be something in the tales of Messer Raj being touched by the Spirit.

"I could do better execution with more tubes, *mi heneral*," he said.

They had fifty-five guns along, and they were all reconcentrated now that the raiding parties had joined forces.

Raj shook his head, his stone-hard face still turned to the gates where men screamed and died and the corpses tossed under the hammer of the shells.

"Not for this," he said. "We don't have the ammunition to expend."

True; they were limited to what they'd brought along. He made a mental note to shift things around to even out the reserve supplies between batteries before they broke camp. A glance at his watch told him it was still early, barely 0800.

"And speaking of which," the general went on, "give them another three rounds per gun and cease fire. Another few minutes and the guns on the walls will have you registered here."

As if to punctuate the thought, a heavy shell buried itself in the earth a hundred meters ahead of them and exploded, throwing clods of dirt as far as the second hillock.

"And then limber up and get out of range," Raj said.

"Si, mi heneral."

seventy-six rounds per gun, Center said.

Ah, Raj thought. About his own offhand estimate. Strange, that so much of Center's advice was a refinement of what he'd have done anyway.

of course. otherwise i would not have selected you.

Which was reassuring. There were times he doubted he was the same man who'd blundered into the centrum beneath the Gubernatorial Palace.

that youth would be gone forever by now in any case.

Raj shrugged and looked down at the field of battle with a mixture of distaste and the sensation a farmer had looking back over an expanse of grain cut and stooked in good time. The Colonials had finally gotten their gates shut and the cannon on the wall active; but that left most of their garrison trapped outside the wall and exposed to fire.

"Signal cease-fire. And get a truce flag ready."

"What terms?" Staenbridge said.

"The usual. Parole not to participate further in this campaign, and one gold FedCred per head."

One advantage of fighting the wogs was that they and the *Gubernio Civil* had been locked in combat so long they'd developed an elaborate code of military etiquette and generally observed it for sound reasons of mutual long-term advantage. One provision often used was releasing prisoners on parole, when the alternative was killing them for want of time and facilities. It put them out of action for the remainder of the war in question, and was about as profitable as selling them for slaves, which was the other choice. Granted that they could be used on some *other* frontier, which freed up troops to be used against you; on the other hand, both powers had an interest in keeping the barbarians at bay.

and the cause of civilization is served, as well.

Kaltin Gruder came up. Raj nodded. "Nice turning movement, Kaltin."

"Work of the day, *mi heneral.* Are we going to take their parole?"

Raj nodded. Kaltin's mouth tightened, but he nodded unwillingly.

"Ali might not keep it," he pointed out. Reluctantly: "Of course, it wouldn't *matter*, with these handless cows."

"There are no bad soldiers, Kaltin, only bad officers. But these have had their morale fairly thoroughly shattered, and they won't be any use to anyone for a good long while. See to it."

Another party rode up; this one included a number of bandaged and bleeding men. The most senior seemed to be a captain; Raj didn't recognize him, which probably meant he was from Osterville's command.

captain fillipo swarez, 51st mazatlan.

Thank you, Raj thought. Aloud: "Captain Swarez."

The man blinked at Raj through red-rimmed, exhausted eyes,

holding his bandaged arm against his chest to limit the jarring of his dog's movement.

"General Whitehall. I am reporting as senior officer in . . . as senior officer of the other field force battalions."

Raj raised an eyebrow. "Major Gonsalvez?"

"Dead, sir."

"Colonel Osterville?"

observe:

A brief vision this time: Osterville's muddy sweating face, bent low over the neck of his dog and slashing behind with his riding crop. A string of remounts followed, and several servants, and pack dogs with small heavy crates strapped to their carrying saddles.

Swarez spat. "That for the *hijo da puta*! Nobody saw him after the shelling started, and his dogs and personal servants are missing."

One of the lieutenants behind him spoke. "*Heneralissimo*, let me send a patrol after him—let me *take* a patrol after him. I guarantee, he'll never trouble you again."

Growls of assent rose from the survivors; their mounts snarled in sympathy, scenting their masters' mood. *No zealot like a convert,* Raj thought.

He shook his head. "Messer Osterville" —he omitted the military rank— "suits me well enough where he is." He looked back at the captain.

"Captain Swarez, how many survivors?"

"Six hundred in all, sir. Two hundred wounded."

Half Osterville's original force, but that included several hundred who'd defected to Raj during the night, and the Spirit alone knew how many who'd bugged out this morning.

"How many of those in your 51st Mazatlan?"

"Two hundred twenty-six. Fit for duty, that is, sir."

Which meant they'd kept together fairly well. "All right. Tell the remainder that those who wish may transfer to your unit, or to any of my other battalions that'll take them—some of them are severely under strength. Have everyone ready to move shortly."

Swarez saluted, relief on his face. A soldier's battalion was his home and family, and his had just been spared from disbandment.

The other survivors could count themselves lucky to have open slots waiting for them.

Raj watched the party with the white flag riding up to the gates of Ain el-Hilwa. He doubted the negotiations would take long; they'd be too hysterically thankful not to face a storm and sack, which they now lacked the men to stop. Say until noon to get the wounded sorted, police up and destroy the enemy weapons, collect the ransom . . .

Demand some fast sprung wagons as part of it, he decided. There were good roads all the way from here to the bridgehead opposite Sandoral. Then . . .

"Meeting of the command group at midday," he said. "Now let's get this wrapped, gentlemen."

He looked down at the field again before he reined about. A good workmanlike day's effort. Unpleasantly final for several thousand Colonials.

It wasn't going to stay this easy. This was a sideshow so far. Ali's main attention was focused on Sandoral.

CHAPTER NINE

"Fwego!"

Corporal Minatelli opened his mouth and put his hands over his ears. His firing slit was close enough that the fortress gun would hurt his hearing if he didn't.

BOOOOMM.

"Reload, canister!"

The big soda-bottle-shaped fortress gun surged backward on its pivot-mounted carriage, muzzle wreathed in smoke. The wooden friction blocks squealed against their screw tighteners as they slowed the multitonne weight of cast iron and steel. It slowed to a stop at the end of the low ramped carriage, and the militia crew sprang into action. Two men leaped in with a bundle of soaked sponges on a long pole and rammed it down the barrel. There was a long *shhhhhhhhhhh* as the water met hot metal and flashed into steam. They pulled the pole out and flipped it, presenting the wooden rammer head. Two more men were lifting the round in, a big dusty-looking linen bag of coarse gunpowder nailed to a wooden sabot, with a tin canister full of lead balls on the other end.

Minatelli shuddered as he turned away. Canister from a light field gun was bad enough. Canister from a 150mm siege weapon . . .

The gun rumbled like thunder as the gunners released the blocks and it ran down the carriage to lift the iron shutter and poke its muzzle out the casement wall. Bronze wheels squealed as the four men at the rear threw themselves at the handspikes in response to the master gunner's hand signals. The gun carriage was mounted on a pivot in the center, with the front and rear running on wheels that rested on an iron ring set into the concrete floor.

"Bring her up two—they'll be trying again," the master gunner said. He accompanied it with hand signals, for the ones who had lumps of cotton waste stuffed in their ears. His crew spun the big elevating wheel at the breech two turns, and the massive pebbled surface of the gun elevated smoothly at the muzzle.

Keep to your trade, Minatelli told himself, stepping up to the firing parapet. He usually didn't have much time for militia, but these gunnery boys knew their business. He peered through; the sunlight made him squint, after the shade of the wall platform with its overhead protection of timber and iron. The stone of the wall was cool against his cheek.

Outside, six hundred meters from the wall, the wog trench was still swarming. Men were dragging away the dead and wounded, the smashed gabions, wickerwork baskets with earth inside them. He could see flashes of heads and shoulders as picks and shovels swung. The trench was big, a Z-shaped zigzag running back to the main wog bastion twelve hundred meters out; that was a continuous earthwork fort all the way around the city now. Cannon flashed from it, and he could feel the massive stone-fronted walls tremble rhythmically under him as the heavy solid shot pounded selected spots. Dust puffed up, making him sneeze. He wiped his nose on his sleeve and spat.

There were hundreds of the assault trenches worming their way toward the walls, but this one was his section's particular tribulation.

The enemy guns boomed again. One bolt struck right beneath him, and his rifle quivered against the stone it rested on with a harsh tooth-gritting vibration. It would be difficult for them to make a breach; Sandoral's walls were twenty meters thick counting the earth backing, and sunk well behind the moat so that only a lip showed . . . but it would happen in time.

Shells screeched by overhead, exploding behind him among the empty houses. The ragheads didn't seem to be worrying about ammunition supplies. He'd helped defend the walls of Old Residence against a hundred thousand Brigaderos, twice the number that the wogs had, but this felt worse. Back then they'd had Messer Raj, and the MilGov barbs had wandered around with their thumbs up their bums while the Civil Government force wore them down. The towel-heads weren't that kind of stupid.

He hopped down and walked along the space of wall his section held, and the platoon of garrison infantry they were supporting. One of those was stretched out on the walkway, most of the top of his head missing and brains spattered all over his firing niche.

"*Fuck* it!" Minatelli screamed. "You—y'fuckhead—didn't y'*tell* him?"

The dead man's corporal looked up. "Couldn't make 'im listen."

The wogs had big bipod-mounted sniper rifles working from their forward lines, single-shot weapons as heavy as the sauroid-killers the Skinner nomads used. They had telescopic sights, too.

"Well, git t'body out of t'way," Minatelli said angrily. Two of the man's squadmates dragged it away as it dribbled. Bad for morale to have corpses lying around if you didn't have to. It was a pity you couldn't remove the smell; it was hot and close here, and the blood began rotting almost at once.

Everyone else was keeping their head away from the firing slit until told. Rifles were lying in the flat stone bottoms of the slits, with their levers open to keep the chambers as cool as be. Each niche had a couple of wooden strips set into troughs in the stone, with rows of holes drilled in the wood. Each hole held a cartridge, base-up and ready to hand. Two thousand-round ammunition crates rested on ledges between firing positions, their tops loosened and the protective tinfoil curled back to show the ten-round bundles, one hundred bundles per box. Buckets of water and dippers hung from iron hooks; there was a wooden box of hand bombs by every man's firing position, round cast-iron balls the size of an orange, with a ring on top to arm the friction fuse. There were even some spare rifles in a rack, for the men disarmed by the jams that would be inevitable once firing got heavy and the weapons heated up.

The only thing missing was enough men to fill all the firing niches, plus the reserve that doctrine called for. What they had was one rifleman for every three slots, one man for nine meters of front. The Colonials had enough troops to attack anywhere along four kilometers of wall, without warning.

The lieutenant blew his whistle. Men tensed, thumbing rounds into their rifles and working the levers to shut the actions. Minatelli sprang back into his niche and licked his thumb to wet the foresight. Enemy pom-poms raked the line of firing slits. The infantryman jerked his head down and squeezed his eyes shut as grit blasted through his, then blinked them open.

"Make 'em count, boys!" he shouted. "Thems *cavalry* you're shootin'."

Men were swarming out of the forward Colonial works, men in djellabas and spiked helmets. Their carbines were slung; most carried long ladders, and some lugged small mortars with folding grappling hooks and reels of cord attached. Others pushed wheeled bridging equipment to get them across the moat. Pairs carried little cohorn mortars, adapted to hurl grappling hooks at the end of a reel of iron cable.

Spirit, there's a lot of them. His narrow slit showed *thousands,* and more pouring out of the trenches like ants out of a kicked-over burrow.

White-painted iron stakes marked the ranges outside. The ramp sight on the rear of Minatelli's rifle was set for four hundred meters. He steadied the forestock against the stone and curled his finger around the trigger, taking a deep breath. The first enemy crossed by the four-hundred-meter-mark, two files holding a ladder between them. He dropped the sight onto the front-right man, let it down to the man's knees, and stroked the trigger. A soft click sounded as the offset, the first slack, took up.

Gentle, like it was a tit, he told himself, and squeezed.

Bam. The wog stopped as if he'd run into a stone wall and dropped, the ladder sagging and swinging broadside onto the city defenses as his teammates staggered and tripped. *Last one I know for certain,* Minatelli thought. Rifles barked in a stuttering crash all along the wall, smoke erupting from the slits. Men in the attacking force fell, and other men replaced them. Minatelli worked the lever of his rifle and thumbed in rounds. Spent brass tinkled around his feet.

BOOOOMMM. The big cannon a few meters down took him by surprise this time; he'd been too involved in his personal war to notice the master gunner's orders. He did see the result, as the malignant wasp-whine of the canister round spewed out its hundreds of ten-gram lead balls. It caught the mouth of the assault trench with a fresh wave of ragheads just clambering over the gabions. They vanished, swept away in the storm of hundreds of marble-sized shot. Dust and fragments of wicker spurted up all over the face of the trench. When the dust cleared, the dirt was covered with a carpet of men pulped into an amorphous mass, a mass that still heaved and moaned in places.

"Reload, canister!"

Minatelli himself reloaded, pausing to snap the ramp under his rear sight down to two hundred meters. The rifle was foul after more than two dozen shots, and the metal scorched his callused thumb as he shoved home the next round. The recoil was worse now too, and his shoulder would be sporting a fine bruise tomorrow, assuming he was here to feel it. Massed carbine fire pecked at the rock outside, some of it uncomfortably close. A round whined through the firing slit, the flattened lead going *whip-whip-whip* as the miniature metal pancake sliced air. It could slice him as easily. He bounced back up, picked a target, fired, ducked back down to reload.

Spirit. He was glad he was in here and not out there. There were as many wogs down as moving.

"Hold 'em, boys, or we're all hareem guards!" he called, and fired again.

Again. The cannon fired a third time, or was it the tenth? No way to tell. Smoke hung dense and choking, turning the ground outside the walls into a fog-shrouded mystery where crimson shapes dashed and bunched. The Colonials were nearly to the edge of the outer works, kicking their way through the caltrops—triangles of welded nails scattered through grass deliberately left to grow knee-high.

Some distant part of Minatelli was amazed that men would slow down in the face of rifle fire to avoid getting a nail in the foot, but many did.

Then the cannon from the projecting bastions cut loose. Each V-shaped protrusion took hundreds of meters of wall in enfilade, dozens of cannon sweeping the ground with loads of heavy canister. Most of them were carronades, short big-bore weapons like gigantic shotguns. Not much range, but they didn't need it.

Minatelli paused to let his rifle cool a bit with the lever open, gulped water from a bucket down a throat as raw as if it had been reamed out with a steel brush. Drops fell on the metal of the breechblock and sizzled. When the smoke cleared enough for him to see again, he reloaded and aimed at one of a pair of Arabs dragging a wounded comrade back with them. He shot, reloaded . . .

"Cease fire! Cease fire!"

The bugles reached him where the shouted command did not. His finger froze on the trigger, and he worked the lever and caught the ejected shell. His fingers were black with powder residue, and it coated his lips, tasting of sulfur when he licked them. There were more dead wogs outside than he could count, coating the ground in sprays and swaths back toward the enemy works, bobbing in the moat below amid the wreckage of wooden bridging equipment and ladders. More up and down the foot of the wall. In places the carpet of bodies stirred and moaned; there were so many he could smell the blood-and-shit stink of ripped-open bodies all the way up here.

He took another drink of water and left his rifle lying on the stone firing slot, lever open. "Sound off!" he called. Then he trotted over to the platoon commander's station.

"Sor! Two dead, three wounded serious." That included the two sections of garrison infantry his eight men were overseeing. "Ev'ryone else ready for duty."

The lieutenant was a good enough sort, a bit young. He looked out through the slit next to him and returned his unused revolver to its holster. Perhaps because he *was* young, he spoke aloud:

"They thought they could rush us. No respect."

"Plenty now, sor."

The young officer nodded, unconsciously smoothing down a wispy mustache. "Yes. Now they'll try starving us out."

Spirit, Minatelli thought.

There hadn't been much but men, dogs, weapons, and ammunition in the trains that brought them east. Sandoral had been full of hungry refugees for a week before they got here, and the invasion had disrupted the harvest.

"Messers, to fallen comrades."

As youngest of the senior officers present, Bartin Foley gave the toast in the three-quarters diluted wine. They all drank.

"Messers, the Governor." Raj gave that, and they tossed aside the clay cups.

As if to remind them of the fallen, a man screamed from the tent nearby where the wounded were being tended. Casualties had been light by every reasonable standard except that of the men whose own personal flesh had been torn and bones been shattered. Suzette was present, but her sleeves were rolled to the elbows and there was still blood spattered down the front of her jacket.

"I gather we won't be trying to take Ain el-Hilwa, *mi heneral,*" Staenbridge said.

"Of course not; what would we do with it?" Raj said. He tapped the map on the table before them. "Messers, we'll split up into the same three raiding parties—Major Swarez, you'll accompany the center group with me" —Osterville's ex-follower nodded—"and Major Hwadeloupe, you'll be attached to Major Gruder's command.

"We'll head south by southeast along this axis." He traced it on the map. "Keeping west of the Ghor Canal."

"Our objective is the railway?" Staenbridge said, tracing it with one finger.

The scouts had given them a definite bearing; it came straight west from the main Colonial line along the Gederosian foothills.

observe, Center said.

A train screeched to a halt, sparks fountaining out from the tall driving wheel of the locomotive. It was a new machine, painted in black and silver, with Arabic calligraphy along the sides in gilt paint and up the tall slender smokestack. Behind it were a dozen cars, the last an armored box with a pom-pom mounted on a turntable behind a shield; thirty or so riflemen poked their weapons out of slits in the boilerplate that sheathed it. The other cars held sections of track, already spiked to cross-ties, piled up in stacks and secured by chains. Another train halted behind the first. This one had boxcars full of men and tools.

They boiled out, their officers waving the ceremonial lash and shouting; there was more noise than a comparable group of Civil Government soldiers would have made, but no more confusion. Teams jogged forward and undogged the chains holding the first train's cargo. They set up a light folding crane and lowered the sections of preformed track to the ground; other teams lifted them with iron hooks and trotted forward, keeping step with a wailing chant.

Ahead of the two trains was a section of wrecked track a quarter-kilometer long. Engineers gave the roadbed a quick check with levels and transit; gangs of workers shoved the burnt, twisted ties and rails to one side. The prefabricated sections were dropped in place and the hookmen went back for another load at the same steady trot. Another team slewed the tracks into alignment with long poles like gunners' handspikes and bolted them together.

Raj shook his head. "There aren't enough of us, and we don't have enough time," he said. "The Colonial sappers can repair track faster than we can tear it up—until Tewfik can get back here. The major bridges will be heavily guarded. But we want him to *think* we're a threat to the railway line, and by all means tear up any stretch you reach."

"What news from Sandoral?" Staenbridge said.

"Ali put in a quick attack when he arrived in force, and when that didn't work he tried a full assault with engineering and artillery support. Total losses of four to five thousand, including wounded too badly hurt to return to duty soon. Our casualties were very light."

"My, my. I wouldn't like to be on Ali's staff right now,"

Visions crawled beneath the surface of Raj's vision; beheadings, impalements. Ali was quite mad.

"Gerrin," he said, "neither would I. He's still got forty thousand effectives, not counting his infantry garrisons." They had seven thousand cavalry, and three thousand infantry in all.

"More goblets than bottles at this banquet," Staenbridge agreed.

If there wasn't enough wine to fill all the glasses at table, beyond a certain point juggling the liquid from one glass to another wouldn't help.

"We might take their supply dump at the railhead," Dinnalsyn said thoughtfully. "That would embarrass them considerably."

"It's fortified, and there are ten thousand men in there," Raj said. "Not first-rate troops, but they're expecting trouble and they've got considerable artillery."

They all nodded. You might be able to take a position like that by a sudden unexpected *coup de main*, or if it was held by barbarians too dim to take the proper precautions. Not otherwise, not with a larger enemy field force free to operate against your rear.

"If that's all, gentlemen, we'd better see to business. Tewfik's banner hasn't been reported back at Sandoral either."

The main column trotted down a roadway through the early morning cool. It was twenty feet broad, well-graded dirt surfaced with gravel, winding down through terraced barley fields from a low ridge planted with a mix of olives and almond trees. Gullies running down toward the flat were full of reddish-green native scrub; a flock of sheep-sized bipedal grazing sauroids fled honking and gobbling into the bush as the troops passed. Dew still laid the dust on the rolling hillside. Beyond were flat fields, irrigated and intensively cultivated. The villages were deserted, ghostly, not a human or a domestic animal in sight. The peasantry had had warning enough to flee by now, driving their herds before them.

Raj finished a pear and tossed the core aside, squinting ahead. Then he stiffened and flung up one hand.

"*Halto*. Silence in the ranks."

The bugles snarled, and the column came to a dead stop in less than three strides. Silence fell, broken only by the occasional jingle of harness as a dog shifted.

There. A dull thudding sound, like a large door being slammed far away. It echoed, and was repeated. Again. Again.

"Artillery, by the Spirit," Staenbridge said softly.

Raj nodded, closing his eyes to concentrate.

civil government field guns, Center said. **two batteries, approximately 8.7 kilometers south-southeast of your present position.**

"Well, that's something serious," Bartin Foley observed flatly.

Ain el-Hilwa had been the only action hot enough to need artillery support so far. The officers around Raj exchanged glances, and so did the men in the long ranks zigzagging back up the hill. The military picnic was over.

"Kaltin," Raj said. That was where Kaltin Gruder's *kampfgruppe* was operating.

He called up the maps of the area. A low ridge on either side, running east-west, more flat ground to the south.

"Sound *Reverse Front,*" he said. "Then *Trot.*"

The bugle screamed again, and the dogs turned in place. They waited the thirty seconds necessary to turn the gun-teams and broke into a rocking trot back up the slope.

"Messengers to the raiding parties, immediate concentration here," Raj began. "Colonel Staenbridge, establish your banner there" —he pointed to the notch where the road crossed the hill— "with a firing line on the reverse slope, ready to move up. Major Bellamy, that'll be your 1st and 2nd, and the 1/591st. Gerrin, anchor your left there" —he pointed to a reservoir— "and re-fuse your right with the raiding parties as they come in. Grammek, get your guns on the reverse crest too, but keep the teams close."

The artilleryman nodded. That was dangerous—risking immobilizing the weapons if the teams were injured—but gave essential seconds of extra time if you had to pull out fast.

"No fieldworks, but put up some quick sangars for the splatguns. Suzette, have those Church people ready to triage the wounded and move them back immediately; we won't be staying. Captains M'lewis,

Foley, I'll be taking a company of the 5th and the Scouts forward with me. And one splatgun. Questions?"

Heads shook. "Good. To your positions, please. Gerrin." Staenbridge reined in. "I've got an unpleasant feeling we'll be coming back faster than we go. Be ready to stop them hard." Even veteran troops could turn unsteady if it looked like a rout.

Staenbridge nodded; they leaned toward each other and slapped fists, inside of the wrist and then back. "We'll be here, *mi heneral.*"

Raj met Suzette's eyes for a moment. No words were necessary. *"Waymanos!"*

They trotted through a land silent and deserted, warming towards the crippling heat of a Drangosh Valley summer morning. Raj's little force rode in column, with a spray of pickets out ahead. The dogs kept up a steady canter-trot-walk-trot-canter, eating the kilometers. Their tongues lolled, but their ears were pricked forward, all but Horace's, which were a hound's floppy style. The guns sounded much closer now, thudding bangs. The terrain hereabouts was mixed, fingers of high *doab* running from the clay bluffs along the Drangosh into the lower, flatter country to the east that extended past the Ghor Canal to the foothills of the Gederosian Mountains. From the sound, the guns were firing on the next ridge south.

All the men had heard the sound before, and most of the dogs. The troopers rode with their rifles across their thighs.

Whistles came from up ahead. One of the Scouts came down the road at a quick lope.

"Courier comin', ser," he said.

The messenger's dog was panting. He pulled a sweat-dampened paper from a jacket marked with the shoulder-flashes of the 7th Descott Rangers. A smell of scorched hide came from the leather scabbard in front of his right knee, the smell a hard-used rifle made when it was slapped into the sheath still hot.

"Ser," he said, "Major Gruder reports we'ns ran inta a patrol. Thought't were a patrol, turned out t'be more wogs'n we could handle."

Raj read quickly; it was a request for reinforcements, with a quick sketch map of the action. He shook his head. Kaltin was a first-class tactician, but he had a tendency to over-narrow focus, to lock his teeth in a situation and try to beat it to death.

"My compliments to Major Gruder, and tell him I'll be there shortly. And to be ready to move position, quickly."

"Ser!"

"Barton, bring them up to a lope."

The messenger pulled his mount around and clapped heels into its flanks. The sound of the guns grew sharper as the ground rose. He could see powder-smoke rising above the higher terrain to the south. A trickle of wounded passed them, riding-wounded leading dogs with more badly injured men slung over them—it was all you could do, in a situation like this.

POUMPF. POUMPF. POUMPF. The guns were firing steadily; he could see them now, spaced out amid spindly native whipstick trees on the ridge. They were firing from the top crest, the crews pushing them back every time they recoiled. Raj pulled off the roadway, leaning forward in the saddle as Horace took the ditch with a bound and swung up the hill.

Kaltin Gruder met him. "Ran into a patrol," he said. "Company strength—one *tabor*. I jumped them, more of them came up, I called in my raiding parties, then even *more* showed up. There's a battle group of two thousand down there now, and they're not stopping for shit. These aren't line-of-communications troops. Regular cavalry, and good ones."

Raj grunted in reply, sweeping his binoculars over the slope below. It was sparsely wooded with whipsticks, tall spindly trees with branches that drooped up and away from the main stem on all sides, dangling fronds of featherlike leaves.

POUMPF. POUMPF.

The eight guns on the ridgeline kept up their steady shelling, the pressure-wave of the discharges slapping at faces and chests. At least twenty Colonial artillery were firing in reply from the lower ground to the front, half pom-poms and half 70mms. They weren't attempting a counter-battery shoot, just searching the edge of the treeline to try and beat down the fire of the Civil Government riflemen. All across the open ground Colonial dragoons were moving forward on foot, line after line of them in extended skirmish order.

Gruder went on: "I've got the 7th in the center, with Poplanich's Own and the 1st Rogor to the right and left and the Maximilliano over there."

He pointed to the east, where smoke and the steady crackle of small arms indicated action. "Whoever the wog commander is, he knows his hand from a hacksaw—started trying to work around my flanks as soon as he got a feel for the depth of my firing line here. I moved the Maximilliano out to extend the line, but it thinned me here badly."

Raj nodded curtly. Gruder's three battalions—a thousand men or so, all under strength—were keeping up a steady crackle of independent fire. Down below figures in red djellabas were scattered on the ground or hobbling, limping, and crawling back toward the guns and the banners grouped around them. Advancing against veteran riflemen cost heavily. A splatgun gave its ripping *braaap* and a file of Colonials nearly a thousand meters away went down as the spread of rifle bullets hit them. Several of the enemy guns shifted aim; Raj could see the splatgun team trundling their light weapon to a new position just ahead of the pompom and field gun shells.

But more and more of the Colonials were making it to their own firing line close to the woods. Their repeaters were just as deadly as the heavier Civil Government weapons at ranges under a hundred meters, and they fired much faster. A haze of off-white powder smoke was drifting away from the thickening Colonial position. Even as he watched, several platoons rose and dashed forward for the woods. Many fell, but others went to ground in the scrub along the edge of the savannah. Once in among the trees, their repeaters would slaughter men equipped with single-shot rifles.

"We can crush them like a tangerine if you swing in with the main force, *mi heneral*," Gruder said.

Kaltin does *tend to get too focused,* Raj thought. His own mind was moving in cool precise arcs and tangents, like something scribed on a drawing-board by an engineer's compasses and protractors. Like a mental analogue of the way you felt when fencing; perhaps a little like the way Center felt all the time, if Center had subjective experience.

He felt more alive than anywhere else. It was a pity he could only feel this on the battlefield, that his art could only be practiced as men died. There were times when he lay awake at night, wondering what that said about him. But not now. Not now.

"No, Major, a full-scale meeting engagement isn't what I have in mind. If there's one Colonial battle group around, there's going to be others."

He considered for a few seconds. "This will have to be quick. We'll withdraw by leapfrogging battalions. Move Poplanich's Own back half a klick to that rise, and the guns. You'll take the 7th and the others back to join the main force. I'll hold the rearguard." Gruder didn't like retreating. "M'lewis, detach two men to each of the battalion commanders to guide them to the main-force position. Follow with the rest."

Gruder nodded briskly; he didn't like it, but that would make no difference to his obedience. Antin M'lewis turned and barked orders. Pairs of men galloped off.

"Trumpeter!" Raj went on. "Relay. Half-kilometer withdrawal. On the signal."

The complex call went out, was echoed. A single long note followed.

The battery on the rise fired one last *stonk* and let the guns roll downhill to their limbers. The teams snatched up the trails and slapped them on; retaining pins went home with an iron clank, the six dogs of each team rose, and the guns set off down the open slope at a trot. Three men rode the offhand dogs of the team; there were two seats on the gun axles and two on the limber, and the remainder had dogs of their own. Up from the savannah came the splatguns, hauled by four-dog teams; lighter, they overtook the field pieces despite the smaller draft.

The crackle of small-arms fire intensified. "Barton. We'll give the wogs a going-away present. Standing saddle-volley, use the crestline. Place the splatgun."

Company A of the 5th was nearest to full strength, eighty men, only forty down from regulation. They fanned out behind Raj, heeling their dogs a meter and a half downslope. The dogs turned and faced the crest, then crouched. The men crouched with them, squatting. It was an inelegant and uncomfortable posture—you couldn't let your full weight rest on the dog—but the men moved into a flawless double line with the ease of a housewife slapping dough for tortillas. Three-meter spacing between each, and the rows staggered so that the rear row matched the intervals in the front. He looked at their faces: stolid, immobile under the film of sweat, a few chewing tobacco and spitting. Every one of them knew what was about to happen.

Below, the Colonials hesitated a crucial handful of seconds when the fire from the Civil Government troops ceased. Just long enough to let them dash back to their waiting dogs. Center unreeled numbers as the depleted battalions trotted up the slope, rallied, and cantered northward. He winced slightly. Those units had been under strength before. A lot of them were still down there in the burning grass and shattered whipstick trees, and would never leave. Long curled trumpets sounded, shriller than his own. Half the Colonials turned and started to jog back towards their dogs. The others opened fire on the retreating raiders; not many went down, but some men and dogs fell out of line.

"Reacting fast," Raj murmured.

The Colonial commander was sending his mounted reserve forward, galloping up the hill. Two *tabor*, a little under three hundred men, with a pair of pom-poms galloping behind. Galloping guns was risky, especially on uneven ground like this. A few men, wounded or just extremely brave, had stayed behind among the dead. One rose to a knee and shot the off-lead dog of a pom-pom team. It collapsed, biting at its wounded leg. The gun slewed around, then tipped over and spun. The massive torque spun through the trail and the harness, turning the team into a thrashing pile of twisted metal and shredded meat that bounced downslope and scattered the dismounted Colonials who followed.

Raj watched the mounted Colonials approach. Numbers scrolled across his vision. The Arabs were keening as they charged. If they could prevent his men from breaking contact . . .

500 meters. 450. 400.

"Now!" he barked.

"Tenzione!" Bartin Foley called, his clear tenor pitched a little higher to carry. The men rose from their squat to stand straddling their dogs. The long Armory rifles came up to their shoulders in smooth curves, the muzzles dead level except for the minute individual quivers as they picked their targets. The slope had concealed them, and to the enemy it must have appeared as if the heads and shoulders popped up out of nowhere.

The Colonials reacted with veteran reflexes, crouching in the saddle and sloping their scimitars forward. Their dogs bounced into a full gallop, throwing themselves forward to get through the killing zone as fast as possible.

"*Fwego!*" Foley's sword chopped down in a bright arc.

BAM. Eighty rifles fired within a half-second of each other. *Braaaaaap.* The splatgun fired from its position in enfilade to one side.

The charging Colonials seemed to stagger. Dogs went down all across their front. It was only three-hundred-odd meters, and at that distance most of the 5th's long-service men could hit a running man, not to mention a thousand-pound dog. Men flew out of the saddle, and rear-rank dogs leaped and twisted desperately to avoid the thrashing heaps ahead of them.

"Rear rank, *fwego!*"

BAM.

"Reload!"

"Front rank, *fwego!*"

BAM.

"Reload!"

Braaaaap. Braaaaap.

"Rear rank, *fwego!*"

BAM.

Braaaaap. The crew worked the splatgun like loom-tenders in one of the new steam-driven factories. Its load struck like case-shot, but far faster and more accurate.

A Colonial trumpet brayed and drums sounded. The mounted Colonials withdrew, leaving their dead and wounded; the thick screen of dismounted men down in the woods ceased to wait for their comrades to bring up their dogs and started up the slope once more. Field gun shells went overhead with a ripping-canvas sound.

He's putting in an enveloping attack, Raj decided, feeling through the movements for the enemy commander's mind. *He's decided this is a sacrificial rearguard.* Half the enemy were mounted already; the dismounted thousand or so would swamp a small rearguard like this in moments, and then the Arab troopers could pour after the fleeing Civil Government soldiers. They were lighter men on fast desert-bred dogs, slender-limbed Bazenjis; they would catch what they chased, and with a two-to-one edge in numbers and more in guns the issue could not be in doubt.

"Waymanos," Raj said.

The dogs rose under the men and turned, and the splatgun crew hitched their weapon and leaped to the saddles and limber-seats. Ten seconds later Company A was moving downslope and north at a trot that turned into a rocking gallop.

They were two hundred meters away when the dismounted Colonials crested the hill. Carbine bullets cracked around their ears; the bannerman's staff jerked in his hand, and a man went out of the saddle with a coughing grunt.

"Don't mask their fire," Raj cautioned.

Foley flicked his saber to the left, and the block of men shifted course. Raj leaned forward against the rush of hot air, the banner snapping and crackling next to him. He looked back; the Colonials were re-forming on the hill, mounting up as their comrades led their dogs forward. North were flat open fields, marked with dust plumes where the retreating Civil Government battalions moved north toward his main force. A slight rise topped by a mosque and grove of cypress trees stood about a kilometer ahead.

Metal flashed there. Raj looked over his shoulder again. The Colonials were coming now, in solid blocks of mounted men; moving at a fast trot and deployed in double line abreast, for speed when they had to go into action. *Sensible.* They'd had a bloody nose twice this morning. He took a quick squint at the sun; 1100 hours. And about now . . .

There was a puff of smoke from the cypress grove ahead. A whir went by overhead, like heavy canvas being ripped in half. A malignant *crack* behind, and another puff of smoke, as the time-fused shell burst over the charging Colonials.

"Hope none of them fire short," Bartin Foley shouted, grinning.

Raj felt himself showing teeth in response. "Take them home, Bartin," he called.

He shifted the pressure of his knees and turned Horace directly for the left end of the formation ahead—Poplanich's Own, four hundred men strong. Plus two batteries of 75s, now firing as fast as the gunners could ram the shells home, reckless both of the barrels and the ammunition supply. Rounds whined by overhead and burst, in the air, or throwing up fountains of dirt if the time fuse failed. He crouched over the dog's neck and set his teeth as the battalion's splatguns opened up; no need to look behind. Closer, and he could see the two staggered rows of men in prone-and-kneeling formation. Then rifles came up and the steady BAM . . . BAM . . . of platoon volleys started. The smoke was thick enough to half-mask the troops as he pulled up in a spurt of gravel by the battalion commander's position.

The Colonials were closer than he expected, four hundred meters but wavering under the unexpected hail of fire. *Yes, about two thousand of them still,* Raj thought; and their artillery was coming over the hill, pompoms and field guns both.

As he watched, blocks of mounted Colonials veered to left and right, moving to flank the Civil Government blocking force. Without prompting, each battery ceased fire for an instant and heaved its guns around to deal with the new threat; the flanking forces moved farther out, but the Colonials in front seemed to disappear. Raj read their trumpet signals: *Dismount* and *At the Double.* The line shrank as the dogs crouched, then turned into a long double rank of men on foot coming forward at a uniform jog-trot.

"In a moment, Major Caztro," Raj said.

The Major—he was a cousin on his mother's side of the late Ehwardo Poplanich—nodded.

"The gunners aren't happy about it," he said.

"Better grieving than dead," Raj said dryly, taking a drink from his canteen; the day was already very hot.

"And . . . *now!*" he said. The major relayed the order to his buglemen.

The gunners fired a last round from their weapons. He could hear one sergeant cursing as he wrenched the breechblock free and tossed it to one of his men. Then he jammed a shell backwards into the opening, stuck a length of slowmatch into the hole where the fuse would normally go, and lit it with the last of the stogie clamped between his lips.

"Fire in the hole!" the noncom shouted. It was echoed down the gun line. "Ten seconds!"

The troopers were already double-timing back to their dogs and swinging out the rear of the cypress grove around the mosque.

"Retreat by platoon columns, at the gallop!" Major Caztro shouted.

Raj looked to either side as he touched his heels to Horace's ribs. The flanking parties were still well back, and the main Colonial force were just remounting and kicking their beasts into a gallop—which must be rather frustrating for them.

The noon sun was blinding-bright. The white dust of the road reflected its heat, and sweat rolled down his forehead out of the sodden sponge-and-cork lining of his helmet. Horace was panting, his black coat splotched with dust. Raj uncorked his canteen and rubbed a little of the water into the dog's neck; if it went down with heat prostration, he was deeply out of luck. Another check behind: the Colonials were coming on fast, but they were staying in line and bringing up their guns with them.

Cautious, but smart, Raj decided.

Barreling in hell-for-leather might have caught him quicker, but he'd already given them the back of his hand twice. There was nothing to show that he didn't have the battalions who'd retreated from the meeting engagement waiting at intervals to mousetrap an unwary pursuit.

Which is our margin, he knew. The Colonials would have won a flat-out gallop.

"How far, *mi heneral*?" the major asked, swerving his dog over to Raj's side.

"Just under seven kilometers," he said. The nearest Colonials were half a klick back, now. "Twenty minutes at this rate."

Caztro looked back as well. "Just long enough for them to get convinced we're going to run all the way to Sandoral?"

"Exactly, Major."

If everyone hasn't bugged out when Kaltin's men came in hell-for-leather.

"*Halto!*"

Raj pulled Horace to a stop, then let him crouch to the ground. His wheezing pant sounded half-desperate, and he was a strong-winded dog. Some of the others were collapsing outright; men brought buckets of water and sloshed them across the moaning, gasping animals. Raj pulled off his sweat-damp neckerchief and turned to trot for the command group below the crest of the hill.

"They're right on my heels," he said.

And everything looks klim-bim, he thought, with a wave of relief so enormous that he felt slightly dizzy. The ground was good—he'd picked it himself—and Gerrin hadn't been wasting his time. The men were spread out along the ridge, well back from the crest and invisible from the other side. Officers lay prone at the top, with their flags furled and laid flat among the scattered olives; inconspicuous rock and earth sangars had been prepared for the guns and splatguns. Back north behind him there was an aid station waiting for field surgery, and relays of men were bringing up buckets of water from the irrigation canal. Kaltin's battalions had watered their dogs and moved up into the firing line, all but Poplanich's Own; two more were on the far right flank, waiting still mounted. Farther north, a small force trotted away dragging brush on the end of their lariats to simulate the dust of a much larger body retreating towards Sandoral.

"And they're coming on like there was no tomorrow," Staenbridge said.

Raj knelt beside him and looked south. The Colonials were

advancing at a round trot, deployed for action in two double-file lines with their guns and command group between.

"Message to Colonel Dinnalsyn," Staenbridge went on. A runner bent near. "My compliments, and the first stonk should be directed at the enemy artillery, before it has a chance to deploy."

Raj looked up and down the long curving line. "Guns?" he said.

"Splatguns forward, and the bulk of the field guns to either side." Staenbridge pointed downslope, to a clump of greenery around a small manor house. "Masked battery there."

Raj's breathing slowed. "Good work keeping everything calm when Kaltin's men came galloping in," he said.

"He had them well in hand, and Suzette and her helpers were there with bandages and water," Staenbridge said judiciously. "I doubt anyone in this army would dare panic while she was looking."

Raj nodded. *Still good work, Gerrin.* He leveled his binoculars and took another swig from the canteen, remembering to follow it with a salt tablet; the last thing he needed was heat prostration.

leading elements at 2300 meters, Center said helpfully. **closing rapidly.** A set of numbers appeared in the upper right corner of his vision, scrolling down as the enemy trotted nearer.

"Wait until their scouts stumble over us?" Staenbridge said.

"Agreed."

Damned if I'm needed here at all, he thought ruefully. I could go take a nap.

you are the source of overall direction, Center reproved. **you have chosen and trained competent subordinates.**

I'm not the only one, Raj thought.

"Keep the initial reception low-key," he added aloud.

A screen of scouts preceded the Colonial main body. A dozen of them came loping up the roadway toward the crest, eyes restless. Raj saw their officer half-check as he neared, looking to right and left. *What spooked him—*

it is too quiet. no birds or pterosauroids except the scavengers.

Raj looked up. Huge wings circled at the limit of vision, supporting long-beaked heads and patient, hungry eyes. Slightly lower were the true birds men had brought with them from lost Earth, crows and naked-necked vultures.

Damn. "I wonder what they do when there's no war?" he said.

Staenbridge looked up too for an instant. "When isn't there war?"

The Colonial scouts came closer. Their leader spurred over the crest of the rise not a hundred meters from Raj, and froze in horrified shock, his bearded mouth dropping open into an O of surprise.

Braaaap. A splatgun fired point-blank, and the scouts went down into a tangle of kicking, howling dogs and wounded men. Troopers swarmed over them in a flurry of shots and bayonet thrusts. Several broke for the rear. Picked marksmen were stationed along the crest; they fired with slow care. One Colonial went down, another . . . and then the third, already crouched wounded over his saddle.

Raj turned his binoculars to the Colonial banner; it was his first glimpse of the enemy commander. A square middle-aged face beneath the spired helmet, dark and hawk-nosed, with a gray-shot forked beard. Not Tewfik, but a junior product of the same hard school. *Come on, be a good wog,* Raj thought urgently.

He'd done it by the book twice now, stopped and deployed when meeting a rearguard. Both times it had cost him time, time for the enemy force which had ravaged his country to escape with their plunder. And there were those dust plumes. If he did it again, the Civil Government troops might escape altogether. Overruning a small rearguard without putting in an attack on foot would force him to spend lives, but that was a cost of doing business.

Yes. The Colonial trumpets brayed and the enemy force rocked into a slow gallop, the front rank drawing scimitars and officers their pistols.

"He's going to try and roll right over us," Staenbridge said with a cruel smile. "But this pitcher will find himself catching, nonetheless."

Raj nodded tersely. He looked to the right. "You kept the . . ."

"1/591st as strike reserve—they're at full strength, their dogs are fresh, and they're fond of the sword," Staenbridge said. He turned back to the front. "Not long now."

750 meters. 700 meters. 650 meters.

Raj nodded. Staenbridge jerked a hand at the signalman, who bent to touch his cigarette to the blue paper of the rocket. It arched skyward and went *pop*.

The banners of eleven battalions rose over the crest of the ridge in a single rippling jerk. Four thousand men rose and took six paces forward, the front rank dropping to one knee and the rear standing. Gunners heaved at the tall wheels of their weapons until the muzzles showed over the ridge. Splatgun crews pulled the concealing bushes away from their dug-in weapons.

The Colonial formations halted as if they had run into a brick wall. They were all veteran troops, and they realized instantly and gut-deep what the sight before their eyes meant; it meant they had all just been sentenced to death.

The battalions opened fire independently, but within a few seconds of each other. All the enemy were on the long gentle upslope, which meant that even if a bullet was over head-height when it reached the enemy formation—high trajectories were inescapable with black-powder weapons—there would probably be someone in front of it before it struck the earth. The platoon volleys rippled up and down the Civil Government line in an instant fogbank of dirty-gray gunsmoke, an endless BAM*bambambambambam* of sound. Brass sparkled in the bright sunlight as the troopers worked their levers and ejected the spent rounds. A steady, metronomic round every six seconds; forty thousand rounds in a minute. The four splatguns per battalion added half as many again.

The masked battery down on the flat opened fire simultaneously with the riflemen above, since they didn't have to manhandle their guns into position. The range was nearly point-blank; eight shells fired at minimum elevation whistled down the corridor between the first and second waves of the Colonial force. Two burst early, slashing shrapnel into the backs of the men and dogs of the first wave. One arched over and burrowed into the soft alluvial soil, sending up a nearly harmless plume of black dirt that collapsed and drifted on the wind. Five airburst within a hundred meters of the enemy command group amidst the limbered-up guns. Five black puffballs, each with a momentary snap of red fire at its heart. The green banner went down, and there was a circle of wounded dogs snapping at their hurts around the place where it lay in the dust.

Ten seconds later, the forty-eight guns of the massed artillery reserve fired from either end of the ridge. Their fire wasn't nearly as accurate as the masked battery; the range was longer, and the gunners had less time to estimate the range and adjust their pieces. The shells were contact fused. Many gouged the earth short, or fell long; both did damage enough. The score or so that fell on target hammered into the Colonial artillery train, still tied to limbers and teams. Dogs died or were wounded into howling agony—and a half-tonne of berserk carnivore was much more hindrance than a dead beast. Ammunition limbers exploded in globes of red fire, flipping wheels and barrels and bits of men dozens of meters into the air. Even then the crews of the surviving guns tried to unhitch them and swing the muzzles around to bear on the enemy who were slaughtering them.

Futile. The crews were within easy small-arms range of the ridge; dozens went down in the few seconds he watched. More shells burst among them, and overhead as the Civil Government artillery switched to time-fused shells that flailed them with shrapnel from above. More ammunition limbers exploded. He saw Colonial artillerymen cut dogs loose from their surviving teams and spur to the rear; officers who tried to stop them were ridden down. The whole crimson-uniformed mass was in full flight, those who could still move. The men on the fastest dogs were first, with the dismounted running or limping or dragging themselves afterwards.

Smoke drifted across the Civil Government line, thick even though a stiff breeze was blowing. Crewmen crawled forward from the splatguns, staying low and calling targets and distances back to their fellows. Officers directed the troopers' volleys with their swords.

Gerrin Staenbridge raised an eyebrow at Raj, who nodded. Another signal rocket hissed skyward, and this time the starburst puff of smoke was blue. A trumpet snarled six notes out on the right flank of the Civil Government force, and the cry of cease firing ran down the battalions on that end of the line. The 1/591st trotted their dogs over the ridge and down the slope, speed building. The swords came out in a single ripple of sun-struck silver as the speed of the charge built. Slowly at first—those were big men on heavy dogs, huge-pawed Newfoundlands and Alsatians sixteen hands at the shoulder. They growled as they charged, a sound like massed millstones grinding away in a cave, and the men shouted:

"*UPYARZ! UPYARZ!*"

"Nicely done," Raj said. "Oh, *nicely* done."

The charge swept down the hill and crashed through the flank of the disintegrating Colonial formation. The ex-Brigaderos held their ranks with fluid precision, stabbing and hacking and shooting with the revolvers most of them wielded in their left hands; the dogs were well enough trained to need no guidance but knees and voice and their place in ranks. The lighter Arab cavalry would have had trouble meeting a charge like that mounted at the best of times. With half their men down and unit cohesion gone, they reacted the way a glass jar did dropped on a flagstone floor. Men spattered in every direction; the 1/591st rode through their line, rallied to the trumpet call, dressed ranks and charged through again in the opposite direction. Hundreds of dismounted Colonials were holding up reversed weapons or helmets, asking quarter.

The barbarians in Civil Government service were whooping like boys as they cantered up the slopes again, despite a few empty saddles; shaking bloodied swords in the air and chanting their guttural Namerique war cries.

"Damn, but that's frightening," Raj said, shaking his head and scanning the enemy.

"Frightening?"

"One mistake, and two thousand disciplined troops with an able commander get creamed."

"*Their* mistake, fortunately."

Raj nodded grimly. "*Un*fortunately, Tewfik has enough men that he can afford to make a mistake—and he won't make this one again. If we make one mistake like this, the campaign is lost and so is Sandoral and the war. We'd lose everything south of the Oxheads as far west as Komar."

Staenbridge blinked. "It must hurt, thinking ahead like that all the time," he said. "General pursuit, *mi heneral*? I think we can take the lot of them, here."

Raj nodded. "That would be best. I hate to see so many good soldiers wasted like this, though."

wait. listen.

"Wait," Raj said automatically. Then: "Sound *Cease Fire* and *Silence in the Ranks*."

Staenbridge looked at him oddly, then signed to the trumpeters. The call rang out, and silence fell—silent enough so that the sounds of wounded men and dogs were the loudest things on the battlefield.

And off to the northeast, a muffled thudding sound, very faint.

"Guns," Staenbridge said. "You've got good ears, *mi heneral*."

distance 18 kilometers.

An hour or two at forced-march speed. "All a matter of knowing what to listen for," Raj said. Center had to use his ears, but it could pay attention to *everything* they detected, however faintly. "We went looking for Tewfik, and we've bloody well found him, haven't we?"

"You think that's him?" Staenbridge said.

"It's another battle group of Colonial cavalry meeting one of the raiding parties I called in," Raj said. "And where there's two, there'll be more. Tewfik's here, and if he's got less than twenty thousand men with him, I'm a christo. He's probing to find out where we are, and once he knows he'll pile on."

He tapped one fist into the palm of the other hand. "Messenger, ride to the sound of the guns; that's probably Major Zahpata's group. Tell him to withdraw as quickly as possible and rejoin on the route north. Gerrin, let's get ready to move out of here, and do it *now*. Hostile-territory drill."

"We have to move anyway," Raj said, preparing to rein Horace around.

The doctor's shoulders slumped. Suzette moved over two steps and laid her blood-spattered hand on Raj's knee. The dog bent its head around and snuffled at her. She shoved it gently away as she looked up at her husband.

"We'll do what's necessary," she said. He nodded wordlessly and pulled on the reins with needless force.

Suzette moved back to the line of wounded. *Not this one,* the Renunciate's eyes said.

Suzette looked down at the soldier sweating on the litter. His olive face was gray with shock, his eyes squeezed tightly shut. There was a tourniquet around the upper thigh of his right leg, and a pressure bandage over a wound below the ribs. He *might* have survived the leg wound, although he'd have lost the limb—there were fragments of bone sticking out of the mass of red-and-gray flesh below the tight wound cloth. There was a faint sewer smell from the stomach wound, though.

"Here, soldier," she said in Namerique—from his coloring the man was MilGov. "Take this, it'll help with the pain."

The blue eyes fluttered open, wandering, the pupils dilated. She lifted a shot-glass sized dose of liquid opium to his lips; enough to knock a war-dog out, and fatal for a man.

Better than leaving them for the Colonials, she thought. It was bleak comfort.

"Yes!" Major Hadolfo Zahpata said. "Pour it on, *compaydres.* Give those wogs hell!"

He walked down the firing line—more like a C with the wings bent back, now. *Fifteen hundred if it's a man,* he thought, squinting into the bright sunlight. *I have perhaps three hundred fifty. And we had to run into them facing the sun.*

Twigs fell on his uniform coat from the apricot trees of the little orchard, cut by the bullets of the Colonial dragoons to his front. More went overhead with flat cracking sounds; he looked down and saw the left sleeve of his jacket open to the elbow, sliced as neatly as by a tailor's shears. One millimeter closer, and . . .

They were advancing by squad rushes across the open grainfields; several hundred were behind the lip of an irrigation ditch about a hundred fifty meters to the front. That gave them cover, which was very bad. His guns were firing over open sights, trying to suppress them, which meant that they had to more or less ignore the steady flow of men *over* the embankment and into the open ground—although, thank the Spirit, they had knocked out the brace of pom-poms there. And the enemy were working around his flanks, both of which were now re-fused.

A body of the enemy stood to charge. A few meters down the line a splatgun crew slammed another iron plate of rounds into their weapon and spun its crank. *Braaaaap.* Two more of the rapid-fire weapons joined it. The Colonials staggered, the center punched out of their ranks. Company and platoon officers redirected the troopers' fire, and volleys slammed out. The Arabs sank back to the ground, opening fire once more. A splatgun crewman went *ooof* and folded over at the middle, dropped, his legs kicking in the death-spasm. Another stepped up from the limber to take his place. Bullets flicked off the slanting iron shield in front of the weapon with malignant sparks.

Thank the Spirit for the splatguns, and for Messer Raj who made them, Zahpata thought. He was a pious man—most who lived on the Border were—and Messer Raj was living proof that the Spirit of Man of the Stars watched over Holy Federation. *Despite our sins,* he added, touching his amulet.

A Colonial shell screeched overhead to explode behind him. There was a chorus of screams after it, men flayed by the shrapnel, and howls from wounded dogs. A revolver banged, putting down the crippled or dangerously hysterical among the animals. Beside him his aide ducked involuntarily at the shell's passage. Zahpata smiled and stroked his small pointed black chin-beard.

Spent brass lay thick around the troopers prone in the shade of the fruit trees; wasps and eight-legged native insects crawled over the shells, intent on the windfallen apricots scattered in the short dry grass. Their sickly sweet scent mingled with the burnt sulfur of powder smoke and the iron-and-shit smell of violent death.

"I'm glad to see you're not concerned, sir," the aide said as Zahpata lowered his binoculars and leaned on his sheathed saber.

Zahpata smiled thinly; the aide was his nephew, something not uncommon in the Civil Government's armies and very common in the 18th Komar Borderers. All of them were recruited from the same tangle of valleys in the southern Oxheads five hundred kilometers west of here, and half the battalion were relatives of one sort or another. The aide—his mother was Zaphata's older sister—was a promising youngster, but inexperienced at war. Except for the continual war of raid and skirmish and ambush with the Bedouin along the frontier, but all Borderers were born to that.

"I am not as concerned, *chico*, as I was before I saw that," he said, pointing. "The unbeliever commander must be so delighted at the prospect of our destruction he did not notice."

He pointed. The aide leveled his own binoculars, squinting against the sun. Zahpata knew what he was seeing; a line of slivers of silver light. Sun on sword-blades.

"Are they ours?"

"Would reinforcements for the sand-thieves advance with drawn blades?" Zahpata asked. By the length of front, that was two battalions—his City of Delrio and Novy Haifa Dragoons, reconcentrating as he'd ordered before this began. Doubtless they'd stepped up their pace to the sound of the guns. "In a moment—"

There was a frantic flurry of trumpet-calls from where the enemy commander's banner stood. Zahpata grinned like a war-dog scenting blood as the Colonial artillery ceased fire and began to limber up with panic speed.

"Sound *Fix Bayonets!*" he said.

The bugle's brassy snarl sounded. Surprised, men checked their fire for an instant; then there was the long rattle and snap as the blades came out and the men slid them home. The enemy had checked their advance; now they rose and turned to retreat. Fire slashed into their backs. Out in the fields beyond, the two Civil Government battalions glinted again as the sabers came down and the charge sounded.

"Sound *General Advance with Fire and Movement*," he said happily. A good many enemies of the Spirit were going to the Starless Dark today.

The troops rose and dressed their ranks by company and battalion standards; the men at either end of the line double-timed to turn their C into a bracket with the open end facing the enemy.

Hammer to the anvil, he thought. The oncoming battalions spread wider, and their artillery wheeled about to unlimber and open fire.

Zahpata frowned. *Hope they're not overconfident.* Any shells that overshot would be coming straight at his men; and if he had many casualties from friendly fire, there would be floggings.

An orderly led up his dog; Zahpata put one hand on the saddlehorn and vaulted up. A whistle brought his head around.

The messenger was a Descotter, with the shoulder-flashes of the 5th. "Ser," he said, in the grating nasal accent of his home County. "T'*heneralissimo* sends his compliments, an' yer t'rejoin immediate—on t' road headin' north. Fast, loik, ser."

Zahpata's aide moved his dog closer as the major read the slip of paper the messenger pulled out of his glove.

"Messer Raj has been *defeated*?" he asked incredulously.

"Don't be more of a fool than your mother made you, Hezus," Zahpata snorted, reading. "Ah—a great victory. Another infidel group, defeated with small loss."

He wrote on the reverse of the first message. "My compliments to the *heneralissimo*, and we expect to intersect the northern road at . . ." What was the heathen name? Ah, yes. ". . . at Mekrez al-Ghirba."

That should put him on an intercept course, or even get there ahead of time. The messenger saluted, pulled his dog's head around, and clapped his heels to its ribs.

"If we're not defeated, sir, why are we pulling back?"

Zahpata looked at the eager young face and sighed inwardly. The boy was here as a military apprentice, and you expected the young to be fools. *Although Messer Raj was only a few years older when he had his first independent command.*

"Messer Raj met and defeated one enemy column; perhaps two thousand men, twenty-five hundred. With twenty guns. We met and defeated another—fifteen hundred men, ten guns. What do you think will happen next?"

"Oh," the aide said.

Zahpata clouted him alongside the head, half-affectionately; his helmet *bonged*. "Live and learn, boy—or don't learn and die." He looked around. "Messenger, to battalion commanders. 18th Komar will lead; City of Delrio follows, Novy Haifa to rear. Scout-screens on all sides, maximum alertness. *Hadelande!*"

CHAPTER TEN

It was dark, with the sun down and only Miniluna in the sky. The earth gave back the day's heat, radiating from the bare clay of the badlands in the Drangosh bend; the darkness turned the ochers and umbers of the canyons to a uniform gray. Pterosauroids cheeped and mewed overhead, swooping after night-flying insects; Raj caught a gleam from the huge round eye of one, a vagrant trace of starlight. Earth-descended bats passed more silently. Off in the tangle of gullies and sinkholes something roared on a rising note, ending in a pierced-boiler screech; there was a rattle along the lines of dogs as the big animals raised their heads and cocked ears toward it. Some carnosauroid; they were hard to eliminate, in any area without a dense population, and the Civil Government force was into the belt of uncultivated land that extended from just west of Ain el-Hilwa along the river north to the border.

Raj sat, wrapping his officer's cloak around his shoulders and looking up at the stars that stretched in a thick frosted band across the sky. The Stars where man had once dwelt, before the Fall—and would again, if Center's plan succeeded.

The unFallen had the powers of gods, Raj thought. Yet from what Center tells me, they were still men—not sinless, as the Church teaches. They had their wars and their intrigues, as we do; their tragedies and defeats, as we do.

true, the voice in his mind said. **my analysis is that such are inherent in the nature of your species.**

Raj leaned back against the clay and lit a cheroot. What's the point, then? he asked. If all I'm doing is letting people make mistakes on a bigger scale and a broader canvas?

Center was silent for half a minute. **this is a difficult question, and one at the limits of my powers of analysis. i was not constructed so as to be capable of philosophical doubt.**

Another pause. **in your terms: the fall represented a limitation of human choice due to suboptimal decisions. the greater capacities of a unified and technologically advanced civilization free humans from the determinism of nature. both their triumphs and their failures become matters of choice.**

Ours aren't?

only to a very limited degree. the vast majority of humans on bellevue are peasants, because you lack the productive capacity to organize yourselves otherwise. this precludes forms of government and social organization less authoritarian, because the civilized regions depend too heavily on coercion to produce the surplus on which cities and a literate leisure class depend. if the fall continues, even agriculture-based societies will collapse and maximum entropy will be reached at a hunter-gatherer level. the survival of human life on this planet will then be in doubt.

As if to illustrate the point, the carnosauroid's retching scream sounded again through the night.

a new civilization may eventually emerge; but it will lack any continuity with the ancestral culture. and fifteen thousand years of savagery means hundreds of generations of human lives without the opportunity to exercise their capacities.

Raj nodded. Peasants were old at forty, and every day in their lives was pretty much the same, except when something went badly wrong. The Church said it was punishment for men's sins—which seemed to be literally true in Center's terms as well—but there was no reason for the punishment to go on forever.

He shivered slightly, despite the warmth of the earth at his back.

The fate of the human race for the next fifteen millennia rests on me, then. And our chances of pulling it off are no better than even.

correct.

He stood and flicked the stub out into the darkness, a solitary ember that arced away and was lost in the night. He turned. Behind him the command group was gathering about the pool of light cast by a kerosene lantern, the undershadow putting the bones of their faces into hard relief. They were unfolding maps, munching on hardtack and pieces of jerked meat; their smiles and eyes looked as feral as so many war-dogs in the yellow light.

"Well, sooner started, sooner finished," Raj said. He strode into the light. "Right, gentlemen. Tewfik's main force is rather smaller than I'd expected—about sixteen thousand men, according to Captain M'lewis's report."

"Countin' banners, sir. Couldna' git closer. Them wogs is screened tighter 'n a cherry inna raghead's hareem."

Everyone nodded. Colonial units were less standardized in number than their Civil Government equivalents. One reason for that was a deliberate attempt to make it harder for observers to get a quick, accurate tally of a Colonial army's numbers by counting the unit standards.

"We'll take sixteen thousand as a ballpark figure—which worries me, Messers. We're here" —he put his finger on a spot west of Ain el-Hilwa— "and we have to cut the bend of the Drangosh to get back to our bridgehead opposite Sandoral. I hope you all realize that after leaving Ali's main army—"

He moved his finger to the west bank, and north almost to Sandoral, then south again to the Colonial pontoon bridge.

"—he could have dropped forces off to cross the river and take up blocking positions *north* of us."

By their expressions, the thought was an unpleasant surprise to a few of the battalion commanders—although not to his Companions.

"That depends on Tewfik's estimate of our numbers and intentions. We'll let the men rest another hour, then start out at Maxiluna rise." With both moons in the sky, there would be more than enough light for riding. "We'll make use of every hour of darkness we can; it'll be cooler, too.

"Colonel Staenbridge," he went on, "you take the three companies of the 5th and lead the way. Spread out but move fast. Captain M'lewis, you'll be the scout screen for the scout screen. Gerrin, if you run into anything you think you can handle, punch through. If not, go around if *that's* possible, screening our retreat. Major Zahpata, you and your 18th Komar will follow in column of march right behind. Exercise normal caution, but rely on Colonel Staenbridge for your intelligence. Gerrin, if you run into anything you *can't* handle, Major Zahpata is to move up immediately and support the 5th at your direction. Understood?"

Both men nodded. *At least I don't have to wonder who'll take orders from whom,* Raj thought thankfully. That sort of thing had nearly gotten him killed in the Southern Territories campaign, at the hands of the late unlamented Major Dalhousie. The problem was that the Civil Government didn't have permanent field armies or a structure above the battalion level—large concentrated field forces were too tempting to ambitious generals. By now, all these men had been on campaign with him long enough to work smoothly together, and he'd disposed of the purblind idiots, one way or another.

"The rest of you will be following in double column up these roads," he said, tracing the route northwest with two strokes of his finger. "They're never more than a kilometer apart, so you'll be close enough for mutual support. If Colonel Staenbridge runs into a major block-force, you'll flank and go round—taking a lick at them from the rear in passing. Boot their arse, don't pee on them; we *cannot* afford to get tangled up in a meeting engagement."

"My oath no," Staenbridge said mildly, still studying the map. "Not with Tewfik and sixteen thousand wogs after our buttocks."

"Exactly."

"What's the source of our intelligence on these pathways through the badlands?" Zahpata asked.

Raj had drawn those in himself. "Personal sources, Major. You may rely on them." *Center can do more with my eyes than I can,* he added silently.

"Major Gruder, I have a special tasking for your command. Otherwise, the order of march will be as follows—"

When the other officers dispersed to their units, Raj lead Kaltin Gruder out into the mouth of the notch.

"Kaltin, I want you to execute a battalion ambush on Tewfik's lead elements here," he said.

Gruder squinted up at the eroded clay hills, comparing them with his memory of the same scene by daylight. "Good ground," he said. "And we've given them a couple of bloody noses—he'll be more cautious this time."

"Probably. Time is exactly what I want you to gain; but *not* at the price of your battalion. Understood?"

Gruder nodded. Raj went on: "Tewfik knows he has two ways to win this campaign. The quick way is to catch us and smash us up before we get back to Sandoral. He's got numerical superiority, but it'd still be expensive. On the other hand, a quick victory is always preferable; the sooner you win, the less time the other side has to come up with something tricky. The slow way is to chase us back into Sandoral and starve us out. So he'll probably be willing to take a swipe at you to save time, but it won't be a reckless one."

Raj reached a space of flat sand, coarse outwash detritus from the bluffs above. He smoothed it further with his boot and drew his sword to sketch in it.

"This is your position. More or less of a very broad V, with the open end facing south. Have your men dig rifle pits at the foot of these hills; I'll detail the City of Delrio to help before they pull out. Scatter the dirt, and it'll be difficult for them to estimate your numbers before they get close. I suggest you place them by companies like this." He traced lines. "With your dogs reasonably close to hand, here and along here. I'll also have the Delrio leave you their splatguns—that'll give you eight total. Put them down here—here—here—here, in pairs."

His sword marked spots along the face of the V. Gruder frowned. "Down on the flat?"

"They're not artillery, Kaltin— those are bullets they're shooting, not shells."

Gruder nodded thoughtfully; a bullet was dangerous all along its trajectory if it was fired at a formation with any depth. Fired from above, it either hit the target it was aimed at or plunked harmlessly into the dirt; fired on the level, it went much farther.

"That'll give you crossfire from both infantry and splatguns, like this." The tip of Raj's saber traced X marks across the sand.

"Now," he went on, moving the sword to left and right on either side of the notch, "this terrain is pretty well impassable to formed bodies of troops. Certainly to artillery. Put observers *here* and *here*. Tewfik may try to work dismounted troopers around your flanks in those areas. If he does, block them with your reserve company—it ought to be easy, in that ground.

"Over here, about twenty klicks, is the only other path suitable for artillery and large formations of troops. That's where he'll go when he decides he can't just rush you out. Put a relay of men between here and there; when his flanking force gets there, pull out."

He raised his head and met the other man's eyes, his own flat and hard. "I give you *no discretion* concerning that. When his men reach there, you bug out. Understood?"

"*Si, mi heneral,*" Gruder said. He grinned. "I have learned something over the past five years."

"I certainly hope so, because I can't spare you *or* your battalion," Raj said.

"Hmmm. Artillery here?" Kaltin's saber pointed to the apex of the V.

"Yes, and start the guns out first. Also, walk all that ground tonight, and have your company commanders do it too. Ranging marks, all the bells and whistles."

"*Si.*" Kaltin studied the improvised sand-table. "I'll have them come and look at this, too. You have a good memory for terrain, *mi heneral.*"

Which was true, and even more so with Center's assistance. "*Waya con Ispirito del Homme,*" Raj said. They gripped forearms. "Get me an extra half-day."

"The Spirit with you also, General. Consider it done."

(••) (••) (••)

Tewfik ibn'Jamal, *Amir* of the Host of Peace, lowered his binoculars and cursed. Arabic was the finest of all languages for that, as for all else—as would be expected for the language God chose to dictate His word in—but the rolling, guttural obscenities did not relieve his feelings.

"And may the fleas of a thousand mangy feral dogs infest the scrotum of the *kaphar* general Whitehall," he concluded.

Ahead was a broad slope five thousand meters across at its mouth, narrowing down to barely a hundred where the roadway snaked into the badlands. The hills behind and to either side were not high, but they were steep as the sides of houses, crumbly adobe scored and riven by the rare cloudbursts of the Drangosh Valley winter. The roadway was graded dirt—a secondary road. The main highway—Allah torment in the flames of Eblis the souls of the engineers who laid it out—ran parallel to the Ghor Canal, through the populated districts farther east and towards Ain el-Hilwa. *That town of fools and dotards.*

Taking that would mean two days' delay, more than enough time for the invaders to scuttle back to the walls of Sandoral—and take any hope of concluding this accursed war quickly with them.

Another *tabor* of dismounted troopers trotted up into the V, angling for the enemy's foremost position on that side—if they could dislodge the outer rim, they could unravel it up the foot of the hills. A steady *braaaap . . . braaaap* sounded, and men fell. Figures in crimson djellabas dropped into the hot white dust of the valley floor, to lie still or twitching and moaning. He could see puffs of dust where the bullets struck, smoke pouring from the positions of the new rapid-fire weapons, a steady crackle and bang from the rifle-pits where the infidel troopers kept up a continuous hail of well-aimed fire. A pom-pom galloped up to support the soldiers.

The rapid-fire weapons from both sides of the V shifted to it. The dogs of its team went down in a tangle, and the gun's long slender barrel slewed around in futility. He watched a survivor drag a wounded comrade into its shelter. Bullets fell on it like a rain of hail to ricochet off in sparks and whining fragments.

In the gun-line directly before him crews heaved at the trails of

70mm field guns and pom-poms. More smoke billowed out as they fired, a ripple of red tongues of fire from left to right. Dirt fountained skyward along the enemy lines, and a spare team was galloped out to retrieve the pom-pom and the wounded.

"Can you not suppress those Shaitan-inspired weapons?" he asked.

His artillery chief shrugged unwillingly. "Insh'allah," he said. "*Amir*, whatever they are, they do not recoil as artillery pieces do—so they can be deeply dug in. All we see is the muzzle and the top of an iron shield. To make good practice we must draw close—and you saw the result of *that*. Also they have a battery of field guns above, with a two-hundred-meter advantage in height. If I push our gun line forward, they will come under artillery fire from the heights as they try to deploy, as well as from small arms."

"Move guns to the left, concentrate on the outer arm of the enemy defenses."

"As the *Amir* commands," the gunner said.

Tewfik turned back to the map table. Sweat dripped from the points of his beard onto the thick paper, reminding him of how thirsty he was. The goatskin *chaggal* at his side was half-empty; his men's would be worse, and there was no source of good water sufficient for fifteen thousand men within a half-day's ride.

"Muhammed," he said, and one of his officers bowed. "Sound the recall."

"Another push and we will be through, *Amir*," the man said stubbornly.

"Another push and we will lose another hundred men dead," Tewfik said. Just then a pair of stretcher bearers trotted by. Their burden moaned and tried to brush at the flies crawling on the ruin of his face. "Or like *that*. I do not continue with a plan that has failed."

"I obey."

"And start men moving here." He traced a line to the eastward on the map. "The going's passable for men on foot. Put some of those Bedouin hunters to use; the sand-thieves do nothing but sit on their arses and eat better men's food. They should know the footpaths. Work around toward the rear of the enemy position.

"Anwar," he went on. "You will take the reserve brigade and go" —he moved the finger in a looping circle far to the west— "twenty kilometers. A tertiary road—passable for wheels, according to the reports. Push all the way through to open country on the other side of these badlands, secure the route, and I will follow. Mutasim, you will put a blocking force across the mouth of this deathtrap; I'll leave you thirty guns. When the *kaphar* pull out, pursue, slow them if you can; we'll see if whoever Whitehall left in charge has sense enough to flee quickly as we flank him."

Mutasim scowled. "So far we have accomplished little," he said, tugging at his beard.

"There is no God but God; all things are accomplished according to the will of God," Tewfik said. He fought the urge to grind his teeth. "We were sent to stop the enemy's ravaging of our land; this we have done. We will pursue him. If we catch him, we will destroy him; if not, we will besiege him in Sandoral, which has not the supplies to support his men for long. In a week, they must begin to eat their dogs—which destroys all hope of mobility. After that, it is merely a matter of time. This was a damaging raid, no more. Insh'allah."

"As God wills," the others echoed.

"Go. Move swiftly."

The officers departed, and trumpets began to sound. Only the aides, messengers, and the *Amir*'s personal mamluks were left, silently awaiting his will. Tewfik stood and stared up the valley again, unconsciously fingering his eyepatch. It had never stopped him seeing into the heart and mind of an enemy commander before. *Whitehall, Whitehall, what is your plan? What dream of victory do you cherish in your secret heart?*

That was what bothered him. He remembered the El Djem campaign; he'd caught Whitehall there, beaten him—although the fighting retreat had been stubbornly effective, preventing him from finishing the young *kaphar* commander off without paying a price that seemed excessive. He'd bitterly regretted that decision a year later, when the Colony's forces met Whitehall's army.

May the Merciful, the Lovingkind, have pity on your soul, my father, he thought. Jamal had been a hard man and a good Settler, but no great general. You ordered that we attack directly into the kaphar guns, and we paid for it, Tewfik thought bitterly. Jamal had paid with his head, the House of Islam with thousands of its best troops and a legacy of civil war. All Whitehall's doing; it had been a good day's work for Shaitan when Whitehall had been born among the infidels of the House of War instead of a believer.

Since then Whitehall had made war in the West, while Tewfik repaired the Host of Peace and prepared for the next round of battle. This time there should be no doubt about the outcome. He had overwhelming numbers, and even Ali wasn't going to force him into the sort of error their father had made.

Yet the Faithful had good intelligence sources in the western realms. Tewfik had followed Whitehall's campaigns closely, and spoken with eyewitnesses. *Why this raid?* By bringing his force out from beyond Sandoral's walls, Whitehall had exposed them to the risk of defeat—without any countervailing chance of decisive victory. True, he had ravaged rich lands; true, he had inflicted stinging tactical reverses on the Muslims. *Our losses were greater than his. But we can absorb them without strategic consequence, and he knows this.* Nor were burnt-out villages in this one little corner of the Settler's domains any sort of strategic loss; yes, a tragedy for those who suffered, and enough to wake screams of rage from the nobles whose estates were ravaged, but nothing mortal. At least once in the past *kaphar* hosts had ravaged their way to the walls of Al Kebir itself, and the House of Islam still stood—there were vast and rich lands south and east of the capital to draw on. This was nothing by comparison.

Whitehall must have *something* in mind, something decisive. But *what*?

Tewfik plucked at his beard again. "He threw as many troops as he could into Sandoral before we reached the walls," he muttered to himself. "Yet it would have been better to send one-third as many, and use the other trains for supplies." Sending all the civilians out of the fortress city had been a shrewd move, but not enough. And why so many cavalry, when the issue would be settled by fighting from behind strong works?

"He has too many troops to hold the walls, and not enough food to feed the numbers he brought—yet not enough men to meet us in the field."

Three pounds of food per man per day, fifteen per dog; Whitehall knew the importance of logistics as well as any man. What was his plan?

There was something else here, something beyond a young *kaphar* chieftain with a genius for war. The infidels whispered that their false god rode at Whitehall's elbow.

He shrugged off the notion. There was no God but God. "Insh'allah," he said again, snapping his binoculars back into the case at his waist. "We waste no more time."

"Hadelande!"

Robbi M'Telgez pulled the rifle free from the scabbard and kicked his feet free of the stirrups. Dirt clouted the soles of his boots as Pochita crouched; he turned and ran up the crumbly slope, coughing in the dust Company A kicked up in their scramble. He chopped the butt of his rifle into the dirt to help the traction, feeling the dirt sticking to the sweat on his face, blinking his eyes against the sting and thanking the Spirit for the chain-mail avental riveted to the back of his helmet. It might or might not turn a swordstroke, but the leather backing of the mail protected your neck from the sun pretty good.

Captain Foley reached the top and his bannerman planted the company pennant. The officer stood with arm—hook arm—and sword outstretched, to give the alignment. M'Telgez flopped down on his belly and crawled the last three paces to the ridgeline, because bullets were already cracking overhead. *Got guts, that one,* he thought.

Foley stayed erect until the unit was in place, then went to one knee only a little back from the crest. Some men in other units gave them a hard time for having the colonel's boyfriend as company commander. He didn't care weather Foley banged men, women, bitch-dogs or sheep—as long as he knew his business, which he did.

There were plenty of wogs making for the same crestline from the other side, hundreds of them. The slope was steeper there, though;

he could see clumps of them falling back in miniature avalanches of rocks and clay, down to where their dogs milled about in the dry streambed below. Others were prone on the slope, firing at the Civil Government banners that had appeared on the ridge above. M'Telgez flipped up the ladder sight mounted just ahead of the block of his Armory rifle and clicked the aperture up to 800 meters.

"Pick your targets!" the ensign in command of his platoon shouted.

He did, a wog with fancywork on his robe walking around at the base of the hill and followed by signalers. A long shot, and tricky from up here, but he had the ground for a firm rest. He worked the rifle into the dirt, fingers light on the forestock, and took up the first tension on the trigger.

"*Fwego!*"

BAM. Eighty rifles fired. The butt punched his shoulder; a measurable fraction of a second later the wog in the fancy robe folded sideways under the hammering impact of the heavy 11mm bullet. He fell, kicking. *Not goin' t'git up, neither,* M'Telgez thought. Not with a hollowpoint round blowing a tunnel the size of a fist through his stomach and intestines. The Descotter whistled tunelessly through his teeth as he worked the lever and reloaded, the spent brass tinkling away down the slope to his rear. Most of the others had picked closer targets; bodies were sliding back down the steep slope. Live ones, too, as the more sensible wogs decided that toiling slowly up a forty-degree slope of crumbling dirt under fire wasn't the way to a long life.

BAM. He picked another hard target, a Colonial prone behind a slight ridge and firing back. The djellaba blended well with the clay, but he aimed up a little. The wog jerked up seconds later, clawing at his back. Lever, reload.

"Five rounds, independent fire, rapid, *fwego.*"

M'Telgez's hand went back to his pouch; he pulled four bullets out of the loops and stuck their tips between his lips like cigarettes. Another went into the chamber, and he snapped the ladder-sight back down to the ramp.

Damn. There were too many wogs who'd decided to chance it. *Bam.* One down. Out one of the rounds between his lips. *Bam.* A miss, but the target yelled and danced sideways. *Bam*. Head shot, and the spiked helmet went end-over-end downslope in a splash of blood and brains. *Bam*. Couldn't tell, smoke too thick. *Bam*.

The oncoming enemy wavered, then fell back; most of them turned over onto their backsides and tobogganed down the slope, controlling the slide with their feet. There were boulders and rocks enough at the bottom to take cover behind, if they were careful.

"Dig in!"

The order came down the line. M'Telgez cursed; like most cavalry troopers, he hated digging—back home in Descott, a *vakaro* resented any sort of work that couldn't be done from the saddle. Resignedly, he spoke to his squad:

"Even numbers! Odd numbers on overwatch. C'mon, lads, 'tain't yer dicks yer grabbin', put yer backs inta it."

He reached to the back of his webbing belt and undid the leather pouch that held the head of his entrenching tool. It was a mattock-and-pick if you put the head in the central hole, a shovel if you put it into the slot behind the broader section. He unhooked the wooden handle that hung from his belt by the bayonet on his left side and knocked it into the main hole. A few swift blows cut through the hard crust of the adobe; it came up in chunks, and he piled those and handy rocks ahead of him, working down the slope behind to make a cut that would let him lie comfortably and fire through a couple of notches.

The afternoon was savagely hot, and the sweat ran down his body in rivulets that he could feel collecting where his shirt and jacket met the webbing belt. The damp cotton drill cloth clung and chafed. A carbine bullet went by overhead now and then with a malignant wasp-whine, encouraging him. A man came by with extra ammunition slung in canvas bandoliers from the pack-dogs; M'Telgez snagged an extra fifty rounds and cut a notch to support them with a few quick strokes of the mattock.

"M'Telgez! Report to the captain!"

Shit. Jest whin I wuz gettin' comfortable, loik, the corporal thought resignedly. "Smeet, y'got it fer now. Don't fook up too bad, will yer?"

"We'll a' git kilt, but it'll na be *my* fault, corp," the older trooper said cheerfully.

M'Telgez wiped his hands on the swallowtails of his jacket and picked up his rifle, then stepped-slid downhill a pace or two; running crouched, his head was below the ridgeline. The crunch of entrenching tools in the dirt marked his passage, and the steady crackle of fire from the alternate numbers keeping up harassment against the wogs. He also passed a few dead men; head and neck wounds were generally quickly fatal.

"Ser," he said when he came to the company pennant.

Barton Foley braced his pad across his knee with the point of his hook and wrote. "You have the way back to battalion, Corporal?"

"Yesser," M'Telgez answered.

He had a good eye for that sort of thing; and it was an officer's job to remember what his men could do.

"Detail one man of your squad to accompany you, and take this to Colonel Staenbridge."

"*No problemo, seyhor.*" He'd take M'tennin, the lad was young, eager and a good shot. Smeet could handle the squad—he was a good junior NCO, when there was no booze around. Drunk, he didn't know a sow from his sister or an officer from an asswipe.

"Verbally, add that we can handle it for the present but would appreciate reinforcements. Report back immediately with his reply— and watch out, there may be wogs in these ravines."

M'tennin screamed.

M'Telgez took one look over his shoulder and clapped his heels to Pochita's ribs. The thing already had the younger man's shoulders in its jaws and one clawed foot hooked into his dog's side, ripping downward in a shower of blood and fur and loops of pink-gray gut. Pochita needed no urging; she brought her hindpaws up between her front and leapt off in a bounding gallop, teeth bared, ears flat, and eyes rolled back, right down the narrow floor of the canyon. Her rider whipped his head around as something screeched behind him, a sound like a steam-whistle gone berserk.

He could *smell* its breath, like a freshly-opened tomb in hot weather. It was bipedal and longer than a war-dog, probably heavier, but it ran with a birdlike stride—lightly, on the toe-pads of its three-clawed feet, so lightly that the shotgun blast of dirt and stones spraying back from each impact was a surprise. The body was a dusty orange-yellow, striped irregularly with vivid black; the open mouth was mottled purple and crimson. Teeth the size of his fingers reached for him, and the clawed forefeet on either side. Behind it another much like it—hunter's reflex told him they were probably a mated pair—was tearing at the bodies of M'tennin and his mount with impartial gluttony. Its muzzle went skyward, the long narrow jaws dislocating as it swallowed a leg and hip.

"*Hingada tho!*" M'Telgez screamed. "Fuck ye!" The carnosauroid shrieked back at him, another carrion-scented blast.

His rifle was in the crook of his left arm. He snatched the pistol out of his boottop with his right and thrust it backward, not three meters from the thing's mouth. Even so half the rounds missed. Three did hit; none of them seemed to do much good. A blood-fleck appeared on the shiny black skin between the angry red of the nostrils, and one fang shattered into fragments of ivory. That got the beast's attention, at least; it spun sideways for an instant, snapping and rearing on one leg as the other slashed at whatever had struck it.

Then it realized *he* had hurt it. Some of the bigger carnosauroids were too dumb to do anything but kill and eat; the smaller agile ones like this could be a lot smarter. There was more than simple hunger in the cry it gave as it bounded after him once more, body horizontal and long slender tail snapping behind it at the tip like a bullwhip.

"Fuck *me*," M'Telgez muttered through a dry mouth, and hurled the revolver at the beast. *That* hadn't been such a good idea.

He leaned left and then right as Pochita took the curves of the narrow gully at dangerous speed. The carnosauroid didn't let little things like turns slow it down; it just ran right up the wall of the cut, letting momentum keep it upright with its head parallel to the ground for an instant. The man wound the sling of his rifle around his right forearm with desperate speed. He'd have only one chance, and that wasn't much with a single shot rifle. Reloading at the gallop . . . he might as well try to fly like a pterosauroid by flapping his arms.

The sides of the gully opened out a little. The carnosauroid screamed again and speeded up, half-overtaking the fleeing human.

Right. Likes t'knock yer over afore it bites.

Normally holding the long Armory rifle out one-handed would have made M'Telgez's arm tremble. Now it was steady, everything diamond-clear to his sight. Even the sideways lunge of the predator seemed fairly slow, an arc drawn through the air to meet the questing muzzle of his weapon.

Bam. The shock of recoil was a complete surprise, hard pain in his arm. The weight of the carnosauroid slammed into Pochita's haunches, and the dog skittered in a three-sixty turn before resuming its gallop. The torque of the outflung rifle nearly dislocated M'Telgez's shoulder, but the pain was negligible next to the horrifying knowledge that he'd failed. Footfalls still ripped the earth behind him, only a little further back—and Pochita's tongue was hanging out in exhaustion.

He rounded another curve—

—and nearly ran into a screen of mounted men in blue jackets and round bowl-helmets. Their guns flicked up, but their eyes were behind him.

"Shoot, ye dickheads!" he screamed, as his dog braced its forelegs and sank down on its haunches to stop.

They didn't. Bent over his pommel, gasping and wheezing, M'Telgez looked behind to see why.

The carnosauroid lay prone not five meters behind him, its muzzle plowing a furrow in the dry gritty dirt. One leg was outstretched and the other to the rear, as if it had done the splits in mid-stride. Tail and head beat the ground in an arrhythmic death-tattoo, then slumped into stillness. A neat hole drilled in the yellow scales just behind and above one ear-opening showed why.

"Well, fuck me," M'Telgez mumbled again. It took three tries to return his rifle to the scabbard, and two to get his canteen open.

"There's one'll na try it, dog-brother," one of the troopers said admiringly. Two rifles cracked as the corpse of the sauroid went through another bout of twitching, the jaws clashing with an ugly wet metallic sound. Carnosauroids took a good deal of killing.

A jingling and thump of paws sounded in the draw; the battalion standard came up. M'Telgez pulled himself erect with an effort and saluted.

"Colonel, message from C-captain Foley," he said. "Ah, we're, ah—"

"Take it easy, lad," the Colonel said, not unkindly, looking at the dead predator and then at M'Telgez's dog. "You had a close shave, there, Corporal."

M'Telgez followed the lifted chin. Pochita's tail was half-missing, ending in a bloody stump; now that the dog wasn't running for its life it was trying to twist around and lick the injury. He dismounted and reached automatically into his saddlebags for ointment and bandages, a cavalry trooper's reflex, and a lifelong *vakaro*'s.

One bite closer . . . he thought. The image must have been clear on his face, because the Colonel leaned down and clapped him on the shoulder.

"Good shot," he said. "Anything with this?"

"Ah, t'Captain 'uld want some reinforcements, loik," M'Telgez said. In an effort to clear his mind: "We'nz goin' t'push through 'em, ser?"

In many line outfits that might have been insolence; Descotters had an easy, unservile way with their squires, though. And he was a long-service man with a good record.

"No, Messer Raj knows a way around," Colonel Staenbridge said. "We just have to block them while the main force gets through. I'll come myself. Lead the way, Corporal."

M'Telgez looked around at the bewildering tangle of blind canyons, sinkholes, and ragged hills. *The Spirit* must *be wit 'im,* he decided. Which was a comforting thought.

"Cheer up, lad," Staenbridge said, as the column formed up and passed the dead predator.

One of the troopers tossed him a fang as long as his hand, with a lump of bloody gum still on the base. M'Telgez dropped it into his haversack; it'd be something to show the girls, cleaned up and worn around his neck on a thong. Might as well get something out of that; that poor *fastardo* M'tennin wasn't going to, not even a burial. There wouldn't be anything left of him or much of his dog by the time they got there.

"Cheer up. Could have been worse—it could have been wogs."

M'Telgez looked down at the four-meter length of tiger-striped deadliness lying in the dirt. He nodded. That was true enough. The carnosauroid had only wanted to kill and eat him.

Wogs might have taken him alive.

"Good," Raj said. "That was clever of Tewfik, but he had to split his covering force up into too many detachments—there are a lot of badlands out there."

Staenbridge nodded. "Only two or three hundred men on the route we actually took," he said. "Still, it might have gotten sticky if we couldn't go around—they had an excellent position. How *did* you know that section of earth was thin enough to cut through behind them?"

An angel told me, and it *could tell the thickness of the gully walls by measuring how inaudible sounds passed through,* Raj thought sardonically. He wondered what Staenbridge would make of the explanation. Raj didn't understand a word of it himself.

sound waves are—

Forget it. I know it works, I don't have to know how or why.

"Lucky guess, Gerrin." The tone ruled out any further questions. "We're about—"

two point six kilometers.

"—two and a half klicks from the bridgehead, now. This is going to be tricky."

"You expect Tewfik to catch us crossing?" Staenbridge said, raising a brow.

"No, but he's not the only competent commander in the Colonial army, and he'll be in heliograph contact with their main body. What I want you to do is—"

CHAPTER ELEVEN

"Come on lads, put your *backs* into it," Colonel Jorg Menyez shouted. "Messer Raj needs this finished and ready to go by full sunrise!"

Arc lights hissed and kerosene lanterns cast their softer light across the chaos on the riverbank quays of Sandoral. Miniluna and Maxiluna were both on the horizon, paling to translucence as the sun cast bands of yellow and purple up into the fading dusk of night.

At least it's a little cooler, the infantry officer thought. That should speed things up. He'd had the preparations going on all night, what could be done without attracting attention.

There was no more point in trying for silence now, not with two thousand men splashing and clattering as they moved the big boxlike pontoon barges into position. Most of the supports had been beached along Sandoral's long waterfront, just outside the river wall. Teams of men grunted and heaved, some pushing, others prying with beams and planks. One by one the square shapes surged out into the river, then jerked to a halt as the anchor-ropes caught them. Other ropes were payed out and men hauled in groaning unison to pull the barges to the growing eastern end of the bridge. North of it was a line of cable floating between barrels; each marked a line dropping down to an anchor on the riverbed. Naked boatmen swam out with more lines to secure the barges to the cable.

As each was tied off against the current, notched beams went into the cutouts in the bulwarks, and sections of planking were pegged down on top. Men scrambled forward to the next even while the mallets were still pounding on the one they ran on; water slopped over the upstream side as the weight of scores of infantrymen and their burdens of timber and cordage rested on the end barge alone. Down in the hulls others threw buckets of water overside and screamed abuse at the work teams above.

A long hollow *boooom* sounded from the southward, from where the nearest part of the Colonial siege line had anchored itself with an earthen fort on the riverbank. A long whirring crash followed, and men froze as a heavy roundshot hit the water and skipped like a thrown rock across the surface of the water by a playful boy. Once . . . twice . . . three times, and the final plume of water was shorter than the others. The Drangosh drank down the big cast-iron ball as easily as it would the boy's pebble. Menyez blew out the breath he had not been aware of holding.

Two kilometers. A little too far. There were ironic cheers from some of the men, and the hammering clatter of work resumed. He looked eastward. The bridge was nearly to the other shore, where a company of infantry was heaving at winches anchored in the dirt, hauling the last few barges. *Nice fast piece of work,* he thought. It helped that they'd done it before, of course.

Booooom. A little sharper this time, a rifled piece. The sound of the shell was higher as well. It came much closer, only a few hundred meters south, but struck the water only once. A tall fountain of spray reached skyward, high enough that its top was touched red by the light of the sun rising in the west.

"Close, but that only counts with handbombs," he said.

Far off and faint, trumpets spoke on the eastern bank. A message began to flicker in from the heliograph station there, as the light strengthened enough for the tripod-mounted mirrors to catch it.

The problem was that there were other heliograph relays farther down the river—Colonial ones.

"Come on, *mi heneral*," Menyez said under his breath.

He looked back over his shoulder at Sandoral. The city was eerily quiet, hardly even a thread of smoke marking the hushed stillness of the morning. Not even a cock crowing; all the chickens had gone into the stewpots several days ago.

And nearly the whole garrison out here working on the bridge, he added to himself. Pretty soon that thought was going to occur to somebody else.

Ali ibn'Jamal lowered his telescope. "My so-brilliant brother has let them escape," he said bitterly. "Allah requite him for it. And their bridge of boats is nearly finished to receive the ravagers of the House of Peace."

Everyone else in the clump of nobles and commanders maintained a tight silence. A cool morning wind ruffled robes and beards and the peacock and egret plumes in turbans and helmets, but many of them were sweating nonetheless.

Cowards, Ali thought, and raised the telescope again. The *kaphar* were working like men possessed on their bridge, getting the surface laid before Whitehall appeared. Tewfik was going to let him ride back into Sandoral like a conquering hero!

"Commander of the Faithful."

It was one of the cavalry generals, a protégé of Tewfik's. Who cannot be Settler. But who could rule from behind the Peacock Throne, with a puppet Settler. It had happened before.

The man knelt and touched his forehead to the floor. "The deserters have told us the *kaphar* are on half-rations—they have been for a week. With another eight thousand men and eight thousand dogs within the walls, they will eat their stores bare in a few days. Then the city must fall."

Eight thousand. Tewfik hadn't killed more than a few hundred of them, after they spent more than a week ravaging his lands. *His* lands! *I do not want them to surrender. I want them to* die.

Of course, they could die after they surrendered . . . but if he allowed them terms, it would be unwise to break them. Not with Tewfik and his officers so close around him—not when they absurdly, blasphemously valued a word given to an unbeliever.

He raised the telescope again. It was incredible how quickly the infidels had gotten their bridge put back together. Cannon were firing from the walls of the earth fort around him, but doing no damage—the range was so great that only sheer luck or divine intervention would land a shell where it could accomplish anything.

They must have their whole garrison working on that, Ali thought. He could see them clearly now that the sun had risen.

Ali smiled suddenly. Those watching his face flinched and looked away, then forced themselves to turn their heads back; it was not safe to be unaware of the ruler's moods.

Ah, Tewfik my brother, you did not think of that. All his life he had been in Tewfik's shadow in matters of war; blundering and hacking his way through the complex problems of the battlefield in confusion, while Tewfik cut to victory with a lambent clarity. But this time, he was the one to see.

"You," he said to the kneeling officer. "Ubaydalla Said. I order an assault on the walls—an immediate assault. Rise, take command of the forward troops, and execute my commands."

"I hear and obey, Settler of Islam," the officer said. He paused thoughtfully. "That is an excellent suggestion. But the preparations—"

It was the expression on his face that moved the Settler; the surprise, that Ali could have come up with a workable plan. He plucked the ceremonial whip out of the man's belt and lashed him across the face with it. An upflung hand saved Said's eyes from the nine pieces of jagged steel on the ends of the thongs, but blood dripped heavily into his beard and from his gashed mouth.

"Are you a coward as well as a fool, pig? Are you *deaf*? I said immediately! If you have time to prepare, so will the enemy! And you are to lead the attack, personally."

"As God wills," the officer said quietly. He bowed again, blood dripping on the priceless carpets, and wheeled away sharply, calling for his subordinates.

A whistle blast jarred Corporal Minatelli out of exhausted sleep. It was much like waking up after a payday in Old Residence. For a moment he lay blinking in puzzlement. It must be Star Day, why were they calling him to work at the quarry already?

The whistle went on and on, sharp repeated calls. A trumpet joined in, sounding: *Stand to, Stand to* over and over again. Then he knew exactly where he was: on the parapet of the wall at Sandoral, with hot white sunlight slashing through the firing slits. He erupted up out of his blanket roll and grabbed his rifle and webbing in either hand, running to his duty station. His muscles ached from a night of hard labor, and the two hours of sleep seemed to have dumped a skullful of hot sand behind his eyes. He was hungry too, mortally hungry with the aching need of a man who had been using twice as many calories as he took in. None of it mattered.

He buckled his belt and leaned back slightly from the wall to make sure that everyone in the squad was at their posts—seven men to hold a section of wall that had been undermanned with forty. Seven men and the six militiamen left of the dozen that usually operated the big gun to his left. Probably the rest of the walls were just as empty. Spirit!

"Oh, *scramento*," he said as he knuckled the crust out of his eyes and looked out the slit.

From left to right across his field of vision the Colonial earthworks were belching jets of smoke with lances of red fire at their hearts; the siege guns were cutting loose. Underneath their deep booms he could hear the sharper sounds of the field guns in the forward bastions, and the rapid *pom . . . pom . . . pom* of the quick-firers. Much of the ground between the Colonial outworks and the city moat and wall was still covered by bloating bodies, and the ripe oily stink was thick—the wog commanders had refused the usual truce to remove the dead. That didn't seem to be slowing down the men who boiled out of the forward ends of the assault trenches any.

In the days since the first attempt at an escalade, the Colonials had braved constant sniping to rig overhead covers for the last few hundred meters of the trenches—platforms of palm logs and sandbags that wouldn't stop a heavy shell but did quite well against rifle bullets and case shot. Now the last ten meters or so of that were jerked down, and the soldiers in crimson came out like red warrior ants. They didn't seem to be as well organized this time, but there were an awful lot of them.

"Ready for it," Minatelli called, clearing his eyes with the thumb of one hand. The fabric of the fortifications quivered underneath him as the heavy solid shot rammed into the granite facing of the concrete-and-rubble wall. Dust quivered up from every crack and crevice. He took an instant to gulp water from a dipper, stale and welcome as a mother's love.

The wogs were running forward with their long ladders, built to cross the moat and not break even at an acute angle to the ground. The walls of Sandoral were not very high; they could not be, and be thick enough to resist modern rifled cannon. Others carried grapnel-throwing mortars.

"Now!" he shouted, and fired. Shots were crackling out all along the walls, and the deeper roar of cannon.

Booom. The fortress gun fired. A swath of the enemy went down, but the scratch crew were cursing with the shrillness of panic as they struggled to reload and relay the huge piece; there just weren't enough of them. Minatelli fired again and again, as fast as he could work the lever—worry about overheating and extraction jams later. Wogs fell, to lie among the bloated, swollen remnants of the previous attack, but they kept coming. Grapnels thumped out of the mortars and blurred up to the ramparts, trailing snakes of cable with knotted hand- and footholds. A shadow fell across his eyes as a ladder toppled toward the wall, slanting out to the ground beyond the moat. He dropped his rifle on the stone ledge for a moment and reached into a bin, pulling out a hand bomb and snagging the ring on top on a hook set into the wall. A quick jerk freed the ring, and the bomb began to hiss as the friction primer within burned.

Toss. A vicious *crack* over towards the base of the ladder. Men fell, and the heavy eucalyptus poles of the construct swayed. A dozen men cut loose with their repeaters at Minatelli's gunslit. Thousands were kneeling all along the edge of the moat, bringing the fighting platform under direct aimed fire. A little way down from Minatelli a lucky pom-pom shell blasted right into a gunslit and exploded; an instant later so did the hand bombs in the bin there, blowing chunks of stone and flesh out into the moat and back down into the cleared zone below the city walls. He ducked down and back as ricochets buzzed through the narrow space, then dashed to the next slit. A file of wogs was already running up the ladder—it was no steeper than some stairways—toward the roof of the fighting platform overhead. He fired again and again. Men fell tumbling off the ladder and down into the foul water of the moat; some of them bobbed limply, others swam for the shore.

Boom. The fortress gun cut loose again, and another swath of wogs went down back toward the assault trench—but there were far too many already near the wall. Almost at the same time an enemy shell struck right underneath the muzzle of the gun. The huge banded barrel jumped backwards; a trunnion cracked, and the weapon pivoted sideways with a squeal of ripped bronze and crackling timbers. A gunner's legs were caught in the way, and the man smeared against the pavement and the iron guide-ring like liver paste on bread.

More carbine rounds flicked at Minatelli's firing slit. He ducked back again, fixed the bayonet on his rifle, then slung it across his back. He filled his hands with hand bombs, slipping his fingers through the rings to carry them—dangerous, but fuck *that* right now for a game of soldiers.

"Saynchez! Hold 'em!" he screamed, and ran back down the covered walkway to the dismounted gun.

The other five militia gunners were standing gaping, looking at their dead comrade.

"Get yor fukkin' *guns*," Minatelli screamed. His hands were full, so he kicked one of the gunners in the arse to get his attention; the man whirled, gaped, then went for his personal weapon. The gunners were equipped with shortswords, revolvers, and double-barreled shotguns: just the thing for the sort of short-range scrimmage that was all too likely in a moment. He could hear boots on the roof overhead.

"The wogs is over the wall," Minatelli shouted, and leaped for the top of the gun.

There was a circular hole above it, with an iron ladder and an octagonal observation-point of timber and boilerplate above, usually for the master gunner. Minatelli scrambled up it, stuck his head out of the hatch, and began throwing hand bombs. There were wogs clambering up onto the roof of the fighting platform by the score—though many were cut down by the enfilade fire of the light swivel guns on the bastion towers to either side—and thank the *Spirit*, none of them looking at him!

The cast-iron bombs clattered on the stone flags; he ducked back down as they burst with rending *crang* sounds, and bits of casing peened off the outside of the observation point. He rose again and threw the last of them; wogs were shooting at him from the outer edge, pausing at the top of their scaling ladders.

He dropped back down. Case shot hammered the boilerplate outside as a swivel gun tried to sweep the ramparts clear.

"Hingada tho!" he cursed at the unseen gunner in the tower, and dropped back to the gun. He could feel the heat of it through the soles of his hobnailed boots.

"Follow me!" He jumped down to the decking with a clash and spark of nails on the concrete.

The militia gunners ran behind him as he dashed back. A wog with his carbine slung and a long curved knife between his teeth swung down from the lip of the overhead, hung by both hands and jacknifed himself in to land on the very edge of the platform, with a fifteen-meter drop behind him. Minatelli shouted and lunged; he had just time enough to meet the Colonial's eyes, black and unafraid. The man was trying to draw the revolver tucked through his sash when the point of Minatelli's bayonet thumped into his chest. The steel didn't penetrate the breastbone, but it was enough to send the man backward over the edge, snarling in frustration.

Another landed beside him. A militiaman fired his shotgun from behind Minatelli, powder scorching his side. The spreading buckshot caught the wog in the gut, blasting him over the edge with his limbs flailing like a jointed doll. Another was hanging from the lip of the roof—it was deliberately made with an overhang beyond the fighting platform below, to make this sort of thing difficult. Minatelli lunged again, this time between the dangling legs. The wog let go with a scream and plunged downward. His drop revealed another kneeling above, aiming a carbine. Minatelli fired from the hip; the Colonial threw himself backward out of the line of fire.

The infantryman pivoted. Two of the militiamen were down, and a pair of wogs he hadn't even noticed stood on the deck. Two more were fighting another; one blocked his scimitar with the barrel of his shotgun, then reeled away wailing over fingers hanging by threads of flesh. That gave his comrade time enough to draw a revolver and fire five times with the muzzle almost pressed against the Arab swordsman's back.

The body hit the ground with a thump. The survivors of Minatelli's squad were at their firing slits, shooting and throwing hand bombs. No, one was stabbing outward with his bayonet. The corporal started towards that slit, hands reloading his rifle of their own volition. The last militiaman shouted from behind him, warning in the tone.

Minatelli turned. Another wog was coming at him, carbine clubbed. He caught it on the bayonet, pivoted the rifle and buttstroked the wog in the face; turned with frantic speed and caught another through the throat with the point. The militiaman was at his side, but more and more wogs were dropping down to the firing platform, some coming through the observation hatch over the gun. His men turned from the firing slits. He shouted to them to rally.

Something flashed very brightly, and there was a soft floating sensation. A heavy pressure. Blackness.

Raj drew up beside Menyez at the western end of the pontoon bridge. The infantry commander grabbed at his stirrup-iron. "Wogs over the wall," he said. "Everything's committed—no more reserve!"

"I'll handle it," Raj replied. "Organize this end and get the remainder and the artillery concentrated in the plaza. *Waymanos!*"

The lead cavalry were coming over the bridge at a round trot, the fastest safe pace.

"Bugler," Raj snapped. "Sound *Charge!*"

The man obeyed instantly, but his eyes went wide. The troops responded as if the call were playing directly on their nervous systems, clapping their heels to their dogs and plunging forward. The floating bridge rocked and shuddered under the sudden impact of thousands of half-tonne dogs accelerating to their running pace.

Howls and shouts rose over the massive thudding and creaking; Raj ignored them, drew his sword and spurred Horace across the Maidan, the empty space by the riverside, to the main water gate. It was broad, thank the Spirit; more than broad enough for cavalry to take in four-abreast column, and there was a wide straight avenue from there to the *Plaza Real*.

He looked westward, squinting into the sun and straining to hear the sounds of combat from the city walls. Green arrowed vectors painted themselves over his vision.

major penetrations at these locations.

"There!" he yelled, pointing with his sword.

Gerrin Staenbridge went by with the banner of the 5th Descott; his reply was a flourish of his own saber, and the men followed his abrupt curve with fluid precision.

"There!" Raj directed the next battalion. "There! There!"

A fourth. "Follow me!"

Not only over the wall, they're into the bloody city, Staenbridge thought, as the column of the 5th Descott burst out of the street into the harsh light of the open ground just inside the city wall. Broad stairways angled up from the roadway to the fighting platform; right now they were swarming with Colonials, their crimson djellabas a solid blotch of color in the dark shade, an occasional helmet-spike or officer's plume glinting. More were milling about on the ground at its foot, the survivors of the first wave. They were disorganized—not many in any unit would have made it this far—but that wouldn't last. Men who'd made it through the killing ground outside and over the wall in the first wave would be too aggressive to sit around waiting for orders.

"Deploy in line of companies!" he roared. Buglers relayed the order every man half-expected.

The column of mounted troopers pouring out of the mouth of the street split on either side of him, fanning out like the arms of an outstretched capital Y with his banner as the dividing point. In thirty seconds they were in a line facing the wall, and moving forward three hundred strong.

"Dismount! Fix bayonets!"

The dogs crouched and the men stepped free, drawing their rifles from the scabbards. Steel glinted as the long blades snapped home.

"Advance with fire, volley fire by platoon ranks!"

BAM. The men moved forward at the double. Colonial officers were hustling the wogs at the foot of the wall into makeshift firing lines, moving them forward in turn. *Can't give them room to deploy.* He'd be outnumbered too badly if he did. Unless more troops arrived up from the river, and he couldn't count on that.

BAM. BAM. BAM. The 5th could double forward and volley-fire at the same time, something possible only with endless practice. There weren't many Colonials at the foot of the wall . . . yet . . . and more of them were reloading than firing, pulling rounds out of the loops across their chests and thumbing them through the loading gates of their carbines. Men fell on both sides, stumbling out of his line, flopping backward when the heavy 11mm Armory rounds punched them in the Colonials ahead.

A sound of iron wheels on flagstones. A splatgun crew wheeled their weapon around and ran it forward. Staenbridge pulled his dog aside.

"The stairway!" he barked.

The master gunner nodded and spun the elevating screw down to maximum. The honeycombed muzzle of the weapon rose like the nose of a hunting dog sniffing the wind. Two more crewmen moved the trail to his direction as he crouched over the breech. He snarled satisfaction and spun the crank.

Braaaaap. Thirty-five rounds punched into the mass of Colonials on the stairway. A bubble of dead and dying sprang into existence in the thick crowd, instantly filled as more pressed down from above. *Braaaap.*

Staenbridge spurred back to his banner, dismounted. The rest of the command group followed. He drew his revolver, tossed it into his left hand, then drew his saber and filled his lungs. Bartin was beside him, hook ready, his double-barreled coach gun in his good hand. Their eyes met for an instant.

"*Charge!*" he shouted, and broke into a run forward.

With a bellow, the 5th Descott threw themselves after their Colonel.

"Charge!" Raj barked.

The trumpeter sounded it; the brassy clamor echoed back from the silent walls of the houses on either side.

"UPYARZ! UPYARZ!" the men bellowed in reply.

Raj snarled silently and leaned forward, point outstretched beyond Horace's neck. The 1/591st filled the street from wall to wall; some of them were riding down the sidewalks, inside the line of plane trees and gaslights that separated the brick walkway from the granite paving blocks of the street. The heavy paws of the big Newfoundlands made a drumming muffled thunder, and the column filled the road for better than two hundred meters back. Even at a slow gallop it was insanely risky; he gritted his teeth against the memory of what men looked like after a hundred war-dogs trampled over them.

Just have to be careful.

Horace was a little ahead of the pack, beside Raj's personal bannerman; the battalion standard and Teodore Welf were to one side. Ahead was a thin scattering of Colonials, running down the road; except for the ones turning to run away when they saw that juggernaut of huge black dogs and white fangs, bared swords and shouting barbarian faces. One officer—a high-ranking one, from the spray of plumes at the front of his helmet—had managed to find a dog, in Civil Government–issue harness. It was highly restive under its new rider. Dogs were like that; you had to train with them a good long while before they accepted you, if they had any spirit. He was keeping the reins and the cheek-levers they controlled tight, and slapping at men's shoulders with the flat of his scimitar as he hustled them into a semblance of a firing line.

His eyes grew wide as he saw Raj's banner. He turned to meet the onrush, drawing an ornate silver-inlaid revolver with his other hand. He clapped spurred heels to the dog's flanks; it bounded forward and a little to one side, crabbing against the ruthless skill of the rider as he forced it forward.

"Whitehall!" he cried in Arabic. "Shaitan waits for thee, Whitehall—and God is great!"

Crack. The bullet scorched past Raj's face. *Going to have a coal miner's tattoo from that one,* a distant corner of his mind recorded. The Arab had bleeding wounds across his face in a nine-line pattern, but his eyes were utterly intent. One well-placed shot or slash, and the heart would be out of the Civil Government force.

All the rest of his attention was on the point of his saber. Luck as well as skill saved the Colonial; his restive dog jibed at the last instant, and the swords crossed in a unmelodious skirring of steel on steel. Nimble, the Colonial's dog pivoted in its own length and started back to avoid the trampling rush of the Brigaderos. The dismounted men ahead had no such option. They managed one volley, an eruption of smoke and red fire. The whole front of the attacking line seethed as men and dogs went down across the fifteen-meter front. Men arched through the air to smash with bone-shattering force against the hard stuccoed stone of the house walls or crumple on the pavement; one landed with gruesome accidental accuracy on the crossbar of a gaslight and hung impaled and twitching like a shrike's prey on a thorn.

But there was too much momentum behind the charge for a single volley to halt, and many of the wounded dogs kept their feet. The light 10mm bullets of the Colonial carbines were deadly to men, but it took a lucky hit to kill a twelve-hundred-pound dog with one shot. Riderless dogs were almost as dangerous as the ones with swordsmen on their backs; one seized a Colonial by the head in its half-meter mouth and flipped him over its tail with one flex of its massive neck. The rear files squeezed by the thrashing chaos of the front rank, and the thin Colonial line went down in a flurry of swordstrokes and two-inch fangs.

The Colonial officer was very much alive. He took aim again; Raj threw himself down on the right side of his dog, holding on to the pommel with one heel. A trick a Skinner nomad had taught him, and it paid off . . . the pistol bullet went snapping through the air where his body had been an instant before. He drew his pistol and shot underneath Horace's belly, into the stomach of the Colonial's dog. The animal hunched itself up in an astonishing leap that made the

Arab release the gun and grab for the reins; then two 1/591st troopers were on him. The scimitar flashed against the heavy MilGov broadswords for one stroke, two, three; he slashed one trooper across the face even as the other slammed his heavy blade through the Arab's stomach.

Raj heaved himself upright. That had been *close.* For a moment there were no wogs in sight except the ones running away—and running away from a dog in a straight line was a losing proposition. Then they were out into the cleared zone just inside the wall. The main city gate—the one with the railway entrance—was just to his right; it was wreathed in smoke, but the Civil Government's banners were still flying above it, and the cannon mounted there were a constant rolling *booom* of thunder. Ahead of him a thin line of Civil Government troopers—the three companies of the 5th he'd left as the main reserve—were holding against a growing tide of wogs pouring down from their foothold on the wall. Just barely holding, and not for long; the Colonials had lost all unit cohesion coming over the wall, but they were forming up again like crystals accreting in a saturated solution, and more every minute.

The 5th's volleys rang out, crisp and unhurried, but as he watched, they were losing men like a sugar lump under a stream of hot tea.

Teodore Welf drew rein beside him as the 1/591st fanned out into line. "Dismount?" he asked.

Raj shook his head. "Not enough time. We've got to hit them before they get organized."

These MilGov knights liked cold steel, and this was the situation for it. The whole scene in front came in glimpses, flashing through gaps in the drifting clouds of sulfurous smoke. More every second, as cannon and rifle fire pumped it out. Bullets went by with an ugly *crack* sound. Five men down the line a trooper gave a grunt and toppled slowly out of the saddle.

A captain of the 5th dashed up, breathless. "Sir?"

"Get them out of the way, Fittorio, then re-form on my left and give me fire support. Welf, get those splatguns out to the right now we've got room for them. *Move!*"

The bugles sounded. The Descotters ahead gave one last volley and turned, moving back at the double. The ragged line of Colonials beyond them gave their yelping cheer and charged in turn, unaware of what awaited behind. Unaware until the bugle sang, and the dogs of the Brigaderos howled in unison. The screams of their riders were only slightly more human. There was just space enough to build up momentum, but plenty of room to deploy in the drill manual's double line. The cavalry came looming up out of the smoke, big men on big dogs, their swords bright. They crashed into the dismounted Colonials like a baulk of timber swinging at high speed; men went down, slashed and stabbed and bowled over by sheer momentum.

Now we see how well their training has sunk in, Raj thought. Aloud: "*Halto!* Dismount, fix bayonets, forward with fire and movement, independent fire!"

One or two of the troopers vanished into the throng ahead, eyes fixed and froth dripping from their mouths. The rest halted and stepped off their crouching dogs, sheathing swords and drawing their firearms—although some might not have, if the dogs hadn't stopped automatically. *Click,* and the long bayonets snapped onto the Armory rifles. The men walked forward in a steady line, not quite straight— more like a very shallow C—taking their dressing from the battalion standard and Raj's beside it. The front of their formation showed level for an instant, then vomited smoke. The sheet of fire smashed into the Colonials clustered at the base of the stairway.

The detachment of the 5th moved into place on the left flank, swinging in like a hinged door. The splatguns wheeled by at a trot and unlimbered, pushing into place to cover the gap between the end of the line on his right and the bare ground around the gate, swept by fire from the bastion towers.

Raj took a step forward. "Charge!" he shouted.

The troopers leveled their bayonets and ran in pounding unison; he ran along with them. The Colonials wavered, and then fled. *The bayonet's a terror weapon,* Raj knew. It didn't really *kill* all that many people, not in this age of breech-loaders, but there were times when it could make men *run.* Or try to run; the stairway that slanted down along the wall was too jammed with men for the ones on the ground to make much headway. Figures in crimson djellabas began to fall from the stairs in ones and twos, caught and squeezed out when the pressure from above and below forced the thick torrent of men to buckle sideways.

"*Halto!* Volley fire!"

The order relayed down the chain of officers. One rank knelt, the other firing over their heads. The rifles came up, aiming upward into the press. BAM. BAM. BAM. Rippling down the line, rounds whanging and keening off the stone, punching through three and four men at a time.

"Platoon column," Raj roared. "Welf, feed them up after us—you men, follow me!"

"To hell with *that*," the young MilGov noble said, and relayed the command. A column of forty troopers formed, with the banners only a few ranks from the front.

"Hadelande!"

"Upyarz!"

Many of the first Colonials went down with the bayonets in their backs. The troopers to the rear of the column fired over their comrades' heads, up the broad stairway. From the foot of it, six hundred men did likewise, and the splatguns with their muzzles raised to maximum elevation. Trapped, the Colonials on the stair turned to fight.

Raj found himself shoulder to shoulder with Teodore Welf; bayonets bristled on either side of them, and the banners waved behind. *Up a step.* Raj caught a scimitar on the guard of his saber, shot under it into his opponent's body. It tumbled down underfoot, and he nearly went over himself, with no room for his feet. An Armory rifle shot next to his ear, leaving it ringing. He threw himself back into swordsman's stance, right foot forward, and lunged again. Again. Welf was fighting with a long dagger in his right hand, using the heavy single-edged broadsword in his left like a ribbon saber; blond hair flew about his shoulders as he howled some Namerique war chant with every other breath. Fire swept the stairs ahead of them; Raj's hair crawled on the back of his neck at the thought of what would happen if somebody aimed a little low.

Or if these wogs had the time to reload. One did. Center's green aiming-grid slapped down across Raj's vision, outlining the figure in strobing light. He moved the red dot onto the center of mass and pulled the trigger, and the man spun away with the carbine flying out of his hands. Another target designated; he turned slightly, the pistol outstretched, squeezed the trigger. It was a hand bomb beginning its arc downward towards him, an impossible target . . . impossible without Center. Left-handed, at that. The iron sphere exploded less than a meter from the thrower when the bullet struck it.

A lot of men had seen that, seen his arm like a pointer and the result. It was close enough to a miracle as no matter, to anyone with practical experience of firearms. Welf shouted:

"Spirit with us! Spirit of Man for Messer Raj!"

The Brigaderos behind him took it up; and some of the stubborn fight went out of the Colonials ahead. More and more were running back up, trying for the grappling lines and ladders over the walls. Raj chanced a look over his shoulder; more banners in the open ground beneath the wall: the 18th Komar, the 7th Descott. The stone was slippery underfoot, slippery with red rivulets running down from above. Fire from the ground was raking the firing platform above, deliberately built with little rear cover.

Not often you actually see that, see ground running with blood. The last time had been in Port Murchison, when Conner Auburn's fleet had sailed into his ambush.

Suddenly he was staggering onto level ground, the fighting platform on the wall; fire from below ceased, and a huge cheer went up as the bannermen waved their flags back and forth. Bodies heaped the pavement. Men poured out of the bastion towers before and behind him, shooting and wielding bayonet and rifle butt, shotguns and clubbed ramrods for the gunners. Ladders toppled as men thrust with poles or the points of their bayonets, through the firing slits and from the roof above.

Silence fell—comparative silence: only the cannonade and the screams of the wounded that littered the platform and stairs and the ground on both sides of the wall. He stepped up to a gunslit and looked out. The Colonial artillery was firing again; shells whined by overhead and crashed into the city behind.

"Get—" he turned and croaked; then stopped, realizing that he didn't recognize the man holding his banner. There were always volunteers for that job, and a continuous need for them. One of the runners was still there, though, reloading his pistol with a hand that dripped blood. "Verbal order to the battalion commanders. Pull their men back into cover. Get me Menyez. And then get that seen to."

"Ser."

The staircase was emptying; men rushed up it to take positions at the firing slits. Others helped or carried the wounded back below; the enemy went over the side to fall like bundles of discarded clothing to the hard-packed earth below. Except that bundles didn't scream on the way down, sometimes . . . *Well, no time for niceties.*

A voice spoke in Namerique: "Otto, this whore's son is alive—shoot!"

Raj looked up sharply and said in the same language: "Check there isn't one of ours alive under there first, man."

The big trooper braced himself and then began dragging bodies away by their legs; two of his comrades waited to either side, bayonetted rifles poised, and an ensign joined them with his revolver drawn. Half a dozen of the bodies were Colonial regulars, the remainder Civil Government infantry—24th Valencia, by the shoulder-flashes.

24th's been taking it on the chin, Raj thought. They died hard, though, by the Spirit.

Suddenly he had time to notice his own panting exhaustion, and the way his harness seemed to squeeze at his ribs. He felt for the canteen at his belt and found it empty, the bottom half ripped open in a flower of jagged tinned iron. Somebody made a joke as he tossed it aside, and he felt his testicles trying to draw up. He wasn't afraid of death, much—it was more that he had so much to *do*—but there were some wounds that were much more terrifying. A trooper handed him another canteen and he rinsed out his mouth, spat, and drank; it was water cut with vinegar, cutting through the dust and phlegm in his throat.

"*Tenk,*" he said—the Namerique word for thanks—and handed it back.

He started to wipe his mouth on the back of his sleeve, then stopped when he realized it was still sodden with blood. There was a little less on his left arm, so he used that instead. Now he could feel the sting of a half-dozen minor wounds, mostly superficial cuts, and a couple of bone-bruises. He broke open the revolver, ejected the spent brass and reloaded, then cleaned his saber a little, enough to resheath it. A trooper swore from the pile of dead.

"This one *is* alive, and he's one of ours!"

Raj moved over. His brows rose; that looked like a minor miracle. The infantryman was even more covered with blood than Raj, although—just like the stuff all over Raj—most of it didn't seem to be his own. A huge bruise covered one side of his face; a rifle lay beside him, the butt shattered and bayonet bent. The rings of a half-dozen handbombs were still on his fingers.

Raj whistled silently, and a number of the cavalry troopers nodded. He went on one knee and extended his hand; someone put another canteen in it, and he used that and his neckcloth to wipe some of the crusted blood from the man's face. He was young, no more than his early twenties, and rather light-skinned.

corporal minatelli, Center supplied. **enlisted in old residence two years ago. literate, watch-stander.** Details from the service record ran through his mind with the icy certainty of the ancient computer's data-transfer.

Damn, if he's as good as he looks, make that Ensign Minatelli, Raj thought.

The noncom's eyes snapped open, and he started violently, hand reaching for the knife in his boot. Raj caught it with irresistible strength.

"Easy there, fellow soldier," he said.

Minatelli controlled a dry retch. Raj checked his pupils; no noticeable difference in the dilation, so the concussion couldn't be too bad. A day's weakness and a bad headache. Lucky: any blow strong enough to knock you out was a real risk to life and limb.

"Sor," he said. The situation seemed to be sinking in. "Anyone else, sor?" he said hoarsely, with a clipped Spanjol accent under the Army dialect of Sponglish.

Definitely Ensign Minatelli, Raj decided. He looked up at the 1/591st junior officer with a question in his face.

"One other, sir—we're giving him first aid now. Looks fairly bad but he might make it."

"Sorry, son," Raj said.

"Spirit," Minatelli whispered. "Did our best, sor, but t'ere was just too many."

"You did fine, soldier. You held them long enough for us to get here."

He slapped the young man gently on the shoulder and rose. Teams of stretcher bearers were coming up the stairs at a run, now that they were a little clearer. A messenger preceded them.

"Ser. From Colonel Staenbridge—wogs back on their sida t'wall. Same frum Major Belagez."

That was a relief, though not unexpected. This had been the most dangerous penetration, the one nearest to the main gate.

"Raj!"

He looked around quickly; it was Suzette, with Fatima in tow and a Renunciate nun-doctor, who was bending over the wounded men being loaded onto the stretchers. Raj looked down at himself . . . well, it *was* a little alarming. She finished helping tie off a bandage and picked up her kit, walking over to him with a determined expression.

"It's not mine," he said, slightly defensive.

"Well, what about *this*?" she asked.

Raj looked down in genuine surprise. There was a long slash down his right arm, starting just above the wrist and running to his elbow. He worked the fingers. Not deep enough to really hurt, and it was with the grain of the muscle anyway. The soft scab broke and fresh blood oozed out along the path the scimitar had traced. *Must have been a good one,* he thought absently. They had some really fine swordsmiths in Al Kebir and Gedorosia, who made blades you could cut through a floating scarf of *torofib*-silk with; ones that would keep the edge when they hacked through bone.

"Take that jacket off right now."

Suzette's voice was determined. Raj obeyed automatically, and caught some of the soldiers concealing grins. *All part of the legend,* he thought resignedly. Even Horace had his place in it, and they all had to follow their roles willy-nilly. He swore mildly as she swabbed out the cut with iodine and washed down the arm before bringing out a roll of bandages.

"Is all that necessary?" he said.

"It *should* have some stitches," she said tartly. "Try not to use it too hard."

"I'll try," he promised. Then he smiled. "I couldn't let you be the only one to collect a scar from this campaign, now could I? Think of my reputation."

She gave an unwilling snort of laughter. "Your reputation will suffer even more if you get killed doing a lieutenant's work. Let the younger men have a chance."

"When you stay home and do embroidery, my dear, it's a deal."

He levered himself erect from his seat on a ledge and looked up. *0900*, he thought. Less than two hours past dawn.

Looking down from the fighting platform, he saw that the cleared ring inside the walls was mostly empty. Except for the enemy dead, of course. *Burial parties.* He'd look in on the wounded . . . *Get those fires under control.* The Colonial shelling had started more; luckily, Sandoral was mostly a city of adobe, brick, and stone with tiled roofs supported by arches—timber had always been expensive here, and he'd ripped out most of it for the bridge.

"Back to work," he said, and walked toward the staircase. Flies rose in a buzzing cloud from the stone, amid the faint sweetish smell of blood beginning to rot in the hot morning sun. A severed hand lay almost in his path; he started to kick it aside, then shook his head and walked down the stairs.

The flags crackled in the wind as his bannermen followed.

CHAPTER TWELVE

Suzette was pale. Fatima looked up in alarm; neither of them was a stranger to field-hospitals after all these years, so it couldn't be that. With a shudder, the Arab girl remembered her first time here, the first battle, four years ago. *Then* there had been huge wooden tubs set up at the feet of the operating tables, to hold the amputated limbs. And they had been full, all that endless day. Bartin had lost his hand that day; she'd held his shoulders down while the surgeon worked.

This was mild, by comparison. Only a few dozen shattered limbs to come off, with plenty of time to dose the worst cases with opium. A few hundred others, and more than half would live. But Suzette *did* look ill as she walked among the cots set up in the main chamber of Sandoral's cathedron. The air smelled of old incense and wax, under the stink of disinfectant and blood.

She was still Messa Whitehall. She finished the conversation, turned on her heel, and walked without running to the door. Fatima followed, grabbing up a towel. Retching sounds came from the cubicle; it was a priest's vesting room, in normal times. Suzette knelt and vomited into a bucket. Fatima hurried up beside her and handed her the towel, then went back for water.

"I don't understand it," Suzette said, wiping her face and slumping back in the chair.

Fatima put a hand on her forehead. "You're not running a fever, Messa."

"No, I'm not. And I feel fine, most of the time; just these last couple of mornings I—" She stopped. "What *date* is it?"

"Second of *Huillio*. Why do you want to . . . oh!"

Suzette's eyes went round. She turned her head slowly and met Fatima's gaze. The younger woman's mouth dropped open; she squeaked before managing to get out a coherent word:

"I thought . . . I thought you couldn't, that is—" She stopped in embarrassment.

"No, there wasn't enough time," Suzette said dazedly. Then her face firmed. "This is *not* to go beyond these walls, understand?"

"Of course, Messa," Fatima said soothingly. "But wouldn't Messer Raj want to know?"

"Not while he's got so much to worry about," Suzette said.

The flat rooftop terrace of Sandoral's District Offices made an excellent observation post, being close to the river and higher than the tops of the maidan wall; it was also far enough in from the defenses that Colonial shells were unlikely to land in the vicinity. The noon sun pounded down, turning the blue tile of the floor pale, drawing knife edges of shadow around the topiaries and pergolas. City administrators had held their receptions here, amid the potted bougainvillea and sambuca jasmine that had already begun to wilt without care. The iron heel plates of the officers' boots sounded on the floors, harsh and metallic. A heliograph station occupied one corner, and a map table and working desk had been set up by the railing nearest the river.

"Well, he's not wasting any time," Raj said.

Through the tripod-mounted heavy binoculars the east bank showed plainly. Tewfik's seal-of-Solomon banner waved from the highest ground; around it several thousand men worked with pick and shovel.

Grammek Dinnalsyn was using a telescope, also mounted; he made a few precise adjustments to the screws and sketched on a pad.

"That's not intended for his whole force," he said. "About three, four hundred men, perhaps."

Raj nodded agreement and took another bite of his sandwich. *Which reminds me . . .*

"Jorg," he said. "You've had your men on half-rations while we were away?"

"*Si*. Mostly hardtack and jerky, some fish and dried fruit."

"The whole command is back on full rations as of now," he said. "Bait the dogs properly, too. Muzzaf, get me a complete inventory of supplies. And fuel."

"*Si*," the little Komarite said. "*Seyhor*, I can tell you immediately—we have less than a week's supply at that rate of expenditure."

"Excellent," Raj said with a smile. The others looked at him oddly. "I presume Ali knows?"

"The outlines," Menyez said. "We've had a few deserters, mostly from the garrison units. Presumably they've 'taken the turban' and told him what they know."

Raj nodded thoughtfully. "Any the other way?"

"Three—two from their transport corps, claim to be Star Church believers conscripted for supplies. The other's a Zanj."

The Colony had conquered some of the outlying city-states there, but was fiercely resented. The Zanj were of different race than most of the Colonials, and followed a branch of Islam the conquerors thought heretical.

"They're probably spies, of course," Menyez concluded. "I've kept them in close confinement."

"I'll talk to them; I can usually get the truth out of a man," Raj said. He was conscious of sidelong glances; another part of the myth, that it was impossible to lie to Messer Raj. *It is when Center's looking through my eyes,* he thought. "In any case, it doesn't matter what Ali knows. Or even what Tewfik knows."

Barton Foley pointed. "They're bringing men across."

Everyone raised their glasses. An overloaded fishing skiff labored across the current, on a trajectory that would land it just south of Sandoral's walls on the western bank. Heads and V-marks of ripples showed where dogs on lead-halters swam in the boat's wake. On the riverbank it had left, men were building an earth ramp down to the water's edge and putting together a raft from bits and pieces, date-palm logs and thin boards that looked as if they'd come from some sheep fence.

"It'll take him a while to get his men back to Ali," Gerrin Staenbridge said, examining his nails. The way the Civil Government forces had scavenged up every small boat and all available materials was handicapping their enemies badly. "You have something in mind, don't you, *mi heneral*?"

Raj grinned at him. "Possibly. Can you think what?"

Staenbridge shook his head. Raj nodded amiably.

"And that's an excellent thing too," he said. "Because you're an extremely perceptive officer, and you have *all* the information. If you can't figure it out, probably Tewfik can't either. Gentlemen, I want you to spend the rest of today and tomorrow reorganizing. Don't let your men settle in too tight—I want full readiness to move at a moment's notice. Those units that've been hit hard, do the necessary shifting around immediately. Weapons maintenance, ammunition issues, the lot—again, immediately, please. Understood?"

Nods. "Grammeck, this afternoon I want to go over some matters with you; bring the complete plans for the pontoon bridge, please. If there aren't any questions, Messers?"

There was obviously one burning one, but nobody was going to ask it. Jorg Menyez remained when the others had left the flat rooftop.

"Colonel?" Raj asked. It wasn't like Jorg to talk for reassurance sake. He was obviously a little embarrassed.

"*Heneralissimo*," he said. "Ah . . . I thought you'd want to know about Osterville."

"Osterville?" Raj asked. It was an effort to remember the man; he hadn't thought of him since Ain el-Hilwa. *And good riddance.* "It's enough that he isn't here, making trouble."

"No, he won't be doing that," Menyez said. "It was unpleasant, but as you said, it was necessary."

Raj looked at him. Menyez flushed. "All right, *mi heneral.* I destroyed the letter and your seal, and he went into the Drangosh with a sixty-kilo roundshot tied to his ankles . . . but I still don't like it."

Raj nodded. "Of course, Jorg." *Only Suzette has my seal.* "I understand."

He shivered slightly, despite the heat of the day.

A dot of red light arched over the wall, trailing fire through the darkness. *Thud.* It exploded among the vacant houses—hopefully vacant houses—and a column of fire rose into the night. Another spark. *Thud.*

"That makes six the past hour," Raj murmured to himself.

in the past fifty-five minutes thirty seconds, Center added. **harassing fire.**

"Ali's obviously decided to starve us out," Raj agreed.

An image drifted across his eyes: his own emaciated body, still living, naked and covered with weals and burns. Pairs of dogs were hitched to chains attached to each ankle and wrist. The drivers urged the dogs forward slowly, gradually taking up the slack. Ali ibn'Jamal sat watching, pounding his fist on the arm of his portable throne and laughing with pleasure, licking his full lips. Tewfik stood to one side, arms crossed and a look of faint disgust on his face, echoed by most of the noblemen and officers around him. Behind him a gallows stood skeletal against the sky, with the bodies of the Companions dangling from it—by meathooks through their ribs. Several of them were still writhing . . .

Raj made a grimace of distaste. "Even by the standards of Mihwel the Terrible, Ali is a prime case."

a subjective judgment, but accurate. child-rearing practices among the colonial royal family are conducive to severely dysfunctional personalities.

A step sounded on the tiles behind him. There had been no challenge and response from the sentries on the stair below, so it could be only one person.

Suzette leaned on the railing beside him, looking out over the city and the glistening water. "Full circle, my love," she said. "Sandoral, and a battle to come."

"And men dying unexpectedly," he said.

She turned her face towards him, drawn and pale beneath the moons. "Osterville couldn't lead and wouldn't follow and wouldn't get out of the way and let you work, either. Can you imagine the sort of havoc he'd have created back here, with everything depending on Jorg keeping things running smoothly? We'd have ended up *swimming* across, while Osterville tried to make everyone do things his way."

"Jorg—"

"Jorg is good man and a good officer, but he doesn't have your talent for facing men down—especially not men higher on the chain of command. You know that." A little anger crept into her voice: "How many better men have been killed on this campaign so far?"

Raj smiled ruefully and shook his head. "You always could out-argue me," he said. A shrug. "I just don't like having a fellow officer killed like that. It's the sort of thing Tzetzas does."

Suzette sighed. "I don't like it either," she said quietly. "But it had to be done."

Raj nodded. They watched another Colonial shell come over the walls.

"It's cold," Suzette said in a small voice.

Raj extended his arm and the long military cloak he wore. Suzette came under it and laid her cheek against his chest.

"We can't afford any mistakes this time, can we?" she said after a moment.

"No," Raj replied. He looked up at the moons. They'd be rising late, tomorrow evening. *Victory or death,* he thought. *All men die, but this has to be done.* "Let's turn in."

"Precisely this bearing," Raj said.

He drew a line in the dust with the stick. Behind him the artillerymen staked down their frame—two sets of rigid beams at right angles, with a slanted piece across the arms. They aligned it with the mark in the dust; once it was firmly in place, they pushed the gun up the slanted fronting of the frame and tied off the wheels at a chalk mark on the wood.

"Range is exactly 3,525 meters," Raj said. "Load contact, two-second delay."

"Sir," the gunner said, giving him a glance.

How could you know? Raj read in his face. And a trace of awe; men knew he didn't make empty boasts.

Raj walked on to the next gun's position as the iron clang of the breechblock sounded behind him. All fifty-eight surviving field guns were lined up just inside the north wall of Sandoral, all up on the frames; all aligned along the precise vector he'd drawn in the dirt for them. Every single one, as far as Center could judge, was now aiming at the exact midpoint of earth above Ali's command bunker, behind the Colonial outworks—where he invariably retired after the sunset prayer. All the fortress guns in the fixed positions on the wall were aligned as well, those of them that would bear on the target.

Irregularities—wear on the rifling of guns, slight differentials in shell loading and drag, whatever—would spread the projectiles. It ought to be an unpleasant surprise, nonetheless.

Dinnalsyn looked back at the long row of guns. "Think we'll get him, *mi heneral?*"

"No," Raj said. "That's a very secure bunker. The last thing I want to do is put Tewfik in full command. But it'll certainly get his attention, and Ali's got a short temper. If I know my man, he'll do something stupid."

The limbers stood in a row five meters behind the guns, the dog teams in traces and lying down.

"Are the rafts ready?" Raj said.

"Ready and waiting, sir," Dinnalsyn said. "The planking and decking from the pontoon bridge was exactly as much as we needed . . . I suppose that's no coincidence?"

"You might say that," Raj replied. He clapped him on the shoulder. "Stay ready for it."

The last of the cavalry battalions on special duty were sitting by the wall, finishing their evening meal: beans and pigmeat and onions, dished out from kettles over camp fires and scooped up with tortillas. It was the 5th Descott. They were professionals enough to concentrate on eating, but he could feel the tension crackling off them. He walked over and made a beckoning gesture. They crowded around him and crouched or sat at his hand signal; only about three hundred fifty left—and the battalion had been at double strength when he took it west to fight the Brigade.

"All right, dog-brothers," he said quietly. That forced them to listen carefully and lean closer; it also made each man feel as if he was talking to that one alone, as an individual. "You've guessed that something's up. Two hours after sundown—"

The sun was just touching the western horizon.

"—the guns are going to cut loose with a five-round stonk. The second the last gun fires—but not before—you give the wogs five rounds rapid. Then you come back down from the wall, ride your dogs to the docks, get on the rafts and off we go."

He paused a moment. "You're all fighting men and all Descotters," he went on. "My father and grandfather and great-grandfather fought the wogs, and so did yours."

Nods; Descotter *rancheros* held their land on military tenure, paying their tax in men rather than money. Fathers and sons and brothers followed each other into the same battalions time out of mind; comrades were neighbors at home, officers the squire's sons.

"There's a lot of Descotter blood and bone buried around here. Now we have a chance to end it." That caused a rustle, men coming forward in their crouch and leaning on their rifles. "If we win this one, we break them—not just push them back, but wreck them for all time. If we lose . . ." He grinned. "Well, we haven't done much losing while we've been together, you and I, have we?"

A low snarl of agreement. "Everything depends on the wogs thinking we're still here, at least for a while. You'll move back to the docks quickly and you'll do it quietly, and with no foul-ups. Understood?"

Gerrin Staenbridge stepped forward. "You can count on us, *mi heneral*," he said solemnly. Another growl from the ranks.

"Keep it quiet, keep it quiet," Ensign Minatelli said.

There were only fifteen men left in his platoon, now—several of them lightly wounded—so it wasn't very different from running his squad. The star on the front of his helmet still felt like a weight of lead to his spirit, though. They formed up outside their bivouac, in the forecourt of what had been a nobleman's house. Minatelli walked down his platoon, giving everything a final check. The men's haversacks were full, three days' rations—smoked pork and hardtack, dried apricots and figs—and extra ammunition in their blanket rolls.

"Company G, fall in."

The men found their places by instinct, in column of twos back from the company pennant. It was *dark* outside: the city gaslights were out, of course—nobody left to shovel coal and tend the tank-farms—and all torches and fires had been forbidden.

Just as well, he thought. It was frightening how few of them were left; the main Colonial attack had come right over their sector of the wall yesterday. Forty men in the company, barely a full platoon.

The battalion colors came by, and Major Felasquez carrying a shuttered bull's-eye light. His one eye gleamed a little as he turned, stopped for a brief murmur with Captain Pinya and stepped closer to the men.

"All right, lads," he said, a little louder.

Don't expect the wogs could hear even if we shouted, Minatelli thought. On the other hand, it gets everyone thinking quiet.

"We've had enough from the towel-heads; now we're going to give it back, the way the monkey gave it to the miller's wife, by surprise and from the rear. Mind your orders, do it right, and with the Spirit's help and Messer Raj's plan, we'll whip them." He stepped back. "24th Valencia Foot—*Waymanos!*"

The column moved forward jerkily; it was strange to the point of being dizzying not to step off to the beat of the drum, and the troops had been told not to march in step. The uniform clash of hobnails on stone pavement was like nothing else on earth, and it carried. Instead they walked, with an occasional quiet curse as somebody stepped on the heels of the man ahead. Guides stood at intersections, their lanterns the only light in the deserted city. Minatelli kept his hand on the hilt of his new sword and ignored the eerie quietness.

Through the river gate the darkness lifted a little; a one-quarter

Miniluna and the stars reflected off the rippled surface of the water. Gravel crunched, then planks boomed a little under their boots. The column halted.

"24th Valencia?" someone asked ahead, a dim figure against the water. "*This* way."

They waited; the men ahead melted away company by company. "Company G, this way."

The men scrambled through the knee-high water and into the barge; it was one of the boxlike constructs he'd helped to cobble together out of wood salvaged from wrecked houses. A long steering-oar marked the notional stern, and there were men standing to the sweeps on either side, six to a flank. They had only a single shuttered lantern to work with, but despite the darkness and the crowding only an occasional thump and oath marked someone tripping as they clambered down from the planking to the hold of the crude vessel.

"You'll be pulling the outermost raft," Captain Pinya said.

"That one, sir?" Minatelli said, pointing.

"That's right, Ensign."

Ensign. Spirit. My folks will never believe it.

He shook himself back to the present. There were so many more ways to fuck *up* at a higher rank. Right now, that could get *everyone* killed.

He saluted and climbed down himself, a little awkward with no rifle on his shoulder and a sword and pistol at his belt. He turned around as soon as he was at the bow, making sure everyone's equipment was blacked as ordered. *Right. Nothing showing but eyeballs.*

"Cast off," he said quietly.

The ropes were undone and the barge began to drift. "That way," he said, pointing.

The rowers were from the Sandoral District garrison; they'd all had some experience moving these damned things around. They dug their clumsy oars into the water and heaved, grunting. One step forward, lower the oar, haul it one step back. Minatelli thumped the boards beside him softly to keep the beat, peering ahead to his target. It was almost invisible until they were on top of it, two sections of the pontoon bridge decking with some timbers in between.

"*Halto,*" he said.

Hands and poles on the raft fended them off and turned the barge around. Ropes were made fast to both sides of the stern, and then the barge released to drift slowly downstream. It halted with a slight jerk, held by the cables that anchored the row of rafts. Minatelli looked back along them, back to the shore and the black silhouette of the city wall. The sun had been down at least an hour and a half. More and more of the pontoon barges and every other type of boat available on the Sandoral docks—the ones that hadn't had a chance to get upstream when the news of the invasion got here—put out into the darkening water, anchoring or sculling up to the rafts. The docks were a moving carpet of men, helmets and furled banners and the muzzles of slung rifles.

Not long now.

"Rest easy, boys," he said. "Rest a bit."

"Gently, gently," Suzette whispered.

The infantrymen assigned as stretcher bearers were well-meaning but clumsy. There were enough of them to manhandle the stretchers into the bottom of the barge and fit them into the crude racks the carpenters had made, turning them into improvised bunk beds. The wounded were dosed heavily with opium to dull the pain of movement, but now and then a man would moan in his delirium. The Renunciates and priest-doctors moved quickly among them, checking pulses.

"Spirit have mercy, this one's dead," a nun said.

"Leave him be," Suzette replied. *Damn.*

The final load came from the carriages and handcarts they'd pressed into service as ambulances.

She looked west, towards the ramparts.

"Drop it in, don't throw it!" Jorg Menyez hissed.

An officer relayed the order. Endless files of infantrymen passed sacks of hardtack and crates of dried meat and fruit from hand to hand, out from the wagons to the end of the pier. Once there, they knelt and let their burdens drop into the water. The current caught them, the hardtack floating for a few minutes before waterlogging dragged it down with a scatter of bubbles, the pierced casks and boxes sinking faster.

A good thing this is fresh water. There would be downdraggers in a feeding-frenzy if they tried this in a harbor. Doubtless the plesiosauroids out in the deeper water would be feeding full tonight, as it was.

"Colonel. Major Tormidero sends 'is compliments, and is 'e to load tha wine?"

"No," Menyez said, biting off the *damned fool* with an effort. "Tell him Ali's men may drown their sorrows as they wish, if they don't fear Allah's wrath."

But not a scrap of food will they find in Sandoral, he thought with hard glee. He sneezed into his handkerchief, not too badly; there weren't any dogs in the immediate neighborhood. It was pitch black. He looked anxiously over the river to the Colonial fortlet planted where the pontoon bridge had been. Evidently *they* hadn't seen anything unusual, either. *It's a siege. They don't* expect *anything to happen.*

"Spirit, but this is a madman's gamble," he whispered to himself, lips barely moving. The only chance at victory . . . but what a chance.

"And what a story to tell the grandchildren, if we pull it off!"

If they didn't . . .

Ali ibn'Jamal took another handful of rice and grilled lamb, belching politely. It was surprisingly good, considering what the cooks had to work with; the army was on preserved rations wagoned up from the bridgehead. His own cook had priority on what little the foragers were bringing in, of course. The bunker had been made quite homelike: silk tapestries and silk-and-gold thread Al Kebir carpets, embroidered cushions about low tables of chiseled brass, incense in crescent-shaped burners on tripods about the walls. The lamplight had been turned down to a civilized level, and zebec and zither played melodiously from behind a screen in one corner. Ali ate, and held out his hands for the slave to wash with rosewater and towel dry.

"Your appetite should be better, Tewfik my brother," he said, and belched again. "Think of how the *kaphar* pigs within Sandoral's walls would drool and slaver at the sight of such a feast!"

Tewfik turned from a low-voiced conversation with his officers. "Indeed, Settler of the House of Peace," he said. "They are very short of supplies. That is why I fear some new trick of this Shaitan's-seed Whitehall."

Ali scowled for a moment, then gestured expansively. "Whitehall is trapped," he said. "He cannot sortie—our men outnumber his and are strongly entrenched; our rear, even, is protected by great works, even though no relieving force of any numbers can approach. He cannot build his bridge of boats again, with your fort and its guns covering the opposite bank. What can he do but starve?"

"Commander of the Faithful, I do not *know* what he can do. And that is what—"

"My lord." One of the duty officers of the Settler's guard came up to Tewfik and bowed. "You commanded that we notify you: the infidel have launched a signal rocket from the walls. One blue starburst."

A gun boomed in the distance. They all ignored it; the Colonial artillery was lobbing a steady round every twenty minutes into Sandoral, to keep the infidels from sleeping easily.

Another boom, and another; and the explosion of a shell, far too close. Another junior officer dashed down the stairs into the bunker.

"From the walls!" he shouted. "Lords, *all* the *kaphar* guns are firing from—"

"Fwego!"

Grammeck Dinnalsyn swept his saber downward. POUMPH. The first of the field guns vomited a long tongue of red flame into the night, backlighting the cloud of smoke that swirled away from the muzzle. Like a ripple, the line of explosions swept down the row of guns, repeated fifty-eight times. The noise was deafening, shock-waves echoing back from the high flat surface of the city wall like pillows of hot air smacking into face and chest. Already the stairways were showing running men, the militia gunners; one per gun on the walls, each to pull the lanyard on a weapon pre-laid on its target.

The first field gun had already fired its second round by the time the last piece discharged at the other end of the line. The crews moved with smooth, metronomic precision. The guns couldn't recoil, up on the elevating frames—although he hated to see the trails overstressed like this; it was asking for trouble later. Each piece had a stack of five extra shells next to it, with preset fuses. Swing the lever and wrench the breech aside; the brass shell clanged out, with a puff of sulfur-reeking smoke. Loader shoved the next round in, breechman pushed the interrupted-screw block home and slapped the lever down, master gunner clipped his lanyard to the toggle, and *fire.*

Six rounds, and silence except for the ringing of abused ears. The master gunners of the two central pieces slashed the ties holding the wheels to the elevating frames with their swords, and the pieces ran down the sloped timbers. The crews snatched up the trails before the pieces could slow, running them back to the limbers and slapping the locking-rings down. The pins went home with an iron clank, men leaped into the saddle or swung onto the axletree seats, and the guns rumbled off down toward the docks at a round trot. An instant later the sound changed to a hard rattle as the metal rims of the wheels rose onto the cobblestones. The maneuver was repeated again and again, each gun out from the first two cutting loose and limbering up to follow.

Dinnalsyn neck-reined his dog around. The guns were vanishing into the night, and small-arms fire crackled from the ramparts above. Alone but for his aides and messengers, he saluted the walls.

"Here's to you, *heneralissimo*," he said. "I don't know how the hell you manage it, but it's never dull. *Waymanos!*"

He clapped heels to his dog.

Corporal M'Telgez was acutely conscious of Messer Raj standing quietly behind him as the artillery bellowed. It was blacker than a meter up a sauroid's butt here on the wall's fighting platform; and it smelled of old death, rotting blood and bits of bodies. He willed himself to ignore the smell, and the feeling of confinement—he was a dog-and-saddle man, not a mole or a town-dweller—and the far more nerve-wracking presence of the *heneralissimo*. Not that he was one to interfere with a man doing his work, far from it. It was just a little disconcerting to have Messer Raj and the Colonel and the Captain all pick *your* spot to pause when the balloon went up. There was a gap in the gabions he'd picked earlier for his first aiming point. Invisible in the darkness now, but pretty soon—

"*Fwego!*"

The stubby mortars on the towers chugged. Starshells burst over the wog entrenchments, throwing a flickering blue-white magnesium light. He exhaled and squeezed the trigger. *Crack*. His rifle punched his shoulder. He worked the lever and reached for one of the rounds in the wooden holder beside his hand. *Crack*. A Colonial gun fired from the forward trenches. He adjusted his sights and aimed for it, with any luck a round might ricochet off the barrel and into one of the crew. *Crack. Crack. Crack*.

"Cease fire! Rearward, on the double!" he called out.

His squad was closest to the staircase. They double-timed down it, through the hot dark and the faint reflected light of the starshells, while the field guns blazed away to their right. Eyes and teeth glimmered from the dogs crouching in neat rows in the open space within the walls; they were too well trained to move when they'd been told to stay, but the noise made them eager and uneasy. They rose with a surge as their riders straddled them. M'Telgez's feet found the stirrups, and he slid his rifle into the scabbard, taking the reins in tightly with his left hand. More and more men poured down the stairways by the gates, until the whole battalion was mounted.

No trumpet calls, but the men fell in—every dog knew its place by smell, if nothing else. M'Telgez saw the shadowy length of the battalion standard go by, and an arm flash up. He tapped his heel to Pochita's flank, and the whole column broke into a fast walk that turned into a slow loping trot. They moved south of the last of the guns, under the arc of the last shells, then turned eastward toward the docks. The sky ripped above them. M'Telgez felt his shoulders hunch; his hindbrain knew what that meant, only too well.

CRUMP. A heavy shell sledged into the empty space behind him. Seconds later dirt pattered down out of the air. At least they weren't firing airburst; it must be too difficult with no observation of the fall of shot. *CRUMP. CRUMP. CRUMP.* The last one fell on a gun that was moving parallel to the column of the 5th Descott, and the limber went up too in a huge ball of red-orange flame. Men screamed and dogs wailed ahead of him. An officer rode out; his pistol cracked as the dogs were put down, and the men swung up behind comrades, no time for first aid now. *CRUMP. CRUMP. CRUMP.* More shells went by overhead and blasted into the upper stories of empty houses. Adobe brick and fragments of roof tiles and burning planks cataracted into the streets. He kept his head down and followed the man ahead of him, hoping that the officers knew where they were going. Shells were coming overhead in a continuous stream, but a whole city was a big target.

Mother, he thought. This was worse than a battle; then you could *do* something.

Horace knew he was being ridden toward another boat ride. He turned nose-to-tail and circled. Raj cursed, but he didn't bother yanking on the reins; you could pull until the levers gouged a hole right through his cheeks, and Horace wouldn't pay much attention. Instead he let the knotted reins fall on the pommel and leaned forward, thumping the hound's neck with the flat of his hand.

"Come *on*, you son of a bitch," he said firmly. "We've got places to go and things to do. Stop this nonsense."

Horace lowered his ears and head and turned, breaking into a shambling trot. Raj's banner snapped in the night air; the Colonial shells went by overhead with their mechanical wails, a continuous diminuendo punctuated by the crash of the bursting charges. He pressed with his heels as a barricade of brick and burning rubble closed the way. Horace took it in a single long leap, then checked a pace to let the others come through. Heat slapped at him as they passed over the flame; a dog yelped suddenly as it stepped on a hot ember.

Raj grinned into the darkness. *Well, we certainly got their attention,* he thought.

all colonial guns are firing at maximum speed, Center noted. **even with ample ammunition reserves, this will degrade performance and shorten the life of the barrels.**

Raj nodded. Wasteful. The hotter a gun got, the worse the wear on the lands of the rifling. After a while it had to be sent back to the foundry to have a new sleeve fitted into the barrel and rifled, and it was never quite as good after that. The third time it had to be scrapped.

"Want to do the honors, *mi heneral?*" Jorg Menyez said.

He waved to the lines of slowmatch that snaked away among the warehouses and boatyards of Sandoral's docks. The raw smell of kerosene and gunpowder was thick in the air.

"Dinnalsyn assures me that it will all go off at about the same time."

Raj looked around with grim satisfaction. When the warehouses and shipyards went up, it would also take all the remaining timber in Sandoral suitable for boats or rafts or bridging materials. Ali might get the city, but he was damned if there'd be anything immediately useful in it when he did. No food, no building materials.

"I wouldn't dream of denying you the pleasure, Jorg," Raj said.

Menyez ceremoniously puffed on his cigarillo and applied the end to the slowmatch. It lit with a sullen hiss and trail of blue smoke.

"And now we bid farewell to beauteous Sandoral: land of exotic giant cockroaches, intolerable sticky heat-rash, and picturesque, hairy wogs with razor-sharp gelding knives," the infantryman mock-quoted. East Residence had enough of a middle class to support a tourist trade, mostly steamboat excursions to the Bay Islands. Guidebooks were common, too. *"Hadios, mi heneral."*

It probably did the men good to see their commanders relaxed and confident. *It does me good. Jorg's usually a worrier. Morale's probably as high as it should be.* Possibly higher than it should be . . . *Now who's worrying?*

"Hadios, Jorg. See you downriver."

He turned Horace. Raft after raft was heading downstream, casting off behind its towing-barge. Sweeps tossed up small chuckling ripples of green water, a faint sheen under the crescent of Miniluna. As each loosed its ties to the anchor cables, another cluster of dogs and guns would trundle out across the linked rafts to the outermost.

War-dogs whined as chain staples fastened their bridles to pins in the decking; the wheels of guns and limbers were lashed down, and another raft and barge combination was under way. Beyond the rafts boats speckled the water, sloops and ferries, and score after score of the pontoon barges.

Messengers trotted up, reported, left. *Damn. Amazing. Only one traffic jam.* And that caused by rubble blocking a street and the battalion assigned to it swerving into another's route. Paws and feet and wheels filled the night with a low rumble of purposeful noise, none of it as loud as the whistle and crash of two hundred Colonial guns bombarding the city. More starshells lightened the sky to the west, Colonial this time, put up so their artillery had better visibility.

"Shall I order a cease-fire?"

"No, Hussein," Tewfik replied, also in a whisper.

The central roof of the bunker had caved in, but the beams had not given way completely. They sagged to the floor, their jagged breaks splintered, like bone-white teeth. Dry dirt poured down still, pooling and spreading; soldiers dug bodies out of the pile, some wounded and some dead, and carried them up the stairs. Ripped down and stamped in a pile, the tapestries still smoldered from the burning kerosene that falling lamps had sprayed across them—sprayed across men, as well.

Although not, unfortunately, across my brother, Tewfik thought. It would be a disaster if Ali died just now. It might be salvation if he were struck down by an incapacitating injury; the longer, the better. *There is no God but God, and all things are accomplished according to the will of God.* But sometimes it was difficult to understand His tactics. He wrinkled his nose at the smell of burning carpets. More waste. The cost of them was enough to pay a brigade of cavalry for a year, and now they would be replaced. Transport would be commandeered to replace them, while the guns ate a month's reserve of ammunition.

"*Amir,* we will lose guns soon if we keep up this rate of fire," the officer warned. "The barrels are so hot we'll have cook-offs during reloading."

"Reduce the rate, but not so much that *he*" —he nodded to the other chamber of the bunker; Ali's sputtering curses could still be heard there, and occasionally a woman's scream— "will notice. Better to shoot the lands out of the barrels than have more executions."

The officer stroked his beard and leaned close. "*Amir*, it is time to consider if the House of Peace can stand, with this man at the head of it."

Tewfik stared into the other man's face for a moment; the brown eyes met his single one unflinching. *Good. I have no cowards on my staff.*

"He has no sons," he said quietly. "Nor do I."

"The Prophet Muhammed had no sons; but many rulers sprang from his daughters."

"And many wars sprang from the claims of his daughters' descendants and the orthodox caliphs, beginning with Kharballa," Tewfik pointed out. That had started a split that echoed down millennia, not even ending with the Last Jihad. "There are also too many nobles with enough of the Settler's blood to make a fair claim. Ali is no fool, he's killed the only ones with indisputable claims or great ability, or both. If we have civil war now, the *kaphar* and the Zanj and the northern savages will race each other to pick our bones. We must continue."

"For the present."

"For the present," Tewfik agreed. *Until Ali alive becomes more a menace to the House of Islam than Ali dead,* went unspoken between them. "Now go, and have the gunners reduce their rate of fire by one-third. On my authority."

I control the Host of Peace, but I cannot rule, he knew bitterly. Not in his own name. If only there were a male heir, a regency might be possible—but there was not. The mullahs would not issue the Friday prayer for one-eyed Tewfik; men would not obey, not without a soldier standing behind them. He would shatter what he most wished to preserve, if he tried that.

"Insh'allah."

The acrid gloom of the bunker was stifling. Left hand on the hilt of his yataghan, he strode up the stairs, past the protective curves and the intermediate guardroom. The blue-white sputtering light of starshells made him slit his eyes at the dark motionless bulk of Sandoral's low-slung walls. They mocked him from behind the moat, tantalized him. Men and dogs labored to bring the ammunition forward to the siege guns from the bombproofs set behind the main line, along pathways sunk into the ground with protective berms on either side. The gunners toiled, stripped to the waist, their faces and torsos black with powder smoke. Many had balls of cotton wool stuffed in their ears, but they courted deafness as well as death with every shot. It did not stop the smooth choreographed sequence of laying, swabbing, loading, ramming, firing.

A heavy shell bit a section out of the firing parapet in a clap of orange flame and rumble of sound. Water spurted up where the stone fell into the moat, leaving a ragged gap in the concrete core. No fire replied from the city.

"Was that your plan, Whitehall, to weaken our artillery? Did you know how my brother would respond to your taunt?"

The stonk on the command bunker had been wickedly well-placed. Whitehall was well served, good officers, brave and well-trained troops, well equipped. *Does he know us well enough to predict that my brother would waste ammunition and guns like this?* He nodded. Certainly.

"Yet it cannot affect the outcome of the war," he mused.

Could it be cover for another raid? Unlikely. With a pontoon bridge for rapid withdrawal and a secure fortified base, Whitehall had still been unable to do more than divert him temporarily. Now the land across the river was unfit to support moving troops. What could the infidel accomplish with the smaller number of men they could smuggle across the river now?

That was the problem. He did not know.

"Lord *Amir*. The Settler requires your presence."

Tewfik ground his teeth. *He has beaten enough women to feel brave again,* he thought. *Now he must play at commander. And waste my time!*

With an enemy like Whitehall, time was one thing you never had a surplus of. From all reports, Barholm Clerett was almost as difficult a master to serve as Ali ibn'Jamal—but at least he was far away.

(•·ı) (•·ı) (•·ı)

The little galley Raj was using as his HQ had been some rich merchant's toy before war came to Sandoral, or perhaps belonged to a landowner with estates on the riverbank who wanted to be able to commute to his townhouse in the district capital. For a moment Raj wondered where he was, that little provincial oligarch. On the road west, grumbling in his carriage with a nagging wife and the nurse fussing with the children and a train of baggage carts behind? Perhaps already in East Residence, imposing on some distant relative or dickering with a lodging-keeper not at all impressed by anything from beyond the walls of *the* city. Or caught on his country property by Colonial raiders, and now tumbled bones in a ditch.

We must be making ten klicks per hour, he thought.

a range of 9.7 to 10.1, averaging 9.9 overall, Center said.

Tonight and tomorrow to reach their destination, traveling with the current. The men in the barges and boats were sculling, but more to keep station and direction than for propulsion. There were enough in each vessel to change off at frequent intervals, too.

"Over to Major Bellamy," Raj said, pointing.

The galley came about sharply, bringing a protesting whine from Horace and Harbie on the foredeck. The crew were all ex-boatmen and used to the shattering labor at the oars; one side dug theirs in hard, the other feathered, and the man at the tiller pushed it over. The slender boat turned in almost its own length and stroked eastward. Beside a raft crowded with troops and dogs it halted; Raj leaned over the side, one hand on the rail.

"There's your destination, Major," he said, pointing southward, downstream. "Remember the timing's crucial."

Bellamy waved back wordlessly, his bowl-cut blond hair bright in the darkness. His rowers bent to their work, and several of the other barges followed. Raj's galley curved back toward the main body of the straggling armada, like a sheepdog with its flock.

More like a pack of carnosauroids, Raj thought, watching the dull glint of moonlight on the barrels of the field pieces on a raft.

Suzette came up beside him, a cigarette glowing in its holder of carved sauroid ivory. "The waiting's the hardest part," she said.

"No, just the longest," Raj said. "Having to send others out, that's hardest."

She put an arm around his waist and leaned her head on his shoulder.

CHAPTER THIRTEEN

"Stake the dogs," Ludwig Bellamy said.

His second-in-command blinked at him. "It's more than a kilometer to the objective," he said in surprise.

"*Ni, migo,*" Bellamy said in Namerique. "Walking that far won't kill us."

He shook his head as the man walked away to spread the order by whisper. Messer Raj had taught his Squadrone followers that fighting on foot was no disgrace, but they'd still rather ride ten kilometers than walk one.

He squinted at his map; an aide lit a match and held it over the paper. Messer Raj had penciled in the route with his own hands. *Yes. That's the gully.* There was a roadway of sorts along the river's edge, but it was entirely too visible from the other side, back around Sandoral. His scouts gathered around, holding the reins of their dogs.

"Lead the way," he said, tracing out the branchings of wash and ravine. "It's only a klick; but keep an eye out for wog pickets."

He looked up at the bulk of the unit; nearly everyone was ashore from the beached barges and rafts, although many were soaked to the waist. Water squelched in his own high boots. The last few came in sight, holding their rifles and bandoliers over their heads as they waded to the muddy riverbank.

"Fall them in," he said quietly.

The 1st Mounted Cruisers formed up in ranks four deep, and the rabble of militia gunners behind them. They'd have no part in the immediate action, but they were important if everything worked right.

"*Migos,* Messer Raj trusts us to do this job right without holding our hands. Let's show him he's right. Keep it quiet and move quickly."

"Right face. At the double, forward *march.*"

They swung off into the night, rifles at the trail. Bellamy trotted up along the line to the head, where the battalion banner was. His aide was leading his dog, back at the rear; the men would march with a better will if they saw the commander on foot too. Some of them grinned and shook their rifles in the air as he passed.

They're pumped, Bellamy decided. This had all the earmarks of one of Messer Raj's sauroid-out-of-the-helmet tricks. They trusted their leader's luck. And they hated being cooped up inside walls, no matter how strong.

He looked ahead. *You have to earn your luck.* It was much darker here, where most of the sky was blocked out by the clay walls of the badlands on either side. They panted up steep slopes, scrambled down others, slogged through sand and deep dust that sucked at their boots, splashed through a few wet spots where water from the spring floods still lay. Men panted, sweated, cursed in low voices. The ground rose toward the hills where the road from the east met the river, where Tewfik had planted his fortlet.

A scout came cantering back and pulled his dog up on its haunches. "As you thought, Lord," he said, leaning down. He was one of the old-fashioned ones, with his hair pulled up in a knot at the side of his head. "There is only a shallow ditch and berm on the landward side—my dog could jump it. And all the cannon point to the water."

Bellamy grunted with relief. Messer Raj had said that was the logical thing for Tewfik to do, but you couldn't count on an opponent having good sense.

He paced back along the column, personally giving the command to halt. The battalion came to a stop with a few lurches that ran one group of men onto another's heels, but nothing major. The company commanders gathered around him.

"Come," he said, leading them westward up a final line of ridge. Beyond was rolling open ground, sparsely bushed with thorny native scrub and some cacti. "There."

In the open, the moonlight was enough to make the Colonial works plain enough. He used his binoculars: not much of a ditch, and there were no obstacles—no timbers studded with old sword-blades, no thorn zariba. Doubtless those would have been added in time, but there had been no time. Across the water red specks crawled through the air and the endless flat thudding of the bombardment continued. There were enough fires in Sandoral now to cast a reddish glow across the great river, expanding and uniting into columns of flame without men to fight them.

"Spread your men out along this ridge, and order fixed bayonets," Bellamy said. "Every man may load his rifle, but no reloading once we're into the enemy camp."

Nods, enthusiastic from the *Squadrones*, less so from the Civil Government officers seconded to the battalion. Fighting at close quarters in the dark, friendly fire would be a greater threat than the enemy. Their repeaters gave them an advantage in a close-range firefight, anyway. Better to rely on impetus and cold steel.

"Nothing fancy," Bellamy said, repeating Messer Raj's words. "Just raise a shout and go in on my signal."

Across two hundred meters of open ground. But the Spirit was with them, and the initiative.

He lay on the ridgeline. "Uncase the colors," he said to his bannermen; they pulled the leather tubes off the standards and gently shook the heavy silk free, taking care to keep both flags—the unit and the Civil Government blazon—below the ridgeline. To either side came rustling, crunching sounds as the men filed up company by company. Starlight glittered as they fixed their bayonets and then lay prone at the word of command. He could see one or two praying, among those closer; others were waiting, stolid or eager as their temperament took them.

And I don't think of glory, he realized. A few years ago that would have been his main concern in a situation like this; that men see him add honor to his name. *Now I'm just worried that nothing go wrong.* Messer Raj was right: civilization was contagious. It was more efficient than the old ways, but it took much of the color out of life. He swallowed water and vinegar from his canteen and loosened his sword in its scabbard, flipped open the cylinder of his revolver and checked the loads.

Marie will enjoy hearing about this. His Brigadero wife still thought war was glorious, and envied warriors. She'd probably have made a good soldier if she'd been born male—her cousin Teodore certainly did—provided she survived the seasoning. *I'd rather go through a battle than pregnancy, at that.* Strange to think of having children—legitimate children; byblows by peon girls didn't count. Stranger still to think of them growing up in East Residence; nobody had said he couldn't move back to the family estates in the Southern Territories, but he could take the hint.

He grinned. That would be terminally dull, anyway. At least Marie could sit out the war in a city with plenty of balls and theater and opera, or bullfights and baseball stadiums.

If we win this war, will there be wars for my sons to ride to? Possibly not; and was that a good thing, or the end of all honor?

Thud. Thud. Thud. There were explosions across the river, along the docks of Sandoral. Plumes of red fire rose into the night, spreading with startling suddenness. In less than thirty seconds the whole waterfront went up in a wall of flame, as the time-fused incendiaries caught among kerosene-soaked wood and spilled cooking oil. There was enough underlight to see the pillars of smoke, roiling and black and red-tinged by the fires.

He took a deep breath. "*Gittem!*" he roared, the old Squadron war shout. The trumpeters were playing *Charge*, over and over again, a raw brazen scream.

The flags went forward. The 1st Mounted Cruisers rose to their feet and threw themselves forward at a pounding run, their bayonets leveled. Ludwig Bellamy ran at their head, sword held forward like a pointer.

"GITTEM! GITTEM!" they bellowed.

Wogs all looking at the show, he thought with hammering glee. The wall stayed empty for long seconds. Then a few carbines began to crack, muzzle flashes like fireflies in the night. Men fell, but not many. He jumped down into the ditch, felt the jar as his boots landed in the muck at the bottom, scrambled in the chunky raw adobe of the berm. It was less than man-height; a Colonial appeared on the top, aiming a long-barreled revolver downward. It snapped a spike of fire, and the bannerman with the battalion standard went down. Somebody else grabbed it up, used the butt as a climbing-prop. Ludwig braced one hand on the berm and chopped with his saber, felt the edge slam into ankle-bone. The Colonial toppled and rolled down toward him, shrieking and trying to draw a dagger. Ludwig slammed the guard of his sword into the man's face and climbed over his body onto the top of the berm.

Cookfires lit the interior of the fortlet, and the glare of burning Sandoral across the river. Men in crimson djellabas streamed back from the gun line that faced the water, firing as they came. Ludwig gave a quick glance to either side; the berm's broad top was solid with his men. Company commanders were planting their pennants, platoon officers taking three steps forward and turning to face their men with outstretched arm and sword as a bar to give their commands the dressing.

"Sound *Kneel and Stand,*" he snapped.

The front rank dropped to one knee and leveled their rifles. The men behind them stood and aimed. Here and there a trooper dropped as the Colonial fire began to thicken a little, falling forward to tumble loose-limbed to the foot of the berm. He waited an instant, until the target had time to thicken.

"*Fwego!*" Ludwig shouted. Then: "*Charge!*"

BAM. One long sound, like a single impossibly long shot. A bright comb of fire reached out towards the dim shapes of the Colonials, five hundred threads of it. On the heels of the volley the troopers ran forward through the thick curls of smoke, their steel glinting red in the reflected light. The Colonials wavered, then ran back the way they'd come, screaming their panic. A few stood and fought, emptying their carbines and drawing their scimitars, but they died quickly—spitted on dozens of points, beaten down with the butt, simply trampled.

Ludwig slashed at a man crawling out of a pup tent, hurdled another. Up the slope to the gunline that was this fortlet's main purpose, set here to command the river and prevent the rebuilding of the pontoon bridge. The guns had been dug in, set in revetments with V-shaped notches forward for their barrels. One group of Colonials, braver or better-led than the rest, was trying frantically to manhandle a pom-pom around to face the menace from the rear. He stopped, braced his legs and began to fire. *Crack. Crack. Crack. Crack. Crack.* Two men down in the confusion around the light gun, and then his troopers were past. Steel clashed on steel for a moment, replaced by the butcher's-cleaver sound of metal slamming into flesh.

Silence fell. 1st Cruiser troopers were standing on top of the fortlet's western wall, firing down—firing at the backs of the fleeing survivors of the post's garrison.

"Sound *Rally*," Ludwig said. "Benter," he went on to his younger brother. "To Captain Marthinez, and his Company A is to man the parapet. Get me a count of the casualties. Hederbert, find those militiamen and put them on the guns, right now. Mauric, see that those dead wogs are all really dead."

He walked as he spoke, over to the flagstaff before the Colonial commander's tent. The dead man lying by the flagstaff was probably the tent's owner, by the scrollwork on his djellaba; he'd been hit by three or four Armory 11mm rounds, and was very thoroughly dead. The smell of death was spreading on the cool night air, like raw sewage and a butcher's shop combined. Ludwig slashed the cord of the flagpole with his saber. The green banner of Islam fluttered to the ground; he used it to clean the sword before sliding it back into its scabbard.

His bannerman needed no prompting. Seconds later, the blue-and-silver Starburst of Holy Federation fluttered up the rough staff and streamed out, almost invisible in the darkness.

Let Ali take a look at that, when he gets tired of shelling an empty city, Ludwig thought, grinning.

The Cruisers cheered at the sight of the flag, man after man taking it up, shaking their rifles in the air or putting up their helmets on the points of their bayonets:

"Hail! Hail! Hail! Hail! HAIL! HAIL!"

Ludwig felt a rush of pride: less than six minutes from the moment he'd given the order to charge. Then he looked up at the flag. *The banner of the Gubernio Civil,* he thought. Four years ago most of these men had fought against the army that Messer Raj led under that banner. There were perhaps half a dozen Sponglish-speaking natives of the Civil Government in the 1st Mounted Cruisers; the rest were MilGov and heretic to a man.

And here they were, crying the banner hail as if . . . *well, it* is *their own. Now.* Messer Raj had given them that.

Mustafa al-Kerouani jerked himself awake and checked his watch. Good, it was still a few minutes until the next status check. He bent to the eyepiece of the telescope and waited. Nothing from the relay to the north, the second from the siege lines around Sandoral. He frowned. They should give him three flashes from their carbide lantern; that was regular procedure. Allah might be merciful if they were all asleep, but neither their *tabor* commander nor Tewfik would. Besides, there was the honor of the engineering corps to consider. What were they, real soldiers or the *fellaheen* conscripts of infantry, who couldn't be trusted to remember to wipe their arses with their left hands unless an officer reminded them every time they shat?

He reached out and squeezed the handgrip of his own lantern. The slotted shutters over the front clacked open, revealing the brilliant chemical light amplified by the hemisphere of mirror behind it. Three long, two short—*acknowledge.*

Nothing. He swore again, looking around the little hilltop camp. A dozen men, eight of them sleeping, around a low-coal campfire with a brass *kave*-pot standing over it on an iron stand. Their riding- and pack-dogs, picketed out on a line. Two sentries, the telescope, heliograph, lanterns for night work, and their personal baggage. One of dozens strung between the bridgehead at Gurnyca and the Settler's headquarters outside the *kaphar* city. Paralyzingly boring duty; there weren't even any of the infidel *fellaheen* left around here, which meant no fresh provender except for some sauroid meat, and no women.

Three long, two short. Still no acknowledgment. *Ibrahim ibn'Habib is a lazy, wine-swilling son of a pig, but he isn't that negligent.* Best send someone over to take a look.

Mustafa blinked out into the darkness where the sentry paced. The bright light killed his night vision, but he could see the outline.

"Moshin?" he said. The other man was Qahtan ash-Shabaai, and much taller. "Moshin, take your dog and check those bastards on Post Three. They must be asleep, or dead."

"Dead," Moshin said—but it was not Moshin's voice, and the word was so thickly accented that he could barely understand it.

Mustafa al-Kerounai reached for his sidearm. He felt the bayonet that punched through his jaw, tongue and palate only as a white flash of cold. Then the point grated through brain and blood vessels within his skull, and the world ended in a blaze of light.

Antin M'lewis withdrew the blade with a jerk. Around him there was a flurry of movement; bayonets and rifle butts struck, and the pick end of an entrenching tool went into the back of a sleeping man's skull with the sound an axe made striking home in hard oak. Talker stamped on a neck with an unpleasant crunching sound, like a bundle of green branches snapping. Dogs wuffled and snarled, dragging at their picket chain as they smelled death. He ignored them and swiveled telescope and signal lantern around on their mountings. The alignment was marked in chalk on the fixed baseplate of the equipment, and he had the code for *acknowledge 0100 hours all is well* on his pad. He clacked it out carefully and waited for the return signal.

Good. There it was. They *still* didn't suspect anything. He used one tail of his uniform jacket to shield his hand and picked up the pot of *kave*, pouring a cup into his messtin.

"Throw summat more wood on t'fire," he said. It might arouse suspicion if the sentinel fire went out during the night. He tossed aside the spiked Colonial helmet. "'N git back ter yer dogs. We'ns'll see how many more ol t' wogs is overconfident."

"Fwego!"

BAM. The single massive volley turned the supply convoy's night encampment into a mass of screaming men and howling dogs, with the oxen's frantic bawling as accompaniment. Major Peydro Belagez smiled, a cruel closed upturn of the lips. He could see the scene quite well, with the watchfires as background.

BAM. Men rose from their blankets and slapped backward instantly, punched down by the heavy Armory bullets. BAM. Maddened by pain and the smell of blood, an ox-team pulled over the wagon to which they'd been tethered and ran off into the night. The wagon's tilt fell across a fire and the dry canvas flared up brightly.

"Forward, *compaydres*," he said.

The two companies of the 1st Rogor Slashers moved forward in line, with a crackle of platoon volleys. Less than thirty Colonial troops had guarded the convoy, and they were infantry—support troops, hardly fighting men at all. The few who lived ran into the night, or knelt and raised their hands in surrender.

As Belagez watched, the platoon commanders called the cease-fire. Two surviving Colonials bolted when they saw the Civil Government troops more clearly; their dark complexions and the shoulder-flashes made it clear they were Borderers, men whose feud with the Colony was old and bitter. A bet was called, and two troopers stepped forward and knelt, adjusting the sights of their rifles. The running Colonials jinked and swerved as they fled; the two Slashers fired carefully. On the third shot one of the Arabs flopped forward, shot through the base of the spine. His face plowed into the dirt, mercifully hiding the exit wound. The other went down and then rose again, hobbling and clutching his thigh as if to squeeze out the pain of his wounds.

"*Hingada thes Ihorantes!*" the first rifleman said. Death to the Infidel, the Slashers' unit motto. "You should do better than that, Huan!"

"Malash. The Spirit appoints our rising and our going down," the other man grunted. He breathed out and squeezed the trigger. *Crack*. Measurable fractions of a second later, dust spurted from the back of the Arab's djellaba. He went down and sprawled in the dirt.

Meanwhile the others had been rounded up. They sat, hands behind their heads, staring at their captors with the wide-eyed look of men who wanted very badly to wake from an evil dream and couldn't. The toppled wagon was burning fiercely now, with a thick flame that stank like overdone fish three days dead to begin with—*advocati*, no mistaking the stench. Sun-dried, they were oily enough to burn like naphtha.

Belagez pointed with his saber. "Get moving—push the other wagons over and tip them into the fire. Break open those crates, that'll be hardtack." The Colonial version came in thin sheets about the size of a man's hand; it would burn too, in a hot fire.

He switched to Arabic, accented but fluent enough. "You, you unbelieving sons of whores. Get to work."

The teamsters and surviving guards joined his men in heaving more of the supplies onto the growing blaze. Another wagon toppled onto it, and the smell of frying apricots joined the stink, enough to make his stomach knot a little. The blaze would be visible for kilometers, but there was nobody alive to witness it—not unless a survivor or two from the last convoy they'd hit had run very fast. The twenty-wagon parties had been spaced quite evenly at four-kilometer intervals along the road, commendable march-discipline and very convenient for the battalions the *heneralissimo* had landed on the west bank. He looked at his watch; it was bright as day now, and hot enough to make him step back.

0300. This would be their last, they'd have to ride hard to make the rendezvous with the river flotilla by dawn. He certainly didn't want to miss the end of this campaign. The fire grew swiftly; his men were in a hurry too, and the prisoners worked very hard.

Idly, he wondered if they knew they were building their own funeral pyres. Probably. Still, it was the Spirit's blessing that men were reluctant to abandon hope while they still breathed.

> "*Oh night that was my guide*
> *Oh night more loving than the rising sun*
> *Oh night that joined the lover*
> *To the beloved one,*
> *Transforming each of them into the other.*"

Raj opened his eyes, then started awake. Suzette laid aside her *gittar* and smiled at him, handing over a cup of *kave*.

"This yacht has all the conveniences, my love," she said.

"What—"

"Absolutely nothing has happened except what you said would. Belagez and the other landing parties made rendezvous. The Colonials have no idea what's going on—we're moving faster than the news. It's noon."

"Ah."

He took the cup and sipped. He felt less jangled than usual on waking, less of the sense that something catastrophic had happened and had to be turned around immediately. *How long has it been since I slept without worry?* he thought.

Five years, one month seven days. defining "worry" as your subtextual intent rendered the term.

Thank you very much, he thought. Aloud: "Thank you, my sweet. You must have fended them off like a mother sauroid on a rookery."

Suzette smiled; not her usual slight enigmatic curve of the lips, but widely as if at some private joke. She shook her head.

"You've had five years to train them, Raj; and they're good men. They wanted you to rest while you could. They can carry out your orders, but we all want—need—you to be at your best when you're needed. Besides" —she dimpled slightly— "you look so young and vulnerable when you're asleep."

Raj laughed softly. *I'm committed,* he realized. *One turn of pitch and toss, winner take all.* It would either work or it wouldn't, and if it didn't he wouldn't be around to worry about it. There was nothing behind them but Ali and his fifty thousand men, barring the road to the border.

"What was that song?" he asked, finishing the coffee. Suzette poured him another and handed him breakfast—toasted hardtack, but she'd found some preserves for it, somehow.

"Very old. My tutor taught it me when I was a girl; Sister Maria, that was."

"Doesn't sound religious," Raj said.

the song is derived from the devotional poetry of st. john of

the cross, Center said. **the musical arrangement was made approximately two thousand four hundred years ago on earth.**

"Ahem." A voice from behind the door of the little stern cabin, out on deck. "I hate to interrupt this touching domestic scene, but . . ."

"Coming, Gerrin," Raj said ruefully.

He stamped into his boots and fastened on his equipment, then scooped up the map he'd been working on late into the night. The sun outside was blinding, the shadow of the awning above hard-edged and utter black by comparison. Raj blinked out over the sparkling green waters of the Drangosh. For a kilometer either way, out of sight behind bends in the high banks, it was covered with rafts and barges and boats. With men and guns and ammunition . . . *nine thousand men*. Nine thousand, to decide the fate of empires. *Nine thousand men relying on* me *to pull it off*. The thought was less crushing than usual. *If there was any force this size on Earth—*

bellevue.

—Bellevue, then, you pedant, this was it.

Raj smiled. Staenbridge and the other battalion commanders grinned back at him. Bartin Foley chuckled.

Raj raised his brows. "Your thoughts, Captain?"

He spread the rolled paper on the deck; the officers and Companions crowded around it, kneeling, staking down the corners with daggers.

"*Mi heneral*, I was just thinking how much less pleasant this morning must be for our esteemed friend Tewfik, when he finds out we've left the party and stiffed him with the drink tab."

A snarling ripple of laughter went around the map. "True enough." Raj rested one hand on his knee and spread the fingers of the other over the map. It was his drawing, with Center supplying a holographic overlay for him to work with. "Gentlemen, this is our latest intelligence on the enemy's bridgehead camp and the pontoon bridge over the Drangosh. You'll note—"

Bompf. The little mortar chugged, and a grapnel soared up through a puff of smoke.

Why? Tewfik thought. The fires had raged all through the night, as if the *kaphar* did not care that the city burned around their ears. No fire from the walls and towers, not all through the night and the bombardment. Now they were ignoring his herald under a flag of truce, for the whole hour since dawn. *Since I could finally free myself from my brother's whining and threats.*

The sun was bright in the east, eye-hurting. He shaded his eye with one hand, the other hooked through the back of his sword belt. The breeze blew from the river and fluttered his djellaba; it snapped out the blue-and-silver Starburst of the Federation from the gate towers of Sandoral, as well. The air was heavy with the sickly scent of things that should not burn—one of the constants of war. He had smelled the same in Gurnyca, and in burnt-out cities down on the Zanj coast. Worse, once, when they had shelled a warehouse full of holdouts in Lamoru and the dried copra inside had caught fire.

"Lord Amir, a lucky sniper from the wall—"

"I do not think this is a plot to assassinate me, Hussein," Tewfik said. *Allah alone knows what it* is, *but not that, I think.*

Men climbed up the cable the mortar had thrown. The first of them had a stick with a white rag attached to it thrust through the shoulder harness of his webbing gear; a flag of truce, by the one and only God. Let Whitehall respect it; he had a name for being scrupulous in such things.

The men climbed in through a narrow window high above the bridge that carried the railway over the moat and through the city wall. Tewfik waited with iron patience. A mirror flashed from the parapet.

Tower apparently empty, he read. He clawed at his forked beard, nostrils flaring instinctively as if to smell out a trap. More silent waiting, until there came the muffled *thud* of an explosion behind walls, and very faintly, a scream.

The officers around him tensed. A half-minute later, the mirror blinked again.

Boobytrap, six casualties. Tower deserted. Walls deserted. No enemy in sight.

A hubbub of oaths and excitement broke out around him; the

word spread along the siege lines as the great gates swung open and revealed the dogleg passage beyond. A long slow roar like heavy surf welled up, as men climbed out of the entrenchments and onto the gabions, and others dashed from the tents and the cooking-fires behind.

"The city is ours!" someone shouted. "The *kaphar* have fled!"

Tewfik felt a great hand reach into his chest and squeeze. Azazrael's wings brushed darkness over his eyes. Almost, he prayed that the dark angel would come for him now; surely this would count as dying for the Faith, in the Holy War. Hussein and one of his mamluks cried out in shock and rushed to support him; he brushed them aside and staggered forward to the edge of the main works.

Fled? he thought. "Fled? Where? Northeast, to the valleys of the Borderers? To hide in their mud-built forts and make little raids, while we bottle them up with one-tenth of our strength and march to the gates of East Residence with the rest? Whitehall?"

"But . . ." The aide's face was fluid with shock. "If not north, then where?" He looked at his commander's face, and fear replaced the shock. "What is it, Lord *Amir*?"

"Kismet," Tewfik said. "Fate. If not north, then south . . ."

"But, Lord *Amir*, the message stations, the outposts along the road—we have heard nothing!"

"Exactly." He whirled. "Hussein. Twenty men, each with three led dogs. Kill the dogs with haste if they must, but make such speed as men may. To the commandant of the railhead camp; maintain maximum alertness, enemy in your vicinity."

Hussein gaped. Tewfik seized him by the shoulder-straps of his harness and shook him. "Fool born of fools, the entire raid across the Drangosh was a diversion—their bridge a disguise for boats and rafts to *float their force south.*"

"May the Lovingkind have mercy upon us!"

"Go!" He turned to the others. "Sound the alert. Mobilize the cavalry, *all* of it—"

"Lord *Amir*," one officer said urgently. "The Settler . . ."

The Settler, who will delay for hours before he grasps the necessities. And with him every one of the great noble houses, and the orders of the Maribbatein and ghazis, all of whom will jealously insist on being consulted before a major move is made.

He raised his hands. "Allah! One day! That is all I ask of You, *one day.*"

Never had he prayed with such sincerity.

CHAPTER FOURTEEN

"Messers, the garrison is ten thousand men, not counting civilian laborers."

The Companions bent over the sand-map for the last briefing. Antin M'lewis hung back slightly, although his scouting this afternoon had provided the last-minute updates. Considerations of social rank aside, he didn't have a line command; his men would be split up and acting as trail guides for the actual units.

Raj went on, pointing with his sword. The wet sand allowed a surprising amount of detail; he'd spent about an hour getting it right, just possible with Center to overlay holograms and make each motion perfectly efficient. The long shadows of evening brought it out well.

"As you can see, it's a square earth fort; two-meter ditch, two-meter palisade and earth rampart, chevaux-de-frise in the ditch. Pentagonal bastions at each corner, gun lines along the fighting parapet, and four gates at each of the compass points. The railroad leads in from the east, and the pontoon bridge out from the west side. There are ten-meter watchtowers on either side of each gate; the gates are spiked timber barriers. Most of the artillery is concentrated in the bastions, which are as usual higher than the main berm; they bear along each wall."

"Ten thousand men," Jorg Menyez said thoughtfully. "*Heneralissimo,* that's a Starless Dark of a lot of firepower."

Raj nodded. "If we let them apply it, which we won't. They're line-of-communications troops, railroad labor battalions and engineers and supply specialists. Also they're not expecting us. We're not going to give them time to get ready, either; and there's one last little surprise to distract them.

"We're here." He moved his sword point north on the sand map, tapping a point on the east bank of the Drangosh. "Less than two klicks north of the objective as the pterosauroid flies. We'll move separately, by battalion columns, marching on foot, as follows."

He named the battalions, moving from left to right, east to west. "17th Kelden County Foot and the 24th Valencia on the extreme left—they'll have the farthest to go, but they're better foot-marchers. Cavalry battalions in the center, Sandoral infantry on the right, nearest the river. The 5th Descott and the 18th Komar will take the median and assault the camp's north gate. Colonel Menyez, you will have overall command of the left wing; Colonel Staenbridge, of the center; Major Gruder, of the right. I'll accompany the central command.

"Colonel Dinnalsyn, you'll split your guns into two Grand Batteries. One will accompany the 24th, one the Sandoral garrison battalions. Your objective will be to neutralize the enemy artillery in the corner bastions for the duration of the assault. One fast hard stonk, then shift fire to support, and when our banners are over the berm and palisade, cease fire and prepare to move up as directed. Understood?"

The artillery commander stroked his thin mustache with his thumb. "It can be done, *mi heneral.* But to be effective, I'll need time for ranging fire."

"I'll provide precise range data when we arrive," Raj said.

"That will be satisfactory, of course, *heneralissimo*," Dinnalsyn said carefully, the crisp East Residence vowels sounding a little strained. From the glances, everyone knew what it meant: *it's bloody eerie.* "You have an excellent eye for it."

Raj continued: "Messers, your approaches will be by the following paths." His sword sketched them out, through the maze of badland cliffs, naming the battalions. "I hope I don't need to emphasize the absolute necessity of caution as you approach the edge of the badland zone and the low country directly north of the enemy camp. There's a company of the Rogor Slashers in place, guided by members of the Scout Company. They'll take out the Colonial watchposts immediately before you debouche into the plain, and there'll be very little time after that—the attack, and the usual rocket, will be your signal. Come out of the hills in column, deploy as you move, and hit the wall running. By that time, the artillery will have the bastions under fire. Nothing fancy, gentlemen; we go in with the bayonet and one round up the spout, climb the wall and sweep" —his sword moved from north to south— "the wogs out of their camp. Then we stop for the night."

He drew his watch and opened the cover. "Synchronize, please. It's 1900 at . . . *mark*." There was a subdued clicking as stems were pressed home. "Two and a half hours to full dark. Colonel Dinnalsyn, move your guns out now. All battalions will be on their way by 19:30. I expect the artillery preparation to begin at 20:15 and the troops to go in at 20:30. It's only a kilometer and the Scouts have the paths clearly marked, so despite the night march that's plenty of time. Questions?"

There were only one or two, technical matters. The plan was simple—startlingly simple. *It's the* strategy *on this one that's complicated,* he thought.

"Then it's all settled bar the fighting. May the Spirit of Man be with us, Messers."

"It is," someone said softly. "The Sword of the Spirit of Man."

Embarrassed, Raj cleared his throat and nodded curtly. The Companions slapped fists in a pyramid of arms and moved away. Junior officers moved in to study the sand table for a few moments, then returned to their units.

Raj walked down the shoreline; it was hard here, rocks lacing the clay of the bank. The barges and rafts were beached as high as human muscle and dogs dragging at the ends of lariats could move them. They weren't planning to go any farther on the water. Many of the men were preparing escalade ladders: simple balks from the rafts, with crosspieces nailed along them, a spike at the top to hold the pole against the sloping surface of an earth berm, and cross-braces at the bottom to keep it from turning. Not very heavy—they hadn't far to go. One standard part of Civil Government training was carrying logs cross-country, units competing against each other—it taught teamwork on a very practical level.

The rest of the men were waiting, some double-timing or stretching under the direction of their platoon officers, getting out the kinks and stiffness of the long crowded voyage. Raj stopped now and then, calling a man by name or slapping a shoulder.

"Ensign Minatelli," he said to one very junior officer. The man's under-strength platoon was twisting their torsos with their rifles held over their heads.

"Sir," the young westerner said, bracing to attention. The men froze. He saluted with a snap.

"No names, no pack drill," Raj said easily. *Serious, but that's all to the good,* he thought appraisingly. Lower middle-class, not a social grouping you found many of in the Army and certainly not in the officer corps, but that was less of a disadvantage in the infantry.

"Ready for your first engagement at commissioned rank?" he said.

"Lot more to worry about, sir," the young man blurted. His sincerity was transparent.

Raj nodded. "The mental comfort level goes down as the rank goes up," he said. "If you take your work to heart. Carry on, son."

He walked on, to where detachments of the 5th were snapping the bridles of their dogs to a picket line. The cavalry troopers straightened, but they didn't come to attention; there was profound respect in their stance, but no formality.

"*Bwenya Dai,* dog-brothers," Raj said.

He smoothed a hand over the neck of one bitch-dog; it turned and snuffled at him, then licked its chops, satisfied at the scent of *Army* that marked ultimate pack-boundaries to a military dog.

"Nice beast," he said sincerely. Descotter farmbred, about a thousand pounds, lean and agile-looking but with powerful shoulders and chest. "Fifteen hands?"

"Ah, the best, that Pochita is, ser," the corporal said. "Frum m'own kin's *ranchero.* Fifteen one, seven years old."

"Robbi M'Telgez," Raj said. "Southern edge of Smythe Parish, yeoman-tenants to Squire Fidalgo? Near Seven Skull Spring?"

"Yesser." M'Telgez visibly expanded a little. "'Tis true we're attackin' t' wog supply base, ser?"

Raj nodded. "A little stroll in the cool evening, and then we collect everything but Ali's underwear. The wogs may not like us helping ourselves, though."

The troopers grinned; catching the scent, the tethered dogs behind them showed their teeth in a distinctly similar expression.

"Carry on," he repeated.

Suzette was waiting beside Harbie and Horace. Seven thousand dogs would take up an intolerable amount of space in the strait confines of the badlands—that was why the operation was going in on foot—but he and his senior officers needed the extra mobility. Raj swung into the saddle and watched the last of the artillery moving out, teams disappearing into the canyon southward. Dust smoked up behind them, but not too much. Later in the summer it would have been a kilometer-high plume. Another reason to send the men in on foot and by widely separated paths.

"This is it, isn't it?" Suzette asked softly.

Raj nodded. "If it works, it's all over bar the shouting. If not . . ." He shrugged. "Well, we won't have to worry about that."

"And if it works, there's Barholm. Raj, he'll kill you the minute he doesn't need you any more."

Raj laughed, full and rich. "My sweet, at the moment that is the last thing on Bellevue I'm worrying about." *I'm not worrying about anything.* The operation was underway, and now all he had to do was deal with the unexpected; think on his feet and use his wits. He felt loose and easy, mind and body working together at maximum efficiency.

His face went blank. "Anyway, I'll have left some accomplishments behind, something that was worth doing."

Suzette touched his elbow; they'd reined a little aside from the bannermen and messengers. "Raj, speaking of things left behind . . . there's something you should know, just in case."

The boatman shivered. He was naked save for his loincloth and covered in soot mixed with tallow, the smell of the grease heavy about him. Ahead the little galley stroked its oars again, then came alongside. He could just see it in the growing dusk, the water lighter where the oars curled it into foam. Their careful stroke went *shush . . . shush . . .* through the night.

The Army officer lit the slowmatch and gave him a salute before vaulting over to the galley. It turned and stroked rapidly back upstream. He knelt on a burlap sack folded on the rough timbers of the raft and took the steering oar. It twisted in his hands, the familiar living buck of the Drangosh, the substance of all his days. He'd never steered a cargo like this before, though. The whole surface of the raft was covered with kegs of gunpowder, lumpy under the dark tarpaulin that covered them, outline broken by palm-fronds and branches. Iron hooks and spikes stood out all around the square vessel, anchored in the main balks.

The current was fast here in midstream, the banks just lines in the darkness to left and right. *Somebody* had to steer, though; otherwise the raft might swirl in towards the banks. He worked the oar carefully, never letting the end break free of the water. From a distance, in the dark, the raft would look like just another piece of river trash caught in the current. The fuse hissed.

There. Lights on the east bank, to his left. The wog camp. A scattering to his right: the ruins of Gurnyca. He bared his teeth. He'd had kin there, before the press-gang enlisted him in the Army. That was why he'd volunteered for this—though the thousand gold FedCreds and the land and the tax exemption for him and his family didn't hurt. But you had to live to enjoy those; revenge was a dish you could eat in advance.

And that Messer Raj. The priest is right. The Spirit *was* with him, you could see it in his eyes. For the Spirit, all men were the tools of Mankind.

A string of lights across the water: sentinel-lanterns along the wog pontoon bridge. Much bigger barges than the ones they'd used to build their own bridge up at Sandoral, with real prows and neat planking. The torches were oil-soaked bundles of rag on the ends of long sticks of ironwood, fastened to the railing of the roadway every fifteen meters or so. He crouched lower, tasting sour bile at the back of his mouth. There was a sheathed knife through the back of his loincloth, but that was for himself if he looked like being captured.

Closer, and he could see the spiked helmets and turbans of the soldiers pacing along the bridge. Cables swooped up out of the water to anchor the upstream prows of the pontoons, dark curves against dark water. Firelight glittered on patches of wave. He braced one foot against a timber, bare callused toes gripping, and threw the weight of back and shoulders against the tiller. The raft moved across the current, slowly, always slowly. His breath tried to sob out past tight-clenched teeth.

One of the wogs was singing, sounding like a man biting down on a cat's tail. It was hard dark outside the circles of firelight the torches cast, both moons down, only the arch of stars above. *Yes.* The raft was heading right between two pontoons. It might have gone right through without him aboard.

He waited until the shadow of the timbered deck above cut off the sky; there was reflected light enough from the torch on one of the pontoons. Then he raised a pole whose other end was set into the deck of the raft. The ironshod point sank deeply into the timber balk above as the weight of the raft and the force of the current drove it. Weight and current pushed the raft sideways, pivoting around the anchor driven deep into the hardwood above. The hooks along the side grated into the hull of the pontoon; he winced at the noise, but there was thick timber and three feet of earth on the roadway above. The raft heeled a little beneath him as they set fast and held against the long slow push of the water.

The boatman dove overside into the water and let the current take him out the south side of the pontoon bridge and a hundred meters downstream. Then he began to stroke in a fast overarm crawl, and the Starless Dark take secrecy. He had less than a minute to get out of killing range.

"Change off," Ensign Minatelli said.

The next platoon came up and took the escalade ladder off his men's shoulders. The shuttered bull's-eye lantern in his hand provided just enough light, although there were whispered curses and cries of pain in the tight confines of the dry wash.

"Let's get moving."

In a way it was fortunate that the wash was so narrow; there wasn't any way to get lost. He moved at a quick walk, stumbling occasionally over a clod or a rock. Men waited at junctions, directing the traffic along the proper path. A few minutes later he ran into the heels of the men ahead.

"*Halto!*" he hissed back.

Captain Pinya came down the line, identifying himself with a quick flick of his own lantern under his face. "We're there," he said. "Halt in place, prepare for action. Wait for the signal, then we go out in column, deploy into line on the move, and keep moving. There's a little more light out in the open."

I hope so.

He was starting to get some idea of how complicated it was to get hundreds of men moving in the same direction and have them arrive when you wanted them to. It was a lot more difficult than it looked when all you had to do was march when someone said, "By the left, forward."

All an ensign had to do in a field action was relay the orders, though. He was very glad of that.

"Fix bayonets. Load. Keep the muzzles *up*."

The last thing they needed was somebody getting stuck or shot because they fell over their feet. It was up to *him* to see that didn't happen.

Spirit.

1018. Raj shut his watch with a snap.

Can't wait much longer. With their outposts gone, the enemy camp would be waking up *soon*. A last iron clank came from the artillery position to his left, about twenty meters away, it was dark enough that he could only see vague traces of movement there. The gunners moved with exaggerated care, setting the fuses behind a screen of blankets that would conceal the brief flashes of light from the enemy. They'd be firing blind, essentially, except for the directions he'd given—Center had given—although the wogs were displaying a pleasant abundance of lamps and watchfires.

Another messenger trotted up.

"Major Gruder reports right wing in position, ser." He handed over a note.

Raj flicked a match between thumb and forefinger. *This herd of handless cows is ready to stampede,* he read. Kaltin was *not* happy at having five battalions of second-rate garrison infantry under his direction besides the 7th.

"Tsk."

Kaltin wouldn't expect to get the best out of a force of Descotter cavalry with that attitude; why did he think infantry would respond any better? A good tactician and very loyal, but there were some jobs you just wouldn't give him. Raj grinned mirthlessly. The chances were he wouldn't be giving anyone any jobs, after this.

He turned to look to the right, toward the river. The tiny dots of the torches along the pontoon bridge glittered like stars in the darkness. *I would have left it farther south,* he thought. Better roads here, and what was left of Gurnyca gave a secure anchorage for the western end, but putting a point-failure source closer to your enemy was a terrible risk. *Ali's doing. He tends to arrogance.* He began a gesture to the messenger beside him; there wasn't any more time.

Smaller torches were running along the center section of the pontoon bridge. He pulled the binoculars from their case on Horace's saddlebow and focused them. Men leaned over the edge of the roadway, looking at the water below and pointing.

Raj turned his head aside. Even looking away, the flash of the explosion was bright; it lit the earthen walls of the Colonial fort the way a flash of lightning might, but for much longer. When he looked back a huge section of the pontoon bridge was *gone*, gone as if a vast mouth had bitten it away. There was a crater in the water, foaming as the river rushed back to fill the hole the blast had momentarily forced into it. Pieces of burning, shattered timber were describing parabolas through the night for thousands of meters all around. The sound hit like a giant rumbling thud, felt on the skin of the face and in the chest cavity as well as through the ears.

An alarm siren began to wail in the fort. More men were running out of it, heading through the west gate and onto the pontoon bridge, or what was left of it—large sections on either side of the gap had torn away their anchoring cables and were beginning to drift southward with the current. That threw more and more stress on the undamaged sections, cable and timber creaking and yielding as the two unconnected segments bent back. He could hear the gunshot cracks of materials yielding as they were pushed past their breaking strain. Parts of it were on fire, too; the sections above water would be tinder-dry, in this climate.

The officer in command of the base was probably an engineering specialist. His first thought would be to save the bridge. As if to confirm the thought, a fire engine pulled by six hitch of dogs thundered out onto the pontoon, dropped a hose overside and began spurting steam-driven water at the fires. Men dropped overside with ropes, swimming out for the anchor points. Others set up winches on the decking.

Raj chopped his hand downward. An aide put his cigarette to the touchpaper of a signal rocket and stepped back. The paper sizzled and the little rocket went skyward with a *woosh*, popping into a blue starburst high overhead.

POUMPF. POUMPF. POUMPF. POUMPF. Over and over again.

Tongues of fire shot into the blackness. Fifty-five guns, massed in two grand batteries of twenty-eight and twenty-seven pieces. Warm pillows of air slapped at his face from the nearby position. The night filled with the whirring ripple of shell fire, and seconds later the snapping *crack* of bursting charges and the red firefly wink over the bastions at each corner of the fortress walls. At three rounds a minute the shellbursts came at more than one per second over each target, an endless ripple of fire. The second stonk contained a proportion of contact-fused shells. The guns were firing at maximum elevation and nearly maximum range, their shells dropping down out of the sky at high angles. Dirt fountained up, and then a mammoth secondary explosion from the eastern bastion.

Somebody left his ready reserve ammunition exposed, he thought. He could imagine the scene in the redoubts, men running half-dressed from their bombproofs into the storm of razor-edged, high-velocity metal as they tried to crew their pieces.

"Dinnalsyn's on time and target," Raj said to himself, gathering the reins. *"Hadelande."*

He clapped heels to Horace's side and swung into a loping gallop down the slope. The flags crackled behind him, harness creaked, a bugle clanked rhythmically against the webbing buckles on a signaler's chest. Rock and dust spurted up under the dogs' paws, with a scent of bruised native scrub like bergamot. Trumpets sounded ahead of him—no point in keeping quiet after this—as the battalions poured over the ridgeline and down the last slope toward the flat fields. The routes he'd picked left them widely spaced, to minimize collisions in the dark, and the flaming chaos at each end of the north face of the Colonial base would help with the alignment.

The dense columns of men flowed forward onto the open ground, double-timing in battalion columns. Starlight glittered on a forest of bayonet points, sheened on the silver Starbursts at the top of the flagstaffs of their colors. He leaned back slightly, and Horace shifted to a swinging trot; they were coming up on the 5th Descott's position. The men gave a short roaring cheer as his flag went by to swing into position near the battalion commander's, a harsh male undertone to the crash and flicker of the guns.

He looked at his watch. 1040 hours. *Nearly on time. Amazing.* A memory prickled at him; nothing he'd ever experienced, but one of the holographic scenarios from Earth's long history of war that Center showed him. Not Hannibal this time, but someone else, and the battle had also been against Arabs . . .

lieutenant-general garnet wolseley, Center said. **tel el-kebir. twenty-five hundred years ago.** A pause. **the similarities are disquieting.**

Why? Raj thought. *This fellow Wolseley won, didn't he?* A night march and an attack on earthwork fortifications, as he remembered.

i was programmed to believe that a progressive improvement of human capacities is a priority, Center said. **the fact that two such**

similar engagements have occurred at this distance in time might support a cyclical rather than linear explanation of human history.

Some things never change.

that, raj whitehall, is precisely the problem—and what we are attempting to change.

The 5th's buglers blew a six-note call and repeated it. Raj turned in the saddle to watch; the fires on the pontoon bridge were out of control, and the easternmost Colonial bastion was a column of flame, giving enough light to turn the night to dusk. The solid column of troops suddenly opened, like a man's outstretched hand when he flared his fingers. Each of the four companies of the 5th turned at an angle to the axis of advance and double-timed outward, following the pennant of the company commander. Thirty seconds later the bugle sounded again, and the company columns spread likewise into platoons, and the platoons flared out like opening fans. In less than four minutes what had been a dense column of men was a double line, rippling as the veterans dressed their ranks on the move with unconscious skill.

This was what the endless parade-ground drill was for: the movements had to be unconscious. So instinctive that they could be done exhausted, or under killing fire—or here, in darkness so bad you could barely see another man at twice arm's length. A line of men couldn't advance at speed for long, not on anything but absolutely flat table-top terrain. A column could maneuver, but it was a hideously vulnerable target with no offensive capacity to speak of.

Gerrin Staenbridge reined in beside him. "After that march, I'm never going to make a joke about the blind leading the blind again, *mi heneral.* If it hadn't been impossible to get lost, we would have."

There was strain in his voice. The possibilities for confusion were enough to turn a man's hair gray . . . which reminded Raj of the silver dusting he saw in his own every time he shaved.

The splatguns had been bouncing along behind the infantry. Now they trotted forward, drawing ahead. One hundred meters, two, three, then the teams wheeled. The crews leapt down and spun the elevating screws to maximum.

"About now," Raj said.

The cannonade lifted for an instant, and starshells burst over the ramparts of the fort. Raj stood in the stirrups and looked right and left, halfway between dread and hope under the wavering blue-white light. *All honor and glory to the Spirit of Man of the Stars,* he thought sincerely. No major units seemed to be missing, as far as he could see— although the right flank was mostly hidden, and that was the one he was most worried about. A long, wavering double line of men stretched across the plain, with gaps of several hundred meters between battalions. Several of the battalions *were* severely out of alignment with their target, marching at angles that would have tangled them with their neighbors eventually. As he watched they started to correct.

"Signaler," he said. The man dropped out of the saddle and set two rockets. They hissed aloft and burst.

Staenbridge drew his sword. "Battalion—"

"Company—" Manifold, down the line.

"Charge!"

The trumpets sounded and kept up their shrilling, a long brass screaming in antiphonal chorus as all the signalers caught up the note. A long swelling shout rose from one end of the field to the other. Flags slanted forward as the whole formation broke into a steady uniform trot.

Braaaaap. The splatguns fired, shot arching down at extreme range to spray the parapet. They kept firing over helmets as the troopers swept by. A pom-pom opened up from the wall ahead, and the flicker of muzzle flashes showed there were *some* wogs on the parapet, at least. The little quick-firer's shells went overhead with a nasty *whack-whack-whack* as it emptied its clip, and burst on the soil behind. Raj drew his revolver, tossed it to his left hand and drew his sword, letting the reins fall to Horace's neck. The dog stepped up the pace to a slow canter, keeping level with the men. The berm ahead loomed up with shocking speed, and the skeletal shapes of the watchtowers on either side. Company A of the 5th kept pace with them on either side, their boots crunching on the gravel of the roadway that ran into the gate.

A carbide searchlight flickered alight from one tower, stabbing into his eyes with hurting brilliance. Seconds later it disintegrated in a shower of fragments as five or six splatguns turned their attention to it. The observation platform at the top of the wooden tower came apart in a shower of splinters and began to burn. The trumpets shrilled on, and the men started to run.

They reached the edge of the ditch. Fire stabbed down at them and some tumbled into it, to lie still or shrieking on the spiked timbers there. More slid down into the ditch on their backsides, clambered carefully through the obstacles and the mud, and began climbing the steep slope on the other side. They scrambled in the heavy clay, chopping their rifle butts into the dirt. Others brought up the escalade ladders, setting their triangle-braced bases at the edge of the ditch and letting them topple forward. The spikes at the upper end hammered into the dirt and men ran up the crossbars, climbing one-handed with their rifles in the other.

"Not much fire!" Raj said exultantly. *We caught them with their pantaloons down, and now it's too late!* Surprise was the best force multiplier there was, and it was working in his favor.

Staenbridge nodded. He turned to Bartin Foley and laid a hand on his shoulder. "Now."

The younger man grinned and leaned out of the saddle, extending his hook. One of his platoon commanders dropped the loop of a leather satchel over it. Then he lit a length of fuse-match that extended from under the buckled cover.

"Ha!"

Foley clapped his heels into his dog's flanks, heading for the timber gate that barred the northern entrance to the Colonial fort. Men were fighting hand-to-hand on the wall to either side, shooting and stabbing and swinging clubbed rifles; there had to have been Colonials on duty at the gate, at least, if not all around the walls. Bodies tumbled down the steep slope of the berm, dead or wounded. Troopers in Civil Government uniform shot through the stubby planks of the palisade at the top, or joined to pull the wood aside, or boosted their comrades over the pointed tops. Probably the towers on either side of the gate had held swivel guns as well as searchlights, but they were both blazing torches now, burning hard enough to make the heat noticeable at a hundred meters.

Foley covered the distance to the gate in a few seconds. A mounted man drew attention, even in the melee above him. Bullets kicked the gravel roadbed around him; once he swayed in the saddle and Staenbridge stiffened beside Raj. The satchel arched through the air and thumped into the dirt at the base of the gate, its momentum wedging it under the palm-log timbers where they swung at ankle height above the roadway. At the same instant he pulled the dog's head around; the beast whirled so quickly that it reared almost upright on its hind legs, with Foley hanging on like a jockey. It landed facing the way it had come, and running. The rider's display of skill would have been worthy of attention in itself, in any other context.

"Damned good man," Raj said, easing back the hammer of his revolver with the thumb of his right hand. Horace tensed under him.

". . . Five, six," Staenbridge said. "Yes, he is, and I wish to the Starless Dark he'd stop *volunteering* for this sort of shit, the hand's enough. Seven, eight—"

Barton Foley had covered three-quarters of the distance back to their position when the satchel charge blew. There were twenty-five kilos of powder in it; the gates disappeared from sight, and chunks of wood flew past them. Foley's dog yelped and leaped forward so quickly that he had to slug the reins back with brutal force to stop it. A splinter a double handspan long stuck out of one haunch; the animal kept trying to turn and reach the wound with its tongue.

Two of Foley's troopers grabbed the bridle while he dismounted; one of them threw a neckerchief over the dog's eyes while the other pulled the splinter out with a single swift yank. The dog's howl of agony was loud even by comparison with the noises of battle.

"Go!" Staenbridge barked. "Go, go, *go*."

The dust billowed away from the gate, showing a shattered ruin that sagged back out of the way. Bartin Foley was first through again, his riot gun in one hand; at his shouted direction a dozen men threw their shoulders against the splintered wreckage and walked it clear. Raj heeled Horace through a dozen paces, then drew him up with the pressure of his knees.

The interior of the camp was a checkerboard of stores in huge pyramids under tarpaulins, interspersed with tents. Some of the tents were on fire, and there was also light from iron baskets of burning greaseweed at the intersections. His head whipped left and right. To the left the Civil Government troops were already over the wall and down into the roadway that circled just inside it. The inner face of the berm was sloped dirt, or broad steps cut into the clay and faced with palm logs. Men poured down in, rallied around unit flags on the flat, moved off. There was a thick scattering of dead Arabs on the roadway, a few on the inner slope, more living ones running like blazes southward. To his right, toward the river, the fighting was still on the parapet itself. In a few places Civil Government banners waved from the parapet.

"All right," he said. *Just what I expected.* That section had had fewest of his veterans, and most of the Sandoral garrison troops. "Gerrin, let's collect some men and go help out. *Waymanos!*"

The issue of the day was no longer in doubt. Now he'd make sure the butcher's bill wasn't any higher than it had to be.

CHAPTER FIFTEEN

Breakfast was astonishing. *Well, we did just overrun a supply dump,* Raj thought, looking over the collection of delicacies.

He spooned up more potted shrimp. Peydro Belagez was eating them mixed with candied dates, which was something only a Borderer would do; Gerrin watched him with the horrified fascination of a gourmet, or a priest witnessing blasphemy. The commanders were seated at a long table in the huge pavilion tent that had been the base HQ. The Colonial engineers, left with time on their hands, had gone a little berserk. There were even *baths*, complete with kerosene-fired water heaters, enough for several hundred men at a time.

The morning air was fresh and hot, still a little smoky with the fires they'd spent half the night putting out. A bugle sounded outside, and a pair of mounted troopers trotted by with a long string of dogs on a leading rein: more of the force's mounts from the site where they'd landed. The barges and rafts were mostly here by now too, grounded on the riverbank or against the stub of the pontoon bridge that still extended halfway across. On the tall flagpole outside the HQ tent the Starburst banner snapped in the breeze.

The commander of the Rogor Slashers went on:

"And they still haven't stopped running, *heneralissimo*. They've split up into small parties and none of them show fight." Belagez's dark leathery face showed a combination of exhaustion and satisfaction. "Your instructions?"

"Ignore them," Raj said. "They weren't a problem in here, and they're not going to be one out there, either."

He swallowed another mouthful of excellent-quality *kave*—the Colony sat astride the trade-route from Azania and kept the best for itself—and looked at Suzette. She had peeled an orange and then set it aside untouched, looking a little pale. *Damnation. Think about that later.*

"Casualties?"

"Less than two hundred," Staenbridge said, sounding slightly surprised. "That's not counting walking wounded fit for duty. We only had twenty dead."

"Most of the live ones will pull through," Suzette added. "There are plenty of medical supplies here, and some excellent Colonial doctors, besides our own. Working under guard, of course."

"Prisoners?"

Kerpatik thumbed through his lists. "Over two thousand, *heneralissimo*. That is, two thousand military personnel. There were substantial numbers of camp followers here as well. The families of the soldiers have mostly fled. The, ah, commercial elements—" he rubbed thumb and the first two fingers of his hand together, "—they care little about the coinage as long as the metal is good."

Raj nodded. Where you had a military base, you got knocking-shops. He'd be willing to bet there was alcohol for sale too, Koranic prohibitions or not.

"Jorg, issue *Guardia* armbands to some of your footsoldiers and get that under tight control. We're still in the field, even if we've captured all the comforts of home. Let's not let the troops relax just yet."

"What about the prisoners?"

"Strip them down to their loincloths and let them go; tell them to start walking south. Now, we captured a good many documents here, including the daily logistics summaries."

Several men exclaimed in delight. That meant they would know the Colonial army's situation in detail, right down to the names of the units and their muster strength.

"Evidently they've been having problems getting the supplies from the railhead to the siege lines outside Sandoral—plenty here, but they're short of draft oxen and fodder over on the west bank."

Dinnalsyn nodded. "They were trying to use locomotive engines to rig up a couple of spare pontoons as steam tugboats, to pull raftloads up to Sandoral," he said. "I had a look; it would have worked, more or less. Whoever was in charge knew his business."

Raj nodded acknowledgment. "In any case, the Colonials have virtually nothing in the way of reserve with their field army. They were living from day to day on what their convoys brought in, once the countryside was laid waste. Now, Messers, here's what we'll do. Jorg, you're in charge here. How many dogs did we capture?"

Muzzaf Kerpatik looked up from a mass of papers. "Over twenty-five hundred, not counting gun teams, sir," he said.

"Good. Jorg, I'm leaving you all the infantry. Mount half of them—the best half—on the captured dogs. You'll also have, hmmm, Poplanich's Own and the 21st Novy Haifa for stiffening. And half the field guns. Move them north in parties of a couple of hundred; keep in continuous contact. Your objective is to prevent Tewfik from making any lodgment on the east bank. Shouldn't be difficult; there isn't much in the way of boats over there, and it would take weeks to put enough material together for another bridge. Which they couldn't build in the face of our artillery, anyway—but keep a sharp lookout; we don't want to get as overconfident as the previous tenants."

"Patrol the vicinity?"

"Vigorously. The infantry in good spirits?"

"Any better and they'd want to march on Al Kebir, *mi heneral.* Their tails are up."

"Deservedly so. Now, I'll take the rest of the cavalry, and the guns, over to the west bank. There are probably still intact supply trains on the road north, and I want to sweep those up immediately."

He rose, picking up his sword belt from the back of the chair. "I want to be on the move in no more than five hours. Tewfik is crazy like a ferenec, and Ali is just plain crazy; let's not give them time to think up any way out of their predicament. *Waymanos*."

"That will not work, Ali my brother," Tewfik said.

His voice was dangerously calm, and he left out the honorifics. Ali turned his head slowly, the great ruby that held the clasp of his turban winking in the stray beams of light that came through ventilation slits in the ceiling of the pavilion high above.

The nobles and officers sitting on cushions around the carpet looked at Tewfik as well, mostly with the same expression they might have used if a man kicked a carnosauroid in the snout.

"Dog will not eat dog," Tewfik went on. "This has been proven many times, as any fool of a soldier would know. Rather," he corrected himself, "most dogs will not. Nine in ten. So we will lose all our cavalry at once, and cannot preserve a portion of our mobility by sacrificing the rest."

Ali's face went a mottled color. It had been a very long time since anyone had dared to call him a fool to his face, even by implication. Even his brother.

"Go!" he said, pointing with a trembling hand. "You are dismissed from the *durbar*. Return when you learn manners!"

Tewfik rose and bowed deeply, hand going to brow and lips and chest; the other clenched on the plain, brass-wired hilt of his scimitar.

His officers fell in about him. That brought another round of silent glances around the council carpet. It was also unheard-of for men to leave the Settler's presence without word. And Ali looked suddenly thoughtful, conscious of the gaps. The nobles remained, and the heads of the religious orders . . .

In the harsh sun outside, Tewfik halted, beyond earshot of the mamluks who stood like ebony statues around the Settler's tent.

"How long?" he said, to an elderly officer with a green-dyed beard.

"There is no reserve. None. The camp is on quarter-rations, but we have fifty thousand men, as many dogs, and twenty thousand camp followers here. There was no food to be had in Sandoral, none at all. I have set men to fashioning nets, and we may gain a little fish by trolling the river; but the *kaphar* hold the fort you planted on the eastern bank opposite the city, and the guns there command much of the water surface. There will be hunger by sundown, starvation by tomorrow's night. Our dogs will be too weak to carry men in three days, and dying in six. By then the men will be dying as well."

Tewfik's hand withdrew the scimitar a handspan, then rammed it home again. "If we lose this army, our people will perish," he said. "And we cannot maintain discipline, even, if we cannot feed the troops."

He looked around. "Ibrahim, put the camp on one-quarter rations—and the camp followers are to receive nothing. Confiscate *all* private supplies of food. Hussein, mount ten thousand men and be ready to ride within the hour."

"Glad to be out of the ruins," Staenbridge said, looking back at the walls of Gurnyca.

Raj nodded. The faint stink of the piles of heads still clung to the inside of his nose, an oily thing like overripe bananas. Almost as bad had been the rats and the scavenging sauroids, rabbit-sized scuttling things all spidery limbs and teeth. One had gone past him with a desiccated arm in its mouth, still wearing the lace-cuffed sleeve of a lady's day-dress.

"That sort of thing has to stop," he said quietly.

"I don't think the wogs will be invading us again in the near future," the other man said with a predatory smile.

Raj shook his head. "I mean it's got to *stop*. We did pretty much the same to the country around Ain el-Hilwa. Look at this!"

He gestured at the territory around them. A few weeks before it had been among the richest land in the Civil Government. Now the fields lay waste, empty except for the ragged scraps of sheep and cattle that the scavengers had left. Burnt stumps marked the remains of orchards, tall date palms and spreading citrus lying amid drifting ash. The adobe of the roofless peasant huts was already crumbling; the fired brick and stone of the burnt-out manors would last only a little longer. Weirs and sluice-gates and the windmills that watered the higher land were blackened wreckage as well. The long column of

Civil Government troops rode through silence, amid a hot wind laden with sand. The sand would reclaim everything to the river's edge, in time.

"There are enough barbarians to fight, without wrecking civilization," Raj said. "*That's* why Ali has to be stopped. Barholm wants to unite the planet, even if it's only so he can rule it himself. Ali's a sicklefoot and he destroys for the love of it."

Staenbridge glanced around instinctively, with the gesture anyone in East Residence—or in the officer corps—learned to use when a too frank opinion of the Governor was voiced. Raj nodded silently. Staenbridge had a family to protect.

Raj's lips tightened. Suzette should be in no danger even if Barholm killed her husband; her family was old and well-connected. A child, though . . .

"Well, this will simplify *our* logistics," Bartin Foley said happily.

The wagons stood abandoned but not empty in the middle of the road, their trek-chains lying limp like dead snakes. From the sign, the teams had been driven on ahead with the dogs of the escort, but no attempt had been made to damage the cargoes.

"Which is fortunate," he murmured, taking off his helmet.

It was surprising; even now he had to remind himself not to scratch his head with his left . . . well, left hook. He juggled the bowl-shaped steel headpiece and ran a hand through sweat-damp black curls. His scalp felt cooler for an instant, then hot again as the noon sun struck it. He heeled his dog and rode slowly down the line of wagons. Half the loads were ammunition, loads for heavy siege guns. *Very* fortunate that the teamsters had been struck by blind panic. The other half was wheat biscuit and bundles of dried *advocati*.

"Ser."

A plume of dust was coming up the road from the south; the banner of the 5th and Messer Raj's personal flag at its head. He kneed his mount over to the side of the road, smiling to himself. Suzette wasn't along this time, and he suspected why. He knew the signs Fatima had borne her first in Sandoral, during the winter Raj spent preparing to meet Jamal's invasion. The whole process was rather disturbing, like a good many things female, but the end product was delightful.

It was also pleasant not to be facing destruction at the hands of an army that outnumbered them seven to one.

The command group pulled up, the battalion fanning out into the fields on either side. "Drag it all down to the river?" Gerrin said.

Foley shook his head. "It's about half ammunition. If we push everything together and set a fuse . . ."

Troopers came in by squads and pulled out bales of *advocati* to bait their dogs, filling their own haversacks with Colonial hard tack and strips of dried mutton. It was a little past noon and intensely hot, the land and sky turned white in the blaze of the sun.

"Ser." A much smaller plume of dust this time, approaching from the north.

The officers corked their canteens and waited with a stolid patience that ignored the discomfort. Their dogs twitched ears and tails against the omnipresent Drangosh Valley flies. Antin M'lewis pulled up at the head of ten of his Scouts.

"Ser," he said, with a casual wave that approximated a salute. "'Bout a thousand wogs comin', all cavalry, six guns. Five klicks off an' closin' fast."

Raj nodded, wiping sweat and dust from his face with his neckerchief. "We'll give them a reception," he said. To a messenger: "My compliments to Majors Bellamy and Gruder, and would they close up quickly, please." He looked around at the terrain. "This should do; Gerrin, set up along this crestline."

"Guns to the left?" Staenbridge asked, pointing to the snags of a citrus orchard that ran down the gentle slope east of the road.

"By all means."

"I presume we don't intend to stay here long."

"No," Raj said. "The last thing we want is a general engagement; we'll just show them they have to stay bunched up and slow them down."

He turned to Foley. "Barton, how many wagon trains does this make?"

"Altogether? Including the ones wrecked when we were coming

downstream?" At Raj's nod he continued: "Twenty-seven; four hundred twenty-two wagons of all sizes. Mostly these standard models," he concluded, waving a hand at the ones in the road.

"That means they shouldn't have recovered more than twenty or thirty tons of supplies altogether," he said. Softly: "Most excellent."

The messengers went out; on either side the 5th's troopers fanned out, sending their dogs back and unlimbering their entrenching tools for hasty heaped-earth *sangars* to their front. A few minutes later Ludwig Bellamy and Kaltin Gruder trotted up the roadway with their banners fluttering in the hot wind, the dust clouds of their commands behind them.

"*Mi heneral*," Bellamy said, his beard-stubble golden against the brown tan of his face. "Dispatches from Colonel Menyez."

Raj took them and broke the seal; the wax was as soft as butter. "Ah. The Colonials are breaking camp outside Sandoral. I think friend Ali has just realized how badly his testicles are caught in the mangler."

The commanders grinned like a group of carnosauroids contemplating a dying sheep.

"This is their vanguard, then," Raj said, looking north. "All right. We'll punch them back, then move southward—they'll be substantially slower, but I don't want to take any chances with Tewfik. Messenger: to Colonel Menyez. I want enough barges to take us off held in constant readiness. We can always duck back across the river if they lunge."

"We'll have to keep a very close eye on them," Staenbridge said thoughtfully.

Raj tapped his chin with one thumb. "Constant patrols," he agreed. "I don't think they'll want to wear down their dogs with skirmishing, hungry as they are."

The carnivore grins widened. Gruder began to laugh; after a moment, the others joined in.

Center drew a graph across Raj's vision, of consumption balanced against maximum possible reserves. At the back of his consciousness there was a trace of feeling, a satisfaction colder and more complete than a human mind could feel.

(⋅⋅⋅)   (⋅⋅⋅)   (⋅⋅⋅)

"Hold your fire!" Raj snapped.

He blinked into the setting sun; four days in the saddle had left his eyes red-rimmed and sore, the Drangosh Valley was hell for dust. He wiped his sleeve across his face and brought up his binoculars. Around him on the hillock the platoon of the 5th lowered their rifles, and the crew of the splatgun looked up from their weapon. Horace stood under the shade of the carob tree and panted, washcloth-sized tongue hanging down, and drooping ears almost covering his eyes.

"Easy target, ser," the gunner said, hopefully.

Raj raised his binoculars. The main Colonial army was several kilometers away; this encampment was notably more ragged than the last. Hardly an encampment at all, with no baggage train; the animals had all been eaten, to judge from the cracked bones left in their campfires. Most of their cavalry were walking and leading their dogs behind them. Some were carrying the saddles as well.

It was the patrol riding towards his men on the hilltop that interested him now. There were two banners at its head, hanging limp in the hot still air. He waited patiently; a gust of breeze flapped them out. One was pure white; the other, black with a Seal of Solomon in red.

"Tewfik," Raj whispered. The sweat down his spine turned clammy.

"Ensign," he said. "We're staying for a moment; they're coming under a truce flag. Get something white and wave it on a stick. Water the dogs, but keep a careful look-out. And have someone set out a blanket, with a piece of hard-tack and some salt."

They were out of extreme field gun range of the Colonial camp, but you never knew.

"Sir," the Ensign said, relaying the orders.

A detail trotted downslope to the well in the courtyard of a burned-out steading. A trooper unstrapped the rolled blanket from behind his saddle, spread it on the scraggly twistgrass beneath the carob tree, and set out a canteen, two cups and a piece of Colonial flat biscuit with a small twist of gray salt on it.

The men were looking at Raj curiously. "What does it mean, sir?" the young officer asked.

"I think," Raj said slowly, "it means the war is over. Escort our guest to me."

Raj saw Tewfik's eye widen in surprise as he recognized the Civil Government commander. The Colonial was much as Raj remembered him from the parley just before the first battle of Sandoral five years ago, perhaps a little grayer. Looking a little gaunt from five days on quarter-rations, but still stocky and strong. Like a scarred bull in a pasture, confronting a younger rival and twitching his horns. Raj knew that Tewfik would be seeing far greater changes in him.

"*Salaam aleikoum,*" the Arab said, bowing slightly.

"*Aleikoum es-salaam,*" Raj replied in accentless Arabic. Center had given him that, and practice made it come smoothly. "And upon you, peace, Tewfik ibn'Jamal."

"Shall it be peace, then?"

"If the Spirit wills. Come, let us talk."

Raj gestured, and the troopers retreated down the slope, out of immediate earshot and with their backs to the supreme commanders. The two men walked into the shade of the carob. Tewfik's eye caught the bread and salt; also the fact that they hadn't yet been offered to him. There was wary respect on his face as he turned to face his enemy and let the saddlebags he carried over one shoulder drop to the ground.

Carefully, carefully, Raj told himself. Take no chances with this man.

indeed, Center said. A brief vision flashed before Raj's eyes: the same meeting, but with the relative positions reversed. **if my physical centrum had been located in al kebir, rather than east residence . . .**

I'd be the one trying to salvage something from the wreck, Raj acknowledged.

"I will not waste words," Tewfik said abruptly, into the growing silence. "You have won this campaign. Without even fighting a major battle. My compliments, young *kaphar*; it is a feat for the manuals and the historians to chew over."

"More than the campaign," Raj said quietly. "The war. And I would betray my ruler and my State, if I did not use this advantage to ensure the Colony is no longer a threat to the Civil Government. We have fought you every generation for nearly a thousand years; it's irrelevant who was at fault in any given war. It must cease."

Tewfik nodded, his face still cat-calm. "Yet it is said that *Heneralissimo* Whitehall fights also for the cause of civilization on Bellevue," he said. "We of the House of Islam brought man to this world. We built its first cities. We preserved much of what learning survived the Fall, and we are the other half of civilized life on this world. Would you see our cities burn and the books with them, while the howling peoples camp in the ruins?"

Raj inclined his head. "You admit that the Colony is ruined if your army is destroyed?"

"That is as God wills; but too many of our high nobles are with us, our best commanders and the leadership needed to maintain the unity of our state. And our best troops; we left nothing but garrison forces on the frontiers. If they do not return, there will be civil war— fourscore separate civil wars; instead of one Settler, we will have a hundred *malik al'taifas,* petty kings ruling factions. They will not be able to maintain the irrigation canals, nor guard the frontiers against the Skinners and the Zanj."

"Or us," Raj pointed out.

Tewfik shook his head. "Conquering a hundred splinter realms would be impossible. You would have to garrison them heavily and there would be constant revolt; our people will not tolerate direct rule by unbelievers, not without such punishment as would destroy what you tried to govern."

"What do you propose?"

The Arab nobleman took a deep breath. "I cannot rule," he said, touching his eye. "And Ali . . . he is my brother, but he is a disaster for all Muslims. One way or another, sooner or later, he would have ruined the Colony. Already he has killed many of our best men—and anyone else who was there at the wrong time.

"What I propose is this: half our army to be disarmed and sent to East Residence. I suggest that you use them to garrison the

Southern and Western Territories; there they will be hostages against the Colony's good behavior. I will take the other half back with me to Al Kebir, and there rule as Vice-Governor in Barholm Clerett's name. My daughter Chaba will go to East Residence and wed Governor Barholm."

He shrugged, and for the first time smiled slightly. "I have no sons, and I fear I have been too indulgent with her—even allowing her to be taught to read. Perhaps it will be better for her thus."

Well, Raj thought, slightly dazed. *That's emphatic enough.* Center's sensor-grid came down over Tewfik's face, tracing blood flow, temperature, pupil-dilation.

subject tewfik is sincere, the computer-angel said. **probability 82%±7.**

Raj was slightly startled. Usually the percentage was much higher, one way or another.

subject tewfik has an unusual degree of control over autonomic body functions. in your vernacular, a poker face.

"A moment," Raj said.

He turned and looked out over the dusty plain of the Drangosh. Then he turned back.

"That sounds acceptable, in outline," he said. "We'll have to settle a few details. Release of all Civil Government prisoners in the Colony, for instance; and an annual tribute sufficient to pay the twenty-five thousand men you'll be giving us. Customs, tariffs, that sort of thing the bureaucrats can settle."

Tewfik nodded, hesitated, then stroked his beard. "My offer, of course, would apply to any *other* Governor as well," he hinted. "From all reports, Governor Barholm is somewhat preferable to my brother Ali . . . but that is not a strong recommendation."

Meaning, take the Chair yourself and rule the world, Raj thought.

interpretation of subtext correct, probability 98%±1, Center clarified.

"How do I know this isn't a ploy to save Ali and half your army?" Raj said. "You could be planning to write the other half off. It'd still be a larger force than I have in the field, and campaigning down to the

Drangosh delta would be a nightmare, particularly with this area too devastated to use as a base."

Tewfik smiled grimly and opened the saddlebag he'd brought. His curly-toed boot hooked it over to lie at Raj's feet. A head rolled out; fairly fresh, although the flies were already crawling around the hacked stump of the neck and the staring eyes. Raj did not need the ruby-clasped turban that rolled from the shaven skull to identify it.

"That for Ali," Tewfik said, and kicked the head to one side. "I should have done that years ago."

Raj raised his brows slightly. *I shouldn't be surprised if he's . . . decisive,* he decided. He gestured to the blanket. They sat down across from each other cross-legged, and shared the bread and salt. Raj laid the sword between them and Tewfik touched his hand to the hilt and blade.

"There shall be peace," Raj said. "I accept . . . in Governor Barholm's name."

"Wa sha' a-l-lah," Tewfik said, the formula full of a tired sincerity. He shrugged and spat on the head. "May God will it."

CHAPTER SIXTEEN

"All off!"

Raj swung down off the train. The East Residence station was crowded, full of the heat and smoke and steam of a busy summer's day. It felt humid after the Drangosh Valley; he rested his eyes on the hints of green higher up the hill and the fleecy clouds scattered across the sky. It was after 1900, near sunset, with Miniluna and Maxiluna both up, huge translucent globes hanging in a purpling sky.

"Move it, soldier!" the conductor said.

Raj smiled wryly and hopped down, ignoring the wooden steps the Central Rail slave was putting by the passenger car. He had a bandage over half his face, and he was dressed in common soldier's clothing—as a Descotter cavalry sergeant, which was probably what he'd have been if he hadn't been born to a noble family. The uniform brought a few cheers and careful claps on the back as he walked out through the station, a garrison bag slung over one shoulder.

That *was* unusual. Questions flew at him:

"Is it true *Heneralissimo* Whitehall cut off Ali's head with his own hand?"

"Are they going to march the prisoners through the streets?"

He smiled lopsidedly and pointed to his bandage; somebody thrust a goatskin of wine into his hand, and a free ticket to the bullfights. He dropped both of them off at the porticoed entrance to the train station—another of Barholm's construction projects—and plunged into the streets. They were thick with people, even though it was still normal working hours. Municipal flunkies were hanging ribbons and streamers from the standards of the gaslights, and a great cheer went up as an ox-wagon piled with huge wine casks halted at a corner.

The full treatment, he thought wryly. He nodded as the crowd began to chant his name when the wine cask was unloaded at the corner. *Barholm's not going to ignore that sort of thing.* It was bad enough that he'd been popular with the troops. Having the capital city mob on his side, no matter how he'd put down the Victory riots six years ago, would be the final nail in the Governor's coffin. *I wonder if they know they're condemning me to death?* he wondered.

Probably not. They'd been very frightened, and the euphoria of relief would be all the stronger for it.

Well, at least the troops won't have any problems getting a drink and a lay when they get in. They deserved that.

He was close enough to hear two of the men dipping their cups into the head of the broached wine cask. They wore the knee breeches, full-sleeved shirts, and leather aprons of prosperous artisans; their shoes had good pewter buckles.

"To Messer Raj and the damnation of all wogs," one said, drinking. "Ah, not bad."

"Looks like Barholm pulled it off again," the other replied. "This'll keep the Chair under his fundament until the day he dies."

"That might be thirty years."

"Thirty more years of Barholm. Spirit. Ah, his wine's good, anyway, and we deserve it—our taxes paid for it. To Messer Raj, Mihwel."

"To the Sword of the Spirit of Man—we won't see his like again, worse luck."

Raj ducked into the tiled entrance of a public bathhouse. *Where . . .*

Center strobed an indicator above one door. Not surprising that a bathhouse had a connection to the catacombs; all this section of the city was underlain by the Ancient tunnels.

"Raj!"

Thom Poplanich stirred to life in the mirrored sphere that was Center's physical being.

He gripped his friend's shoulders. "You did it!" His eyes noted the fresh creases, and the leathery tan of the Drangosh Valley's sun and sand-laden wind. "You did it!"

Raj returned the *embrahzo*.

"I did my duty," he said quietly. He shook his head, as if the magnitude of it was only now striking him. "I've reunited Earth—"

bellevue.

"—Bellevue under Holy Federation and the Spirit of Man of the Stars."

"The Fall is over," Thom whispered, awed. "After a thousand years, it's over."

the next cycle has begun, Center clarified. **this is only a beginning, but the direction of maximum probability has been reversed. there is no longer a strong drive to maximum entropy here on bellevue; and from bellevue, the human universe may be reclaimed in time. fifteen thousand years of barbarism have been reduced to a maximum of another five centuries. beyond that, stochastic analysis is no longer adequate. my projections indicate that human capacities will have increased beyond my ability to analyze.**

Raj laughed and ran a hand through his gray-shot curls. "I feel like a man who's been running down stairs and didn't notice that the staircase ended," he said. "The troops and the Colonials are on their way back; it'll take a while, but the first trains should arrive in hours. I came to say goodbye, before . . ."

Thom's smile died. "Before what?" he asked sharply.

Raj looked up in surprise at the tone of command in the other man's voice. "Before I report to the Governor," he said.

"Who no longer needs you. Who fears you," Thom said.

Raj shrugged. "I've done my duty to the Spirit of Man. I'm not going to flinch at the end. Barholm can't kill me deader than a Colonial bullet or a Brigadero's broadsword might have. It's not a safe profession, soldiering."

Thom turned, a terrible anger on his face. "There's no need for that! There's no need for that now—and even if there was, a ruler who treats a faithful servant that way doesn't deserve to rule, doesn't deserve to *exist*. Hasn't he done enough? More than any other man could have done?"

The shout rang in the strait confines of the sphere, then sank away as if the material had changed to absorb it.

raj whitehall has one further duty to the plan.

Raj put a comforting hand on Thom's shoulder. "I know. I said I was willing to die."

not that.

Both men started.

for six years, i have been training your friend here to rule as i trained you to fight. now it is time to put him on the throne of the reunited planet. you should find that easy, in comparison to the things you have already accomplished in my service.

The mirrored sphere flashed and vanished. They were disembodied viewpoints watching a huge crowd surge through the gardens of the Gubernatorial Palace, crying out and eddying around the iron order of the troops who guarded it. Raj recognized the shoulder-flashes of the 5th Descott and the Rogor Slashers, of Cruisers and Brigaderos units . . . and Colonials, still in their crimson djellabas but carrying Armory rifles.

The great ebony doors with their hammered silver Starbursts swung open. Barholm Clerett came through; bandaged and bruised, his hands bound before him. Gerrin Staenbridge walked beside him with drawn pistol, Bartin Foley on the other side, and a file of Descotters with fixed bayonets on either side. They hustled the blank-faced Barholm into a closed carriage at the foot of the marble stairs. Mounted troopers of the 1st Cruisers with drawn swords fell in around it, and the driver touched the white greyhounds of the team into action. The crowd parted reluctantly; a few rocks and lumps of dogshit flew at the carriage.

"To the frying post with the tyrant Barholm!"

"Death to Barholm the tax-eater!"

"Dig up Barholm's bones!"

The clamor might have turned to riot, but trumpeters blew a ceremonial fanfare from the balcony above. Tall windows swung open, and Raj Whitehall walked out and halted, his hands clasped behind his back.

Silence fell gradually, although the noise of the crowd was like distant surf or the rustling of leaves in dense forest.

Raj heard his own voice; the superb acoustics of the semicircular frontage of the Palace carried it out over the heads of the crowd.

"Citizens of Holy Federation! The tyrant Barholm is de-Chaired!"

Massed cheering broke over him like thunder, and cries hailing him governor. He raised his hand again.

"I am the Sword of the Spirit of Man, but not the Spirit's viceregent on Earth. Citizens, I give you your Governor. Governor Poplanich, grandson of Governor Poplanich, legitimate heir to the Chair."

In the slow, hieratic pace that the regalia imposed, Thom Poplanich paced out to stand beside his General. The sunlight blazed on metallized robes, on the Stylus and Keyboard in his hands.

"My people—" he began.

observe:

The sphere blinked. Raj saw himself standing under the great dome of the Cathedron that Barholm had built. A wedding was being held, a man and a woman standing in shimmering robes before the Patriarchal Arch-Sysup of East Residence, their hands entwined and bound with the sacred Cable. The man was Thom Poplanich; the woman was dark and round-faced, plain, with intelligent black eyes that sparkled with excitement. Raj saw himself step forward to give the groomsman's responses. It was obviously a great occasion of state; besides the nobles and clerics, his Companions were there, and Suzette . . .

Tewfik ibn'Jamal stood on the other side of the couple, in the place reserved for the father of the bride. His eye met the image-Raj's for an instant, and winked.

observe:

Chancellor Tzetzas stood and contemptuously turned his face to the pockmarked brick wall. Behind him the officer of the firing squad raised his sword. The rifles leveled and vomited smoke . . .

observe:

Raj stood in a testing room in the Armory, examining a rifle. He was older, his hair mostly gray. The weapon in his hands was one the younger self did not recognize; chunky and short, with a box-magazine protruding below the stock and a cocking-lever at the side. He raised it and fired at the target downrange. The rifle fired again and again, spitting spent brass to the right, without any motion but pulling the trigger. And there was no smoke from the barrel . . .

observe:

A crowd of gaping peons stood at the edge of a wheatfield—somewhere in the Central Provinces, from the flat terrain and broad treeless horizons. Behind them were the mud hovels they dwelt in; in front of them a huge clanking machine snorted and backed, then surged out into the ripe grain. It moved slowly, a whirring contraption like a skeletal cylinder of boards bending down the heads of the stalks. Beside it went an ox-wagon, and threshed grain poured out of a spout into it as the machine chewed its way into the wheat. As Raj watched, it reaped as much land as a dozen peons could do in a day; from the sun, scarcely an hour had passed.

observe:

Sullen, shaven-headed Skinner nomads surrendered their huge sauroid-killing rifles to an officer in Civil Government uniform. A huge engine on linked treads of steel stood behind the officer, quivering with mechanical life; the twin trails of its passage stretched off into the distance, and weapons bristled from its armored hull. Overhead a flying machine circled, with stiff wings like a soaring pterosauroid and a buzzing propeller at the rear.

observe:

An older Raj stood in the Cathedron once more. Suzette was with him, older as well, but smiling. The groom walked to his place beneath the dome; for a moment Raj thought it was Thom, but then he saw the differences, the darker complexion and the beak nose. *Thom's son,* he realized.

The image of a Raj twenty years older stepped forward, the bride's fingers resting on his arm. The young woman's green eyes glowed.

observe:

Bartin Foley as an old man, in a nobleman's formal civil clothes. He stood in the presentation room of the Palace, and bowed his head as an official Raj didn't recognize placed a gold-chain medallion over his head. Beside him on the table rested a book. On the cover, embossed letters read: *Raj Whitehall and His Times.*

observe:

He was looking down from the roof of a great shed. The dust motes in the air shook with the force of the energies below. Incomprehensible machines crawled by on a conveyor-belt. Men and women in overalls swarmed about them, fastening on parts with tools that hummed and screeched and whirred and sent showers of sparks across the concrete floor.

A siren whooped. The noise ended as if cut off with a knife, and the workers downed tools and turned to troop out of the huge building.

observe:

A crowd gathered around a plinth in East Residence. They were just familiar enough to be disturbing, men with their hair in pigtails, women in skirts scandalously short, to their knees. A poster read: *Elections to the Consultative Senate to be held.* Beneath: *Vote Reform! The Anti-Peonage Act needs your support!*

observe:

A train streaked by. Raj *thought* it was a train. It floated above the tracks with no visible support, and the locomotive was shaped more like a rifle bullet or an artillery shell than anything he recognized. The hum of its passage lingered in the air long after it had passed the horizon.

observe:

An avenue in East Residence, with a view down to the harbor. Raj could recognize a few of the buildings: the Cathedron, the Palace. Most of the rest had changed, in styles totally foreign. Before him was a mausoleum. The viewpoint swooped closer. The walls around the base were sculpted in bas-relief, and they showed his troops. Marching, making camp, charging with leveled bayonets. The central column held high-relief bronzes; here he recognized faces, Gerrin, Bartin, Kaltin—all his Companions, and Suzette. Their clasped hands ringed the broad pillar.

Atop it was a statue. A rider, on a great black hound. He was armed, but his outflung hand was empty, pointing to the sky. Below in gold letters was set:

raj whitehall. the conqueror of peace.

Beyond, from the bay where East Residence's harbor lay, something huge was lifting toward the heavens on pillars of pale fire.

Pigeons rose in a massed flutter of wings about the statue as the thunder of the starship's drive rolled across the plaza.

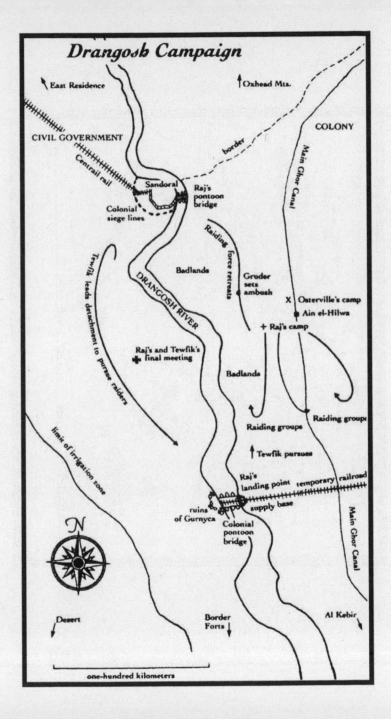

Drangosh Campaign

East Residence

CIVIL GOVERNMENT

Central rail

Oxhead Mts.

COLONY

border

Main Ghor Canal

Sandoral

Raj's pontoon bridge

Colonial siege lines

Raiding force retreats

DRANGOSH RIVER

Badlands

Gruder sets ambush

X Osterville's camp

Ain el-Hilwa

+ Raj's camp

Tewfik leads detachment to pursue raiders

Raj's and Tewfik's final meeting

Badlands

Raiding groups

Raiding groups

Tewfik pursues

limit of irrigation zone

Raj's landing point

temporary railroad

ruins of Gurnyca

supply base

Colonial pontoon bridge

Main Ghor Canal

N

Desert

Border Forts

Al Kebir

one-hundred kilometers

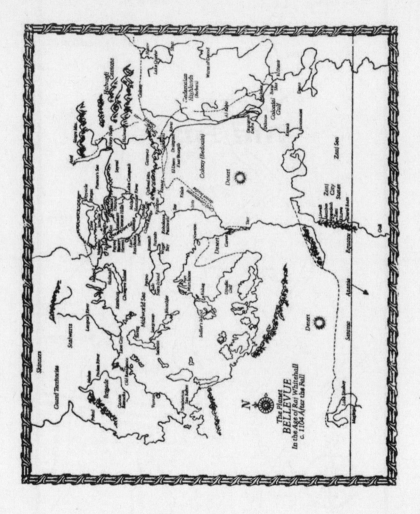

The Planet
BELLEVUE
In the Age of Rai Whitehall
c. 1104 After the Fall

❂ VI ❂
THE CHOSEN

❀ ❀ ❀

To Jan, with love.
And to Steve's dad, who did a good job.

❀ ❀ ❀

GET USED TO IT . . .

Jackboots walked over the kitchen floor above Jeffrey and Lucretzia, making the planking creak and sending little trickles of dust down into the cellar. To Jeffrey, the dark basement slowly took on a flat, silvery tone as Center boosted his perceptions.

The voice of Raj echoed in Jeffrey's mind: **to the right of the door.**

Jeffrey's hand reached out to the knob, moving with an automatic precision that seemed detached and slow. He jerked it backward, and the Land soldier stumbled through. A grid dropped down over his sight, outlining the enemy. A green dot appeared right under the angle of the man's jaw. His finger stroked the trigger, squeezing.

Crack. The soldier's head snapped sideways as if he'd been kicked by a horse. Jeffrey was turning, turning, the pistol coming up. The second soldier was leveling her rifle, but the green dot settled on her throat.

Crack. The woman fell back and writhed, blood spraying. The soldier behind her was jumping back, out of sight, almost, but the green dot settled on his leg.

Crack. A scream, as the third soldier tumbled out of sight. The grid outlined a prone figure against the planks of the entranceway, and an aiming point strobed. Jeffrey squeezed the trigger four times. But there was one more soldier, and the bark of the rifle was much deeper than Jeffrey's pistol. The nickel-jacketed bullet ricocheted, whining around the stones of the cellar like a giant lethal wasp.

Jeffrey tumbled back down the stairs, snapping open the cylinder of his revolver and shaking out the spent brass.

"Christ," Jeffrey muttered, staggering. *I just killed four human beings.*

this is what the world will be, for the rest of your life, Center said.

CHAPTER ONE

Visager
1221 A.F. (After the Fall)
305 Y.O. (Year of the Oath)

Commodore Maurice Farr lifted the uniform cap from his head and wiped at the sweat on his forehead with a handkerchief. He was standing on the liner docks on the north shore of Oathtaking's superb C-shaped harbor. Behind him were the broad quiet streets of Old Town, running out from Monument Square behind his back. There the bronze figures of the Founders stood, raised weapons in their hands—the cutlasses and flintlocks common three centuries ago. The Empire-Alliance war had ended an overwhelming Imperial victory. The first thing the Alliance refugees had done was swear a solemn oath of vengeance against those who'd broken their ambitions and slaughtered everyone of their fellows who hadn't fled the mainland.

After three years in the Land of the Chosen as a naval attaché, Farr was certain of two things: their descendants still meant it, and they'd extended the future field of attack from the Empire to everyone else on the planet Visager. Perhaps to the entire universe.

West and south around the bay ran the modern city of Oathtaking, built of black basalt and gray tufa from the quarries nearby. Rail sidings, shipyards, steel mills, factories, warehouses, the endless tenement blocks that housed the Protégé laborers. A cluster of huge buildings marked the commercial center; six and even eight stories tall, their girder frames sheathed in granite carved in the severe columnar style of Chosen architecture. A pall of coal smoke lay over most of the town below the leafy suburbs on the hill slopes, giving the hot tropical air a sulfurous taste. A racket of shod hooves sounded on stone-block pavement, the squeal of iron on iron and a hiss of steam, the hoot of factory sirens. Ships thronged the docks and harbor, everything from old-fashioned windjammers in with cargoes of grain from the Empire to modern steel-hulled steamers of Land or Republic build.

Out in the middle of the harbor a circle of islands linked by causeways marked the site of an ancient caldera and the modern navy basin. Near it moved the low hulking gray shape of a battlewagon, spewing black smoke from its stacks. His mind categorized it automatically: *Ezerherzog Grukin*, name-ship of her class, launched last year. Twelve thousand tons displacement, four 250-mm rifles in twin turrets fore and aft, eight 175mm in four twin-tube wing turrets, eight 155mm in barbette mounts on either side, 200mm main belt, face-hardened alloy steel. Four-stacker with triple expansion engines, eighteen thousand horsepower, eighteen knots.

The biggest, baddest thing on the water, or at least it would be until the Republic launched its first of the *Democrat*-class in eighteen months.

Farr shook his head. *Enough. You're going home.* He raised his eyes.

Snow-capped volcanoes ringed the port city of Oathtaking on three sides. They reared into the hazy tropical air like perfect cones, their bases overlapping in a tangle of valleys and folds coated with rain forest like dark-green velvet. Below the forest were terraced fields; Farr remembered riding among them. Dusty gravel-surfaced lanes between rows of eucalyptus and flamboyants. A little cooler than down here on the docks; a little less humid. Certainly better smelling than the oily waters of the harbor. Pretty, in a way, the glossy green of the coffee bushes and the orange orchards. He'd gone up there a couple of times, invited up to the manors of family estates by Chosen navy types eager to get to know the Republic's naval attaché. Not bad oscos, some of them; good sailors, terrible spies, and given to asking questions that revealed much more than they intended.

Also, that meant he got a travel pass for the Oathtaking District. There were some spots where a good pair of binoculars could get you a glimpse at the base if you were quick and discreet. Nothing earthshaking, just what was in port and what was in drydock and what was building on the slipways. Confirming what Intelligence got out of its contacts among the Protégé workers in the shipyard. That was how you built up a picture of capabilities, bit by bit. He'd been here three years now, he'd done a pretty good job—gotten the specs on the steam-turbine experiments—and it was time to go home.

For more reasons than one. He dropped his eyes to the man and woman talking not far away.

What did I ever see in him? Sally Hosten thought.

Her husband—soon to be ex-husband—stood at parade rest, hands clasped behind his back. Karl Hosten was a tall man even for one of the Chosen, broad-shouldered and narrow-waisted, as trim at thirty-five as he had been twelve years ago when they married. His face was square and so deeply tanned that the turquoise-blue eyes glowed like jewels by contrast; his cropped hair was white-blond. He wore undress uniform: gray shorts and short-sleeved tunic and gunbelt.

"This parting is not of my will," he said in crisp Chosen-accented Landisch.

"No, it's mine," Sally agreed, in English.

She'd spoken Landisch for a long time, her voice had been a little rusty when she went to the Santander embassy to see about getting her Republican citizenship back. She'd met Maurice there. And she didn't intend to speak Karl's language again, if she could help it.

"Will you not reconsider?" he said.

Twelve years together had made it easy for her to read the emotions behind a Chosen mask-face. The sorrow she sensed put a bubble of anger at the back of her mouth, hard and bitter.

"Will you give John back his children?" she said.

A brief glance aside showed that her son John wasn't nearby anymore. Where . . . twenty feet or so, bending over a cargo net with another boy of about the same twelve years. Jeffrey Farr, Maurice's son.

Karl Hosten stiffened and ran a hand over his stubbled scalp. "The law is the law; genetic defects must be—"

"A clubfoot is not a genetic defect!" Sally said with quiet deadliness. "It's a result of carriage during pregnancy"—a spear of guilt stabbed her—"which can be, was, corrected surgically. And you didn't even *tell* me you were having him sterilized in the delivery room. I didn't find out until he was eleven years old!"

"Would you have been happier if you knew? Would he?"

"How happy would he be when he found out he couldn't be Chosen?"

Karl swallowed and looked very slightly away. *He is my son too,* he didn't say. Aloud: "There are many fine careers open to Probationers-Emeritus. Johan is an intelligent boy. The University—"

"As a *Washout*," Sally said, using the cruel slang term for those who failed the exacting Trial of Life at eighteen after being born to or selected for the training system. It was far better than Protégé status, anything was, but in the Land of the Chosen . . .

"We've had this conversation too many times," she said.

Karl sighed. "Correct. Let us get this over with."

She looked around. "John!"

John Hosten felt prickly, as if his own skin were too tight and belonged to somebody else. Everyone had been too quiet in the steamcar, after they picked him up at the school. He'd already said good-bye to his friends—he didn't have many—and packed. Vulf, his dog, was already on board the ship.

I don't want to listen to them fight, he thought, and began drifting away from his mother and father.

That put him near another boy about his own age. John's eyes slid back to him, curiosity driving his misery away a little. The stranger was skinny and tall, red-haired and freckled. His hair was oddly cut, short at the sides and floppy on top, combed—a foreigner's style, different from both the Chosen crop and the bowl-cut of a Proti. He wore a thin fabric pullover printed in *bizarre* colorful patterns, baggy shorts, laced shoes with rubber soles, and a ridiculous looking billed cap.

"Hi," he said, holding out a hand. Then: "Ah, *guddag.*"

"I speak English," John said, shaking with the brief hard clamp of the Land. English and Imperial were compulsory subjects at school, and he'd practiced with his mother.

The other boy flexed his fingers. "Better'n I speak Landisch," he said, grinning. "I'm Jeffrey Farr. That's my dad over there."

He nodded towards a tall slender man in a white uniform who was standing a careful twenty meters from the Hosten party. John recognized the uniform from familiarization lectures and slides: Republic of Santander Navy, officer's lightweight summer garrison version. It must be Captain Farr, the officer Mom had been seeing at the consulate about the citizenship stuff.

I wish she'd tell me the truth. I'm not a little kid or an idiot, he thought. That wasn't the only reason she was talking to Maurice Farr so much. "John Hosten, Probationer-hereditary," he replied aloud.

A Probationer-hereditary was born to the Chosen and automatically entitled to the training and the Test of Life; only a few children of Protégés were adopted into the course. Then he flushed. He wasn't going to be a Probationer long, and he could never have passed the Test, not the genetic portions. Not with his foot. He couldn't be anything but a Washout, second-class citizen.

"You don't have to worry about all that crap any more," Jeffrey said cheerfully, jerking a thumb over his shoulder at the liner *Pride of Bosson.* "We're all going back to civilization."

The flag that fluttered from her signal mast had a blue triangle in the left field with fifteen white stars, and two broad stripes of red and white to the right. The Republic of Santander's banner.

John opened his mouth in automatic reflex to defend the Land, then closed it again. He was going to Santander himself. To live.

"Ya, we're going," he said. They both looked over towards their parents. "Your mother?"

"She died when I was a baby," Jeffrey said.

There was a crash behind them. The boys turned, both relieved at the distraction. One of the steam cranes on the *Bosson*'s deck had slipped a gear while unloading a final cargo net on the dock. The Protégé foreman of the docker gang went white under his tan—he'd be held responsible—and turned to yell insults and complaints up at the liner's deck, shaking his fist. Then he turned and whipped his lead-weighted truncheon across the side of one docker's head. There was a sound like a melon dropping on pavement; the docker's face seemed to distort like a rubber mask. He fell to the cracked uneven pavement with a limp finality, as if someone had cut all his tendons.

"Shit," Jeffrey whispered.

The foreman made an angry gesture with his baton, and two of the dockers took their injured fellow by the arms and dragged him off towards a warehouse. His head was rolled back, eyes disappeared in the whites, bubbles of blood whistling out of his nose. The foreman turned back to the ship and called up to the seamen on the railing, calling for an officer. They looked back at him for a moment, then one silently turned away and walked towards the nearest hatch . . . slowly.

The gang instantly squatted on their heels when the foreman's attention went elsewhere. A few lit up stubs of cigarette; John could smell the musky scent of hemp mingled with the tobacco. A few smirked at the foreman's back, but most were expressionless in a different way from Chosen, their faces blank and doughy under sweat and stubble. They were wearing cotton overalls with broad arrows on them, labor-camp inmates' clothing.

"Hey, that crate's busted," Jeffrey said.

John looked. One wood-and-iron box about three meters on a side had sprung along its top. The stencils on the side read *Museum of History and Naturel Copernik*. He felt a stir of curiosity. Copernik was capital of the Land, and the Museum was more than a storehouse; it was the primary research center of the most advanced nation on Visager. He'd had daydreams of working there himself, of finally figuring out some of the mysterious artifacts of the Ancestors, the star-spanning colonizers from Earth. The Federation had fallen over a thousand years ago—it was 1221 A.F. right now—and nobody could understand the enigmatic constructs of ceramic and unknown metals. Not even now, despite the way technology had been advancing in the past hundred years. They were as incomprehensible as a steam engine or a dirigible would be to one of the arctic savages.

"What's inside?" he said eagerly.

"C'mon, let's take a look."

The laborers ignored them; John was in a Probationer's school uniform, and Jeffrey was an obvious foreigner—an upper-class boy could go where he pleased, and the Fourth Bureau would be lethally interested if they heard of Protégés talking to an *auzlander*. Even in the camps, there was always someplace worse. The foreman was still trading cusswords with the liner's petty officer.

John grabbed at the heavy Abaca hemp of the net and climbed; it was easy, compared to the obstacle courses at school. Jeffrey followed in an awkward scramble, all elbows and knees.

"It's just a rock," he said in disappointment, peering through the sprung panels.

"No, it's a meteorite," John said.

The lumpy rock was about a meter across, suspended in an elastic cradle in the center of the crate. It hadn't taken any damage when the net dropped—unlike a keg of brandy, which they could smell leaking—but then, from the slagged and pitted appearance, it had survived an incandescent journey through the atmosphere. John was surprised that it was being sent to the museum; meteorites were common. You saw dozens in the sky, any night. There must be something unusual about this one, maybe its chemical composition. He reached through and touched it.

"Sort of cold," he said. Not quite icy, but not natural, either. "Feel it."

Jeffrey stretched a long thin arm through the crack. "Yeah, like—"

The universe vanished.

Sally looked over her shoulder. Where *was* John? Then she saw him, scrambling over the cargo net with another boy. With Maurice's son. She opened her mouth to call them back, then closed it. *It's important that they get along.* Maurice hadn't made a formal proposal yet, but . . . She turned back.

Karl had his witnesses to either side: his legal children, Heinrich and Gerta, adopted in the fashion of the Chosen. Heinrich was the son of a friend who'd died in an expedition to the Far West Islands; they were dangerous, and the seas between, with their abundant and vicious native life, even more so. The other had been born to Protégé laborers on the Hosten estates and christened Gitana. Karl had sponsored her; she was a bright active youngster and her parents were John's nurse and attendant valet/bodyguard respectively.

Maria and Angelo stood at a respectful distance; their daughter ignored them. Ex-daughter; no Chosen were as strict as those Chosen from Protégé ranks. She was Gerta Hosten now, not Gitana Pesalozi.

A Chosen attorney exchanged papers with the plump little Santander consul, then turned to Sarah.

"Sarah Hosten, née Kingman, do you hereby irrevocably renounce connubial ties with Karl Hosten, Chosen of the Land?"

"I do."

"Karl Hosten, do you acknowledge this renunciation?"

"I do."

"Do you also acknowledge Sarah Hosten as bearing full parental rights to John Hosten, issue of this union?"

"Excepting that John Hosten may continue to claim my name if he wishes, I do." Karl swallowed, but his face might have been carved from the basalt of the volcanoes.

"Heinrich Hosten, Gerta Hosten, Probationers-adoptee of the line of Hosten, do you witness?"

"We do."

"All parties will now sign, fingerprint and list their *geburtsnumero* on this document."

Sally complied, although unlike anyone born in the Land of the Chosen she didn't have a birth-number tattooed on her right shoulderblade and memorized like her name. The ink from the fingerprinting stained her handkerchief as she wiped her hands.

The consul stepped forward. "Sarah Jennings Kingman, as

representative of the Republic of Santander, I hereby officially certify that your lapsed citizenship in the Republic is fully restored with all rights and duties appertaining thereunto; and that your son John Hosten as issue of your body is accordingly entitled to Santander citizenship also. . . . Where is the boy?"

The universe vanished. John found himself in a . . . place. It seemed to be the inside of a perfectly reflective sphere, like being inside a bubble made of mirror glass. He tried to scream.

Nothing happened. That was when he realized that he had no throat, and no mouth. No body.

No body no body nobodynobody—

The hysteria damped down suddenly, as if he'd been slipped a tranquilizer. Then he became conscious of weight, breath, *himself*. For a moment he wanted to weep with relief.

"Excuse me," a voice said behind him.

He turned, and the mirrored sphere had vanished. Instead he saw a room. The furnishings were familiar, and *wrong*. A fireplace, rugs, deep armchairs, books, table, decanters, but none of them quite as he remembered. A man was standing by a table, in uniform, but none he knew: baggy maroon pants, a blue swallowtail jacket, a belt with a saber; a pistol was thrown on the table beside the glasses. He was dark, darker than a tan could be, with short very black hair and gray eyes. A tall man, standing like a soldier.

"Where . . . what . . ." John began.

"Attention!" the man said.

"Sir!" John barked, bracing. Six years of Probationer schooling had made that a reflex.

"At ease, son," the dark man said, and smiled. "Just helping you get a grip on yourself. First, don't worry. This is real"—he gestured around at the room—"but it isn't physical. You're still touching the meteorite in the crate. Virtually no time is passing in the . . . the outside world. When we've finished talking, you'll be back on the dock and none the worse for wear."

"Am I crazy?" John blurted.

"No. You've just had something very strange happen." The smile grew wry. "Pretty much the same thing happened to me, lad. A long time ago, when I wasn't all that much older than you are now. Sit."

John sank gingerly into one of the chairs. It was comfortable, old leather that sighed under his weight. He sat with his feet on the floor and his hands on the arms of the chair.

"My name's Raj Whitehall, by the way. And this"—he waved a hand at the room—"is Center. A computer."

Despite the terror that boiled somewhere at the back of his mind, John shaped a silent whistle. "A *computer*? Like the Ancestors had, the Federation? I've read a *lot* about them, sir."

Raj Whitehall chuckled. "Well, that's a good start. My people thought they were angels. Yes, Center's a holdover from the First Federation. Military computer, Command and Control type. Don't ask me any of the details. Where I was brought up, experts understood steam engines, a little. Look there."

John turned his head to look at the mirrored surface. Instead, he was staring out into a landscape. It wasn't a picture; there was depth and texture to it. Subtly different from anything he'd ever seen, the moons in the faded blue sky were the wrong size and number, the sunlight was a different shade. It cast black shadows across eroded gullies in cream-white silt. Out of the badlands came a column of men in uniforms like Raj's. They were riding, but not on horses. On *dogs*, giant dogs five feet high at the shoulder. They looked a lot like Vulf, except their legs were thicker in proportion. John whistled again, this time aloud.

The column of men went by, and a clumsy-looking field gun pulled by six more of the giant dogs. Then Raj Whitehall pulled up his . . . well, his giant hound. A woman rode beside him, not in uniform. Her face was dusty and streaked with sweat, and beautiful. Slanted green eyes glowed out of it.

The vision faded, back to the absolutely perfect mirror. John looked back to Raj. "Where was that?" he said. Then, slowly: "When was that?"

Raj nodded, leaning his hips back against the table and crossing his arms. "That was Bellevue, the planet where I was born. About a hundred and fifty years ago."

"You're . . . a ghost?"

"A ghost in a machine. A recording that thinks its a man. It's a convincing illusion, even to me."

John sat silently for what felt like a minute. "Why are you talking to me?"

"Good lad," Raj said. John felt an obscure jolt of pride at the praise. Raj went on. "Now, listen carefully. You know how the Federation collapsed?"

John nodded. Visager had preserved the records; he'd seen them in school. Expansion from Earth, then rivalries and civil war. Civil war that continued until the Tanaki Nets were destroyed and interstellar travel cut off, and then on Visager itself until civilization was thoroughly smashed. After that a long process of rebirth, slow and painful.

"That happened all over the human-settled galaxy. On Bellevue, the collapse was even worse than here. Center was left in the rubble underneath the planetary governor's mansion. Center waited a long, long time for the time to be right. More than a thousand years; then it found me. Bellevue's problem was internal division. We were set to slag ourselves down again, this time right back to stone hatchets, all the more surely because we were doing it with rifles and not nukes. I was a soldier, an officer. With Center's help—and some very brave men—I reunited the planet. Bellevue's the capital of the Second Federation, now."

"You want me to *unite Visager*?" John felt his mouth drop open. "*Me?*" His voice broke embarrassingly, the way it had taken to doing lately, and he flushed.

Raj shook his head. "Not exactly. More to *prevent* it being unified, at least by the wrong people." He leaned forward slightly. "Tell me honestly, John. What do you think of the Chosen?"

John opened his mouth, then closed it. Memories flickered through his mind; ending with the blank, caved-in faces of the dockers as the unconscious man was carried away.

"Honestly, sir—not much. Mom doesn't, either. I tried talking to Dad about it once, but . . ." He shrugged and looked away.

Raj nodded. "Center can foresee things. Not *the* future always, but what will probably happen, and how probable it is. Don't ask me to explain it—I've had three lifetimes, and I still can't understand it. But I know it works."

maintenance of your personality matrix is incompatible with the modifications necessary to comprehend stochastic analysis.

John started and put his hands to his ears. The voice had come from everywhere and nowhere. It felt *heavy*, somehow, as if the words held a greater freight of meaning than any he'd ever heard. The sound of them in his head had been entirely flat and even, but there were undertones that resonated like a guitar's strings after the player's fingers left them. The voice felt . . . sad.

"Center means that if I was changed that much, I wouldn't be me," Raj said.

john hosten, the ancient, impersonal voice said, **in the absence of exterior intervention, there is a 51% probability ±6%, that the chosen will establish complete dominance of visager within 34 years. observe.**

John looked toward the mirrored wall.

An endless line of men in tattered green uniforms marched past a machine-gun nest manned by Land troops, Protégé infantry, and a Chosen officer. Two plainclothes police agents stood by, in long leather coats and wide-brimmed hats, heavy pistols in their hands. Every now and then they would flick their hands, and the soldiers would drag a man out of the line of prisoners, force him down to his knees. The Fourth Bureau men would step up and put the muzzles of their guns to the back of the kneeling man's head . . .

conquest of the empire, Center said. **observe:**

A montage followed: cities burning, with their names and locations somehow in his mind. Ships crowded with slave laborers arriving in Oathtaking and Pillars and Dorst. A group of Chosen engineers talking over papers and plans, while a line of laborers that stretched beyond sight worked on a railway embankment.

consolidation. further expansion.

A burning warship sank, in an ocean littered with oily guttering flames, wreckage, bodies, and men who still tried to move. Hundreds of them were sucked backwards and down as the ship upended and sank like a lead pencil dropped into a pool, its huge bronze propellers still whirling as it took the final plunge. Through the smoke came a line of battlewagons, with the black-and-gold banner of the Chosen at their masts. Their main batteries were scorched and blistered with heavy firing, but silent; their secondary guns and quick-firers stabbed out into the waters.

destruction of santander.

Even without Center's information, he recognized the next scene. It was Republic Hall in Santander City. The great red-granite dome was shattered; a man in the black frock coat and tall hat of Republican formality stood before a Chosen general and handed over the Constitution of the Republic in its glass-cased box. The general threw it down and ground the heel of his boot into it while the troops behind him cheered.

consequences.

A shabby tenement street in a Chosen city. Figures clustered about the steps, talking, falling silent as a strange-looking steamcar bristling with weapons hummed by.

"But those are *Chosen*," John exclaimed.

Raj spoke: "What do carnivores do when they've finished off the game?"

metaphorical but correct, Center's passionless non-voice said. **once consolidation is complete, the chosen lines would fall out with each other. the planet cannot support so large a ruling class in conditions of intense competition, not indefinitely; and the social system resulting from conquest and slavery cannot be rationally adjusted to maximize productivity. internal reorganization would lead to the creation of a noble caste and the exclusion of most chosen lines.**

Armies clashed, armed with strange, powerful weapons. Machines swarmed through the air, ran in sleek low-slung deadliness over the earth. Men died, Protégé soldiers, civilians.

the new nobility would fight among themselves, first with protégé armies. rivalry would build.

A long sleek shape dropped on a pillar of white fire into a desert landscape. Landing legs extended, and a hatchway opened.

technological progress would continue to an interplanetary-

transport level, then fossilize. none of the contending factions on visager could afford to divert sufficient resources to reestablish stardrive.

A huge city, buildings reaching for the sun. It took a moment for John to recognize it as Oathtaking, and then only by the shape of the circular harbor and the volcanoes that ringed it. Suddenly one of the giant towers vanished in an eye-searing flash.

one party among the nobility attempts to use the fallen chosen lines against the other. instead they rise against the nobility planet-wide, attempting to restore the old system. the protégés revolt. maximum entropy results.

Rings of violet fire expanded over the sites of cities, rising until the fireballs spread out against the top of the atmosphere.

probability 87%, ±6%, Center added.

John sat, shaken. *I'm just a kid,* he thought. Not even good enough to make the Test of Life, a gimp. *What'm I supposed to do about all this?*

"Why can't you do something?" he asked. "You came from the stars, you've got another Federation—land a starship and *tell* people what to do!"

"We can't," Raj said. "First, we don't have the resources. There are only four worlds in the Federation, so far. There are *thousands* needing attention. And even if we could, that would just set us up for another cycle of empire, decline and war like the First Federation. The new worlds have to climb out on their own with minimal interference, and do so in the right way."

correct, Center said. **a true federation may achieve stability in an dynamic and mobile sense. a hegemony imposed from without could not.**

"You want me to . . . somehow to stop the Chosen from taking things over," John said.

He felt a flush of excitement. It was a little like what he'd felt last week, when the housemaid looked back over her shoulder at him as she plumped the pillows and smiled, and he knew he *could* right there and then if he wanted to. But it was stronger, deeper. *He* could affect the destiny of a whole planet. *Save* the whole world. He, John Hosten with a pimple on his nose and a foot that still ached when he used it too hard, despite all the surgeons could do.

specifically, you will act to strengthen the republic of santander, Center said. **with my advice and that of Raj Whitehall, you will rise quickly and be in a position to influence policy. such intervention will drastically increase the probability of the republic emerging as the dominant factor in the cycle of wars which will begin in the next two decades.**

"The Republic will conquer . . . unite the world?"

no. that probability is less than 12%, ±3. observe:

Troops in the brown uniforms and round hats of the Republic marched out of a city: Arena, in the Sierra. Crowds lined the streets, hooting and whistling. Sometimes they threw things.

santander lacks the organizational infrastructure to forcefully integrate foreign territories.

"No staying power," Raj amplified. "They can get into wars, and if you push them to the wall they can mobilize like hell, but when it's less vital than that, they don't like paying the butcher's bill or the money either. They'll get into wars occasionally, and piss away men and equipment and then decide it's no fun and go home."

correct. santander will exercise a general hegemony, increasingly cultural and economic rather than military. this will inaugurate a period of intense competition within a framework of minimal government. such episodes are unstable but tend to rapid technological innovation.

"The Republic will go into space because it gives you as much glory as war and it's less frustrating," Raj explained.

observe:

A cylinder taller than a building lifted into the air in a blue-white discharge. The next view was strange: a white-streaked blue disk floating in utter blackness, ringed by unwinking stars. It wasn't until John saw the outline of a continent that he realized he was seeing Visager from space.

From space! he thought. A construct of girders floated across the vision. Men in spacesuits flitted around it and incomprehensible machines with arms like crabs.

**a tanaki displacement net, Center said. in this scenario, visager
would enter the second federation without prior political
unification. an unusual development.**

The visions ceased, leaving only a mirrored wall at the end of a
strange study.

Raj handed him a glass and sat in the chair facing him. John took
a cautious sip of the sweet wine.

"Lad, you can leave here with no memories of what you've seen
and heard," he said calmly. "Or you can leave here as Center's agent—
as I was Center's agent—to help get this planet out of the dead-end
it's trapped in and set its people free."

"I'll do it," John blurted, then flushed again.

The words seemed to have come directly from his mouth without
passing through his brain.

Raj shook his head. "This isn't a game, John. You could die. You
quite probably *will* die."

The mirrored wall dissolved into its impossibly real pictures. This
time they were much more personal. John—an older John—lay
beside a hedgerow. His face was slack, eyes unblinking in the thin
gray mist of rain. One hand lay on his stomach, a blue bulge of
intestine showing around the fingers.

John sat stripped to the waist in a metal chair, waist and limbs
and neck held by padded clamps; another device of levers and screws
held his mouth open. A single bulb shone down from the ceiling. A
Fourth Bureau specialist dressed in a shiny bib apron stepped up to
him with a curved tool in his hands.

"Shame, Hosten, shame," he said. "You have neglected your
teeth. Still, I think this nerve is still sensitive."

The curved shape of stainless steel probed and then thrust. The
body in the chair convulsed and screamed a fine mist of blood into
the cellar's dark air.

Another John stood in the dock of a courtroom. The Republic's
flag stood on the wall behind the panel of judges. They whispered
together, and then one of them raised his head.

"John Hosten, this court finds you guilty as charged of treason
and espionage. You will be taken from this place to the National

Prison, and there hung by the neck until dead. May God have mercy on your soul."

The visions died. John touched his tongue to his lips. "I'm not afraid to die," he whispered. Then aloud: "I'm not afraid, and I know my duty. I'll do what you ask, no matter how long it takes, no matter what the risks."

"Good lad," Raj said quietly, and gripped his shoulder. "You and your brother will both do your best."

Jeffrey Farr looked at the mirrored sphere. "Seems like I'm going to be in action a lot," he said.

He tried to sound calm, but the quaver was in his voice again. Those scenes of himself dying—gut-shot, burned, drowned, the Chosen executioners with whips made of steel-hook chains—they were more real than anything he'd ever seen. He could *feel* it. . . .

"If you say yes," Raj said. "I'm not going to lie to you, son. Soldiering isn't a safe profession; and if you refuse, the final war between the Land and your country may not be for a generation or more, possibly two."

"Yeah, and the horse might learn to sing," Jeffrey said. He was a little surprised at Raj's chuckle. "And if I had kids, they'd be around when it happened,, anyway. I'll do it. Somebody's got to. A Farr does what has to be done."

Unconsciously, his voice took on another tone with the last words; Raj nodded approvingly and handed him the balloon snifter.

"Good lad."

"There's just one thing," Jeffrey said. He looked up; the . . . computer . . . wasn't there—wasn't anywhere, specifically, while he was in its mind—but that helped.

"Just one thing. If, ah, Center can predict things, and manipulate them the way you're saying, couldn't you change the Chosen? You showed me what would happen if the Chosen took over by *themselves*, didn't you? Left to themselves, on their own."

correct. Raj nodded.

"So, you could help *them*, and sort of twist things around so that _they_ built a star-transport system? It'd be easy enough, with you showing all the technical stuff they had to do every step of the way, not like reinventing it, not really. And you could get whoever you picked to the top in Chosen politics, couldn't you? Make 'em next thing to a living god."

Raj leaned back in his chair. "Smart lad," he said admiringly. "But then, you've got a different perspective on it than your brother—your brother to be, I mean."

probability of medium-term success with such a course of action is 62%, ±10, Center said. **unusually high degree of uncertainty due to stochastic factors. we cannot be certain of coming into contact with a suitable chosen representative. this course of action is contraindicated by other factors, however.**

Raj nodded, his hard dark face bleak. "It might be possible to get Visager back into interstellar space with the Chosen running things," he said. "But you couldn't change them into something we'd _want_ in interstellar space—not without redesigning their society from the ground up, and that would be impossibly difficult."

impressionistic but correct. observe:

The blank hemisphere cleared. Once again Jeffrey saw the blue-white shape of a planet from space, but this time it was not Visager. A shimmering appeared, and spots blinked into existence in the darkness above the planet, tiny until the perspective snapped closer. That showed huge metal shapes—spaceships, he supposed—with the sunburst of the Land on their flanks. Doors opened in their sides, and smaller shapes fell towards the cloud-streaked blue world, shapes with wings and a sleek shark-shape to them. The viewpoint followed them down in a dizzying plunge, through atmosphere and cherry heat, down to the ground. They landed amid flames and rubble, burning vegetation, and shattered buildings. Ramps slid down, and gun-tubs in the assault transports fired bolts that cut paths of thunderous vacuum through the air to clear the perimeter of the landing zone. War machines slid down the ramps on cushions of air, their massive armor bristling with weapons and sensors.

A head appeared in the turret of one of the war machines as it slid to earth and nosed up, dirt howling from around its skirts. The man's helmet visor was flipped up, and his grin was like something out of the deep oceans.

"Let's do it, people," he said. "Let's *go*."

probability of successful redesign of chosen culture is 12%, ±6, Center said.

"We could put them on top; we could even get them out to the stars," Raj said. "But they'd still attack anything that moved—it's their basic imperative."

"Yeah, I can see that," Jeffrey said, linking and cracking his fingers—then looking down suddenly, conscious that his *real* hands weren't moving at all, somewhere he couldn't see. Raj nodded wryly. *And for him, it's like this all the time. It felt* real, *but . . .*

"Yeah," he went on. "They've got to be stopped, here and now."

"You and your brother will do it," Raj said. "With our help."

—and the meteorite was smooth under his fingers.

John Hosten half fell to the dock. *Raj?* he thought. *Center?* Was this some sort of crazy dream? Maybe he was realty back in his bunk at school, waiting for reveille.

The dockers were looking at him, dull curiosity, or simply noting that he was something moving. Jeffrey Farr three-quarters fell down the net after him, his face stunned and slack. John caught him automatically, pushing the limp form against the cargo net so that he could cling and support himself. "*You too?*"

do not show distress, the machine-voice said in his mind.

Pull yourselves together, lads, Raj continued. The voice was equally silent, but it had the modulation of human speech, without the sense of cold bottomless depth that Center's carried.

"John! Jeffrey!"

There was anger in the adults voices. Jeffrey's face was pale enough that the freckles stood out like birthmarks, but he smiled his gap-toothed grin.

"Hey, we're in some shit now, man." "Lets go."

"Say good-bye to your father," Sally Hosten said.

John stepped forward. "Sir."

Karl gave a tiny forward jerk of his head. "*Min sohn.*"

He extended his hand; John stared at it in surprise for an instant. That was the greeting among equals. Then he bowed and took it. The impersonal power clamped briefly on his. A servant came forward at Karl's signal.

"Here," Karl said. He handed John a cloth-wrapped bundle. Within was a gunbelt and revolver. "This was my father's. You should have it. This and my name are all that Fate allows me to leave you."

Thh . . . thank you, sir," John said.

His eyes prickled, but he fought the feeling down. *Why now?* Even by Chosen standards, Karl had never been a demonstrative man.

"You are a boy of good character," Karl said. "If I have ever been less than a father to you, the fault is mine. Your mother and I have parted but for reasons each thinks honorable. Obey your mother; work hard, be disciplined, be brave."

"Yes sir," John said.

Karl hesitated for an instant, began to turn away. Then he swallowed and continued: "You will always be welcome among the Chosen, boy, while I live."

He saluted, fist outstretched. John answered it for the first time— *for the last time,* he realized, as his father strode away with the same stiff-backed carriage.

"Good-bye, sib," Gerta Hosten said. She drew him into a brief hug, leaving him speechless at the display of emotion. "Watch your back among the Santies."

Heinrich clasped hands and thumped him on the shoulder. "The Land's loss but maybe your gain," he said. "Come visit sometime, sprout, when you're rich and famous."

John watched them leave and took a deep breath. "Good-bye, Maria," he said to the Protégé nursemaid.

She folded him to her broad bosom. "Good-bye, little master. Call Maria if you ever need her," she said in her slurred lower-class Landisch.

Her husband bowed and touched John's hand to his forehead.

He was a bear-broad man with grizzled black hair. "I, too, young master. Now, go. Your mother waits for you."

John did an about-face and began walking towards the gangplank, his face rigid. His mother's hand took his; he squeezed it for a moment, then freed himself.

No more tears, he thought. That's for kids. I have to be a man, now.

CHAPTER TWO

1227 A.F.
310 Y.O.

"People are going to think we're weird," Jeffrey said, panting.

"Hell, we *are* weird, Jeff," John replied.

They fell silent as they raced up the slopes of Signal Hill, past picnicking families and students—it was part of the University Park. The switchbacks were rough enough, but John cut between them whenever there weren't any flowerbeds on the slopes. At last they stood on the paved summit, amid planters and trees in big pots and sightseers paying twenty-five centimes apiece to look through pivot-mounted binoculars at the famous view over Santander City. Jeffrey threw his hand-weights to a bench and groaned, ducking his head into a fountain and blowing like a grampus before he drank.

John stood, concentrating on ignoring the ache in his right foot, drinking slowly from a water bottle he carried at his waist. Signal Hill was two hundred meters, the highest land in the city and right above a bend in the Santander River. From here he could see most of the capital of the Republic: Capitol Square to the northwest, and the cathedral beyond it; the executive mansion with its pillars and green copper roof off to the east, at the end of embassy row. The Basin District, the ancient beginnings of Santander City, was below the hill in an oxbow curve of the river, and the canal basin was on the south bank, amid the factories and working-class districts. Southward the urban sprawl vanished in haze; northward you could just make out the wooded hills that carried the elite suburbs.

The roar of traffic was muted here, the hissing-spark clatter of streetcars, the underground rumble of the subway, the sound of horses and the increasing number of steamcars, even the burbling roar of the odd gas-engine vehicle. He could smell nothing but hot stone and the cool green smells of the park, also a welcome change from most of the city. The sun was red on the western horizon, still bright up here, but as he watched the streetlights came on. They traced fairy-lantern patterns of light over the rolling cityscape, amidst the mellow golden glow of gaslights and the harsher electric glare along the main streets.

He grew conscious of someone watching him: a girl about his own age, but not a student—her calf-length dress was too stylish, and the little hat perched on one side of her head held a quetzal plume. She smiled as he met her eyes, then turned to talk to her matronly companion.

"Looking you over, stud," Jeff said.

John half-grinned. Objectively, he knew he was good-looking enough; tall like his father, with yellow-blond hair and a square-chinned face. And he kept himself in good enough shape . . . *but they don't know.* His foot twinged.

He punched his brother on the arm. "Like Doreen down in the canteen?" he said. They sat on the grass and passed a towel back and forth. "Thank me for it, bro. If I hadn't gotten you into this weird Chosen stuff you'd still be a weed and skinny. She's eating you with her eyes, my man."

Jeffrey Farr had filled out, although he'd always be slimmer than the son of his foster-mother. Only a trace of adolescent awkwardness remained, and his long bony face was firming towards adulthood.

"Doreen? *All* she'll do is look. Her folks are Reformed Baptist, you know; I've got about as much chance of seeing her skirt up as I do of getting the Archbishop flat. I tried pinching her butt and she mashed my toe so hard I dropped my tray."

John clucked his tongue. "The Archbishop's butt? Hell, I didn't know you had a taste for older women. . . . Pax, pax!"

Jeffrey lit a slightly sweat-dampened cigarette. "Those things will kill you," John said, refusing the offered pack.

"And the other Officers Training Corps cadets will think I'm a pansy if I don't smoke," Jeffrey said, leaning his elbow on his knee and looking out over the city. "I'll admit, the phys ed side of it is easier because of all this exercise shit you talked me into."

"How's Maurice taking you going into the army?"

Jeffrey shrugged. "Dad's just surprised, is all. Every Farr for five generations has been navy."

"Since the days of wooden ships and iron men," John agreed.

The Republic hadn't had a major land war in nearly seventy years, and the army was tiny and ill-funded. The navy was another matter, since it had always been policy not to let the Empire gain too big an edge.

"More like iron cannon and wooden heads. When do you hear from the diplomatic service?"

"Next week," John said. "But I'm pretty confident."

"You've got the marks for it."

Thanks to Center, he said silently.

Jeffrey's green eyes narrowed and he shook his head. *Even Center can't make a silk purse out of a sow's udder,* he replied, through the relay that the ancient computer provided.

correct, Center said. **i have merely shortened the period of instruction and made possible a broader-based course of study.**

Think we'll have enough time before the Chosen take on the Empire? Jeff thought.

chosen-imperial war within the next two years is a 17% ±3 probability. within the next four, 53% ±5. within the next six, 92% ±7.

"I should have my commission in a year," Jeff said. "You'll be a member in good standing of the striped-pants-and-spooks brigade."

"Much good it'll do the Empire," John said gloomily, splitting a grass stem between his thumbs.

North lay the rest of the Republic, and the Gut—the narrow

waterway that divided the mainland along most of its width. North of the Gut was the Universal Empire, largest of Visager's nations, potentially the richest, and for centuries the most powerful. Those centuries were generations gone.

"And we're doing fuck-all!" Jeff said. "I know politicians are supposed to be dimwits, but the staff over at the Pyramid are even worse, and the admiralty isn't much better, apart from Dad."

"*We're* doing all we can," John said calmly. "The *Republic* isn't doing much yet, but some people see what's coming—Maurice, for example. And he's a rear admiral, now. We ought to have some time after they attack the Empire."

"I suppose so," Jeff sighed. "Hey, you keep me on an even keel, did I ever tell you that? Yeah, even the Chosen aren't crazy enough to take on us and the Empire at once. When that starts, people will sit up and take notice—even *them*." He nodded towards the capitol building's dome.

"Maurice sometimes doubts they'd notice if the Fleet of the Chosen steamed up the river and began shelling them," John said lightly.

"Dad's a pessimist. C'mon, let's get back to the dorm, shower, and grab a hamburger. Maybe Doreen will take pity on me."

"Teamwork, teamwork, you morons!" Gerta Hosten gasped, hearing the others stumble. "Johan, your turn on point."

The jungle trail was narrow and slick with mud. The improvised stretcher of poles and vines was awkward, would have been awkward even without the mumbling, tossing form of the boy strapped to it. His leg was splinted with branches; the lianas that bound it to the wood were half-buried in swollen-purple flesh.

Gerta dug her heels in and waited until the stretcher came level, then sheathed her knife and took the left front pole. The man she was relieving worked his fingers for a moment, drew his bowie and plunged forward to slash a way for his comrades. She took the left front pole, Heinrich carried both rear poles, and Elke Tirnwitz was on the right front. Johan Kloster moved farther ahead, chopping his way through the vines. Etkar Summeldorf was getting the free ride; he'd broken a leg spearing a crocodile that tried to snack on them while they forded a river yesterday.

They'd eaten a fair bit of the croc. You got nothing supplied in the team-endurance event that concluded the Test of Life. Well, almost nothing: a pair of shorts, a pair of sandals, a cloth halter if you were a girl, and a bowie knife. Then they dropped you and four teammates down a sliderope from a dirigible into the Kopenrung Mountains along the north side of the Land, and you made the best time you could to the pickup station. Nobody told you exactly where that was, either. The Chosen of the Land didn't need to have their hands held. If you couldn't make it, the Chosen didn't need you— and you had better *all* make it. The Chosen didn't need selfish grandstanders, either.

"Leave me," Etkar mumbled. "Leave me. Go."

"We *can't* leave you, you stupid git," Elke said in a voice hoarse with worry and fatigue—they were an item, and besides, Etkar had probably saved their lives at the river. "This is a team event. We'd all drop a hundred points if we left you behind."

They'd *all* saved each other's lives.

It was hot: thirty-eight degrees, at least, and steambath humid. Bad even by the Land's standards. The Kopenrungs were in the far north, nearest to the equator. That was one reason they'd never been intensively developed, that and the constant steep slopes and the lateritic soils. And the leeches, the mosquitoes, the wild boar and wild buffalo and leopards and constant thunderstorms and tornadoes.

Sweat trickled down her skin, adding to the greasy film already there and stinging in the insect bites and budding jungle sores. The rough wood pulled at her arm and abraded the calluses on her palm. Muscles in her lower back complained as she leaned back against the weight of the stretcher and the slope. Branches and leaves swatted at her face.

"Heinrich, *min brueder*," Gerta said, pacing the words to the muscular effort. "Tell me again how wonderful it is to be Chosen."

Elke made a sharp hissing sound with her teeth. The Fourth Bureau was unlikely to be listening, but you never knew. Heinrich grunted a chuckle.

"*Shays,*" Johan swore. "Shit." There was wonder in his tone.

"What is it?" Gerta asked. She couldn't see more than a few paces through the undergrowth; this section of hillside had burned off a while ago, and the second growth was rank.

"We made it."

"*What?*" in three strong young voices.

"We made it! That *was* the clearing we saw back on the crest!"

None of them spoke; they didn't slow down, either. Gerta managed a sweat-blurred glimpse at the mist-shrouded, jungle-covered mountains ahead. They looked precisely like the mist-shrouded, jungle-clad mountains she'd been staring at for the entire past week.

When they broke out of the cover onto the little bench-plateau they broke into a trot by sheer reflex. There were pavilions ahead, and a crowd of people—officers, officials, Protégé servants. A doctor ran forward at the sight of the stretcher.

"How is he?" Elke said.

The doctor looked up and frowned. "The leg doesn't look too bad. Now. He'd have lost it in another twenty hours."

Protégés held out trays. Gerta grabbed at a ceramic tumbler and drank, long and carefully. It was orange juice, slightly salted. She shut her eyes for an instant of pure bliss.

A man cleared his throat. She opened her eyes and snapped to attention with the other members of her team; all but Ektar, who was out with a syringe of morphine in his arm.

The man was elderly, bald, stringy-muscular. He had colonel's pips on the shoulders of his summer-weight uniform, and a smile like Death in a good mood on his wrinkled, bony face. She was acutely conscious of the ring on the third finger of his left hand, an intertwined circlet of iron and gold. The Chosen ring.

"Gerta Hosten, Heinrich Hosten, Johan Kloster, Elke Tirnwitz, Etkar Summeldorf. The ceremony will come later, of course, but it is my honor to inform you that each of you has achieved at least the minimum necessary score in the Test of Life. Accordingly, at the age of eighteen years and six months, you will be enrolled among the Chosen of the Land. Congratulations."

One of the others whooped. Gerta couldn't tell which; she was too busy keeping herself erect. Six months of examinations, tests, psychological tests, tests of nerve, tests of intelligence, tests of ability to endure stress; all topped off with seven hellish days in the Kopenrung jungles—and it was *over*.

I'm not going to be a Washout. She'd decided long ago to kill herself rather than endure that; a large proportion of Washouts did. *Born in a Protégé cottage, and I'm* Chosen *of the Land.*

She snapped off a salute, arm outstretched and fist clenched. A blood-boil burst and left red running down her mouth as she grinned; the pain was a sharp stab, but she didn't give a damn.

"You are a very wealthy young man," the River Electric Company executive said, looking down at the statement in surprise.

"I had some seed money from my stepfather," John explained. "The rest of it comes from commodities deals, mainly." Courtesy of Center's analysis; that made things childishly easy. "And investment in Western Petroleum."

His formal neckcloth felt a little tight; he suppressed an impulse to fiddle with it. The room was on the seventh story of one of the new office buildings between the Eastern Highway and the river, with an overhead fan and shuttered windows that made it cool even on the hot summer's day. The River Electric exec had very little on the broad ebony expanse of his desk, just a blotter and a telephone with a sea-ivory handset. And the plans John had sent in.

"This . . ."

"Mercury-arc rectifier," John supplied helpfully.

"Rectifier, yes, seems to be very ingenious," the executive said.

He was a plump little man with bifocals, wearing a rather dandified cream-colored jacket and blue neckcloth. There was a parrots feather in the band of his trilby where it hung on the rack by the door.

"However," he went on, "at present the River Electric Company is engaged in an extensive, a very extensive, investment program in primary generating capacity. Why should we undertake a risky new venture which will require tying up capital in new manufacturing plant?"

John leaned forward. "That's just it, Mr. Henforth. The rectifier will *save* capital by reducing transmission losses. The expense of installing them will be considerably less than the savings in raw generating capacity. *And* the construction can be subcontracted. There are a lot of firms here in the capital, or anywhere in the Eastern Provinces—Tonsville, say, or Ensburg—who could handle this. River Electric's primary focus on hydraulic turbines and turbogenerators wouldn't be affected."

Henforth steepled his fingers and waited.

"And," John went on after the silence stretched, "I'd be willing to buy say, five hundred thousand shares of River Electric at par. Also licensing fees from the patent would be assigned."

"It's definitely an interesting proposition," Henforth said, smiling. "Come, we'll go up to the executive lounge on the roof and discuss this further with some of our technical people." He shook his head. "A young man of your capacities is wasted in the diplomatic service, Mr. Hosten. Wasted."

"Skirmish order!"

The infantry platoon fanned out, three meters between each man, in two long lines. The first line jogged forward across the rocky pasture, their fixed bayonets glittering in the chilly upland air. Fifty meters forward they went to ground, taking cover behind ridges and boulders. The second line moved up and leapfrogged forward in turn.

Ensign Jeffrey Farr watched carefully through his field-glasses. The movement was carried out with precision. *Good men,* he thought. The Republic's army wasn't large, only seventy thousand men. It wasn't particularly well-paid or equipped, either; the men mostly enlisted because it was the employer of last resort. Bottle troubles, wife troubles, farm kids bored beyond endurance with watching the south end of a northbound plowhorse, sheer inability to cope with the chaotic demands of civilian life in the Republic's fast-growing cities. They could still make good soldiers if you gave them the right training, and trained men would be invaluable when the balloon went up. The provincial militias were supposed to be federalized in time of war, but as they stood he had little confidence in them.

He raised his hand in a signal. The platoon sergeant blew a sharp blast on his whistle and the men rose from the field, slapping at the dust on their brown tunic jackets. Their stubbled faces looked impassive and tired after the month of field exercises through the mountains.

"Good work, Ensign," his company commander nodded. Captain Daniels was a thickset man of forty—promotion was slow in the peacetime army—with a scar across one cheek where a Union bullet had just missed taking off his face in a skirmish twenty years ago.

"Very good work," the staff observer said. "I notice you're spreading the skirmish line thinner."

"Yes, sir," Jeff said. He nodded at an infantryman jogging by with his weapon at the trail. It was a bolt-action model with six cartridges in a tube magazine below the barrel. "Everyone's getting magazine rifles these days, except the Imperials, and new designs are coming fast and furious. We've got to disperse formations more."

Although to hear some of the fogies talk, they expected to fight in shoulder-to-shoulder ranks like Civil War troops equipped with rifle-muskets.

"Yes, I read that article of yours in the *Armed Forces Quarterly,*" the staff type said. "You think nitro powders will be adopted for small arms?"

major belmody, Center said. A list of biographical data followed.

The major looked pretty sharp, if a little elegant for the field in his greatcoat and red throat-tabs and polished Sam Browne. And being a younger son of the Belmody Mills Belmodys probably hadn't hurt his rise through the officer corps either; thirty-two was damned young to get that high.

"I'm certain of it, sir," Jeff said. The Belmodys were big in chemicals and mining explosives. "No smoke, less fouling, and much higher muzzle velocities, flatter trajectories, smaller calibers so the troops can carry more ammo."

Captain Daniels spoke unexpectedly. "*I* don't trust jacketed bullets," he said. "They have a tendency to strip and then tumble when the barrel's hot."

"Sir, that's just a development problem. Gilding metal can't take the temperatures of high-velocity rounds. Cupronickel, or straight copper, that's what needed."

The older officer smiled. "Ensign, I wish I was half as confident about anything as you are about everything."

"God knows we could use some young firebrands in this man's army," Major Belmody said. "In any case, you and Ensign Farr must dine with me tonight."

"After I see the men settled in, sir," Jeff said. The major raised an eyebrow and nodded, returning his juniors' salutes.

"You'll do, Farr," Captain Daniels said, grinning, when the staff officer's car had bounced away over the pasture with an occasional *chuff* of waste steam. "You'll go far, too, if you can learn to be a little more diplomatic about who you deliver lectures to."

Lieutenant Gerta Hosten leaned back against the upholstery of the seat and watched out the half-open window as the train clacked its way across the central plateau. The air coming in was clean; this close to Copernik the line had been electrified, and the lack of coal smoke and the pounding, chuffing sound of a steam locomotive was a little eerie. There was plenty of traffic on the broad concrete-surfaced road that flanked the railway, too, steam or animal-drawn. This was the most pleasant part of the Land, a rolling volcanic upland at a thousand meters above sea level, cooler and a little drier. The capital had been moved here from Oathtaking only a generation after the first wave of Alliance refugees arrived. Copernik's beginnings went back before the coming of the Chosen, right back to the initial settlement of Visager, but nothing remained of the pre-conquest city. Over the past generation as geothermal steam and then hydropower supplemented coal, it had also become a major manufacturing center.

Gerta watched with interest as rolling contour-plowed fields of sugar cane, rice, soya, and maize gave way to huge factory compounds. One of them held an airship assembly shed, a hundred-meter skeletal structure like a Brobdingnagian barn. The cigar-shaped hull was still a framework of girders, with only patches of hull-cladding where aluminum sheet was being riveted to the structure.

She buttoned the collar of her field-gray walking-out uniform, buckled on her gunbelt with the shoulder-strap, and took up her attaché case. Normally she'd have let her batman carry that, but there were eyes-only documents in it. Nothing ultra-secret, or she wouldn't be carrying them on a train, but procedure was procedure.

Behfel ist Behfel, she recited to herself: orders are orders. She also had a letter from John Hosten in there. Evidently he was doing well down in the Republic; he'd gotten some sort of posting in their diplomatic service.

It was a pity about John.

"Wake up, *feldwebel,*" she said.

Her batman blinked open his eyes and stood, taking down the two bags from the overhead rack. Pedro was a thickset muscular man in his thirties, strong and quick and apparently loyal as a Doberman guard dog. Also about as bright; in fact, she'd owned dogs with more mother-wit and larger vocabularies. It was policy to exclude the upper two-thirds of the intelligence gradient when recruiting soldiers and gendarmes from the Protégé caste. She had her doubts about that, and she'd always preferred bright ones as personal servants. More risk, but greater potential gain.

Behfel ist behfel.

Hie train lurched slightly as it slowed. The pantograph on the locomotive clicked amid a shower of sparks as they pulled into the Northwest Station. There were many tall blond young men in uniform there, but not the one she instinctively sought. Heinrich wouldn't be waiting for her; that wouldn't be seemly, and anyway she had to report to Intelligence HQ for debriefing.

My lovely Heinrich, she thought. I'd fuck you even if you were my birth-brother. An exaggeration, but he was a dear, and of course incest taboos didn't apply to adoptee-kin. And this time when you ask me to marry you, I'm going to say yes.

The implications of the documents in her attaché case were clear, if you could read between the paragraphs. It was time to do her eugenic duty to the Chosen; even with servants, infants took up a lot of time and effort. Best do it while there was time.

In a couple of years, they were all going to be very, very busy.

CHAPTER THREE

1233 A.F.
317 Y.O.

Looks different from a Protégé's point of view, John Hosten thought, carefully slumping his shoulders.

He was walking the streets of Oathtaking in the drab cotton coat and breeches of some middling Protégé worker. He could have been a warehouse clerk, or a store-checker; his hair had been dyed brown, but the best protection was sheer swarming numbers and the fact that nobody *looked* at an average Proti.

He'd forgotten how *hot* the damned place was, too. Hot, the air thick and wet and saturated with coal smoke and smells. Bigger than he remembered from his childhood; the villas went further up the slopes of the volcanoes, the factories were larger and the smokestacks higher, there were more overhead power lines, workers hanging out the sides of the overburdened trolley cars. And many, many more powered vehicles on the streets. Most of them were in army gray, steam-powered trucks and haulers built to half a dozen standard models. A fair number of luxury cars, too, some of them imported models from the Republic. Half a dozen Protégés went by on a gang-bicycle, which was a very clever invention, when you thought about it.

Too heavy for one to pedal—it takes six. Factory workers can use them to commute, but they don't get personal mobility.

Cleverness wasn't a wholly positive quality. . . .

He ducked into the brothel's front door; it wasn't hard to find, having BROTHEL #22A7-B, PROTÉGÉ, CLASS 6-B printed on the front door, with a graphic symbol for illiterates. Inside was a depressingly bare waiting room with a brick floor and girls sitting around the walls on wood-slat benches, naked save for cotton briefs, folded towels beside them, and a number on the wall above each head below a lightbulb. They didn't look as run-down as you'd expect, but then few of them were professionals. Temporary service in a place like this was a standard penalty for minor infractions of workplace regulations. A staircase led to cubicles above, and a clerk sat behind an iron grille just inside the door; the place smelled of sweat, harsh disinfectant, and spilled beer.

A hulk stood nearby, an iron-bound club thonged to his massive wrist, picking at his teeth with the thumbnail of his other hand. Probably a retired policeman; he looked John over once, and tapped the head of the club warningly against the stucco. John cringed realistically, turning and ducking his head.

"Prices are posted," the clerk said in a monotone; she was in her fifties, flabby with a starchy diet and lack of exercise. "You want I should read 'em? Booze is extra."

John pushed iron counters across the table and through the scoop trough beneath the iron grille. Fingers arranged them in a pattern; they were from Zeizin Shipbuilding AG, one of the bigger firms.

recognition, Center said. Pointers dropped across the clerk's pasty face indicating pupil dilation and temperature differentials. **97%, ±2.**

That was about as definite as it got; now the question was whether this was his real contact, or whether the Fourth Bureau had penetrated the ring and was waiting for him. His palms were damp, and he swallowed sour bile, eyes flickering to the doors. He wasn't carrying a weapon; it would have been insanely risky, here—a Protégé caught armed would be *lucky* to be executed on the spot. And when they found his *geburtsnumero* . . .

subject is contact, Center reassured him. **anxiety levels are compatible. 73%, ±5.**

A whole *hell* of a lot less certain than the first projection, but still reassuring. A little.

The clerk nodded and pressed a button on her side of the counter. A light went on with a *tick* over the girl closest to the stair; she stood with a mechanical smile and picked up her towel.

The upper corridor was fairly quiet, in midafternoon; a row of cubicles stood on either side, with curtains hung before them on rings and a shower at one end. John's guide pulled aside a numbered curtain and ducked through.

He followed. Within was a single cot, a washstand and tap, and a jar of antiseptic soap . . . and crouched in a corner, the burly form of Angelo Pesalozi. He stood, bear-burly, more gray than John remembered.

"Young Master Johan," he rumbled.

John extended his hand. "No man's master now, Angelo," he said, smiling.

The hand of Karl Hosten's driver and personal factotum closed on his with controlled strength. John matched it, and Angelo grinned.

"You have not grown soft," he said. "Come, we should do our business quickly."

The girl put her foot on the cot and began to push on it, irregularly at first and then rhythmically; with vocal accompaniment, it was a remarkably convincing chorus of squeaks and groans.

"A minute," John said. "My life is at risk here, too, and will be again, and I must understand. Karl Hosten is a good master, and your own daughter is one of the Chosen. Why are you ready to work against them?"

Brown eyes met his somberly. "He is a good master, but I would have no master at all, and be my own man. I have four children; because one is a lord, should the others be slaves, and my grandchildren? There are more bad masters than good."

He jerked his head towards the girl. "She dropped a tray of insulator parts, and so she must whore here for a month — is this justice? If a man speaks against the masters when they send his wife to another plantation, or take his children for soldiers, his brother for the mines, he is hung in an iron cage at the crossroads to die—is this justice? No, the rule of the Chosen is an offense against God. It must cease, even if I die for it."

John met his eyes for a long moment. **subject is sincere; probability**—He silenced the computer with a thought. *I know.*

And Angelo had always been kind to a boy with a crippled foot . . .

"Yes," John said. "That is so, Angelo."

The Protégé nodded and produced folded papers from inside his jacket; they were damp with sweat, but legible.

"These I took from the wastebasket, before the daily burning," he said. "Here is an order, concerning five airships—"

"I worry about that boy," Sally Farr said.

"I don't," Maurice Farr replied.

They were sitting on the terrace of the naval commandants quarters, overlooking Charsson and its port. This was the northernmost part of the Republic of Santander, hence the hottest; the shores of the Gut were warmer still, protected from continental breezes by mountains on both sides. The hot, dry summer had just begun; flowers gleamed about the big whitewashed house, and the tessellated brick pavement of the terrace was dappled by the shade of the royal palms and evergreen oak planted around it. The road ran down the mountainside in dramatic switchbacks; there were villas on either side, officers' quarters and middle-class suburbs up out of the heat of the old city around the J-shaped harbor.

The roofs down there were mostly low-pitched and of reddish clay tile; it looked more like an Imperial city from the lands just north of the Gut than like the rest of Santander. Much of the population was Imperial, too—there had been a steady drift of migrant laborers in the past couple of generations, looking for better-paid work in the growing mines and factories and irrigation farms.

Farr's eyes went to the dockyards. One of his armored cruisers was in the graving dock, with a cracked shaft on her central screw. The other four ships of the squadron were refitting as well; when everything was ready he'd take them up the Gut on a show-the-flag cruise.

"John," he continued, "is on his way to becoming a very wealthy young man. *And* he's doing well in the diplomatic service.

"Thank you," he went on to the steward bringing him his afternoon gin and tonic. Sally rattled the ice in hers.

"He has no social life," she said. "I keep introducing him to nice girls, and nothing happens. All he does is study and work. The doctors say he should be . . . umm, functional . . . but I worry."

Maurice turned his head to hide a quick smile. From what Jeffrey told him, John had been seen occasionally with girls who *weren't* particularly nice. Enough to prove that the infant vasectomy the Chosen doctors had done *hadn't* caused any irreparable harm in that respect, at least.

"Do you know something I don't?" Sally said sharply.

"Let's put it this way, my dear: there are certain things that a young man does not generally discuss with his mother."

"Oh."

Smart, Maurice thought fondly. *Pretty, too.*

Sally was looking remarkably cool and elegant in her white and cream linen outfit and broad straw hat, the pleated skirt daringly an inch above the ankle. Only a little gray in the long brown hair, no more than in his. You'd never know she'd had four children.

"Besides," he went on, "he's been assigned to the embassy in Ciano. From what I know of the tailcoat squadron there, social life is about all he'll have time for—it's a diplomat's main function. Count on it, he'll meet *plenty* of nice girls there."

"Oh." Sally's tone wavered a little at the thought. "Nice *Imperial* girls. Well, I suppose . . ." She shrugged.

She looked downslope in her turn. There were fortifications there, everything from the bastion-and-ravelin systems set up centuries ago to defend against roundshot to modern concrete-and-steel bunkers with heavy naval guns.

"John seems to think that there's going to be war," she said. "Jeffrey, too."

Maurice nodded somberly. "I wouldn't be surprised. War between the Chosen and the Empire, at least."

"But surely we wouldn't be involved!" Sally protested.

"Not at first," Maurice said slowly. "Not for a while."

"Thank goodness Jeffrey's in the army, then," she said. The Republic of Santander had no land border with either of the two contending powers. "And John's safe in the diplomatic corps."

"You dance divinely, Giovanni," Pia del'Cuomo said. "It is not fair. You are tall, you are handsome, you are clever, you are rich, and you dance so well. Beware, lest God send you a misfortune."

"I've already had a few from Him," John Hosten said, keeping his tone light and whirling the girl through the waltz. The ballroom was full of graceful swirling movement, gowns and uniforms and black formal suits, jewels and flowers and fans. "But He brought me to Ciano to meet you, so he can't be really angry with me."

Pia was just twenty, old for an Imperial woman of noble birth to be unmarried, and four years younger than him. Also unlike most Imperials of her sex and station, she didn't think giggles and inanities were the only way to talk to a man. She was very pretty indeed, besides, something he was acutely conscious of with their hands linked and one arm around her narrow waist.

No, not pretty—beautiful, he thought.

Big russet-colored eyes, heart-shaped face, creamy skin showing to advantage in the glittering low-cut, long-skirted white ballgown, and glossy brown hair piled up under a diamond tiara. Best of all, she seemed to like *him*.

The music came to a stop, and they stood for a moment smiling at each other while the crowd applauded the orchestra.

"If jealous eyes were daggers, I would be stabbed to death," Pia said with a trace of satisfaction. "It is entertaining, after being an old maid for years. My father has been muttering that if I wished to do nothing but read books and live single, I should have found a vocation before I left the convent school."

John snorted. "Not likely."

"I would have made a *very* poor nun, it is true," Pia said

demurely. "And then I could not have gone on to so many picnics and balls and to the opera with a handsome young officer of the Santander embassy. . . ."

"A glass of punch?" he said.

Pia put her hand on his arm as he led her to the punch table. The white-coated steward handed them glasses; it was a fruit punch with white wine, cool and tart.

"You are worried, John," she said in English. Hers was nearly as good as his Imperial, and her voice had turned serious.

"Yes," he sighed.

"Your conversations with my father, they have not gone well?"

Even for an Imperial commander, Count Benito del'Cuomo was a blinkered, hidebound. . . . With an effort, John pushed the image of the white muttonchop whiskers out of his mind.

"No," he said. "He doesn't take the Chosen seriously."

Pia sipped at her punch and nodded to her chaperone where she sat with the other matrons against one wall. The older woman—some sort of poor-relation hanger-on of the del'Cuomos—frowned when she saw that Pia was still talking with the Republic's young chargé d'affaires. They began walking slowly towards the balcony.

"Father does not think the Land will dare to attack us," she said thoughtfully. "We have so many more soldiers, so many more ships of war. Their island is tiny next to the Empire."

"Pia—" He didn't really want to talk politics, but she had reason to be concerned. "Pia, their note demanded extraterritorial rights in Corona and half a dozen other ports, control of grain exports, and exclusive investment rights in Imperial railroads."

Pia checked half a step. She *was* the daughter of the Minister of War. "That . . . that is an ultimatum!" she said. "And an impossible one."

John nodded grimly. "An excuse for war. Even if your emperor and senatorial council were to agree to it, and you're right, they couldn't, then the Chosen would find some new demand."

"Why do they warn us, then? Surely they are not so scrupulous that they hesitate at a surprise attack."

"Scarcely. I have a horrible suspicion that they *want* the Empire to be prepared, so you'll have more forces in big concentrations where they can get at them," John said.

They walked out into the cooler air and half-darkness of the great veranda. Little Adele and huge Mira were both up and full, flooding the black-and-white checkerwork marble with pale blue light, turning the giant vases filled with oleander and jessamine and bougainvillea into a pastel wonderland. The terrace ended in a fretted granite balustrade and broad steps leading down to gardens whose graveled paths glowed white amid the flowerbanks and trees. Beyond the estate wall, widely spaced lights showed where the townhouses of the nobility stood amid their walled acres, with an occasional pair of yellow kerosene-lamp headlights marking a carriage or steamcar. Westward reached a denser web of lights, mostly irregular—Ciano had a street plan originally laid out by cows, except for a few avenues driven through in recent generations. Those centered on the Imperial palace complex, a tumble of floodlit white and gilded domes.

From here they could just make out the glittering surface of the broad Pada River; the dockyards and warehouses and slums about it were jagged black shapes, no gaslights *there.* Above them two lights moved through the sky, with a low throbbing of propellers. An airship, making for the west and the great ocean port of Corona at the mouth of the Pada.

"Chosen-made," John said, nodding towards it. "Pia, your soldiers are brave, but they have no conception of what they face."

Pia leaned one hip against the balustrade, turning her fan in her fingers. "My father . . . my father is an intelligent man. But he . . . he thinks often that because things were as they were when he was young, so they must remain."

"I'm not surprised. My own government tends to think the same way." *If not to quite the same degree,* he added to himself.

They were silent for a few minutes. John felt the tension building, mostly in his stomach, it seemed. Pia was looking at him out of the corner of her eyes, the beginning of a frown of disappointment marking her brows.

"Ah . . . that is . . ." John said. "Ah, I was thinking of calling on your father again."

Pia turned to face him. "Concerning political matters?" she asked, her face calm.

An excuse trembled on his lips. Yes. *Of course.* That would be all he needed, to add cowardice to his list of failings. A crippled soul to join the foot.

"No," he said. "About something personal . . . if you would like me to."

The smile lit up her eyes before it reached her mouth. "I would like that very much," she said, and leaned forward slightly to brush her lips against his.

probability of sincerity is 92% ±3, with motivations breakdown as follows—Center began.

Shut the fuck up! John thought.

He could hear Raj's amusement at the back of his mind. ***Damned right, lad.***

Jeff's voice: *God, but that one's a looker, isn't she?* He must be getting visual feed from Center, through John's eyes.

Will you all kindly get the hell out of my love life?

"Giovanni, there are times when I think you are talking to God, or the saints, or anyone but the person you are with!"

John mumbled an apology. Pia's eyes were still glowing. "The only question is, will he consent?"

"He'd better," John said. Pia blinked in surprise and slight alarm at the expression his face took for a moment. He forced relaxation and smiled.

"Why shouldn't he?" he said. "He knows I'm not a fortune hunter"—the del'Cuomos were fabulously wealthy, but he'd managed to discreetly let the Count know the size of his own portfolio—"and if he didn't like me personally, he'd have forbidden me to see you."

Pia nodded. "Well, I do have three younger sisters," she said with sudden hard-headed shrewdness. "It isn't seemly for them to marry before me—and also, my love, I think Father thinks he can beat you down on the dowry by pretending that the marriage is impossible because you are not of the Imperial Church."

John grinned. "He's right. He *can* beat me down."

Some cold part of his mind added that Imperial properties weren't likely to be worth much in a little while.

He took a deep breath. It was like diving off a high board: once you were committed, there was no point in thinking about the drop.

"Pia, there is something I must tell you." She met his eyes steadily. "I am . . . I was born with a deformity." He averted his eyes slightly. "A clubfoot."

She let out her breath sharply. His glance snapped back to her face. She was smiling.

"Is it nothing more than that? The surgeons must have done well, then—you dance, you ride, you play the . . . what is the name? Tennis?" She flicked a hand. "It is nothing."

Breath he hadn't been conscious of holding sighed out of him. "It's why my father never accepted me," he said quietly.

She put a hand up along his face. "And if he had, you would be in the Land, preparing to attack the Empire," she said. "Also, you would not be the man I love. I have met Chosen from their embassy here, and beneath their stiff manners they are pigs. They look at me like a piece of kebab. You are not such a man."

He took the hand and kissed it. "There is more." John closed his eyes. "I cannot have children."

Pia's fingers clenched over his. He looked up and found her eyes brimming, the unshed tears bright in the starlight—and realized, with a shock like cold water, that they were for *him.*

"But—"

He nodded jerkily. "Oh, I'm . . . functional. Sterile, though, and there's nothing that can be done about it." He turned his head aside. "It was done, ah, when I was very young."

"Then you too have reason to hate the Chosen," Pia said softly. "Look at me, Giovanni."

He did. "You are the man for whom I have waited. That is all I have to say."

Jeffrey Farr smiled.

"You find our ships amusing?" the Imperial officer asked sharply. The steam launch chuffed rhythmically along the line of anchored battlewagons. He'd noticed the same attitude often in Imperial naval officers. Unlike the Army—or the squabbling committees in Ciano who set policy and budgets—they had to have *some* idea of what was going on abroad. Not that they'd admit the state their service was in, of course. It came out in a prickly defensiveness.

"Quite the contrary," Farr said smoothly. "I smiled because I recently received news that my brother, my foster-brother, is going to be married. To a lady by the name of Pia del'Cuomo."

And I don't think your ships are funny. I think they're pathetic, he added to himself.

The Imperial officer nodded, mollified and impressed. "The eldest daughter of the Minister of War? Your brother is a lucky man." He pointed. "And there they are, the pride of the Passage Fleet."

Ten of the battleships floated in the millpond-quiet bay of the military harbor, flanked by the great fortresses. Lighters were carrying out supplies, much of it coal that had to be laboriously shoveled into crane-borne buckets and hoisted again to the decks for transfer to the fuel bunkers. The ships were medium-sized, about eleven thousand tons burden, with long ram bows and a pronounced tumblehome that made them much narrower at the deck than the waterline. They each carried a heavy, stubby single 350mm gun in a round cheesebox-style turret fore and aft, and their secondary batteries in a string of smaller one-gun turrets that rose pulpit-style from the sides. Each had a string of four short smokestacks, and a wilderness upperworks of flying bridges, cranes, and signal masts.

They'd been perfectly good ships in their day. The problem was that the Empire was still building them about twenty years after their day had passed.

correct, Center observed. **roughly equivalent to British battleships of the 1880s period.**

Eighteen . . . ah. Center used the Christian calendar, which nobody on Visager did except for religious purposes. For one thing, it was based on Earth's twelve-month year, nearly thirty days shorter than this planet's rotation around its sun. For another, the numbers were inconveniently high.

Jeffrey shivered slightly. The period Center named was two thousand years past. Interstellar civilization had been born, spread, and fallen in the interim, and a new cycle was beginning.

"You're loading coal, I see," he said to the Imperial officer . . . Commodore Bragati, that was his name. "Steam up yet?"

"No, we expect to be ready in about a week," Bragati said. "Then we'll cruise down the Passage, and show those upstarts in the Land who rules those waters."

Two weeks to get ready for a show-the-flag cruise? Raj thought with disgust. *I'd say these imbeciles deserve what's probably going to happen to them, if so many civilians weren't going to be caught in it.*

"The main guns are larger than anything the Land has built," Bragati said.

low-velocity weapons with black-powder propellant, Center noted with its usual clinical detachment. **the chosen weapons are long-barreled, high-velocity rifles using nitrocellulose powders.**

He thought he detected a trace of interest, though, as well. Jeffrey smiled inwardly; the sentient computer wasn't all that much different from his grandfather and the cronies who hung around him— military history buffs and weapons fanciers to a man. Center was a hobbyist, in its way.

"And the main armor belt is twelve inches thick!"

laminated wrought iron and cast steel plate, Center went on. **radically inferior to face-hardened alloy.** Which both the Land and the Republic were using for their major warships.

None of the battleships looked ready for sea. Less excusably, neither did the scout cruisers tied up three-deep at the naval wharves, or the torpedo-boat destroyers. Or even the harbor's own torpedo boats, turtle-backed little craft.

On the other hand . . . "Well, the fleet certainly looks in good fettle," Jeffrey said diplomatically.

So they were, painted in black and dark blue with cream trim. Sailors were scrubbing coal dust off the latter even as he watched. He shuddered to think of the amount of labor it must take to repair the paintwork after a practice firing. If they did have practice firings, he had a strong suspicion that some Imperial captains might simply throw their quota of practice ammunition overboard to spare the trouble.

"Thank you for your courtesy," he said formally to the Imperial commodore.

At least he'd learned one thing. Bragati wasn't the sort of man he wanted to recruit into the stay-behind cells he and John were setting up. Too brittle to survive, given his high rank.

"Damn, I hate dying," John said as the scene blinked back to normalcy.

Or Center's idea of normalcy, which in this scenario was a street in a Chosen city—Copernik, to be specific—during the rainy season. There was no way to tell it from the real thing; every sensation was there, down to the smell of the wet rubberized rain cape over his shoulders and the slight roughness of the checked grip of the pistol he held underneath it. Watery rainy-season light probed through the dull clouds overhead, giving a pearly sheen to the granite paving blocks of the street. Buildings of brick and stone reached to the walkways on either side, shuttered and dark, frames of iron bars over their windows.

John looked down for a second at his unmarked stomach. There hadn't been any way to tell the impact of the hollowpoint rifle bullet from the real thing, either—Center's neural input gave an *exact* duplicate of the sensation of having your spleen punched out and an exit wound the size of a woman's fist in your lower back. The machine had let the scenario play through to the final blackout. His mouth still felt sour and dry. . . .

"Do you have to make it quite that realistic?" he muttered, sidling down the street, eyes scanning.

"For your own good, lad." Raj's voice was "audible" here. "Priceless training, really. You can't get more rigorous than this; and outside, you won't be able to get up and start again."

"I still—"

A sound alerted him. He whirled, drawing the pistol from the holster on his right hip and firing under his own left arm, into the planks of the door. His weight crashed into it before the ringing of the shots had died, smashing it back into the room and knocking the collapsing corpse of the Fourth Bureau agent into his companions. That gave John just enough time to snapshoot, and the secret policeman's weapon flew out of a nerveless hand as the bullet smashed his collarbone. . . . . . blackness.

The street reformed. "I still really hate dying. One behind me?"

correct. Center did not bother with amenities like speaking aloud. scanning to your right as you entered the room was the optimum alternative.

"I hated it, too," Raj said unexpectedly.

The street scene faded to the study where they'd first . . . John supposed "met" was as good a word as any. Raj puffed alight a cheroot and poured them both brandies.

"Hunting accident—broke my neck putting my mount over a fence," he said. "Quick, at least. I was an old, old man by that time, and the bones get brittle. Still, I had enough time to know I'd screwed the pooch in a major way. The real surprise was waking up—" He indicated the construct. "I was expecting the afterlife, the *real* afterlife." He frowned. "Although this isn't precisely my soul, come to think of it. Maybe I'm in two heavens . . . or hells."

"At least you got to see your own funeral," John said.

His body-image still carried the revolver. He opened the cylinder and worked the ejector to remove the spent brass, then reloaded and clicked the weapon closed with his thumb. The action was wholly automatic, after thousands of hours of Center's instruction—and Raj's, too. The personality of the general gave the training an immediacy that the machine intelligence could never quite match, one that remembered the flesh and the unpleasant realities to which it was subject.

"My grandchildren were touchingly grief-stricken," Raj said, his grin white in the dark face. "And now, back to work."

"This is play?" John asked.

His own bedroom in the embassy complex snapped back into view; it was private, with the door locked, and big enough for his body to leap and move in puppet-obedience to what his mind perceived in Center's training program. Experience had to be ground into the nerves and muscles, as well as the mind and memory. The rest of the staff thought he had an eccentric taste for calisthenics performed in solitude.

The phone rang, the distinctive two long and three short that meant it was from the ambassador.

John sighed silently as he picked it up. There were times when it was easier to deal with the Chosen; they were more straightforward.

Gerta found the embassy of the Land of the Chosen in the Imperial capital of Ciano reassuringly familiar, down to the turtle helmets and gray uniforms and brand-new magazine rifles of the guards at the gate. They snapped to present as her car halted; an officer checked her papers and waved her through, past two outward-bound trucks. In the main courtyard, staff were setting up fuel drums and shoveling in a mixture of file folders and kerosene distillate. The smoke was rank and black, towering up into the sky over the pollarded trees and the slate-roofed buildings. The guards at the entrance gave her a more detailed going-over.

"Captain Gerta Hosten, Intelligence Section, General Staff Office, *geburtsnumero* 77-A-II-44221," she said.

"Sir," the embassy clerk said, after a moments check of the tallysheet before him. "Colonel von Kleuron will see you immediately."

I should hope so, Gerta thought with perfectly controlled anger as she walked through the basalt-paved lobby of the main embassy building. *After dragging me out here for Fate-knows-what when the balloon's about to go up.*

It was busy enough that several times she had to dodge wheeled carts full of documents being taken down to the incinerators. Not so busy that several passersby in civilian dress didn't do a slight check and double-take at her Intelligence flashes; probably the Fourth Bureau spooks were about as happy to see her here as they would be to invite Santander Intelligence Bureau operatives in. The air was scented with the smell of paper and cardboard burning, and with fear-sweat.

She repeated the identification procedure at the Intelligence chief's office. This time it was a Chosen NCO who checked her against a list.

"Welcome to Ciano, Captain," he said. "No problems at the airship port?"

"Walked straight through, barely looked at my passport," she said. "The colonel?"

The NCO hopped up from his desk—it was covered with files being sorted—opened the door and spoke through it, then opened it fully and stepped aside.

Gerta marched through, tucked her peaked cap precisely under her left arm. Her heels clicked, and her right arm shot out at shoulder-height with fist clenched.

"Sir!"

Colonel von Kleuron turned out to be a middle-aged woman with a long face and pouches under her eyes. *Her* office, with its metal filing cabinets, table with a keyboard-style coding machine, and plain wooden desk, seemed to still be in full operation. All in military gray, nothing personal except a photograph of several teenage children on the desk.

"At ease, Captain," She looked at Gerta with a slight raise of her eyebrow. "You seem to be throttling a considerable head of steam, Hosten."

"Sir, Operation Overfall is scheduled to commence shortly. My unit is tasked with an important objective, and we've been training for nearly a year. Nobody's indispensable, but I'll be missed."

"We should have you back shortly, Captain," von Kleuron said. "Not to waste time: give me your appraisal of Johan—John—Hosten, your foster-brother."

Gerta blinked in surprise. That she had *not* expected. Von Kleuron tapped the folder open before her; a picture of John was clipped to the front sheet. Gerta recognized it; it was a duplicate of one she'd gotten from him. She also recognized the correspondence tucked into the inner jacket of the file; of course, she'd submitted all her letters for approval before sending, and turned over copies of all his immediately. Plus, the Fourth Bureau would have their own from the censors in the postal system, but that was another department.

"As in my reports, Colonel. Intelligent and resourceful, and, as I remember him as a boy, with considerable nerve and determination. Certainly he overcame his handicap well. From what he's accomplished in the Republic over the last twelve years, he's become a formidable man."

"His attitude towards the Chosen?"

"I think he had reservations even as a boy. Now?" She shrugged. "Impossible to say. We don't discuss politics, only family matters."

"Weaknesses?"

"Sentimentality." The Landisch word she used could also mean "squeamishness."

"Are you aware that Johan Hosten has become an operative for the Republic's Foreign Intelligence Service? As well as a diplomat." The last was a little pedantic; in Landisch, diplomat and spy were related words.

Gerta's eyebrows went up slightly. "No, sir, I wasn't aware of that. I'm not surprised."

"It has been decided at a high level to attempt to enlist the subject as a double agent. We are authorized to waive Testing and offer Chosen status, and appropriate rank."

Gerta frowned. It smacked of an improvisation, not a good idea on the eve of a major war. On the other hand, John *would* be an asset if he could be turned . . . and it would be pleasant to have him on-side. If possible. It was obvious why she'd been brought in; she was the only Chosen intelligence operative with a personal link to John. Heinrich had known him as well, but he was a straight-leg, an infantry officer. *And* far more conspicuous in Ciano; her height and physical type was far more common in the Empire than his.

On the other hand, women who could bench-press twice their own weight were *not* common here, and she hoped very much she wouldn't have to try looking like an Imperial belle in a low-cut dress. She didn't even know how to walk in a skirt.

Behfel ist Behfel. "How am I tasked, sir?"

John tapped his walking stick against the front of the cab. "Driver, pull up."

The horses clattered to a halt, and the driver set the brake and jumped to the cobblestones to open the door.

"Signore?" he said, looking around.

They were in a district of upper-middle-class homes, about halfway between the theater district north of the main railway station and the apartment John kept near the Santander embassy.

"I've changed my mind, I'm going to walk home," he said.

Shameless self-indulgence, he thought. He *should* make up for taking an evening off at the opera with Pia by going straight home and reading files. On the other hand, he had his cover as a effete diplomat to maintain. The Santander diplomatic service was supposed to be a harmless dumping ground for well-connected upper-class playboys. Many of them were, and the rest found it useful camouflage.

He paid the cabbie the full value of his intended trip, and the horses clattered off through the dark.

Ciano was a pleasant city to walk through, this part at least, on a warm spring night. The sidewalk was brick, with trees at four-meter intervals—oaks, he thought—and cast-iron lampstands rather less frequently. Most of the houses on either side had wrought-iron railings separating them from the street, often overgrown with climbing roses or honeysuckle. The gaslights gave a diffuse glow to the scene, soft yellow light on the undersides of the trees; the street had a melancholy feel, like most of the Imperial capital, a dreamy sense of past glories and a long sleep filled with reverie.

John twirled the walking stick and strolled, unclasping his opera cloak and throwing it over his left arm. It was very quiet, the air smelling of dew and roses. Quiet enough that he heard the footsteps not long after Center's warning.

four following, the computer said. **there are two more at the junction ahead.**

John was suddenly, acutely conscious of the feel of the brick beneath his feet, the slight touch of the wind on his face beneath the glossy black topper. Twelve years of Center's scenarios and Raj's drill had given him a training nobody on the planet could match, but he'd never had anyone try to kill him before. *Odd, I'm not really frightened.* More like being extremely alert and irritated at the same time.

There was a double-edged steel blade inside his walking stick, the gold head made a very effective bludgeon, and a small six-shot revolver nestled under one armpit. It didn't seem like much, right now, but it would probably be enough if these were street toughs out to roll a toff.

The wall by his side was brick. John turned casually and set his back against it, like a man pausing to admire the view toward the north and the Imperial Palace.

Four men came up the sidewalk behind him. They were dressed in double-breasted jackets and bag-hats, peg-leg trousers and ankle-boots; middle-class streetwear for Ciano. Their faces were unremarkably Imperial as well, rather swarthy and blue-stubbled for the most part. There was something about the way they moved, though, the expressions on the faces—or rather the lack of them. Big men, thick-shouldered. With flat bulges under their left armpits; one of them was holding his right hand down by his side, as if something was resting in the loosely curled fingertips. The hilt of a knife, perhaps, or a lead-weighted cosh.

Protégés, he thought. Tough ones, at that. Operatives. Fourth Bureau, or Military Intelligence.

correct, Center said. **97%, ±2.**

Well, it was some comfort to know his judgment was good.

The men halted and spread out, waiting with a tense wariness. One spoke:

"Excuse, sir. You will please to come with us." A guttural accent in the Imperial, one natural to someone who'd grown up speaking Landisch.

Four of them, and two more waiting close by. *Not good odds.* And if they'd wanted him dead, he'd be dead. A steamcar and a couple of shotguns, no problem and no fuss. Or someone waiting in his apartment, the Chosen could certainly find a good shooter when they needed one. This was a snatch team, not hitters.

"All right," he said, turning and walking ahead of them.

Two closed in on either side. One quietly relieved him of the walking stick. Another leaned over, put a hand under his jacket and took his revolver, dropping it into his own coat pocket. A few seconds later, fingers plucked the little punch-dagger out of the collar of his dress coat. There was a sound at that, something like a very quiet chuckle smothered before it began. The men closed in on either side of him—nobody in front, of course. This lot had been fairly well-trained.

They all halted under the streetlight at the T-shaped intersection. The two men waiting there both threw their cigarettes into the center of the road. Seconds later a quiet hum of rubber tires sounded as a steamcar came down the road and halted—a big Santander-made four-door Wilkens in plain blue paint, with wire-spoke wheels and two sofa-style seats facing each other in the rear compartment. The head of the snatch team signaled John to enter.

There was a woman sitting in the front seat, with her back to the driver's compartment. The interior of the Wilkens was fairly dark, only the reflected light of the streetlamps. That was enough to show the oily blued sheen of a weapon in her hand; it gestured him back to the rear of the vehicle. He obeyed silently. Two of the Protégé gunmen sat on either side of him, wedging him into position. The front door *chunked* closed. Just for insurance, the Protégé beside John had a short double-edged blade in his hand, under the limp hat. That put the point not more than a couple of millimeters from his short ribs. John's lips quirked. They certainly weren't taking any chances with him; but then, the preferred Chosen method of dealing with ants was to drop an anvil on them.

The woman leaned out the window and spoke to the other members of the team. "Report to the safe house," she said. Gray uniform tunic, Captain's rank-tabs, red General Staff flashes, Military Intelligence insignia.

The motion left the light on her face for a second. She was in her late twenties, not much older than he; a dark brunette, black hair cropped to a plush sable cap, black eyes, high cheekbones, and a rather full mouth. An Imperial face or Sierran, except for the hardness to it, the body beneath close-coupled and muscular but full-bosomed. He blinked, surprise tugging at his mind.

"Gerta!" he blurted.

probability subject identity not gerta hosten is too low to be

meaningfully calculated, Center noted, overlaying the woman's face with a series of regressions that took it back to the teenager who'd said good-bye to him on the docks of Oathtaking twelve years ago.

She sat back and let the pistol rest on her knee; it was a massive, chunky, squared-off thing, not a revolver.

recoil-operated automatic, magazine in the grip, Center said. **11mm caliber, six to eight rounds.**

"Hi, Johnnie," she said in Landisch. "Nice to see you again."

John took a deep breath. "If you wanted to talk, you could have invited me more politely," he said in a neutral tone.

"Behfel ist behfel, Johnnie."

"I'm not under Chosen orders."

She smiled and waggled the automatic.

"All right, I grant that. I presume you're not going to kill me?"

"I'd really regret having to do that, John," she said.

veracity 95% ±3, Center observed. A brief flash showed pupil dilation and heat patterns on Gerta's face.

Of course, the way she phrased it implied that she might have to kill him anyway. Looking at her, he didn't have the least doubt she'd do it—regrets or no.

"How're the children?" he asked after a moment.

"Erika's just starting school, and Johan's at the stage where his favorite word is *no*," she said. "We've adopted two more, as well. Protégé kids, a boy and a girl. The boy's a byblow, probably one of Heinrich's."

"Two?" John said, raising his eyebrows.

"Policy."

Which was information, of a sort. The Chosen Council must be anticipating casualties . . . and not just in the upcoming war with the Empire, either.

He didn't try to look out the windows as the wheels hammered over the cobblestones, then hummed on smoother main street pavement of asphalt or stone blocks. Gerta uncorked a silver flask. John took it and sipped: banana brandy, something he hadn't tasted in a long time.

"*Danke,*" he said. "Anything you can tell me?"

"The colonel will brief you, Johnnie. Just . . . be reasonable, eh?"

"Reasonable depends on where you're sitting," he said, returning the flask.

"No it doesn't. When someone else holds all the cards, reasonable is whatever they say it is."

He looked at the pistol. She shook her head.

"Not just this. The Chosen hold all the cards on Visager; it'd be smart to keep that in mind."

He was almost relieved when they pulled into a side entrance to the Chosen embassy compound. The Wilkens was as inconspicuous as a steamcar in Ciano could be—powered vehicles weren't all that common here, even now—and the rear windows were tinted. The embassy itself was fairly large, a severe block of dark granite from the outside, the only ornamentation a gilded-bronze sunburst above the ironwork gates. The area within was larger than the Santander legation, mainly because all the Land's diplomatic personnel lived on the delegation's own extraterritorial ground. It might have been something out of Copernik or Oathtaking inside, boxlike buildings with tall windows and smooth columns, low-relief caryatids beside the doors. Fires were burning in iron drums in the open spaces between, while clerks dumped in more documents and stirred the ashes with pokers and broomsticks.

Christ, he thought. The sight hit him in the belly like a fist, more than the danger to himself had. War was *close* if the embassy was torching their classified papers.

He was hustled through a doorway, down corridors, finally into a windowless room with a single overhead light. It shone into his eyes as he sat in the steel-frame chair beneath it, obscuring the two figures at a table in front of him. One of them spoke in Landisch:

"Let's dispose with the tricks, shall we, Colonel?" Gerta said. "This isn't an interrogation."

The overhead light dimmed. He blinked and looked at the two Chosen officers. Both women—nothing unusual with that, in the Land's forces—in gray Army uniforms. Intelligence Section badges. A middle-aged colonel with gray in her blond brushcut and a face like a starved hound.

"Johan Hosten," the senior officer said. "We have arranged to speak with you on a matter of some importance."

John nodded. He could guess what was coming.

"The Land of the Chosen has need of your services, Johan Hosten."

"The Land of the Chosen rejected me rather thoroughly when I was twelve," he pointed out. "I'm a citizen of the Republic of Santander."

"The Republic is a democracy with universal suffrage," the colonel said. "Hence, weak and corrupt, with no real claim on your allegiance." She spoke in a flat, matter-of-fact tone, as if commenting on the law of gravity. "Your father is second assistant of the general staff of the Land and a member of the Council. The implications are, I think, plain."

They certainly were. "I'm not Chosen and not qualified to be so," he said. *Think, think.* If he rolled over too quickly, they'd be suspicious.

"The regulations governing admittance have been waived or modified before," the intelligence officer said. "I am authorized to inform you that they will be again, in your case. Full Chosen status, and appropriate rank."

"You want me to defect?" he said slowly.

"Of course not. You will remain as an agent in place within the Santander intelligence apparat—of course, we know that your diplomatic status is a cover—and provide us with information, and your nominal superiors with disinformation which will be furnished. We can feed you genuine data of sufficient importance so that you will rise rapidly in rank. At the appropriate moment, we will bring you in from the cold."

She nodded towards Gerta. *Ah. They sent Gerta along as an earnest of good faith.* The offer probably *was* genuine. And to the Chosen's way of looking at it, perfectly natural. Perhaps if he'd never been contacted by Center, it might even have been tempting.

There were times he woke up at night sweating, from dreams of the man he might have become in the Land.

"Let me think," he said.

"Agreed. But not for long."

He dropped his head into his hands. *Jeff, you following this?*

You bet, brother. You going to ask them for something in writing?

Out of character, he answered. A Chosen officer's word is supposed to be good. I don't have much time.

Although surely *they* knew that *he* knew he'd never leave the room alive if he refused. The embassy could be relied upon to have a way of disposing of bodies.

He raised his head again. No problem in showing a little worry, and he could smell his own sweat, heavy with the peculiar rankness of stress.

"I'm engaged to be married to an Imperial," he said.

The colonel shrugged. "Marriage is out of the question, of course, but after the conquest, you can have your pick for pleasure. Take the bitch as you please, or a dozen others."

Gerta winced and touched her superior on the sleeve, whispering in her ear.

John shook his head. "Anything that applies to me, applies to Pia. Or no deal."

The colonel's eyes narrowed. "You have already been offered more than is customary," she warned.

"No. Pia, or nothing."

Gerta touched the colonel's sleeve again. "We should discuss this, sir," she said.

"Agreed. Hosten, retire to the end of the room, please."

He obeyed, facing away from the table. The two Chosen leaned together, speaking in whispers. Far too softly for anyone to overhear . . . anyone without Center's processing power, that was. The computer was limited to the input of John's senses, but it could do far more with them than his unaided brain.

"What do you make of it, captain?" the colonel asked.

"I'm not sure, sir. If he'd agreed without insisting on the woman, I'd have said we should kill him immediately—that would be an obvious fake. The woman . . . that makes it possible he's sincere . . . but he'd also know that *I* know him well."

Thanks a lot, Gerta.

"As it is, I still suspect he's lying. Immediate termination would be the low-risk option here."

"I was under the impression that you thought highly of this Johan Hosten."

"I do. Heinrich and I named a son after him. I respect his courage and intelligence; which is why he's too dangerous to live unless he's on our side."

"He seems inclined to agree to the proposition."

"He'd have to anyway, wouldn't he?"

"What evidence do you have to suppose he lies?"

"Gestalt. I lived with him until he was twelve and we've corresponded since. He's committed to the Republic, absurd though that may sound. He *believes*. And John Hosten would never betray a cause in which he believed."

A long silence. "As you say, the Republic's ideology is absurd—and he is, from the records, not a stupid or irrational man. Termination is always an option, but it is irrevocable once exercised. We will test him; his position is potentially a priceless asset. And we are offering him the ultimate reward, after all."

"Colonel, please record my objection and recommendation."

"Captain, this is noted." Aloud: "Johan Hosten, attend."

When he was standing beside the chair, she continued: "We will concede this woman Probationer-Emeritus status."

Second-class citizenship, but if married to one of the Chosen her children would be automatically entitled to take the Test of Life. Although they'd know he could sire no children. He blinked, keeping his face carefully neutral. Pia had wept when he told her that, and he'd been afraid, really afraid.

"This is . . ." He stopped and began again. "You understand, I've been growing more and more frustrated with Santander. You must know that, if your sources inside the Foreign Office are as good as I suspect. I keep *telling* them the risks, and they ignore them." He shrugged. "As you said, it makes no sense to fight for those who won't fight for themselves." He stood, and gave the Chosen salute. "I agree. Command me, colonel!"

The colonel returned the gesture. Gerta stared at him with cold appraisal, biting at her lip thoughtfully. Then she shook her head and made a small gesture to the senior officer, a thumb-pull, much the same as one would make to cock a pistol before shooting someone in the back of the head.

Colonel von Kleuron looked at them both and then shook her head.

John fought back an impulse to let out a long sigh of relief. *They aren't going to kill me now.* Thanks, *Gerta, thanks a lot.*

Although he should have expected it. He'd always known his foster-sister was smart, and she *did* know him well.

"Johan Hosten."

The basset-hound face of the colonel allowed itself a slight smile.

"You have made a wise decision. You will be dropped at some distance, and contacted when appropriate. May your service to the Chosen be long and successful."

"Welcome back, Johnnie," Gerta said. "I'm sure you'll make a first-class operative. You've got natural talent."

Lucky bastard, Jeffrey said silently.

No, it's Chosen arrogance, John replied from half a continent away. A faint overlay of the controls of a road steamer came through the link, beyond it a long dusty country road.

Jeffrey smiled, imagining serious expression and the slight frown on his stepbrother's face.

Have they contacted you since? he said/thought.

No. It's only been three days, and they're very busy. The whole Land embassy staff left on the last dirigible.

Jeffrey lifted his coffee cup. It was morning, but some of the other patrons in the streetside cafe had already made a start on something stronger. Many of them were settling in with piles of newspapers or books, or just enjoying the perennial Imperial sport of people-watching. The coffee was excellent, and the platter of pastries extremely tempting; you had to admit, there were some things the Imperials did very well. His contact should be showing up any minute.

Give me a look at the activity in the harbor, John requested.

Jeffrey turned slightly in his seat and looked downhill; Center would be supplying the visual input to John.

Awful lot of Chosen shipping still there, his stepbrother commented.

They're still delivering cod, Jeffrey replied. To the naval stockpiles, no less.

My esteemed prospective father-in-law, John thought dryly, assures me that the Imperial armed forces are ready down to the last gaiter button. Quote unquote.

Is the man a natural-born damned fool?

No, he just can't afford to face the truth. I think he wishes he'd died before this . . . and he's glad Pia will be safe in Santander.

Speaking of which, we should—Jeffrey began. Then: Wait.

A dirigible was showing over the horizon, just barely. Jeffrey was in officer's garrison dress, which included a case for a small pair of binoculars as well as a service revolver. He drew the glasses and stood, looking down the long street leading to the harbor. The airship wasn't in Land Air Service colors, just a neutral silvery shade with a *Landisch Luftanza* company logo on the big sharkfin control surfaces at the rear. A large model, two hundred meters in length and a quarter that in maximum diameter. One of the latest types, with the gondola built into the hull and six engines in streamlined pods held out from the sides by struts covered in wing-like farings.

"That isn't a scheduled carrier," he said to himself.

correct. vessel is land air service heavy military transport design. A brief flash of a report he'd read several months ago. **sharkwhale class.**

"I have a bad feeling about this," he said. "John, I'm going to be busy for a while."

I suspect we all are, his brother answered. Better try and make it to the legation.

CHAPTER FOUR

"Coming up on Ciano. Airspeed one hundred and four kilometers per hour, altitude one thousand four hundred. Windspeed ten KPH, north-northwest. Fifteen kilometers to target."

The bridge of the war dirigible *Sieg* was a semicircle under the bows, with slanting windows that gave a 180-degree view forward and down. Gerta Hosten was the only one present not in the blue-trimmed gray of the Landisch Air Service; she was in army combat kit, stone-gray tunic and pants, webbing gear and steel helmet. Her boots felt a little insecure on the stamped aluminum panels of the airship's decking, unlike the rubber-soled shoes the crew wore. The commanding officer, Horst Raske, stood by the crewman who held the tall wheel that controlled the vertical rudders. Another wheel at right-angles turned the horizontal control surfaces. Ballast, gas, and engines all had their own stations, although each engine pod also held two crewmen for repairs or emergencies.

"Off superheat," Raske said.

A muted *whump* went through the huge but lightly built hull of the airship. Vents on the upper surface of the ship were opening, releasing hot air from the ballonets that hung in the center of the hydrogen cells. The dirigible felt slower and heavier under her feet, and the surface of the water began to grow closer. Land was a thick line of surf ahead, studded with tiny doll-like buildings. The broad estuary of the Pada River lay southward, to the right; just inside it were the deep dredged-out harbors of Corona, swarming with shipping.

"All engines three-quarter, come about to one-two-five." Ranke's voice was as calm and crisp as it had been on the practice runs on the mockup. Nobody had ever flown a dirigible into a real combat situation like this before; airships had only existed for about forty years. "Commencing final run."

He turned to Gerta. "Thirty minutes to target," he said. "The observer"—in a bubble on top of the airship—"reports the rest of the air-landing force is following on schedule. Good luck."

Gerta returned his salute. "And to you, Major."

You'll need it, she thought. *She* was getting off this floating bomb; into a firefight, granted, but at least she wouldn't have a million cubic meters of hydrogen wrapped around her while she did it.

The catwalk behind the bridge led down through crew quarters, past the radio shack, and into the hold. That was a huge darkened box across the belly of the *Sieg,* spanned with girders higher up; the only vertical members were several dozen ropes fastened to the roof supports and ending in coils on segments of floor planking. Crouched on the framework floor were her troops, three hundred of the Intelligence Service Commando, special forces, reporting directly to the general staff and tasked with the very first assault. Most of the dirigibles and surface ships following were crowded with line troops, Protégé slave-soldiers under Chosen officers. The Protégé infantrymen were getting four ounces of raw cane spirit each about now. The IS Commando were all-Chosen, only one candidate in ten making the grade.

The sergeant of the headquarters section handed her a Koegelmann machine-carbine. Half the commando was armed with them or pump-action shotguns rather than rifles, for close-in firepower. She slapped a flat disk drum on top of the weapon and ran the sling through the epaulet strap on her right shoulder so that it would hang with the pistol grip ready to hand.

"Right," she said in a voice just loud enough to carry. "This is what we've all been training for. We're the first in, because we're the *best*. It looks like the Imperials are sitting with their thumbs up their butts . . . but once we land, even they'll realize what's going on. Remember the training: hit hard, hold hard, and by this time tomorrow Corona will belong to the Chosen. Corona, and then the Empire. Then the *world*. And for a thousand years, they'll remember that *we* struck the first blow."

A short growl rippled over the watching faces, not quite a cheer; the sort of sound a pack of dires would make, closing in on a eland herd. The company and platoon leaders grouped around her as she knelt.

"No clouds, not much wind, unlimited visibility," she told them. "And no last-minute screwups from Intelligence, either."

"Meaning either everything's as per, or the reports were totally fucked in the first place and nobody's found out better," Fedrika Blummer said.

"Exactly. Fedrika, remember, *don't* get tied up in the scrimmage. Get those Haagens set up on the perimeter, or the Imperials will swamp us before the main force arrives. Kurt, Mikel, Wilhelm, all of you remember this—we're going to be heavily outnumbered. The only way we can pull this off is if we hit so hard and so fast they never suspect what's coming down. Go through them like grass through a goose and don't leave anyone standing."

"*Ya*," Wilhelm Termot said. The others nodded.

"Let's do it, then."

Jeffrey Farr dumped the papers in the cast-iron bathtub and sprinkled them with lamp oil. He flicked a match on his thumb and dropped it onto the surface. The mass of documents flared up in a gout of orange flame and black smoke and a coarse acrid smell. He retreated from the bathroom into the bedroom.

Jeffrey began throwing things into a satchel—his camera, spare ammunition for his revolver—and checked the bathroom. It was full of smoke, but the papers were burning nicely. They held the details of the network he'd been setting up here in Corona—but Center was the perfect recording device, and one that couldn't be tapped. For that matter, he'd carefully refrained from memorizing them himself. What he didn't know he couldn't tell, and Center could always furnish him with the details. It put need-to-know in a whole different category. He waited until the tub held nothing but flaky ash, then quenched it with a jug of water from the basin before he jogged up to the flat roof of the apartment building. It was four stories tall, and the roof was set with chairs and planters; nothing but the best in this neighborhood.

He got out the heavier pair of binoculars and focused on the dirigible. It was close now, slowing. Heading for Fort Calucci at the outer arm of the military harbor, from the looks of it.

What in the hell are they going to try there? he thought. That was HQ for the whole Corona Military District.

an assault with air-transported troops, Center said. **probability 78%, ±3. observe:**

—and troops in gray Land uniforms slid down ropes on to the roof of the HQ complex—

Looks like it, Raj said. The bastardos have nerve, I'll grant them that.

"Oh, shit," he whispered a moment later.

What's the matter? John's voice.

"Lucretzia," he said.

Well—

"I know, I know, she's not the girl you bring home to mother— but she's down by the portside."

the legation would be the lowest-risk area for temporary relocation, Center hinted.

"Yeah, but I've got to do something about her," Jeffrey said. "It's personal, and besides, she's a good contact."

Good luck, John said.

And watch your back, lad, Raj added.

The fabric of the *Sieg* groaned and shivered with a low-toned roar.

Valving gas, Gerta thought. Negative buoyancy.

As if to confirm it, the falling-elevator sensation grew stronger.

The nose of the dirigible tilted upwards and the engines roared as the captain controlled the rate of fall with the dynamic lift of air rushing under the great hull. She tasted salt from the sweat running down her face. Any second now.

"Ready for it!"

The commandos were bracing themselves with loops set into the aluminum deck planking. Gerta snugged the carrying strap of the carbine tight and ran both arms and a foot through the braces. The engine roar died suddenly, down to idle. Into the moment of silence that followed came a grinding, tearing clangor. The ship wrenched brutally, struck, bounced, struck, flinging her body back and forth. Then it came to a queasy, rocking halt with the floor at an angle. The bellow of valving gas continued.

"Now! Go, go, go!"

Booted feet slammed against quick-release catches. Two dozen segments of floor plating fell out of the belly carrying the coils of rope with them; light broke into the gloom of the hold, blinding. Men and women moved despite it, in motions trained so long that they were reflex. Twenty-four jumped, wrapped arms and legs around the sisal cables, and dropped out of sight. Others followed them with the regular precision of a metronome. Gerta and the headquarters section went in the third wave, precisely thirty-five seconds after the first.

Noise hit her as she slid out of the hold, into the giant shadow of the huge structure overhead. The *Sieg* was shifting, beginning to bob up a little as the weight left it. The pavement of the tower's flat roof was only eight meters down, less than a third the distance the teams sliding down into the fortress courtyard had to cover. There were half a dozen Imperials below her, gaping and pointing at the dirigible overhead. They didn't start to move until shots and screams broke out below. There was a moment of controlled fall and she struck the ground, rolling off the segment of decking and reaching under the horizontal drum magazine of the Koegelmann to jack the slide back. The blowback weapon was new; it had a grip safety that was supposed to keep the bolt from racking forward.

She'd found that the safety wasn't completely reliable. A really sharp jar could send it forward, chambering and firing a round. *Not a good idea* to arm it just before you jumped down a rope.

Gerta came down in a perfect four-point prone position and stroked the carbine's trigger. It roared and hammered backward into her shoulder, spent brass tinkling on the painted metal surface of the towers top. The bullets were pistol-caliber but heavy, 11mm, and they were H-section wadcutters. They punched into the Imperials with the impact of so many soggy medicine balls, blasting out exit wounds the size of teaplates. The rest of the section was firing as well. Seconds later, the area was clear of living enemies.

Something whirled by overhead, towards the heavy disk-shaped metal hatch that led from the rooftop down into the main section of the tower. A man was standing on the ladder below. His face was gray with shock, but he was struggling with the massive covering. The stick grenade struck his hands where they rested on the locking wheel of the hatch. He screamed and sprang backwards off the ladder, falling out of sight. The grenade hit the lip of the entryway, spun twice and then toppled out of sight down the shaft after the Imperial soldier.

The hatch fell, too, pulled past its balance point before the Imperial noticed the grenade. Gerta came off the ground like a spring-launched missile, diving forward to try and jam the butt of her carbine into the gap. Halfway through the movement the grenade went off below, but though dust and grit billowed out, the pressure wasn't enough to slow the several hundred kilos of mass. It whumped down into the locking collar and the butt-plate of her carbine rang against it with a dull clank. She flipped up to her knees and reached for the small close-set wheel in the top of the mushroom-cap hatch. Three others joined her, but the wheel turned irresistibly under her fingers, and she could hear the holding bars sinking into their sheaths. The locking wheel on the inside was much larger than the topside equivalent, with greater leverage.

Damn, she thought, coming erect and looking around. Somebody down there must be able to find his dick without a directory.

Water pattered down, thick as a Land thunderstorm in the rainy season. The great bulk of the *Sieg* was rising and turning, dumping ballast as she went for extra lift. The dirigible seemed to bounce upward, the shadow falling away from the fortress, turning southward for the river estuary with a roar of engines. Ropes fell away from it like writhing snakes to lie draped across walls and pavement.

The tower roof held only live Chosen and dead Imperials; mostly dead, one with a chunk of skull missing was still sprattling like a pithed frog. She duckwalked quickly to the edge of the roof, avoiding the spreading pools of blood—the last thing she needed was slippery boots—and looked down. There were a few bodies in the courtyard. Gunfire came from the buildings that ringed it: shotgun blasts, rifle fire, the distinctive burping chatter of machine carbines. Then a long ripping burst; that could only be one of the tripod-mounted, water-cooled machine guns the heavy-weapons platoon had brought in.

Good. Fedrika must have gotten out to the perimeter.

"Right, Elke, Johan, pop it."

They'd come prepared. Two years after Gerta was born, construction started on a complete duplicate of this fortress in the jungles of the Kopenrungs. The Chosen believed in planning ahead. Fort Calucci had been built back when bronze smoothbore cannon were the most formidable weapons available, but it had been updated continuously since. The last building program had been fifteen years ago, after some sea skirmishes between the Empire and the Republic of Santander. The whole complex had been girdled with five- to fifteen-meter thick ferroconcrete, and the tower clad with the armor of several scrapped battleships. Even modern high-velocity naval rifles would have problems with it.

Fortunately, every fortress had its weaknesses.

The two Chosen trotted over to the hatchway with the charge between them. It was a cone, broadside down, supported on stubby iron legs to give an exact distance from the target. She didn't know precisely how it worked—the principle was suicide-before-reading secret—but she'd seen models tested. The bomb clanged as it dropped to the center of the hatch.

"Fire in the hole!" the two commandos shouted as they triggered the fuse and dove away.

All the force of the explosion went straight down, like a welding-torch jet. Or *almost* all. The sheathing was thin metal and would disintegrate with an *almost* complete lack of shrapnel. Almost was not a very comforting word, when you were on a flat steel pie plate with no cover at all. She pressed her back against the bulwark around the rim, curled her knees up against her chest, tucked her chin down to her throat and held the Koegelmann over her body.

BWAAMP. Shock picked her up and slammed her down on the decking. A spatter of hot steel dropped across her; she cursed and scrabbled with a gloved hand to get the gobbets off her clothing. The smell of scorched hair, uniforms, and wood added its bit to the stink; someone yelled as a droplet struck a spot too tender for self-control.

Metal pinged and scattered. Before the noise died, the explosives experts were on their feet and racing towards it. Smoke was pouring out of a round melted-looking hole in the middle of the metal hatch. The wheel was frozen, either still locked from below or warped by the blast. The sappers stuffed rods of blasting explosive into the gap; it would have been futile to try it against the unbroken surface, since the force of the explosion would dissipate along the line of least resistance, into the open air.

"Fire in the hole!"

A flare soared up into the air from the courtyard below and popped green. Gerta looked at her watch. *Five minutes.* The company tasked with taking the gates and powerplant had succeeded. Good fast work. . . .

The blasting sticks made the whole top of the tower flex like a giant tympanum. This time a *lot* of metal went flying. Trapped inside the pierced hatchway the fast-moving gasses of the explosion had plenty of leverage and no place else to go. Bits and pieces went *ting* against the armored rooftop, or the bulwark around her. Somebody screamed once and then fell silent. The force picked her up and slammed her down painfully, items of equipment ramming themselves into her with bruising force. She blinked watering eyes.

A few bent and twisted remnants of the hatch stood up, like the lid of a badly opened tin can.

Two grenades arched into the gap. Three seconds later they

exploded, and the Chosen commandos began dropping through the way the blasting charges had opened.

"Shit," Jeffrey Farr whispered again.

He ducked into the little Sherrinford and stamped repeatedly on the foot-pump, building pressure for the fuel and water feeds. When the bell rang, he flicked the switch for the spark-starter. A muted *whump* sounded as the flash boiler lit, sounding a bit breathy without the force-pump draft that ran off the flywheel. Red fluid began rising in the glass columns set into the dashboard that showed steam temperature, boiler pressure, water, fuel, battery condition, and air reservoir. Plenty of fuel and the battery was new, thank God. Thirty seconds later another bell rang and the steam temperature and pressure gauges rose over the operating minimum level. He eased the engine into reverse with the engaging lever beside the wheel, backed out cautiously into traffic and headed south.

There were *dozens* of big dirigibles coming in from the southwest, huge elongated teardrop shapes moving like clouds to a grating roar of engines. No attempt at disguise with these; they had the Land sunburst on their flanks. The first wave passed overhead at two thousand meters, heading east. The second slowed and began turning in formation over the harbor and defenses. Slots opened in the bottoms of the hulls. Dark objects tumbled out. Oblong shapes rained down, like torpedoes with fins.

aerial bombs, Center said. **not aerodynamically optimum, but functional.**

"I'll say," Jeffrey muttered.

A large dirigible could carry *tons* of cargo; some of the latest models had forty or fifty tons useful lift.

Crump. Crumpcrumpcrumpcrump—

They probably sailed empty from the Land, then took on their loads from ships over the horizon, Raj observed.

probability 76%±4, Center said.

"Damn. I'd better get to the—"

A long whistling roar. Jeffrey jerked at the wheel, going up on the sidewalk with two wheels and scattering yelling pedestrians. Dust fountained over him through the open windows of the canvas-topped car, and the road seemed to drop out from under him for a second. Coughing, he saw the apartment block three buildings down fall into the street in a slow-motion avalanche. That was bad aiming, they were probably trying for the gasworks about a kilometer away, but he supposed it didn't matter if you had *enough* bombs. He spat dust-colored saliva and watched as the shark-shape of the dirigible slid away overhead, explosions following it like a trail of monstrous eggs. A dozen of them, and then a huge globe of fire rising over the rooftops; they *had* gotten the gas-storage tanks.

Time to go, lad.

"No argument."

He let the throttle out, up to fifty kilometers an hour—well over the speed limit, but that was purely theoretical in Corona at the best of times. There were a few people milling around, but not many. The crowds were standing and pointing, open-mouthed; a few were crowding towards the broken apartment building, but there was fire in the rubble—broken gas mains, and water spurting from severed pipes. A horse-drawn fire engine went by with clanking bells and sparks flying from its hooves. An Imperial officer with gold epaulets and a spiked wax mustache rode by in the other direction. He had his pistol in his hand and he was riding towards the harbor, although what he planned to do there was a mystery. The naval dockyards three kilometers away were a mass of fire and smoke, with columns of fire from the secondary explosions showing red through the black clouds.

One mother was holding her child up to see the explosions, apparently under the impression they were some kind of fireworks.

Not many seemed to be panicking as yet—which showed ignorance, not steady nerves. He could catch glances in between dodging trolley cars and pedestrians. Half a dozen Land merchantmen had beached themselves by the harbor forts on either side of the entrance from the Pada estuary. It was too far away to see men, but the hulls were darkened in a spiderweb pattern, boarding nets dropped over the side so that embarked troops could climb down to the corniche road. Sections of their hull sides dropped open, revealing pedestal-mounted guns. The flat *whump* of the cannon joined the rising chorus of small-arms fire.

Something else was firing, a little like a gatling gun but not much. Trotting out all the novelties for the party, he thought. But they'll have to do better than this.

The streets grew narrower as he got down onto the flats where there were older buildings, sometimes leaning out over the cobbles. The rough street hammered at the car's suspension, and he had to squeeze the bulb of the horn—and keep his speed up—to get through the crowds. When he stopped, it was beneath a leaning tenement where laundry flapped from lines strung across the street. The balconies were crowded with chattering tenants pointing southward.

Jeffrey leaned out the window and flourished a coin. "*Eh, bambino!*" he called.

A barefoot urchin with pants held up by a single suspender elbowed through to him. "Tell Lucretzia Collossi that Jeffrey is here to see her," he said. "And tell her to bring her jewels. Another one of these if she's here in five minutes."

The boy—he was about nine—grinned, showing gaps in his teeth, and disappeared in a flash of bare heels. Jeffrey got out of the car and waited tensely, one hand on the butt of his revolver. He didn't expect trouble; there were few Imperials his size, people in this neighborhood avoided uniforms, even unfamiliar ones, and it wasn't really all that rough anyway. Still, no sense in taking chances.

The spectators were disappearing from the balconies. *Finally showing some sense,* he thought. A trickle of traffic appeared, heading north and uphill away from the harbor. Then a woman hurried out of the tenement's front doors. She was a year or two younger than him, dressed much better than the neighborhood standard, and extremely pretty in a dark full-figured way. She smiled at him, but there was a nervous wariness in her eyes; she carried her jewel box, and a small suitcase, moving like a dancer even now. Of course, she *was* a dancer, and quite a good one. Nice girl, even if she wasn't a nice girl, so to speak. And very useful. To recruit agents, he had to have respect; and to an Imperial, if Jeffrey didn't have a woman, he wasn't manly enough to take seriously. It generally paid to talk to people in their own language, he'd found.

Jeffrey flicked another coin to the boy and slid behind the wheel. Lucretzia kissed him as she took the passenger's seat.

"Is it the war?" she said.

"It is," Jeffrey replied. "With a vengeance."

"Where are we going?" Her voice rose.

Jeffrey did a sharp right and headed south down the alleyway. "The corniche. It's likely to be the quickest way to the consulate, and short of getting out of town, that's the safest place right now."

The growing crowd parted before the bow of the Sherrinford. The bumper rapped sharply against the wheel of a pushcart full of fruit; it spun away, showering oranges and melons into the crowd, and the owner screamed curses after the car. Jeffrey slid his revolver free and held it in his lap.

"Why . . ." Lucretzia licked her lips. "Why don't we do that, leave town?"

"Because a big flotilla of those dirigibles went right over when this all started," Jeffrey said grimly. "One gets you nine they dropped troops right on the main roads and the railway to Ciano."

probability 88%, ±2, Center said.

"But that would mean . . . that would mean a real *war*," she said.

Her voice rose a little again; Lucretzia was nobody's fool. She had her career path planned out, down to the dressmaking shop she intended to buy, and her previous "friend" had been a post-captain in the Imperial Navy. The Imperials had been expecting a few skirmishes in the Passage, perhaps a raid or two, followed by some diplomatic chair-polishing. That had happened before.

The scenario had changed.

A new series of *thud* sounds punctuated the thought.

They came out of the narrow alleyway and onto the broad paved esplanade, and Lucretzia crossed herself. Battleship Row was plainly visible from here. Or would have been, if the warships between here and the naval docks hadn't been spewing so much black coal smoke from their sharply raked funnels.

"Damn," he said mildly. "Must be two dozen of them."

twenty-six, Center said. **including two which are damaged beyond minimal functionality.**

They were all the same type, slim little craft throwing plumes of water back from their sharply raked bows. Built for speed, with smooth turtlebacks over their forward decks to shed water; a light gun-turret behind that, and a multibarreled weapon of some sort aft. Alongside the funnels were pivot-mounted torpedo launchers, each with four U-shaped guide tubes fastened together.

None of the battlewagons had managed to get their main or secondary batteries into action. The heavy guns wouldn't have done much good, anyway, since they took so much time to train and reload. Several of them *had* gotten their quick-firers working; four-barreled cannon firing little two-pound shells at one per second per barrel, worked by lever-actions and fed from hoppers. The light weapons were a continuous crackle of noise and red tongues of flame along the sides of the big warships, with a pall of dirty gray smoke rising to the sky. Two of the Land vessels were dead in the water, burning and listing, with quick-firer shells sending up spurts of water all around them. The others bored in like wolves slashing at aurochos. Their speed was amazing, almost impossible.

thirty-one knots, Center said.

They must be turbine-powered, Jeffrey thought. He was vaguely conscious of driving, and of Lucretzia's nails digging into his shoulder. The Chosen had been experimenting with steam turbines for more than a decade now. Santander was doing the same, as a possible way to generate electric power. It was obvious that the Land had had other applications in mind.

Another Chosen destroyer was hit. This one staggered in the water, then vanished in a globe of fire that sent water and steel scrap and probably—undoubtedly—body parts up in a plume hundreds of meters high. The quick-firers must have hit the torpedo warheads. When the spray and smoke cleared the bow and stern of the light craft were already disappearing under the water.

Now the first flotilla of destroyers was within a thousand meters of the battleships. They peeled off, turning, heeling far over with the momentum of their charge. As each came to a quarter off their original course the torpedoes lanced overside in a hiss of steam from the launching cylinders. The long shapes splashed home into the still waters of the harbor and streaked towards their targets. The muzzles of the quick-firers depressed, trying to detonate the torpedoes before they struck, but they were only a few hundred meters away, and the destroyers' own weapons were raking the open firing positions. Jeffrey saw four tin fish strike the *Empress Imelda* from stern to three-quarters of the way to her bow.

Each of the warheads held over a hundred kilos of guncotton. Confined by the water, the explosions would punch holes big enough for two or three men to walk in abreast . . . and Imperial warships had lousy internal compartmentalization. For that matter, safe at anchor the watertight doors would be dogged open for convenience sake while they made ready for sea. He let out the throttle lever and braked to a stop.

"What are you *doing?*" Lucretzia asked.

"Taking a better look. Shut up for a second."

He pulled back the fabric top of the car and stood with his binoculars, bracing his elbows against the metal rim of the frame holding the windscreen. The *Empress* rolled over as he watched, shedding ant-tiny men. A few managed to run up onto the bottom as the weed- and barnacle-encrusted plates came into view, but the ship was settling fast as well as capsizing. Most of the rest of the heavy warships were listing or sinking. As he watched the *Emperor Umberto* blew up with a violence that was stunning even at this distance. Jeffrey shook his head and ignored the ringing in his ears, letting the binoculars thump down on his chest and sliding behind the wheel.

There were Land merchantmen heading in towards the docks, with uniformed figures crowding out from the holds onto the decks. He didn't want to be here when they arrived. His watch read 10:00. Barely an hour after the first dirigibles arrived overhead.

The Republic's legation in Corona was not far from the liner docks; most of its business was linked to the maritime trade. The highway up from the corniche was mostly empty now, except for a couple of craters and gasfires. Unfortunately, one of the craters occupied the site of the legation. From the looks of it, at least two or three six-hundred-kilo bombs had landed around it in a tight group. Nothing was left but shattered pieces of the limestone blocks which had made up the walls.

Christ.

His mind felt numb. Everyone he'd worked with for the past year was probably in there—most of them at least. The consul lived there, with his family. Captain Suthers. Andy Milson . . .

The instructors were right. Masonry doesn't have much resistance to blast damage.

"Christ," he said aloud.

He looked over at Lucretzia. She was looking at *him*.

CHAPTER FIVE

"Telegraph center under control, Captain," the runner said.

Gerta nodded. The troops assigned to that task included several who could duplicate the "fist" of the Imperial Navy signalmen.

She dabbed at the wound on her cheek with the back of her hand. Not serious, just a slice from a grenade fragment—you had to follow on quickly, to catch the opposition while they were still stunned from the blast. She'd been a little *too* quick, that was all. It just stung a little, no real damage, not worth taking time to bandage.

A deep breath. The Imperial commandant's office—he was an admiral, technically—was a segment of a wedge, one level down from the top of the tower. A window was dogged shut; the shutter was a half-meter of armorplate, but it was still a silly thing to do, weakening the structural integrity of the building that way. There was a fine Union rug, an ornate desk with several telephones—Imperial technology didn't run to efficient exchanges yet—and a smaller desk for the admiral's aide. He sprawled backward over it, most of his face missing and his brains leaking over the edge in a gelatinous puddle. The thin harsh smell of the new nitro powder was heavy in the room, under the stink of death.

Two signalers were working at the locking wheel of the window. They got it open, sliding it back like a pie-wedge of steel, and set up a heliograph.

377

"Send phases one and two completed on schedule," Gerta said.

A telephone rang, three sharp clatters. She picked it up.

"Yes, Vice-Admiral del'Gaspari," she said, holding a neckerchief over the pickup and pitching her voice low. With luck, her soprano would come across as a bad connection. "Admiral del'Fanfani will be here shortly. Speak louder, please, I cannot—" She pushed the receiver down. It began to ring again immediately.

Her Imperial was good enough, at least, complete with Ciano upper-class accent. But she hoped—ah.

The admiral came through the door, hands bound behind him; he was a tall thin man, balding, with white walrus mustaches. His eyes were fixed and blank, the stare of a man who is rejecting all the input his senses deliver. Behind him was a short fat woman, and a dark slim girl in her mid-teens. His wife and daughter; she recognized them from the files. Half a dozen troopers followed them.

"Sir. Commandant's quarters are secure."

Gerta nodded. The whole complex was in Chosen hands now. She looked at her watch. Twenty-seven minutes from start to finish. Amazing; it had actually gone *better* than planned. She'd expected it to take an hour at least.

"Good work, Sergeant." Then, more sharply: "Admiral del'Fanfani."

The old man straightened and blinked. "What is the meaning of this?" he said. "I demand—"

Gerta gestured. A trooper slammed the butt of his rifle home over the Imperial officer's kidneys; not too hard, but the man collapsed forward, his mouth working. The Chosen commandos hauled him upward. She stepped closer.

"It is necessary that you cooperate with us," she said. *Or at least be useful.* Nothing vital depended on it, but it would be handy. "You will speak as I direct."

The admiral drew himself up. "Never!" he said hoarsely.

Gerta shrugged. One of the ones holding the Imperial drew her knife and raise her eyebrows.

"No, I don't think a shank will make him sufficiently cooperative," she said. "We'll stick with the plan."

Intelligence had very complete dossiers on the Imperial command staff, and a fair grasp of their psychology. Imperials were odd about certain bodily functions.

One of her troopers swept a table clear of documents and oddments; they crashed to the floor with a tinkle of glass. Two more picked the daughter up and slammed her down on it, on her back.

"Papa!" she screamed, flailing and kicking her legs.

Then just screamed, as the troopers each grabbed a leg and bent them back until the knees nearly touched her shoulders. Another stepped up and grabbed the collar of her dress, running his dagger under it and slitting the heavy fabric down until it peeled off her. A few more strokes and the undergarments were cut. The soldier grinned, sliding the knife back into its sheath and unbuttoning his fly. He spat into one hand. Gerta spared them a glance—the girl was quite pretty, but female bodies did nothing for her erotically, and besides, this was business—and then turned back to the Imperial officer.

The girl's mother hit the ground with a heavy thud, her eyes rolling up in her head in a dead faint. The admiral was quivering like a racehorse in the starting gate, opening and closing his mouth.

"I will—" he began.

The girl gave a shrill cry. "Stop," Gerta said. The soldier did, which said a good deal for Chosen discipline.

"I will speak! Leave her alone!"

Gerta made a gesture, and the commandos released his daughter. The girl jackknifed into a fetal shrimp-curl on her side, face to knees, whimpering quietly. Gerta put a hand on the telephone.

"As long as you cooperate," she said. "You will speak as follows . . ."

"Damn!" Jeffrey said.

There was a barricade ahead, wagons and furniture and ripped-up paving blocks. Behind it were fifty or so Imperial soldiers and some sailors in their striped jerseys and berets. They all had rifles, and there was a six-barrel gatling on a field-gun mount. He looked up at the buildings on either side. More men there. *Somebody* around here had some faint conception of what he was supposed to be doing, but it was probably a junior officer. He braked and began to turn the car around.

"Alto!"

Men ran out from either side, pointing rifles. Single-shot rifles, but it only took one, and there were half a dozen pointing at him—

"Here's one of the Chosen dog-suckers now!"

The Imperial seaman who shouted that and poked his bayonet close had probably never seen a Land military uniform. On the other hand, he'd probably never seen one from the Republic of Santander, either.

"Take me to your officer!" Jeffrey said, loudly and clearly. "Immediately."

Reflex warred with hysteria in the young man's face. Jeffrey stepped down from the car, keeping his movements brisk but not threatening, and handed Lucretzia down to the pavement. She was a little pale, but she adjusted her hat and laid her hand on his arm in fine style. That probably pulled the soldiers out of their combination of funk and bloodlust; their mental picture of an invader didn't include a young Imperial woman dressed like a lady—not quite like a lady, but they wouldn't have the social skills to pick that up. They walked behind the pair up to the barricade, not quite hustling them.

The Imperial in charge was a naval lieutenant, about nineteen, with INS *Emperor Umberto* on his cuff. He also had acne, a pathetic attempt at a mustache, and the fixed look of a man doing his damndest in a situation he knew was utterly beyond him.

Lucky fellow, Jeffrey thought. For now.

"Lieutenant," he said. "Captain Jeffrey Farr, Republic of Santander Army."

"Captain," the young man said, saluting. "You will excuse me, but—"

"I understand," Jeffrey said smoothly. "Now, if you'll excuse *me*, I'm responsible for this young lady's safety and the consulate has been destroyed."

"The consulate? The Chosen have declared war on the Republic?"

The young Imperial lieutenant looked hopeful for a moment. Jeffrey felt slightly guilty.

"No, I'm afraid not—accident of war, but the rest of the consular staff are dead enough for all that. My government will doubtless lodge a complaint, but in the meantime, I'm a neutral."

"Then I will not detain you, sir," the lieutenant said.

Jeffrey hesitated for an instant. "Lieutenant . . . as one fighting man to another, are you in contact with your superiors?"

The lieutenant swallowed. "No, sir, I am not. The city telegraph and telephone lines appear to be inoperable or under enemy control."

"The Chosen are landing in force at the docks." That was less than half a kilometer away. "Lieutenant, without support, you haven't a prayer. I'd strongly advise you withdraw until you *do* get in contact with your chain of command."

It would be an even better idea to ditch the uniforms and weapons and hide in a cellar, then pretend to be harmless laborers, but he didn't think the young Imperial would take that sort of advice.

"If I have no orders, I have my duty; but thank you, Captain Farr. There are better than thirty thousand Imperial military personnel in Corona. If we all do something, the situation may yet be salvaged. You'd better go, this isn't your fight."

The hell it isn't. It wasn't his *battle*, though. If every Imperial officer had this one's aggression and instincts, Corona could have been saved. That was very unlikely.

He looked over his shoulder. Two of the Imperial soldiers were driving the car up to the barricade, and others were pushing aside a cart to give it room to pass.

"You understand, of course," the lieutenant went on, "I must commandeer your vehicle."

Jeffrey hadn't understood anything of the sort—although it would be invaluable, particularly with the communications network down. Cars weren't common in Corona. And it didn't make much sense to object, not when the Imperial had fifty or sixty armed men at his back. Lucretzia seemed more inclined to argue; Jeffrey took her by the arm and hurried her past.

"Where can we go without the car?" she hissed.

"Where could we go *with* it? The main roads are blocked. I'm trying to get to a safe house. Now *move*."

They walked quickly up the street. The crowds were thicker here, but milling around as if they weren't sure where to go. That included numbers in Imperial military uniforms. Columns of smoke were rising to the air from dozens of points in the city now. He looked at his watch. 11:00 hours.

BAAAAMM. A volley from the barricade a hundred meters behind them. The gatling there cut loose with a slow *braaaap . . . braaaap* as the operators turned its crank. Jeffrey half-turned, then recognized the next sound.

"Down!" he shouted, and pancaked, carrying the woman with him.

The whistling screech ended in a sharp *crack* about twenty meters back. Someone fell thrashing across Jeffrey's legs. He pushed at them with his feet, but the body resisted with the boneless slackness of a sack of rice; he had to roll onto his back and push with one boot to get the twitching weight free. That gave him an excellent view of what was coming up the roadway. Even at several hundred meters it looked huge, a rhomboid shape of riveted steel armor leaking steam along its flanks, with the Land's sunburst on its bow. Endless belts of linked metal plates supported it on either side. Between the top and bottom track each flank held a sponson-mounted cannon; 50mm by the look, light naval quick-firers. On the top of the boxy hull was a round turret mounting two thick shapes that must be the new water-cooled automatic machine-guns Intelligence had been reporting.

They were. The turret swiveled and the muzzles of the automatics flashed, with a sound like endless ripping canvas. Bullets chewed into the Imperial's barricade in a continuous stream, ripping wood into splinters and silencing the ineffectual rifles. Men turned and ran; the lieutenant waved his sword in their faces, trying to rally them. Then the other side-mounted cannon in the Chosen tank cut loose. The shell landed nearly at the Imperial officer's feet, exploding in a puff of smoke with a malignant red snap at its core. One of the lieutenants boots was left, toppling over slowly. The rest of him was splashed across the paving blocks. In the silence that followed they could hear the tooth-grating squeal of steel on stone as the Chosen fighting vehicle ground up the slope towards them.

For a long moment, he was paralyzed. Instinct tugged at the small hairs along his spine. He'd seen war machines far worse in Center's scenarios, but this was *here*, lurching and grinding its way towards him. He didn't blame the Imperials for bugging out at all.

"Come on!" Lucretzia was tugging at his sleeve.

Good idea. Jeffrey took her hand and ran.

The basement room was hot and close, stuffy with their breath and sweat. Jeffrey put a cautious eye to the slat-covered cellar window, looking out. The firing had stopped, the slow banging of the Imperial rifles and the fast flat cracks of the Land repeaters. He could see one Imperial soldier trying to crawl away in the kitchen-garden outside, dragging his limp legs. Boots stepped up behind him, jackboots with gray uniform trousers tucked into them. A rifle with a knife-bayonet attached followed, pointed to the back of the wounded man's head. It barked, and the body slumped forward, hidden by the thigh-high corn.

Damn. It was pure bad luck, to get right to the edge of town— they were in a straggling suburb of market-gardens and villas—and then get caught up in a skirmish.

The Land soldier kneeled and went through his victim's pockets; then he paused to reload his rifle, pulling the bolt back and up, then thumbing in two stripper-clips of five rounds from the pouches on his webbing. He was a dark-tanned man of medium height, the helmet clipped to his belt revealing a shaven skull. The face below it was beetle-browed and hard; he looked to be exactly what he was, a highly-trained human pit bull. Savage, not too bright, but abundantly deadly. He smacked the bolt forward, chambering a round, and turned to shout a question over his shoulder. Someone answered in the same Protégé-accented Landisch, and three more joined him. Unseen others pounded away in lockstep, a platoon column by the sound of it.

Lucretzia had her hands locked over her mouth, eyes wide. *Been a hard day for her. Hell, for both of us.* He sincerely hoped she wouldn't scream.

They heard a door burst open above. Things smashed, crockery, glass. There was a sudden overpowering smell of wine. *Bad.* The Protégé soldiers must be so wrought up they weren't even stopping to loot more booze. He eased the revolver out of his holster and slowly, quietly thumbed back the hammer. It was a double-action, but saving a fraction of a second on the pull might be worthwhile. Jeffrey swallowed through a mouth gone cotton-dry. When they didn't find anything upstairs, they might just move along, probably they had a lot of territory to cover . . . they might not shoot at someone in the uniform of a neutral third country . . .

probability 8%, ±2.

Thanks. Just about his own calculation of the odds on Protégés understanding what "neutral" meant, or caring if they did.

Jackboots walked over the kitchen floor above them, making the planking creak and sending little trickles of dust down into the cellar. Slowly, the light in the basement took on a flat, silvery tone. Jeffrey set his teeth; he'd experienced what Center could do with his perceptions before, but he'd never liked it.

Neither did I, but you use what's to hand, Raj said. **To the right of the door.**

That stood at the top of a flight of stairs. It was thin pine boards; if there had been only one Land soldier, Jeffrey would have fired through them when the knob began to turn. But there were at least four.

The catch clicked, but the door didn't open immediately. Instead there was a slight *shink* sound . . . exactly what the point of a bayonet would sound like, touching on dry planking. Jeffrey's hand reached out to the knob, moving with an automatic precision that seemed detached and slow. He jerked it backward, and the Land soldier stumbled through. A grid dropped down over his sight, outlining the enemy. A green dot appeared right under the angle of the man's jaw. His finger stroked the trigger, squeezing.

Crack.

The soldier's head snapped sideways as if he'd been kicked by a horse. His helmet went flying off into the dimness of the cellar, dimness that made the muzzle flash strobe like a spear of reddish fire. It hid the flow of brain and bone that followed, but blood spattered back into Jeffrey's face. He was turning, turning, the pistol coming up. The second Land soldier was levelling her rifle, but the green dot settled on her throat.

Crack.

The woman fell back and writhed for an instant, blood spraying over everything, him, the stairs, the ceiling . . . The soldier behind her was jumping back, face slack with alarm. Out of sight, almost, but the green dot settled on his leg.

Crack.

A scream as the Land soldier tumbled out of sight. The grid outlined a prone figure against the planks of the entranceway and an aiming-point strobed. Jeffrey squeezed the trigger four times.

Oh shit. There was another one—

The bark of the rifle was much deeper than his pistol. The nickel-jacketed bullet was also much heavier and faster; it punched through the thin planking and ricochetted, whining around the stones of the cellar like a giant lethal wasp. Jeffrey tumbled back down the stairs, snapping open the cylinder of his revolver and shaking out the spent brass. He snapped the three-round speedloaders into the cylinder and flipped it closed—bad practice normally, but he was in a hurry—and skipped back two steps before firing again through the overhead planks. The soldier fired back the same way, three rounds rapid, and Jeffrey threw himself down again as the ricochettes spun through the cramped confines of the basement before thumping home into the piled-up firewood and potatoes.

Lucretzia was scrambling at the belt of the fallen Land soldier. *Damn, what's she doing?* Then: *Damnation, I should have taken his rifle!*

He scrabbled over to the corpse, ignoring what he was crawling through. Just before he reached it, Lucretzia figured out how to pull the tab on one of the potato-masher grenades the dead soldier had been carrying in loops at his belt. Her toss was underhand and rather weak; the grenade landed spinning on the top step of the cellar stairs

and hung for a moment before it tumbled over the lip of the doorsill
into the kitchen.

. . . three, four, five—

The confined space of the room upstairs magnified the blast, not
nearly as much as having it go off in the cellar would have, of course.
Jeffrey pounded up the stairs on the heels of the sound, caromed off
the doorway and into the kitchen. The Land soldier was just staggering
to her feet, blood running from her nose and ears. The green spot
settled on the bridge of her nose, and Jeffreys finger tightened.

Crack.

The flat brightness faded from his eyes. "Christ," he muttered,
staggering. *I just killed five human beings.* He'd been in skirmishes
before, minor stuff, but this . . .

this is what the world will be, for the rest of your life, Center
said.

"You sure?" Jeffrey said.

Lucretzia nodded, looking down the street. "I am a danger to you.
And you to me. Alone, I can fade into the city. Alone, you can move
quickly—or find an enemy officer who will respect your neutrality."

The Imperial woman leaned forward and kissed him lightly. "I
have the code. I will be in touch, Jeffrey. And thank you."

"You're welcome," he muttered, shaking his head.

a prudent decision, Center observed. **chances of survival are
optimized for both individuals.**

"I still don't like it," Jeffrey said.

You'll like what comes next even less, lad, Raj said at the back of
his mind. *You'd better find an officer and turn yourself in.*

**chances of personal survival roughly equivalent to attempted
flight in that scenario,** Center said. **mission parameters—**

"I know, I know, mission first," he said. "Let's do it."

Reluctantly, he laid down the rifle he'd taken from the body of
the Protégé trooper. Logically, he should already be inside the Chosen
unit's skirmisher screen. Depending on how closely they were
following Land doctrine, and how screwed up things had gotten . . .

He began ghosting down the street, staying close to the buildings and pausing to listen. It was late afternoon, the sun cruelly beautiful as it slanted through the hazy air. He could hear the heavy *crumping* of explosions from the south, down towards the river basin and the factory district. And closer, a rhythmic tramping.

He ducked into a doorway, the carved jamb and edge providing a little cover. A platoon of Land infantry were coming down the street, on alternate sides by eight-trooper squads; jog-trotting effortlessly with their bayonetted rifles across their chests at the port. And yes, an officer with them.

"*Gestan!*" he called out in Landisch. "Wait! *Nie shessn!* Don't shoot!"

A whistle blew, and the platoon went to earth in trained unison, weapons bristling outward. He stepped forward, hands in the air and uneasily conscious of how his testicles were trying to crawl up into his stomach.

"Attention!" he barked at the two Protégé riflemen who came running up at a crouch.

They stiffened instinctively at the bark in upper-class Landisch.

"Take me to your officer immediately," he went on, walking past them at a brisk stride and tucking his swagger stick under his left arm. He could hear the silence of hesitation behind him, and then the clack of hobnails on the brick pathway as they followed. Doubtless the points of the bayonets were hovering an inch or so from his kidneys. *Got to maintain the momentum.*

The officer was waiting with a folded map in her hand and a bulky automatic pistol in the other. Blue eyes narrowed as they recognized his brown Santander uniform, and he could sense thoughts moving behind them. *She's in the middle of a mission and doesn't need complications,* Jeffrey thought. The hand holding the pistol gave a slight unconscious twitch. *One bullet in the head, and there's no complication at all.* If anyone found his body, it would be an unfortunate accident.

"Captain, Jeffrey Farr, Army of the Republic," he said, saluting casually with a touch of the swagger stick to the brim of his peaked cap. "Congratulations, *fahnrich*, on a soldierly job of work—taking a city this size by storm is quite an accomplishment!"

He extended his hand. The Chosen officer took it automatically; at close range he could see that she wasn't more than twenty, under the cropped hair and hard muscularity. There was a trace of baffled hesitation at this glib stranger who spoke the tongue of the Chosen like a native. He gave a firm squeeze and pumped the hand up and down once.

Good work, Raj said. **Personal contact always makes it a little more difficult to shoot someone.**

"Most impressive. Now, since you've got the situation well in hand, if I could trouble you for an escort to your colonel?"

"Jeffrey Farr?" the Chosen colonel said. His square, blond-stubbled face split in an unexpected smile. "Well, I'll be cursed. We're relatives, of a sort—Colonel Heinrich Hosten, at your service, Captain."

The command post was set up in a small park, a few officers grouped around tables carried out from nearby houses. Heinrich Hosten was a big man, easily an inch or two over Jeffrey's six feet, and broad-shouldered, slab-built. A pair of field glasses were hanging around his neck, and there was a square of surgical gauze lightly spotted with blood taped to the side of his bull neck.

He spoke fairly loudly; a battery of mule-drawn field guns was trotting by on the stone-block pavement beyond the park; Jeffreys mind catalogued them automatically, M-298's, the new standard piece—75mm calibre, split trail, shield, hydropneumatic recuperators that returned the tube to battery position after every round. Behind them came a brace of field ambulances, also mule-drawn—the animals looked as if they'd been commandeered locally—that pulled aside to let stretcher-bearers take their contents to a church being used as an aid station. More troops were marching up from the harbor, passing the banner and waiting motorcycle couriers of the regimental HQ.

Jeffrey smiled back at the Chosen colonel. *Damned dangerous man,* he thought, remembering John's description. Not at all the guileless bruiser he looked. *Smart. Dedicated.*

Bet he's glad of an audience, Raj said. **These johnnies haven't**

fought a war in a long time. They're good, but they want to show off, too.

"Looks like you caught the dagoes asleep at the tiller," Jeffrey said, turning and shading his eyes with his hand. He touched the cased glasses at his side with his hand. "If you don't mind?"

"*Klim-bim,*" Heinrich said; a useful Chosen expression which could mean anything from *affirmative* to *all's right with the world*.

Jeffrey focused the glasses. Nothing was left of the Imperial fleet that he could see; black stains on the surface, the protruding masts of a couple of battlewagons. Fire and billowing columns of dark smoke marked the naval basin; warships and merchantmen were burning, sinking, or listing all over the harbor. Black flags with golden sunbursts marked both the great fortresses at the entrance to the harbor, although Fort Ricardo on the south had the burnt-out skeleton of a dirigible draped over it. The Land's flag also flew over the governor's palace off to the west, and the city hall and railway station directly south. Fires were burning out of control in a dozen places, vivid against the dusk of evening, and there was a continuous staccato crackle of small-arms fire over the mass of tile rooftops.

"Looks like you've cut them up into pockets," Jeffrey said.

"*Ja.* Easier than we anticipated. Speed and planning and impact. There were a lot of them, but we had the jump from the beginning. Light casualties."

"And you had those . . . what are they called, those moving fortresses?"

"*Tanks.*" Heinrich snorted, and a few of the other officers smiled sourly. "Terrifying when they work, which is less than half the time. We're supposed to have one here."

Jeffrey turned his glasses northward; the city suburbs thinned out from here, although it was harder to see since there wasn't a slope over the intervening ground.

"You're preparing for counterattack?" he said.

Heinrich laughed again and jerked a thumb at the dirigible passing overhead. "I love those things," he said. "We dropped battalion-sized task forces with lots of automatic weapons at the road-rail junctions halfway to Veron. The wops have something like six divisions concentrating there, but there's no way they can do a damned thing for a week—and by then we'll have linked up with the airborne forces, plus we'll have landed the better part of an army corps."

Jeffrey nodded, pasting a smile on his face. That seemed like a very good analysis. But there were times when you wanted so *badly* to be wrong.

"Impressive," he said.

Heinrich laughed heartily. "Stay with us for a while," he said. "And we'll show you impressive."

CHAPTER SIX

"In the sight of Almighty God, God the Parent, God the Child, God the Spirit, I pronounce these two as one. What God has joined, let none dare put asunder."

John Hosten gripped Pia's hand, conscious that his own was slightly damp and sweaty. The long embroidered cord was bound around their joined hands and wrists in the ritual knot. Incense rose towards the tall vaulted ceding of the cathedral. The wedding party was small and sparse, old Count del'Cuomo in his dress outfit, a few other men in Imperial field uniform, some friends from the embassy. They rattled like a handful of peas in the huge, dim, scented stone bulk of the place, lost in the patterns of light from the stained-glass windows that occupied most of its walls.

He raised her veil and kissed her, soft contact and a scent of verbena.

The priest raised his staff for the blessing, then halted, listening.

They all did, and looked upward. A dull *crump . . . crump . . .* came in the distance; everyone in Ciano knew that sound now. Hundred-kilo bombs from a Chosen dirigible bomber, working its way across the sky at two thousand meters.

"Down by the docks," John whispered to himself, "trying for the gasworks."

probability 93%, ±2, Center said.

"John!"

He looked down at Pia. Her lips were fixed in determination. "This is my wedding day. I will not let those *tedeschi* pigs interfere with it."

Pia's tone was conversational, but it carried in the stillness of the cathedral. A murmur of approval went through the watchers. John could feel Raj smiling at the back of his mind.

You're a lucky man.

"I *am* a lucky man," John murmured aloud.

count no man lucky until he is dead, Center observed.

The open-topped car hummed down the roadway, gravel crunching under the hard rubber of its wire-spoked wheels, throwing a rooster-tail of dust behind it. Shade flicked welcome across John's face from the plane trees planted beside it, each one whitewashed to the height of a man's chest. Through the gaps he could see the fields, mostly wheat in this district, with the harvest just finishing. Stocks of shocked grain drew a lacy pattern across the level fields; here and there peasants were finishing off a corner of a poplar-lined field with flashing sickles. Ox-drawn carts were in the field, piled high with yellow grain, hauling the harvest to the barns and threshing floors; the laborers would spend the rainy winter beating out the grain with flails.

Damn, but that's backward, John thought, holding the map across his knees with his hands to keep the wind from fluttering it. At home in Santander, all the bigger farms had horse-drawn reapers these days, and portable steam threshing machines had been around for a generation.

Downright homelike for me, Raj said. *Except that there weren't many places on Bellevue as fertile as this. Fattest peasants I've ever seen.*

The road climbed slightly, through fields planted to alfalfa, and then into hilly vineyards around a white-painted village. He scrubbed at his driving goggles with the tail-end of his silk scarf and squinted. The guidebooks said the village had a "notable square bell tower" and a minor *palazzo*.

"Castello Formaso," John called ahead to the driver. "This ought to be it."

It was; most of an Imperial cavalry brigade were camped in and around the town. Cavalry wore tight scarlet pants and bottle-green jackets, with a high-combed brass helmet topped with plumes, and they were armed with sabers, revolvers, and short single-shot carbines. You could follow those polished brass helmets a long way; there were patrols out all across the plain to the west of town, riding down laneways and across fields and pastures, disappearing into the shade of orchards and coming out again on the other side. The troopers closer to hand were watering their horses or working on tack or doing the other thousand and one chores a mounted unit needed.

The road was thick with mounted men, parting reluctantly to the insistent *squeeee-beep!* of the car's horn. Animals shied or kicked at the unfamiliar sound; one connected with the bodywork in an expensive and tooth-grating crunch of varnished ashwood.

Then the car swerved under a brutal wrench at the wheel. John looked up from his map in the back seat as it flung him against the sidewall; his broad-brimmed hat went over into the roadside dust. A dirigible was passing overhead, nosing out of a patch of cloud at about six thousand feet. A six-hundred-footer, *Eagle*-class, reconnaissance model. Some of the Imperial cavalry were popping away at the airship with their carbines, and in the village square ahead they had an improvised antiaircraft mounting for a gatling gun—a U-shaped iron framework on a set of gears and cams. The carbines were merely a nuisance, but letting off six hundred rounds a minute straight up was a *menace*.

"You there!" John barked, tapping the shoulder of his driver. The car came to a halt with a tail-wagging emphasis as the man stood on the brakes. John vaulted out over the rear door and strode towards the gatling.

"You there!" John continued, rapping at the frame with his cane for emphasis. The Imperial NCO in charge looked up. "That thing is out of range, and you'd be dropping spent rounds all over town. Do *not* open fire."

The soldier braced to attention at a gentleman's voice. John nodded curtly and turned to where the cavalry brigade's command group were sitting under a vine-grown pergola in the courtyard of the village *taverna*.

Nothing wrong with their nerves, John thought. The portly brigadier had his uniform jacket unbuttoned, his half-cloak across the back of his chair, and a huge plate of pasta and breaded veal in front of him. Several straw-wrapped bottles of the local vintage kept the food company. He looked up as John rapped out his orders at the gatling crew, his face purpling with rage as the stranger strode over to his table.

"And who the hell are you? *Teniente,* get this civilian out of here!"

John bowed with a quick jerk of his head, suppressing an impulse to click heels. Showing Chosen habits was *not* the way to make yourself popular around here right now.

"I am John Hosten, accredited chargé d'affaires with the Embassy of the Republic of Santander," he said crisply. He pulled out a sheaf of documents. "Here are my credentials."

"I don't care shit for—" The Imperial officer stopped, paling slightly under his five o'clock shadow. "The signore John Hosten who married Pia del'Cuomo?"

Who is the favorite daughter of the Minister of War, yes, John thought. "The same, sir," he continued aloud. "Here to observe the course of the war."

"Excellent!" the brigadier said, a little too heartily, mopping his mouth on a checkered linen napkin. "We drove these pig-grunting beasts into the sea once before centuries ago, and you can watch it done again!"

A murmur of agreement came from the other officers around the table, in a wave of wineglasses and elegant cigarette holders. Polished boots struck the flagstones in emphasis. John inclined his head.

Considering that we're four hundred kilometers west of Corona and he doesn't know fuck-all about where the enemy's main force is, I'd say that was just a little over optimistic, Raj commented dryly.

"Brigadier Count Damiano del'Ostro," the portly cavalryman said, extending a hand. "At your service, *signore.*"

John shook the plump, beautifully manicured hand extended to him in a waft of cologne and garlic, and looked up. The Land dirigible was gliding away on a curving pathway that would take it miles to the east, down the road to the capital and then back towards the Pada River near Veron. According to the newspapers, a strong Imperial garrison was holding out in that river port, preventing the Land's forces from using it to supply their forward elements.

You could believe as much of that as you wanted to. John did know that at least ten Imperial infantry divisions and two of cavalry were concentrating—slowly—at a rail junction about fifty miles east; he'd driven through them that morning. The dirigible was doing about seventy-five miles an hour. It would be there in three-quarters of an hour, and reporting back in two. John looked back at the cavalry commander, who was supposed to be locating the Land's armies and screening the Imperial forces from observation.

"You've located the enemy force, Brigadier del'Ostro?" he said.

The brigadier twirled at one of his waxed mustachios. "Soon, soon—our cavalry screen is bound to make contact soon. The cowards refuse to engage our cavalry under any circumstances. Why, *their* cavalry are mounted on *mules,* if you can believe it."

"The Land doesn't have any cavalry, strictly speaking," John pointed out gently. "They have some mounted infantry units on mules, yes. One mule to two men; they take turns riding. They march very quickly."

Del'Ostro laughed heartily and slapped a hand to his saber. "Without cavalry, they will be blind and helpless. Desperate they must already be; do you know, they let *women* into their army?"

John smiled politely with the chorus of laughter. I hope you never meet my foster-sister, he thought. Then again, considering that you're partly responsible for this, I hope you do meet Gerta.

"Come, I'll show you how my men scout!" del'Ostro said.

He threw the napkin to the table and strode out, buckling his tunic and calling orders. He and his staff headed towards four Santander-made touring cars, evidently the mechanized element of this outfit. Guards crashed to attention, a drum rolled, a bugle sounded, and Brigadier Count del'Ostro mounted to the backseat, standing and holding the pole of a standard mounted in a bracket at the side of the car.

"Hate to think what those spurs are doing to the upholstery," John murmured to himself—in Santander English, which the driver did not speak. "Follow," he added in Imperial. "But not too close."

"Si, *signore*," the driver said.

John opened a wicker container bolted to the rear of the front seat and brought out his field glasses; big bulky things, Sierra-made, the best on the market.

"Halt," he said after a moment.

Steam chuffed, and the engine hissed to a stop. The car coasted and then braked to one side of the road, under the shade of a plane tree. John pushed up his driving goggles again and leaned his elbows on the padded leather of the chauffeur's seat.

Brigadier del'Ostro had forgotten his foreign audience in his enthusiasm. His party swept down the long straight road in a plume of dust and a chorus of loyal cries; the mounted units using the road scattered into the ditches, not a few troopers losing their seats. One light field gun went over on its side, taking half its team with it, and lay with the upper wheel spinning in the cars' wake. John ignored them, scanning to the west over the rolling patchwork of grainfields and pasture. There weren't any peasants in that direction; he supposed they were too sensible to linger when the Imperial cavalry screen arrived.

There *were* spots of smoke on the skyline: burning grain-ricks, perhaps, or buildings. He didn't think that the Land's forces would be burning as they came, too wasteful and conspicuous, but fires followed combat as surely as vultures did.

Ah. A dull thudding noise, like a very large door being slammed some distance away. It repeated again and again, at slow intervals. Artillery.

Over a rise a mile away came a bright spray of Imperial cavalry; some of them were turning to fire behind them with their carbines. Little white puffs of smoke rose from their position. Then came a long rattling crackle. A shape lurched over the rise, and two more behind it. John focused his glasses; it was a big touring car, with a carapace of bolted steel plate on its chassis, and a hatbox-shaped turret on top. Two fat barrels sprouted from the turret's face: water-cooled machine guns. They fired again, a long ripping sound, faint with distance. Men and horses fell in a tangled, kicking mass, and the screaming of the wounded animals carried clearly. The Sierra binoculars were excellent; he could see carbine slugs ricochetting off the gray-painted metal in sparking impacts, leaving smears of soft lead and bright patches where bare metal was exposed.

"Driver, reverse," John said calmly. Because this is no longer near the front. I think it's just become a salient about to be pinched off.

Nothing happened. He looked down; the driver was staring westward, too, hands white-knuckled on the wheel of the car.

"Driver!"

He rapped a shoulder, and the chauffeur came out of his funk like a man broaching deep water, shaking his head.

"Get us out of here, man. *Now.*"

"Si, signore!"

He wrenched at the wheel and reversing lever, got the long touring car around without putting it into either of the roadside ditches although one wheel hung on the edge for a heart-stopping moment. John reversed himself, kneeling and looking back along the road.

More and more of the Imperial cavalry were pouring back towards the village of Castello Formaso; the ones there were streaming out of town heading east, or dismounting and deploying around the town. The party with Brigadier del'Ostro were trying to backtrack as well, but two of the cars had collided and blocked the road. As he watched, machine-gun fire raked the tangle, punching through the wood and thin sheet metal of the vehicles as easily as it did the brightly uniformed bodies that flopped and tumbled around them. Brigadier del'Ostro was still standing on the seat, waving his sword when his car exploded in a shower of parts and burning gasoline. The wreckage settled back, rocking on the bare rims of the wheels, and men ran flaming from the mass.

And over the hill where the armored cars had appeared came a column. John focused on it: Land troops, half mounted on mules, the other half trotting alongside, each soldier holding on to a stirrup leather. As he watched they halted, the mounted half dismounted, handlers took the mules by the reins, and the whole column shook itself out into a line advancing in extended order. Behind them, teams were unloading machine guns with their tripods and boxes of ammunition belts from pack mules.

He could imagine the *clink-clank-snap* sounds as the heavy weapons with their fat water-filled jackets were dropped onto the fastenings and clamped home; the operators raising the slides, feeding the tab at the end of the belt through, snapping the slide back down, jerking back the cocking lever and settling in with their hands on the spade grips and thumbs on the butterfly trigger while the officer looked through his split-view range finder . . .

"Faster," he said to the driver, licking salt off his upper lip.

His hand went to check the revolver under his left armpit; there was a pump-action shotgun in a scabbard on the back of the driver's seat. Nothing much, but it might come in handy if worst came to worst.

"Uh-oh," he mumbled involuntarily, looking ahead. Castello Formoso was a solid jammed mass of riders, horses, carriages and carts and field guns and ambulances.

Shoomp. His head came up and looked eastward, beyond the village. *Whonk!* An explosion on the road; nothing dramatic, not nearly as large as a field-gun shell, but definitely something exploding. John tracked left and right with the binoculars. More armored cars.

Those things couldn't mount a cannon! he thought.

examine them again, please. Center thought.

The war machines were insectile dots, even with the powerful glasses. A square appeared before John's eyes, and the image of the car leaped into it, magnified until it seemed only a few yards away. The picture was grainy, fuzzy, but grew clearer as if waves of precision were washing across it several times a second.

maximum enhancement, Center said. The round cheesebox turrets of these held only one machine gun; beside it was a tube, canted up at a forty-five degree angle.

mortar, Center said. **probable design—**

A schematic replaced the picture of the armored car. A simple smoothbore tube, breaking open at the breech like a shotgun, with a brass cup to seal it, firing a finned bomb with rings of propellant clipped on around the base. *Shoomp. Whonk!* They were dropping mortar shells on the main road, stopping the outflow of men and carts from the village. The mounted troopers were spilling out into the vineyards on either side in a great disorderly bulge, but the trellised vines were a substantial obstacle even to horses. A few officers were trying to organize, and a field gun was being wheeled out to return fire at the war-cars.

And as sure as death, there's a flanking force ready to put in an attack to follow up those armored cars, Raj thought.

It all happened so quickly! John thought.

It always does, when somebody fucks the dog big-time, Raj thought grimly. *I knew officers like del'Ostro well. Mostly because I broke so many of them out of the service; and whoever's running the show on the enemy side is a professional. Those aren't bad troops, but they're dogmeat now. Get out while you can, son.*

Good advice, but it looked easier said than done. John took two deep breaths, then stood in the base of the car and held onto one of the hoops that held the canvas top when it was up.

"Driver," he said. "Take that laneway." It was narrow and rutted, but it led east—and at at an angle, southeast, away from where the Land war-cars had appeared.

"Signore—"

"Do it."

It would *not* be a good thing to be captured, particularly given what was strapped up in the luggage in the rear boot of the car. He doubted, somehow, that diplomatic immunity would extend to not searching him, and Land Military Intelligence would be *very interested* to find out what he had planned.

"Jeffrey, I hope you're doing better than I am," he muttered.

CHAPTER SEVEN

"Watch this," Heinrich said. "This is going to be funny, the first bit."

Jeffrey Farr took a swig from his canteen—four-fifths water and one-fifth wine, just enough to kill most of the bacteria. The machine gunner ahead of them made a final adjustment to her weapon by thumping it with the heel of her hand, then stroked the bright brass belt of ammunition running down to the tin box on the right of the weapon.

The command staff of the Fifteenth Light Infantry (Protégé) was set up not far behind the firing line, on a small knoll covered in long grass and scrub evergreen oak. The infantry companies of the regiment were fanning out on either side, taking open-order-prone positions; many were unlimbering the folding entrenching tool from their harnesses, mounding earth in front of themselves, as protection and to give good firing rests.

He looked behind. An aid station was setting up, a heavy weapons company was putting their 82mm mortars in place, a reserve company was waiting spread out and prone, ammunition was coming down off the packmules and being carried forward. . . .

"Very professional," he said.

Heinrich nodded, beaming, as pleased as a child with an intricate toy. "*Ja*. Although this hasn't been much of a challenge so far. I do wish we still had those armored cars assigned to us, though."

Jeffrey took another swig at the canteen. He was parched, and his feet hurt like blazes, even worse than the muscles in his calves and thighs. The weather was hot and dry, and the spearhead of the Land forces had been moving *fast*. Everyone was supposed to be able to do thirty miles a day, day in and day out, with full load, and the Chosen officers were supposed to do *better* than their Protégé enlisted soldiers. After four weeks with them, he was starting to believe some of the things the Chosen said about themselves. Company-grade officers and up were entitled to a riding animal—mules, in this outfit—but he'd rarely seen one using a saddle except to get around more quickly during an engagement. Heinrich's light-infantry regiment moved even faster than the rest, and they treated the dry, dusty heat of a mainland summer as a holiday from the steambath mugginess of the Land.

Through his field glasses, the approaching Imperial force looked professional too, in its way. The cavalry were maintaining their alignment neatly, despite the losses they'd had in the last few engagements, in blocks a hundred wide and three ranks deep, with a pennant at the center of each, advancing at a trot. Light field guns and gatlings bounced and rattled forward between each regiment of horse; the whole Imperial line covered better than two kilometers, and infantry were deployed behind it, coming forward at the double in a loose swarm.

"How many would you say?" Jeffrey asked.

"Oh, four thousand mounted," Heinrich said. "The foot—"

He turned to another officer, one stooping to look through a tripod-mounted optical instrument.

"Better part of two brigades, from the standards, sir," she said. "Say seven to nine thousand, depending on whether they were part of the bunch that tried to force the line of the Volturno."

Jeffrey looked left and right; three battalions, less losses; say fifteen hundred rifles, with one machine gun to a company and a dozen mortars.

"Rather long odds, wouldn't you say?" he said.

"Oh, it'll do," Heinrich replied. He began stuffing tobacco into a long curved pipe with a flared lip and a hinged pewter cover. "Mind you"—he struck a match with his thumbnail and puffed the pipe alight, speaking around the stem—"I wouldn't mind if the rest of the brigade came up, or at least that *ferdammt* artillery we're supposed to have, but it'll do."

The Chosen colonel turned his head slightly. "*Fahnrich* Klinghoffer; mortars to concentrate on enemy crew-served weapons, commencing at two thousand meters. Automatic weapons at fifteen hundred, infantry at eight hundred; flank companies to be ready to swing back. Runner to General Summelworden, and we're engaged to our front; attempted enemy break-out. Dispositions as follows—"

Messengers trotted off on foot; one stamped a motorcycle into braying life and went rearward in a spray of dust and gravel. That would be the message to rear HQ—there were only three of the little machines attached to the regiment and they were saved for the most important communications.

"Wouldn't a wireless set be useful?" Jeffrey asked.

Heinrich gestured with his pipe. "Not really. Too heavy and temperamental to be worth the trouble; telegraphs are bad enough—the last thing any competent field commander wants is to have an electric wire from Supreme HQ stuck up his arse. Let them do their jobs, and we'll do ours."

I wouldn't have minded having this fellow working for me, Raj thought.

chosen staff training ensures uniformity of method, Center noted. **this reduces the need for communications.**

"Twenty-two hundred," the officer at the optical said. "Picking up the pace."

"Still, twelve thousand to two . . ." Jeffrey said.

Heinrich grinned disarmingly. "We're holding the neck of the bag. All we have to do is delay them long enough for the rest of the corps to come up, and they've lost better than two hundred thousand men. Worth a risk."

Jeffrey nodded. Down below the riflemen finished digging and were snuggling the stocks of their weapons into their shoulders; a few pessimists were setting out grenades close to hand. The machine gunners sat behind their weapons, elbows on knees, bending to look through the sights: all Chosen, he noticed—one Chosen NCO as gunner, five Protégé privates to fetch and carry and keep the weapon supplied with ammunition and water.

The Imperial field gunners halted their teams, wheeling the guns and running them off the limbers. The clang of the breechblocks was lost under the growing, drumming thunder of thousands of hooves. Elevating wheels spun. The Imperial guns were simple black-powder models with no recoil gear; they'd have to be pushed back into battery after every shot, but there were a lot of them.

Behind Jeffrey, hands poised mortar bombs over the muzzles. The Chosen officer at the optical raised her hand, then chopped it downward.

Schoonk. Schoonk. Schoonk. Twelve times repeated.

The mortar shells began dropping. Each threw up a minor shower of dirt, like a gigantic raindrop hitting silt. The first rounds dropped all across the axis of the Imperial advance, some ahead of it, some behind; four or five plowed into the mass of cantering horsemen, sending animals and men to the ground. The ranks expanded around the casualties, then closed up again with a long ripple.

The observers called corrections. *Schoonk. Schoonk* . . . This bracket landed much closer to the Imperial field guns. One landed on a limber, which went up in a giant globe of orange fire, shells whistling across the sky like fireworks. The noise was loud even at this distance. Another went up a second later.

"Tsk, tsk," Heinrich said. "Sympathetic detonation—too close together. Careless."

In Landisch, saying someone was sloppy was a serious moral criticism, worse than theft, although not quite as bad as eating your children. The Chosen assumed courage; what they really respected was an infinite capacity for taking pains.

An Imperial gun cut loose in an enormous puff of off-white smoke. Something went overhead in a tearing rising-pitch whistle and exploded behind them, sending a poplar tree shape of dirt into the air. The next shell hammered short, just beyond the Land infantry line. One over, one under, which meant . . .

Heinrich made a small gesture with one hand; everyone whose job permitted it went to ground, including Jeffrey Farr. He wished he had one of the Land helmets; even a thin layer of stamped manganese-nickel steel was a comforting thing to have between you and an airburst.

Crack. The next shell *was* an airburst, a little off-center and a bit high up. Imperial fuses weren't very modern, either, so that was good shooting with what they had available. Somebody screamed nearby, and a call went up for stretcher-bearers. Guns were firing all along the Imperial line now, but the hooves were louder.

Much louder. The cavalry were swinging into a gallop, and as he watched the sabers came out, a thousandfold twinkling in the hot sunlight, like slivers of mirrored glass. The troopers swung the swords down, holding them forward along the horses' necks with the blades parallel to the ground. On his belly, Jeffrey could feel the thunder of thousands of tons of horseflesh thudding into the ground on metal-shod hooves.

"Steady now, steady," Heinrich murmured to himself, glancing left and right at his regiment.

Jeffrey stared at the approaching Imperials with a complex mixture of emotions. If they overran this position, he'd probably die . . . and he'd like nothing better than to see the Chosen stamped into the earth by the hooves, cut apart by those sabers, pistoled, annihilated. But he didn't want to share the experience, if possible.

Beneath that his mind was calculating, measuring distances by the old trick of how much you could see—so many yards when a man was a dot, so many when you could make out his arms, his legs, the belts of his equipment. The Land soldiers were doing the same. Behind them the mortars kept up a steady *schoonk . . . schoonk . . .* stopping now and then to adjust their aim.

The machine gun cut loose with a stuttering rattle, faster and more rhythmic than the gatlings he was familiar with. Every fourth round was tracer, and they arched out pale in the bright sunlight. More of the automatics opened up along the regiment's line. The closest gunner traversed smoothly, tapping off four-second bursts, smiling broadly to herself.

Jam, Jeffrey prayed. Jam, damn you, jam tight!

But they didn't jam. The cavalry charge disintegrated instead, hundreds of horses and men falling in a few seconds. At the gallop there was no time to halt, no chance to pull aside. The first rank went down as if a giant scythe had cut their legs from beneath them, and the succeeding ones piled into them in a kicking, rolling, tumbling wave of thousand-pound bodies that reached three layers high in places. He could see men thrown twenty feet and more as their mounts ran into that long hillock of living flesh, saw them crushed under tons of thrashing horse. The sound was indescribable, the shrill womanish shrieking of the horses and the desperate wailing of men.

Tacktacktacktacktacktacktack—

A shell landed near one of the machine guns, probably by sheer chance, leaving a tangle of flesh and twisted metal. The others continued, concentrating on the main mass of stalled horsemen; individual riders came forward, and dismounted men—horses were bigger targets than humans. Some of them were firing their carbines as they came. Far beyond their range, but not that of the Landisch magazine-rifles, with high-velocity jacketed slugs and smokeless powder. Land riflemen opened up, the slower *crack . . . crack . . .* of their weapons contrasting with the rapid chatter of the machine guns.

Imperials fell; the Land infantry could fire ten or twelve aimed rounds a minute, and they were all good shots. More green-uniformed soldiers crowded forward, some crawling, others running in short dashes. There were infantry in peaked caps among them now, as well as the dismounted cavalry. One of the big soft-lead slugs whipcracked by Jeffrey, uncomfortably close; he hugged the dirt tighter. Not far away a Land soldier sprawled backwards kicking and blowing a froth of air and blood through his smashed jaw. Others crawled forward to drag the wounded back to where the stretcher-bearers could get at them, then crawled back to their firing positions.

"Hot work," Heinrich said, propping himself up on his elbows. "Ah, I expected that."

More and more Imperials were filtering up, taking cover behind the piles of dead horses and men, working around the edges of the Land regiment. Steam hissed from the safety cap on the top of the jacket of the machine gun in front of the knoll; a Protégé soldier rose to fetch more water and pitched back with a grunt like a man belly-punched, curling around the wound in his stomach. He sprawled open-eyed after a second's heel-drumming spasm, and another rose to take his place. The Chosen gunner wrapped her hand in a cloth and unscrewed the cap. Boiling water heaved upward and pattered down on the thirsty soil, disappearing instantly and leaving only a stain that looked exactly like that left by the soldiers blood. Soldiers poured their canteens into the weapon's thirsty maw, and the gunner took the opportunity to switch barrels.

"Sir! *Hauptman* Fedrof reports enemy moving to our left in force—several thousand of them. Infantry, with guns in support."

Jeffrey saw Heinrich frown, then unconsciously look behind to where the supports would be coming from . . . if they came.

"Move one company of the reserve to the left. Refuse the flank, pull back a little to that irrigation ditch and laneway. Tell the mortars to fire in support on request. And *Fahnrich* Klinghoffer, get me a report on our ammunition reserves."

"Hot work," Jeffrey said.

"*Watch* it!" John barked involuntarily as the left wheels of his car nearly went into the ditch.

The refugees were swarming on both sides of the road, trampling through the maize fields on both sides and gardens. Every once and a while they surged uncontrollably back onto the roadway, blocking the westbound troops in an inextricable snarl of handcarts, two- and four-wheeled oxcarts, mule-drawn military supply wagons, guns, limbers . . .

"Take the turnoff up ahead," he said, as the vehicle inched by a stalled sixteen-pounder field gun.

The gun had a six-horse hitch, with a trooper riding on the off horse of every pair. They looked at him with incurious eyes, glazed with fatigue, bloodshot in stubbled, dirt-caked faces. The horses' heads drooped likewise, lips blowing out in weary resignation. From the looks of them, the men had already been in action, and somebody had gotten this column organized and heading back towards the fight. For that matter, there were plenty of Imperial soldiers in the vast shapeless mob of refugees heading eastward away from the fighting—some in uniform and carrying their weapons, others shambling along in bits and pieces of battledress, a few bandaged, most not.

The car crept along the column, the driver squeezing the bulb of the horn every few feet, heading west and towards the blood-red clouds of sunset. It was *risky*—the chances of meeting an officer who wasn't particularly impressed with the son-in-law of the war minister increased with every day, and a car was valuable, even one with hoof-marks in the bodywork.

Better than going the other way. When he was heading away from the fighting, the refugees kept trying to get aboard. It was really bad when the mothers held up their children; a few had even tried to toss the infants into the car.

They turned up a farm lane, over a low hill that hid them from the road, past the encampments of the refugees; some were lighting fires, others simply collapsing where they stood. The sun was dropping below the horizon, light turning purple, throwing long shadows from the grain-ricks across the stubblefields. The lane turned down by a shallow streambed, into a hollow fringed with trees. An old farmhouse stood there, the sort of thing a very well-to-do peasant farmer would have, built of ashlar limestone blocks, with four rooms and a kitchen. Outbuildings stood around a walled courtyard at the back; a big dog came up barking and snarling as the car pulled into the stretch of graveled dirt in front of the house.

Two men followed it, both carrying shotguns. One shone a bull's-eye lantern in John's face.

"You are?" the man behind the lantern said.

"John Hosten," he said.

"Arturo Bianci," the man with the lantern said. His hand was firm and callused, a workingman's grip. "Come."

They went into the farmhouse, through a hallway and into the kitchen; there was a big fireplace in one end, with a tile stove built into the side, and a kerosene lantern hanging from a rafter. Strings of garlic and onions and chilies hung also; hams in sacks, slabs of dried fish scenting the air; there were copper pans on the walls. Four men and a woman greeted him.

"No more names," John said, sitting at the plank table. "This group is big enough as it is, by the way."

Silence fell as the woman put a plate before him: sliced tomatoes, cured ham, bread, cheese, a mug of watered wine. John picked up a slab of the bread and folded it around some ham; it was an important rite of hospitality, and besides that, meals had been irregular this last week or so.

"We wondered if you could get through, with the refugees," Arturo said slowly, obviously thinking over the implications of John's remark.

"Fools." Unexpectedly, that was the woman; she had Arturo's looks in a feminine version, earthy and strong, but much younger. "Do they think they can run faster than the *tedeschi?* All they do is block the roads and hamper the army."

John nodded; it was a good point. "They're afraid," he said. "Rightly afraid, although they're doing the wrong thing."

"Not only them," Arturo said. "Our lords and masters have—" he used a local dialect phrase; John thought he identified "sodomy" and "pig," but he wasn't sure. "You think we will lose this war, *signore?*"

"Yes," John confirmed. "The chances are about—"

92%, ±3, Center said helpfully.

"—nine to one against you, barring a miracle."

The other men looked at each other, some of them a little pale.

"I don't understand it—we are so many, compared to them. It must be treason!" one said.

"Never attribute to treason or conspiracy what can be accounted for by incompetence and stupidity," John said.

Arturo rubbed a hand over his five o'clock shadow, blue-black and bristly. The sound was like sandpaper.

"I knew we had fallen behind other countries," he said. "I have relatives who moved to Santander, to Chasson City, to work in the factories there. I might have myself, if I had not inherited this land from my father. That was why I joined the Reform party"—somewhat illegal, but not persecuted very stringently—"so that we might have what others do, and not spend every year as our grandfathers did. I did not know we had become so primitive. These devil-machines the Chosen have . . ."

"Their organization is more important, their training, their attitude," John said. "They've been planning for this for a long time. Your leadership has what it desires, and just wants to keep things the way they are. The Chosen . . . the Chosen are *hungry,* and eating the whole world wouldn't satisfy them."

Arturo nodded. "All that remains is to decide whether we submit, or fight from the shadows," he said. "We fight. Are we agreed?"

"We are agreed," one of the men said; he was older, and his breeches and floppy jacket were patched. "But I don't know how many others we can convince. They will say, what does it matter who the master is, if you must pay your rent and taxes anyway?"

The woman spoke again. "The Chosen will convince them, better than we."

The men looked at her; she scowled and banged a coffee pot down on one of the metal plates set into the top of the stove.

"It is true," Arturo said. "If half of what I have heard is so, that is true."

"It's probably worse than what you've heard," John said grimly. "The Chosen don't look on you as social inferiors; they look on you as animals, to be milked and sheared as convenient, then slaughtered."

Arturo slapped his hand on the plank. "It is agreed. And now, come and see how we have cared for what you sent us!"

He took up the bulls-eye and clicked the shutter open. They went out the back door, into a farmyard with a strong smell of chickens and ducks, past a muddy pond and into a barn. Several milch-cows mooed from their stalls, and a pair of big white-coated oxen with brass balls on the tips of their horns. Their huge mild eyes blinked at the light, and then went back to meditatively chewing their cuds. The cart they hauled was pushed just inside the door, its pole pointing at the rafters; tendrils of loose hay stuck down through the wide spaced boards of the loft. Towards the rear of the barn were stacked pyramids of crates, one type long and thin, the other square and rectangular.

Arturo opened one whose nails had been pulled. "Enough of us know how to use these," he said, throwing John a rifle.

It was the standard Imperial issue, but factory-new, still a little greasy from the preservative oil. A single-shot breechloader, with a tilting block action and a spring-driven ejector that automatically tipped the block down and shot the spent cartridge out to the rear when the trigger was pulled all the way back. Not a bad weapon at all, in its day, and it could still kill a man just as dead as the latest magazine rifle. The smaller crates were marked AMMUNITION 10MM STANDARD 1000 ROUNDS.

"Two hundred rifles, and revolvers, blasting powder, a small printing press," Arturo said.

"Where were you planning on hiding them?" John said, looking around at the set peasant faces, underlit by the lamp Arturo had set down on the packed earth floor of the barn.

"The sheep pen. Under hard dung, six inches thick."

"Good idea, for some of them," John said, easing back the hammer of the rifle. The action went *click*. "But you shouldn't put more than a dozen in one place. Nor should any one of you *know* where the rest are. You understand me?"

Arturo seemed to, and his daughter, possibly a few of the others. John went on.

"You know what the Chosen penalty is for unauthorized possession of weapons—so much as one cartridge, or a knife with a blade longer than the regulations allow?"

"A bullet?" one of the peasants asked.

"Not unless they're in a real hurry. Generally, they hang you up by the thumbs and then flog you to death with jointed steel whips made out of chain links with hooks on them. Small hooks, about the size of a fishhook, and barbed. I've seen it done; it can take hours, with an expert." Silence fell again.

"You want to frighten us?" one of the men asked.

"Damned right," John replied. "You'll stay alive longer, that way; and hurt the Chosen more."

Watch out, lad—you want to get them thinking, not terrorize them, Raj said. *Time enough for realism when they're committed.*

Arturo nodded thoughtfully. "We will have to organize . . . differently. Nothing in writing. Small groups, with only one knowing anyone else, and that as little as possible."

Good. We don't have to explain the cell system to him, at least, John thought.

Although the idea of the Fourth Bureau getting its hands on these amateurs . . . needs must. If nobody fought the Chosen, they'd win. That meant you had to accept the consequences.

"And then," Arturo said, "when we are ready—when enough are ready to follow us—we can start to hurt them. Blowing up bridges, picking off patrols, perhaps their clerks and tallymen, sabotage. We will have *some* advantages: we know the ground, the people will hide us."

"You'll have to strike fairly far from your homes, though," John said.

"Why?"

"Because the Chosen reprisals will fall hardest on the location where guerilla activity flares up. You strike away from where you live, and it kills two birds with one stone; you get the people who suffer the reprisals hating the Chosen, and you protect your base."

Arturo tilted the lantern to shine the light on John's face. That emphasized the structure of it, the slabs and angles.

"You are a hard man, *signore*," he said. "As hard as the Chosen themselves, perhaps."

John nodded. "As we all will need to be, before this is over," he said. *Those of us still alive.*

The Chosen officer's blue eyes stared unblinking up at the moonlit night sky. It was bright, full moon, the disk nearly as large as the sun to the naked eye and almost too bright to look at, so Jeffrey could see them clearly. Her helmet had rolled away when the bullet went in through the angle of her jaw and out the top of her head; fortunately the shadow hid most of what the soft lead slug had done when it lifted off the top of her skull. Jeffrey was glad of that, and the bit of extra cover the body provided. Bullets thudded into the loam of the little hillock, or keened off stones with a *wicka-wicka* sound like miniature lead Frisbees.

Every minute or so a shell would burst along the Chosen gunline, stretched back now into a U-shape with the blunt end towards the enemy. The shellbursts were malignant red snaps in the night, a flash of light and the crack on its heels. Every few minutes a Land hand-grenade would explode where the Imperials had gotten close, but the invaders were running short on them. Short on everything.

The night air was colder, damper, and it carried the smell of cordite, gunpowder and the feces-and-copper scent of violent death. Bodies lay scattered out from the line, sometimes two-thick where automatic weapons or concentrated riflefire had caught groups charging forward—the Imperials' training kept betraying them, making them clump together. The field of the dead seemed to move and heave as wounded men screamed or whimpered or wept, calling for water or their mothers or simply moaned in wordless pain. Through it darted the living, more and more of them filtering in. Their firepower was diffuse compared to the Land's rapid-fire weapons, but it was huge, and the sheer weight of it was beating down resistance.

Goddamn ironic if I die here, Jeffrey thought. He'd devoted his whole life to the defeat of the Chosen. . . .

"I think the next push may make it this far," Heinrich said. "You can't claim our hospitality's been dull."

He was chewing the stem of his long-dead pipe as he unbuckled the flap of his sidearm. Most of the surviving command group had armed themselves with the rifles and bayonets of dead Protégé soldiers, those who hadn't gone out to take charge of units with no officers left alive.

"Damn," Heinrich went on. "We must have killed or crippled a good third of them. Didn't think they'd keep it up this long."

"Here they come again," someone said quietly.

The forward Imperial positions were no more than a hundred yards away. The firefly twinkling of muzzle flashes sparkled harder, concentrating on the surviving machine guns, and men rose to charge. A bugle sounded, thin and reedy. The machine guns were fewer now, firing in short tapping bursts to conserve ammunition. Jeffrey could feel something shift, a balance in his gut. This time they would make it to close quarters.

Listen, Raj said. **Is that—**

airship engines, Center said. **probability approaching unity. approaching from the southwest, throttled down for concealment; the wind is from that direction. four kilometers and closing.**

Heinrich turned his head. A light flashed in the darkness above the ground, a powerful signal-lamp clicking a sequence of four dots and dashes.

"Damn," Gerta Hosten said mildly.

The muzzle flashes down below and ahead outlined the Land position as clearly as a map in a war-college *kriegspiel* session; you could even tell the players, because the Imperials' black-powder discharges were duller and redder. It was fortunate that dirigibles had proven to be more resistant to fire than expected; punctures in the gas cells tended to leak up, rather than lingering and mixing with oxygen . . . usually.

A night drop—another first. Well, orders were orders, and it *was* Heinrich down there. She'd really regret losing Heinrich.

"We could do better with a bombing run," the commander of the dirigible muttered. "And parachuting in the ammunition they need."

"With a four-thousand-meter error radius, Horst?" Gerta asked absently, tightening a buckle on her harness.

"That's only an average," he said defensively. "The *Sieg* usually does better than that."

Airdrops of supplies to cut off forces had proven invaluable; unfortunately, an embarrassing percentage had dropped into enemy positions.

"*Behfel ist behfel,*" she said, which was an unanswerable argument among the Chosen.

"Coming up on drop," the helm said. "Five minutes."

The *Sieg* was drifting with the wind and would come right in over the position, if the wind stayed cooperative.

This is going to be tricky, she thought as she ducked back down the corridor and into the hold. The lights cast a faint greenish glow over it; there was little spare space, even though her unit had taken heavy casualties—the problem with being a fire brigade was that you got sent to a lot of hot places. A good deal of the crowding was the cargo load: rifle ammunition, boxes of machine-gun belts, mortar shells, grenades. *Just* what you wanted to drop with you into the darkness and a firefight,

"Ready for it. On the dropmaster's signal," she said.

The waiting . . . she'd expected it to get better, after the first time. It didn't; you didn't ever get used to it.

"Now!"

A brief roar of propellers as the engines backed to kill the *Sieg*'s drift. They all swayed, and the pallets of crates creaked dangerously. Then the hatchways in the floor of the gondola snapped open.

The ground was *close* below, even in the gloom. Crates strapped to cushioned pallets slid out the gaping holes in the decking, to crash down and set the airship surging upward. Gas valved with a hollow booming roar as she leaped for the dangling line and slid downward, the ridged sisal of the cable biting into gloved hands and the composition soles of her boots.

"Oh, *shays*," she muttered.

It was a good thing that Land military doctrine called for decentralized command, particularly in all-Chosen units, because unless her eyes deceived her she was sliding right down on top of an Imperial gatling-gun crew. An alert one, because they were turning the muzzle of their weapon towards her, the line of flashes strobing as it turned . . .

Thump. She hit the ground and rolled reflexively, then rolled again, trying for dead ground where the gatling could not bear. Chosen died behind her, seconds too slow. The gatling ceased fire for an instant as another group hit the ground and opened up with rifles and machine carbines. Gerta unslung her own weapon and jacked the slide.

"Hell!"

Jeffrey Farr rolled frantically as a one-ton pallet of cargo crashed out of the sky towards him. It landed, slithered downslope, and pitched on its side, resting against a gnarled dead grapevine. The outline of the dirigible was suddenly clear against the stars, the diesels bellowing and the exhausts red spikes in the night. For an instant the heavy oily stink of the exhaust overrode the other smells of the night battle, the fireworks scent of black powder and death.

He rolled again as a dark figure lunged out of the shadows at him behind the point of an eighteen-inch socket bayonet, an Imperial infantryman. Jeffrey's pistol came free in his hand as the bayonet went *skunk* into the rocky clay next to him, and his finger tightened on the trigger. In the red light of the muzzle blast he could see the contorted face of the Imperial soldier for a flickering second, before the man dropped away, folding around his belly. Jeffrey froze for an instant; he'd just killed a man, an ally . . .

Happens more often than you'd think, Raj thought/ said crisply. ***Get moving, lad. Time enough for nightmares later.***

Something went *pop* overhead. Actinic blue-white light flooded the field.

The man behind the gatling pitched forward; his face jammed the mechanism as the cranker kept grinding for an instant. Several of the crew turned, snatching up their carbines. Gerta went down on one knee, snuggled the butt of the machine-carbine into her shoulder, and began shooting. The range was less than thirty meters, point-blank if you knew the weapon. Someone was shooting at the crew from the other side, a rifle by the sound of it. That distracted them the few seconds necessary to cut down half of them with four short bursts. Muzzle flare from the Koegelman was blinding in the darkness, enough to make her eyes water and leave afterimages of a bar of fire dancing before them.

The drum of the machine-carbine clicked empty just as the parachute flare went off overhead; whoever had been supporting her wasn't anymore, and the Imperials stopped trying to get their jammed gatling going again. Six of them charged her; no time to reload one of the cumbersome drums. She blinked her eyes frantically in the jerky shadows, waiting tensely.

They were trying for her with cold steel, probably out of ammunition or saving their last shots for point-blank range in this uncertain light. The first lunged, almost throwing himself forward behind the point, eyes wild. Gerta buttstroked aside the bayonet and slammed the steel plate into his throat. Cartilage crunched in and he fell backward, choking, knocked off his feet by the combined impetus of her blow and his own rush. She dropped the carbine and drew the long fighting knife slung at the small of her back with one hand and her automatic with the other.

One. Coming at her with his carbine clubbed, grasped by the barrel. Wait, wait. She went in under the blow, felt it fan the air inches from her forehead, and ripped the long blade upward. It slid in under the left ribs, sawing upward until the point was through lung and heart. Weight slumped onto her right hand.

Gerta pivoted with the body before her, and the man behind hesitated an instant. She shot over the shoulder of the twitching corpse. The bullet hit the bridge of the Imperial's nose and snapped his head backward as if it had been kicked by a mule. A bullet thumped into her meat-shield; she fired again, again, until the twelve rounds in her automatic were exhausted.

I'm alive, she thought, staggering and letting the dead weight slip off the end of her knife. She took a step and stumbled; something had gouged a groove across her left thigh and she hadn't even noticed. Gerta pushed away the pain while her hands automatically ejected the spent clip and reloaded the pistol. She moved forward, limping, up the slope to where the bulk of her unit should—should—be. Another parachute flare burst, and she threw herself down and crawled as machine-gun bullets whipcracked through the air where she had been. Spurts of sand and rock flicked into her face, and the wound was starting to *hurt.* The Land position ought to be just ahead . . . assuming there was anyone left alive besides that trigger-happy gunner who'd just come within a hair of sawing her in half.

"What a ratfuck."

Boots nearly landed on him as the dirigible turned away. Something whipped across his body, hard enough to hurt: a sisal cable. Dozens of others were dropping down out of the night, and human forms were sliding down them. Two more nearly trampled on him, ignoring Jeffrey and the corpse in their rush; they *did* use the body of the man he'd just killed as a springboard. A half-dozen grappled with the big pallet that had nearly crushed him. Seconds later they were stripping out a heavy water-cooled machine gun with its tripod and ammunition, slapping it down and opening up on the masses of Imperial infantry caught charging to finish off the Land blocking force. Tracers whipped out through the darkness, iridescent green, like bars of St. Elmo's fire. Infantry shook themselves out into their units and swept down the Land line, winkling out Imperials who'd made it that far.

Damn, I've never seen troops move that fast, he thought. They were in full marching kit, and they moved like leopards.

an all-chosen unit, Center observed. Jeffrey's vision took on a flat brightness. **identifying markers**—The brightness strobed over unit badges.

They've been culling out the weakest ten percent of their own breed every generation for four hundred years, Raj said. *And skimming off the top one or two percent of their Protégés at the same time. You'd expect it to show.*

Jeffrey shuddered, even with rounds still splitting the air above him. *It's a good thing there aren't more of them,* he thought. *There'd be no stopping them.*

if there were more, Center observed, **it would be impossible to support so large and so specialized a nonproductive class.**

Always a lot fewer carnosauroids than grazers, Raj amplified.

The image that came with the thought made him shudder a moment even then: something man-sized and whip-slender, leaping to slash a bloody gouge in an ox's side with a sickle-shaped claw on its hind foot, like a fighting cock grown big enough to scythe his belly open.

Heinrich was back on his feet, bellowing orders. Protégé troopers broke open boxes of ammunition, dashing back to their positions with cotton bandoliers around their necks and boxes of machine-gun belts in their hands.

Jeffrey did a three-point spin at a sound behind him, landing on hip and one hand. He froze as he found himself looking down the use-pitted muzzle of a Land automatic. A Chosen woman with captain's insignia on her field-gray rose; short for one of that race, and dark, he could tell that even in the moonlight. Blood was runneling black down one thigh, where the uniform had been ripped open by a grazing shot.

"What the hell is a Santy doing here?" she said, standing, favoring the wounded leg a little.

"You!" Heinrich said, turning, a broad grin on his square face. "I might have known."

"I was the closest—the marching reliefs ought to get here about dawn," the woman said. "What the hell is a Santy officer doing with you, Heinrich?"

Closer, he could see the General Staff Intelligence Commando flashes on cuff and collar. *Must be—*

gerta hosten, captain, intelligence branch, Center supplied helpfully.

A dangerous one, son, Raj said. *Be very careful.*

Jeffrey could have told that. The eyes fastened on him were the coldest he'd ever seen, colder than the far side of the moon.

"Oh, we picked him up in Corona," Heinrich said.

"You should have turned him over to us, or the Fourth Bureau."

"Well, he's a neutral—and a relative of sorts, Johan's foster-brother. At loose ends, the Santy legation in Corona stopped a couple of thousand-kilo bombs with its roof."

"Jeffrey Farr," Gerta said; she seemed to be filing and sorting information behind her eyes. "He's a *spook,* Heinrich. You ought to shoot him."

"I haven't been showing him the plans for the new torpedo," Heinrich said, a slight exasperation in his voice.

Gerta shrugged, and holstered her automatic. Jeffrey felt a slight prickle of relief. Unlikely that she'd just shoot him down as he stood—

probability 27%, ±7, Center said.

—but it was still a relief. She shrugged.

"It's your command. Let's get this ratfuck organized, shall we?"

"Ya." Heinrich turned his head slightly, towards Jeffrey: "My wife, Captain Gerta Hosten." Back to her: "What's the theater situation?"

"FUBAR, but we're winning—not exactly the way we expected to, but we are. Once this position's blocked, General Summelworden's got them in the kettle and we can turn up the heat; Ciano next. Where do you want my machine guns? And get me something to stop this leak, would you? I can't keel over just yet."

"Automatics over by—"

The conversation slid into technicalities. Heinrich waved at a passing medic who then knelt to put a pressure bandage on Gerta's thigh.

Ciano next, Jeffrey thought. That's going to be ugly.

CHAPTER EIGHT

Everything was calm and unhurried in the Imperial situation room. There was a huge map of the Empire on one wall, stuck with black pins to represent Land forces and green ones for Imperial. A relief map of the same territory stood in a sunken area in the center of the floor, with a polished mahogany rail around it, and enlisted men pushed unit counters with long-handled wooden rakes. One wall of the big room was all telephones and telegraphs, their operators scribbling on pads and handing them to decoders.

Aides in polished boots and neat, colorful uniforms strode back and forth; generals frowned at the maps; the Emperor tugged at his white whiskers and bunked sleepy, pouched eyes. Behind him stood guards in ceremonial uniform, and several civilians . . .

No, John Hosten thought, appraising them. *Their eyes flickered ceaselessly over the room, appraising, watching. Waiting. The real guards. And by their looks, the only people in this room who're doing their jobs.*

John Hosten approached, flanked by two ushers, and made his bow. Behind the surface of his mind he could feel Raj and Center examining the maps, the computer's passionless appraisal and Raj's cold scorn.

Systematic lying, Raj thought. ***All the way up the chain of***

command. It's always the commander's fault when that happens.
Once you let people start telling you what you want to hear, you're
fucked—and everyone else with you.

"Rise, *Signore* Hosten," the Emperor said.

He was an old man, but John was slightly shocked at his appearance; there was a perceptible tremble to his hands now, and a faint smell of sickness. Count del'Cuomo beside him looked even worse, if possible—but then, he probably had better information available, as Minister of War.

"Your Majesty," John said.

He handed over the folder of documents, neatly tied with a green-and-red ribbon.

"My credentials, Your Majesty. And my regrets, but my government requires my services at home. I will be returning to Santander City."

The Emperor smiled absently. "And taking one of our fairest flowers with you . . . where is young Pia?"

"Currently, she's working as a volunteer nurse," John said. *Against my advice.*

The Emperor frowned. "Not . . . not really *suitable*, I'd have thought," he murmured.

Count del'Cuomo shrugged. "She was always too much for me, your Majesty," he said. He looked up at John. "But my son-in-law will take good care of her, and return in happier times, when we have driven the *tedeschi* back to their island, as we did before."

John bowed again, more deeply, and took the required four paces backward. That nearly ran him into an aide with a stack of telegrams, but he ignored the man. Ignored everything, until a turn down the corridor gave him a view down over the city. Then he took in a sharp breath.

It was early morning, still almost dark. The news of the fall of Milana must have reached the people in the hour or so he'd spent waiting. Not from a courier or coded message, surely; the Imperial armies hadn't fallen apart quite that drastically . . . yet. More probably from a refugee on a fast riverboat. As for official statements, by this time they just confirmed what they denied. Even when they were sincere, and he'd bet it just meant that the lower-level functionaries writing them had been suckered by their own propaganda.

John Hosten stood for a moment looking down at the rioting and the fires, past the gardens of the palace and the cordon of Guard troops stationed along the perimeter. A man of thirty, tall and a hard-faced, in a diplomat's black morning coat, wing collar and dark-striped trousers. A servant almost walked into him, saw his face and silently stood aside.

"Back to the embassy," John said to himself; then aloud, to the driver of his car.

"Don't know if we can, sir," the driver said. He was an embassy man himself, diplomatic service, and quite capable. *Harry. Harry Smith,* John reminded himself. It was too easy to forget about people, when you spent time looking at the world through Center's eyes.

Too true, son, Raj said. *And if you think it's a problem for you . . .*

"Lot of the streets looked to be blocked," Smith went on. He shrugged. "Kin find m' way through, maybe."

"Mr. Smith," John said.

The driver twisted around to look at him; he was a slight, grizzled man, with blue eyes and wrinkles beside them. There was a slight eastern twang in his Santander. John recognized it, and the manner.

"My wife is down near the train station, working in the emergency hospital," he said. "I have to get to the embassy to get some help so I can get through to her. If you don't think you can make it through, I'll drive."

The blue eyes squinted at him. "Nossir. You watch our back, I'll drive." He reached under the front seat and pulled out a pump-action shotgun. "You know how to use one of these, sir?"

Smiling, John took it and racked the action. A shell popped out; he caught it one-handed and fed it back into the gate in front of the trigger. A wary respect came into Smiths eyes; it increased when John tucked the weapon under a traveling rug on the seat beside him.

"I'll bring it out if we need to use it, or show it to somebody," he said. "Now let's get going."

((•)) ((•)) ((•))

"I need some volunteers," John said. "To get someone out of the city."

He nearly had to shout over the clamor of the crowd outside the gilded wrought-iron gates of the embassy compound. There were thousands of them, more crowded down the street, surging and screaming. Marine guards in blue dress uniforms were stationed inside the gate and along the walls, carrying rifles with fixed bayonets. A little ceremonial saluting cannon had been wheeled out and faced the main entranceway, just as a hint in case the crowd decided to try and batter the metal down. That was unlikely; under the gilding the bars were as thick as a woman's wrist. The Marines were discouraging those trying to break through with the butts of their rifles, or short jabs with their bayonets. Nothing more was needed, not yet.

A slow trickle was getting in, through the postern gate beside the main ones; people with valid Santander papers, or spouses, or embassy personnel who'd gotten trapped out in the city.

"Sir?" The Marine captain looked around incredulously.

"Captain, my wife is out there, and I need some volunteers to help me get through the crowd."

The captain opened his mouth; John could see the snap of refusal forming. He looked the man in the eye.

"This is *very important* duty," he said meaningfully.

It wasn't much of a secret in the compound that John was with the Secret Service. Nor that he was immensely rich, or that he had connections at the highest levels, military and civilian.

"I'm not sending any of my men out into that," the officer said bluntly, jerking a hand towards the near-riot beyond the gate. Just then was a barked order, and the dozen troopers by the gate fired a volley into the air. The crowd surged back with screams of panic, then ran forward again when nobody fell.

"I wouldn't ask you to," John said. "I'm going, whether anyone wants to come with me or not. I'd appreciate some help, but I don't expect you to *order* anyone out."

The Marine officer hesitated. "My responsibility is to guard the perimeter."

"And to assist the staff in their functions."

Decision crystallized. "All right, sir. You can *ask*. Sergeant!"

A thickset man with a shaven head covered in a network of scars looked up. The Santander Marines saw a lot of travel, mostly to places where the locals didn't like them.

"Sir!"

"Mr. Hosten needs some volunteers to accompany him into the city and pull someone out. See if anybody feels like it."

What was left of the sergeant's eyebrows—they'd evidently been burned off his face at some point—rose. He looked appraisingly at John and smiled like a dog worrying a bone.

"Hey, Sarge."

John looked around; it was the driver.

"Yeah, Harry?"

"It's righteous, Sarge. I'm going."

The noncom looked down at the driver's legs, and the graying man shrugged.

"Hey, we're driving—I don't have to sprint."

"You always were a natural-born damned fool, Harry," the sergeant said. He looked back at John. "I'll pass the word, sir."

John stripped off the morning coat as he waited, switching to the four-pocket hunting jacket his valet brought and gratefully throwing aside the starched collar of his dress shirt. Smith glanced at the shoulder rig that lay exposed.

"Guess I shouldn't have asked about the scattergun, sir," he said.

"How could you know?" John pointed out. "Look, am I likely to get anyone?"

"Besides me?" Harry shrugged. "I've been out of the corps a while now, but Berker knows me—hell, Berker carried me out when I got a slug through both legs. He'll—"

The bald sergeant returned, with five men behind him. They were all armed, and several of them were stuffing gear into field packs.

"Sir!" he said. "Corporal Wilton, privates Goms, Barrjen, Sinders, and Maken." In a whisper: "Ah, sir, I sort of hinted there'd be some sort of reward, you know?"

"There certainly will be," John said. To the men: "All right, here's the drill. We're heading for the main train station and the emergency hospital that's been set up there. We're going to pick up Mrs. Hosten—Lady Pia Hosten—and then we're either coming back here, or getting out the city to the east, depending on which looks most practical. I expect anyone who comes with me to follow orders and not be nervous about risks. Understood?"

A chorus of *yessirs*, a couple of grins. None of the men looked like angels, but then they were Marines, and assignment to the embassy guard in Ciano had been something of a plum, reserved for men with something on their records besides a decade of well-polished boots.

He looked up. Something was flying through the pillars of smoke that reached up into the sky over Ciano. A huge shark-shape, three hundred meters long, a shining teardrop droning through the air to the sound of motors. Dozens more followed it, a loose wedge coming in from the west like the thrust of a spearpoint.

"Let's do it, then."

Wounded men screamed in fear as the building shook. Pia Hosten grabbed a pillar and held on as the stick of bombs rattled the iron girders of the roof. The fitted stone swayed slightly under her touch, a queasy feeling. Half the nursing sisters were gone, and there were wounded everywhere—hundreds in this room, thousands in the building, the heat mounting under the tall arches and the smell of puss and gangrene mounting, and more still coming in. The gas was off, and the mains.

"Water . . . water . . ."

I should have done as John said, she thought, hurrying over with a dipper.

She raised the man's head and put the rim to his lips. He drank, then choked and began to thrash.

"Sister Maria!" Pia called.

The man arched, then slumped; his eyes rolled up and went still.

The nun arrived, then scowled. "He is dead."

"He wasn't when I called you!" Pia snapped, then leaped up to hold the older woman as she sagged. "I am sorry, Sister."

"There are so many," the nun whispered. "My God, my God, why have you forsaken us?"

"Where is Doctor Chicurso?"

"Gone—most of them are gone. The guards at the entrances, they are gone also. Only the ambulances keep arriving."

"The guards are gone?" Pia asked sharply.

"Yes, yes. An officer came, and said they were needed. But many had just left, I think, taken off their uniforms and . . ."

She made a weary gesture towards the rest of the city.

Pia swallowed and stood, walking quickly towards her work station, taking off the hideously stained apron that covered her plain gray dress. If the guards were gone, it would be very bad.

John was right. I should have left for the embassy yesterday. There was no more she could do here. But it was hard, very hard, to leave the Sister standing slumped amid the impossible need of the hurt.

She walked quickly along the aisle that separated the rows of men lying on the floor, through to the cubicle that had served her and a dozen other volunteers and nurses. She heard a scream and a crash before she arrived, and men's voices.

The door was half-open; she slammed it back. The sharp reek of medical alcohol hit her like a wave; the three army hospital orderlies had been drinking it. The scream had come from Lola Chiavri, one of the volunteers; two of them had her pressed down on a table, her dress ripped open to the waist. The third was wrestling with her thrashing legs, trying to rip down her underdrawers, laughing and staggering. They turned to stare at her, open-mouthed. One sniggered.

"Hey, Gio', somebody new for d'party."

Pia drew herself up. "Release that lady at once! Where is your officer?"

The one at the foot of the table was a little less drunk than the others. He released the other woman's legs and turned, grinning like a dog worrying a bone.

"Officers all run away, missy, 'fore the *tedeschi* gets here. Why shou' the *tedeschi* get all the liker an' cooze? C'mere!"

He turned towards her, his pants obscenely unbuttoned,

laughing and fondling himself with one hand and reaching for her with the other. Pia drew the four-barrel derringer from her pocket and pointed it.

"Y'gonna *hurt* me with that little thing?" the man laughed. "Oh, don' *hurt* me, missy!"

Snap. The sound was like a piece of glass breaking in the tiny room. A black dot appeared between the would-be rapist's eyes, precisely 5.6mm in diameter, turning red as she watched. The expression slid off his face like rancid gelatin, and he toppled forward to lie at her feet. His skull struck the stone floor with a final-sounding *thock*.

Pia hid her surprise. She'd been aiming at his stomach, and he was only four feet away. The other two orderlies were backing towards the far wall, their hands held out palm-up, making incoherent sounds.

"There are three more bullets in this gun," she said crisply, backing up two paces and standing aside. "Go!" They hesitated, unwilling to approach any closer. "Go now, or I will shoot."

The two men sidled past her and ran blundering down the corridor, eyes fixed on the four muzzles of the little gun. Pia waited until they were out of sight before letting the hand that held the derringer drop. Acrid-tasting bile forced itself up her throat as she looked down at the man she'd killed.

"It was so *quick*," she whispered, and forced herself to swallow.

Just then Lola struck her, clinging and whimpering. Pia shook her sharply. "Get dressed! We have to get out of here!"

Back to the palace district; the embassy was there, or at least there wouldn't be total anarchy.

Pia remembered John pleading with her not to go to the hospital today. *I should have listened.*

"Sweet Jesus on a crutch," Harry Smith muttered.

A thousand yards down the hill a crowd was tipping a car over. It was an aristocrat's vehicle—few others could afford them, in the Empire, and this was a huge six-wheeler—strapped all over with luggage. The owners were still inside; a woman tried to crawl out one of the rear windows and was met with sticks, fists, pieces of cobblestone. She screamed and slumped, and hands dragged her limp and bleeding body back inside. A gun spoke; the noise covered the report, but John could see the puff of smoke.

"Stupid," he whispered.

Half a dozen rifles answered the shot; there were scores of Imperial army deserters in the crowd, many with their weapons. John could see sparks flying as bullets hit the metalwork of the car. Some ricochetted into the densely packed ranks of the rioters. One must have punctured the fuel tanks, because a deep soft *whump* and billow of orange flame drove the mob back, some of them on fire. Both the figures that tried to crawl out of the burning automobile were on fire, and probably would have died even without the hail of rocks that beat them back.

"All right, Harry," he went on. "What's your plan?"

"Well, sir, there's a side route," the driver said thoughtfully. "But its a bit narrow."

"You're the expert," John said.

For once, he was glad that diplomatic corps conservatism stuck the embassy with steamers; they had less pickup than the latest petrol-engine jobs, but they were *quiet*. Smith spun the wheel away from the main avenue, down a side-street, and into a maze of alleyways. Some of them were old enough to date back to the founding of Ciano, to the centuries right after the Collapse, when men first started building again in stone. The wheels drummed on cobbles and splashed through refuse and waste, throwing him lurching into the four Marines packed into the rear of the touring car. Normally the district would have been crowded, but most of the people were missing.

Probably out rioting. Not that it would do them any good when the Chosen showed up, but he supposed it was more tolerable than sitting and waiting. The ones who were left were mostly children, or old. They slammed shutters and ducked aside at the sight of an automobile filled with uniforms and armed men.

"Uh-oh."

The hill was steeper here, and it gave them an excellent view south over the river to the industrial section—the prevailing winds in the central Empire were always from the north, which meant that residential properties were on the north bank of the Pada. They could see the Land airships coming in over the flatter southern shore at two thousand feet, only a thousand feet above their own position.

Probably aligning on landmarks, Raj thought at the back of his mind.

probability near unity, Center confirmed.

John felt a spurt of anger. *God damn it, that's my* wife *down there,* he thought coldly.

I could never keep mine out of it, either, Raj thought. *And she was a lot less of a romantic than yours.*

The dirigibles were coming in fast, seventy miles an hour or better; the lead craft seemed to be aimed straight at him. The bomb bay doors were open, but nothing was coming out. John looked out of the corners of his eyes; the Marines looked a little tense, but not visibly upset. They kept their eyes on the buildings around them, only occasionally flicking to the approaching bombers.

"Smith, pull in here. We'll wait it out and then continue."

Here was a nook between two walls, both solid. Bad if the buildings come down, good otherwise. You paid your money and you took your chances. . . .

"Anyone who wants to can get out and take cover," John said in a conversational tone.

Nobody did, although they squatted down. The dirigibles were over the river now, moving into the railyards and the residential sections of Ciano. Their shadows ghosted ahead of them, black whale-shapes over the whitewashed buildings and tile roofs.

"Hey," one of the Marines said. "Why aren't they bombing south? That's where the factories and stuff are."

Smiths hands were tight on the wheel. "Because, asshole, they don't want to damage their own stuff—they'll have it all in couple of days. *Shit!*"

Crump. Crump. Crump . . .

The bombs were falling in steady streams from the airships; the massive craft bounced higher as the weight was removed.

"Fifty tons load," John whispered, bracing his hand on the roof-strut of the car and looking up. "Fifty tons each, thirty-five ships . . . seventeen hundred tons all up."

"Mother," someone said.

"Won't kill y'any deader here than back at the embassy."

"They wouldn't bomb the embassy."

"Yeah, sure. They're gonna be *real* careful about that."

"Can it," the corporal said. "For what we are about to receive . . ."

The sound grew louder, the drone of the engines rasping down through the air. John could see the Land sunburst flag painted on their sides, and then the horseshoe-shaped glass windows of the control gondolas. A few black puffs of smoke appeared beneath and around the airships; some Imperial gunners were still sticking to their improvised antiairship weapons, showing more courage than sense. The pavement beneath the car shook with the impact of the explosions. Dust began to smoke out of the trembling walls of the tenements on either side. The crashing continued, an endless roar of impacts and falling masonry.

"Here—" someone began.

The shadow of a dirigible passed over them, throwing a chill that rippled down his spine. There was a moment of white light—

—and someone was screaming.

John tried to turn, and realized he was lying prone. Prone on rubble that was digging into his chest and belly and face. He pushed at the stone with his hands, spitting out dust and blood in a thick reddish-brown clot; more blood was running into his left eye from a cut on his forehead, but everything else seemed to be functional. And someone was still shouting.

One of the Marines, lying and clutching his arm. John came erect and staggered over to the car, which was lying canted at a three-quarter angle. The intersecting walls of the nook they'd stopped in still stood, but the buildings they'd been attached to were gone, spread in a pile of broken blocks across what had been the street.

the angle of the walls acted to deflect the blast, Center said. **chaotic effect, and not predictable.**

Good thing for the plan it did what it did, John thought as he rummaged for the first-aid kit.

your death at this point would decrease the probability of an optimum outcome from 57% ±3 to 41% ±4, Center said obligingly.

"Nice to know you're needed," John said.

The ringing in his ears was less, and he could see properly. Good, no severe concussion; he squatted beside the wounded Marine.

"Hold him," he said to the others. "Let's take a look at this."

Two men held the shoulders down. The arm was not broken, but it was bleeding freely, a steady drip rather than an arterial pulse. He slipped the punch-dagger out of his collar and used it to cut off the sleeve of the uniform jacket; not the ideal tool—it was designed as a weapon—but it would do. The flesh of the man's forearm was torn, and something was sticking out if it. John closed his fingers on it. A splinter of wood, probably oak, from a structural beam. Longer than a handspan, and driven in deep.

"This is going to hurt," John said.

"Do it," the Marine gasped, gray-faced.

One of the others put a rifle sling between his teeth. John gripped firmly, put his weight on the hand that held the man's wrist to the ground, and pulled. The Marine convulsed, arching, his teeth sinking into the tough leather.

The finger-thick dagger of oak slid free. John held it up; no ragged edges, so there probably wasn't much left in the wound—hopefully not too much dirty cloth, either, since there was no time to debride it.

"Let it bleed for a second," he said. "It'll wash it clean."

There was medicinal alcohol and iodine powder in the kit. John waited, then swabbed the wound clear with cotton wool and poured in both. This time the Marine simply swore, and John grinned.

"You must be recovering." He packed the wound, bandaged it, and rigged a sling. "Try not to put too much strain on this, trooper."

"Yessir. Ah . . . what the hell do we do now, sir?"

They all looked at him, battered, bruised, a few bleeding from superficial cuts, but all functional. He looked down the street; there was a breastwork of stones four feet high in front of them, and more behind, but the road downslope looked fairly clear. Smoke was mounting up rapidly, though; the fires were out of control; the waterworks were probably hit and the mains out of operation. It lay thick on the air, thick between him and Pia.

"First we'll get this road cleared," he said briskly, spitting again. "Goms"—who looked worst injured—"there's some water in the boot of the car, see to it. Smith, check the car and see what it needs. Wilton, Sinders, Barrjen, Maken, you come with me."

He studied the way the rocks interlocked in the barrier ahead of them. "We'll shift this one first."

"Sir? Prybar?" corporal Wilton said. The crusted block probably weighed twice what John did, and he was the heaviest man there.

"No *time*. Barrjen, you on the other side, there's room for two."

Barrjen was three inches shorter than John, but just as broad across the shoulders, and thick through the belly and hips as well; his arms were massive, and the backs of his hands covered in reddish hair. He grinned, showing broad square teeth.

"If'n you say so, sor," he said, and bent his knees, working his fingers under the edges of the block.

John did likewise and took a deep, careful breath. "*Now*."

He lifted, taking the strain on back and legs, exhaling with the effort until red lights swam before his eyes and something in his gut was just on the edge of tearing. His coat *did* tear across the back, the tough seam parting with a long ripping sound. The stone resisted, and then he felt it shift. Shift again, his feet straining to keep their balance in the loose rubble, and then it was tumbling away down the other side like a dice from the box of a god, hammering into the pavement and falling into the gutter with a final *tock* sound.

Barrjen staggered backward, still grinning as he panted. "You diplomats is tougher'n you looks, sor," he said, in a thick eastern accent.

John spat on his hands. Center traced a glowing network of stress lines across the rockfall, showing the path of least resistance for clearing it.

"Let's get to work."

"I want to go home," Lola said—whimpered, really.

Pia fought an urge to slap her. The other woman's eyes were still round with shock; understandable, and she was less than twenty, but . . .

"Up here."

The staircase was empty; it filled the interior of the square tower, with a switchback every story and narrow windows in the cream-colored limestone. Smoke was drifting through them, enough to haze the air a little. The light poured in, scattering on the dust and smoke, incongruously beautiful shafts of gold bringing out the highlights and fossil shells in the stone. Pia labored upward, feeling the sweat running down her face and soaking the nurse's headdress she wore, thanking God that skirts had gone so high this year—barely ankle-length.

"Come on," she said. "We'll be safe up here."

"Safe for a little while," Lola said. Then: "Mother of *God*," as they came out onto the flat roof of the tower.

Ciano was burning. The pillars of fire had merged into columns that covered half the area they could see. Heavy and black, smoke drifted down from the hillsides, covering the highways that wound through the valleys running down to the Pada. The warehouse districts along the river were fully involved, the great storage tanks of olive oil and brandy bellowing upward in ruddy flame like so many giant torches.

"Nobody's fighting the fires at all," Pia whispered to herself. The waterworks must have been finally destroyed. And the streets by the docks, they were stuffed with timber, coal, cotton, so much tinder. She could feel the heat on her face, worse even in the few moments since they had come out onto the flat rooftop.

Lola looked around. "What can we do?"

"Wait," Pia said. "Wait and pray."

Thunder rumbled from the eastward. Pia's head came around slowly. The sky was summer blue, save for the great pillars of black smoke. Rain would be a mercy, but God had withheld His mercy from the people of the Empire. The sound rumbled again, then again—too regularly spaced for thunder, in any case.

The rain was not coming. The Chosen were, and those were their guns. She slipped to her knees and crossed herself, bringing the rosary to her lips.

Come to me, John, she thought. Come quickly, my love.

Then she began to plan.

CHAPTER NINE

"Ciano's burning," Jeffrey Farr said, opening his eyes.

Get out of there, he added silently to his brother. Afterimages of buildings sliding into streets in sheets of fiery rubble washed across his vision as the link through Center faded.

"Ya," Heinrich Hosten said cheerfully. "Maybe we shouldn't have bombed it quite so heavy."

He looked eastward, toward the smoke that hazed the horizon. The distant *thump . . . thump . . .* of artillery sounded, slow and regular.

"Street fighting," the Chosen officer went on. "We may have trapped them too well—there are a quarter of a million troops in there, less what's getting out, the net's not watertight."

"Why not just let it burn?" Jeffrey asked.

"The High Command may do that for a while. Praise the Powers That Be, *we* won't be pitchforked into it right away."

The survivors of Heinrich's regiment had been pulled into reserve, not completely out of action, but things would have to take a decided turn for the worse before they were put back into the line any time soon. More than a third of the roster had died blocking the Imperial breakout for those crucial hours, and as many again were wounded. The survivors were billeted now in the grounds of a nobleman's country estate; they could see the smoke-shadowed buildings of Ciano in the distance to the east. Heinrich had spent the last couple of days rounding up supplies for the celebration that bellowed and sprawled across the gardens: oxen and whole pigs roasted on spits, barrels stood at the ends of tables heaped with food. A roar went up from the troops—the male majority, at least—as a crowd of women were herded through the gates.

Jeffrey averted his eyes and ignored the screams. Nothing he could do, nothing at all . . . for now. Heinrich beamed indulgently down at the scene below the terrace and bit the last meat off the turkey drumstick in his hand.

"They've earned a little rest," he said, idly stroking the hip of the naked girl who poured his glass full again. "Did damned well."

The rest of the surviving officers were grouped around the tables on the balustraded terrace, paying serious attention to the feast the villa's staff had prepared for the new overlords. Most Chosen ate rather sparingly at home; in the food-poor Land red meat was a luxury except for the wealthiest among the upper caste. Jeffrey remembered John telling him how the Friday pork roast was the high point of the week, and that was for an up-and-coming general's family. Now that they had the biggest area of rich farmland on Visager under their control, the Chosen were making up for lost time.

The thought made the food taste a little better. *Maybe they'll get soft.*

probability 87% ±3, defining "soft" as significantly reduced militechnic functionality, Center supplied.

After more than a decade, Jeffrey could sense overtones of meaning in the words, even though they seemed machined out of thought the way engine parts were lathed from bar stock.

But? he supplied.

significant reduction would require 7 generations, plus or minus—

Never mind.

Heinrich tore off another drumstick and pulled the girl into his lap. "Victory, it is wonderful!" he said.

"Yeah," Jeffrey Farr replied. *It will be.*

((•)) ((•)) ((•))

"Are you sure this is a good idea?" Lola asked, ripping up the last of her petticoat.

"No," Pia said. "But the only other thing I can think of is to wait here for the Chosen. My Giovanni will come—but *look* at that out there!"

Ciano was the largest city in the world; for centuries, it had been the *capital* of the world, when the Universal Empire had been what its name claimed for it, leading humanity on Visager back from the Fall. Now it was dying, and mostly by its own hand.

"We've gotta find some broad in *this*?" Goms said.

Probably more crowded a couple of hours ago, John thought.

"Jesus," the marine finished, coughing in the thick air, a compound of smoke and explosion-powdered brick and stone.

"Back! Back!" the driver shouted, as half a dozen men in Imperial uniforms rushed towards the car.

They ignored him, if they heard at all; their faces had the fixed, carved-wood look of utter desperation sighting a chance of survival. A marine raised his rifle, cursed, lowered it again.

"If they get to the car, we're all dead," John said.

"He's right," Harry said. "Shit . . ."

The rifle blasted uncomfortably close to John's ear. He stood motionless, his hand resting on the top of the windscreen. It had been a warning shot; he could hear the sick whine of the ricochet, see the bright momentary spark where jacketed metal hit the cobblestones. The Imperials ignored it. More from the milling crowd were following; none of them looked to be armed—the Imperial army had regarded this as the ultimate rear area until a day or two ago—but there were a lot of them, all convinced that the car represented their chance to get *out*. They probably weren't thinking much beyond that.

"Damn," the marine said softly, and worked the bolt.

"Five rounds rapid!" Corporal Wilton said.

The marines had been waiting with their second finger on the trigger and their index lying under the bolt. *BAM* and five rounds blasted out. *Click* and the index finger flipped up the rear-mounted bolt handle of the rifles. Spring tension shot the bolt back halfway through its cycle as soon as the turning bolt released the locking lugs; a quick pull back and the shell was ejected; a slap with the palm of the hand and *chick-Chack!* the next round was in. Well-trained men could fire twelve aimed rounds a minute that way, and all the marines had "marksman" flashes on their shoulders.

Face frozen, John watched the first Imperial double over like a man punched in the belly—even at point-blank range the marines were aiming for the center of mass, as they'd been taught. The Imperial slumped forward and slid facedown, blood flowing over the cobbles. The shots cracked, quick careful firing with a half-second pause to aim. He didn't have to order *cease-fire* when the survivors turned and ran.

Wilton pulled the bolt of his rifle back and pushed a five-round stripper clip into the magazine with his thumb. The zinc strip that had held the cartridges tinkled against the side of the car. The crowd surged away from the car, milling aimlessly.

John didn't think anyone else would try to steal it for a while. It stood in one of the narrower laneways leading into the big plaza that stood before the train station; the station building itself wasn't burning . . . yet . . . but a stick of bombs had left a series of craters across the plaza, leading towards the twenty-meter high columns of the facade like an arrow on a map. The plaza had been crowded with mule- and horse-drawn wagons and ambulances, supply vehicles, even a few powered staff cars.

Most of the vehicles were abandoned, some burning or overturned. Wounded animals screamed, their voices shrill over the calling of hundreds—thousands—from within the great building, adding the last touch of hell. Wounded men were pouring out of the tall blushwood portals and out into the square, all of them who could move. Or could stagger along grasping at the walls, or support each other, or crawl. The stink of death and gangrene came with them in waves, strong enough that even a few of the marines gagged at it.

"Sir," Henry said, "we'd never have made it down if we'd left half an hour later. And there's no way in hell we're going to drive back to the embassy."

"No," John said, smiling slightly as he checked his pistol and then slid it back into the shoulder-holster under his frock coat. "But I don't think we'll have much of a problem finding my wife."

He nodded towards the left-hand tower. Someone on top had strung two strips of brightly colored cloth from corner windows to the middle of the front facing, and another straight down from the point at which they met. Together they formed an arrow—>, pointing upward at the tower-top. He took his binoculars out of the dashboard compartment and focused on the tiny figure waving at the apex of the signal.

"Let's go," he said.

The driver cleared his throat. John released Pia and stepped back; even then, in that charnel house of a place, the marines were grinning. Pia blushed and tucked strands of hair back under her snood.

"Sir," Harry said, "We're not going to get back to the embassy."

"No, we have to get out of the city entirely," John said thoughtfully.

They were in one of the loading bays of the station; fewer bodies here, fewer of the moaning, fevered wounded. None of the marines was what you'd call squeamish—they'd all seen action in the Southern Islands—but several of them were looking pale. So did Pia's friend; a couple of the troopers were courteously handing her safety pins to help fasten up her ripped dress.

"Sure you're all right?" John asked again.

"As right as can be," Pia said stoutly. "We cannot go to the embassy?"

John shook his head. "The fires are out of control, and there's fighting in the streets. The Chosen are close to the western end of the city, too."

Pia shivered and nodded. John turned his head slightly.

"Sinders," he said, "didn't you say you worked for the North Central Rail before you joined the corps?"

Sinders blinked at him. "Lord love you, sir, so I did," he said. "Locomotive driver. Had a bit of a falling out with the section foreman, like."

Someone spoke sotto voce: "Had a bit of a falling down with his daughter, you mean."

"Follow me," John said. He hopped down from the platform; cinders crunched under his boots. They handed down the women and walked over the tracks to the other side of the vast shed. "There, that one. Could you drive it?"

A steam engine and its fuel car stood pointing eastward; vapor leaked from several places, hiding the green-and-gold livery of the Imperial Pada Valley line.

"Sure, sir. It's Santander made, anyway—standard 4–4–2, rebuilt for the Imperial broad gauge. That's if we got time to raise steam, that could take a while."

"It has steam up," John said. Center drew a thermal schematic over his sight.

"But where would we go on it, sir?"

"East a ways, at least."

The marines looked uncertain. "Ah, beggin' yer pardon, sir," the corporal said "But ain't those Land buggers all around?"

"Maybe not to the east. And if we do run into them, we've got a better chance of standing on diplomatic immunity when they're in the field and under control by their officers than when they're turned loose on the city. I can speak Landisch and I've got the necessary papers."

And code words to prove he was a double agent working for Land Military Intelligence, if it came to that. Useful with the army, although the Fourth Bureau would probably kill him. Military Intelligence was as much the Fourth Bureau's enemy as anything in Santander was.

"Let's go," he finished.

They jogged over to the engine, grateful when its clean smell of hot iron, oil and soot overcame the slaughterhouse stink of the abandoned dying. John lifted Pia up with both hands on her waist, then her friend. Three of the Marines scrambled up onto the heap of broken coal that filled the fuel car; the rest of the party jammed themselves into the cab.

"Going to be a bit crowded," Sinders said, tapping at gauges and studying the swing of dials and the level of fluid in segmented glass tubes. "She's hot, though—plenty of steam. Could use a little coal . . . not that way, ye daft pennyworth!"

One of the marines jerked his hand back from the handle of the firebox set into the forward arch of the cab's surface.

"Use the shovel!" Sinders said. "Lay me down some, and I'll get this bitch movin'—beggin' your pardon, ma'am," he said to Pia.

John took the worn, long-handled tool down from the rack, sliding through the press of men and women. The ashwood was silky-smooth under his hands; he flicked the handle of the firedoor up and to the side, swinging the tray-sized oblong of cast iron open until it caught on the hook opposite. Hot dry air blasted back into the cab of the locomotive, with a smell of sulfur and scorched metal.

"Wilton, you get back with the others on the fuel car, I'm going to need some room here. Darling, could you and—"

"Lola. Lola Chiavri," the other woman said.

"Miss Chiavri get on those benches." Short iron seats were bolted under the angled windows at the rear sides of the cab, so that an off-duty fireman or stoker could sit and watch the track ahead.

John spat on his hands and dug the shovel into the coal that puddled out of the transfer chute at the very rear of the cab.

"Spread it around, like, sir," Sinders said, turning valve wheels and laying a hand on one of the long levers. "Not too much. Kind of bounce it off that-there arch of firebrick at the front of the furnace, you know?"

John grunted in reply. The second and third shovelfuls showed him the trick of it, a flicking turn of the wrists. *Have to get someone to spell me,* he thought. He was amply strong and fit for the task, but his hands didn't have the inch-thick crust of callus that anyone who did this for a living would develop.

WHUFF. WHUFF. Steam billowed out from the driving cylinders at the front of the locomotive.

"Keep it comin', sir. She's about ready." Sinders braced a foot and hauled back on another of the levers. "Damn, they shoulda greased this fresh days ago. Goddam wop maintenance."

There was a tooth-grating squeal of metal on metal as the driving wheels spun once against the rails, the smell of ozone, a quick shower of sparks. Then the engine lurched forward, slowed, lurched again and gathered speed with a regular *chuff. . . chuff. . .* of escaping steam. Pia grinned at John as he turned for another shovelful of coal; he found himself grinning back.

"Did it, by God," he said, then rapped his knuckles against the haft of the shovel in propitiation.

Sunlight fell bright across them as they pulled out of the train station; he flipped the firedoor shut and slapped Sinders on the shoulder.

"Halt just before that signal tower and let me down for a moment," he half-shouted over the noise into the Marines ear. "I'll switch us onto the mainline."

The trooper looked dubiously at the complex web of rail. "Sure you . . . yessir."

John leaped down with the prybar in hand. The gravel crunched under his feet, pungent with tar and ash. A film of it settled across the filthy surface of what had once been dress shoes; he found himself smiling wryly at that. He looked up for an instant and met Pia's eyes. She was smiling too, and he knew it was at the same jape.

That's some woman, he told himself, as he turned and let Center's glowing map settle over his vision. She recovered fast.

connections are here . . . and here.

Thanks, he thought absently.

you are welcome.

He drove the steel into the gap between the rails and heaved. After all these years, I'm still not sure if Center has a sense of humor.

Neither am I, if it's any consolation, Raj replied.

Chunk. The points slid into contact. He sprinted down the line a hundred yards and repeated the process, then waved. The locomotive responded with a puff of steam and a screech of steel on steel as Sinders let out the throttle. At his wave, it kept going; he sprinted alongside and grabbed at the bracket, grunted, took two more steps and swung himself up into the crowded cabin.

He looked ahead, southeastward. The track was clear. "Let's go home," he said.

"Home," Pia whispered. She buried her head against John's chest, and his arm went around her shoulders.

Pia went pale as she slid down from the saddle, biting her lip against the pain. Lola was weeping, but silently, and he was feeling the effects of days of hard riding himself. The marines were in worse condition than John; they were fit men, but they were footsoldiers, not accustomed to spending much time in the saddle.

"See to the horses," John said, looking upslope to the copse of evergreen oaks.

They were only a hundred miles from the Gut, and the landscape was getting hillier; the deep-soiled plain of the central lowlands was behind them, and they were in a harder, drier land. Thyme and arbutus scented the air as he climbed quickly to the crest of the hill; the other side showed rolling hills, mostly covered in scrub with an occasional olive grove or terraced vineyard or hollow filled with pale barley stubble. Occasional stands of spike grass waved ten meters in the air. The rhizome-spread native plant was almost impossible to eradicate, but individual clumps never expanded beyond pockets where the moisture level and soil minerals were precisely correct. And a dusty gray-white road, winding a couple of thousand yards below them. On it, coming down from the north . . .

John relaxed. That was no Chosen column. A shapeless clot of humanity grouped around half a dozen two-wheeled ox carts, a few men on horseback, mostly civilians on foot, some pulling handcarts heaped with their possessions.

"Refugees," he said, as Pia and several of the Marines came up. "We can cut—wait."

He pressed himself flat again and raised his field glasses. There was no need to say more to the others; four weeks struggling south through the dying Empire had been education enough for all of them. The troops pouring over the hills on the other side of the road were ant-tiny, but there was no mistaking the smooth efficiency with which they shook themselves out from column into line. Half were mounted—on mules—the other half trotting on foot beside, holding on to a stirrup iron with one hand.

Chosen mobile-force unit, Raj said. *You can move fast that way, about a third again as fast as marching infantry.*

The Land troops were all dismounting now, mule-holders to the rear, riflemen deploying into extended line. There was a bright blinking ripple as they fixed bayonets. Others were lifting something from panniers on the backs of supply mules, bending over the shapes they lifted down.

machine guns, Center commented.

"Christ on a crutch," Smith whispered. "They're gonna—"

The refugees had finally noticed the Chosen troops. A spray of them began to run eastward off the road about the same time that the Land soldiers opened fire. The machine guns played on the ones running at first; the tiny figures jerked and tumbled and fell. The rest of the refugees milled in place, or threw themselves into the ditches. Two mounted men made it halfway to where John lay, one with a woman sitting on the saddlebow before him. The bullets kicked up dust all around them, sparking on rocks. The single man went down, and his horse rolled across him, kicking. The second horse crumpled more slowly. A group of soldiers loped out toward it, and the male rider stood and fired a pistol.

The long jet of black-powder smoke drifted away. Before it did the man staggered backward; three Land rifles had cracked, and John saw two strike. He dropped limply. The woman tried to run, holding something that slowed her, but the Protégé troopers caught her before she went a dozen strides. She seemed to stumble, then fell forward with a limp finality. There was a small *snap* sound. One of the troopers slammed his bayonet through her back and wrenched it free with a twist; the body jerked and kicked its heels. Another kicked something out of her outstretched hand, picked it up, then flung it away with an irritable gesture. It landed close enough to the ridge for him to see what it was—a pocket derringer, a lady's toy in gilt steel and ivory.

John turned his head aside, shutting his ears to the screams from the road, and to the whispered curses of Smith and the marines. That showed him Pia's face. It might have been carved from ivory, and for a moment he knew what she would look like as an old woman—with the face sunk in on the strong bones, one of those black-clad matriarchs he'd met so often at Imperial soirees, and as often thought would do better at running the Empire than their bemedalled spouses.

The Land soldiers kept enough of the refugees alive to help drag the bodies and wrecked vehicles off the roadway. Then they lined them up with the compulsive neatness of the Chosen and a final volley rang out. The column formed up on the gravel as the slow *crack* ... *crack* ... of an officer's automatic sounded, finishing the wounded. Then they moved off to the Santander party's left, heading north up the winding road through the dun-colored hills.

John waited, motioning the others down with an extended palm. Five minutes passed, then ten. The sun was hot; sweat dripped from his chin, stinging in a scrape, and dripped dark spots into the dust inches below his face with dull *plop* sounds. Then ...

"Right," he muttered.

Two squads of Land soldiers rose from where they'd hidden among the tumbled dead and wagons, fell into line with their rifles over their shoulders and moved off after their comrades at the quickstep.

"Tricky," Smith said. "What'll we do now, sir?"

"We go down there," John said, standing and extending a hand to help Pia up. "Pick up supplies and head south along that road toward Salini just as fast as the horses can stand."

Pia looked down towards the road and quickly away. Smith hesitated. "Ah, sir ... if it's all the same ..."

"Do it," John said. Smith shrugged and turned to call out to the others.

No harm in explaining, as long as it isn't a question of discipline, Raj prompted him.

John nodded; to Raj, but Smith caught the gesture and paused.

"We can move faster on the road," John said. "Also if we don't have to stop for food, including oats for the horses. That detachment was clearing the way for a regimental combat team. With our remounts, we can outrun them."

Smith blinked in thought, then drew himself up. "Yessir," he said, with a small difficult smile. "Just didn't like the idea of, well—"

Pia's hand tightened in John's. "That was what happens to the weak," she said unexpectedly. "We're all going to have to become .. . very strong, Mr. Smith. Very strong, indeed."

The Santander party moved forward over the crest and down the slope towards the road, leading their horses over the rough uneven surface speckled with thorny bushes. The shod hoofs thumped on dirt, clattered against rocks with an occasional spark. None of the humans spoke. Then Johns head came up.

What's that noise? he thought.

A thin piping. Pia stopped. "Quiet!" she said.

John put up his hand and the party halted. That made the sound clearer, but it had that odd property some noises did, of seeming to come from all directions.

the sound is—Center began.

Pia released John's hand and walked over to the body of the woman who'd shot herself rather than be captured by the Land soldiers. John opened his mouth to call her back, then shut it; Pia had probably—certainly—seen worse than this in the emergency hospital back in Ciano.

The Imperial girl rolled the woman's body back John could see her pale; the soft-nosed slug from the derringer had gone up under the dead woman's chin and exited through the bridge of her nose, taking most of the center of her face with it. Not instantly fatal, although it would have been a toss-up whether she bled out from that first or from the bayonet wound through the kidneys.

—an infant, Center concluded, as Pia picked up a cloth-wrapped bundle from where the woman's body had concealed it. She knelt and unbound the swaddlings. John came closer, close enough to see that it was a healthy, uninjured boychild of about three months—and reassured enough by the contact to let out an unmistakable wail. Also badly in need of a change; Pia ripped a square from the outer covering and improvised.

"There's a carrying cradle on the saddle of that horse, I think," she said, without looking up. "Why doesn't someone get it for me and save the time?"

Don't even try, kid, Raj said at the back of John's mind.

Nightmare images of himself trying to convince Pia that it was impossible to carry a suckling infant on a forced-march journey through the disintegrating Empire flitted through John's mind. He smiled wryly, even then.

Besides, he thought, looking down at the road, there's been enough death here.

"Sinders, do that," he said aloud. "Let's get moving. And if there's a live nanny goat down there, somebody truss it and put it over one of the spare horses."

CHAPTER TEN

The throng filling the Salini waterfront had the voice of surf on a gravel beach: harsh, sometimes louder or softer, but never silent. A mindless, inhuman snarl.

The bridge of the protected cruiser *McCormick City* was crowded as well. Many of those present were civilians whose only business was to speak with Commodore Maurice Farr, Officer Commanding the First Scouting Squadron. The situation didn't please Farr. Captain Dundonald, the flagship's captain, was coldly livid, though openly he'd merely pointed out that the admiral's bridge and cabin in the aft superstructure would provide the commodore with more space.

Farr sympathized with his subordinate, but "subordinate" was the key word here. He had no intention of removing himself to relative isolation while trying to untangle a mare's nest like the evacuation of Santander citizens and their dependents from Salini. Farr was sleeping in the captain's sea cabin off the bridge, forcing Dundonald to set up a cot in the officers' library on the deck below.

"Commodore Farr," said Cooley, spokesman for the captains of the five Santander freighters anchored in the jaws of the shallow bay that served Salini for a harbor, "I want you to know that if you don't help us citizens like your orders say to, you'll answer to some damned important people! Senator Beemody is a partner in Morgan Trading, and there's other folk involved who talk just as loud, though they may do it in private."

Three of the other civilian captains nodded meaningfully, though grizzled old Fitzwilliams had the decency to look embarrassed. Fitz had left the navy after twelve years as a lieutenant who knew he'd never rise higher in peacetime. That was a long time ago, but listening to a civilian threaten a naval officer with political consequences still affected Fitzwilliams in much the way it did Farr himself.

"Thank you, Captain Cooley," Farr said. "I'll give your warning all the consideration it deserves. As for the specifics of your request . . ."

He turned to face the shore, drawing the civilians' attention to the obvious. The Salini waterfront crawled with ragged, desperate people for as far as the eye could see. The *McCormick City* and two civilian ferries hired by the Santander government were tied up at the West Pier. A hundred Santander Marines and armed sailors guarded the pierhead with fixed bayonets.

Behind them, the six staff members of the Santander consulate in Salini sat at tables made from boards laid on trestles. The vice-consuls poured over huge ledgers, trying to match the names of applicants to the register of Santander citizens within the Empire.

The job was next to hopeless. No more than half the citizens visiting the Union had bothered to register. The consulate staff was reduced to making decisions on the basis of gut instinct and how swarthy the applicant looked.

Every human being in Salini—and there must have been thirty thousand of them as refugees poured south as the Shockwave ahead of unstoppable Chosen columns—wanted to board those two ferries. Farr's guard detachment had used its bayonets already to keep back the crowd. Very soon they would have to fire over the heads of a mob, and even that wouldn't restrain desperation for long.

"Gentlemen," Farr said, "the warehouses on Pier Street might as well be on Old Earth for all the chance you'd have of retrieving their contents for your employers. If I landed every man in my squadron, I still couldn't clear the waterfront for you. And even then what would you do? Wish the merchandise into your holds? There aren't any stevedores in Salini now. There's nothing but panic."

Farr's guard detachment daubed the forelocks of applicants with paint as they were admitted to the pier. It was the only way in the confusion to prevent refugees from coming through the line again and again, clogging still further an already cumbersome process.

A middle-aged woman with a forehead of superstructure gray leaped atop a table with unexpected agility, then jumped down on the other side despite the attempt of a weary vice-consul to grab her. She sprinted along the pier. Two sailors at the gangway of the nearer ferry stepped out to block her.

With an inarticulate cry, the woman flung herself into the harbor. Oily water spurted. One of the Santander cutters patrolling to intercept swimmers stroked to the spot, but Farr didn't see her come up again.

"There's a cool two hundred thousand in tobacco aging in the Pax and Morgan Warehouse," Cooley said. "Christ knows what all else. Senator Beemody ain't going to be pleased to hear he waited too long to fetch it over."

This time he was making an observation, not offering a threat.

Salini's Long Pier was empty. The two vessels along the East Pier, itself staggeringly rotten, had sunk at their moorings a decade ago.

The wooden-hulled cruiser *Imperatora Giulia Moro* still floated beside the Navy Pier across the harbor, but she was noticeably down by the stern. The *Moro* had put out a week before along with the rest of the Imperial Second Fleet under orders from the Ministry in Ciano. The Second Fleet was a motley assortment. Besides poor maintenance and inadequate crewing levels, all the vessels had in common was their relatively shallow draft. That made operation in the Gut less of a risk than it would have been for heavier ships, since the Imperial Navy's standard of navigation was no higher than that of its gunnery.

The *Moro* had limped back to her dock six hours later. She hadn't been out of sight of the harbor before her stern seams had worked so badly that she was in imminent danger of sinking. Now her decks were packed with refugees to whom the illusion of being on shipboard was preferable to waiting on land for Chosen bayonets.

The *Moro*'s crew had vanished in the ship's boats, headed across the Gut to Dubuk in Santander. Farr couldn't really blame them.

Those men were likely to be the fleet's only survivors—unless the other vessels had cut and run also.

A steam launch chuffed toward the *McCormick City's* port quarter, opposite the pier. A Sierra flag hung from the jackstaff. Diplomats? At any rate, another complication on a day that had its share already. For the moment, Captain Dundonald's crew could deal with the matter.

The remaining civilian present on the bridge was the one Farr had sent armed guards to summon: Henry Cargill, Santander's consul in Salmi and the official whose operations Farr was tasked to support. Turning from the bridge railing—brass at a high polish, warmly comforting in the midst of such chaos—Farr fixed his glare on the haggard-looking consul.

"Mr. Cargill," Farr said, "if we don't evacuate this port shortly there will be a riot followed by a massacre. I have no desire to shoot unfortunate Imperial citizens, and I have even less desire to watch those citizens trample naval personnel. When can we be out of here?"

"I don't know," the consul said. He shook his head, then repeated angrily, "I'm damned if I know, Commodore, but I know it'll be sooner if you let me get back to the tables. I'm supposed to be spelling Hoxley now—for an hour. Which is all the sleep he'll get till midnight tomorrow!"

Cargill waved at the waterfront. The refugees stood as dynamically motionless as water behind a dam—and as ready to roar through if a crack appeared in the line of Santander personnel.

"They're coming from the north faster than we can process the ones already here," he continued. "Formally, I have orders to aid the return of Santander citizens to the Republic. *Off* the record, I have an expression of the governments deep concern lest large numbers of penniless refugees flood Santander."

A party of armed men had pushed their way through the crowd to the pierhead. Farr tensed for a confrontation, then relaxed as the guard detachment passed the new arrivals without even painting their foreheads. There were women among them, and unless the distance was tricking Farr's eyes, some of the men wore portions of Santander Marine *dress* uniforms.

Cargill bitterly quoted, "The Ministry trusts you will use your judgment to prevent a situation that might tend to embarrass the government and draw the Republic into quarrels that are none of our proper affair.' The courier who brought that destroyed the note in front of me after I'd read it, but I'm sure the minister remembers what he wrote. And the president does, too, I shouldn't wonder!"

Farr looked at the consul with a flush of sympathy he hadn't expected to feel for the man who was delaying the squadron's departure. Consular officials weren't the only people who were expected to carry the can for their superiors in event an action had negative political repercussions. "I see," he said. "I appreciate your candor, sir. I'll leave you to get back to your—"

Ensign Tillingast, the *McCormick City's* deck officer, stepped onto the bridge with a look of agitation. Behind him were a pair of armed marines and a bareheaded civilian wearing an oilskin slicker.

Tillingast looked from Farr to Captain Dundonald, who curtly nodded him back to the commodore. Farr commanded the squadron, but he *didn't* directly control the crew of the flagship. He tried to be scrupulous in going through Dundonald when he gave orders, but the natural instinct of the men themselves was to deal directly with the highest authority present in a crisis.

"Sir, he came on the launch," Tillingast said, "I thought I should bring him right up."

The stranger took off his slicker and folded it neatly over his left forearm. Under it he wore the black-and-silver dress uniform of a lieutenant in the Land military service, with the navy's dark blue collar flashes and fourragére dangling from his right epaulet. To complete his transformation he donned the saucer hat he'd carried beneath the raingear.

"I am not of course a spy," the Land officer said with a crisp smile to his surprised audience. He was a small, fair man, and as hard as a marble statue. "The ruse was necessary as we could not be sure the animals out there—"

He gestured toward the crawling waterfront.

"—would recognize a flag of truce."

Drawing himself to attention, he continued, "Commodore Farr,

I am *Leutnant der See* Helmut Weiss, flag lieutenant to *Unterkapttan der See* Elise Eberdorf, commander of the Third Cruiser Squadron."

He saluted. Farr returned the salute, feeling his soul return to the stony chill that had gripped it every day of his duty as military attaché in the Land.

"I am directed to convey *Unterkapttan* Eberdorf's compliments," Weiss said, "and to inform you that she is allowing one hour for neutral shipping to leave the port of Salmi before we attack."

"I see," Farr said without inflection.

The ships of Farr's squadron were almost as heterogeneous a group as the Imperial Second Fleet. The *McCormick City* was a lovely vessel—6,000 tons, twenty knots, and only five years old. She mounted eight-inch guns in twin turrets fore and aft, with a secondary battery of five-inch quick-firers in ten individual sponsons on the superstructure. The *Randall* was five years older, slower, and carried her four single eight-inch guns behind thin gunshields at bow and stern. Farr was of the school that believed armor which wasn't at least three inches thick only served to detonate shells that might otherwise have passed through doing only minor damage.

At least the *Randall's* secondary battery had been replaced with five-inch quick-firers during the past year. Guns that used bagged charges instead of metallic cartridges loaded too slowly to fend off torpedo attack.

The *Lumberton* was older yet, with short-barrelled eight-inch guns and a secondary battery of six-inch slow-firers that had been next to useless when they were designed—at about the time Farr was a midshipman. Last and least, the *Waccachee Township* wore iron armor over a wooden hull much like the poor *Imperatora Giulia Moro* across the harbor. She'd never in her career been able to make thirteen knots.

"Attack what?" Captain Dundonald said. "Good God, man! Does this look like a military installation to you?"

Lieutenant Weiss chuckled. "Yes, well," he said "You must understand, gentlemen, that though it will doubtless take a year or two to reduce the animals to a condition of proper docility, we must first close the cage door. Besides, the squadron needs target practice. We were escorting the transports at Corona."

He eyed the *Moro*. The brightly clad refugees gave the impression that the ship was dressed in bunting for a gala naval review of the sort the Empire had so dearly loved. "From what those who were present at Corona say, the Imperial main fleet wasn't much more of a danger than that hulk will be."

Farr tried to blank his mind. The image of shells slamming home among the mass of humanity on the *Moro* was too clear; it would show on his face. And if he spoke, something unprofessional would come out of his mouth.

"Commodore—" said a breathless Ensign Tillingast, bursting onto the bridge again.

"Ensign!" Farr shouted. "What the *hell* do you think you're doing, breaking in on—"

"Your son, sir," Tillingast said.

"Jeffrey?" Farr blurted. He wished he could have the word back as it came out, even before John Hosten stepped through the companionway hatch.

John was limping slightly. He'd lost twenty pounds since Farr last saw him; and, Farr thought, the boy had lost his innocence as well.

"Sir, I'm sorry," John said. "I became separated from Jeffrey in Ciano. He was in Corona when—"

John appeared to be choosing his words with as much care as fatigue and sleeplessness allowed him. Farr had seen his son's eyes flick without lighting across Weiss' uniform.

"When we last spoke," John resumed, "Jeffrey intended to present himself to a Chosen command group. He felt association with Land forces was of more benefit to his professional development and that of the Republic's army than remaining with the Imperials would be."

Lieutenant Weiss allowed himself a tight smile. Captain Dundonald ostentatiously turned his back.

"I'm confident that so long as my sons live, they'll do their duty as citizens of the Republic of the Santander," Farr said, his voice as calm as a wave rising on deep water. "As will their father."

If at full strength—probable since Weiss said they hadn't seen action—the Land's Third Cruiser Squadron would be four nearly identical modern vessels. They were excellent sea boats and faster than even the *McCormick City*—unless their hulls were foul; don't assume the enemy is ten feet tall, though be prepared in case he is.

On the other hand, the cruisers were small ships, less than 3,000 tons standard displacement. The ten ten-centimeter quick-firers each carried in hull sponsons were no serious gunnery threat to Farr's squadron . . . but the three torpedo tubes were another matter. Corona had proved how effective Chosen torpedoes could be.

"Lieutenant Weiss," Farr said. "I have orders to give to my command before I reply to your message. I'd like you to remain present so that you can provide your superior with a full accounting."

Weiss clicked his heels to emphasize his nod.

"Commander Grisson," Farr said to his staff secretary, "Signal the squadron, 'Under way in ten minutes.'"

That was a bluff. His ships had one or at most two boilers lighted to conserve coal at anchor. Peacetime regulations. . . . Still, Eberdorf had kept her cruisers over the horizon, so by the time Weiss returned with Farr's reply more than the "hour's deadline" would have passed.

"Make it so, Ryan!" Dundonald snapped to his own signals officer, staring wide-eyed from the wheelhouse. The *McCormick City*'s captain had no intention of standing on ceremony now.

"Gentlemen," Farr continued to the freighter captains watching from the starboard wing of the bridge, "as senior military officer present, I'm asserting federal control over your vessels. You will dock—"

"You can't do that!" Captain Cooley said.

"I *have* done it, Captain," Farr said without raising his voice. "And if you want to return to Santander in the brig of this vessel, just open your mouth once more."

Cooley started to speak, took a good look at the commodore's face, and nodded apology.

Bells rang through the *McCormick City*'s compartments. A gun fired a blank charge as an attention signal; yeomen tugged at the flag halyards, relaying the commodore's orders to the rest of the squadron.

"You will take on board as many civilians as possible," Farr resumed. "By that I mean as many as you can cram on board with a shoehorn. I don't care if you've only got a foot of freeboard showing—it's just eighty miles to Dubuk and the forecast is for calm. Mr. Cargill—"

"Yes." There was a trace of a smile on the consul's worn visage.

"Your personnel will direct civilians onto the transports. Any processing can be done after we dock in Dubuk. I'll leave you forty men for traffic control, which I trust will be sufficient."

"Giving those poor wops their lives back should be sufficient in itself, sir," Cargill said. "Thank you."

"The remainder of the shore party will be broken down into five twelve-man detachments, Grisson," Farr said. "They will board the federalized transports in order to aid the civilian crews in recognizing naval signals."

"In view of the need for haste, sir," Grisson said, "I assume the signal detachments will proceed directly to their new assignments rather than returning to their home vessels to deposit their sidearms?"

"That's correct," Farr said. Grisson was a nephew of Farr's first wife; a very able boy.

"Commodore," Captain Fitzwilliams said, "I don't guess I've forgotten the signal book in the twenty years I been out. Don't short your gun crews for the sake of the *Holyoke*. We'll be where you put us."

Farr returned his attention to Lieutenant Weiss. The Land officer's face had somehow managed to become even harder and more pale than it had been when he arrived.

"Lieutenant," Farr said, "I regret that I will be unable to comply with Commander Eberdorf's request because it conflicts with my orders to aid the consular authorities to repatriate Santander citizens from Salini. As you've heard, I've taken measures to streamline the process. I'm afraid the loading will nonetheless continue until after nightfall."

Weiss' eyes were filled with cold hatred. Farr suppressed a wry smile. His own feeling toward the Chosen officer was loathing, not hatred.

"Until the process is complete, I must request that Land military forces treat Salini as an extension of the Republic of the Santander," Farr continued. With age had come the ability to sound calm when the world was very possibly coming apart. "I regret any inconvenience this causes Commander Eberdorf or her superiors. Do you have any questions?"

"I have no questions of a man who doesn't know his duty to his country, *Kommodore*," Weiss said.

"When I have questions about my duty, Lieutenant Weiss," Farr said in a voice that trembled only in his own mind, "it will not be a foreigner I ask for clarification."

Weiss began to put on his oilskins methodically. His eyes were focused a thousand miles beyond the bulkhead toward which he stared.

The freighter captains had been exchanging looks and whispers. Now Captain Cooley spat over the railing and said, "Commodore? The rest of us reckon we can figure out naval signals, too, until this business gets sorted out back home."

He nodded toward the waterfront and added, "Only don't count on that lot being on board by nightfall. If we're not still at the dock at daybreak, then my mother's a virgin."

The Land officer strode for the companionway without saluting or being dismissed.

"Lieutenant Weiss?" Farr called. Weiss stopped and nodded curtly, but he didn't turn around.

"Please inform your superior that if she's dead set on having a battle," Farr said, "we can offer her a better one than her colleagues appear to have found at Corona."

Weiss trembled, then stepped down the companionway.

Farr had never felt so tired before in his life. "Commander Grisson," he said, "Signal the squadron, 'Clear for action.'"

"This is the first time I've seen Corona, Jeffrey," Heinrich said.

"The regiment dropped north of town and we never had occasion to work back." He chuckled. "Not such a tourist attraction as I'd been told."

A tang of smoke still hung in the air ten weeks after Land forces overran the city. Work gangs had cleared the streets, using rubble from collapsed structures to fill bomb craters, but there'd been no attempt to rebuild.

There was no need for reconstruction. The port city's surviving civilian population had been removed from what was now a military reservation closed to former citizens of the Empire.

Corona was the node which connected the conquering armies to their logistics bases in the Land. Protégés from the Land performed all tasks. Labor here was too sensitive to be entrusted to slaves who hadn't been completely broken to the yoke. Convoys of vehicles were pouring up from the docks: steam trucks, Land military-issue mule wagons, and a medley of impressed Imperial civilian transport pulled by everything from oxen to commandeered race horses. There was little disorder; military police were out in force directing traffic, wands in their hands and polished metal brassards on chains around their necks. Troops marched by the side of the road, giving way to Heinrich and Jeffrey on their horses. The Chosen officer exchanged salutes with his counterparts as they passed, running a critical eye over the Protégé infantry.

It wasn't the smoke that made Jeffrey Farr's nose wrinkle as he dismounted and handed the reins to the Protégé groom who'd run at his stirrup from the remount corral at the edge of town. Nobody'd made an effort to find all the bodies in the wreckage either. Some of them must be liquescent by now. Well, he'd smelled plenty of other dead bodies in the past weeks. Humans weren't as bad as horses, and nothing was as bad as a ripe mule.

"So," the Chosen colonel said with a grin, "I hope our honored guest found his tour of our new territories to have been an interesting one?"

"Rather a change from the round of embassy parties I expected when I was posted to Ciano, that's true, Heinrich," Jeffrey said. Part of him wanted to bolt for the gangplank of the *City of Dubuk*, the three-stack liner chartered by the Santander government to repatriate its citizens through Corona. There was no need to do that. Heinrich liked him.

And, God help him, he liked Heinrich. The blond colonel epitomized the virtues the Land inculcated in its Chosen citizens: courage, steadfastness, self-reliance, and self-sacrifice.

You don't have to hate them, lad, said Raj Whitehall in Jeffrey's mind. *Just crush them the way you would a scorpion.*

Though Jeffrey'd seen plenty to hate as well.

Jeffrey lifted the rucksacks paired to either side of his saddlehorn and threw them over his left shoulder. He'd picked up his kit on the move. Clothing, mostly; all of it Land-issue. Life with Heinrich's fire brigade was dangerous enough without being mistaken for an Imperial infiltrator. He'd replace it on board if possible. Already late arrivals boarding the *Dubuk* were giving him hard looks.

"Very luxurious, no doubt," Heinrich said, eyeing the liner critically. "Well, I don't begrudge you that. I'm looking forward to a transient officers' hostel with clean sheets tonight myself. And a few someones to warm them with me, not so?"

The *City of Dubuk*'s whistle blew a two-note warning: a minute till the gangplank rose. Crewmen were already taking aboard lines preparatory to undocking. If Jeffrey had missed this ship, he would have had to take a freighter to the Land and there transship to Santander. At least for the present the Chosen had embargoed all regular trade between their newly conquered territories and the rest of Visager.

a pity, that, said Center. **but clandestine supply routes into the area will be sufficient to support our low-intensity guerilla operations**.

Jeffrey was very glad he was here to board the *Dubuk*. After the campaign he'd just watched, he didn't want to be around the Chosen any longer than necessary.

"Thank you for your hospitality, Heinrich," he said. "And your help in getting me here in time to save a long swim home."

Heinrich laughed and leaned from his saddle to clasp Jeffrey Chosen-fashion, forearm-to-forearm with hands gripping beneath one another's elbow. "An excuse to take my troops out of the field," he said as he straightened. "I'm not the only one who appreciates a little rest and recreation."

The *Dubuk's* whistle blew its full three-note call. Heinrich kicked his horse forward so that its forehooves rested on the gangplank. The animal whickered nervously at the hollow sound. A sailor on the deck above shouted a curse.

"Go then, my friend," Heinrich said. He smiled. "And tell the person who just spoke that if his tongue wags again, I will ride aboard and add it to my other trophies."

Jeffrey started up before someone on shipboard said the wrong thing in trying to clear the gangplank. He knew Heinrich too well to take the threat as a joke.

Nor would I count on the fact he likes you making much difference in the way Heinrich carries out his duties, lad, Raj said. *Nor should it, of course.*

A middle-aged civilian and the *Dubuk's* purser waited for Jeffrey at the head of the ramp. Their grim expressions faded to guarded question when they viewed the diplomatic passport he offered them.

Jeffrey tugged the sleeve of his Land uniform tunic. "I was in the wrong place when the fighting broke out," he said in a low voice. "If you can help me find the sort of clothes human beings wear, I'd be more than grateful."

"Jeffrey, my friend?" Heinrich called as he let his nervous horse step back. A hydraulic winch immediately began to haul the gangplank aboard. "When you have rested, come visit me again. These animals will be providing sport for years, no matter what the Council says!"

Jeffrey waved cheerfully, then moved away from the railing. If Heinrich could no longer see him, he was less likely to shout something that would put Jeffrey even more on the wrong side of an us-and-them divide with everyone else aboard the *City of Dubuk.* "Needs must when the Devil drives," he murmured to the men beside him.

"You're related to John Hosten, I believe, sir?" the civilian asked in a neutral voice.

his name is beemer, Center said. **he is deputy director of the ministry's research desk, though his cover is consular affairs.**

"John's my brother," Jeffrey said thankfully. "Stepbrother, really, but we're very close."

Beemer nodded. "I'll see about replacing your clothes, sir," he said. To the purser he added, "Ferrington? I only need one of the rooms in my suite. I suggest we put Captain Farr in the other one. I know his brother."

The purser still looked puzzled, but he shrugged and said, "Certainly, Mr. Beemer. Captain Farr? That'll be Suite F on the Boat Deck. Would you like a steward to take your luggage there?"

The *City of Dubuk* blew a deep blast. The pair of tugboats on the vessel's harbor side shrilled an answer. Their propellers churned water, taking up the slack in the hawsers binding them to the liner.

Jeffrey hefted his saddlebags with a wan smile. "Thank you, I think I'll be able to manage on my own," he said. "If you gentlemen don't mind, I'll watch the undocking from the bow."

"Of course," said Beemer equably. "I hope you'll have time during the trip to chat with me about your recent experiences."

"Whatever you'd care to do, captain," the purser said. "So far as the crew of the *City of Dubuk* is concerned, this is an ordinary commercial voyage. We're here to assist you."

Jeffrey paused. "For a while there," he said, "I didn't think I'd ever see home alive."

And *that* was the truth if he'd ever told it. He bowed to the two men and walked forward. The deck shivered with the vibration of the tugs' engines.

Center? he asked. Did Dad think Eberdorf would attack the harbor while he was there?

There was no chance of that, lad, Raj said. *Commander Eberdorf spent the past three years at a desk in the navy's central offices in Oathtaking. She's too politically savvy to start a second major war while the first one's going on.*

The *City of Dubuk* swayed as she came away from the dock. The lead tug signaled with three quick chirps.

But did Dad know that? Jeffrey demanded.

your father does not have access to the database that informs your decisions—and those of raj, Center replied after a pause that could only be deliberate. **nor does he have my capacity for analysis available to him. he viewed the chance of combat as not greater than one in ten, and the risk of all-out war resulting from such combat as in the same order of probability.**

Jeffrey put his hand on the wooden railing. It had the sticky roughness of salt deposited since a deckhand had wiped it down this morning.

Dad thought the risk was better than living with the alternative.

At the time Jeffrey's link through Center had showed him the scene on the bridge of the *McCormick City,* his own eyes had been watching Heinrich and two aides torturing a twelve-year-old boy to learn where his father, the town's mayor, had concealed the arms from the police station.

The ship swayed again, this time from the torque of her central propeller as she started ahead dead slow.

I was so frightened . . . but I'd never have spoken to Dad again if he'd permitted a massacre like the ones I watched.

I had men like your father serving under me, Raj said. **They could only guess at the things Center would have known, but they still managed to act the way I'd have done.**

The *City of Dubuk* whistled again, long and raucously, as all three propellers began to churn water in the direction of home.

I've always thought those people were the greatest good fortune of my career, Raj added.

CHAPTER ELEVEN

Gerta Hosten spat in the dry dust of the village street.

"*Leutnant,* just what the *fik* do you think you're doing?" she asked.

"Setting the animals an example!" the young officer said.

"An example of what—how to show courage and resistance?" she asked.

The subject of their dispute hung head-down from a rope tied around his ankles and looped over a stout limb of the live oak that shaded the village well. He spat, too, in her direction, then returned to a cracked, tuneless rendition of "Imperial Glory," the former Empire's national anthem. Two hundred or so peasants and artisans stood and watched behind a screen of Protégé infantry; the town's gentry, priests, and other potential troublemakers had already been swept up. The packed villagers smelled of sweat and hatred, their eyes furtive except for a few with the courage to glare. The sun beat down, hot even by Land standards on this late-summer day, but dry enough to make her throat feel gritty.

Gerta sighed, drew her Lauter automatic, jacked the slide, and fired one round into the hanging man's head from less than a meter distance. The flat elastic *crack* echoed back from the whitewashed stone houses surrounding the village square and from the church that dominated it. The civilians jerked back with a rippling murmur; the

Protégé troopers watched her with incurious ox-eyed calm. Blood and bone fragments and glistening bits of brain spattered across the feet of the Protégé who had been waiting with a barbed whip. He gaped in surprise, lifting one foot and then another in slow bewilderment.

"Hauptman—"

"Shut up." Gerta ejected the magazine, returned it to the pouch on her belt beside the holster, and snapped a fresh one into the well of the pistol. "Come."

She put her hand on the lieutenant's shoulder and guided him aside a few steps, leaning toward him confidentially. Young as he was, she didn't think he mistook the smile on her face for an expression of friendliness; on the other hand, she was a full captain and attached to General Staff Intelligence, so he'd probably listen at least a little.

"What exactly did you have planned?" she said.

"Why . . . ammunition was found in the animal's dwelling. I was to execute him, shoot five others taken at random, and then burn the village."

Gerta sighed again. "*Leutnant,* the logic of our communication with the animals is simple." She clenched one hand and held it before his nose. "It goes like this: 'Dog, here is my fist. Do what I want, or I will *hit* you with it.'"

"Ya, Hauptman—"

"Shut up. Now, there is an inherent limitation to this form of communication. You can only burn their houses down *once*— thereby reducing agricultural production in this vicinity by one hundred percent. You can only kill them *once.* Whereupon they cease to be potentially useful units of labor and become so much dead meat . . . and pork is much cheaper. Do you grasp my meaning, boy?"

"Nein, Hauptman."

This time Gerta repressed the sigh. "Terror is an effective tool of control, but only if it is applied *selectively.* There is nothing in the universe more dangerous than someone with nothing to lose. If you flog a man to death for having two shotgun shells—loaded with birdshot, he probably simply forgot them—then *what incentive is left to prevent them from active resistance?*"

"Oh."

The junior officer looked as if he was thinking, which was profoundly reassuring. No Chosen was actually *stupid;* the Test of Life screened out low IQs quite thoroughly, and had for many generations. That didn't mean that Chosen couldn't be willfully stupid, though—over-rigid, ossified.

"So. You must apply a *graduated* scale of punishment. Remember, we are not here to exterminate these animals, tempting though the prospect is."

Gerta looked over at the villagers. It was *extremely* tempting, the thought of simply herding them all into the church and setting it on fire. Perhaps that would be the best policy: just kill off the Empire's population and fill up the waste space with the natural increase of the Land's Protégés. *But no. Behfel ist behfel.* That would be far too slow, no telling what the other powers would get up to in the meantime. Besides, it was the destiny of the Chosen to rule all the rest of humankind; first here on Visager, ultimately throughout the universe, for all time. Genocide would be a confession of failure, in that sense.

"No doubt the ancestors of our Protégés were just as unruly," the infantry lieutenant said thoughtfully. "However, we domesticated them quite successfully."

"Indeed." Although we had three centuries of isolation for that, and even so I sometimes have my doubts. "Carry on, then."

"What would you suggest, *Hauptmann?*"

Gerta blinked against the harsh sunlight. "Have you been in garrison here long?"

"Just arrived—the area was lightly swept six months ago, but nobody's been here since."

She nodded; the Empire was so damned *big,* after the strait confines of the Land. Maps just didn't convey the reality of it, not the way marching or flying across it did.

"Well, then . . . let your troopers make a selection of the females and have a few hours' recreation. Have the rest of the herd watch. From reports, this is an effective punishment of intermediate severity."

"It is?" The lieutenant's brows rose in puzzlement.

"Animal psychology," Gerta said, drawing herself up and saluting.

"Jawohl. Zum behfel, Hauptman. I will see to it."

Gerta watched him stride off and then vaulted into her waiting steamcar, one hand on the rollbar.

"West," she said to the driver.

The long dusty road stretched out before her, monotonous with rolling hills. Fields of wheat and barley and maize—the corn was tasseling out, the small grains long cut to stubble—and pasture, with every so often a woodlot or orchard, every so often a white-walled village beside a small stream. Dust began to plume up as the driver let out the throttle, and she pulled her neckerchief up over her nose and mouth. The car was coated with the dust and smelled of the peppery-earthy stuff, along with the strong horse-sweat odor of the two Protégé riflemen she had along for escort.

Wealth, I suppose, she thought, looking at the countryside she was surveying for her preliminary report. Warm and fertile and sufficiently well-watered, without the Land's problems of leached soil and erosion and tropical insects and blights. Room for the Chosen to grow.

"We're in the situation of the python that swallowed the pig," she muttered to herself. "Just a matter of time, but uncomfortable in the interval." That was the optimistic interpretation.

Sometimes she thought it was more like the flies who'd conquered the flypaper.

"Mama!"

Young Maurice Hosten stumped across the grass of the lawn on uncertain eighteen-month legs. Pia Hosten waited, crouching and smiling, the long gauzy white skirts spread about her, and a floppy, flower-crowned hat held down with one hand.

"Mama!"

Pia scooped the child up, laughing. John smiled and turned away, back toward the view over the terrace and gardens. Beyond the fence was what *had* been a sheep pasture, when this house near Ensburg was the headquarters for a ranch. Ensburg had grown since the Civil War, grown into a manufacturing city of half a million souls; most of the ranch had been split up into market gardens and dairy farms as the outskirts approached, and the old manor had become an industrialists weekend retreat. It still was, the main change being that the owner was John Hosten . . . and that he used it for more than recreation.

"Come on, everybody," he said.

The party picked up their drinks and walked down toward the fence. It was a mild spring afternoon, just warm enough for shirtsleeves but not enough to make the tailcoats and cravats some of the guests wore uncomfortable. They found places along the white-painted boards, in clumps and groups between the beech trees planted along it. Out in the close-cropped meadow stood a contraption built of wire and canvas and wood, two wings and a canard ahead of them, all resting on a tricycle undercarriage of spoked wheels. A man sat between the wings, his hands and feet on the controls, while two more stood behind on the ground with their hands on the pusher-prop attached to the little radial engine.

"For your sake I hope this works, son," Maurice Farr said sotto voce, as he came up beside John. He took a sip at his wine seltzer and smoothed back his graying mustache with his forefinger.

"You don't think this is *actually* the first trial, do you, Dad?" John said with a quiet smile.

The ex-commodore—he had an admiral's stars and anchors on his epaulets now—laughed and slapped John on the shoulder. "I'm no longer puzzled at how you became that rich that quickly," he said.

If you only knew, Dad, John thought.

wind currents are now optimum, Center hinted.

"Go!" John called.

"Contact!" Jeffrey said from the pilots seat, lowering the goggles from the brow of his leather helmet to his eyes. The long silk scarf around his neck fluttered in the breeze.

The two workers spun the prop. The engine cracked, sputtered, and settled to a buzzing roar. Prop-wash fluttered the clothes of the spectators, and a few of the ladies lost their hats. Men leaped after them, and everyone shaded their eyes against flung grit. Jeffrey shouted again, inaudible at this distance over the noise of the engine, and the two helpers pulled blocks from in front of the undercarriage wheels. The little craft began to accelerate into the wind, slowly at first, with the two men holding on to each wing and trotting alongside, then spurting ahead as they released it. The wheels flexed and bounced over slight irregularities in the ground.

Despite everything, John found himself holding his breath as they hit one last bump and stayed up . . . six inches over the turf . . . eight . . . five feet and rising. He let the breath out with a sigh. The plane soared, banking slowly and gracefully and climbing in a wide spiral until it was five hundred feet over the crowd. Voices and arms were raised, a murmured *ahhhh.*

The two men who'd assisted at the takeoff came over to the fence. John blinked away the vision overlaid on his own of the earth opening out below and people and buildings dwindling to doll-size.

"Father, Edgar and William Wong, the inventors," he said. "Fellows, my father—Admiral Farr."

"Sir," Edgar said, as they shook his hand. "Your son's far too kind. Half the ideas were his, at least, as well as all the money."

His brother shook his head. "We'd still be fiddling around with warping the wing for control if John hadn't suggested moveable ailerons," he said. "*And* gotten a better chord ratio on the wings. He's quite a head for math, sir."

Maurice Farr smiled acknowledgment without taking his eyes from where his son flew above their heads. The steady droning of the engine buzzed down, like a giant bee.

"It works," he said softly. "Well, well."

"Damned toy," a new voice said.

John turned with a diplomatic bow. General McWriter probably wouldn't have come except for John's wealth and political influence. He stared at the machine and tugged at a white walrus mustache that cut across the boiled-lobster complexion . . . or that might be the tight collar of his brown uniform tunic.

"Damned toy," he said again. "Another thing for the bloody politicians"—there were ladies present, and you could hear the slight

hesitation before the mild expletive as the general remembered it—
"to waste money on, when we need every penny for *real* weapons."

"The Chosen found aerial reconnaissance extremely useful in the
Empire," he said mildly, turning the uniform cap in his fingers.

McWriter grunted. "Perhaps. According to young Farr's
reports."

"According to *all* reports, General. Including those of my own
service, and the Ministry."

The general's grunt showed what he thought of reports from
sailors, or the Ministry of Foreign Affairs' Research Bureau.

"They used dirigibles, you'll note," McWriter said, turning to
John. "What's the range and speed? How reliable is it?"

"Eighty miles an hour, sir," John said with soft politeness. "Range
is about an hour, so far. Engine time to failure is about three hours,
give or take."

The general's face went even more purple. "Then what bloody f
. . . bloody *use* is it?" he said, nodding abruptly to the admiral and
walking away calling for his aide-de-camp.

"What use is a baby?" John said.

"You're sure it can be improved?" the elder Farr said.

"As sure as if I had a vision from God"—*or Center*—"about it,"
John said. "Within a decade, they're going to be flying ten times as far
and three times as fast, I'll stake everything I own on it."

"I hope so," Farr said. "Because we are going to need it, very
badly. The navy most of all."

"You think so, Admiral?" another man said. Farr started slightly;
he hadn't seen the civilian in the brown tailcoat come up.

"Senator Beemody," he said cautiously.

The politician-financier nodded affably. "Admiral. Good to see
you again." He held out a hand. "No hard feelings, eh?"

Farr returned the gesture. "Not on my side, sir."

"Well, you're not the one who lost half a million," Beemody said
genially. He was a slight dapper man, his mustache trimmed to a
black thread over his upper lip. "On the other hand, Jesus Christ with
an order from the President couldn't have saved those warehouses,
from my skipper's reports . . . and you're quite the golden boy these

days, after facing down that Chosen bitch at Salini. We can offer her a better one than her colleagues appear to have found at Corona,'" he quoted with relish. The senator's grin was disarming. "What with one thing and another, grudges would be pretty futile. And I have no time for unproductive gestures, Admiral. You think we'll need these?"

"Damned right we will. Knowing your enemy's location is half the battle in naval warfare. Knowing where he is while he doesn't know where you are is the other half. We've relied on fast cruisers and torpedo-boat destroyers to scout and screen for us, but the Chosen dirigibles are four times faster than the fastest hulls afloat. *Plus* they can scout from several thousand feet. We need an equivalent and we need it very badly, or we'll be defeated at sea in the event of war."

"Which some think is inevitable," Beemody said thoughtfully. "I'm not entirely sure—but the news out of the Empire certainly seems to support the hypothesis. Admiral. John."

"People can surprise you," Farr said reflectively as the senator moved through the crowd, shaking hands and dropping smiles.

"Beemody knows when to jump on a bandwagon," John said. "And he's big in steel mills, heavy engineering—a naval buildup will be like a license to print money, to him. And he's no fool; I've done enough business with him to know that."

"Darling," Pia's voice broke in. She hugged his arm; the nursemaid was behind her with the child. "Father." Her eyes went up to the aircraft that was circling downward above them. "I would *love* to do that someday."

John put an arm around her shoulders. "Maybe in a few years," he said. "Here comes Jeffrey."

The plane ghosted down, seemed to float for an instant, then touched with a lurching sway. The Wong brothers ran out to grip the wingtips and keep its head into the wind; other workers brought cords and tarpaulins to stake it down. Jeffrey Farr swung down from the controls, pulling off his helmet and waving to the cheers of the crowd. He vaulted the fence easily with one hand on a post, then walked towards his father and stepbrother. One arm was around the waist of a pretty dark girl who clung and looked up at him, laughing.

"I see you've already found a way to profit from the glamour of flight, Jeff," John said, bending over her hand.

"Too late," Jeffrey replied. "Meant to tell you, you're going to be best man."

John looked up quickly, to find Pia laughing at him. "Some things even the wife of your bosom doesn't tell you," he said resignedly.

And I told Center not to tell you, either, Raj said. There was a smile in the disembodied voice.

"Well, I haven't told Mother yet, either," Jeffrey said. "There are limits to even *my* courage."

"I'm sure your mother will be delighted," the elder Farr said, bending over Lola's hand in his turn. "But not surprised, after the last year. The Empire has conquered both her sons, it seems."

Pia's face went rigid for an instant, and then she forced gaiety back to it. "A fall wedding, perhaps?"

Jeffrey nodded. "And John won't escape mine—although I should bar him from the church, the way he got hitched without me there, the inconsiderate bastard."

John chuckled. "I'm sure you could see it as vividly as if you'd really been there," he said dryly. "How does she fly?'

"Too businesslike, that's your problem." Jeffrey shrugged. "Sweet, for a machine that underpowered. Very maneuverable, now that the movement of the flaps is extended. The canard keeps the stalling speed low, but I think it'll have to go when you move to an enclosed cockpit; the eddy currents around it close to the ground are tricky. Apart from that, she needs a better engine and something to cut the wind."

"And you must make a speech about it," Pia said, putting her hand through John's elbow.

"Damn," he muttered, looking at the assembly.

About fifty people. Important people, high-ranking military officers, industrialists, reporters for the major papers and wire services, politicians on the military committees.

"It is part of your job," Pia said relentlessly.

John sighed and straightened his lapels. Nobody had ever said the job would be agreeable.

"So much for reports that it could not be done," Karl Hosten said, looking down at the summaries.

Gerta Hosten closed her own file folder with a snap. "Well, sir, it was scarcely a secret that powered heavier-than-air flight was possible. We are here, and not on ancient Terra, after all."

"But our ancestors did not arrive in winged vehicles with propellers," the Chosen general said with a sigh.

Gerta looked up with concern. There was more white than gray in her foster-father's face now, and his face looked tired even at ten in the morning. *Duty is duty,* she reminded herself. Not all the work of conquest was done out on the battlefield.

She was back in Corpenik for a while herself. There wasn't much in the way of fighting left in the Empire—*former Empire, now the New Territories*—for one thing, and for another she was pregnant again, enough months along to rate desk duty for a while. The whitewashed office in the General Staff HQ building was on the third floor; she could see out over the courtyard wall from here, to a vast construction site where gangs of slave labor from the New Territories dug at the red volcanic earth of the central plateau, filling the warm damp air with the scent of mud. Some office building, she supposed; bureaucrats were a growth industry these days. The Land's government had always been tightly centralized and omnicompetent, and there was a lot more for it to do. Or it might be factories. A lot of those were going up, too.

She looked down at the folder. "According to John's report, the Santies are going to push these heavier-than-air craft mainly because their experiments with dirigibles have been such a disaster."

General Hosten nodded and pushed a finger at a photograph. It was a grainy newspaper print, showing the ghost outline of a wrecked and burned airship strewn across a bare grassy hillside with mountains in the distance.

"I am not surprised. Success or failure in airship design is mostly a matter of details, and an infinite capacity for taking pains is our great strength."

Whereas our great weakness is obsession with details at the expense of the larger picture, Gerta thought, silently. There were things you didn't say to a General Staff panjandrum, even if he was your father.

"Still, we'll have to follow suit," Gerta said. "Dirigibles are potentially very vulnerable to aircraft of this type, and they could be very useful in themselves."

Karl nodded thoughtfully, running a finger along his heavy jawline. "I will raise the matter in the next staff meeting," he said. "The Air Council must be informed, of course." Looking down at the folder: "Johan has done good service here."

He was frowning, nonetheless. Gerta noted the expression and looked quickly away. *Not completely comfortable with it,* she thought. *Didn't expect Johnny ever to be false to a cause, even for the Chosen.* She agreed, for completely different reasons, but again, it wasn't the time to mention it.

"Sir, the next item is the Far Western Islands appropriation."

Karl nodded and opened the file. "It seems clearcut," he said. "The islands have a climate that is, if anything, more difficult than the Land; the distance is extreme"—over eight thousand miles—"and the value of the minerals barely more than the cost of extraction."

Gerta licked her lips. "Sir, with respect, I would strongly advise against abandoning the base there at present."

Karl's eyebrows rose. "Why? It scarcely seems cost-effective, now that the Empire is ours."

"Sir, the Empire is poor in minerals, particularly energy sources. Our processing industries here in the Land will be expanding dramatically and the petroleum in the Islands may come in very useful. Besides, I just don't like giving up territory we've spent lives in taking."

He nodded slowly. "Perhaps. I will take the matter under advisement. Next, we have the report on our agents in the Union del Est." He smiled bleakly. "The Republic of Santander is not the only party who can play the game of stirring up trouble on the borders."

〈(◦◦)〉 〈(◦◦)〉 〈(◦◦)〉

"*Fuck* it!"

Jeffrey Farr swore into the sudden ringing silence within the tank. The only sound was a dying clatter as something beat itself into oblivion against something equally metallic and unyielding.

He pushed up the greasy goggles and stuck his head out of the top deck. Black oily smoke was pouring up out of the grillwork over the rear deck; luckily there was a stiff breeze from the east, carrying most of it away. The rest of the four-man crew bailed out with a haste bred of several months' experience with Dirty Gerty and her foibles, standing at a respectful distance with their football-style leather helmets in their hands.

Jeffrey climbed down himself, conscious that he was thirty-one years old, not the late teens of the other crewmen. Not that he wasn't as agile, it just hurt a little more; and he was tired, mortally tired.

"Filter again?" said the head mechanic of Pokips Motors, the civilian contractors.

"I think," Jeffrey replied, spitting the smell of burning gasoline and lubricating oil out of his mouth and taking a swig from the canteen someone offered. "Then that tore a fuel line or broke the oil reservoir."

The military reservation they were using was on the southern edge of the Santander River valley, two hundred miles west of the capital. A stretch of flatland, then some tree-covered loess hills leading down to the floodplain, ten thousand acres or so. A holdover from days before land prices rose so high; this was prime corn-and-hog country—cattle, too—all around. Most of *this* section was now torn up by the jointed-metal tracks of Gerty and her kindred, and by the huge wheels of the steam traction engines that winched them home when they broke down, which was incessantly. Gerty was the latest model: a riveted steel box on tracks, about twenty feet long and eight wide, with a stationary round pillbox on top meant to represent a turret. The engineers were still working on the turret ring and traversing mechanism, and hopefully close to finishing them.

"Th' prollem is," the mechanic said, "yer overstrainin' the engines somethin' fierce. Got enough *horsepower*, right enough—two seventy-five-horsepower saloon-car engines, right enough. But the torque loads more'n they wuz designed to stand."

"Well, we'll have to *redesign* them, won't we?"

Jeffrey kept his voice neutral. The man was trying his best to do his job; it wasn't his fault that engineering talent was so much thinner on the ground here in the western provinces of Santander. It was yeoman-and-squire country here, and always had been. Outside the eastern uplands, manufacturing was mostly limited to the port cities and focused on maritime trade and textiles. The problem was that this was prime tank country; the provincial militias here were actually *interested* in the prospect of armored warfare. Nobody but a few dinosaurs like General McWriter thought much of the prospects of horsed cavalry anymore, not after what had happened in the Empire.

Jeffrey felt his skin roughen. The machine guns flickered in his mind, and the long rows of horsemen collapsed in kicking, screaming chaos . . .

"Transmission," he said. "We need a more robust transmission."

"What've yer got in mind?"

Jeffrey pulled out a diagram. "Friction plate," he said. "It's not elegant, but I think it won't keep breaking like this chain drive setup. Like you say, these tanks just have too much inertia for a system designed for three-ton touring cars."

"Hmmmm." The mechanic studied the diagram. "Interestin'."

He looked up at Gerty. A couple of his men had gotten the engine grille up and were spraying water on the flames flickering there.

"How'd them Chosen bastids keep theirs going?" he asked. "Heavier'n this, I hears."

"They use steam engines and mostly they *don't* keep going," Jeffrey said. "We need something reliable enough to do exploitation as well as breakthrough."

The mechanic looked down at the diagram again. "Need some fancy machinin' fer this."

"Hosten Engineering can do you up a model, and jigs," Jeffrey said. "They've got the plans."

((•)) ((•)) ((•))

John Hosten leaned back in the chair and sipped his lemonade. Oathtaking was hot, as usual, and sticky-humid, as usual, and the air was thick with coal smoke. The hotel was close by the docks; they'd extended hugely since his last visit, new berths extending further into what had been coastal forest reserve and farmland. In fact, he could see one freighter unloading now from this fourth-floor veranda. It was a smallish ship of fifteen hundred tons, swinging sacks of grain ashore with its own booms and steam winches. As he watched the net fell the last four feet to the granite paving blocks of the wharf. Half the bottom layer split, spraying wheat across the stone and into the harbor. Screams and curses rang faintly as the cable paid out limply on top of the heap. Stevedores scurried about, overseers lashing with their rubber truncheons. Eventually a line formed, trotting off with the undamaged sacks on their backs. Others started sweeping up the remainder with brooms and dumping it in a collection of boxes and barrels.

God, I'm glad I don't have to eat that, he thought silently. In this heat and humidity, they'd be lucky not to get ergot all over it.

He nodded towards the dock. "You'd get less spoilage if you moved to bulk-handling facilities," he said mildly. "Elevators, screw-tube systems, that sort of thing."

Gerta Hosten raised her eyes from the diagrams before her. "We're not short of labor," she said, with a smile that didn't reach the cold, dark eyes.

Meaning they are short of the type of labor that bulk transport would need, Raj said thoughtfully.

An image drew itself at the back of John's consciousness: short, dark-skinned men with iron collars around their necks loading a train—an unbelievably primitive train, with an engine like something out of a museum, an open platform and a tall, thin smokestack topped with sheet-metal petals. Each staggered sweating under a bundle of dried fish secured in netting, heaving it painfully onto the flatcars. Other men watched them, soldiers with single-shot rifles mounted on giant dogs. Occasionally a dog would snap its great jaws with a door-slamming sound and the laborers would shuffle a little faster.

Who needs wheelbarrows when you've got enough slaves? Raj said with ironic distaste. *We got over that, eventually. Thanks to Center.*

and to you, raj whitehall, Center replied.

John reached into the inner pocket of his light cotton jacket and took out his cigarette case. From what he'd described, the centralized god-king autocracy Raj Whitehall had been born into had been almost as nasty as the Chosen—more desirable only because Center and Raj could put their own man on the throne and use that as the fulcrum to move society off dead center. *There seem to be more wrong paths than right,* he thought.

correct. high-coercion societies locked in stasis alternating with barbarism are the maximum probability for postneolithic humanity, Center observed dispassionately. **the original breakthrough to modernity on earth was the result of multiple low-probability historical accidents, observe—**

Later we may have time for lectures, Raj observed. *Meanwhile, John has a job of work to do.*

Gerta looked up again, stacking the reports neatly on the hotel room's table, and took a long drink of water.

"This . . . Whippet?"

"It's a type of racing dog," John said helpfully.

"This Whippet looks like a very useful *panzer,* if you . . . if the Santies can get it working," she observed.

"True enough," John said. "There's a lot of controversy. The western provinces are pushing it, but the easterners want more effort to go into aircraft. And they have most of the internal-combustion manufacturing capacity."

"Yes, I read the speech of this . . . Senator Damian? The representative from Ensburg, in any case—you thoughtfully supplied it with the latest reports. 'I put my faith in our mountains'; a very colorful phrase."

Her strong, calloused fingers turned the sheaf of papers over. "Now, this, this *Land-Cruiser,* it's going to give the Army Council's engineers hives."

The blueprints on the table showed a massive boxy machine,

mounting a six-inch gun on its centerline, a two-inch quick-firer in a turret above, and six machine-guns in sponsons on either side.

"What a monstrosity," she went on. "If the Santies are having trouble making the Whippet go, how do they expect this . . . this *thing* to move?"

John leaned forward. A lot of work, mostly Center's, had gone into the Land-Cruiser. It was no easy task to design something beyond Visager's current technological level, but *just* beyond, close enough that competent engineers would be kept busy on the tantalizing quest for this particular Holy Grail. Disinformation was much more than simple lying.

"Each bogie has its own engine," he pointed out.

The huge machine rested on four bogies on either side, each riding on a pivot with bell-crank springs. "See, there's a drive train run through this flexible shaft coupling, and then through meshed gears to the toothed sprocket here between the load-bearing wheels."

"Porschmidt will love this. Unfortunately."

At John's glance she went on: "The new head of Technical Development. He's brilliant, but he keeps trying to make bad designs good instead of junking them—he'd rather design three force pumps and an auxiliary circulation system into an engine rather than just turn a part over to keep it from leaking. You should see what he did to the heavy field gun. It's enough to make a Test of Life examiner cry. He's the sort who gives engineering a bad name; convinced that just because its his, his shit doesn't stink."

"Well, if the Republic's wasting its time, so much the better," John said with a smile.

"*Ya.* Only, is the Republic wasting its time, or are you wasting ours?"

John kept the expression on his face genial, as his testicles tried to climb back into his abdomen. It was impossible to have a cold sweat in Oathtaking's climate, but you could feel clammy-nauseated.

"Gerta, *min soester,* do you think so little of me?"

"Johan, *min brueder,* I think very highly of you. I think somehow you're fucking Military Intelligence up the butt and making them like it." She grinned, and this time the expression went all the way through. "But you're giving us so much real information to sweeten the pot that I can't convince anyone of it . . . yet."

She sighed, relaxed, and put the documents away in her attaché case, spinning the combination lock. Then she poured some banana gin from the carafe into her water, and a dollop into his lemonade. "Now I'm officially off-duty."

He sipped; the oily-sweet kick of the distillate seemed to match the surroundings, somehow. And one wouldn't affect his judgement noticeably.

"So, I hear you've adopted a child," Gerta said.

"Yes. See, I *am* practicing Chosen custom, as far as I can." They both laughed. "How's your youngest?"

"A shapeless lump of protoplasm, the way they all are at that age," Gerta said.

She pulled a picture from her uniform tunic. A baby looked out, with one chubby hand stuffed in its mouth; the fuzzy background was probably a Protégé wetnurse, from the linen bodice.

"Young Sigvard. That's four, now; I think I've done my duty by the Chosen, don't you? It's an interesting experience, pregnancy, but I wouldn't want to overindulge."

"And the adoptees?"

"Good children, every one," Gerta said. "The one good thing about desk duty is that I get to see more of them; they've been practically living in Father's house most of the time, the last two years, what with the war."

John produced a snapshot of Pia and Maurice junior; Gerta looked at it critically. "Sound enough stock," she said . . . which was a high compliment, by the standards of the Land.

"I hear Heinrich made brigadier?"

"*Ya*, same dispatch-and-notice list that bumped me to full colonel," Gerta said, leaning back and stretching. "They added another six divisions to the regular roster, lots of new hats to go around. Especially with all the demotions and such after the Campaign Study."

John nodded. The General Staff had high standards; there had been a lot of shaking up after the campaign in the Empire. Mere success wasn't good enough . . .

Mark of a good army, lad, Raj said. *Anyone can learn from his mistakes. It takes sound doctrine to be able to learn from winning.*

"Enough other compensations to go around, I suppose," he said aloud.

Gerta chuckled. "Well, the Council *has* been handing out estates fairly liberally. Mostly in the west, around Corona, to start with. Too much unrest for it to be safe for us to scatter ourselves around widely, just yet." A shrug. "We'll deal with that in due course."

CHAPTER TWELVE

"Christ, how do I git myself inta these things?" one of the marines behind him in the longboat muttered.

John smiled in the darkness. That was Barrjen. The stocky marine had managed to volunteer—unofficially, the whole mission was highly off the record—despite his loud relief at making it home last time. In fact, the ones who'd been with him from Ciano to Salini had *all* volunteered, even Smith with his gimp foot. Some of them had been pretty shamefaced about it, as if they were mentally kicking themselves, but they'd all done it.

It was a moonless night and overcast, typical weather for winter in the Gut. The whaleboat glided silently over the dark water; they might as well have been rowing in a closet, for all that he could see. Water purled under the muffled oars, breath smoked. Only the radium dial of his compass guided them, that and . . .

"*Down!*" he hissed quietly.

The dozen men in the boat shipped oars and turned their cork-blackened faces downward in the same motion. A few seconds later the quiet thumping of a marine steam engine came over the water. A searchlight stabbed out into the darkness, blinding bright, the arc light flicking over the waves. Behind it was a gaggle of other boats. Fishing boats; the Chosen couldn't shut down the Gut fishery, it was too important to the economy, and too many of the important pelagic species were best caught in darkness. They *did* send out a gunboat to make sure nobody tried to make a break for the Santander or Union shores, and probably kept the families of the fishermen hostage, too.

The light flicked past them. Weaker lights were breaking out among the fishing boats, lure lanterns strung out over bows and sides. John waited tensely until they were surrounded by the other boats, several dozen of them spread out widely.

"Wait for it . . ."

A thrashing of whitewater as something big broached and snapped for the dangling lantern of a boat, something with a long head full of white teeth. Yells drifted over the water, and he could see a man poised with a harpoon, backlit against the oil lamp. He struck, and a monstrous three-lobed tail came up out of the water. Other boats were closing in, to help with the first catch and wait for the others that would be drawn by the commotion and the blood in the waters.

"Now! Stroke, stroke!"

The Land gunboat was out further in the Gut, hooting its steam whistle and scanning with the searchlight . . . but it was guarding against attempts to get *away,* not looking for boats making for the ex-Imperial shore. John kept his right hand on the whaleboat's tiller, flicking an occasional glance down at the compass in his left. That was mostly for show; Center kept a ghostly vector arrow floating before his gaze.

there are now echoes from cliffs of the configuration indicated, the machine said. **distance one thousand meters and closing.**

Thump. John's head whipped around. That was the gunboat's cannon . . . ah. "Just a big 'un," he whispered to the crew.

You got an occasional one of those, even in the shallow waters of the Gut. Nothing like the monsters that made sailing the outer seas hazardous, but too much for a harpooner to handle. There had been very little life on land when humans arrived on Visager, but the oceans more than made up for it. The Chosen officer on the gunboat probably thought of it as sport, something to break the dull routine of night escort work. And very good cover for John.

"We'll be coming up on the cliffs soon," he said quietly. "Half-stroke . . . half-stroke . . ."

The oars shortened their pace, scarcely dipping into the water. He could hear the slow boom of surf now, thudding and hissing on rock. John held up his signal lantern and carefully pressed the shutter: two long, two short, one long.

A flicker answered him, two shorts, repeated—all that they dared use, with the light pointing out to the Gut.

"Yarely now," the lead marine in the head of the boat said. There was a quiet *plop* as he swung the lead. "By the mark, six. Six. Five. Six. Four. Four."

Rock loomed up on either hand, just visible as the waves broke and snake-hissed over it. A river broke the cliff near here, cutting a pathway that men or goats could use.

"By the mark, seven. Ten. No bottom at ten."

The pitching of the boat changed, calmer as they moved into the sheltered waters. John felt sweat matting his hair under the black knit stocking cap. The guerillas would be waiting; the guerillas, or a Fourth Bureau reaction squad.

"Rest oars," he said.

The poles came in, noiseless. The boat coasted, slowing . . . and the keel crunched on shingle. Four men leapt overboard into thigh-deep water, fanning out with their weapons ready. The rest followed them a second later, putting their shoulders to the whaleboat's sides and running it forward. John drew the revolver from his shoulder rig and ran forward to leap off the bow.

there, Center said, reading input from his ears too faint for his conscious mind to follow.

He walked forward, sliding his feet to avoid tripping on the uneven surface. A match glowed, cupped in a hand, just long enough for him to recognize the face. Arturo Bianci, the *cotadini* he'd shipped the arms to, back when the war began. Two years looked to have aged the man ten, which wasn't all that surprising.

A hand gripped his. "No lights," John warned.

Bianci made a sound that was half chuckle. "We have learned, *signore.* Those of us who live, have learned much."

They had; there were ropes strung from sticks to guide up the steep rocky path. Guerillas joined the Marines in unloading the crates and lashing them to their shoulders with rope slings. John swung crates down from the boat, pleased with the silence and speed . . . and waiting for the moment when lights would spear down from the clifftop and voices sound in Landisch. At last the boat rode high and empty, rocking against the shingle.

"This way," John said.

Harry Smith nodded, and together they pushed it upstream, under an overhang of wild olive and trailing vines. Smith reached in, rocking it to one side with his weight, and pulled the stopper. Water gurgled into the whaleboat, and it sank rapidly in the chest-deep stream.

"I'll put a few rocks in her," Smith said. "She'll be here when y'all get back. So'll I be. Good luck, sir." He racked a shell into the breech of his pump shotgun.

"Thanks. To you, too—we're all going to need it."

Heinrich Hosten looked at the thing that twitched and mewled on the table. The Fourth Bureau specialist smiled and patted it on what was left of its scalp.

"Yes, I'd say they're definitely planning on something to do with the train," she said. "Can't tell you exactly where, though—the subject didn't know, that's for certain."

Heinrich nodded thanks as he left. Outside he stood thoughtfully beside his horse for a while, looking around at the buildings of the little town, then pulling a map from the case at his side and tilting it so that the lantern outside the Fourth Bureau regional HQ shone on the paper. When he mounted, he turned towards the barracks, his escort of riflemen clattering behind him through the chill night.

"No, don't wake Major van Pelt," he said to the sentry outside the main door. It had been a monastery before the conquest, perfect for its new use; a series of courtyards with small rooms leading off, and large common kitchens, refectories for mess halls. "Who's the officer of the day?"

That turned out to be a very young captain. Heinrich returned her salute, then smiled as he stuffed tobacco into his big curved pipe.

"*Hauptman* Neumann, what's a junior officer's worst nightmare?"

"Ah . . ." Captain Neumann knotted her brow in thought. "Surprise attack by overwhelming numbers?" she said hopefully.

"Tsk, tsk. That would be an *opportunity* for an able young officer," Heinrich said genially. "No, a nightmare is what you are about to undergo; an operation conducted with a senior officer along to look over your shoulder and jog your elbow. What forces are stationed here in Campo Fiero?"

"One battalion of the Third Protégé Infantry, currently at ninety-eight percent of full strength, and a squadron of armored cars—five currently ready, three undergoing serious maintenance. That is not counting," she added with an unconscious sniff, "police troops. Plus the usual support elements."

"Troops so-called," Heinrich said, nodding agreement. He turned to the map table that filled one corner of the ready room. "Ah, yes. Now, find me a train schedule. While you're at it—I presume your company is on reaction status? Good. While you're at it, get your troops ready to move, full field kit, but no noise. Nobody to enter or leave the barracks area."

He stared at the map, puffing with the pewter lid of the pipe turned back. *Now,* he thought happily, *if I were a rebellious animal, where would I be?*

"Good choice," John said.

Bianci grunted beside him. "The bridge would have been better, but there are blockhouses there now—a section of infantry and a couple of their accursed machine guns at each end. With signal rockets always at the ready."

John nodded. Oto was up; the smallest of Visager's three moons also moved the fastest, and although it was little more than a bright spark across the sky, it did give *some* light. Enough to see how the railway track curved around a steep rocky hill here, falling away to a stretch of marsh and then a small creek on the other side. The guerillas numbered about sixty; Bianci hadn't offered to introduce anyone else, which was exactly as it should be.

"We got quite a few trains at first," Bianci said. "But then the *tedeschi* began making villagers from along the lines ride in carriages at front."

"You can't allow that to stop you," John said.

Bianci glanced his way, a shadowed gleam of eyeball in the faint moonlight, the smell of garlic and sweat.

"We didn't," he said. "But the villagers began to patrol the rail line themselves . . . to protect their families, you understand. So now we pick locations far from any habitation. Like this."

"Good ground, too," John said.

One of the Marines came up the hill, trailing a spool of thin wire. Another squatted next to John, placing a box next to him. It had a plunger with an handbar coming out of the top, and a crank on the side. Bianci leaned close to watch as the Marine cut the wire and split it into two strands, stripping the insulation with his belt knife. The raw copper of the wire matched the hairs on the backs of his huge freckled hands, incongruously delicate as they handled the difficult task in near-darkness.

"Ahh, *bellissimo,*" the Imperial said. "We've been using black powder with friction primers—and since they started putting a car in front of the locomotive, that doesn't work so well."

"We can get detonator sets to you," John said. "But you'll have to come up with the wire—telegraph wire will do well enough."

Bianci nodded again. "That we can do." He looked down at the track hungrily. "Every slave in the rail yards tells us what goes on the cars. This one has military stores, arms and ammunition, medical supplies, and machine parts for a new repair depot north of Salini; the *tedeschi* have been talking of double-tracking the line from the Pada to the coast . . . why, do you think?"

"They'll be reopening the trade with the Republic and the other countries on the Gut, soon," John replied. "And to be able to move supplies and troops faster. They have   "

Far away to the northwest, the mournful hoot of a locomotive's steam whistle echoed off the hills. Bianci laughed, an unpleasant sound. "Right on time. The trains run on time, since the *tedeschi* came . . . except when we arrange some delays."

John burrowed a little deeper behind a scree of rock. *I have to be here, dammit,* he thought. The guerillas had to see that they were getting some support, however minimal. The problem was that the Santander government wasn't ready to really give that support, not yet. It was surprising what you could do with some contacts and a great deal of money, though.

Silence stretched. Bianci raised himself on an elbow. "Odd," he said. "They should be on the flat before this stretch of hills by now."

"Glad you stopped," Heinrich said, shining his new electric torch up at the escort car.

"Yessir." The vehicle was a standard armored car, fitted with outriggers so that it could ride the rails, and a belt-drive from the wheels to propel it. Doctrine said that fighting vehicles had to have a Chosen in command; in this case, a nervous young private, showing it by bracing to attention in the turret and staring straight ahead, rigid as the twin machine guns prodding the air ahead of him.

"At ease," the Chosen brigadier said. "Now, we want to do this quickly," he added to Captain Neumann. "Unload boxcars four through six."

Greatly daring, the commander of the armored car spoke: "Sir, those are—"

"Military supplies. I'm aware of that, Private." The rigid brace became even tighter. He turned back to Neumann. "Then get the I-beams rigged and we'll load the cars."

Luck had been with him; there had been a stack of steel forms, the type used to frame the concrete of coast-artillery bunkers, in Campo Fiero. Used as ramps, they could get an armored car onto the train . . . with ropes, pulleys, winches, and a lot of pushing. Getting down would be easier, he hoped.

Orders barked sotto voce had the hundred-odd troopers of Neumann's company slinging crates out of boxcars, the Chosen officers pitching in beside their subordinates. Others were unstrapping the steel planks from the armored cars waiting where the little dirt road crossed the rail line. Heinrich moved forward as the crew of sweating Protégé infantry staggered; they were still panting from the five-mile forced march to intercept the train.

But nobody saw us get on, the Chosen officer thought a little smugly, catching the corner of the heavy metal shape. Muscle bulged in his arms and neck as he braced himself and heaved it around, teeth clenched around the stem of his pipe.

"Dominate that piece of equipment!" he barked as the Protégés took up the strain.

They obeyed, looking at him out of the corners of their eyes. A slightly awed look; he'd taken two strong men's load for half a minute. The steel clanged down on the side of the flatcar, and the armored vehicle's driver started to back and fill, aligning his wheels with the ramp.

Heinrich stepped back, dusting his palms. Somewhere south of here waited a pack of animals with delusions of grandeur. Somehow that reminded him of Jeffrey Farr, Johan's foster-brother. A good man: sound soldier, a bit soft, but sound. A great pity they'd probably have to kill him someday.

"And I was right," he muttered to himself. "There is going to be good sport here for years."

"The sun sets, but it also rises," Bianci whispered, putting his hand to the pushbar of the detonator set.

"Hmmm?" John said, startled out of reverie.

"An old saying, *signore.*"

The train whistle hooted again, louder. *Always a melancholy sound,* John thought, taking a swig from his canteen. Oto was nearly down, but Adele was up, brighter and slower as it rose over the horizon. An armored car running on the rails came first, buzzing along with the belt from its rear wheels slapping and snarling. The turret moved restlessly, probing the darkness. A light fixed above the machine guns swept across the slope. John tensed.

Nothing, he thought, breathing in the scent of the dew-damp thyme crushed beneath his body. *Good fire discipline.* Not one of the men on the slope had been detected, and not one moved.

"Now," Arturo breathed, spinning the crank on the side of the detonator. Then he pushed down on the plunger.

WHUMP. WHUMP. WHUMP.

Three globes of magenta fire blossomed along the curving stretch of rail. One before the escort car; it braked desperately, throwing roostertails of sparks from its outrigger wheels. Not quite fast enough. The front wheels tumbled into the mass of churned earth and twisted iron that the dynamite had left, and the hull toppled slowly sideways, accelerating to fall on its side and skid down the gravel and earth of the embankment. The locomotive was a little more successful, braking in a squeal of steel on steel that sent fingers of pain into John's ears even half a thousand yards away. The front bogie dropped into the crater the explosive mine left, tipping the nose of the locomotive down. That jacknifed the coal car and first boxcar upward off the tracks, leaving them dangling by the couplings that held them to the engine. The rest of the boxcars jolted to a crashing halt. Most of them partially derailed, lunging to the right or left until brought up by the inertia of the car ahead, leaving the whole train of two dozen cars lying in a zigzag. But none were thrown on their sides. . . .

"Going too slow," Arturo said, puzzled.

Realization crystallized, like a lump in John's gut. "*Trap!*" he shouted. "Get—"

Schoonk. A mortar threw a starshell high into the sky above them. Blue-white light washed over the stretch of hill and swamp, actinic and harsh to their dark-adapted eyes. *Schoonk. Schoonk.*

A rippling crackle of small-arms fire broke out across the hillside and from guerillas concealed in the swamp across the embankment; they'd learned that an ambush worked best with two sides. A captured machine gun was in place there, too, its brighter muzzle flashes contrasting with the duller, redder light of the ex-Imperial black-powder rifles most of the partisans carried.

"Pull back!" John shouted into Arturo's ear. "Get out, leave a rearguard and *get out now.*"

The guerilla leader hesitated. With a sound like a giant ripping canvas across the sky, more than a dozen belt-fed Haagen machine guns cut lose from the train. The guerillas' rifle fire was punching through the thin pine boards of the boxcars, but John could see it sparking and ricochetting from steel within. Gunshields; the machine guns were fortress models, with an angled steel plate to protect the gunner. Their fire beat across the hillside like flails of green tracer, intersecting hoses of arched light through the night. Sparks scattered as the high-velocity jacketed bullets spanged off stone; little red glows showed where rounds had cut reeds in the swamp, like the mark of a cigarette touched to thin paper. Scores of Protégé infantry were tumbling out of the cars, too, some falling, more going to ground along the train and returning fire.

And the doors of the rear boxcars were thrown open from within. Steel planks clanged down, and the dark lurching shape of armored cars showed within. The first skidded down the ramp, landing three-quarters on, almost going over, then steadying. Its engine chuffed loudly as the wheels spun and spattered gravel against the side of the train, and then the turret traversed to send more machine-gun fire against the hillside. Squads of infantry rose and scurried into its shelter, advancing behind it as the car nosed towards the lower slopes of the hill. A grenade crunched with a malignant snap of light. Three more of the war-cars thudded to the ground, crunching through the trackside gravel.

John grabbed Arturo's shoulder. "*Get the fuck out of here!*" he screamed in the partisan's ear. Then to Barrjen: "Collect the rest. Time to bug out."

"Yes *sir*."

With a long dragon hiss, a rocket rose from the wrecked train. It kept rising, a thousand yards or more, then burst in a shower of gold—the colors of the Chosen flag, yellow on black.

"Sound the *halt in place*," Heinrich Hosten said, standing with his hands on his hips. "And remember, live prisoners."

Troopers were moving down the hillside under the glare of the arc light, prodding at bundles of rags with their bayonets. Occasionally that would bring a response, and the soldiers would pick up the wounded guerilla, cautiously, after the first one who'd stuffed a live grenade under his body was found.

The trumpet sounded, four urgent rising notes. A slow crackle of skirmish fire in the hill country to the west died down. In the comparative silence that followed he could hear the relief train that the signal rocket was intended for, with the rest of the battalion and its equipment. Plus the equipment and workers to repair the track, of course. It was surprisingly difficult to do lasting damage to a railway track without time or plenty of equipment.

"Shall we pursue when the rest of the battalion comes up, Brigadier?" Captain Neumann said.

"*Nein*," he said. "Too much chance of ambushes in the dark." He got out his map case. "But it would be advisable to push blocking forces *here* and *here*. Then in a few hours, we can sweep and see how many of these little birds we can bag."

Captain Neumann looked at the emergency aid station where her wounded were being looked after. There were four bodies with their groundsheets drawn over their faces.

"We only killed twenty or so of them," she said. "This is a bad exchange rate."

"The operation is not over," Heinrich said. "And we have taught them a little lesson, I think."

"That is the problem—when we teach them a lesson, they *learn*," Neumann said unexpectedly.

Heinrich shrugged. "We must see that we learn more than they," he added, knocking the dottle out of his pipe.

The cave smelled bad: damp rock, and the wastes of the survivors, since they hadn't dared go outside for the last three days. Weak daylight was leaking through, enough penetrating this far into the cave to turn the absolute blackness into a gray wash of light.

"We failed," Arturo said bitterly.

"We survived," John replied. "Enough of us. Next time we'll do better."

"So will they!" the guerilla said.

"We'll just have to learn faster," John said. "Besides, there are more of us than of them."

He looked toward the light. "Now we'd better check if their patrols are still looking," he said. "It's a fair hike back to the cove."

John Hosten's wasn't the biggest steam yacht under Santander registry, by a considerable margin; they were a common status symbol among the rising industrial magnates of the Republic. The *Windstrider* was only about twelve hundred tons displacement. It *was* the most modern, with some refinements that Center had suggested and John had made in the engineering works he owned. One of them was a wet-well entrance on the side that could be flooded or pumped dry in less than a minute, as well as turbine engines, something no vessel in the Republic's Navy had yet. The little ship lay long and sleek against the morning sun, a black silhouette outlined in crimson.

"Row! Bend yer *backs* to it, y'scuts!"

Smith's voice had a hard edge from the bows. John knew why; he could hear it without turning from his position at the tiller. A deep chuffing, the hollow sound steam made when exhausted into the stack of a light ship, and the soft continual surf noise of a bow wave curving away from the prow, just on the edge of hearing. The gunboat had picked them up twenty minutes ago, and it had grown from a dot on the horizon to a tiny model boat that grew as he watched, shedding a long plume of black coal smoke behind from its single cylindrical funnel.

"Stroke!" he barked, willing strength to flow from his voice through the crew to the oars. "Stroke! Almost home! Stroke!"

Sweat glistened on their faces, mouths gasping for air. A new sound came through the air, a muffled droning.

"Smith!"

One-handed, John tossed the binoculars to the ex-marine. He took them and looked upward. "Oh, shit, sir. One of them gasbag things. Just comin' into sight, like."

"How many engine pods?"

"Four. No, four at the sides an' one sort of at the back."

"Skytiger. Patrol class," John said. Center helpfully offered schematics and performance specifications. "They've got a squadron of them operating out of Salini now."

The *Windstrider* was very close. John felt himself leaning forward in a static wave of tension, and grinned tautly at himself. If things went badly, the yacht was no protection at all, merely a way to get a lot of other people killed with him. And his subconscious *still* felt as if he was racing for absolute safety. A ghost-memory plucked at him, something not his own. Raj Whitehall spurring his riding dog for a barge, with enemies at his heels. . . .

Damn, he thought. You seem to have had a much more picturesque life than me.

Adventure is somebody else in deep shit, far, far away, Raj said. ***And I think you're about to be that somebody. Focus, lad, focus.***

The long hull loomed up. John threw his weight on the tiller and the whaleboat heeled sharply, turning in its own length to curve around the bow and come down the side away from the Land gunboat. The narrow black slit of the loading door came up fast, perhaps too fast. . . .

"Ship oars!" he called.

The long ashwood shafts came inboard with a toss; Marines were well-trained in small-boat operations. One caught the edge of the steel slit nonetheless, snapping off and punching a rower in the ribs with enough force to bring an agonized grunt. The whaleboat shot into the gloom of the inner well; the overhead arc light seemed to grow brighter as the metal door slid shut. The air was humid, hot, with a smell of machine oil and sweat.

The crew collapsed over their oars, wheezing, faces red and dripping. John vaulted onto the sisal mats that covered the decking— an irony there, since the fiber had probably been imported from the Land—nodded in return to the crew's salutes, and took the staircase three rungs at a time. The hatchway to the boat chamber clanged shut below him; someone dogged it shut below, and a crewman threw matting over the hatch, leaving it looking identical to the rest of the corridor. He stepped through a doorway, and suddenly he was in the passenger section of the yacht. Soft colorful Sierran carpets underfoot, walnut panelling . . . by the time he reached his cabin, his valet was already towelling down his torso. He changed with rapid, precise movements, stuck a cigarette into a sea-ivory holder, and strolled out on deck.

"About bloody time," Jeffrey observed, making a show of looking at the approaching Chosen gunboat with his binoculars. "How'd it go?"

"You saw it—a damned ratfu—er, walking disaster."

Pia came up and took John's arm. "*Tedeschi* pigs," she muttered under her breath. Her eyes were fixed on the Chosen vessel, as well.

Good thing she's not on the guns, John thought.

There were four guns on the yacht, port and starboard forward and aft of the mid-hull superstructure. Nothing too remarkable about that; any vessel on Visager's seas had to have some armament, given the size and disposition of the marine life. The two-and-a-half-inch naval quick-firers on pedestal mounts were not entirely typical, however—nor was the fact that they could elevate to ninety degrees. Two were, their muzzles tracking the leisurely approach of the Chosen dirigible; the other two followed the gunboat. *That* had a three-inch gun behind a shield on the forecastle, another at the stern, and pom-poms—scaled-up machine guns firing a one-pound shell— bristling from either flank. The Chosen captain wouldn't be worried about the purely *physical* aspects of any confrontation, even without the airship. Although that confidence was possibly overstated, since the yacht had an underwater torpedo tube on either side.

"Try to look like a man on his honeymoon," John told his stepbrother.

"I'm trying," Jeffrey replied through clenched teeth. "He's signaling . . ." A bright light flickered from the Chosen gunboat. "*Heave to and prepare to be boarded,*" he read. "Arrogant bastards, aren't they?"

"Jeffrey?" Lola Farr, *nee* Chiavri, came up the companionway to the bridge, holding on to her hat. "Is there—" She caught sight of the Chosen vessels. "Oh!"

"Don't worry," Jeffrey said. He nodded his head upward towards the pole mast in front of the yacht's funnel. The flag of the Republic of the Santander snapped in the breeze. "They're not going to start a war."

Although they might be quite willing to endure an embarrassing diplomatic accident, John thought morbidly. He wished Pia and Lola weren't along, but then, it would look odd if they weren't, given the cover story. *And Pia wouldn't stay if I nailed her feet to the kitchen floor.*

"Captain," John said quietly to the grizzle-bearded man who stood beside the wheel with his hands clasped behind his back. "Signal *Santander ship, International Waters,* and *sheer off.*"

"Sir." He passed along the orders. "Shall I make speed?"

"No, just maintain your course," John said. The *Windstrider* could probably outrun the Chosen gunboat, but not the airship—or a cannon shell, for that matter. "Act naturally, everyone."

Jeffrey grinned. "*Natural,* under the circumstances, would be scared s—spitless."

"Act arrogant, then; the Chosen understand that."

John looked around at the bridge of the yacht. It was horseshoe-shaped, with another horseshoe within it; the inner one was enclosed, a curved waist-high wall of white-painted steel with windows above that, meeting the roof above. That held the wheel, binnacle, engine-room telegraph, and chart table. The outer semicircle was open save for a railing of teak and brass and empty save for the two couples and a few stewards. They were in cream-colored livery; Jeffrey wore a summer-weight brown colonel's uniform, and John white ducks, the sort of outfit a wealthy man might wear for playing tennis . . . or yachting. Pia and Lola were in gauzy warm-weather dresses of peach and lavender, looking expensive and haughty.

Perfect, John thought.

The gunboat was running on a converging course, white water foaming back from its bow. As he watched, it swung parallel to the yacht, almost alongside, and slowed to match speed. John smiled tightly and touched Pia's hand where it rested in the crook of his arm. She gave his arm a squeeze and released it. He took a drag on the cigarette, suppressing a cough, and strolled in a jaunty fashion to the starboard wing of the open space. His hand rested on the railing, casually touching a certain bronze fitting.

The vessels were less than a dozen yards apart—showing good handling on the part of both crews. That meant that the gunboat was less than a dozen yards from the sixteen-inch midships torpedo tube, armed and flooded. The fitting under his hand was connected to a simple bell-telegraph and light; if he pressed it twice, the men crouched behind the little circular door would pull levers . . . and a slug of high-pressure compressed air would shove the tin fish out of the tube. A few seconds and the Chosen gunboat would be a broken-backed hulk sliding under the waters.

Of course, that would ruin his cover; the airship would report back, or someone in the yacht's crew would talk even if they got lucky . . .

"Ahoy there!" a voice bellowed through a speaking trumpet from the low bridge of the gunboat. Its Santander English was accented but fluent. "'Tis iz *Leutnant der See* Annika Tirnwitz. Prepare to be boarded."

Cannon and pom-poms and machine guns were trained with unnerving steadiness on him, ready to rake the *Windstrider* into burning wreckage in seconds—about as many seconds as the torpedo would take to do its work. The gray-uniformed crew waited in motionless tension, all except for a dozen who were shouldering rifles and making ready to swing a launch from its davits. John pitched his voice to carry.

"This is sovereign territory of the Republic of the Santander. You have no authority here and any act of aggression will be resisted."

"That iz un private vessel! You do not diplomatic immunity haff!"

John pointed up to the flag. "*Leutnant,* you may come aboard with no more than one other member of your crew. Otherwise, I must ask you to get out of my way."

Half-heard orders carried from the gunboat to the yacht. Most of the boarding party who'd been preparing the launch grounded arms and stood easy; the little boat slid down into the water, and several figures in Land uniform slid down ropes from the gunboat's deck to man it. Smuts of black smoke broke from the slender funnel at its stern, a small steam engine chugged, and the launch angled in towards the Santander ship.

"Captain," John called over his shoulder. "Party to greet the *Leutnant.* And a rope ladder, if you please."

Whistles fluted as the Chosen officer came over the side. The escort for her and the Protégé seaman who followed behind were distantly polite; the rest of the crew glared. Everyone was wearing a cutlass and revolver, and carbines stood ready to hand.

Aren't you laying it on a bit thick? Jeffrey thought, the familiar mental voice relayed by Center. *You're supposed to be secretly on their side, after all.*

That's exactly it, John replied. *A good double agent plays his part well—and my part is a wealthy playboy who dabbles in diplomacy, but who is secretly a Foreign Office spook and violently anti-Chosen.*

The irony of it was that the best way to convince his Chosen handlers that he was a competent double agent was to act the way he would if he *wasn't* a double agent, except for his reports to them—he was an information conduit, not an agent of influence. Which meant, of course, that they could never be sure he wasn't a *triple* agent, but that was par for the course.

Espionage could make your head hurt.

Annika Tirnwitz was a tall lanky woman of about thirty, with a brush of close-cropped brown hair and a face tanned and weatherbeaten to the color of oiled wood. Her blue eyes were like gunsights, tracking methodically across the yacht, missing nothing. John thought he saw a little surprise at the quality of the crew and the arms, but . . .

correct, Center thought. **subject tirnwitz is surprised.** A holograph appeared over her face, showing temperature patterns and pupil dilation. A sidebar showed pulse rate and blood pressure. **subject is also experiencing well-controlled apprehension.**

"*Leutnant der See* Annika Tirnwitz," the Chosen said, with a slight stiff nod. "Who is in command here?"

John replied in kind. In accentless Landisch he replied: "Johan Hosten, owner-aboard. What can I do for you, *Leutnant?*"

subject's apprehension level has increased markedly.

Nice to know that he wasn't the only one feeling nervous here, and even nicer that he had Center to reveal what was behind that poker face. Of course, only a fool *wouldn't* be a little fearful of the possible consequences of a fight here. Not the physical ones—cowards didn't make it through the Test of Life—but the political repercussions. Relations between the Land and Santander had never been all that good, and since the fall of the Empire they'd gone straight down the toilet. The press back home was having a field day with the atrocity stories the refugees were bringing in; the Chosen were too insular to even try countermeasures, they didn't understand the impact that sort of thing had on public opinion in the Republic. John's own papers were leading the charge . . . and the stories were mostly true, at that.

The Chosen *did* understand status and territory and pissing matches, though. Sinking the yacht of a wealthy, powerful man related to a Santander Navy admiral . . .

"*Herr* Hosten?" Tirnwitz said. She cleared her throat. "My vessel was pursuing a small boat. Carrying subversive terrorist elements."

John made a sweeping wave of his hand. "As you can see, *Leutnant,* there's no boat here except our ship's lifeboats, all of which are secured and lashed down . . . and dry."

His eyes lifted slightly to the dirigible. It was much closer now, but when he'd come aboard it had been too far to the north to see what actually happened.

Tirnwitz's lips thinned in frustration. The *Windstrider*'s boats *were* lashed down and tight in their davits; nobody could have hoisted one aboard in the time they'd had. Nor could a whaleboat have made it over the horizon in the yacht's shelter . . . although possibly the men on one could have scrambled aboard and pulled the plug on their boat.

He could see that thought going through Tirnwitz's head. "I must make inspection and question your crew," she said after a moment.

"Impossible," John replied.

Jeffrey moved up to his side. "And to paraphrase what my father said in Salini last year, if you want to start a war, this is as good a place as any."

Pia waved a steward forward with a tray; it looked rather incongruous when combined with the cutlass and revolver at his waist, and the short rifle slung over his shoulder.

"Perhaps the *Leutnant* would like some refreshments?" she said with silky malice. "Before she returns to her ship."

The sailor behind the Chosen captain growled and half moved, then sank back quivering with rage at a finger-motion from her. She stared at Pia for a moment.

"An Imperial. The animals are less insolent in the New Territories these days," she said. "Teaching them manners can be diverting." She nodded to John. "Someday we may serve Santander refreshments, a drink you'll find unpleasant. *Guten tag.*"

CHAPTER THIRTEEN

The blast furnace shrieked like a woman in childbirth, magnified ten thousand times. A long tongue of flame reached upward into the night, throwing reddish-orange light across the new steelworks. John nodded thoughtfully as the bell-cap was lowered down onto the great cylinder, like a cork into a bottle taller than a six-story building. The flames died down as the cap intercepted the uprush of superheated gases from the throat of the furnace, channeling them through pipes where they were cleaned and distributed to heat ovens and boilers. A stink of cinders and sulfur filled the air, and the acrid nose-crackling smell of heated metal. Gravel crunched under his feet as he turned away, the small party of engineers and managers trailing at his heels.

A train of railcarts rumbled by, full of reddish iron ore, limestone, and black-brown coke in careful proportions. The carts slowed, then jerked and picked up a little speed as the hooks beneath them caught the endless chain belt that would haul them up the steep slope to the lip of the furnace.

"Nice counterweight system you've installed, sir," the chief engineer said. "Saves time on feeding the furnace."

John nodded. *Courtesy of Center,* he thought.

"Saves labor, too," the engineer said. "God knows we're short."

"How are those refugees shaping up?" John said.

"Better'n I'd have thought, sir, for Wop hayseeds. They're not afraid of shedding some sweat, that's for sure."

"Pay's better than stoop work in the fields," John said.

A lot of the Imperial refugees who'd left the camps outside the cities on the south shore of the Gut ended up as migrant workers following the crops across Santander. They'd jumped at the chance of mill work. A couple of them snatched off their hats and bowed as he passed, teeth gleaming white against their soot-darkened olive skins. John touched the gold head of his cane to his own silk topper; luckily white spats were out of fashion, or Pia would be even more upset than she was likely to be with him anyway.

"No damned strikes, either," the plant's manager said.

"Shouldn't be, with the wages we pay," John said.

Off to the left a huge cradle of molten iron was moving, slung under a trackway that ran down the center of the shed. It dropped fat white sparks, bright even against the arc lights, then halted and tipped a stream of white-hot incandescence into the waiting maw of the open-hearth furnace. Further back, beyond the soaking pits for the ingots, the machinery of the rolling mill slammed and hummed, long shafts of hot steel stretching and forming.

The engineer nodded towards them. "We're fully up to speed on the rail mill," he said. "If you can keep the orders coming in, we can keep the steel going out."

John nodded. "Don't worry about the orders," he said. "Plenty of new lines going in, what with the double-tracking program. And the Chosen are buying for their new lines in the Empire."

That brought the conversation behind him to a halt. He looked back at the expressions of clenched disapproval and grinned; it was not a pleasant thing to see.

"You're selling to the Chosen?" the engineer said.

"*I* prefer to think of it as getting the Chosen to finance our expansion program," John replied.

What's more, it's good cover. Several times over. It gave him a good excuse for traveling to the Land, which helped with his ostensible work as a double agent in the employ of the Chosen. The shipments were also splendid cover for agents and arms to the underground resistance.

"And besides the sheet-steel rolls, you'll be getting heavy boring and turning lathes soon. From the Armory Mills in Santander City."

That rocked the man back on his heels. "Ordnance?" he said. "That'll *cost*, sir. We'll have to learn by doing, and it's specialist work."

John nodded. "Don't worry about the orders," he said again. "Let's say a voice whispered in my ear that demand is going to increase."

He touched the cane to his hat brim again and shook hands all around. His senior employees had learned to respect John Hosten's "hunches," even if they didn't understand them. Then walked across the vacant yard to where his car was waiting by the plant gate under a floodlight.

"Back home, sir?" Harry Smith said, looking up from polishing the headlamps with a chamois cloth.

"Home," he said. "For a few days."

"Ah," the ex-marine in the chauffeur's uniform said. "We're going somewhere, then, sir?"

John nodded and stepped into the passenger compartment of the car as Smith opened it for him, tossing hat and cane to one of the seats. There were six, facing each other at front and rear. One held Maurice Hosten, sleeping with his head in Maurice Farr's lap; the older man looked down at his five-year-old namesake fondly, stroking the silky black hair that spilled across the dark blue of his uniform coat. Pia glanced up, with a welcoming smile that held a bit of a frown.

"Even on your son's birthday, you cannot keep from business?" she said.

"Only a little bit of business, darling," he said, settling back against the padded leather of the seat; it sighed for him. "Quietly, or you'll wake him."

Maurice Farr chuckled. "After the amount of cake this young man put away, not to mention the lemonade, the spun candy, the pony rides, the carousel, and the Ferris wheel, a guncotton charge couldn't wake him—you should know that by now."

"He does; he's just using that as an excuse." Pia's hand took John's and squeezed away the sting of the words. "This one, you wave the word 'duty' in front of him, and he reacts like a fish leaping for a worm."

"And the hook's barbed," John said ruefully, nodding to Smith through the window that joined the passenger compartment and the driver's position up ahead. The car moved forward with a hiss of vented steam.

"Your lady's been running an interesting notion past me," Admiral Farr said.

"This Ladies'—"

"Women's," Pia corrected.

"Women's Auxiliary?" John finished.

"Yes. *If* we get into an all-out war with the Land, we could use it. Though I'm not sure how the public would react; there was a lot of bad feeling during the agitation over the franchise, a decade or so ago. People claiming it was the first step to Chosen corruption and so forth."

"I don't think that'll be much of a problem," John said thoughtfully. Center provided the probable breakdown of public sentiment in various combinations of circumstance. "After all, Pia's idea is to have women take jobs that *release* men to fight. There are already plenty of women in the nursing corps—have been since the last war with the Union, you know, whatshername with the lantern and all that."

"And if the big war happens, we'll need every fighting man we can get," the admiral said thoughtfully. "We'll not win that one without a damned big army, and the fleet'll have to expand, too. We won't be able to spare men for typing and filing and whatnot."

"And factory work," Pia said. "First, we must have a committee—women of consequence, to be respectable, but also of . . . energy."

"If it's energy you want, what about your sisters-in-law?" Maurice said. "If it's one thing my daughters have, it's energy . . . oh."

Pia nodded. "Them I talk to first," she said. "They are young, but there is time."

"It'll be a while," John said. Pia nodded; his foster-father looked at him a little strangely, struck by the certainty of the tone. "But it's not too early to get started laying the groundwork."

"Son, for a man of thirty, sometimes you sound pretty damned old," Maurice said. He touched his graying temples. "Maybe I'd better retire, and leave the field to you younger bucks."

"I don't think you can be spared, Father," John said. "And . . . it isn't all *that* long until the balloon goes up."

"Is it indeed?" Maurice Farr said.

"The situation in the Union's getting pretty tense," John said. "The People's Front may win the next election there."

"The Chosen certainly won't like that," Maurice said. "I'm not too certain I do either. The Union's not going to solve its problems by an attack on property . . . although the way the wealthy act there is a standing invitation to that sort of thing."

John nodded. "The Chosen have a lot of influence in certain circles there," he said. "And I don't think those circles are going to lie down and die just because they lose an election. It'll take a couple of years for things to boil over, but the Land is certainly heating up the pot."

Maurice Farr blinked slowly, his face slowly losing the shape of a grandfather's and becoming an admiral's. "They can't get supplies into the Union except by sea," he said thoughtfully.

John shook his head. "We can't fight them over aiding one faction in the Union," he said. "Western provinces wouldn't go for it."

"All that good soil softens the brain, I think," Farr said.

"Amazing what being a couple of hundred miles from the action will do. And they've always resisted the easterners' attempts to get the Republic as a whole involved in Union affairs; it'll take a while for them to realize this is different."

Pia looked up at him. "This is why you must travel to the Union, my love?" she said.

John sighed unhappily. "Jeffrey and I will be in and out of there for years now," he said. "Until the crisis comes. But don't worry, it shouldn't be particularly risky. We're only advising and playing politics, after all."

(((•))   (((•))   (((•))

Jeffrey Farr had never liked the Union del Est very much. For one thing, the waiters, innkeepers, clerks, and such made it a point of pride to be surly, and he'd never liked seeing a job done badly. For another, the women didn't wash or change their underclothes often enough to suit him; he supposed that that was an academic point now that he was a married man with a nine-year-old daughter and another child on the way, but the memory rankled . . . *and she looked so good, before and after she took off her drawers. But phew!*

The men didn't wash much, either, but that was less personal.

Still, the coastal city of Borreaux looked well enough; the terrain was less mountainous than most of the southern shore of the Gut, a long narrow plain flanking a river between low mountains. The plain was covered with vineyards, mostly; the foothills of the mountains were gray-green with olives, and the upper slopes still heavily forested with oak and silver fir despite centuries of cutting for buildings and ship timber and barrels. The town itself sprawled along the river in a tangle of docks and basins, backed by broad, straight streets lined with trees and handsome three-story blocks of buildings in a uniform cream limestone. The slums weren't quite as bad as in most Union cities and were kept decently out of sight. The rooftop terrace of this restaurant was quite pleasant—sun shining through the striped awnings, servers in white aprons bearing food and drink on trays. . .

. . . and just to spoil it, three Chosen officers in gray were at a table nearby, two men and a woman, and two local ladies. The Land aristocrats were plowing their way through a five-course meal, and punishing a couple of bottles of the local wine fairly hard. Or rather, the two men were, and laughing occasionally with their local companions, who were either extremely high-priced talent or the minor gentlewomen they appeared to be. The Chosen woman was sipping at a single glass of the wine and looking around. Medium-height, dark hair and eyes . . .

Christ, it's Gerta! Jeffrey thought, with a jolt of alarm that turned the hunger in his stomach to sour churning. *Why didn't you tell me?*

Would have, lad, if it'd been an emergency. Don't want you to lose your alertness, though. We can't always notice things for you.

He tried to keep a poker face, but Gerta must have seen some change. She raised the wineglass slightly, and an eyebrow with it. The mannerism reminded him of John a little—but then, they'd been raised together. It startled him sometimes to remember that John had been born among the Chosen. If it wasn't for that clubfoot . . .

observe:

A man's looks were more than muscle and bone; the personality within shaped them, everything from the set of his mouth to the way he walked. It took a moment for Jeffrey to realize that the tall man in the uniform of a Land general was John. The face was the same, but full of a quiet, grim deadliness. The city behind him was familiar, too: Borreaux, but in ruins. A dirigible floated overhead, and columns of Land troops were marching up from the docks.

john hosten is in the upper 0.3% of the human ability curve, Center said. **in the absence of his disability, and assuming no intervention on our part, the probability of his achieving general rank by this date in his timeline is 87%, ±4. probability of becoming chief of general staff, 73%, ±6. probability of becoming head of chosen council of state, 61%, ±8. probability of chosen conquest of visager increases by 17% ±5 in that eventuality.**

Jeffrey gave a slight internal shudder. With no clubfoot—and no Center—he and John would probably have spent their lives fighting each other.

correct. probability—

Shut up, Raj and Jeffrey thought simultaneously.

The waiter arrived at last, and laid a bowl of the famous Borreaux fish stew before him; trivalves in their shells, chunks of lizard tail, pieces of fish, all in a broth rich with garlic, tomatoes, and spices. It smelled wonderful; it would have been even more wonderful if the waiter hadn't had a rim of grime under his thumbnail, and the thumb hadn't been dipping into the stew. Jeffrey forced himself to ignore that, and what the kitchen was probably like; he poured himself a glass of white wine and tore a chunk of bread off the end of a long narrow loaf. Say what you liked about the Unionaise, they did know how to cook.

And it was a damned unlucky chance that Chosen officers, and

Gerta of all people, happened to be right here when he was expecting—

A small, slight man came up to Jeffrey's table and sat, taking off his beret and stubbing out a villainous-smelling cigarette in an ashtray. His eyes flicked sideways toward the Chosen three tables away.

"They can't hear us," Jeffrey said. "And we're facing away."

So that they couldn't lip-read. Offhand, he thought that the two male Chosen were straight-legs; Gerta certainly wasn't, though, and might well have been trained in that particular skill. As to what they were doing here . . .

"And we have business," Jeffrey went on, spooning up some of the fish stew. "Damn, but that's good," he said mildly.

"Vincen Deshambre," the thin man said. Jeffrey took his hand for a moment. "Delegate of the *Parti Uniste Travailleur*." He slid a small flat envelope out of his jacket and across the table.

"Colonel Jeffrey Farr," Jeffrey replied, reading it.

He spoke fair Fransay, and read it well; the Union del Est had been the Republic's main foreign enemy until a generation or so ago, with skirmishes even more recently. Santander military men were expected to learn the language, for interrogations and captured documents, if nothing else.

Vincen looked over again at the table with the Chosen. "Bitches," he said, his voice suddenly like something that spent most of its time curled up on warm rocks.

Jeffrey looked up, raising his eyebrow. Only one of the Chosen could possibly qualify.

"Not the foreigners," Vincen said. A light sheen broke out across his high forehead, up to the edge of the thinning hair. "They're just pirates. If we were united, we could laugh at them."

I don't think so, Jeffrey thought. Alone, the Union against the Land of the Chosen would be a match between the hammer and the egg. Not *quite* as easy a victim as the Empire had been, of course. For one thing the terrain was worse, for another it was farther away, and for a third the country wasn't quite so backward. *Still, I see his point.* And the Land wasn't about to simply invade the

Union. That would mean war with Santander, and the Chosen weren't ready . . . yet.

Neither was Santander.

"Those *whores* are what's wrong, them and those like them."

Jeffrey did a quick scan across the other table, then turned and let Center freeze the picture in front of him, magnifying until they all seemed to be at arm's length.

"I don't think they're professionals," he said.

Vincen flushed more deeply; it was a little disconcerting to see a man actually sweating with hate.

"Elite," he said, using the Fransay term for the upper classes. "*Merdechiennes* are losing their power, so they call in foreigners to prop it up for them."

"Well, two can play at that game," Jeffrey said.

The Unionaise gave him a sharp look Santander had taken several substantial bites out of the western border of the Union, in the old wars. Jeffrey smiled warmly.

"We're not territorially expansive . . . not anymore, at least."

Of course, much of the western Union was an economic satellite of the Republic these days, and the *Travailleur*—Worker—party didn't like it one little bit. Despite the fact that without that investment, its members would still be scratching out a living farming rocks as *metayers,* paying half the crop to a landlord.

Vincen grunted. "As you say. We have the evidence now. General Libert is definitely in correspondence with Land agents. They offer transport for his Legion troops back to the mainland."

Center called up a map for Jeffrey. The Union del Est covered a big chunk of the southern lobe of Visager's main continent, between Santander and the sort-of-republic of Sierra. South of it wasn't much but ocean right down to the south polar ice cap, but there were a series of fairly substantial islands, some independent, some held by the Republic or the Union.

"Libert's on Errif, isn't he? That's quite a ways out, seven hundred kilometers or so. Can't your navy squadron in Bassin du Sud keep him bottled up?"

The Legion were the best troops the Union had, and mostly

foreigners at that. They were the ones who'd finally beaten the natives on Errif, after a war where the Union regulars nearly got thrown back into the sea And there were large units of Errifan natives under Union officers on the islands too, now. They'd probably be about as tough fighting against the Union government as they had been in the initial war.

"The navy is loyal to the government, yes," Vincen said. "But the Land, they offer air transport if there is a matching military uprising on the mainland."

Jeffrey whistled silently, remembering the air assault on Corona in the opening stages of the Imperial war. *Can't fault the Chosen on audacity,* he thought. Errif was a lot further from their bases. *Overfly the Union,* he thought, calculating distances. They could at that; the *Landisch Luftanza* had a concession to run a route that way. Refuel at sea, from ships brought round the continent in international waters. *Yes, it's possible. Just.* You had to be ready to take chances in war; otherwise it turned into a series of slugging matches. Big risks could have big payoffs . . . or disaster, if things went into the pot.

"Why don't you recall him and jail him?" Jeffrey asked. "Before he has a chance to rebel."

Vincen clenched his fists. "Because this coalition so-called government has even less balls than it has brains!" His half-howl brought stares from the tables around them, and he lowered his voice. "Us, the damned syndicalists, the regional autonomists—everyone but the twice-damned anarchists and separatists, and name of a dog! We have to keep them sweet, too, because we need their votes in the *Chambre du Delegats.*"

He made a disgusted sound through his teeth, hands waving. Unionaise were like Imperials that way: tie their hands and they were struck dumb as a fish.

"Last year, we could have arrested him. Arrested all the traitors in uniform. What did our so-called government do? Pensioned half of them off! Gave them pensions wrung out of the workers' sweat, so that they could plot at their leisure."

"'Never do an enemy a small injury,'" Jeffrey quoted. "Old Imperial saying." Very old, from what Center said.

Vincen's small eyes were hot with agreement. "We should have executed the lot of them," he said. "Now it's too late. The government is holding off on General"—he virtually spat the word—"Libert in the hopes that if they don't *provoke* him, he'll do nothing."

"Stupid," Jeffrey said in agreement. "They're also probably afraid that if they send troops to arrest him, they'll go over to him instead."

Vincen nodded jerkily. "There are loyal troops—the Assault Guards, for instance—but yes, the ministry is concerned with that."

"Which brings us down to practicalities," Jeffrey said. "If there is a military uprising with Land support, what exactly do you plan to do about it?"

"We will fight!"

"Yes, but what will you fight *with?*"

The little Unionaise linked his fingers on the table. "We have confidence that part of the army at least will remain loyal. Beyond that, there are the regional militias."

Jeffrey nodded. He had no confidence in them; for one thing, they had even less in the way of real training than the provincial militias back home. Some of the states of the Union were run by the conservative opposition parties, and thereby pro-Chosen. Even in the ones that weren't, too many of the militias were under the influence of local magnates, almost all of whom supported the conservative opposition parties, as did the Church here. The Church here *was* a great landed magnate, come to that.

"And we'll hand out arms to the party militias of the coalition, and to the workers in the streets—let's see how the Regulars like being drowned in a *sea* of armed workers."

"It's good to see you're in earnest," Jeffrey said. It all sounded like a prescription for a bloodbath, but that was preferable to another swift Chosen triumph, he supposed. "For my part, I can assure you that my government will declare any outright intervention in internal Union affairs an unfriendly act."

That meant less than it should; semi-clandestine intervention wouldn't provoke Santander retaliation. The Republic simply wasn't ready for war, either physically or psychologically.

"And I think we can guarantee that you'll be allowed to purchase weapons. Speaking in my private capacity, you'll also find some of our banks sympathetic in the matter of loans. Provided your government is equally reasonable."

"I suppose you'll want concessions. . . ."

They settled down to dicker; when Vincen left, the expression on his face was marginally less sour. Fortunately, the Chosen officers left a little later. The men went with their local companions; one of them stopped to say a final word with Gerta Hosten. She laughed and shook her head. The man shrugged, and the girl with him pouted. When they had left, Gerta picked up her wineglass and came over to Jeffreys table.

"You're welcome," he said as she seated herself without asking permission.

The hard dark face showed a slight smile. "We meet again. A pleasure. It would have been an even bigger one if Heinrich had had the sense to shoot you four years ago. I *told* him you were a spook."

"I'm here on vacation," Jeffrey said, smiling back despite himself. "Besides, Heinrich doesn't have your suspicious mind."

"Which is why he's a straight-leg. Too damned good-natured for his own good." Gerta raised her wineglass. "These Unionaise make some pretty things," she said as the cut crystal sparkled in the evening sun. "And they make good wine. But they couldn't organize sailors into a whorehouse."

"Well, that's your problem," Jeffrey said. "You're the ones with the training mission here."

"Purely as private contractors, on leave from our regular duties," Gerta said piously.

"And I'm a tourist," Jeffrey said.

Unwillingly, he joined in Gerta's chuckle.

"You know the best thing about competing with you Santies?" Gerta asked. When he shook his head, she continued: "It's not that you're short of guts, because you aren't, or because you're stupid, because you aren't that, either. It's that you're never, ever *ready*." She finished her wine and rose.

"And we're going to win this round," she said.

"Why's that, the invincible destiny of the Chosen race?"

"Invincible muleshit," she said cheerfully, with a grin that might have come out of deep water, rolling over for the killing bite. "The reason that we're going to win this one is that we're trying to help fuck this place up—and the Unionaise are positive geniuses at that, anyway."

CHAPTER FOURTEEN

Everyone in Bassin du Sud was afraid. John Hosten could taste it, even without Center's quick flickering scans of the people passing by. The narrow crooked streets were less full of people than he'd seen on previous business visits, and the storekeepers stood at the ends of their long narrow shops, ready to drop the rolling metal curtain-doors. Windows were locked behind the scrolled ironwork of their balconies, and similar ironwork doors had been pulled across most of the narrow entranceways that led to interior courtyards. He could still get glimpses down them, the sight of a fountain or a statue in old green bronze, or a line of washing above plain flagstones.

Gerta's smile haunted him, seen through Jeffrey's eyes.

Every time he'd seen her smile like that, people started dying in job lots.

There was something else about the streets, he decided. *I hope Jean-Claude is still there.* Something very odd about the streets, but he couldn't quite put his finger on it.

few military personnel, Center said.

Bassin du Sud had a fair-sized Union garrison, plus a navy base. In fact, if he turned, he could see part of it downslope from the rise he was on. His stepfather would have gone into a cold rage at the knots hanging from the rigging of the three hermaphrodite cruisers at the dock, and the state of their upperworks, but . . .

The sound hit a huge soft pillow of air, knocking him backward. Down by the naval docks a hemisphere of fire blossomed upwards, with bits and pieces of iron and wood and crewmen from the three cruisers. A stunned silence followed the explosion, then a great screaming roar like nothing he had ever heard in his life.

A mob, Raj's mental voice said softly. *That's the sound of a hunting mob.*

Over it came sounds he had no problem recognizing. First a series of dull soft thuds in the distance, like very large doors slamming. Then a burbling, popping sound that went on and on, rising and falling. Artillery and small arms.

"I'm *late,* God damn it," he said, and began to run. Perhaps too late. The rough pavement was slippery and uncertain under his boots; he kept his right hand near the front of his jacket, ready to go for a weapon.

Careful, lad, Raj cautioned. *I don't think foreigners are going to be all that popular around here right now.*

The narrow street widened a little, into a small cobbled plaza the shape of an irregular polygon, with a fountain in the middle spilling water into granite horse troughs around it. A bullet spanged through the air. He dove forward and rolled into the cover of the troughs, ignoring the stone gouging at his back, and came up with the automatic ready in his hand.

A man in a monk's brown robe was staggering away from the little church on the other side of the plaza. He was a thick-bodied man, with a kettle belly and a round, plump face. A few hours earlier it might have been a good-natured face, the jolly monk too fond of the table and bottle of the stories. Now it was a mask of blood from a long cut across the tonsured scalp. Dozens of men and women in the rough blue clothing of city laborers were following the monk, jeering and poking him with sticks, spitting and kicking. The cleric's heavy body jerked to the blows, but his wide fixed eyes looked out of blood wet skin with a desperate fixed expression, as if his mind had convinced itself that the exit to the plaza represented safety.

There was no safety for him. One of the mob tired of the fun. The pried-up cobblestone he swung must have weighed ten pounds; the monk's head burst with a sound much like a watermelon falling six stories onto pavement. He collapsed, his body still twitching beneath the brown robe. John swore softly to himself and rose, letting the pistol fall down by his side. The black crackle finish of the weapon's steel probably wouldn't show much against his frock coat . . . and while the ten rounds in the magazine also wouldn't be much good against a charging mob, he didn't intend to die alone if it came to that.

"Hey, there's one of the Chosen dog-suckers who're in bed with the elite and the Christ-suckers!" someone bawled.

"Santander!" John shouted, in a controlled roar. It cut through the murmur of this little outlier of the mob. "I'm from Santander"—*though I was born in Oathtaking and my father's a general on the Council, but there's no need to complicate matters—*"on diplomatic business."

He pulled out his passport with his left hand and held it up. Half the crowd probably couldn't read, much less recognize official stamps, but his accentless Fransay and his manner made them hesitate.

"I'm on my way to the Santander consulate right now," he went on, and pointed to the northward where the sound of fighting was heaviest. "Don't you people have business up there?"

The crowd milled, people talking to their neighbors; individuals once more, rather than a beast with a single mind and will. John holstered his weapon and trotted past them, past the church where flame was beginning to lick out the shattered stained-glass windows. A quick glance inside showed the chaos of swift incompetent looting and the body of a nun lying spread-eagled in a huge pool of blood from her gashed-open throat.

What lovely allies, he thought dryly, and mentally waved aside Centers comments. *I know, I know.*

The streets broadened as he climbed the slope above the harbor and gained the more-or-less level plateau that held the newer part of the city. The press of people grew too, crowds of them pouring in from the dock areas behind him and from the factory-worker suburbs. He dodged around an electric tram standing frozen in the middle of the street, past another burning church—from the columns of smoke, there were fires all over town—and past cars, lying abandoned or passing crammed past capacity. Those held armed men, in civilian clothes or green Assault Guard *gendarmerie* uniforms with black leather hats, or army and navy gear. All the men in them had red armbands, though, and some had miniature red or black flags flying from their long sword-bayonets. John cursed, kicked, and pushed his way through the crowds, but the press grew closer and closer; it was like being caught in heavy surf, or a strong river current.

Suddenly the crowd surged around him, an eddy this time. He barely cleared the corner onto the Avenue d'Armes when the shooting broke out ahead, louder this time. He was enough taller than the Unionaise crowd to see why. A dozen military steam cars had pulled up and blocked the road fifty yards ahead. They weren't armored vehicles, but they each had a couple of pintle-mounted machine guns. Infantry followed, rushing up and deploying on and around the cars. Their rifles came up in a bristle, and the crews of the machine guns were slapping the covers down and jacking the cocking levers. The fat water jackets of the automatic weapons jerked and quivered with their fearful haste.

John felt a cold rippling sensation over his belly and loins. Everything seemed to move very slowly, giving him plenty of time to consider. A man in front of him was pushing a wheelbarrow full of stones and half-bricks, ammunition for the riot which this no longer was. He squatted—there was no room to bend—gripped the man by waist and ankle, and heaved. The Unionaise pitched forward, flying over the toppling wheelbarrow and into the three men ahead of it, staggering them. They fell backward against the wood and iron in the same instant that John dove forward and down onto the bricks it spilled, into the space it had made, the only open space in the whole vast crowd.

A giant gripped a sheet of canvas in metal gauntlets and *ripped*. John curled himself into a ball behind the wheelbarrow and bared his teeth at the picture his mind supplied of what was happening ahead.

The crowd *couldn't* retreat, not really, not with so many thousands behind them still pressing forward and the high blank walls on either side.

Twenty machine guns fired continuously, and several hundred magazine rifles as fast as the soldiers could work their bolts and reload. Bodies fell over the wheelbarow, over John, turning his position into a mount that kicked and twitched and bled. He heaved his back against the sliding, thrashing mass; if he let it grow he'd suffocate here, trapped beneath a half-ton of flesh. The barricade of bodies shuddered as bullets smacked home. John was blind in a hot darkness that stank with the iron-copper of blood and slimy feces and body fluids. They ran down over him, matting his clothing, running into his mouth and eyes. He heaved again, feeling his frock coat rip with the strain. Bodies slid, and a draft of fresher air brought him back to conscious thought.

Can't attract attention . . .

Through a gap he could see the rooftops beyond the barricade of war-cars. Something moved there, and something smaller flew though the air.

Crump. The dynamite bomb landed between two cars and rolled under the front wheels of one. It backflipped onto the vehicle next to it with a rending crash of glass and metal; superheated steam flayed men for yards around as the flash-boiler coils in both ruptured. Some officer with strong presence of mind was redirecting fire to the rooftops on either hand, but more dynamite bombs rained down. *Crump. Crump. Crump.*

There hadn't been time for panic to infect the whole mob, even though hundreds—thousands—had been killed or wounded. Not even Center could have predicted their reaction. The survivors ran forward, and John ran with them. One machine gun snarled back into action briefly, and then the forefront of the mob was scrambling over the ramp of dead and dying that stood four and five bodies deep in front of the wrecked war-cars. He dove over it headfirst, while the surviving soldiers shot down the rioters silhouetted upright on the edge. The automatic was in his hand as he knelt. A green grid of lines settled over his vision, and the aim strobed red as he swung from one target to the next. *Crack.* A soldier pitched backward from the spade grips of his machine gun with a round blue hole between his eyes and the back blown out of his head by the wadcutter bullet. *Crack.* An officer folded in the middle as if he'd been gut-punched, then slid forward to lie limply among the other dead. *Crack. Crack.* The slide locked back and his hands automatically ejected the empty magazine and replaced it with one from the clips attached to the shoulder-holster rig.

John blinked, breathing hoarsely. His hand shook slightly as he holstered the automatic and he blinked again and again, trying to shed the glassy sensation that made him feel like an abandoned hand-puppet.

I never liked it either, Raj said. There was the momentary image of a room in a tower, with half a dozen men sprawled in death across tables and benches. *It's necessary, sometimes. Brace up, lad. Work to be done.*

John nodded and wiped at the congealing blood on his face. *Well, that didn't work.* He stripped off his businessman's frock coat and used the relatively dry lining instead, cleaning away enough so that his eyes didn't stick shut and spitting to clear the taste out of his mouth. Then he bent to pick up a soldier's fallen rifle and bandolier; the weapon was Land-made or a copy. *No, Oathtaking armory marks.* He thumbed two stripper clips into the magazine and slapped the bolt home before working his way to the edge of the crowd. Not much chance his contact would be at home, but it wasn't far and he had to check.

Snipers were firing from the towers of the Bassin du Sud cathedral. The *Maison Municipal* was directly across from it, with improvised barricades of furniture and planter boxes full of flowers in front of the entrances and people shooting back from behind them, and from the windows above. John went down on his belly and leopard-crawled along the sidewalk from one piece of cover to the next. When he was halfway across an explosion lifted him and slammed him against the wall of the building, leaving him half-stunned as the cathedral facade slid into the square in a slow-motion collapse, falling almost vertically. Quarter-ton limestone building blocks mixed with gargoyles and fretwork and fragments of glass avalanched across the pavement. John pressed his face into the sidewalk and hoped that the plane trees and benches to his right would stop anything that bounced this far. There was a pattering of rubble, and something grazed his buttocks hard enough to sting; then a cloud of choking dust swept across him, making him sneeze repeatedly. The earthquake rumble died down, and he doggedly resumed his crawl.

Willing hands pulled him over the barricade; the crowd behind it included everyone from Assault Guards to female file clerks, armed with everything conceivable, including fireplace pokers and Y-fork kid's catapults. Many of the people there were standing on the piled furniture and cheering the ruin of the cathedral, despite the fact that hostile fire was coming from other buildings around the plaza as well. John prudently rolled to one side before coming erect, grunting slightly as his bruises twinged. An Assault Guard looked at him, unconsciously fingering the pistol at his side.

"Who are you?" he said.

"I'm here to see Jean-Claude Deschines," John replied.

"Just like that?" The *gendarme* had narrow eyes and a heavy black stubble. "I asked who you are."

"And I asked to see Jean-Claude. Tell him John is here with the package he was expecting."

The other man's eyes narrowed; he nodded and trotted off. John set his back against a twisting granite column and wrestled his breath and heartbeat back under control, ignoring the sporadic shooting and cheering and trying to ignore the deadly whine of the occasional ricochet making it through the barricaded windows. Ten years ago he wouldn't have been breathing hard. . . . The entrance hall was dark because of those barricades, just enough light to see the big curving staircase at its rear, and the usual allegorical murals depicting Progress and Harmony and Industry, the sort of thing the *Syndicat d'Initative* put up in any Unionaise town hall. One did catch his eye, a mosaic piece showing Bassin du Sud as it had looked a couple of centuries ago, with only the grim bulk of the castle on its hill, and a small walled village at its feet. That castle had been built as a base to stop Errife corsairs, back when the island pirates had virtually owned the coast, setting up bases and raiding far inland for slaves and loot.

The castle was still there. And it was the garrison HQ for the Bassin du Sud military district. The curtain walls and moats and arrowslits weren't all that relevant anymore, but there were heavy shore-defense mortars in the courtyards, Land-made breechloaders, capable of commanding the harbor if the plotters consolidated their hold on the garrison.

A tall man with a swag belly clattered down the staircase; he had a police carbine over his shoulder and a pistol thrust through the sash around his waist.

"Jean!" he roared genially, and came toward John with open arms for the hug and kiss on both cheeks that was the standard friendly greeting in the Union. At the last moment he recoiled.

John looked down briefly at his shirt. "Most of it's other people's blood," he said helpfully.

"Name of a dog! You were caught in the street fighting?"

John nodded. "Nearly got massacred by some soldiers with car-mounted machine guns, but somebody dropped dynamite on them. There seem to be a lot of explosions going on today." He jerked his head towards the doors leading out onto the plaza.

"My faith, yes," the mayor of Bassin du Sud said happily. "Copper miners. I . . . ah . . . arranged for a special train to bring in a few hundred of them from up in the hills. Ingenious fellows, aren't they?"

John nodded. They were also anarchists almost to a man, those that weren't members of the radical wing of the *Travailleur* party. A few years ago, when the Conservatives had been in power, they'd taken up arms in a revolt halfway between a damned violent strike and outright revolution. The government had turned General Libert's Legionnaires and Errife loose on them when the regular army couldn't put the insurrection down.

"You're going to need more than dynamite and hunting shotguns to get the garrison out of the castle. Especially if you want to do it before Libert arrives. What've you got in the way of ships to stop him crossing?"

"Three cruisers were lost."

"I saw it. Sabotage?'

The mayor nodded. "Time bombs in the magazines, we think. But there's one corsair-class commerce raider, and some torpedo boats. There were nothing but merchantmen in Errif harbor at last report."

"That's last report. He may shuttle men over by air. Chosen 'volunteers' under 'private contract.' In fact, I wouldn't put it past the Chosen to escort his troopships in with a squadron of cruisers."

"That would mean war!" The mayor's natural olive changed to a pasty gray. "War with the Republic."

"Not if they could claim a local government invited them in."

"Nobody could—"

"*Mon ami,* you don't know what Santander lawyers are like. They could argue the devil into the Throne of God—or at least tie everything up on the question for a year or better. Which is why you have to get some transport down to my ship; she's stuffed to the gills with rifles, machine guns, ammunition, explosives, mortars, and field-guns."

Jean-Claude nodded decisively. "*Bon.*" He turned and began to shout orders.

Gerta Hosten put her eye to a crack in the worn planks of the boathouse. It was crowded, with the half-dozen Chosen commandos and the fishing boat pulled up on the ways, and the stink of old fish was soaked into the oak and pine timbers. The rubber skinsuit she was wearing was hot and clammy out of the water; she shrugged back the weight of the air tank on her back and peered down the docks.

"Still burning nicely," she said, looking over to the naval dockyards. "The storehouses and wharfs are burning, too. Considerate of the enemy to use wooden hulls."

Obsolete, but this was a complete backwater in military terms. All the Union's few modern warships were up in the Gut, and it would take weeks to bring any down here. By then this action would be settled, one way or another. Her companions were too well disciplined to cheer, but a low mutter of satisfaction went through them. Then someone spoke softly:

"Native coming." They wheeled and crouched, hands reaching for weapons. "It's ours."

The Unionaise knocked at the door, three quick and then two at longer intervals. One of the commandos opened it enough for him to sidle in; he looked around at the hard-set faces and swallowed uneasily.

"What news, Louis?" Gerta said, in his language. She spoke all four of Visager's major tongues with accentless fluency.

"Our men are pinned in the garrison and the seafront batteries," he said. "The *syndicistes* are slaughtering everyone they can catch— everyone wearing a gentleman's cravat, even, priests, nuns . . ."

The Chosen shrugged. What else would you do, when you had the upper hand in a situation like this? Louis swallowed and went on:

"And they are handing out arms to all the rabble of the city."

"Where are they getting them?" Gerta asked. According to the last reports, most of the weapons in Bassin du Sud were in the castle or the fortified gun emplacements that guarded the harbor mouth.

"There is a Santander ship in dock, one that came in a few days ago but did not unload. The cargo is weapons, all types—fine modern weapons. They are handing them out at the dock and sending wagons and trucks full of others all around the city."

"Damn," Gerta swore mildly. That *would* put a spanner in the gears. "Show me."

She unfolded a waterproof map of the harbor and spread it on the gunwale of the fishing boat. Louis bent over it, squinting in the half darkness until she moved it to a spot where a sliver of sunlight fell through the boards.

"Here," he said, tapping a finger down. "Quay Seven, Western Dock."

"Hmmm." Gerta measured the distance between her index and little fingers and then moved them down to the scale at the bottom of the map. "About half a mile, say three-quarters, as we'll swim."

Bassin du Sud had a harbor net, but like all harbors the filth and garbage in the water attracted marine life. And on Visager, marine life meant death more often than not. They'd already lost two members of the team.

"Nothing for it," she said. "Hans, Erika, Otto, you'll come with me. The rest of you, launch the boat and bring it *here*." She tapped a finger on the map; the others crowded around to memorize their positions. "Function check now."

Everyone went over everyone else's air tanks, regulators, and other gear. Hard hat suits with air pumped down a hose had been in use for fifty or sixty years, but this equipment was barely out of the experimental stage.

"Air pressure."

"Check."

"Regulator and hose."

"Check."

"Spear-bomb gun."

"Check."

"Mines."

"Check and ready."

The last of the foot-thick disks went into the teardrop-shaped container, and the man in charge of it adjusted the internal weights that kept it at neutral buoyancy Gerta pulled the goggles down over her face and put the rubber-tasting mouthpiece between her lips. She checked her watch: 18:00 hours, two hours until sunset. Ideal, if nothing held them up seriously. Lifting her feet carefully to avoid tripping on her fins, she waded into the water.

The *Merchant Venture* had her deck-guns manned and ready when John leapt off the running board of the truck and down onto the dock at the foot of the gangway. She also had full steam up and her deck-cranes rigged to unload cargo.

"Go!" John said, trotting towards the deck.

"Is that *you*, sir?" Barrjen blurted.

The blood on his face must look even more ghastly now that it had a chance to dry.

"Not mine," he said again. "Get the first load down on the dock," he went on. "Get some crewmen up here and form a chain to hand rifles and bandoliers down to anyone who comes up and asks for one."

The ex-marine blinked at that, but slung his own weapon and began barking orders. It was a relief sometimes, having someone who didn't *argue* with you all the time.

Stevedores were pushing rail flats onto the tracks alongside the Santander merchant ship; Jean-Claude had gotten them out of the fighting and moving fast enough. Steam chugged and a winch whirred with a smell of scorched castor oil on the deck ahead of the ship's central island bridge. The crates coming out of the hold were the heavier stuff: field-guns and mortars and their ammunition. More trucks were arriving, honking their air-bulb horns, and growing crowds of people with Assault Guards to shove them into some sort of line.

"Damndest fucking way—begging your pardon, sir—I've ever seen of unloading a ship," Adams, the vessel's first mate, said unhappily.

"No alternative at present," John said.

He lifted his eyes to the hills. *Chateau du Sud* was invisible from here, all but the pepperpot roof of one of the towers. That gave them direct observation for the fall of shot, though; and those 240mm *Schlenki Emma* up there could drop their shells right through the deck. When the stored ammunition and explosives went off, it would make the destruction of the Unionaise cruisers earlier in the day look like a fart in a teacup.

Long narrow crates full of rifles and short square ones full of ammunition began going down the gangways hand to hand, then out into the eager crowd. John restrained an impulse to get into the chain and swing some weight, and another to look up at the castle again. Nothing he could do now but wait. At least there was also nothing the rebels or their Chosen backers could do to him either, except fire those guns . . . and they didn't seem to suspect what was going on. Yet.

The harbor water was murky and dark, tasting of oil and rot. Gerta felt the reach of the tentacle before she saw it, flicking up from the mud and scattered debris of the bottom, thick as a big man's arm and coated on one side with oval suckers and barbed bone hooks. The back of it buffeted her aside, tumbling her through the water like a stick. It wrapped itself around Hans Dieter with the snapping quickness of a frog's tongue closing around a fly. Then it jerked him downward, screaming through the muffling water. Blood and gouting air bubbles trailed behind him; so did the streamlined container of limpet mines, anchored by a stout cord to his waistbelt.

Scheisse, Gerta thought.

Her body reacted automatically, stabilizing her spin, jackknifing and plunging downward as fast as her fins could drive her. The darkness grew swiftly, but the creature was moving upward with its strike. Ten meters long, a torpedo shape with a three-lobed tail; the mouth had three flaps as well, fringed with teeth like ivory spikes around a rasping sucker tongue, with a huge reddish eye above each. The tentacles were threefold. A second had closed around Hans' legs, pulling his legs loose from his torso and guiding them into the sausage-machine maw. The third lashed out at her.

She whirled, poising the speargun, and fired. A slug of compressed air sent the bulbous-headed spear flashing down and kicked her back; she could feel the *schunnnk* as the mechanism cycled in her hands. The spear slammed into the base of the tentacle just as the hooks slashed through her skinsuit and tore at her flesh. She shouted into the rubber of the mouthpiece, tasting water around it, and curled herself into a ball. The shock of the explosion thumped at her, sending her spinning off into the murky water.

It had been muffled by flesh. There was inky-looking blood all around her. She extended arms and legs frantically to kill the spin. That saved her life; the long shape of the killer piscoid floundered by where she would have been, flailing the water with its two intact tentacles, mouth gaping. Gerta fought to control her speargun while the creature bent itself double to attack again. There was a crater in the rubbery flesh where its third tentacle had been, gouting blood into the water, but that didn't seem to be fazing it much. The mouth opened as broad as the reach of her arms, the other two tentacles trailing back in its wake and still holding bits of Hans. Some crazed corner of her mind wondered if it was coming *at* her or *up* at her or *down* . . .

No matter. One last chance . . . she fired.

The mouth closed in reflex as something entered it. Swallowing was equally automatic. This time she had a perfect view of the consequences. The smooth body behind the eyes was as thick as her own torso. Now it belled out like a gun barrel fired when the weapon's muzzle was stuffed with dirt. The mouth flew open the way a flower did in stop-motion photography, with bits and pieces of internal organ and of Hans Dieter shooting out at her. The predator fish drifted downward, quivering and jerking as its nervous system fired at random.

Got to get out *of here,* she thought. The blood and vibrations would attract scavengers from all over the harbor. And then: *Where are the mines?*

Otto swam up pulling the container, Gerta felt her shoulders unknot in relief, enough that she was dizzy and nauseous for an instant before control clamped down. It had been so *quick . . .* and Hans had been a good troop. She grabbed a handhold on the other side of the container and signaled to Elke with her free hand, telling her to take over the watch. It would be faster with two pulling, and they'd lost time.

The additional risk was something they'd just have to take.

"About half done," John said to himself.

He half turned to speak to Adams when the deck surged under his feet. Water spouted up between the dock and the hull, a fountain surge that drenched the whole front of the ship. Seconds later the hull shuddered again, and another mass of water fell across her midships; and a third, this time at the stern. Dead sea-things bobbed to the surface.

John looked up reflexively. But there had been no sound of a heavy shell dropping across the sky. *Torpedo?* his mind gibbered. There wasn't more than a yard or two between dock and hull . . .

a mine, Center said. **attached to the hull by strong magnets, put in place by divers with artificial breathing apparatus. probability approaches unity.**

Crewmen vomited out of the hatches, screaming. A second wave came a few seconds later, dripping and sodden with seawater, some of them dragging wounded crewmates. John stood staring blankly, fists squeezing at either side of his head. Then the deck began to tilt towards the quayside, scores of tons of water dragging the port rail down. His ears rang, so loudly that for a moment he couldn't hear Barrjen's shouted questions.

John shook his head like a wet dog and grabbed Adams' shoulder. "Where are the starboard stopcocks?" he said, then screamed it into the man's ear until the expression of stunned incredulity faded.

"What?"

"The stopcocks! We've got to counterflood or she'll capsize!"

"But if we flood, she'll fookin' *sink*."

"There's only ten feet of water under her keel; we can salvage the cargo and float her later, but if we don't flood she'll capsize, man. *Now!*"

He could feel the force of his will penetrate the seaman's mental fog. "Right," the mate said, wiping a hand across his face. "This way."

"I'll come, sir," Barrjen said.

"Good man. Let's go."

The companionway down from the bridge was steep and slippery with oily soot from the funnels at the best of times. Now it was canted over at thirty degrees, and John went down it in a controlled fall. The hatchway below flapped open, abandoned in the rush to get away from the waters pouring through the rent hull. He dropped through it into water already ankle-deep, bracing himself against the wall with one hand to keep erect on the tilting deck.

"Don't tell me," he said as Adams staggered beside him. "The stopcocks are on the other side of the ship."

"Yessir."

"No time like the present," John said grimly, and gave him a boost forward. The trip across the beam of the ship became steadily more like a climb. Adams staggered ahead, pushed from behind by John and the ex-marine. At last they came to a complex of wheels and pipes.

"That one!" Adams shouted, pointing. Then he looked down the side of the ship. "Oh, Jesus, the barnacles are showing—Jesus Son of God, Mary Mother, she's going to go over."

"No she isn't," John said, fighting off a moments image of drowning in the dark with air only a few unreachable feet away through the hull. He spat on his hands. "Let's do it."

The spoked steel wheel was about a yard in diameter, locked by a chain and pin. Adams snatched it out, and John locked his hands on the wheel. It moved a quarter of an inch, stopped, moved again, halted. John braced a foot against the wall and heaved until his muscles crackled and threatened to tear loose from his pelvis.

"Jammed," Adams said. "Must've jammed—shaft torqued by the explosion."

"Then we'll unjam it."

John looked around. Resting in brackets on the side of the central island of the ship were an ax, sledgehammer, and prybar.

"Jam these through the spokes," he said briskly. "Here and here. Now both of you together, *heave*."

They strained; there was silence except for grunts of effort and the distant shouts on the dock. Then the ax handle snapped across with a gunshot crack. Barrjen skipped aside with a curse as the axhead whipped past him and bounced off the wall, leaving a streak of shiny metal scraped free of paint on the wall.

"Fuck *this*," John shouted.

He snatched the sledgehammer from Adams hands, jammed the crowbar firmly in place, and braced himself to strike. That was difficult; the ship was well past its center of gravity now, A few more minutes, and the intakes for the flood valves would be above the surface. That would happen seconds before she went over.

Clung. The vibrating jolt shivered painfully back up his arms, into his shoulders, starting a pain in the small of his back. He took a deep breath as the sledge swung up again, focused, exhaled in a grunt of total concentration as the hammer came down. *Clung. Clung. Clung.*

Adams' nerve broke and he fled back up the ladder. Two strikes later Barrjen spoke, at first a breathy whisper as he stared at the wheel with sweat running down his face.

"She's moving." Then a shout: "The boor's moving!"

It was; John had to reposition himself as it turned a quarter revolution. Easier now. He flung the sledgehammer aside and pulled the crowbar free, grabbing at the wheel with his hands. Barrjen did likewise on the other side. Both men strained at the reluctant metal, faces red and gasping with the effort, bodies knotted into straining statue-shapes. The wheel jerked, moved, jerked. Then spun, faster and faster.

A new sound came from beneath their feet, a vibrating rumble.

"Either that works, or she's already too far gone," John gasped. "Let's see from the dock."

There was a crowd waiting. They cheered as John and the stocky ex-Marine jumped from the tilted deck to the wharfside, a score of hands reaching to steady them. John ignored the babbled questions. He did take a proffered flask of brandy, sipping once or twice before handing it back and never taking his eyes from the ship.

"She's not tilting any further," Barrjen said.

"And she's settling fast."

Four minutes and the decks were awash. Another and they heard a deep rumbling *bong,* a sound felt through the soles of their feet more than through the ears. The funnels, central island and crane-masts of the merchantman trembled through a thirty-degree arc to a position that was nearly vertical as the relatively flat bottom of the ship rolled it nearly upright on the mud of the harbor bottom.

John flexed his hands and took a deep breath. "Right," he said, when the cheers died down. "Get some small explosive charges here, we'll want to kill off any sea life." Scavengers were swarming in. "We'll need diving suits, air pumps, more ropes. Get moving!"

He looked up into the darkening evening sky, then over towards the castle. He was just in time to see the great bottle-shaped spearhead of flame show over the courtyard walls. The siege howitzers were in action at last. His shoulders tensed as he listened to the whirring, ripping sound of the shell's passage, toning lower and lower as it approached. The three-hundred-pound projectile came closer, closer . . . then went by overhead. John pivoted on one heel, part of a mass movement that turned the crowd like sunflowers following the sun across the sky. A red gout of flame billowed up from the gun batteries holding the approaches to the harbor. Seconds later the other heavy howitzer in the castle fired, and the high-velocity guns in the batteries were in fixed revetments. They couldn't be turned to face the castle, and wouldn't be able to elevate that high if they did. . . .

"I'll be damned," John said softly. "The garrison went over to the government side."

Probably after killing all their officers. The Unionaise regular army was short-service conscript.

Barrjen pounded him on the back. "We won, eh, sir? Goddam."

John shook his head. "We won some time." He looked at the celebrating crowd. "Let's see if we can get the snail-eaters to make some use of it."

CHAPTER FIFTEEN

There were no Land dirigibles in the air over the city of Skinrit. Commander Horst Raske felt a little uneasy without the quiver of stamped-aluminum deckplates beneath his feet. Several of the other Air Service captains around him looked as if they felt the same, and everyone in the Chosen party looked unnatural out of uniform—still more as they were in something resembling Unionaise civil dress. Raske kept his horse to a quick walk and spent the time looking around.

"Bad air currents here," he muttered.

Several of his companions nodded. Skinrit itself was nothing remarkable, a little port about three steps up from a fishing village, smelling of stale water inside the breakwater, and strong stinks from the packing and canning plants that were its main industries—the cold currents down here below the main continent were heavy with sea life. Hundreds of trawlers crowded the quays, and battered-looking tramp steamers to take their cargoes of salted and frozen and canned fish to the north. The area around the town was hilly farmland and pasture; most of the buildings were in the whitewashed Unionaise style and quite new—built since their predecessors were burnt in the Errifean Revolt ten years ago. Around them reared real mountains, ten thousand feet and more, their peaks gleaming salt-white with year-round snow, their sides dark with forests of oak, maple, birch, and pine.

Vicious, he thought. Convection currents, crosswinds, unpredictable gusts. *Oathtaking is bad, but this will be worse.*

None of the crowds in the street seemed to be taking much notice of them, which was all to the good. Most were Unionaise themselves, sailors or settlers here; the remainder Errife in long robes, striped or checked or splotched in the patterns of their clans. Occasionally soldiers would come through, usually walking in pairs with their rifles slung, and always surrounded by an empty bubble of fear-inspired space. They wore the khaki battledress of the Union Legion, and its fore-and-aft peaked cap with a tassel. Raske thought that last a little silly, but there was nothing laughable about the troops themselves; quite respectable, about as tough-looking as Protégé infantry, looking straight ahead as they swung through the crowd.

They moved out of the street into the main plaza of Skinrit, past the legion HQ with its motto in black stone above the door: *Vive le Mart*—Long Live Death. A couple of Errife skulls were nailed to the lintel, with scraps of weathered flesh and their long braided hair still clinging to them. It was a reassuring sight, rather homelike, in fact. . . .

The governor's palace was large and lumpy, in a Unionaise style long obsolete. Errif had been a Unionaise possession in theory for some time, although they'd held little of the ten thousand square miles of rock, mountain, and forest until a few decades ago. Just enough to stop the pirate raids that had once been the terror of the whole southern coast of the continent; a few Errife corsairs had gotten as far north as the Land, although they'd seldom returned to the islands alive.

Servants showed them into a square room with benches, probably some sort of guard chamber.

"Masquerade's over," Raske said.

"Good!" one of his officers said.

She stripped off the Unionaise clothing with venom; back in the Land, only Protégé women wore skirts. They switched into the plain gray uniforms in their packs and holstered their weapons. The lack of those had made them feel considerably more unnatural than the foreign clothing. Gerta Hosten gave him a bland smile.

"You do the talking, Horst," she said.

He nodded stiffly. It wasn't his specialty, airships were. On the other hand, a Unionaise general would probably be more comfortable talking to a man, and they needed this Libert . . . for the moment.

"Why on earth didn't they send an infantry officer?" he asked plaintively.

"*Behfel ist Behfel,* Horst. This is the transport phase. They are going to send an infantry officer, once Libert's on the ground and we start sending in our own people. "'Volunteers,' you know . . ."

"Who's the lucky man?"

"Heinrich Hosten."

Horst Raske smiled blandly at the Unionaise officer. General Libert was a short, swarthy, tubby little man with a big nose. He looked slightly ridiculous in the khaki battledress of the Union Legion, down to the scarlet sash around his ample waist under the leather belt and the little tassel on his peaked cap.

The Chosen airman reminded himself that the same tubby little man had restored Union rule here when the Errife war-bands were burning and killing in the outskirts of Skingest itself, and then taken the war into their own mountains and pacified the whole island for the first time. The way he'd put down the miners' revolt on the mainland had been almost Chosen-like.

Libert abruptly sat behind the broad polished table, signaling to the staff officers and aides behind him. Raske saluted and took the seat opposite; Errife servants in white kaftans laid out coffee. He recognized the taste: Kotenberg blend, relatives of his owned land there.

"We agree," Libert said after a moments silence.

Raske raised an eyebrow. "That simple?"

"You charge a high price, but after the fiasco at Bassin du Sud, time is pressing." He frowned. "You would have done better to be more generous; the Land's interests are not served by an unfriendly government in Unionvil."

"Nor by a premature war with Santander, which is a distinct risk if we back you fully," Raske pointed out. "That requires compensation, besides your gratitude."

Libert allowed himself a small frosty smile, an echo of Raske's own. They both knew what gratitude was worth in the affairs of nations.

"Very well," Libert said. He held a hand up, and one of the aides put a pen in it. "Here." He signed the documents before him.

Raske did likewise when they'd been pushed across the mahogany to him.

"When can we begin loading?" Libert said. "And how quickly?"

"I have twenty-seven *Tiger*-class transports waiting." Raske said. "One fully equipped infantry battalion each; say, seven hundred infantry with their personal weapons and the organic crew-served machine guns and mortars. Ten hours to Bassin du Sud or vicinity, an hour at each end for turnaround, and an hour for fueling. Say, just under two flights a day; minus the freightage for artillery, ammunition, immediate rations, and ten percent for downtime—which there *will* be. Call it four days to land the thirty thousand troops."

Libert nodded in satisfaction. "Good. This is crucial; my Legionnaires and Errife regulars are the only reliable force we have in the southern Union. We should be able to get the first flight underway by sundown, don't you think?"

Raske blinked slightly. Beside him, Gerta Hosten was smiling. It looked as if they'd picked the right mule for this particular journey.

Jeffrey Farr closed his eyes. Everyone else in the room might think it was fatigue—he'd been working for ten hours straight—and he *was* tired. What he wanted, though, was reconnaissance.

As always, the view through his brother's eyes was a little disconcerting, even after nearly twenty years of practice. The colors were all a little off, from the difference in perceptions. And the way the view moved under someone else's control was difficult, too. Your own kept trying to linger, or to focus on something different.

At least most of the time. Right now they both had their eyes glued to the view of the dirigible through the binoculars John was holding. A few sprays of pine bough hid a little of it, but the rest was all too plain. Hundreds of soldiers in Union Legion khaki were clinging to ropes that ran to loops along its lower sides, holding it a few yards from the stretch of country road ten miles west of Bassin du Sud. It bobbled and jerked against their hold; he could see the valves on the top centerline opening and closing as it vented hydrogen. The men leaping out of the cargo doors were not in khaki. They wore the long striped and hooded kaftans of Errife warriors. Over each robe was Unionaise standard field harness and pack with canteen, entrenching tool, bayonet and cartridge pouches, but the barbarian mercenaries also tucked the sheaths of their long curved knives through the waistbelts. John swung the glasses to catch a grinning brown hawk-face as one stumbled on landing and picked himself up.

The Errife were happy; their officers had given them orders to do something they'd longed to do for generations: invade the mainland, slaughter the *faranj*, kill, rape, and loot.

How many? Jeffrey asked.

I think they've landed at least three thousand since dawn, maybe five. Hard to tell, they were deploying a perimeter by the time I got here.

Jeffrey thought for a moment. What chance of getting the Unionaise in Bassin du Sud to mount a counterattack on the landing zone?

Somewhere between zip and fucking none, John thought; the overtones of bitterness came through well in the mental link. They all took two days off to party when the forts in the city surrendered. Plus having a celebratory massacre of anyone they could even imagine having supported the coup.

Don't worry, Jeffrey said. *If Libert's men take the town, there'll be a slaughter to make that look like a Staff College bun fight. What chance do you have of getting the locals to hold them outside the port?*

Somewhere between . . . no, that's not fair. We've finally gotten the ship unloaded, and there's bad terrain between here and there. Maybe we can make them break their teeth.

Slow them down, Jeffrey said. *I need time, brother. Buy me time.*

He opened his eyes. The space around the map table was crowded and stinging blue with the smoke of the vile tobacco Unionaise preferred. Some of the people there were Unionaise military, both the red armbands on their sleeves and the rank tabs on their collars new. Their predecessors were being tumbled into mass graves outside Unionvil's suburbs even now. The rest were politicians of various types; there were even a few women. About the only thing everyone had in common was the suspicion with which they looked at each other, and a tendency to shout and wave their fists.

"Gentlemen," he said. A bit more sharply: "Gentlemen!"

Relative silence fell, and the eyes swung to him. *Christ,* he thought. *I'm a goddamned* foreigner, *for God's sake.*

That's the point, lad. You're outside their factions, or most of them. Use it.

"Gentlemen, the situation is grave. We have defeated the uprising here in Unionvil, Borreaux, and Nanes."

His finger traced from the northwestern coast to the high plateau of the central Union and the provinces to the east along the Santander border.

"But the rebels hold Islvert, Sanmere, Marsai on the southeast coast, and are landing troops from Errife near Bassin du Sud."

"Are you sure?" His little friend Vincen Deshambres had ended up as a senior member of the Emergency Committee of Public Safety, which wasn't surprising at all.

"Citizen Comrade Deshambres, I'm dead certain. Troops of the Legion and Errife regulars are being shuttled across from Errif by Land dirigibles. Over ten thousand are ashore now, and they'll have the equivalent of two divisions by the end of the week."

The shouting started again; this time it was Vincen who quieted it. "Go on, General Farr."

Colonel, Jeffrey thought; but then, Vincen was probably trying to impress the rest of the people around the table. He knew the politics better.

"We hold the center of the country. The enemy hold a block in the northeast and portions of the south coast. They also hold an excellent port, Marsai, situated in a stretch of country that's strongly clerical and antigovernment, yet instead of shipping their troops from Errif to Marsai, the rebel generals are bringing them in by air to Bassin du Sud. That indicates—"

He traced a line north from Bassin du Sud. There was a railway, and what passed in the Union for a main road, up from the coastal plain and through the Monts du Diable to the central plateau.

"Name of a dog," Vincen said. "An attack on the capital?"

"It's the logical move," Jeffery said. "They've got Libert, who's a competent tactician and a better than competent organizer—"

"A traitor swine!" someone burst out. The anarchist . . . well, not really leader, but something close. De Villers, that was his name.

Jeffrey held up a hand. "I'm describing his abilities, not his morals," he said. "As I said, they've got Libert, Land help with supplies and transport, and thirty to forty thousand first-rate, well-equipped troops in formed units. Which is more than anyone else has at the moment."

There were glum looks. The Unionaise regular army had never been large, the government's purge-by-retirement policy had deprived it of most of its senior officers, and most of the remainder had gone over to the rebels in the week since the uprising started. The army as a whole had shattered like a clay crock heated too high.

"What can we do?" Vincen asked.

"Stop them." Jeffreys finger stabbed down on the rough country north of Bassin du Sud. "Get everything we can out here and stop them. If we can keep their pockets from linking up, we buy time to organize. With time, we can win. But we have to stop Libert from linking up with the rebel pocket around Islvert."

"An excellent analysis," Vincen said. "I'm sure the Committee of Public Safety will agree."

That produced more nervous glances. The Committee was more selective than the mobs who'd been running down rebels, rebel sympathizers, and anyone else they didn't like. But not much. De Villers glared at him, mouth working like a hound that had just had its bone snatched away.

"And I'm sure there's only one man to take charge of such a vital task."

Everyone looked at Jeffrey. *Oh, shit,* he thought.

"What now, mercenary?" De Villers asked, coming up to the staff car and climbing onto the running board.

"Volunteer," Jeffrey said, standing up in the open-topped car.

It was obvious now why the train was held up. A solid flow of men, carts, mules, and the odd motor vehicle had been moving south down the double-lane gravel road. You *certainly couldn't call it a march,* he thought. Armies moved with wheeled transport in the center and infantry marching on either verge in column. This bunch sprawled and bunched and straggled, leaving the road to squat behind a bush, to drink water out of ditches—which meant they'd have an epidemic of dysentery within a couple of days—to take a snooze under a tree, to steal chickens and pick half-ripe cherries from the orchards that covered many of the hills. . . .

That wasn't the worst of it, nor the fact that every third village they passed was empty, meaning that the villagers had decided they liked the priest and squire better than the local *travailleur* or anarchist schoolteacher or cobbler-organizer. Those villages had the school burnt rather than the church, and the people were undoubtedly hiding in the hills getting ready to ambush the government supply lines, such as they were.

What was *really* bad was the solid column of refugees pouring north up the road and tying everything up in an inextricable tangle. Only the pressure from both sides kept up as those behind tried to push through, so the whole thing was bulging the way two hoses would if you joined them together and pumped in water from both ends. *And* they'd blocked the train, which held his artillery and supplies, and the men on the train were starting to get off and mingle with the shouting, milling, pushing crowd as well. A haze of reddish-yellow dust hung over the crossroads village, mingling with the stink of coal smoke, unwashed humanity, and human and animal wastes.

"We've got to get some order here," Jeffrey muttered.

The anarchist political officer looked at him sharply. "True order emerges spontaneously from the people, not from an authoritarian hierarchy which crushes their spirit!" De Villers began heatedly.

"The only thing emerging spontaneously from this bunch is shit and noise," Jeffrey said, leaving the man staring at him open-mouthed.

Not used to being cut off in midspeech.

"Brigadier Gerard," Jeffrey went on, to the Unionaise Loyalist officer in the car. "If you would come with me for a moment?"

Gerard stepped out of the car. The anarchist made to follow, but stopped at a look from Jeffrey. They walked a few paces into the crowd, more than enough for the ambient sound to make their voices inaudible.

"Brigadier Gerard," Jeffrey began.

"That's Citizen Comrade Brigadier Gerard," the officer said deadpan. He was a short man, broad-shouldered and muscular, with a horseman's walk—light cavalry, originally, Jeffrey remembered. About thirty-five or a little more, a few gray hairs in his neatly trimmed mustache, a wary look in his brown eyes.

"Horseshit. Look, Gerard, you should have this job. You're the senior Loyalist officer here."

"But they do not trust me," Gerard said.

"No, they don't. Better than half the professional officers went over to the rebels, I was available, and they *do* trust me . . . a little. So I'm stuck with it. The question is, are you going to help me do what we were sent to do, or not? I'm going to do my job, whether you help or not. But if you don't, it goes from being nearly impossible to completely impossible. If I get killed, I'd like it to be in aid of something."

Gerard stared at him impassively for a moment, then inclined his head slightly. "*Bon,*" he said, holding out his hand. "Because appearances to the contrary, *mon ami*"—he indicated the milling mob around them—"this is the better side."

Jeffrey returned the handshake and took a map out of the case hanging from his webbing belt. "All right, here's what I want done," he said. "First, I'm going to leave you the Assault Guards—"

"You're putting me in command here?" Gerard said, surprised.

"You're now my chief of staff, and yes, you'll command this position, for what it's worth. The Assault Guards are organized, at least, and they're used to keeping civilians in line. Use them to clear the roads. Offload the artillery and send the train back north for more of everything. Meanwhile, use your . . . well, troops, I suppose . . . to dig in here."

He waved to either side. The narrow valley wound through a region of tumbled low hills, mostly covered in olive orchards. On either side reached sheer fault mountains, with near-vertical sides covered in scrub at the lower altitudes, cork-oak, and then pine forest higher up.

"Don't neglect the high ground. The Errife are half mountain goat themselves, and Libert knows how to use them."

"And what will you do, Citiz—General Farr?"

"I'm going to take . . . what's his name?" He jerked a thumb towards the car.

"Antoine De Villers."

"Citizen Comrade De Villers and his anarchist militia down the valley and buy you the time you need to dig in."

Gerard stared, then slowly drew himself up and saluted. "I can use all the time you can find," he said sincerely.

Jeffrey smiled bleakly. "That's usually the case," he said. "Oh, and while you're at it—start preparing fallback positions up the valley as well."

Gerard nodded. De Villers finally vaulted out of the car and strode over to them, hitching at the rifle on his shoulder, his eyes darting from one soldier to the other.

"What are you *gentlemen* discussing?" he said. "Gentleman" was not a compliment in the government-held zone, not anymore. In some places it was a sentence of death.

"How to stop Libert," Jeffrey said. "The main force will entrench here. Your militia brigade, Citizen Comrade De Villers, will move forward to"—he looked at the map—"Vincennes."

De Villers' eyes narrowed. "You'll send us ahead as the sacrificial lambs?"

"No, I'll *lead* you ahead," Jeffrey said, meeting his gaze steadily. "The Committee of Public Safety has given me the command, and I lead from the front. Any questions?"

After a moment, De Villers shook his head.

"Then go see that your men have three days rations; there's hardtack and jerked beef on the last cars of that train. Then we'll get them moving south."

When De Villers had left, Gerard leaned a little closer. "My friend, I admire your choice . . . but there are unlikely to be many survivors from the anarchists."

He flinched a little at Jeffrey's smile. "I'm fully aware of that, Brigadier Gerard. My strategy is intended to improve the government's chances in this war, after all."

"So."

General Libert walked around the aircraft, hands clenched behind his back. It was a biplane, a wood-framed oval fuselage covered in doped fabric, with similar wings joined by wires and struts. The Land sunburst had been hastily painted over on the wings and showed faintly through the overlay, which was the double-headed ax symbol of Libert's Nationalists. A single engine at the front drove a two-bladed wooden prop, and there was a light machine gun mounted on the upper wing over the cockpit. It smelled strongly of gasoline and the castor oil lubricant that shone on the cylinders of the little rotary engine where they protruded through the forward body. Two more like it stood nearby, swarming with technicians as the Chosen "volunteers" gave their equipment a final going-over.

"So," Libert said again. "What is the advantage over your airships?"

Gerta Hosten paused in working on her gloves. She was sweating heavily in the summer heat, her glazed leather jacket and trousers far too warm for the sea-level summer heat. Soon she'd be out of it.

"General, it's a smaller target—and much faster, about a hundred and forty miles an hour. Also more maneuverable; one of these can skim along at treetop level. Both have their uses."

"I see," Libert said thoughtfully. "Very useful for reconnaissance, if they function as specified."

"Oh, they will," Gerta said cheerfully.

The Unionaise general gave her a curt nod and strode away. She vaulted onto the lower wing and then into the cockpit, fastening the straps across her chest and checking that the goggles pushed up on her leather helmet were clean. Two Protégé crewmen gripped the propeller. She checked the simple control panel, fighting down an un-Chosen gleeful grin, and worked the pedals and stick to give a final visual on the ailerons and rudder. *I love these things,* she thought. One good mark on John's ledger; he'd delivered the plans on request. And the Technical Research Council had improved them considerably.

"Check!" she shouted.

"Check!"

"Contact!"

"Contact!"

The Protégés spun the prop. The engine coughed, sputtered, spat acrid blue smoke, then caught with a droning roar. Gerta looked up at the wind streamer on its pole at a corner of the field and made hand signals to the ground crew. They turned the aircraft into the wind; she looked behind to check that the other two were ready. Then she swung her left hand in a circle over her head, while her right eased the throttle forward. The engine's buzz went higher, and she could feel the light fabric of the machine straining against the blocks before its wheels and the hands of the crew hanging on to tail and wing.

Now. She chopped the hand forward. The airplane bounced forward as the crew's grip released, then bounced again as the hard unsprung wheels met the uneven surface of the cow pasture. The speed built, and the jouncing ride became softer, mushy. When the tailwheel lifted off the ground she eased back on the stick, and the biplane slid free into the sky. It nearly slid sideways as well; this model had a bad torque problem. She corrected with a foot on the rudder pedals and banked to gain altitude, the other two planes following her to either side. Her scarf streamed behind her in the slipstream, and the wind sang through the wires and stays, counterpoint to the steady drone of the engines.

Bassin du Sud opened beneath her; scattered houses here in the suburbs, clustering around the electric trolley lines; a tangle of taller stone buildings and tenements closer to the harbor. Pillars of smoke still rose from the city center and the harbor; she could hear the occasional popping of small-arms fire. Mopping up, or execution squads. There were Chosen ships in the harbor, merchantmen with the golden sunburst on their funnels, unloading into lighters. Gangs of laborers were transferring the cargo from the lighters to the docks, or working on clearing the obstacles and wreckage that prevented full-sized ships from coming up to the quays; she was low enough to see a guard smash his rifle butt into the head of one who worked too slowly, and then boot the body into the water.

The engines labored, and the Land aircraft gained another thousand feet of altitude. From this height she could see the big soccer stadium at the edge of town, and the huge crowd of prisoners squatting around it. Every few minutes another few hundred would be pushed in through the big entrance gates, and the machine guns would rattle. General Libert didn't believe in wasting time; anyone with a bruise on their shoulder from a rifle butt went straight to the stadium, plus anyone on their list of suspects, or who had a trade union membership card in his wallet. *Anyone who still has one of those is too stupid to live,* Gerta thought cheerfully, banking the plane north.

There were more columns of smoke from the rolling coastal plain, places where the wheat wasn't fully harvested and the fields had caught, or more concentrated where a farmhouse or village burned. Dust marked the main road, a long winding serpent of it from Libert's Legionnaires and Errife as they marched north. The wheeled transport was mostly animal-drawn, horses and mules, and strings of packmules too. That would change when the harbor was functional again; the Land ships waiting to unload included a fair number of steam trucks, and even some armored cars. The infantry was marching on either side of the road in ordered columns of fours; heads turned up to watch the aircraft swoop overhead, but thankfully, nobody shot at her.

The mountains ahead grew closer, jagged shapes of Prussian-blue looming higher than her three thousand feet. There was a godlike feeling to this soaring flight; to Gerta's way of thinking, it was utterly different from airship travel. On a dirigible you might as well be on a train running through the sky. This was more like driving a fast car, but with the added freedom of three dimensions and no road to follow; alone in the cockpit she allowed herself a chuckle of delight. You could go *anywhere* up here.

Right now she was supposed to go where the action was. A faint *pop-pop-popping* came from the north. *Ah, some of the enemy are still putting up a fight.* The resistance in Bassin du Sud and on the road north had been incompetently handled, but more determined than she'd have expected.

Gerta waggled her wings. The other two airplanes closed in; she waited until they were close enough to see her signals clearly, then slowly pointed left and right, swooped her hand, and circled it again before pointing back southward. Her flankers each banked away. *Funny how fast you can lose sight of things up here,* she thought. They dwindled to dots in a few seconds, almost invisible against the background of earth and sky. Then she put one wing over and dove.

Time to check things out, she thought as the falling-elevator sensation lifted her stomach into her ribs.

Somebody screamed and pointed upwards. John Hosten craned his neck to look through the narrow leaves of the cork-oak, squinting against the noon sun. The roar of the engine whined in his ears as the wings of the biplane drew a rectangle of shadow across the woods. It came low enough to almost brush the top branches of the scrubby trees, trailing a scent of burnt gasoline and hot oil strong enough to overpower the smells of hot dry earth and sunscorched vegetation. He could see the leather-helmeted head of the pilot turning back and forth, insectile behind its goggles.

Everyone in the grove had frozen like rabbits under a hawk while the airplane went by, doing the best possible thing for the worst possible reason.

"It's a new type of flying machine," John said. "They build them in Santander, too; that one was from the Land, working for Libert."

The *chink* of picks, knives, and sticks digging improvised rifle pits and sangars resumed; everyone still alive had acquired a healthy knowledge of how important it was to dig in. John still had an actual shovel. He worked the edge under a rock and strained it free, lifting the rough limestone to the edge of his hole.

"Sir," one of his ex-marines said. "They're coming."

He tossed the shovel to another man and crawled forward, sheltering behind a knotted, twisted tree trunk, blushing pink since the cork had been stripped off, and trained his binoculars. Downslope were rocky fields of yellow stubble, with an occasional carob tree. In the middle distance was a farmstead, probably a landlord's from the size and blank whitewashed outer walls. A defiant black anarchist flag showed that the present occupants had different ideas, and mortar shells were falling on it. Beyond it, Errife infantry were advancing, small groups dashing forward while their comrades fired in support, then repeating the process. John shaped a silent whistle of reluctant admiration at their bounding agility, and the way they disappeared from his sight as soon as they went to earth, the brown-on-brown stripes of their kaftans vanishing against the stony earth.

Good fieldcraft, Raj said. Damned good. You'd better get this bunch of amateurs out of their way, son.

"Easier said than done," John muttered to himself.

"Ah, sir?" Barrjen said, lowering his voice. "You know, it might be a good idea to sort of move north?"

There were about three hundred people in the stretch of woodland, mostly men, all armed. There had been a couple of thousand yesterday, when he began back-pedaling from the ruins of Bassin du Sud. He was still alive, and so were most of the Santander citizens he'd brought with him, the crew of the *Merchant Venture*, and all the ex-Marines from the Ciano embassy guard. *Not so surprising, they're the ones who know what the hell they're doing,* he thought. He doubted he'd be alive without them.

"All right, we've got to break contact with them," he said aloud. "The only way to do that is to move out quickly while they're occupied with that hamlet."

Most of the Unionaise stood. About a third continued to dig themselves in. One of them looked up at John:

"*Va.* We will hold them."

"You'll die."

The man shrugged. "My family is dead, my friends are dead—I think some of those *merdechiennes* should follow them."

John closed his mouth. *Nothing to say to that,* he thought. "Leave all your spare ammunition," he said to the others. Men began rummaging in pockets, knapsacks and improvised bandoliers. "Come on. Let's make it worthwhile."

"Damn, but I'm glad to see you."

Jeffrey was a little shocked at how John looked; almost as bad has he had when he got back from the Empire. Thinner, limping—limping more badly than Smith beside him—and with a look around the eyes that Jeffrey recognized. He'd seen it in a mirror lately. There was a bandage on his arm soaked in old dried blood, too, and a feverish glitter in his eyes.

"You, too, brother," Jeffrey said.

He glanced around. The commandeered farmhouse was full of recently appointed, elected, or self-selected officers (or *coordinateurs,* to use their own slang) of the anarchist militia down from Unionvil and the industrial towns around it. Most of them were grouped around the map tables; thanks to John and Center, the counters marking the enemy forces were quite accurate. He was much less certain of his own. It wasn't only lack of cooperation; although there was enough of that, despite the ever-present threat of the Committee of Public Safety. Most of the *coordinateurs* didn't have much idea of the size or location of their forces either.

"C'mon over here," he said, putting a hand under John's arm. "Things as bad as you've been saying?"

"Worse. Those aeroplanes they've got, they caught us crossing open country yesterday."

observe, Center said.

—and John's eyes showed uprushing ground as he clawed himself into the dirt. It was thin pastureland scattered with sheep dung and showing limestone rock here and there.

"Sod this for a game of soldiers," someone muttered not far away.

A buzzing drone grew louder. John rolled on his back; being facedown would be only psychological comfort. Two of the Land aircraft were slanting down towards the Bassin du Sud refugees and the Santander party. They swelled as he watched, the translucent circle of the propeller before the angular circle of pistons, and wings like some great flying predator. Then the machine gun over the upper wing began to wink, and the *tat-tat-tat-tat* of a Koegelman punctuated the engine roar. A line of dust-spurting craters flicked towards him . . . and then past, leaving him shaking and sweating. A dot fell from one of the planes, exploding with a sharp *crack* fifty feet up.

Grenade, he realized. Not a very efficient way of dropping explosives, but they'd do better soon. Voices were screaming; in panic, or in pain. A few of the refugees stood and shot at the vanishing aircraft with their rifles, also a form of psychological comfort, not to feel totally helpless like a bug under a boot. The aircraft banked to the north and came back for another run. Most of the riflemen dove for cover. Barrjen stood, firing slowly and carefully, as the lines of machine-gun bullets traversed the refugees' position. Both swerved towards him, moving in a scissors that would meet in his body.

"Get down, you fool!" John shouted. *Dammit, I need you!* Loyal men of his ability weren't that common.

Then one of the machines wavered in the air, heeled, banked towards the earth. John started to cheer, then felt it trail off as the airplane steadied and began to climb. He was still grinning broadly as he rose and slapped Barrjen on the shoulder; both the Land planes were heading south, one wavering in the air, the other anxiously flying beside it like a mother goose beside a chick.

"Good shooting," he said.

Barrjen pulled the bolt of his rifle back and carefully thumbed in three loose rounds. "Just have t'estimate the speed, sir," he said.

Smith used his rifle to lever himself erect. "Here," he said, tossing over three stripper clips of ammunition. "You'll use 'em better than me."

—and John shook his head. "There I was, thinking how fucking ironic it would be if I got killed by something designed to plans I'd shipped to the Chosen," he said.

Jeffrey closed his eyes for an instant to look at a still close-up of Centers record of the attack. "Nope, they've made some improvements. That was moving faster than anything we've got so far."

correct, Center said to them both. **a somewhat more powerful engine, and improvements in the chord of the wing.**

"I still sent them the basics," John said.

"Considering that your companies have been doing the work on 'em, and they know they have, it would look damned odd if their prize double agent *didn't* send them the specs, wouldn't it?" Jeffrey said. "You know how it is. If disinformation is going to be credible, you have to send a lot of good stuff along with it."

John nodded reluctantly. "I'm getting sick of disastrous retreats," he said.

Jeffrey smiled crookedly. "Well, this *isn't* as bad as the Imperial War," he said. "We're not fighting the Land directly, for one thing."

He looked over his shoulder and called names. "Come on, you need a doctor and some food and sleep. The food's pretty bad, but we've got some decent doctors. Barrjen, Smith, take care of him."

"Do our best, sir," Smith said. "But you might tell him not to get shot at so often."

The two Santanders helped John away. Jeffrey turned back to the map, looking down at the narrow line of hilly lowland that snaked through the mountains.

"We'll continue to dig in along this line," he said, tracing it with his finger.

"Why here? Why not further south? Why do we have to give up ground to Libert and his hired killers?" De Villers wasn't even trying to hide his hostility anymore.

Jeffrey hid his sigh. "Because this is right behind a dogleg and the narrowest point around," he said. "That means he can't use his artillery as well—we have virtually none, you'll have noticed, gentle . . . ah, Citizen Comrades. And the mountains make it difficult for him to flank us. Hopefully, he'll break his teeth advancing straight into our positions."

"We should attack. The enemy's mercenaries have no reason to fight, and our troops' political consciousness is high. The Legionnaires will run away, and the Errife will turn on their officers and join us to restore their independence."

A few of the others around the table were nodding.

"Citizen Comrades," Jeffrey said gently. "Have any of you seen the refugees coming through? Or listened to them?"

That stopped the chorus of agreement. "Well, do you get the impression that the Legion or the Errife refused to fight in Bassin du Sud? Is there any reason to believe that they'll be any weaker here? No? Good."

He traced lines on the map. "Their lead elements will be in contact by sunset, and I expect them to be able to put in a full attack by tomorrow. We need maximum alertness."

He went on, outlining his plan. In theory it ought to be effective enough; he had fewer men than Libert in total, but the terrain favored him, and holding a secure defensive position with no flanks was the easiest thing for green troops to do.

The problem was that Libert knew that too, and so did his Chosen advisors.

CHAPTER SIXTEEN

"What news from the academy?"

Libert's aide smiled. "The report from *Commandant* Soubirous is *nothing to report,* my general."

The pudgy little man nodded seriously and tapped his map. There was enough sunlight through the western entrance of the tent to show clearly what he meant; the Union Military Academy was located at Foret du Loup, out on the rolling plateau country, between the mountains and Unionvil.

"When we have cleared the passes through the Monts du Diable, we must send a column—a strong column—to the relief of the academy. The Reds must not be allowed to crush Commandant Soubirous and the gallant cadets."

Heinrich Hosten coughed discreetly. "My general," he said, in fluent but accented Fransay. "Surely we should be careful not to disperse our forces away from the main *schwerepunkt*? Ah, the point of primary effort, that is."

"I am familiar with the concept," Libert said.

He looked at the Chosen officer; the foreigner was discreetly dressed in the uniform of a Union Legion officer, without rank tabs but with a tiny gold-on-black sunburst pin on the collar of his tunic.

"Yes, my general," Heinrich said.

"However, this will probably be a long war—and it is perhaps better that way," Libert said. The Chosen in the room reacted with a uniform calm that hid identical surprise. The Unionaise commander smiled thinly.

"This is a political as well as a military struggle. A swift victory would leave us with all the elements that brought on the crisis intact. A steady, methodical advance means that we do not simply defeat but annihilate all the un-Unionist elements. And it gives us time and opportunity to thoroughly *cleanse* the zones behind our lines, in wartime conditions."

"As you say, sir," Heinrich said. "That presupposes, however, that we succeed in getting out of this damned valley to begin with."

"I have confidence in the plan you and my staff have worked out," Libert said, turning back to the map.

Heinrich ducked his head and left the tent. "Damned odd way of looking at it," he said to Gerta.

"Sensible, actually," Gerta said, smiling and shaking her head, "when you look at it from his point of view. We could stand being a little more methodical ourselves; this whole operation here has the flavor of an improvisation, to me."

They stopped for a moment to watch Protégé workmen and Chosen engineers assembling armored cars from crated parts sent up by rail.

"It's an opportunity," Heinrich said after a while.

"Its a temptation," Gerta said. "We've had less than a decade to consolidate our hold on the Empire—"

"Nine years, six months, two days, counting from the attack on Corona," Heinrich said with a smile of fond reminiscence.

"Quibbler." She punched him lightly on his shoulder. "We should wait for a generation at least before taking on Santander. And this is probably going to mean war with the Republic eventually, if our little friend"—she jerked her head back at the tent—"wins."

"They're getting stronger, too," Heinrich pointed out. "You know the production problems we're having with labor from the New Territories."

"Yes, but we've got the staying power. *We* don't have an

underlying need to believe the world is a warm, fuzzy-pink playground where everyone's nice down deep except for a few villains who'll be defeated at the end of the story. We can get the animals working well enough, given enough time—and the Santies will go to sleep and let down their guard if we don't make obvious threats."

"We're not threatening them, strictly speaking."

"Land forces on their border? Even a *Santy* can't convince himself that's not a threat. We're waking a sleeping giant, and stiffening his backbone."

Heinrich shrugged. "But if we beat the Santies, everything else is mopping up. Anyway, it's a matter for the Council, *nein?*"

"*Jawohl.* Orders are orders. Let's get this battle done."

Heinrich smiled more broadly. "Actually, you've got a different job."

"Oh?"

"Libert's pretty taken with this academy thing. He'd probably spend six months avenging the place and the gallant cadets if it fell, which would be an even worse diversion of effort than marching to relieve it. So we'd better make sure it doesn't fall. . . ."

"Shays."

"And how are you, sir?" the train steward asked. "Not so great," John mumbled. "Drink, please—water, something like that."

"Sir."

The steward bowed silently as he left the compartment. The revolution hadn't reached this part of the Union yet, evidently. Or perhaps it was just that this was a Santander-owned railway, and close to the border, and John was evidently rich enough to command a whole first-class compartment for himself, and another for half a dozen tough-looking armed men.

The view out the window was much like the eastern provinces of the Republic outside the cities. An upland basin surrounded by mountains with snow gleaming at their tops, the peaks to the west turning crimson with sunset. Grass, tawny with summer, speckled with walking cactus and an occasional clubroot, smelling warm and dusty but fresher than the lowlands to the east. Herds of red-coated cattle and shaggy buffalo and sheep, with herdsmen mounted and armed guarding them. Occasionally a ranch house, with its outbuildings and whitewashed adobe walls; more rarely a stretch of orchards and cultivated fields around a stream channeled for irrigation, very rarely a village or mine with its cottages and church spire.

It looked intensely peaceful. A hawk stooped at a rabbit flushed by the *chufchufchuf* of the locomotive, and the carriage swayed with the clacking passage of the rails. John wiped sweat from his forehead and touched the arm in its sling with gingerly fingers, wincing a little. Better, definitely better—he'd thought he was going to lose it, for a while—but still bad. Thank God the doctor had believed what he said about debriding wounds, but then, a massive bribe never hurt.

Home soon, he thought.

The door to the compartment opened again: the steward, immaculate in white jacket and gloves, with a tray of iced lemonade. Behind him were the worried faces of Smith and Barrjen.

"You all right, sir?"

"I would be if people stopped bothering me!" John snapped, then waved a hand. "Sorry. I'm recovering, but I need rest. Thank you for asking."

The two men withdrew with mumbled apologies as the steward unlatched the folding table between the seats and put the tray on it. John took a glass of the lemonade and drank thirstily, then put the cold tumbler to his forehead.

"Shall I put down the bunk, sir?"

John shook his head. "In a little while. Come back in an hour."

"Will you be using the dining car, sir?"

His stomach heaved slightly at the thought. "No. A bowl of broth and a little *dry* toast in here, if you would." He slipped across a Santander banknote. "In a while."

The steward smiled. "Glad to be of assistance, Your Excellency."

John closed his eyes. When he opened them again with a jerk it was full night outside, with only an occasional lantern-light to compete with the frosted arch of stars and the moons. The collar of his shirt and jacket were soaked with sweat, but he felt much better . . . and very thirsty. He drank more of the lemonade, and pushed the bell for the steward to bring his soup.

I must be reaching second childhood, and I'm not even thirty-five, he thought. Making all this fuss over a superficial wound and a little fever.

Nothing little about a wound turning nasty, Raj said in his mind. *I've seen too much of that.*

There was a brief flash of hands holding a man down to blood-stained boards. He thrashed and screamed as the bone-saw grated through his thigh, and there was a tub full of severed limbs at the end of the makeshift operating table. Unlike Center's scenarios, Raj's memories carried smell as well; the sickly-sweet oily rot of gas gangrene, this time.

You even had Center worried for a while.

calculations indicate a 23% reduction in the probability of a favorable outcome if john hosten is removed from the equation at this point, Center said. **such analysis does not constitute "worry."**

How's Jeff doing? he asked.

observe:

—and he was looking through his foster-brothers eyes.

Evidently Jeffrey was out making a hands-on inspection, riding a horse along behind the Loyalist lines. *Scattered clumps might be a better way to put it than "lines"* John thought.

Oh, hi, Jeffrey replied. *How's it going?*

He pulled up the horse behind a large bonfire. Militiamen and some women were lying around it; a few hardy souls were asleep, others toasting bits of pungent sausage on sticks over the fire, eating stale bread, drinking from clay bottles of wine and water, or just engaging in the universal Unionaise sport of argument. The rifle pits they'd dug were a little further south, and their weapons were scattered about. Perhaps three-quarters were armed, with everything from modern Union-made copies of Santander magazine rifles to black-powder muzzle loaders like something from the Civil War three generations back. One anarchist chieftain had a bandanna around his head, two bandoliers of ammunition across the heavy gut that strained his horizontally striped shirt, three knives, a rifle, and two pistols in his sash.

There was even a machine gun, well dug in behind a loopholed breastwork of sandbags.

Well, somebody knows what they're doing, John observed.

Jeffrey nodded. The Union had compulsory military service; in theory the unlucky men were selected by lot, but you could buy your way out. Any odd collection of working-class individuals like this would have some men with regular army training.

He looked up at the stars; John opened his own eyes, and there was an odd moment of double sight—the same constellations stationary here, and through the window of the moving train four hundred miles northwest. That put Jeffrey in a perfect position to see the starshell go off.

Pop. The actinic blue-white light froze everything in place for an instant, just long enough to hear the whistle of shells turn to a descending ripping-canvas roar.

Jeffrey reacted, diving off the horse into the empty pit behind the machine gun. The guns were light, from the sound of the crumping explosions of the shells, but that wouldn't matter at *all* if he was in the path of a piece of high-velocity casing.

Somebody else slid in with him, in the same hug-the-bottom-of-the hole posture. They waited through seconds that seemed much longer, then lifted their head in the muffled silence of stunned ears. More starshells burst overhead. . . .

"Five-round stonk," Jeffrey said. A short burst at the maximum rate of fire the gunners could manage. Which meant . . .

An instant later he collided with the other occupant of the hole as they both leapt for the spade grips of the machine gun. "Feed me!" Jeffrey snarled, using his weight and height to lever the Unionaise soldier—it must be the veteran, the one who'd dug the weapon in— aside.

There was light enough to see, thanks to the rebel starshell. The nameless Unionaise ripped open the lid of a stamped-metal rectangular box. Inside were folds of canvas belt with loops holding shiny brass cartridges; he plucked out the end of the belt with its metal tab. Jeffrey had the cover of the feed-guide open and their hands cooperated to guide the belt through as if they had practiced for years. The Unionaise yanked his hand aside as Jeffrey slapped the cover down and jerked the cocking lever back twice, until the shiny tab of the belt hung down on the right side of the weapon.

"Feed me!" he snapped again—it was important for the loader to keep the belt moving evenly, or the gun might jam.

The whole process had taken perhaps twenty seconds. When he looked up to acquire a target, figures in stripped kaftans were sprinting forward all across his front, horribly close. Close enough to see the white snarl of teeth in swarthy, bearded faces and hear individual voices in their shrieking falsetto war cry.

Must've crawled up, his mind gibbered as his thumbs clamped down on the butterfly trigger.

The thick water jacket of the gun swept back and forth, firing a spearhead of flame into the darkness; the starshells were falling to earth under their parachutes, none replacing them. Errife mercenaries fell, some scythed down by the hose of glowing green tracer, some going to ground and returning fire. Muzzle flashes spat at him, and he heard the flat *crack* of rounds going overhead. Other rifles were firing, too, where militiamen had made it back to their foxholes or started firing from wherever they lay. One jumped up out of the blankets he'd been sleeping in and ran out into the beaten ground, making it a hundred yards southward before his blind panic met a bullet.

"Jesus, there are too *many* of them!" Jeffrey said, swinging the barrel to try and break up concentrations. The Errife came forward like water through a dam built of branches, flowing around anything hard, probing for empty spots. He fired again and again, clamping down the trigger for short three-second bursts, spent brass tinkling down to roll underfoot and be trodden into the dirt.

A dim figure tumbled into the slit trench with them. The Unionaise soldier dropped the ammunition belt and snatched up an entrenching tool stuck into the soft earth of the trench side and began a chopping stroke that would have buried it in the newcomer's head.

"It's me! Francois!"

With a grunt of effort the first man turned the shovel aside, burying it again in the earth.

"You're late," he panted, turning back to the box. "Get your rifle and make yourself useful."

There was nothing but moonlight and starlight to shoot by now. Just enough to see the stirring of movement to his front.

"What's your name?" Jeffrey said, between bursts.

"Henri," the loader said. "Henri Trudeau." Then: "Watch it!"

Something whirred through the air. They both ducked; behind them Francois stood for a few fatal seconds, still fumbling with the bolt of his rifle. The grenade thumped not far above the lip of the machine gun nest. There was a wet sound from behind them, and Francois' body slumped down. Jeffrey didn't bother to look; he knew what the spray of moisture across the back of his neck came from. Instead, he pushed himself back up while the dust was still stinging his eyes, drawing the automatic pistol at his waist.

An Errife was pointing his rifle at Jeffrey's head from no more than three feet away. He froze for an instant, so close to the enemy trooper that he could hear the tiny *click* of the firing pin. The rifle did not fire. *Bad primer,* Jeffrey thought, while his hand brought up the pistol. *Crack.* The barbarian flopped backwards. *Crack.* A miss, and the next one was on him, long curved knife flashing upward at his belly. Jeffrey yelled and twisted aside, clubbing at the Errife's head with his automatic. It thumped on bone, muffled by the headcloth twisted around the mercenary's skull. Jeffrey grabbed for his knife wrist and struck twice more with frantic strength, until the robed man slumped back against the rear wall of the trench and Jeffrey jammed the muzzle of his pistol into his stomach and pulled the trigger twice.

Out of the corner of his eye, Jeffrey saw Henri's entrenching tool flashing again and again, used like an ax. The impacts were soft blubbery sounds, underlain by crunching.

"*Cochon,*" the Unionaise wheezed. "*Morri, batard—*"

"He is dead," Jeffrey said. Henri wheeled, shovel raised, then let it fall. "Now let's get out of here."

The volume of fire was slackening, but the ululating screech of the Errife rose over it—and other voices, screaming in simple agony. The islanders liked to collect souvenirs.

"You go get things in order," Henri said. Til man this gun. You do your job and I'll do—"

"Jesus Christ in a starship couldn't get any order here," Jeffrey said. "Let's get moving. This isn't going to be the last battle."

Henri stared at him for an instant, his face unreadable in the dark. "*Bon*," he said at last. "*Voyons.*"

CHAPTER SEVENTEEN

"Nothing to report, nothing to report, nothing to *fucking* report—you had me stuck there for three damned months."

Gerta knocked back a shot of banana gin and followed it with a draught of beer, savoring the hot-cold *wham* contrast of flavors. The place had been a nobleman's townhouse before the Chosen took Ciano and the Empire with it, and an officer's transit station-cum-club since. Gerta and her husband were sitting on the outdoor terrace, separated from the street by a stretch of clipped grass and a low wall of whitewashed brick. It was hot with late summer, but nothing beside the sticky humidity of this time of year in the Land, and there was an awning overhead. She reached moodily for another chicken, lettuce, and tomato sandwich. At least it wasn't rotten horsemeat, and she'd gotten rid of the body lice.

"And there wouldn't have been anything but a bloody hole in the ground to report at Libert's precious Academy, if I hadn't been there," she said. "The froggie imbecile supposedly in command didn't even remember elementary tricks like putting out plates of water in the basement to detect the vibrations of sappers trying to dig under the walls. *And* I had to practically stick a knife in his buttocks to get him to listen."

"Still, I hear that got exciting," Heinrich said. "The counter-mining."

"Too exciting," Gerta said dryly, remembering.

—cold wet darkness, water seeping through the belly of her uniform. Squirming down like birth in reverse, and then the dirt crumbling away ahead of her, falling through into the enemy tunnel, slamming against a timber prop, the man's mouth making an O in the dim light of the lanterns as she brought her automatic up . . .

"What took you so long?" she asked again.

"Well, you were the one who thought there was something to Libert's 'methodical' approach," Heinrich said reasonably. He lit his pipe and blew a smoke ring skyward, watching as the shapes of dirigibles heading for the landing field passed across it. "We took so long because every time we took a village we'd stop to shoot everyone suspicious, then everyone Libert's police could winkle out, then waited while Libert appointed everyone from the mayor down to the sewer inspector and checked that things were working smoothly."

"Got stopped butt-cold outside Unionvil, too," Gerta said. "By *Imperials,* of all things."

"By the Freedom Brigades," Heinrich corrected. He closed the worked pewter lid of his S-shaped pipe and reached for a sandwich. "Imperial refugees, Santies, some Sierrans, Santy officers, damned good equipment and so-so training. But plenty of enthusiasm."

"Well, what are we going to do about it?" Gerta demanded. "I've been working internal-security liaison since I got back."

"Two can play at that game," Heinrich said with satisfaction. "That's why I'm back here. We're going to 'Volunteer'—"

Pop.

The small spiteful crack on the sidewalk outside was almost inaudible under the traffic noise. Gerta was out of her chair and halfway across the lawn with a single raking stride; Heinrich was too big a man to be quite as graceful, but he was less than two paces behind her at the start and they vaulted the wall in tandem, landing facing each way with their automatics out.

A woman ran into Gerta, looking back over her shoulder. She bounced off the Chosen as if she had run into a wall; Gerta grabbed and struck twice, punching with clinical precision. Something tinkled metallically, and the Imperial Protégé collapsed to the brick sidewalk, her face turning scarlet as she struggled to suck breath through a paralyzed diaphragm. Behind her the dense crowd had scattered like mercury on dry ice, leaving a Chosen officer lying facedown. He was doggedly trying to crawl forward when Heinrich stooped over him.

"Lie still," he said. The bark of command penetrated the fog of pain; Heinrich cut cloth and wadded it into a pressure bandage. "Bullet wound, left of the spine, just south of the ribs. Looks nasty."

Gerta came up, nostrils flaring slightly at the iron scent of blood. There was no fecal smell, so the intestine hadn't been perforated, but there were too many essential organs and big blood vessels in that part of the body for comfort. She was dragging the Protégé woman by one ankle, and holding something in the other.

Heinrich looked at it and almost laughed. It was like a child's sketch of a pistol; a short tube, a wire outline for a grip and another piece of wire to act as a spring and drive a striker home on the single cartridge within.

"What sort of weapon is that?" he asked.

"It's not a weapon, it's an assassination tool. One shot and you throw it away; just the thing for killing a straw boss, or one of *us* on a crowded street."

Heinrich's features clamped down to a mask. After a moment he said: "Wouldn't have thought the Santies would come up with that."

"They're nasty when they get going," Gerta said. "We've been finding more and more of these. The problem is tracing back the chain of contacts. This animal will tell us something, perhaps."

"Indeed."

They looked up; a medic had arrived, with two Land-born Protégé assistants, and a man in civilian clothes. The long leather coat might as well have been a uniform: Fourth Bureau.

"That was quick," Gerta said neutrally. *Not the time for another intercouncil pissing match,* she told herself. This *was* their turf.

"Not quick enough. We had some information, but clearly it was insufficient."

The woman had recovered enough breath to recognize what was standing over her. She tried to crawl away, then screamed when he stamped on her hand.

It died away to a whimper when he knelt beside her and held up something: a jointed metal like a gynecologist's speculum, but with a toothed clamp on the end. Gerta recognized it, an interrogation instrument designed to be inserted in the subject's vagina, clamped on the uterus and tear it out with one strong pull.

"Now, my dear, I would like to ask you some questions," the secret policeman said. "And you would like to avoid pain . . . and there is so *much* pain you can feel." His hand clamped on her jaw. "No, no, you cannot bite off your tongue. Not yet."

Heinrich stood as the specialists staunched the bleeding of the wounded man, set up a saline drip, and began to ease him onto the stretcher. An unmarked police car drew up as well; the woman was drugged with a swift injection and thrown into the wire cage at the back.

"My oath, but going back into combat down in the Union looks better and better," he said.

Gerta looked morosely at the bloodstain on the deserted sidewalk. "Better and better, but where's it leading?"

"We'll win, of course."

"We won here."

Heinrich hesitated. "You know, you've got a point." He shrugged. "It's the Santies behind all this. If we finish them off, we can pacify successfully."

"Come on baby, you can do it," Jeffrey crooned.

The dogfight had swirled away into patchy cloud to the west; all he could see were two plumes of smoke rising from the ground where planes had augered in. The engine coughed again, a skip in its regular beat that produced a sympathetic lurch in his own heart. He banked gently over the zigzag trenches that scarred the land below, breaking into knots of strongpoints and bunkers in the ruined buildings of the university complex just south of Unionvil. Even now he shivered slightly at the sight of them; the winter fighting there had been ghastly, stopping the last Nationalist offensive in the very outskirts of the capital city.

"Come on," he said again.

Bits of fabric were streaming back from the cowling and upper wing of his Liberty Hawk II, ripping off as the slipstream worried at the bullet holes. That wasn't his main concern; the Mark I had sometimes had the whole wing cover peel off in circumstances like this, giving the remaining fuselage the aerodynamics of a brick in free-fall, but the new model was sturdier. He *really* didn't like the sound the engine made, though. Slowly, carefully, he brought the little fighter around and began to descend towards the landing field. Only a mile or two now . . .

And the engine coughed again and died. "Shit," he said with resignation, and yanked at the tab to cut the fuel supply. Then: "*Shit!*" as he looked down and saw a thickening film of gasoline in the bottom of the cockpit. "I *hate* it when things like that happen!"

Make a note to write to the design team, Raj prompted. If it had been Center, he would have taken that literally. . . .

A few black puffs of antiaircraft fire blossomed around him. Friendly fire, which was just as dangerous as the opposition's. It petered out; someone must have noticed the red-white-and-blue rondels on his wings, the mark of the Freedom Brigades' Air Service. Then the X shape of the field came into view over a low ridge, a ridge uncomfortably close to the fixed undercarriage. He concentrated on the white line of lime down the center of the graded dirt runway, ignoring the crash-truck that was speeding out to meet him with men clinging to its sides and standing on the running boards. A pom-pom in a circular pit near the edge of the runway tracked him, its twin six-foot barrels looking bloated in their water jackets, but at least that bunch seemed to keep their eyes open—a single fighter of Santander design with its prop stationary was hard to mistake for a Chosen or Nationalist raiding group, but every now and then a gun crew with active imaginations managed it.

Lower. Lower. Wind whistling through the wires and struts, flapping his scarf behind him. Lower . . . *touch.* The hard rims of the wheels ticked at the ground in a scurf of dry dirt and gravel, ticked again, settled with a rattling thud. The unpowered aircraft slowed rapidly to a halt. Jeffrey snapped open his belts and swung out to the lower wing, then to the ground, and lumbered away as fast as the weight of the parachute and the fleece-lined leather flight suit would let him.

"Motherfucking son of a *bitch*!" he shouted, throwing the leather helmet and goggles to the ground, followed by the parachute.

"You all right?"

That was one of the Wong brothers. Jeffery rounded on him. "The interrupter gear still isn't working right," he said as the crew from the crash truck swarmed over the Hawk, fire extinguishers at the ready.

"My guns *both* jammed. Which left me a sitting duck. And the fuel lines are still leaking into the pilot's compartment when the integral tank gets cut—do you have any fucking *idea* how good that is for pilot morale?"

Wong made soothing motions with his hands. "As soon as we can get more rubber, we can make the tanks self-sealing," he said.

Jeffrey snorted. The Land had all the natural rubber on Visager—the only places that could grow it were the Land *itself* and the northernmost peninsula of what had once been the Empire. John's factories were just beginning to produce a trickle of synthetic rubber from oil, but it was fiendishly expensive and the Land would cut off the natural type the minute their extremely efficient spies caught Santander using it for military purposes.

Crazy war, he thought. *We're fighting here in the Union, but it's all "volunteers" and normal trade goes on.*

"And the latest Land fighter is still better than ours."

"The triplane?" Wong said with interest.

"Yes, the Skyshark. It's almost as fast as our Mark II and it's got a better turning radius in starboard turns."

Wong took out a notepad and began to scribble as they walked back towards the squadron HQ; behind them the crew hitched up the plane and pulled it away towards the hangar and revetments, half a dozen walking behind with a grip on its wings to steady it. A group was waiting for Jeffrey.

"You should not risk yourself so, General Farr," General Pierre Gerard said.

"You must be really pissed, Pierre, you never call me that otherwise."

The loyalist officer shrugged, a very Unionaise gesture. "Still, it is true. And someone must tell you."

You, John, my wife, and my two invisible friends, Jeffrey thought. And I can never get away from those two.

"I have to have hands-on experience to work effectively with the designers," he said, looking over his shoulder for Wong. The little engineer and ex-bicycle manufacturer was trotting off to take a look at the shot-up Mark II. "Also to help refine our tactics for the pilot schools. We're sending them up with less than thirty hours' flight time, so at least we should be teaching them the *right* things."

They walked into the HQ, a spare temporary structure of boards and two-by-fours. John stripped out of the flight suit, shivering slightly as the chill spring air of the central plateau hit the sweat-damp fabric of his summer-weight uniform.

"What is your appraisal?" Gerard said.

"The enemy have more and better planes than we do," Jeffrey said, sitting down and accepting the coffee an orderly brought. Coffee was another thing they were going to miss if—when—all trade with the Land was cut off. "And better pilots, more experienced. If it's any consolation, we're improving faster than they are, but we're starting from a lower base."

Gerard frowned, looking down at his hands on the rough table. "My friend, this is bad news. Although perhaps the government will listen now when I tell them the offensive on the eastern front is a bad idea."

Jeffrey halted the coffee cup halfway to his mouth. "They're still going ahead with that?" he asked incredulously.

"And they will strip men, guns, aircraft from every other front for it," he said. "The Committee talks of recapturing Marsai and splitting the rebel zone in half."

"The Committee has its head up its collective butt," Jeffrey said.

Gerard's head swiveled around. *Unfair,* Jeffrey chided himself. *He* could say that; the Committee of Public Safety had no jurisdiction over Brigade members, they'd insisted on that from the beginning. Gerard was in high favor after helping to stop Libert's thrust for the capital in the opening months of the war, but even so the Committee's name was nothing to take in vain. Chairman Vincen seemed to think that if he made himself into a worse mad bastard than Libert and the Chosen, he could *beat* Libert and the Chosen. It didn't necessarily work that way, but desperate men weren't the best logicians.

Gerard cleared his throat "And it will be even more difficult if they can continue to use Land dirigibles to shift troops and supplies at will behind their lines."

"They can as long as they can keep our planes from punching through," Jeffrey said. "Those gasbags are sitting targets for fighters, but we don't have the numbers or the range to penetrate their own fighter screens.

Gerard's bulldog face grew longer. "Then they will be able to shift faster than I can—what is that expression you used?"

Jeffrey sighed. "They can get inside your decision curve. I just hope things are going better back home."

Admiral Arthur Cunningham was a big, thickset man, with graying blond hair. Right now his face and bull neck were turning red with throttled rage, and he pulled at his walrus mustache as he stared at the ship model in the center of the glossy ebony table.

The hull was a large merchant variety, an eight-thousand-ton bulk carrier of the type used to ferry manganese ore from the Southern Islands under Santander protectorate. The top had been sliced off and replaced with a long flat rectangular surface; the funnels ran up into an island on the port side, and a section had lowered like an elevator to show rows of biplanes in the huge hold below the flight deck.

"Its an abortion," Cunningham said.

"It's what we need for scouting," Maurice Farr corrected.

The rings on his sleeves and the epaulets on his shoulders marked him as a rear admiral, and kept Cunningham superficially respectful. Nobody could mistake his expression, or the meaning in the look he shot John Hosten where he sat beside his father.

"Farr, I'm surprised. I expect *politicians* to act this way." From his tone, he also expected them to have sexual intercourse with sheep. "You're a navy man and the son of a navy man. Why are you doing this?"

"We *work* for politicians, Cunningham—there's a little thing called the Constitution that more or less tells us to. And in this instance, the politicians are right. We need aerial scouting if we're going to match the Land's fleet; otherwise they'll be able to lead us around like a bull with a ring in its nose."

"We need airships with decent open-sea range, not flying toys on this abortion of a so-called ship!" Cunningham said, his voice rising toward a bellow and his fist making the coffee cups rattle.

John spoke: "We've tried, Admiral Cunningham. Here."

He pulled glossy photographs from an envelope and slid them across the table. "You see the results."

The frame spread across a hillside was just recognizable as a dirigible's, after the fire.

"The Land is too far ahead of us on the learning curve with lighter-than-air craft. They've got the diesels, the hull design, and most of all, plenty of experienced construction teams and crews. We can't match them, not at acceptable cost, not with everything else we're trying to do. And land-based aircraft just don't have the range to give cover and reconnaissance to a fleet at sea. Hence, we need the . . . aircraft carriers, we're calling them."

"Your shipyards need the contracts, you mean," Cunningham said bluntly. "Farr, this is diverting effort from capital ships."

Farr shook his head. "Look, Arthur, you know very well the bottleneck there is the heavy guns and the armor-rolling capacity."

Cunningham rose and settled his gold-crusted cap. "If you will excuse, me, sir—" he began.

"Admiral Cunningham, *sit down!*" Farr barked.

After a moment's glaring test of wills, the other man obeyed. "Admiral Cunningham, your objections are noted. You will now cooperate fully in carrying out the decisions of the Minister of Marine and the Naval Staff, or you will tender your resignation immediately. *Is that clear?*"

Twenty minutes later John Hosten sank back in his chair,

shaking his head as he looked at the door that Cunningham had carefully *not* slammed behind him.

"I hope there aren't too many more like him, Dad," he said.

Maurice Farr sighed. His close-cut hair and mustache were gray now, but he looked as trim as he had when he stood on the docks of Oathtaking nearly two decades before.

"I'm afraid there are quite a few," he said. "A lot of the officers are convinced that this is being forced on the navy by politicians—and Highlander politicians from the east, at that, with their industrialist friends." He smiled. "They're right, aren't they?"

"But—" John began, then caught the look in his stepfather's eye. "You can still get me going, can't you?"

Farr laughed. "You take everything a bit too seriously, son," he said. "Don't worry; Artie Cunningham would rather eat his young than resign just before the first big naval war in a generation. If he has to swallow that"—he nodded at the model of the aircraft carrier that filled the center of the big table—"he'll swallow it, for the sake of the battlewagons."

Farr lit a cigarette. "He's not stupid, just rather specialized," he went on. "I can understand him; I'm a cannon-and-armorplate sailor myself. But I don't like operating blind." He stared at the model. "I *do* hope this concept's as workable as you and Jeffrey say. It looks good on paper, certainly, but I don't like ordering straight from the drawing board."

"Dad, I'm as sure as if I'd seen them fight battles myself."

pearl harbor, Center said helpfully. **the pursuit of the *bismark*. taranto. midway—**

Great, and how do I tell Dad that? John replied. Hastily: That was a rhetorical question.

Maurice Farr rose and began stacking papers in his briefcase. "No rest for the wicked—I've got to get back to HQ and deal with more bumpf. God, for a fleet command."

"Not long, I think, Dad," John said.

A long moment after his stepfather had left John heard the door behind him open.

"Touching," a voice said in Landisch.

"English," John said sharply. "Tradecraft."

"Oh, indeed."

The man—he was dressed in Santander civilian clothes, with a well-known yachting club's pattern of cravat—came and sat not far from John. He looked at a duplicate set of the airshipwreck photos.

"What caused this?"

"The design was overweight and underpowered; they took out a section in the center and enlarged it to take an extra gasbag. The bag chafed against the bolts internally, and they had a terrible problem with leaks. Probably they nosed in on that hill in the dark, or there was a fire from static discharge, or both."

"Sloppy," the Chosen officer said, tucking the pictures away. He nodded to the model of the aircraft carrier. "Will this work?"

"Probably, after a fashion. I can't turn down *all* the good ideas, you know—not and keep my standing with the military and defense industries."

"Indeed."

"I suppose we'll have to build them, too. Dirigibles are so vulnerable to heavier-than-air pursuit planes."

"Perhaps," the intelligence officer said. "And perhaps not."

"Straight and level, straight and level, damn your eyes," Horst Raske said, in a tone that was as close to a prayer as one of the Chosen was likely to get.

The bridge of the *Grey Tiger* was vibrating itself, very slightly, despite the skilled hands on the wheels and controls set about the U-shaped space. Through the vast semicircle of clear window they could see the teardrop shape of the experimental airship carrier *Orca* as she quivered in the clear air over the Land's central plateau, a hundred miles north of Copernik. The craft was huge, nearly a thousand feet from nose to stern, with beautiful swept control fins in an X at the rear, its smooth sheet-aluminum hull showing it to be one of the new metalclads.

Underneath it a small biplane fighter was making another run, first matching speeds with the dirigible, then edging upwards. A strong metal loop was fastened to the biplane's upper wing, and a long trapezoidal hook mechanism dangled below the airship's belly. The fighter swayed and dipped as it rose into the buffeting wake of the huge dirigible, then again as it hit the prop-wash of the six bellowing high-speed diesels. It rose sharply, and the observers on the *Grey Tigers* bridge sucked in their breaths, certain it would crash into the thin structure of the airship's belly.

Instead it pulled nose-up, almost stalling, then slipped into contact with the hook. A cable locked the mechanism shut, and it moved smoothly backwards with the aircraft pivoting and jerking on the hook-and-ring connection. The rise stopped with the biplane just below the entrance hatch intended for it,

"What?" Professor Director Gunter Porschmidt spoke with his usual quick, slightly angry tone. Some of the white-coated assistants around him moved away a little. "What? Why do they wait?"

Gerta Hosten replied. "Because, *Herr Professor,* the plane will only fit into the entrance hatch if aligned precisely with the airship's keel . . . and it is difficult to get it to point that way traveling at ninety miles per hour."

Porschmidt blinked at her. "Oh. Yes, yes, make a note." One of the assistants scribbled busily.

Tiny human figures on ropes dropped out of the airship's belly. Laboriously, they fixed rope tackle to the biplane's wings and body, and the trapeze swung it up once more. On the second try—the first crumpled a wing against the side of the hatch—they got it through. Porschmidt beamed, and there was a discreet murmur of applause from the Research Council officials with him.

"Good, good," the chief scientist said. "But perhaps we should assign a better pilot to the next series of tests?"

"The pilot is Eva Sommers," Gerta said. "Her reflexes were among the ten best ever recorded in the Test of Life; she has fifteen kills to her credit from the war down in the Union and is currently the Air Council's best test pilot."

"Oh." Porschmidt shrugged. "Well, the purpose of operational testing is to improve the product."

"Herr Professor?"

"Yes?"

"While this is undoubtedly a great technical achievement," Gerta said, "given our current quality control problems, don't you think—"

He made a dismissive gesture. "The Chosen Council told me to design a device which would give us greater heavier-than-air scouting capacity than the enemy's new ship-borne aeroplanes. Production is not my department."

Horst Raske waited until they had left his bridge before putting a hand to his forehead and sighing.

"Well, this proves one thing conclusively," Gerta said, watching the *Orca* turn away.

"What?"

"That the Chosen are still Visager's supreme toymakers," she added.

"Brigadier, I do not think that is funny."

"It isn't. Porschmidt falling out a hatchway without a parachute at six thousand feet, *that* would be funny."

"If only the man were an incompetent!"

"If he were an incompetent, he wouldn't have passed the Test of Life," Gerta said. "Unfortunately, that is no guarantee that he will not be wrong—just that he'll be plausibly, brilliantly wrong with ideas that sound wonderful and are just a tantalizing inch beyond realization."

Raske shuddered. "I hope some of his ideas work out better than *that*." He nodded towards the disappearing airship. "When I think of the conventional models we could have made for the same expenditure of money and skilled manpower . . . and you're right, quality control has fallen off appallingly."

"A complete waste of—" Gerta stopped, struck. "Wait a minute. The problem there is hull turbulence, right?"

Raske looked at her. "Yes. No way to eliminate it, that I can see. An airship pushes aside a lot of air, and that's all there is to it."

"But fifty, sixty feet down there's less problem?"

"Of course—but you can't put the hook gear *that* far down. The leverage would snap it off at the first strain."

"Yes, but why do we want to hoist the plane aboard the airship's cargo bay?"

She began to talk. Raske listened, his face gradually losing its hangdog expression.

"Now why can't Porschmidt come up with ideas like that?" he asked.

"Oh, some of Porschmidt's brainchildren work well enough, better than I expected." Gerta said. She smiled. "As our friends to the south will soon find out."

CHAPTER EIGHTEEN

"A great difference from the beginning of the war, *n'est pas?*" General Gerard said with melancholy pride.

Many of the soldiers trudging along the sides of the dusty road cheered as the car carrying Gerard and Jeffrey went by. They were almost all Unionaise on this front, not Freedom Brigades, so they were probably cheering the local officer—although Jeffrey was popular enough.

And they do shape a lot better, Jeffrey thought. For one thing, they were all in uniform and almost all had plain bowl-shaped steel helmets, and they all had the Table of Organization and Equipment gear besides. More importantly, they were moving in coherent groups and not getting tangled up or scattering across the countryside. Infantry marching on either side, horse-drawn guns and mule-drawn wagons and ambulances towards the middle, and a fair number of Santander-made trucks, Ferrins, and big squarish Appelthwaits. Occasionally an airplane would pass by overhead, drawing no more than a few curious stares; the men were accustomed to the notion that they had their own air service, these days.

The air was thick with dust and the animal-dung-and-gasoline stink of troops on the move. Around them the central plateau stretched in rolling immensity, with the snowpeaks of the Monts du

Nora growing ever closer on the northeast horizon. The grainfields were long since reaped, sere yellow stubble against reddish-yellow earth, with dust smoking off it now and then. Widely spaced vineyards of trained vines looking like bushy cups covered many of the hillsides, and there was an occasional grove of fruit trees or cork oaks. The people all lived in the big clumped villages, looking like heaps of spilled sugar cubes with their flat-roofed houses of whitewashed adobe. The peasants came out to cheer the Loyalist armies; Jeffrey suspected that prudence would make them cheer the Nationalists almost as loudly. Not that the government wasn't more popular than the rebel generals, who brought the landlords back in their train wherever they conquered, but Unionvil's anticlerical policies weren't very popular outside the cities, either.

"Everyone seems to be expecting a military picnic," Jeffrey said, leaning back in the rear seat of the big staff car.

It was Santander-made, of course; a model that wealthy men bought, or wealthy private schools. Six-wheeled, with a collapsible top, and two rows of leather-cushioned seats in the rear. Gerard had had the original seats replaced with narrower, harder models, plus communications gear and maps, with a pintle-mounted twin machine gun set between the driver's compartment and the passengers. Henri Trudeau stood behind the grips of the weapons, carefully scanning the sky.

"Morale is good," Gerard acknowledged. "The men know they've gotten a lot better, these past two years."

"You've done a good job," Jeffrey said.

"And you, my friend. Those suggestions for an accelerated officer-training system helped very much."

Ninety-day wonders, courtesy of Raj and Center, Jeffrey thought. Center had a *lot* of records of sudden mobilizations for large-scale warfare.

"Well, combat is the best way to identify potential leaders," Jeffrey said. "It's sort of expensive as a sorting process, but it works."

Henri spoke unexpectedly. "Things wouldn't be going this well if you hadn't got those anarchist *batards* killed off right at the start, sir."

Gerard looked up with a smile; the Loyalist Army was still informal in some respects. Jeffrey shook his head.

"The rebels inflicted heavy casualties on the anarchist militia, that's true," he said judiciously. *I'm becoming a politician like John,* he thought. "But that's scarcely my fault. They wanted to fight, and I put them where they could fight. Besides, you were with them, Henri."

The Unionaise soldier grinned. "I wanted to *win,* sir. Which is why I've stuck with you since. And they were a wonderful example, in their way—everyone could see what came of their notions."

Then his head came up. "Watch it!" The machine gun swiveled around on its pivot.

"Listen up, people."

The selection of Chosen officers who would be supporting the offensive braced to attention inside the green dimness of the tent.

"Colonel Hosten is Military Intelligence for this operation and also our liaison with the Union Nationalist forces. She will conclude the briefing."

Gerta stepped up in front of the map easel. "At ease. The situation is as follows . . ."

She talked for ten crisp minutes, answering the occasional question. *What a relief,* she thought. Liaison work was a strain; foreigners chattered, they didn't know how to concentrate on the business at hand, they wandered off into irrelevancies. At last she finished.

"Now, let's go out there and *kill.*"

"Inspiring and informative," Heinrich said. The double stars of a general rested easy on his shoulders, standing out from the hybrid uniform of the Eagle Legion, the Land "volunteer" force fighting with the Nationalists. "I suppose you'll go collate some reports?"

Gerta smiled. "Well, actually, Copernik wants detailed reports on the performance of the Von Nelsing two-seater," she said.

Heinrich shrugged his shoulders ruefully. "There are times when I think this whole war is nothing but a laboratory experiment," he said.

"It is," Gerta said. "Good on-the-job training, too."

"True." He frowned. "The problem is, the enemy learns as well—and they needed it more than we. So they improve more for an equal amount of experience. If you play chess with good chess players, you get good."

My darling Heinrich, you are extremely perceptive at times, Gerta thought as she ducked out of the tent and headed for the landing field.

The squadron looked squeaky-clean and factory-new, even the untattered wind sock and the raw pine boards of the messhall. Everything but the pilots. They'd all been transferred from Albatros army-cooperation planes to the new Von Nelsings; Gerta walked around hers admiringly. The fuselage was light plywood, a monocoque hull factory-made in two pieces and then fastened together along a central seam, much stronger than the old fabric models and extremely simple to make, which was crucial these days. There were two engines in cowlings on the lower wings, giving the craft a higher power-to-weight ratio than a fighter; it was heavier than the pursuit planes, but not twice as heavy. Six air-cooled machine guns bristled from the pointed nose, and there was a twin-barreled mount facing backwards from the observer's seat. Protégé groundcrew were fastening four fifty-pound bombs under each wing, and then a one-armed Chosen supervisor came along to inspect. Gerta gave the plane a careful going-over herself. They'd set up a multiple checking system, but with all the new camps full of Imperial deportees making components, it paid to be careful.

"All in readiness, sir," the squadron commander said expressionlessly, saluting.

And it would be even more ready if a hot-dogger from HQ wasn't pushing her way in, Gerta finished for him silently. She didn't mind; she *was* a hot-dogger from HQ, and she *was* pushing her way in shamelessly.

She was also a better pilot than any of the youngsters here; she'd been flying since the Land first put heavier-than-air craft into the sky.

"Let's show what these birds can do, then," she said.

The Protégé gunner made a stirrup of her hands and Gerta used it to vault up and climb into the cockpit. Then she stuck a hand down and helped the other woman into the plane. More than half the aircrew were female; they had lower averages on body weight and higher on reflexes, both of which counted on the screening test. This one seemed quite competent, if not a mental giant, and what you needed in an observer-gunner was good eyes and quick hands.

The first planes were already taxiing when she completed her checklist and signaled to the groundcrew to pull the chocks from before the spat-streamlined wheels. This production model seemed very much like the prototypes she'd flown back home, but the airfield was at three thousand feet rather than sea level. She pulled her goggles down over her eyes and followed the crewman with the flags; four more seized the tail of her plane and lifted it around to the proper angle. They held the plane against the growing tug of the motors until she chopped her hand skyward and it leapt forward.

Good acceleration, she noted. There'd been a bit of a tussle between the three aircraft companies over the scarce high-performance engines, with some claiming they were wasted on a cooperation airplane. *Smoother on the ground, too.* The new oleo shock-absorbers on the wheel struts were reducing the pounding a plane normally took on takeoff. The fabric coverings of the wing rippled slightly, as they always did. *Have to see how those experiments with rigid surface wings are going.* No reason in theory why the wings shouldn't be load-bearing plywood on internal frames like the body. That would *really* speed up production.

Up. She pushed the throttles forward and waggled her wings to test the balance of the engines, then banked upward and started glancing down at the ground, smiling to herself with the familiar exhilaration of flight. And there was *nothing* more fun than strafing missions. There was the Eboreaux River, the town of Selandrons . . . and the irregular line of the trenches. Not a solid maze of redoubts and communications lines like some sections of the front, just field entrenchments. Enemy artillery sparkled along it and through it— their offensive was getting off to a good start, penetrating the thin defenses and thrusting for the river.

Ground crawled beneath her, like a map itself from six thousand feet. The cold, thin air slapped at her face, making her cheeks tingle. An occasional puff of black followed the squadron as the converted naval quick-firers the Santies had supplied to the Reds opened up, but there were a *lot* of targets up here today; aircraft were rising from all along the front, swarming up from the front-line airfields by the hundreds. There were planes on either side as far as she could see, black dots against the blue and white of the sky, the drone of engines filling her ears.

Magnificent, she thought. Even better, the fighter squadron assigned to give them top cover was in place.

Ahead, the squadron commander waggled his wings three times and then banked into a dive. At precise ten-second intervals the others followed. Gerta grinned sharklike as she flipped up the cover on the joystick and put her thumb lightly on the firing button.

"Those aren't ours," Gerard said sharply, standing.

No, they aren't, Jeffrey thought with sharp alarm. The Loyalists and Brigades didn't use that double-arrowhead formation.

"Get me some reports," Gerard said sharply to the communications technician.

She—the Union forces had a Women's Auxiliary now, too—fiddled with the big crackle-finished Santander wireless set that occupied one side of the great car. There weren't many other sets for the tech to talk to; wireless small enough to get into a land vehicle was a recent development . . . courtesy of Center. Jeffrey kept his eyes on the growing swarm of dots along the western horizon, but he could hear the pattern of dots and dashes through the tech's headphones. Center translated them for him effortlessly, but he waited until the tech finished scribbling on a pad and handed the result to Gerard.

"Sir. Enemy planes in strength attacking the following positions."

Gerard took it and flipped through the maps on the table. "Artillery parks and shell storage areas and fuel dumps behind our lines."

Another series of dots and dashes. "And our airfields. Fortunate that most of our planes are already up."

Jeffrey whistled, leaning against one of the overhead bars and bracing his binoculars. "I make that over two hundred," he said. "Fighters . . . and there are two-engined craft as well."

"The new Von Nelsings we've heard about. That puts a stake through the heart of this offensive."

"I'd say we've run right into a rebel offensive," Jeffrey said.

"Exactly. And I will advance no further into the jaws of a trap. Driver! Pull over!"

The big car nosed over to the side of the road. Several smaller ones full of aides and staff officers drew up around it.

"No clumping!" Gerard ordered sharply. "You, you, you, come here—the rest of you spread out, hundred-yard intervals." He began to rap out orders.

A fighter cut through the Land formation, the red-white-and-blue spandrels on its wings marking it as a Freedom Brigades craft. The twin machine guns sparkled, and a series of holes punctured the wing to her right; one bullet spanged off the steel-plate cowling of the engine. Behind Gerta, the Protégé gunner screamed with rage as she wrestled the twin-gun mount around, tracer hammering out in the enemy fighter's wake. The Von Nelsing next to her dove after it, but the more nimble pursuit plane turned in a beautifully tight circle, far tighter than the twin-engine craft could manage.

However, Gerta thought, and dove.

That cut across the chord of the Brigade's fighter's circle; the heavier Von Nelsing dove *fast*. For a moment the wire circle gunsight behind her windscreen slid just enough ahead of the Santy Mark II. Her thumb stabbed on the button, and the six machine guns ahead of her hammered. Over a hundred rounds struck the little biplane fighter in the second that her burst lasted, ripping it open from nose to tail like a knife through wrapping paper. It staggered in the air, collapsed in the middle, and exploded into flame all in the same instant. The burning debris fluttered groundward in pieces, the dense mass of the engine falling fastest.

"*And fuck you very much!*" Gerta shouted, banking sharply to the right and heading groundward.

The Brigader had interrupted her mission. *There* was the road, still crowded with troops and transport. The men were running out into the fields on either side, or taking cover in the ditches, but the vehicles were less mobile. She lined up carefully, coming down to less than two hundred feet, ignoring the rifles and machine guns spitting at her. You'd have to be dead lucky to hit a target like this from the ground, plus being a very good shot, and the engines were protected.

Now. She yanked at the bomb release and fought to hold the plane steady as the fifty pounders dropped from beneath each wing. The explosions in her wake were heavier than shells of the same weight; less had to go into a strong casing, leaving more room for explosives. They straddled the roadway, raising poplar shapes of dirt and rock, also wood and metal and flesh. The guns in the nose of her airplane stammered, drawing a cone of fire up the center of the road.

Jeffrey dove for the floor of the car, pulling Gerard after him. Hot brass from the twin mounting fountained over them both. Bullets cracked by and pinged from the metal of the car. There was a fountain of sparks from the wireless and the operator gave a choked cry and slumped down on them with a boneless finality that Jeffrey recognized all too well, even before the blood confirmed it. It was amazing how *much* blood even a small human body contained. A second later there was another explosion, huge but somehow soft and followed by a pillow of hot air; a wagon of galvanized iron gasoline cans had gone up.

The two men heaved themselves erect; Gerard paused for an instant to close the staring eyes of the wireless operator. Henri was still swinging the twin-barrel mount, hoping for another target. The driver slumped in the front seat, lying backward with the top clipped off his head and his brains spattered back through the compartment. Other vehicles were burning up and down the road, and some of the roadside trees as well. A riderless horse ran by, its eyes staring in terror. Other animals were screaming in uncomprehending pain. The officers who'd gathered around Gerard were bandaging their wounded and counting their dead.

"You all right?" Jeffrey asked.

Gerard daubed at his spattered uniform tunic and then abandoned the effort. "*Bien, suffisient.* Yourself?"

"None of it's mine."

"Then let us see what we can do to remedy this—what is it, your expression?"

"Ratfuck."

"This ratfuck, then."

"Damn, they actually got them to work," Jeffrey said, scratching. Damn. Lice again. I may be a lousy general, but I'd rather it wasn't literal.

Two weeks into the latest offensive, and the Loyalists were already back nearly a hundred miles from their start-lines. One of the reasons was parked in the valley below them. It was a rhomboid shape more than forty feet long and twenty wide, thick plates of cast steel massively bolted together. The top held a boxy turret with a naval four-inch gun mounted in it, and each corner of the machine had a smaller turret with two machine guns; a field mortar's stubby barrel showed from the top as well, to deal with targets out of direct line of sight. There were drive sprockets in four places along the top of each tread, and steam leaked from half a dozen apertures. The long shadows of evening made it look even larger than it was, gave a hulking, prehistoric menace to the outline.

A Loyalist field-gun lay tilted on one wheel in front of the Land tank, its horses and men dead around it. Three lighter tanks had clanked on by up the valley towards the tableland, and only a few infantry and crew stood around the monster, the crew pulling maintenance through open panels, inspecting the tracks, or just enjoying spring air that must be like wine from heaven after the black, dank heat of the interior. A thick hose extended from its rear deck to the village well, jerking and bulging occasionally as the pump filled its tanks with water.

"That thing must weight fifty tons." *And we gave them the idea. Some disinformation.* You had to hand it to the Chosen engineers; they were perennially overoptimistic, but their hubris brought some amazing tour-de-force technical feats at times.

the vehicle weighs sixty one point four three tons, Center said. **maximum armor thickness is four inches at thirty degrees slope. estimated range eighty miles under optimum conditions. mechanical reliability and ergonomics are poor. cost effectiveness is low.**

Beside him on the ridge Henri was staring at the Land tank, his mouth making small chewing motions. Jeffrey had a hundred-odd men with him, Brigade troops and Loyalists, whatever had been left when the front broke. Many of them were taking a look and beginning to sidle backwards. There was a phrase for it now: "tank panic." The ordinary ones were bad enough, but these new monsters were worse.

"No movement," he snapped.

Discipline held enough to keep his makeshift battle group from dissolving right there. Then again, the ones who'd felt like quitting had mostly gone in the days since the rebel counterattack and its Land spearheads had broken through the Loyalist front. These were the ones with some stick to them.

"Gather around, everyone but the scouts." He waited while the quiet movement went on; the men had good "fieldcraft, at least. "All right, there's a heavy tank down there. They're dangerous, but they're also slow and clumsy, and the enemy doesn't have very many of them. We're behind their lines now, and they feel fairly safe. As soon as it's dark, I'm leading a forlorn hope down there to take it out with explosives. I need some volunteers. The rest will cover our retreat, and we'll break out to our own front. Who's with me?"

He waited a moment, then blinked in surprise as more than half lifted their hands. A nod of thanks; there was nothing much to say at a time like this.

"Ten men, no more. Henri, Duquesne, Smith, Woolstone, McAndrews—"

Night fell swiftly, and the highland air chilled. The commandos spent the time checking over their weapons, and making up grenade bundles—taking one stick grenade and tying the heads of a dozen more around it. Those who thought several days' stubble and grime insufficient blacked their faces and hands with mud; a few prayed.

"How does a general keep getting himself into this *merde*, sir?" Henri asked, grinning.

"Going up to the front to see what's going on," Jeffrey said. "It's a fault, but then so are women and wine."

He looked up; it was full dark, and still early enough in spring to be overcast.

Rain? he asked.

chance of precipitation is 53%, ±5, Center replied.

"We'll go with it," he said aloud. "Spread out. Avoid the sentries if you can; if you can't, keep it quiet."

The commandos moved down from the ridge, through the aromatic scrub and into the stubblefields of the valley bottom. There was little noise; the men with him had all been at the front for long enough to learn night-patrol work. *I'd have had more posts and a roving patrol here,* he thought.

Whoever was in charge wanted to keep pursuing as fast as he could, Raj said. **He left the minimum possible with the tank when it broke down. Sound thinking. The chances of a Loyalist band big enough to cause trouble being bypassed are low. But even low probabilities happen sometimes.**

There was a low choked cry from off to the left in the darkness, and a wet thudding sound. *We're going to—*

A rifle cracked, the muzzle flash bright in the darkness. Jeffrey could see the crew around the tank scrambling up out of their blankets and heading for their machine; half or better of them would be Chosen and deadly dangerous even surprised in their sleep. He tossed his pistol into his left hand and drew the bundle of grenades out of the cloth satchel at his side, running forward, stumbling and cursing as clods and brush caught at his feet. Abruptly the landscape went brighter, to something like twilight level. *Thanks,* he thought; Center was reprocessing the input of his eyes and feeding it back to his visual cortex. It no longer felt eerie after more than twenty-five years with Center in his brain.

A red aiming dot settled on a panicked Protégé soldier staring wildly about him in the near-complete darkness. Jeffrey fired, then dove and rolled to avoid the bullets that cracked out at the muzzle flash of his weapon. He didn't need to check on the enemy soldier. The dot had been resting right above one ear. A series of vicious blindsided firefights was crackling around the rebel encampment, men firing at sounds and movement glimpsed in *split* seconds. Or firing at what they *thought* was sound or movement.

Chooonk. The mortar in the turret of the Land heavy tank fired. Jeffrey dove to the ground again, squeezing his eyes shut. Reflected light from the ground still dazzled him for an instant as the starshell went off.

What was really frightening was a high-pitched *chuff* and squeal of steel on steel. The tank was live; they must have kept the flash-boilers warm for quick readiness. He'd counted on the half hour it took to bring the huge machine on-line.

One of the corner turrets cut loose, beating the ground with a twin flail of lead and green tracer. Then the four-inch gun in the main turret fired. That must be more for intimidation than anything else, since they didn't have a target worth a heavy shell. It *was* intimidating, a huge leaf-shaped blade of flame, the ripping crash and the *crump* of high explosive from the hillside where the load struck.

He couldn't fault the men he'd left behind on the ridge. They opened fire on the camp and the Chosen tank, dozens of winking fireflies showing from their rifles. Sparks danced over the heavy armor of the panzer as it shed the small-arms bullets like so many hailstones . . . but it *did* force the commander to stay buttoned up, vision limited to whatever showed through the narrow vision blocks that ringed the cupola on top of the tank.

Schoonk. Another starshell. The machine-gun turrets were beating at the ridge, trying to suppress the riflemen there, and doing a good job of it. The enemy infantry were taking cover behind the tank, firing around it Then it began to move, grinding across the little valley towards the ridge. Towards him.

Stupid, Jeffrey thought as he hugged the dusty earth, blinking it out of his eyes. The Loyalist force didn't have anything that could threaten the four-inch armor plate of the Land war machine. *That's the Chosen for you.* Aggressive to a fault, ready to attack whether it was necessary or not.

Of course, if he was unlucky they'd reduce his own personal ass to a grease spot in this stubblefield.

The earth shook as the massive weight ground slowly, slowly towards him. The machine gun bursts from the four turrets and the coaxial weapon blended together into a continuous chattering punctuated by the occasional chugging of the mortar, firing illuminating rounds or high explosive to probe the dead ground behind the ridge. Closer. Closer.

Now it was looming over him. *Good.* No one had noticed him in the dark and the flickering shadows of the descending starshells as they wobbled on their parachutes. Steel screamed in protest and the earth groaned with a creaking sound as the walking fortress rolled towards him, lurching as the driver tried to keep the treads working at equal speeds. His stomach felt watery, and his testicles were trying to crawl up into it for comfort: "tank panic" felt a lot more understandable, even sensible, right now.

Black shadow passed over him as the prow moved by. There should be more than two feet of clearance between the tank's belly and the dirt. More than enough for him, if this was one of the ones without hinged blades fitted to the bottom. He rolled on his back, despite the voice at the back of his head screaming that he should bury his face in the dirt. The pitted, rusty surface of the hull was moving only inches from his face, closer when a bolthead went by: And there were the big eyebolt rings near the rear, fitted for use with a towing line.

He dropped his pistol on his stomach and reached out with both hands. *There,* He pushed the handle of the stick grenade through the bolt. His cap stuffed in beside it snugged it close enough not to move for a few seconds. He scooped up the pistol again with his right hand, and kept hold of the pull-tab at the base of the stick grenade with his left, letting the motion of the tank pull it loose, arming the weapon.

Don't stop now, baby, please, he thought.

It didn't. The commander must have been waiting until he was closer to use the main gun again, and the automatic weapons were reasonably effective on the move. The weight rolled from overhead, like freedom from the grave. Jeffrey began to crawl frantically, then rose and ran two dozen paces.

The first explosion was muffled by the bulk of the tank. It seemed absurdly small beneath the huge bulk of the Land vehicle, but even on something weighing sixty tons the armor couldn't be thick *everywhere*. The tank came to a lurching halt, although one machine-gun turret continued to fire for fifteen seconds. Then there was a second explosion, this one *inside* the tank. Steam jetted from the back deck, then a few seconds later from every opening and crack in the hull, squealing into the night like so many locomotive whistles. Jeffrey could feel his skin crawl slightly at the thought of what it must have been like inside, the sudden wash of superheated vapor flaying the crew alive.

That did not stop his pumping run. A low wall of crumbling stone and adobe showed ahead of him; he hurdled it and went to the ground with his face pressed to the dirt. Hot metal was in contact with ruptured shell casings and vaporized gasoline, and right about—

Whump. The fuel and ammunition went off together, and the Land panzer came apart along the lines where the sheets of cast and rolled armor were riveted together. Chunks plowed into the wall a few feet from him, showering powdered dirt and small stones with painful force. He raised his head cautiously; he could see nothing moving near the twisted wreckage of the tank, although the light from the burning remnants was bright enough to read by. The turret lay on its side a few yards distant; further out still were bodies that lay still. Mostly still.

"I hope none of them were mine," he muttered. His voice sounded faint and faraway in his ringing ears. Louder: "Rally here! Rally here!"

CHAPTER NINETEEN

"Those are their final orders?" Jeffrey asked.

"*Oui.* Unionvil is to be held at all costs. No troops may be diverted; instead we are to commit our strategic reserve. Chairman Deschambre assures me that the political consequences of losing the capital would be 'disastrous,' quote unquote. Minister of Public Education and Security Lebars tells me that they shall not pass."

"Quote unquote," Jeffrey supplied. "What strategic reserve, by the way?"

"The one we pissed away with that misbegotten offensive towards the Eboreaux last year and have never been able to replace," Gerard said.

Jeffrey nodded. His eyes felt sandy from lack of sleep, and his ears rang from too many cups of strong black coffee, the taste sour on his tongue. Outside the tent light flickered and stuttered along the horizon; it might have been thunder and heat lightning, but it wasn't. It was heavy artillery, firing all along the buckling front south and east of Unionvil. The traffic on the road outside was heavy, troops and supply wagons moving up to the front, wounded men coming back—some in ambulances, more hobbling along supporting each other, their bandages glistening in the light of the portable floods outside the HQ tents. A convoy of trucks came through, flatbeds crowded with reinforcements whose faces seemed pathetically young under their helmets. At least the mud wasn't too bad, despite spring rains heavier than usual. They'd had three years to improve the roads around here, three years with the front running through what had been the outermost satellite villages of Unionvil. That didn't look like being true much longer.

"Baaaaaa."

Gerard's head came up, trying to find the man who'd bleated like a sheep. It was fifty yards to the road, and dark.

"*Baa. Baaaa. Baaaa.*" More and more of the wounded along the sides of the road were bleating at the reinforcements, mocking the lambs going to the slaughter. Gerard walked to the door of the big tent.

"Captain Labushange. This is to stop."

Whistles blew and feet pounded; there was always a company of Assault Guards and another of military police attached to the regional headquarters.

"And now I must use the *Assaulteaux* against wounded men for telling the truth," Gerard said. "By the way, my friend, Minister Lebars also assures me that it is better to die on your feet rather than live on your knees."

"Does the woman always talk like that?"

"Invariably. It's not just the speeches." Gerard looked down at the map table. "Leave us," he said to the other officers.

"So I have no choice," he went on, touching a red plaque with a fingertip. It fell on its side, lying behind an arrowhead of black markers. "And how am I different from Libert, now?"

"Libert started it," Jeffrey said, putting a hand on the other man's shoulders. "You couldn't be like him if you tried. We'll do what's necessary."

"I will," Gerard said. "Keep the Freedom Brigade troops in the line. This is a Union matter."

Jeffrey nodded. "Don't hesitate," he warned.

It was probably wise to keep the Brigade troops out of Gerard's coup, although they were just as rabid about the Committee of Public Safety as the native Union soldiers of the Loyalist army. Still, they were foreigners.

"Hesitate? My friend, I have been hesitating for six months. Now I will act."

He strode out of the room, calling for aides and staff officers. Jeffrey remained, looking down at the map. Unionvil was a bulge set into the rebel line, a bulge joined to the rest of the Loyalist sector by a narrow bridge of secure territory.

"I hope you're not acting too late," he said, reaching for his greatcoat.

Heinrich Hosten was in charge on the other side, looking at the same map. Jeffrey knew Heinrich, and he also knew exactly what he'd do in Heinrich's boots at this moment.

Jeffrey ducked out into the chilly night.

"Senator McRuther?"

The meeting was relatively informal. At least, John wasn't being grilled in front of the Foreign Affairs Committee in full, in the House of Assembly, with a dozen reporters following every word. This oak-paneled meeting room was much quieter, redolent of polish and old cigars, not even a stenographer taking notes. Most of the faces across the mahogany table were formidable enough, age and power sitting on them like invisible cloaks.

Senator McRuther was nearing seventy, and he still wore the ruffled white shirts and black clawhammer jackets that had been modish when he was a young man. He represented the Pokips Provincial District in the western lowlands, and he'd done that since he was a young man, too.

"Mr. Hosten," he said—turning the "s" sound almost into a "z" with malice aforethought, the Chosen pronunciation. "What exactly have you accomplished with your policy of 'constructive engagement,' except to get us into a war?"

John nodded. "You're right, Senator. We *are* in a war, although not a declared one. However, I might point out that the Land of the Chosen has over forty thousand of its regular army troops in the Union del Est. They're backing General Libert, and they're *winning*. I suggest that this is not in the national interests of the Republic of the Santander."

"Hear, hear," Senator Beemody said.

A few others nodded or murmured agreement; not all of them were from the eastern highlands, either. John's eyes took tally of them. Beemody's eastern Progressive bloc; a number from the western seacoast cities, which were growing fat on new naval contracts. And a scattering from the rural districts of the western lowlands, some of them McRuther's own Conservatives. The elderly senator hadn't kept office for fifty years by being stupid, even if he was set in his ways.

"As you say, they're winning. Never do an enemy a small injury; you've succeeded in antagonizing the Land without stopping them. If Libert and his Nationalists win we'll have a close ally of the Land on our eastern frontier, a powerful garrison of Land troops keeping him loyal, and we'll have to support this grossly inflated standing army *forever*. I realize that you and the rest of the highlander industrialists would love that, but *my* constituents pay the taxes to keep soldiers in idleness."

"Senator," John said quietly, "the Land is not antagonistic to Santander because we've backed the Loyalist side in the Union civil war. It's antagonistic to us because we're the only thing that keeps the Land from overrunning the whole of Visager. And I hope I don't have to go into further detail about what rule by the Chosen means."

More murmurs of agreement. John's newspapers had been publicizing exactly what that meant for years. Refugees from the Empire, and now from the Union, had been driving home the same message. Militia had had to be called out to put down anti-Chosen rioting when the pictures of the Bassin du Sud massacre came out.

Senator Beemody coughed discreetly. "General Farr"—the high command had confirmed his promotion as soon as he'd stepped back on Santander soil—"I gather you do not recommend an immediate declaration of war."

"No," Jeffrey said. McRuther blinked in surprise, his eyes narrowing warily.

"We're not ready," the younger Farr went on.

Beside him in his rear admiral's uniform, his father nodded. The family resemblance was much closer now that there was gray at

Jeffrey's temples and streaking his mustache. The lines scoring down from either side of his nose added to it as well.

"We're much stronger now than we were four or five years ago," Jeffrey went on. "Military production of all types is up sharply, and now we've got field-tested models. Our latest aircraft are as good as the Land models, and we're gradually getting production organized. The Freedom Brigades've given us a *lot* of men with combat experience, including a lot of officers; besides that, they're thirty-five thousand veterans as formed troops, and if the Union falls they'll retreat over the border. So will a lot of the Loyalist Army. But we're still not mobilized, a lot of the new Regular Army formations are weak, and the Provincial militias need to be better integrated. Admiral Farr can speak to the naval situation."

Jeffrey's father nodded.

"We have a tonnage advantage of three to two," he said. "More in battleships. The Land Navy has more experience, particularly in cruiser and torpedo-boat operations in the Gut, which could be crucial. Still, I'm fairly confident we could dominate the Gut. The problem is that operating further north, in the Passage, we'd be sticking our . . . ah, necks into a potential meatgrinder, with strong Land bases on either side and a long way from our own. If we lose our fleet, we'd be a long way towards losing the war itself. Furthermore, nobody knows what aircraft will mean to naval war. The Chosen have more experience, but only with dirigibles. We need time to finish the aircraft carriers and to train the fleet in their use."

"Senators," Beemody said, "the Republic of the Santander cannot tolerate a Union which is satellite to the Land. Are we agreed?"

One by one the men on the other side of the table lifted their hands. McRuther sighed and followed suit, last and most reluctant.

"Then that is the sense of the Foreign Affairs Committee," Beemody said. "On the other hand, we are not yet ready for full-scale conflict. I therefore suggest that we recommend to the Premier that in the event of the fall of the Loyalist government in the Union, the Republic should declare a naval blockade of all Union ports pending the removal of foreign forces from Union soil."

"But that *means* war!" McRuther burst out.

"Not necessarily. As Admiral Farr has pointed out, we *do* have more heavy warships than the Land. The Gut is closer to our bases than theirs; we can blockade the Union and they'd be in no position to retaliate without risking their seaborne communications across the Passage. And while losing command of the sea *might* be disaster for us, it would *certainly* be a disaster for them. They can lose a war in an afternoon, in a fleet action. With the Union blockaded, they'd be forced to pull in their horns. They can't afford to isolate the expeditionary force they've committed to the Union. It's our hostage."

McRuther pointed to the map on the easel at the end of the table. "They can supply through the Sierra—and the Sierra is neutral."

Senator Beemody looked to the three men sitting across the table, in naval blue, army brown, and the diplomatic service's formal black tailcoat.

"Sirs, there's only a single track line from north to south through the Sierra," Jeffrey said. "Besides that, it's narrow gage, so you'd have to break bulk at both ends, the old Imperial net and the Union's."

"General?" Beemody prompted.

"Assuming that the Union was fully under Libert's control, and that the Chosen went along with a naval blockade?" Beemody nodded. "Supplying their forces would be just possible. Daily demand would go down and they could supply more from Union resources. It would certainly take some time for a squeeze to be effective, in terms of logistics."

"We *can* interdict the Gut," Admiral Farr said. "That I can assure you gentlemen."

"But the role of the Sierra will be crucial," Beemody said. "Senators, I move that the Foreign Ministry be directed to dispatch a special envoy with sealed plenipotentiary powers to secure the assistance of the Sierra Democratica y Populara in a preemptive blockade of the Union to enforce the neutralization and removal of all foreign troops. It's risky," he said to their grave looks, "but I sincerely believe it's our only chance. Otherwise in six months' time we'll be confronted with a choice between a war that might destroy us and accepting a Land protectorate on our border, which is intolerable. A show of hands, please, Senators."

This time the vote was less than unanimous. McRuther kept his hand obstinately down, switching his pouched and hooded blue eyes between Beemody and the Farrs.

"Fifteen ayes. Five nays. The ayes have it. The recommendation will be made. I remind the honorable senators that this meeting of the Foreign Affairs Committee is strictly confidential."

"Agreed," McRuther said sourly. "Its no time for a war of leaks."

"Then if that's all, Senators?"

The big room seemed larger and more shadowy when only Beemody, Farr, and his sons were left. The faces of past premiers looked down somberly from oil paintings on the walls; the old-fashioned small-paned windows were streaked with rain. Branches from the oaks around the building tapped against the glass like skeletal fingers. John Hosten had a sudden image of men—men not yet dead, the dead of the greater war to come—rising from their graves and traveling back to this moment, *tap-tap-tapping* at the windows, pleading for their lives. Tens of thousands, hundreds of thousands, millions.

observe:

Center showed him a vision he'd seen times beyond number, since that year on the docks of Oathtaking. Visager from space, the globes of fire expanding over cities, rising in shells of cracked white until they flattened against the upper edge of the atmosphere and the whole globe turned dirty white with the clouds. . . .

His stepfather cleared his throat. "You don't really think the Chosen will swallow a blockade of the Union?" he said to the head of the Foreign Affairs Committee.

Beemody shook his head. "About as likely as a hyena giving up a bone," he said frankly. "But it's as good a *casus belli* as any, the Senate will swallow it because they're desperate and desperate men believe what they want to, and the public will go along, too. Even McRuther will go along; he knows we can't dodge this much longer. But we *do* need more time, and we *do* need the Sierrans to come in on our side. They should; if we fall, they're next."

"But it's easier to see that when you don't have someone ahead of you in the lineup to the abattoir," Jeffrey said with brutal frankness.

"Hope springs eternal—and the Sierrans aren't just decentralized, they've got the political nervous system of an amoeba. Getting them to agree where the sun comes up is an accomplishment."

"Perhaps," John said slowly, "we could get the Chosen to do our arguing for us."

His foster-father frowned in puzzlement. Jeffrey shot him a glance, then tilted his head slightly towards the older men.

There comes a time when you have to use an asset, John said. If you won't risk it, what bloody use is it?

Center? Jeffrey asked.

probability of success is in the fifty percent range, the machine voice said. **chaotic factors render closer analysis futile at this point. success would increase the probability of a favorable outcome to the struggle as a whole by 10%, ±3.**

John nodded mentally. "Here's what I propose," he said. "First, sir"—he nodded to Admiral Farr—"Senator, you should be aware that we have a very highly placed double agent who the Chosen—Land Military Intelligence, to be precise—think is their mole and who they rely on implicitly for analysis of the Republic's intentions. I can't be more specific, of course. And this is entirely confidential."

The Admiral and Senator Beemody nodded in unison. There was no telling where the real moles were, of course.

"Here's what I think we should do—"

Gerta Hosten was walking stiffly when she entered the room. John stood.

"Are you all right?" he asked, surprised to find the concern genuine, even after all these years.

"Flying accident," she said, looking around.

The little house was a gem, in its own way; patterned silk wallpaper, Errife rugs, inlaid furniture, all discreetly tucked away in a leafy suburb north of the embassy section of Santander City. Just what a millionaire industrialist would use for assignations he wanted to keep thoroughly secret from his wife, which was the cover John was using. *Good tradecraft,* she thought grudgingly; John could read that on her face, even without Center's supremely educated guesses.

"Not serious, I hope." John sat and poured the coffee and brandy.

"Just a wrenched back for me. Thankfully, the plane totaled itself in front of half the Chosen Council. That damned bomber is a flying—just barely flying—abortion. If it'd had a full fuel load, much less bombs, I'd be in bits just large enough to plug a rat's ass."

"The Air Council's finally given up on using airships as strategic bombers?"

"I should hope so, after we lost a dozen trying to hit Unionvil in the last offensive," she said. "But those eight-engine monsters Porschmidt came up with, they're no better. Only marginally faster, the bomb load is a joke, they're unbelievably expensive to build and maintain, and landing them's more dangerous than combat. The bugger's got the Council's ear, though, him and his backers. Now he's throwing good money after bad, trying to *improve* the fuckers." She sighed. "To business."

"Here," John said, sliding the folder across the ivory-and-tortoise-shell of the table.

It had three separate sets of "Top Secret" and "Eyes Only" stamps on it, Army General Staff, Naval Staff, and Premier's Office, the latter a miniature of the Great Seal that only he and his chief aide could use. Gerta whistled silently as she picked it up. Her face went totally unreadable as she finally looked up at him. "This is serious?"

"Totally. Note the Premier's sign-off."

She flipped to the end. *To be implemented, as soon as possible.* "I'll be damned," she said. "I wouldn't have thought the Santies could get their shit together like this."

"Jeff advised it, strongly," John said. "He's quite the fair-haired boy right now, and not just with the general public."

"He deserves it," Gerta said, refilling her cup. "Heinrich was extremely impressed with the way he got most of the Brigades out of Unionvil before we pinched off the pocket there. Excuse me, before General Libert pinched off the pocket with the assistance of volunteer contractors from the Land operating without the approval of the Chosen Council."

She grinned like a wolf. "Heinrich picked up some very pretty things there when we sacked the city."

John matched her expression, although in his case it wasn't a smile. "What'll you recommend?"

"Me? I'm just MilInt's messenger girl," Gerta said.

"You're also the daughter of the Chief of the General Staff," John pointed out. "And you've been carrying the hatchet for them for fifteen years now."

"That's between me and the *vater,* Johnnie," Gerta said, taking out a camera the size of a palm from the street purse resting beside her chair. She opened it, checked the ambient light, and began photographing each page of the folder with swift, methodical care. "Besides, all doing a good job gets you is more jobs—you know how it works.

"I'll tell you, though," she said as she worked, "that I told him we shouldn't get involved in the Union, and that if we had to make another grab so soon it should be the Sierra instead."

"Tougher nut," John observed.

"True, but not one we had to swim to get to," she replied. "Frankly I think the navy flatters its chances when the balloon goes up. The Union thing could leave our tits in the wringer if things go wrong. This"—she nodded to the papers between snaps—"is exactly what the Santies *should* do, after all. But the Union was just too tempting, the political situation. I wish there were more women on the Chosen Council."

John looked up at the irrelevancy. The Chosen had equality of the sexes, but males did predominate slightly at the higher ranks.

"Men never can resist the chance to stick it in an inviting orifice," Gerta said, and finished her pictures. "Heinrich's as smart as a whip, for example, but he spends an unbelievable amount of time and effort improving the Union's genetic material. It's the same with politics. No patience."

"Do I detect a certain note of complaint?"

They both laughed. "Plenty left over," Gerta said. She rose and saluted. "Thanks, Johnnie . . . if it's genuine."

CHAPTER TWENTY

"It's like something out of th' Bible," Harry Smith blurted, looking down from where the car rested on a high track beside a customs station.

Belton Pass was the main overland route between the Union and the Republic of the Santander. The saddle was only seven thousand feet high, and hilly rather than mountainous; on either side the Border Range reared up to twenty thousand feet or better, capped by glaciers and eternal snow above the treeline. There were enigmatic Federation ruins on the slopes, built of substances no scientist could even identify, and tunnels where strange machines crouched like trolls in an ancient tale—some as pristine as the day they were last used, some crumbling like salt when exposed to air or sunlight. In the centuries after the Fall mule trains had used the pass, and border barons had built stone keeps whose tumbled stone had supplied material for shepherds huts in later years. Wars between the two countries had left their legacy of forts, the more recent sunken deep in the rock and covered in ferroconcrete and steel. There was a motorable road now, too, and a double-tracked railway built with immense labor and expense all the way from Alai in the western foothills.

Trains had been coming out of the Union for weeks now. The first had carried the last gold reserves of the Loyalist government, and the most precious records. Later ones had carried everything that could be salvaged from the factories of the Union's western provinces, some with the labor forces sitting on the machine tools. More and more carried people, shuttling back and forth with crowds riding packed so tightly that smothered bodies were unloaded at every stop, and the roofs of the freight cars black with refugees. Even more poured by cart and horse and ox-wagon, scores of thousands more on foot carrying their few possessions on their backs or in handcarts and wheelbarrows. They packed the lowlands in a moving mass of black and dun-brown, dust hanging over them like an eternal cloud. Only behind the Santander border posts with their tall flagpoles did they begin to fray out, as soldiers and volunteers directed them.

Pia Hosten leaned against her husband's long limousine, dark circles of fatigue under her eyes. She pulled off the kerchief that covered her hair and shuddered.

"It will be like a plague out of the Bible if we do not get more of the delousing stations set up. Typhus and cholera, those people are all half-starved and filthy and they have had no chance to wash in weeks."

"We'll do it," John said. "The government's sending in more troops to set up the camps and keep order, and we're shipping in food and medical supplies as fast as the roads and rail net will bear." He looked at his wife, and brushed back a strand of hair that fell down her forehead. "There would be thousands dead, if it weren't for your Auxiliaries," he said. "Nobody else was ready."

She turned and buried her face in his shoulder. "I feel as if I am trying to bail the ocean with a spoon," she said.

"You're exhausted. You've done an enormous job of work, and I'm proud of you."

"Dad!"

Maurice Farr came bounding up the slope, handsome young olive face alight, trim and slender in the sky-blue uniform of the Air Cadets.

"Dad—I mean, sir—Uncle Jeff, I mean General Farr, is coming. With General Gerard!" He stopped. "Mom, are you all right?"

She straightened. "Of course." Then she looked down at her plain dress, stained with sweat and her work. "My God, I can't—"

"It's not a diplomatic reception, darling," John said soothingly. "And I don't think Jeff or Pierre will care much about appearances. Not after what you've been doing."

The car that drew a trail of dust up the gravel road was much less elegant than John's, although it was the same big six-wheeled model. It had patched bullet holes in several places, a few fresh ones, and three whip antennae waving overhead. Rock crunched under the wheels as it drew to a stop and stood, the engine pinging and wheezing as metal cooled and contracted. The men who climbed down were ragged and smelled strongly of stale sweat, and there was dust caked in the stubble on their faces.

Pierre Gerard drew himself up, saluted, and held out his pistol butt-first. "As representative of the Union del Est—" he began.

John took the weapon and reversed it, handing it back to the Union general. *And head of state, don't forget that,* he reminded himself.

"General Gerard, as representative of the Republic of the Santander, it is my privilege to welcome you, your government, your armed forces and your people to our territory. I am instructed to assure you that you will all be welcome until the day when you can return to restore your country's independence, and in the interim the government and people of the Republic will extend every aid, and every courtesy, within their power."

He smiled and held out his hand. "That goes for me, too, of course, Pierre."

The other man took his hand in a strong dry grip for an instant. Then he clicked heels and bent over Pia's. "We've heard what you and your ladies have done for my people," he said quietly. "We are in your debt, forever."

"We're in your debt," John said. "You've been fighting the common enemy for five years. And you'll see more fighting before long, if I'm any judge of events."

Jeffrey Farr nodded. "Damned right."

Both men twisted sharply at the sound of aircraft engine. The planes coming up the valley from the west were Hawk III's, over a dozen of them. They relaxed.

"Most of the aircraft will be crossing further north," Gerard said. "All the troops that are going to make it out here will be across by tomorrow. Except for the rearguard."

John nodded with silent grimness. Those would have to fight where they were until overrun, to let the civilians and what was left of the Brigades and the Loyalist armies break contact and retreat over the border.

"The perimeter around Borreaux's holding for now," he said. "We've got ships shuttling continuously from there to Dubuk with refugees. Navy ships, too. My father created a precedent for that at Salini."

Gerard smiled wryly. "Wars are not won by evacuations, however heroic," he said.

John nodded. "I assume Jeffrey's filled you in on the deployments for your troops?"

"*Oui.* Rather far forward."

Jeffrey spread his hands in embarrassment. "If—when—the enemy attack, we'll need men who can be relied on not to break," he said. "The Brigades won't, and neither will your men."

Gerard nodded. "The civilians, though?"

"We're setting up temporary camps around Alai, Ensburg, and Dubuk," John said. "From there we'll try to move people where there's housing and jobs."

Gerard looked down on the mass of humanity filling the great pass below and the roads to the east. "We come as beggars, but we can fight, and work. Everyone but the children and cripples will. We have a debt to collect, from Libert and his *allies*." He spat the last word. "Does Libert know he's a puppet, yet?"

John shook his head. "There's an old saying," he replied. "If you owe the bank a thousand and can't pay, you're in trouble. If you owe a million and can't pay, the *bank* is in trouble. Libert and his army are saving the Chosen a great deal of trouble and expense, just by existing. I'm sure he'll use that leverage."

Jeffrey nodded. "I think that's why the pursuit hasn't been

pressed more vigorously," he said thoughtfully. "Libert *wants* us to get enough men over the border to be a standing menace. That means that the Chosen have to keep him on, or risk having the whole population go over to the Loyalist side who're waiting to return. They don't have enough troops in the Union to hold it down by themselves, not and keep an offensive capacity. Not yet, at least."

Gerard shrugged and saluted. "I must get back to my men."

John shook his head again. "Visit my home soon," he said. "You won't do your people any good by collapsing."

The shrewd brown eyes studied him. "You will not be there?" he said.

"No. There's . . . trouble brewing. Exactly what I can't say, but I can say that the board's going to be reshuffled thoroughly, and soon."

"Citizens!"

The sixth of the twelve-man Executive Council of the Sierra Democratica y Populara stood to address the seven hundred members of the Board of Cantonal Delegates. One of his colleagues passed him a ceremonial spear, the mark of the speaker, and pushed the button on top of a very modern timer clock.

I do not believe this, Gerta Hosten thought to herself. She and the Land delegation were sitting in the visitors' seats to one side of the Executive Council. An extremely ancient oak in the middle of the beaten dirt of the circle hid many of the delegates from her, and from each other. This was where the first representatives of the people-in-arms had met four hundred years ago to proclaim the Sierra, probably under the parent of this very tree, and so here they *still* met, where the city of Nueva Madrid had grown up. And met, and met, and met; the speeches had been going on for a week and looked good for another two.

Every one of them carried a rifle and wore a bandolier. That was about the only uniformity. Dress ranged from fringed leather to Santander-style business suits, with a predominance of berets and ferocious waxed mustaches. There were no women, since females didn't have the vote in any of the Sierran cantons, although they weren't badly treated otherwise.

Every adult male *did* have the vote, and every delegate here could be recalled at any time by the cantonal voters meeting in open assembly. Any hundred men could call an assembly. The delegates chose the twelve-man executive, but the voters could recall them at any time, and often did.

I do not believe anything this absurd has survived this long, she thought. Whenever I think our councils are cumbersome, I should remind myself of this.

The speaker shouted in an untrained bellow, with a strong up-country peasant accent to his Ispanyol: "Citizens! For four hundred years, no enemy has gotten anything but disaster from attacking us. We drove out the Imperials!"

Well, that's no particular accomplishment, she thought. Then: To be fair, that was when the Empire was a real power. They drove us into the ocean back then.

"We drove out the Union! We threw the Errife back into the sea when their ships ranged every coast! We made the Republic withdraw from our island of Trois! In the Sierra, every one of us is a fighting man, every one!"

Funny, in most places half the population are women, Gerta thought as the delegates cheered wildly.

"So let the cunt-whipped Chosen perverts fuck themselves!" The speaker's mountain-peasant accent grew thicker. "Let the dirty money-grubbing Santanders fuck themselves! The Sierra pisses on all of them!"

Eventually the timer rang, loud and insistent. The president pro tem of the Executive Council—each member held the office in rotation for a week—cleared his throat as he took back the spear.

"We must, in courtesy, listen to the arguments of the honorable Thomas Beemer, Ambassador Plenipotentiary to the Sierra from the Republic of the Santander."

Assistant head of the Research Department of the Foreign Ministry, Gerta reminded herself. That made him the equivalent of the second-in-command of the Fourth Bureau back home, although the Research Department didn't have the internal security functions the Fourth Bureau did. A very high-powered spook. A rabbity-looking little man, bald and peering out through thick glasses. Important not to underestimate him because of that.

"Honorable delegates," Beemer said. "The Chosen took the Empire fifteen years ago. Over the last five they have conquered the Union. Only you Sierrans and we in the Republic remain independent.

"The Republic does not intend to let the Chosen eat the world, not all in one gulp or one nibble at a time. I am here to announce that from this midnight, the Republic of the Santander declares a total naval blockade of the Union. This blockade will be maintained until all foreign troops are withdrawn and a legitimate government chosen by free elections under Santander supervision. The Republic will regard it as a grave breach of friendly relations if the Democratic and Popular Sierra allows overland transit to evade this blockade."

Johnny was telling the truth, Gerta thought, still mildly surprised. First a blockade, and then the seizure of the Sierra in cooperation with pro-Santander and anti-Chosen factions among the cantons. Those slightly outnumbered the neutralists, which wasn't surprising considering the position the Sierra found itself in. Nobody here was actually pro-Chosen, of course. That would be like expecting a pig to be pro-leopard.

This time the roar went on for twenty minutes. Delegates milled, shouted into each others faces, shook their fists or used them and were clubbed down by their neighbors. Occasionally someone would fire his rifle, into the air, thankfully, although the bullet had to come down *somewhere.* The Chosen embassy sat in stolid silence, upright and expressionless, their round uniform caps resting on their knees. When the noise eventually died down, Ebert Meitzerhagen stood, walked forward three precise steps and stood at parade rest.

He was a vivid contrast to Beemer, one reason he'd been chosen for the role. His cropped pale hair and light eyes stood out the more vividly for the deep mahogany tan of his skin; his face and bull-neck were seamed with scar tissue, and the massive shoulders strained at his uniform jacket. The great hands dangling at his sides were equally worn and battered, huge spatulate things that looked capable of ripping apart oxen without bothering with tools. All in all, he looked to be exactly what he was: a brutal, methodical, merciless killer. The Sierrans wouldn't necessarily be intimidated, but they weren't fools enough to believe all their own bombast, either.

"Sierrans," Meitzerhagen said. "We wish no war with you. We have no territorial demands on you."

Yet, Gerta thought. General Meitzerhagen was being truthful enough: the Chosen Council wanted a decade of peace now. If they could get it on their own terms, which did *not* include giving up the fruits of victory in the Union.

"If you join with Santander in attacking us and our allies, do not expect us to meekly endure it. When someone strikes us a blow, we do not just strike back—we crush them."

He held out a hand palm up and slowly closed it into a fist, letting the delegates look at the knuckles, scarred and enlarged.

Gerta called up a mental map of the Sierra. Mountains north and south, high ones—too high for dirigibles, except in a few passes, and they'd have to come uncomfortably close to the ground even there. A spine of lower mountains down the center, joining the two transverse ranges and separating two wedges of fertile lowland on the west and east coasts. The eastern wedge was drained by the Rio Arena, from here at Nueva Madrid to Barclon at the rivers mouth. The Arena valley was the heartland of the Sierra, where most of the agriculture and population and trade lay, although the national mythology centered on the shepherds and hill farmers of the mountain forests.

This is going to be very tricky, she thought. *And we don't have much time.*

Fortunately, good staff work was a Chosen specialty.

Admiral Maurice Farr tapped the end of the polished oak pointer he'd been using on the map into his free hand. "Gentlemen, that concludes the briefing. The blockade begins as of midnight tonight." He looked out over the assembled captains of the Northern Fleet. "Any questions?"

"Admiral Farr." Commodore Jenkins, commander of the Scout Squadron of torpedo-boat destroyers spoke. A thickset, capable-looking man, missing one ear from a skirmish in the Southern Islands. "Could you clarify the rules of engagement?"

"Certainly, Commodore. No ships, except Unionaise fishing vessels, are to be allowed within four miles of any of the Union ports on the list, or to within five miles of the coast, or to offload or load any cargo. You will issue warnings; if the warning is ignored you will fire over the vessel's bow. If the warning shot is disregarded, you may either board or sink the vessel in question at your discretion."

"And if the violator is a warship?"

"You will proceed as I have outlined."

There was a slight rustle among the blue-uniformed men in the flagship's conference room.

"Yes, gentlemen, I am aware that this may very well mean war. So is the Premier."

And not a moment too soon, if there's going to be a war, he thought. The Republic's lead in capital ships was shrinking, as the Chosen finally got their building program under way. At a fairly leisurely pace, since they'd been planning on war a decade hence, but they had some first-rate designs on their drawing boards. One in particular had struck his eye, a huge all-big-gun ship with twelve twelve-inch rifles in four superimposed triple turrets fore and aft of the central island, and a daunting turn of speed. If it worked the way John's intelligence report said it would, nothing else on Visager's oceans could go near it and live. Fortunately, they hadn't even laid down the keel, and this conflict would be fought with existing fleets.

Santander's fleet was as ready as he could make it. That left only the personal question. *Am I too old?* Fleet command in wartime needed a man who could make quick decisions under fatigue and stress. Maurice Farr was within a year of the mandatory retirement age. Should he be at a desk in Charsson, or at home working on the book? *I'm a grandfather with teenage grandchildren.* He took stock of himself. He'd kept himself in trim, and he didn't need to shovel coal or heave propellant charges into a breech. No failure of memory and will that he could detect. *No. I can do it.* He spoke again, into the hush his words had made.

"You will accordingly keep your ships on full alert at all times, with steam raised and ready to weigh anchor at one hour's notice. All leaves are cancelled, and naval and other reservists have been notified to report to their duty stations."

Jenkins nodded. "If I may, Admiral, how are we going to maintain a blocking squadron along the Union's south coast? Bassin du Sud and Marsai are the only good harbors or fully equipped ports between Fursten and Sircusa."

"The Southern Fleet"—a grand name for a collection of candidates for the knackers yard and armed civilian vessels, with only two modern cruisers—"will blockade Bassin du Sud and Marsai. At need, they can be reinforced from the Northern Fleet. Any more questions? No?"

Mess stewards entered, with trays of the traditional watered rum, one for each of the officers. The toast offered by the senior officer present was equally a matter of tradition.

"Gentlemen—the Republic and Liberty!"

"The Republic!"

CHAPTER TWENTY-ONE

"Dammit!"

Commodore Peter Grisson raised his binoculars again. The dawn light was painting the Chosen dirigible an attractive pink, a tiny toy airship at the limit of visibility to the north. Far out of range of anything the ships below it could do. They all had the new high-angle antiaircraft guns, but the distance was far too great.

I hate that bloody thing, he thought, wishing for a storm. You could get some monsters down here south of the main continent, with nothing but the islands between here and the antarctic ice and nothing at all all the way around the planet east or west to break the winds. His ships, some of them at least, could keep station better than that floating gasbag.

But the ocean was like a millpond, only a trace of white at the tops of the long dark blue waves. The *McCormick City* and the *Randall* steamed on, heading east-northeast for their blockade stations off the southern Union coast. They were making eight knots, well below their best cruising speed, because most of the gunboats and naval reserve yachts and whatnot around them couldn't do any better. Certainly the pathetic hermaphrodite—wood-hulled and iron-armored—relics that made up the other six cruisers couldn't. Neither of his two best ships were new, but at least they were steel-hulled and armored, and they'd both had extensive refits recently, virtual rebuilding.

Then a light began to flicker on the nose of the Land dirigible. Grisson smoothed his mustache with a nervous gesture. *What would Uncle Maurice do?* he thought, and looked at the captain of the *McCormick City.*

The captain lowered his own binoculars. "Coded, of course," he said neutrally.

"Of course. But Land scout dirigibles carry wireless." The Land's armed forces didn't make as much use of that on land as the Republic's did, but they had plenty for sea service. "So whoever he's signaling is *close.*"

Grisson thought for a moment. The rules of engagement and his own orders from the Admiralty gave him virtually complete discretion. One thing Uncle Maurice wouldn't do was sit with his thumb up his ass waiting for things to happen to him.

I can't run, he knew. Intelligence on the Land naval forces in the area and their Unionaise allies was scanty, but whatever they had was likely to have the legs on his motley squadron. *Therefore . . .*

"Squadron to come about," he said, giving the new heading. "Signal *battle stations* and sound *general quarters.* My compliments to Commander Huskinson, and the torpedo-boat destroyers are to deploy. Tell him I have full confidence in his ships' scouting ability. No ship is to fire unless fired upon or on my order."

Bells rang, signal guns fired, yeomen hoisted signals to the tripod mast of the *McCormick City.* "Oh, and general signal: *The Republic expects every man to do his duty.*"

Armored panels winched up across the horseshoe shape of the fighting bridge, leaving slits for viewing all around. A signals yeoman bent over his pad near the wireless station, decoding a message.

"Sir. From the destroyers."

Grisson took the yellow flimsy.

Am under attack by Land heavier-than-air twin engine models stop more than a dozen stop smoke plumes detected to northeast eight ships minimum approaching fast stop.

For a moment Grisson's mind gibbered at him. The distance to shore was more than twice the maximum range of any Land-made airplane. *Stop that,* he told himself. *It's happening. Deal with it.*

"Signal: Wait for me stop am proceeding your position best speed stop."

The key of the wireless clicked as the operator rattled it off. Eyes were fixed on him from all over the bridge; he could taste salt sweat on his upper lip. He'd known this moment had to come all his professional life—ever since he was a snot-nosed teenage ensign on this very ship, when Maurice Farr faced down the Chosen at Salini and saved fifty thousand lives. *I expected this, but not so soon.*

"Signal to the fleet. Maximum speed." All of ten knots, if they were to keep together. "Add: We are at war. Expect hostile aircraft before we engage enemy surface forces. Plan alpha. Acknowledge. Stop. Repeat signal until all units have acknowledged receipt."

Some of the reservists would probably be a little slow on signals, and he didn't want anyone haring off on his own.

There was a collective sigh, half of relief. "Yeoman," he went on to the wireless operator, "do you have contact with Karlton?"

"Yessir."

"Then send: Commodore Grisson to Naval HQ. Southern Fleet in contact with Land and Libertist-Unionaise naval forces. Have received unprovoked attack in international waters. Am engaging enemy. Enemy twin engine heavier-than-air attack aircraft sighted at distances exceeding two hundred nautical miles from shore. Long live the Republic. Grisson, Commander, Southern Fleet. Stop. Repeat until you have acknowledgment."

"Yessir."

The rhythm of the engines hammered more swiftly under his feet. The black gang would probably be cursing his name. *Insubordinate bastards,* Grisson thought, the irrelevancy breaking through the tension that gripped his gut. It'd be a relief when the fleet all finally converted to oil-firing and turbine engines. A few score stokers could contribute more disciplinary offenses and Captain's Mast hearings than the entire crew of a battlewagon.

Neither side was going to have heavy ships here . . . at least, that was what the reports said. The Chosen had a complete squadron of modern protected cruisers in Bassin du Sud: six ships, *von Spee*-class, the name ship and five consorts. Seventy-five hundred tons, turbine engines—coal-fired though, the Land was short of petroleum—four eight-inch guns in twin turrets fore and aft, each with a triple six-inch turret behind it superimposed on a pedestal mount. They carried pom-poms and quick-firers as well, of course. There would be a squadron of twelve torpedo-boat destroyers as well, and the cruisers carried torpedo tubes, too. Land torpedoes were excellent.

"Captain," he said. "All right; we're going to be at a disadvantage in weight of gun metal and torpedoes both, but less so in gunpower. We'll try to maintain optimum firing distance with the heavier ships and slug it out, while the lighter craft with torpedo capacity close in. Gunboats and others are to engage their destroyers."

"What about our destroyers, sir?"

"I'm going to send them in at the cruisers. They're outnumbered by their equivalents; we'll just have to hope one of them gets lucky. A couple of hits could decide the action, one way or another."

And thank God the practice ammunition allowance was raised last year. Somebody at Navy HQ had insisted on not putting *all* the increased appropriation into new building.

The *McCormick City* began to pitch more heavily as the northward turn put the sea on her beam. In less than fifteen minutes he could see the smoke from his quartet of three-stacker destroyers, and beyond them a gray-black smudge that must be the enemy. Black dots were circling in the sky over the destroyers, stooping and diving in turn. The little scout ships were curving and twisting to avoid them, their wakes drawing circles of white froth against the dark blue of the ocean. Their pompoms and high-elevation quick-firers were probing skyward, scattering puffs of black smoke against the cerulean blue of the sky.

"Signal to the destroyers," Grisson said. "Ignore those planes and go for the cruisers."

Aircraft couldn't carry enough bombs to be really dangerous, and their chance of hitting a moving target wasn't big enough to be worth worrying about.

The Land cruisers were hull-up now, their own screen of

turtleback destroyers lunging ahead. The smaller Santander craft swarmed forward, disorderly but as willing as a terrier facing a mastiff.

"The signal," Grisson said quietly, "is *fire as you bear.*"

If you only knew how I begged and pleaded to save your sorry ass, Gerta thought, smiling at the dictator of the Union.

At least General Libert had learned to ignore her gender—she suspected he thought of Chosen as belonging to a different species, in any event. He was being polite, today, here in Unionvil. No reason not to; he'd achieved his objectives.

"In short, the Council of the Land expects me to declare war on Santander," he said dryly. "What incentives do you offer?"

Not shooting you and taking this place over directly, Gerta thought. I used every debt and favor owed me to help convince the General Staff that it wasn't cost-effective. Don't prove me wrong.

"General Libert, if you *don't*, and we lose this war, the Santies have a certain General Gerard waiting in the wings to replace you. With his army, now deployed along the Santander-Union frontier. I very much doubt that the Republic is going to distinguish you from us in *its* formal declaration of war, which should get through the House of Assembly any hour now."

Libert nodded. He looked an insignificant little lump against the splendors of carved and gilded wood in the presidential palace, beneath the high ceilings painted in allegorical frescos. The place had the air of a church, the more so since Libert had had endless processions of thanksgiving going through with incense and swarming priests; most of his popular support came from the more devout areas of the Union.

His eyes were cold and infinitely shrewd. "And if you *win*, Brigadier, what bargaining power or leverage do I retain?"

"You have your army," Gerta pointed out. "Expensively equipped and armed by us."

Libert stayed silent.

"And you'll have additional territory. I am authorized to offer you the entire area formerly known as the Sierra Democratica y

Populara. Provided you assist to the limit of your powers in its pacification, and subject to rights of military transit, mining concessions, investment, and naval bases during and after the war. We get Santander. It's a fair exchange, considering the relative degrees of military effort."

Libert's eyebrows rose. "You offer to turn over a territory you will have conquered yourselves? Generous."

"Quid pro quo," Gerta said. *Now, the question is, does Libert realize that we'd turn on him as soon as the Santies are disposed of?* He was more than realistic enough, but he might not understand the absoluteness of Chosen ambition.

Libert sipped from the glass of water before him. "The Sierrans have a reputation for . . . stubbornness," he said. "I have studied the histories of the old Union-Sierran wars. This may be comparable to the gift of a honeycomb, without first removing the bees and their stings."

"We intend to smoke out the bees," Gerta said. "Or to put it less poetically, we intend to depopulate the Sierra, with your assistance. Your people aren't fond of the Sierrans"—that was an understatement, if she'd ever made one—"and after the war, you can colonize with your own subjects. There will be land grants for your soldiers, estates for your officers, a virgin field for your business supporters—including intact factories, mines and buildings. We'll leave enough Sierrans for the labor camps."

"Ah." Libert's face was expressionless. "But in the meantime, the Union would need considerable support in order to undertake a foreign war so soon after our civil conflict."

"Could you be more specific?" Gerta said wearily.

"As a matter of fact, Brigadier . . ."

He slid a folder across the table to her, frictionless on the polished mahogany. She opened it and fought not to choke. Oil, wheat, beef, steel, chemicals, machine tools, trucks, weapons— including tanks and aircraft.

"I'm . . ." Gerta ground her teeth and fought to keep her voice normal. "I'm sure something can be arranged. But as you must appreciate, General, we need to strike *now*."

"That would indeed be the optimum military course," Libert said. *And so you must give me what I ask, or risk unacceptable delay,* followed unspoken.

"I will consult with my superiors," she said. "We must, however, have a definite answer by dawn."

Or we'll kill you and take this place over ourselves, equally unspoken and equally well understood.

Gerta rose, saluted, and walked out.

"Why do we tolerate this animal's insolence?" young Johan Hosten hissed to her as their boot heels echoed in step through the rococo elegance of the palace's halls.

"Because with Libert cooperating, we gain an additional two hundred thousand troops," she said. "Most of them are fit only for line-of-communication work, but that's still nine divisional equivalents we *don't* have to detach for garrison work. Plus another hundred thousand that we *don't* have to use to hold down the Union in our rear while we fight the Santies."

Her aide subsided into disciplined silence—disciplined, but sullen.

I'm going to enjoy our final reckoning with Libert myself, she thought. Aloud: "I'd rather have three teeth drilled than go through another negotiating session with him, that's true," she said.

"Sir . . ."

Gerta looked aside. "Speak. You can't learn if you don't ask."

"Sir, you were against opening our war with Santander this early. Have you changed your mind?"

"That's irrelevant," she said. "We're committed now. Conquer or die." She sighed. "At least my next job is a straightforward combat assignment."

Air assault was no longer a radical new idea. Most of the troops filing into the dirigibles nestled in the landing cradles of the base were ordinary Protégé infantry, moving with stolid patience in the cool predawn air. A few of the most important targets still rated a visit from the General Staff Commando, and she'd ended up on overall command. Gerta looked around at the faces of the officers; they seemed obscenely young. No younger than she'd been at Corona, mostly.

It's déjà vu all over again, she thought to herself.

"That concludes the briefing. Are there any questions?"

"Sir, no sir!" they chorused.

Confident. That was good, as long as you didn't overdo it. Most of them had more experience than she'd had, her first trip to see the elephant. Policy had been to rotate officers through the war in the Union, as many as possible without doing too much damage to unit cohesion.

"One final thing. The Sierrans have much the same line of bluster that the animals did here, before we conquered the Empire. They have a word for it in their language . . . *machismo,* I think it is. There's one crucial difference between the two, though."

She looked around, meeting their eyes. "The Sierrans actually *mean* it. They couldn't organize an orgy in a whorehouse, but they're not going to roll over at the first tap of the whip either. Don't fuck up because you expect them to run."

"Sir, yes Sir!"

As they scattered to their units she wondered briefly if they'd take the warning seriously. Probably. Most of them had enough experience not to take the legends about Chosen invincibility too literally.

"All over again," she murmured aloud.

"Sir?" her aide said.

Fairly formal considering that they were alone and that Johan Hosten was her eldest son, but they were in a military situation, not a social one. And Johan was still stiffly conscious of being an adult, just past the Test of Life. She remembered that feeling, too.

"It reminds me of the drop on Corona," she said.

Half my lifetime ago. Why do I get this feeling that I keep doing the same things over and over again, only every time it's more difficult and the results are less? All the same, down to the smell of burnt diesel oil. The tension was worse; now she knew what they were heading into. She buckled on her helmet, slung the machine-carbine and began drawing on thin, black leather gloves as they walked through the loading zone. Wood boomed under their boots as they climbed the mobile ramp to a side-door of the gondola built into the hull beneath the great gasbags. Crew dodged around them as she walked back to the main cargo bay; Horst Raske wasn't in charge this time, he was with the new aircraft carrier working-up with the Home Fleet based out of Oathtaking.

What a ratfuck, she thought. *The Santies build aircraft carriers, and we waste six months in a pissing match over who gets to build ours.* The Councils had finally decided, in truly Solomonic wisdom—she'd read the Christian Bible as part of her Intelligence training—to split the whole operation. Building the hull was to be Navy; the airplanes and the personnel, plus logistics, training and operations, were done by the Air Council. The Navy would command when the fleet was at sea. *How truly good that's going to be for operational efficiency,* she thought. At least she'd managed to persuade Father to appoint Raske, who didn't confuse territorial spats and service loyalties with duty to the Chosen.

There were a company of the General Staff Commando in the cargo bay, plus a light armored car on a padded cradle that rested on a specially strengthened section of hull. It was one of the new internal-combustion models, and someone had the starter's crank ready in its socket at the front, below the slotted louvers of the armored radiator. Somehow it looked out of place in the hold of an airship, a brutal block of steel in a craft at once massive and gossamer-fragile. They were tasked with taking out the Sierran central command, such as it was. Although she frankly doubted whether that would help or hinder the resistance.

"Make safe," she said. "Lift in five minutes."

They squatted, resting by the packsacks and gripping brackets in the walls and floor. Gerta's station was by an emergency exit; that gave her a view out a narrow slit window. Booming and popping sounds came from above, as hot air from the engine exhausts was vented into the ballonets in the gasbags. More rumbling from below as water poured out of the ballast tanks. The long teardrop shape of the airship quivered and shook, then bounced upwards as the grapnels in the loading cradles released.

The dirigibles were out in force this time; she could see them rising in ordered flocks, one after another turning and rising into the lighter upper sky. The air was calm, giving the airship the motion of a boat on millpond-still water, no more than a slight heeling as it circled for altitude. Down below the airbase was a pattern of harsh arc lights across the flat coastal plain on the Gut's northern shore. The surface fleet with the main army wasn't in sight. They'd left port nearly a day before, to synchronize the attacks. There were biplane fighters and twin-engine support aircraft escorting the airships; as she peered through the small square window in the side of the hull she could see a flight of them dropping back to refuel from the tankers at the rear of the fleet.

You put on a safety line and climbed out on the upper wing with the wind trying to pitch you off—sometimes you did, and had to haul yourself back on. In a single-seater, someone from the airship had to slide on a body-hoop down the flexing, whipping hose. Then you had to fasten the valves, dog them tight, and keep the tiny airplane and huge airship at precisely matching speeds, because if you didn't the hose broke, or the valve tore out of the wing by the roots. If that happened the entire aircraft was likely to be drenched in half-vaporized gasoline and turn into an exploding fireball when it hit the red-hot metal surfaces of the engine. . . .

She raised her voice: "Listen up!

They were over the surface fleet now; hundreds of transports from ports all along the northern shore of the Gut, escorted by squadrons of cruisers and destroyers. The ships cut white arrowheads on the green-blue water six thousand feet below.

"Magnificent," Johan Hosten whispered.

This time Gerta nodded. It *was* a magnificent accomplishment, throwing a hundred thousand troops and supporting arms into action, fully equipped and briefed, at such short notice.

But we were supposed to fight Santander in another five to eight years. With our new battleship fleet ready, and another fifty divisions and a thousand tanks. Now . . . we're reacting, not initiating. The enemy should be responding to our moves, not us to theirs.

"Thirty minutes to drop!"

(••) (••) (••)

"This is a new one," Jeffrey shouted over the explosions.

"Too damned familiar, if you ask me," John said grimly, checking his rifle.

It was a Sierran-made copy of the Chosen weapon. They'd managed a few improvements, mostly because everything was expensively machined. No cost-cutting use of stampings *here,* by God—which meant that only about half of the Sierrans had them. The rest were making do with a tube-magazine black-powder weapon, also a fine example of its type.

"I've been caught in far too many goddamned Land invasions."

"Yes, but it's the first time we've been in one *together,*" Jeffrey pointed out. There was gray in his rust-colored hair, but the grin took years off him.

"Let's go make ourselves useful."

"Yup. No hiding in embassies this time." Jeffrey sobered. "Damned bad news about Grisson. He was a good man; Dad thought a lot of him."

"Going to be a lot of good men die before this one's over," John said.

"Hopefully not us. . . . Watch it!"

The room shook from a near-miss. Dust and bits of plaster fell around them. The Santander embassy was in coastal Barclon, where most of the business was done, rather than in inland Nueva Madrid, the ceremonial capital. Right now that meant it was within range of the eight-inch guns of the offshore Land cruisers, as well as the aircraft. The Sierran antiaircraft militia was putting a lot of metal into the air; too much for dirigibles to sail calmly overhead and drop their enormous bombloads, which was something to be thankful for.

An embassy staffer ran down the stairs. Her face was paler than the plaster dust that spattered her face and dress, and she waved a notepad.

"They're dropping troops on Nueva Madrid," she said, her voice rising a little. "And they're attacking from north and south over the mountains, too. Sanlucar has fallen—the last message said shells were bursting inside the fortress."

John's eyebrows went up. That was the main fortress-city guarding the passes from the old Empire south into the Sierra.

The staffer went on: "And the Chosen Council has issued a statement, demanding that we declare ourselves strictly neutral in the Sierran-Land war, and 'cease all hostile and unfriendly actions.'"

Ambassador Beemer nodded, checking the old-fashioned revolver in the shoulder holster beneath his formal morning coat.

"Not a chance," he said. He looked up at John and Jeffrey. "Admiral Farr is never going to forgive me. I should have sent you home yesterday."

"We both thought the Chosen would wait until the Sierrans voted," John said.

"Why? It was obvious which way it was going to go." He hesitated. "They'll be landing troops here?"

"Sure as they grow corn in Pokips," Jeffrey said. "Coordination is a strong point of theirs. In fact, I'd give you odds they're landing on both sides of the city right now."

Nobody was going to fall for the "merchantmen" full of soldiers, not after the attack on Corona. There wasn't any way to prevent ships loitering offshore, though.

"Then I suppose . . . well, according to diplomatic practice, the Chosen should intern us and exchange us for their own embassy personnel in Santander City."

Beemer didn't sound very confident. John nodded. "Sir, I'd recommend suicide before falling into Chosen hands—and that's assuming you get past the kill-crazy Protégés in the first wave. If the Chosen win, international law won't exist anymore, because there will be only one nation. And if they lose, they don't expect to be around to take the blame."

Beemer's head turned, as if calculating their chances. North and south the armies of the Land were pouring over the mountain passes into the Sierra. West was the Chosen . . .

"Sir, I made arrangements, just in case. If we can get to the docks . . ."

Beemer started to object, then nodded. "You're a resourceful young man," he said mildly. "I'll get our people together."

Luckily there were only about half a dozen Santander citizen staff on hand; most of them had been sent home last week, when the crisis began. None of the Sierran employees were here; they'd all headed for their militia stations and the fighting half an hour ago. Two of the embassy limousines could hold them all, with a little crowding. John took his seat beside Harry Smith, sitting up on one knee with the rifle ready.

"Just like old times, eh?" he said.

Smith grinned tautly. "Barrjen is going to be mad as hell," he said. "I talked him into staying home for this one."

Another salvo of heavy shells went by overhead just as the limousines cleared the gates of the embassy compound. They struck upslope, and blast and debris rattled off the thin metal of the cars' roofs. John had a panoramic view of Barclon burning, pillars of familiar greasy black smoke rising into the air. He could also see the Land naval gunline out in the harbor, cruising slowly along the riverside town. There weren't any battleships, but there *were* a couple of extremely odd-looking ships, more like huge armored barges than conventional warships. Each had a barbette with a raised edge in the center and the stubby muzzle of a heavy fortress howitzer protruding from it.

Well, I guess that explains what happened to the harbor forts, John thought. Coastal forts were designed to shoot it out with high-velocity naval rifles, weapons with flat trajectories. They'd be extremely vulnerable to plunging fire. *We'd better move fast.*

estimated time to chosen landing in barclon itself is less than thirty minutes, Center said.

Land aircraft were circling the city, spotting for the naval guns. John looked up at them with a silent snarl of hatred.

I'd have sworn that dirigible aircraft carrier idea was completely worthless, he thought.

It was, lad, Raj said quietly. ***At a guess, I'd say they retreated to something less ambitious—using the dirigibles to carry fuel and arranging some sort of midair hookup.***

correct. probability approaches unity.

The streets were surprisingly free of crowds; what there were seemed to be moving to some purpose: armed men heading for the docks or the suburbs to the south, women with first-aid armbands or the civil-defense blue dot. Smith kept his foot on the throttle and made good use of the air horn. More barges were appearing from behind the Land fleet, coastal craft hastily converted to military use. They were black with men. Behind them lighter ships, gunboats and destroyers, moved in to give point-blank support to the landing parties with their quick-firers and pom-poms.

"Here!" John shouted.

The limousines lurched to a stop and the Santander citizens tumbled out, white-faced but moving quickly. Jeffrey and Henri brought up the rear; John stopped to drop grenades down the fuel tanks of both. Their pins were pulled, but the spoons were wrapped in tape. John hoped some Land patrol was using the cars by the time the gasoline dissolved the adhesive tape.

They had stopped in front of a boathouse in the fishing section of the port, a typical long shed with doors opening onto the water where a boat could be hauled out on rollers. This one was more substantial than most but just as rundown.

"Do you think a boat can make it out past the Land Navy?" Beemer asked dubiously.

John unlocked the doors. "No, I don't, sir," he said. "Therefore—"

Even with the sound of the bombardment in their ears, a few of the embassy staff paused to gawk. Within the dim barnlike space of the shed was a large biplane; each lower wing bore two engines back to back, with props at the leading and trailing edge. The body of the craft was a smooth oval of stressed plywood, broken by circular windows; the cockpit was separate, with only a windscreen ahead of it. Two air-cooled machine guns were mounted on a scarf ring in the center of the fuselage, where the upper wing merged with it. Bearing the planes weight were two long floats, like decked-over canoes.

"Fueled and ready to go," John said. "Prototype—the navy's ordering a dozen. Jeff! Get some hands on the props!"

Bright sunlight made him blink as the big sliding doors were thrown back. The body of the airplane began to quiver as men spun the props and the engines coughed into life in puffs of blue smoke. He looked back into the body of the aircraft; Jeff's Unionaise bodyguard was stepping up into the firing rest beneath the machine guns. His foster-brother slid into the other seat in front of the controls, while Smith showed frightened embassy staff how to snap their seatbelts shut as they took their places along either side of the big biplane.

"Good thinking," Jeffrey said.

"I like gadgets," John said. He looked ahead. "I didn't think the Chosen could get aircraft here to support a landing, though."

"Neither did I." He ran his hands over the controls. "Shall I?"

"You're the expert, Jeff."

Jeffrey Farr had run up quite a score in the aerial fighting over the Union. It was partly innate talent, but also because Center could put an absolutely accurate gunsight in front of his eyes, one that effortlessly calculated the complex ballistics of firing from one fast-moving plane and hitting an equally elusive target.

The engines bellowed, and the biplane wallowed out onto the surface of Barclon's harbor. The sun was behind them, still low in the east, but the wind was coming directly down the Gut; the corsairs' wind, they'd called it in the old days. Right now it meant charging straight into the line of muzzle flashes from the heavy guns of the Land fleet. One landed not three hundred yards away; the undershot produced a momentary tower of white water and black mud, and a wave that rocked the seaplane on its floats.

"Time's a-wasting," Jeffrey said, and opened the throttles.

The line of gray-painted warships grew with terrifying speed, closer and closer. *Nice spacing,* Jeffrey thought absently. *Dad would approve.* It wasn't easy to get warships moving so precisely and keeping such good station in the midst of action. He supposed this *was* action, although he couldn't see much in the way of shooting back—just an occasional burst from a field-gun shell, militia firing from the harbor mouth streets.

The floatplane skipped across the slight harbor swell, throwing roostertails of spray from the prows of the floats. It was odd and a little unsettling to taxi in a plane that was horizontal and not down at the rear where the tail wheel rested. The craft felt a little sluggish;

probably loaded to capacity with all these people, and the fuel tanks were full, too. But it *was* feeling lighter, the salt spray on his lips less as the floats began to flick across the surface of the waves rather than resting fully in the water. The controls bucked a little in his hands, and he drew back on the yoke.

Bounce. Bounce. Bounce, and *up*. He climbed slowly, not trying to avoid the Chosen ships. *Let 'em think we're one of theirs.* There certainly weren't any Sierran aircraft in the air today. For that matter there hadn't been more than a couple of dozen of them to begin with, and he'd bet the Chosen had taken them all out in the first few minutes of the strike, somehow. Infiltrated a strike commando days ago and activated them at a predetermined time, at a guess.

correct. probability 87%, ±5.

The sheer numbers of ships behind the gunline was stunning, and their upperworks were all gray-black with troops.

"Must be a hundred thousand of them," he said. "That's a big gamble; over fifteen percent of their total strength."

John had worries more immediate than strategy. "Fighter coming down to look us over," he shouted back over the thundering roar of the airsteam.

The biplane swooping towards them had the rounded cowling of a von Nelsing, but the wings looked a little different, plywood covered and with teardrop-section struts instead of the old bracing wires and angle-iron.

"How fast is this thing?" he asked.

one hundred fourteen miles an hour in level flight at three thousand feet, Center said. **the latest mark of von nelsing pursuit plane has a maximum speed of one hundred forty miles an hour.**

"Thank you so much," Jeffrey said.

No chance of outrunning it. He looked down; they were over the tail end of the Chosen fleet, the last straggle of commandeered trawlers rigged for minesweeping or laying, and a screen of four-stacker destroyers. Ahead he could just make out a line of dirigibles, keeping watch up the Gut. Another thirty miles or so and he'd be in sight of the Isle of Trois, the big island that filled most of the eastern end of the narrow sea.

"How long do you think it'll take—"

"For the pilot to twig that we aren't Land Air Service?" John said. "About three minutes."

Land pilots were all Chosen, trained to use their initiative. Not much doubt about what this one would chose to do.

"You tell Henri," Jeffrey said. "We'd better be quick about this."

He pushed the stick forward, putting the big plane on a downward slope. Its weight made it faster thus, and reducing the dimensions the nimble enemy fighter could use also improved the situation. The higher buzz of the von Nelsing's engine grew stronger. He could almost hear the *chick-chack* sound as the pilot armed the twin machine guns in the nose.

The water came closer, until he could see the thick white lines along the tops of the waves, running west to east as they almost always did in the Gut this time of year. The wind was more variable here, gusting and falling away. His hands were busy on stick and rudder pedals, keeping the big aircraft level. In the rearview mirror the machine-gun position was empty, with the guns pointing backward as if locked in their rest positions.

John came back. "He's ready," he said. Reaching down the side of the cockpit, he came up with a pump-action shotgun and held it across his lap. "Whenever you signal."

Jeffrey wished he could spit to clear the gummy texture out of his mouth. This was like trying to fight while stuck neck-deep down a whale's blowhole. The fighter crept up from behind them, a hundred feet or so above. He could see the goggled face craning and bending to get a glimpse of them, and waved cheerfully up at him. *Or her.* Who knew, that might even be Gerta Hosten. . . .

probability 3%, ±1, Center said.

Shut up.

The aircraft grew closer. The Chosen pilot waggled his wings and pointed backward with an exaggerated gesture; he was getting impatient. So—

"Now!"

He banked the plane sideways, towards the enemy. The Chosen pilot acted the way pilots did, on instinct, pulling up sharply for height. Henri erupted out of the open gun mount, slamming the guns up to their maximum ninety degrees. For a moment the bigger biplane seemed joined to the fighter above it by twin bars of tracer, then the von Nelsing staggered in the air and peeled away trailing smoke. John stood in the open cockpit, shielding his eyes with one hand and grabbing at the edge of the cowling to brace the blocky strength of his upper torso against the savage pull of the slipstream.

"Pilot's dead or unconscious," he said aloud as he dropped back. Seconds later the fighter plowed into the surface of the water at full diving speed and a seventy-degree angle. It disintegrated, the engine continuing its plunge towards the shallow bottom of the Gut and the fuselage and wings scattering in fragments of wood, some burning.

Henri shouted in triumph, and the passengers cheered. John continued to crane his head backward and around. "Hope nobody saw that," he said.

Jeffrey nodded. "By the way, brother of mine, where the hell are we headed?"

"I've got a couple of trawlers spotted up the Gut with fuel under the hatches," John said. "All just in case. If they're not there, there's an inflatable dinghy in the baggage compartment."

"And if that doesn't work, we'll swim," Jeffrey said, flying one-handed while he felt in the pockets of his tunic for his cigarettes.

"No, actually, I've got a motor launch hidden in a cove on the east coast of Trois," John said seriously.

Jeffrey laughed. "And a slingshot in your underwear," he said. More soberly: "I hate like hell being cut off like this. What's going on, and who's doing what?"

"I suspect the Chosen are doing most of the doing right now," John replied. "I just hope we're not the only ones keeping our heads while all about are losing theirs."

"If we are, they'll blame it on us," Jeffrey said. "I'll bet Dad's doing something constructive, though."

CHAPTER TWENTY-TWO

Maurice Farr stood at the head of the table in the admiral's quarters of the *Great Republic,* pride of the Northern Fleet, and stared at the messenger.

The captains and commodores along either side looked up from their turtle soup, some of them spilling drops on their ceremonial summer-white uniforms. The overhead electrics blazed on the polished silver, the gold epaulets, the snowy linen of the tablecloth, and the starched jackets of the stewards serving the dinner. It would take news of real importance to interrupt this occasion.

"Gentlemen," Farr said, quickly scanning the message, "Land forces have attacked the Sierra. Preliminary reports are sketchy, but it looks like they caught them completely flat-footed. Hundreds of transports escorted by squadrons of cruisers and destroyers have landed troops around Barclon in the Rio Arena estuary, and up and down the coast. Air assault troops are landing in Nueva Madrid, and the mountain passes on the northern and southern borders are under simultaneous attack."

Another messenger came in and passed a flimsy to the admiral. He opened it and read: *Brothers Katzenjammer have flown the coop. Stop. Never again. Stop. Love, J&J.*

Farr's shoulders kept their habitual stiffness, but he sighed imperceptibly. One less thing to worry about personally . . . and the Republic was going to need both his sons in the time ahead.

A babble of conversation had broken out around the table. "Gentlemen!" Silence fell. "Gentlemen, we knew we were at war yesterday."

When the news of Grisson's disaster had come through. *And the politicians will blame it on him.* Two modern ships and a score of relics and converted yachts against a dozen first-rate cruisers with full support. One of the Land craft had made it back to Bassin du Sud with her pumps running overtime, and several of the others had taken damage. All things considered, it was a miracle the Southern Fleet had been able to inflict that much harm before it was destroyed.

"Now we have a large target. Silence, please."

The tension grew thicker as Maurice Farr sat with his eyes closed, gripping the bridge of his nose between thumb and forefinger.

"All right, gentlemen," he said at last. One or two of the hardier had gone on eating their soup, and now paused with their spoons poised. "Here's what we'll do. I'm assuming that all of you have steam up"—*you'd better* went unspoken—"and we can get under way tonight."

That raised a few brows; a night passage up the Gut would be a definite risk, even after the exercises Farr had put the Northern Fleet through after assuming command six months ago.

"Steaming at fourteen knots, that should place us"—he turned to the map behind him—"*here* by dawn tomorrow. Then . . ."

Admiral der See Elise Eberdorf blinked at the communications technician.

"They report *what?*" she said.

"Sir, the entire Santander Navy Northern Fleet is steaming down the Gut towards us at flank speed, better than fifteen knots. Distance is less than forty miles."

Eberdorf blinked again, staring blindly out the narrow armored windows of the *Grossvolk.*

"Sixteen battleships, twenty-two fast protected cruisers, auxiliaries in proportion," the man read on. "Approaching—"

That is *the entire Northern Fleet,* she thought. Less the *Constitution,* which was downlined with a warped main drive shaft according to the latest intelligence. They were approaching through the southern strait around Trois; they must have left their base last night and made maximum speed all night, ignoring the chance of grounding or mines. Which meant . . .

She looked out at the chaos that covered the waters before Barclon. The Land's gold sunburst on black was flying over most of the city's higher buildings, those still standing. The fires were still burning out of control in some districts, and the forts guarding the harbor mouth were ruins full of rotting flesh. The water was speckled with half the Land's merchant fleet and about a third of its navy, many of them working shore-support and punching out enemy bunkers for the army.

Two-thirds of the Republic's navy was heading this way, and the Republic had a bigger navy to start with.

Fools, she thought with cold anger. I told them that we should concentrate on building battleships.

Enough. Duty was duty; and her duty here was clear.

"Signals," she said crisply. They had waited motionless, but she could sense the slight relief when she began to rap out orders. "To all transports in waves A and B." Those closest to the dock. "Enemy fleet approaching. Beach yourselves upriver."

That way the crews and troops could get off the ships, at least.

"All transports drawing less than five feet are to proceed upriver."

Where they'd be safe from the shells of Santander battlewagons, at least. The animals still held parts of the river not far inland, but that was a lesser risk.

"Waves C through F are to make maximum speed northward." With luck, most of them would have enough time to get under the protection of the guns of the fortresses that marked the seaward junction of the old Sierran border. Imperial forts, but adequately manned and upgunned since the conquest.

"Order to the fleet," she said. Sixty miles . . . just time enough. "Captains to report on board the flagship, with the following exceptions. Battleships *Adelreich* and *Eisenrede* are to make all speed north and rendezvous at Corona." Sending them out of harm's way; the navy would need every heavy ship it had to keep control of the vital passage.

"Mine-laying vessels are to proceed to the harbor channels and dump their cargos overboard. Maximum speed; ignore spacing, just do it. End. Oh, and transmit to Naval HQ."

"Sir."

Her chief of staff stepped up beside her, speaking quietly into her ear. "Sir, the enemy will have seven times our weight of broadside. What do you intend to do?"

Eberdorf's face was skull-like at the best of times, thin weathered skin lying right on the harsh bones. It looked even more like a death's-head as she smiled.

"Do, Helmut?" she said. "We're going to buy some time. And then we're all going to die, I think."

"*Watch* it!" someone said on the bridge.

Maurice Farr didn't look around. He also didn't flinch as the Land twin-engine swept overhead, not fifty feet above the tripod mast of the *Great Republic.* He was looking through the slide-mounted binoculars of the combat bridge as the bombs dropped. One hit squarely on A turret, the forward double twelve-inch gun mount. The ship groaned and twisted, but when the smoke cleared he could see only a star-shaped scar on the hardened surface of the thick rolled and cast armor. Behind him a voice murmured:

"A turret reports one casualty, sir." That was to the *Great Republic's* captain. "Turret ready for action."

"Give me the ranges," Farr said.

"Eleven thousand, sir. Closing."

Farr nodded. They were slanting in towards the Land ships, like not-quite-parallel lines, but there was shoal water between the fleets, far too shallow for his heavy ships, or even for most cruisers.

"Admiral," the captain of the *Great Republic* said, "at maximum elevation, I could be making some hits by now with my twelve-inchers."

"As you were, Gridley," Farr said emotionlessly.

"Yes, sir."

Two more Land aircraft were making runs at the Santander flagship, both twin-engine models. One was carrying a torpedo clamped underneath it; the other carried more of the sixty-pound bombs. He stiffened ever so slightly; the torpedo was a real menace, and he hadn't know that aircraft could be rigged for—

The torpedo splashed into the shallow green water. Seconds later it detonated in a huge shower of mud. The Land biplane flew through the column of spray, its engines stuttering. Just then one of the four-barrel pom-poms on the side of the central superstructure cut loose. It was loud even in comparison to the general racket of battle, and the glowing globes of the one-pound shells seemed to flick out and then float, slowing, as they approached it. That was an optical illusion. The explosion when the aircraft flew into a dozen of the little shells was very real; it vanished in a fireball from which bits of smoking debris fell seaward.

The stick of bombs from the next aircraft fell in a neat bracket over the Santander battleship, raising gouts of spray that fell back on the deck. Tentacled things floated limply on the water, or landed on the deck and lashed their barbed organic whips at the riveted steel.

Thud. *Flash*. Thud. *Flash*. The eight-inch guns of the Land cruisers on the other side of the shoal were opening up on him. He smiled thinly, observing the fall of shot. Water gouted up, just short of the leading elements of his seventeen battleships—the eighteenth, the *President Cummings*, was aground on a mudbank back half a kilometer and working frantically to it. The shell splashes were colored, green and orange and bright blue, dye injected into the bursting charges to let observers spot the point of impact. All were just a little short, although the foremost Santander battleship had probably been splashed. Another flotilla of four-stacker destroyers was darting out from behind the Land heavy ships, surging forward over the shoal water impassable to the deeper keels.

For a moment, he abstractly admired their courage. Then he spoke:

"Secondary batteries only, if you please."

"Yes, sir. Admiral, there may be mines in the channel ahead."

"I don't think so; we rushed them. In any case, damn the mines, continue course ahead."

"Yes, sir."

The *Great Republic* had her weapons arranged as most modern warships did: two heavy turrets fore and aft, in this case twin twelve-inch rifles, and four turrets for the secondary armament, two on either side just forward and abaft the central superstructure. That meant each of the battleships could fire a broadside of four eight-inch secondaries. They bellowed, the muzzle blasts enough to rock every man on the bridge and remind them to keep their mouths open to avoid pressure-flux damage to the eardrums. Shells fell among the Land destroyers, sixty-eight at a time. Four destroyers were hit in the first salvo, disappearing in fire and black smoke and spray as the heavy armor-piercing shells tore into their fragile plate structures.

One destroyer came close enough to the *Great Republic* to begin to heel aside, the center-mounted three-tube torpedo launcher swinging on its center pivot. Every pom-pom on the battleship cut loose at it, hundreds of one-pounder shells striking from stem to stern of the destroyer's long slender hull. So did the six five-inch quick-firers in sponson mounts along the armored side. Afterwards, Farr decided that it had probably been a pom-pom shell hitting a torpedo warhead that started the explosions, but it might have been a five-incher penetrating into a magazine. The light was blinding, but when he blinked back his sight and threw up a hand against the radiant heat there was still a crater in the water, shrinking as the liquid rushed back into the giant bubble the shock wave had created. Of the destroyer there was very little to see.

Another salvo of Land eight-inch shells went by, overhead this time.

All along the line of Santander battlewagons the main gun turrets were turning, muzzles fairly low—they were close enough now that the flat trajectories of the high-velocity rifles would strike without much elevation. Farr didn't trust high-angle fire at long range; it was deadly when it hit, but the probabilities were low given the current state of fleet gunnery.

He smiled bleakly. *I've waited a long time for this,* he thought. Aloud:

"You may fire when ready, Gridley."

Sixty-eight twelve-inch guns spoke within two seconds of each other, a line of flame and water rippling away from the muzzle blast all along the two-mile stretch of the Santander gunline. The *Great Republic* shivered and groaned, her eighteen-thousand-ton mass twisting in protest. The massive projectiles slapped out over the furrows the propellant gasses had dug in the water, reaching the height of their trajectory as the sea flowed back.

Then they began to fall towards the Chosen, multiple tons of steel and high explosive avalanching down. When their hardened heads struck armor plate, it would flow aside like a liquid.

Heinrich Hosten looked out over the harbor of Barclon with throttled fury. The surface of the water was burning, floating gasoline and heavier oils from the sunken tankers still drifting in flaming patches. The masts of sunken freighters slanted up out of the filthy water, among the floating debris and bodies. A few hulls protruded above the surface, nose-down with the bronze propellers dripping into the filth below. Other columns of smoke showed low on the western horizon, where the Santander battleships and their consorts were heading for home. The air stank of death and burnt petroleum, with the oily reek of the latter far more unpleasant.

"At least the enemy are withdrawing," the naval attaché said.

Heinrich swallowed bile. "Captain Gruenwald, the enemy are withdrawing because they have accomplished their mission and there are no targets left which warrant risking a capital ship. Now, get down there and see what assets we have left—if any. Or get a rifle and make yourself useful. But in either case, get out of my sight."

"Jawohl."

The naval officer clicked heels, did a perfect about-face, and left. Heinrich's head turned like a gun turret to his chief of staff.

"Report?"

"We got about ninety percent of the troops and support personnel off the transports," he said. "Half the supplies, mostly ammunition. Very little of the food"—it had been in the last convoys—"and only about one-quarter of the motor fuel. We may be able to recover a little more from tankers sunk in shallow water."

So much for the masterpiece of my career, Heinrich thought. An operation going absolutely according to plan, which was a minor miracle—until the Santander fleet showed up. *It could have been worse. A day earlier, and they'd have slaughtered the entire army at sea.*

Aloud: "Well, then. Immediate general order: All motor fuel to be reserved for armored fighting vehicles. The officers can walk or ride horses. Next, the reports from the other elements."

This was a four-pronged invasion: his, down here in the coastal plain; an air assault on Nueva Madrid and points between here and there; and the two overland drives into the mountains on the Sierras northern and southern flanks.

"Sir. Brigadier Hosten reports successful seizure of the central government complex in Nueva Madrid, most of the personnel on the critical list, of the National Armory, and the refinery. The refinery will be operational within six to ten days. She anticipates no problem holding her perimeter until linkup with the main force. All the other air-landing forces report objectives achieved."

Heinrich grunted with qualified relief. The rhythm of operations would be badly disrupted still, but at least he wouldn't run completely dry of fuel when what he had on hand was gone. When he held the triangle of territory based on the Gut and reaching to Nueva Madrid, the bulk of Sierra's population and industry would be under Chosen control.

The aide went on: "General Meitzerhagen reports that the northern passes are now secured and he is advancing south along the line of the railway. Resistance is disorganized but heavy and consistent. Also, there have already been raids on his line of communication."

Heinrich grunted again, running a thick finger down the line of rail leading towards the central lowlands, with a branch westward along the Rio Arena.

"My compliments to General Meitzerhagen, and his followup

elements are to secure the line of rail by liquidating the entire population within two days foot-march of the railways."

The aide blinked; that was a little drastic, even by Chosen standards. Cautiously, he asked, "*Herr General,* will that not distract from our primary mission?"

"No. Santander can interdict the Gut, but they cannot land significant forces here—they don't have enough to spare from the Union border. Hence, the outcome of this campaign is not in doubt, given the forces available here. For reasons you have no need to know, it is now absolutely imperative that we secure the rail passage across the Sierra to our forces in the Union. Guerillas cannot operate without a civilian populace to shelter and feed them. These Sierrans are stubborn animals, and I have no time to tame them by gentle means. Their corpses will give us no trouble except as a public health problem."

"Zum behfel, Herr General."

"And my compliments to Brigadier Hosten: signal *Well done.*"

"Why, thank you, Heinrich," Gerta muttered to herself, tossing the telegraph form onto her desk.

That had belonged to one of the Executive Council of the Sierra until yesterday morning. There was still a spatter of dried blood across it where a submachine-gun burst had ended that particular politician's term of office; it was beginning to smell pretty high, too. The windows were permanently opened—grenade—which cut it a little; it also let her listen to mop-up squads finishing off the pockets of resistance all across Nueva Madrid.

"Enter," she said; the words were blurred by the bandages across one side of her face, and by the pain of the long gash underneath.

Her son snapped to attention. "Sir. The last fires in the refinery are out. Here are the casualty reports. The technicians say that the water supply can be restarted as soon as we hold the reservoir; Colonel von Seedow asks permission to—"

Colonel von Seedow came in, walking rather stiffly.

"You may go, *Fahnrich,*" she said. Johan was young enough to still be entranced by military formality.

Von Seedow saluted more casually. "It's an easy enough target," she said. "My scouts report that the enemy aren't holding it in force, and I'd rather we didn't give them time to think of poisoning it."

Gerta considered; she was tasked with taking the capital and a set surrounding area and holding until relieved. On the other hand, she had considerable latitude, resistance had been light, and just sitting on her behind waiting had never been her long suit.

Speaking of which . . . "That a wound, Maxine?" she said, as the other Chosen officer sat in a gingerly fashion.

"In a manner of speaking, Brigadier. You don't like girls, do you?

Gerta blinked; it was a rather odd question at this point. "No. About as entertaining as a gynecological exam, for me. Why?"

"Well, in that case my warning is superfluous, but watch out for the ones here. They *bite*."

They shared a chuckle, and Gerta pulled out the appropriate map. "Through here?" she said, drawing a line with her finger to the irregular blue circle of the reservoir.

"*Ya.* And a couple of companies around here. Can you spare me some armored cars?"

"That's no problem, we only lost two in action."

Maxine von Seedow ran a hand over the blond stubble that topped her long, rather boney face. "Good. We did lose more infantry than I anticipated."

"Stubborn beasts, locally."

Von Seedow rose, wincing slightly. "Tell me about it, Brigadier. In my opinion, we should exterminate them. I should have the reservoir by nightfall."

"Good. The last thing I want is an epidemic of dysentery. Or rather, the last thing *you* want is an epidemic of dysentery."

Maxine raised her pale eyebrows.

"In their infinite wisdom, the General Staff are pulling me out. They've got another hole and need a cork."

CHAPTER TWENTY-THREE

"War! Extra, extra, read all about it—Republic at war with Chosen! Admiral Farr smashes Chosen fleet!"

"Well, part of it," Jeffrey Farr said, snatching a copy thrust into his hands and flipping a fifty-cent piece back.

The car was moving slowly enough for that; the streets of Santander City were packed. Militiamen were rushing to their mobilization stations, air-raid wardens in their new armbands and helmets were standing on stepladders to tape over the streetlights, and everybody and his Aunt Sally were milling around talking to each other. Smith pulled the car over to the curb for ten minutes while a unit of Regulars—Premier's Guard, but in field kit—headed towards the main railway station. The newspaper was full of screaming headlines three inches high, and so were the mobilization notices being pasted up on every flat surface by members of the Women's Auxiliary, who also wore armbands.

The crowds cheered the soldiers as they marched. John nodded. "Hope they're still as enthusiastic in a year," he said grimly.

"Hope we're alive in a year," Jeffrey replied, scanning the article. His lips shaped a soundless whistle. "Hot *damn,* but it looks like Dad completely cleaned their clocks. Eight cruisers, a battleship, and half their transports. Good way to start the war."

"Improves our chances," John said. "I wonder if Center—"

admiral farr's actions indicate the limit of stochastic multivariate analysis, Center said. **in your terms: a pleasant surprise, probability of favorable outcome to the struggle as a whole is increased by 7%, ±1.**

Jeffrey nodded. "Wonder what they'll do now," he mused. "What'd you do, in their boots?"

"Stand pat," John said at once. "Fortify the line of the Union-Santander border, concentrate on pacifying the occupied territories, and build ships and aircraft like crazy—taking Chosen personnel out of the armies to do it, if I had to. Absolutely no way we could fight our way through the mountains."

Good lad, Raj said. *That would make their tactics serve their strategy.*

correct, Center replied, dispassionate as always. the strategy john hosten has outlined would give probability of chosen victory within a decade of over 75%; probability of long-term stalemate 10%; probability of santander victory 15%. in addition, in this scenario there is a distinct possibility of immediate and long-term setback to human civilization on visager, as the effort of prolonged total war and the development of weapons of mass destruction undermines the viability of both parties.

"Fortunately, they're not likely to do that," Jeffrey said. "The Chosen always did tend to mistake operations for strategy,"

probability of full-scale chosen attack on santander border is 85%, ±7, Center confirmed.

"They'll try to roll right over us," John said. "The question is, can we hold them?"

"We'd better," Jeffrey said. "If we don't hold them in the passes, if they break through into the open basin country west of Alai, we're royally fucked. The provincial militias just don't have the experience or cohesion to fight open-field battles of maneuver yet."

"The Regulars will have to hold them, then."

Jeffrey's face was tired and stubbled; now it looked old. "And Gerard's men," he said softly. "There in the front line."

John looked at him. "That'll be pretty brutal," he warned. "They'll be facing the Land's army—in the civil war, it was mostly Libert's troops with a few Land units as stiffeners."

Jeffrey's lips thinned. "Gerard's men are half the formed, regular units we have," he said. "We need *time*. If we spend all our cadre resisting the first attacks, who's going to teach the rush of volunteers? We've split up the Freedom Brigades people to the training camps, too."

John sighed and nodded. "*Behfel ist behfel.*"

"Good God, what *is* that?" the HQ staffer said.

Jeffrey Farr looked up from the table. All across the eastern horizon light flickered and died, flickered and died, bright against the morning. The continuous thudding rumble was a background to everything, not so much loud as all-pervasive.

"That's the Land artillery," he said quietly. "Hurricane bombardment. Start sweating when it stops, because the troops will come in on the heels of it."

He turned back to the other men around the table, most in Santander brown, and many looking uncomfortable in it.

"General Parks, your division was federalized two weeks ago. It should be here by now."

"Sir . . ." Parks had a smooth western accent. "It's corn planting season, as I'm sure you're aware, and—"

"And the Chosen will eat the harvest if we don't stop them," Jeffrey said. "General Parks, get what's at the concentration points here, and do it fast. Or turn your command over to your 2-IC." Who, unlike Parks, was a regular, one of the skeleton cadre that first-line provincial militia units had been ordered to maintain several years ago, when the Union civil war began ratcheting up tensions. "I think that'll be all; you may return to your units, gentlemen."

He looked down at the map, took a cup of coffee from the orderly and scalded his lips slightly, barely noticing. The markers for the units under his command were accurate as of last night. Fifty thousand veterans of the Unionaise civil war; another hundred thousand regulars from the Republic's standing army, and many of the officers and NCOs had experience in that war, too. Two hundred and fifty thousand federalized militia units; they were well equipped, but their training ranged from almost as good as the Regulars to abysmal. More arriving every hour.

Half a million Land troops were going to hit them in a couple of hours, supported by scores of heavy tanks, hundreds of light ones, thousands of aircraft.

"None of Libert's men?" Gerard said quietly, tracing the unit designators for the enemy forces.

"No. They're moving east—east and north, into the Sierra."

"Good," Gerard said quietly. Jeffrey looked up at him. The compact little Unionaise was smiling. "Not pleasant, fighting one's own countrymen."

"Pierre . . ." Jeffrey said.

Gerard picked up his helmet and gloves, saluted. "My friend, we must win this war. To this, everything else is subordinate."

They shook hands. Gerard went on: "Libert thinks he can ride the tiger. It is only a matter of time until he joins the other victims in the meat locker."

"I think he's counting on us breaking the tiger's teeth," Jeffrey said. "God go with you."

"How not? If there was ever anyone who fought with His blessing, it is here and now."

"Damn," Jeffrey said softly, watching the Unionaise walk towards his staff car. "I hate sending men out to die."

If you didn't, you wouldn't be the man you are, Raj said. *But you'll do it, nonetheless.*

Maurice Hosten stamped on the rudder pedal and wrenched the joystick sideways.

His biplane stood on one wing, nose down, and dove into a curve. The Land fighter shot past him with its machine guns stuttering, banking itself to try and follow his turn. He spiraled up into an Immelmann and his plane cartwheeled, cutting the cord of his opponent's circle. His finger clenched down on the firing stud.

"*Fuck!*" The deflection angle wasn't right; he could feel it even before the guns stuttered.

Spent brass spun behind him, sparkling in the sunlight, falling through thin air to the jagged mountain foothills six thousand feet below. Acrid propellant mingled with the smells of exhaust fumes and castor oil blowing back into his face. Land and cloud heeled crazily below him as he pulled the stick back into his stomach, pulled until gravity rippled his face backward on the bone and vision became edged with gray.

Got the bastard, got him—

Something warned him. It was too quick for thought; stick hard right, rudder right . . . and another Land triplane lanced through the space he'd been in, diving out of the sun. His leather-helmeted head jerked back and forth, hard enough to saw his skin if it hadn't been for the silk scarf. The rest of his squadron were gone, not just his wingman—he'd seen the Land fighter bounce Tom—but all the rest as well. The sky was empty, except for his own plane and the two Chosen pilots.

Nothing for it. He pushed the throttles home and dove into cloud, thankful it was close. *Careful, now.* Easy to get turned around in here. Easy even to lose track of which way was up and end up flying upside down into a hillside convinced you were climbing. There was just enough visibility to see his instruments' radium glow: horizon, compass, airspeed indicator. One hundred thirty-eight; the Mark IV was a sweet bird.

When he came out of the cloudbank there was nobody in sight. He kept twisting backward to check the sun; that was the most dangerous angle, always. The ground below looked strange, but then, it usually did. Check for mountain peaks, check for rivers, roads, the spaces between them.

"That's the Skinder," he decided, looking at the twisting river. "Ensburg's thataway."

Ensburg had been under siege from the Chosen for a month. So that train of wagons on the road was undoubtedly a righteous target. And he still had more than half a tank of fuel.

Maurice pushed the stick forward and put his finger back on the firing button. Every shell and box of hardtack that didn't make it to the lines outside Ensburg counted.

(o·o)   (o·o)   (o·o)

"Damn, that's ugly," Jeffrey said, swinging down from his staff car.

The huge Land tank was burnt out, smelling of human fat melted into the ground and turning rancid in the summer heat. The commander still stood in the main gun turret, turned to a calcined statue of charcoal, roughly human-shaped.

"This way, sir," the major . . . *Carruthers, that's his name* . . . said. "And careful—there are *Lander* snipers on that ridge back there."

The major was young, stubble-chinned and filthy, with a peeling sunburn on his nose. From the way he scratched, he was never alone these days. He'd probably been a small-town lawyer or banker three months ago; he was also fairly cheerful, which was a good sign.

"We caught it with a field-gun back in that farmhouse," he said, waving over one shoulder.

Jeffrey looked back; the building was stone blocks, gutted and roofless, marked with long black streaks above the windows where the fire has risen. There was a barn nearby, reduced to charred stumps of timbers and a big stone water tank. The orchard was ragged stumps.

"Caught it in the side as it went by." He pointed; one of the powered bogies that held the massive war machine up was shattered and twisted. "Then we hit it with teams carrying satchel charges, while the rest of us gave covering fire."

The ex-militia major sobered. "Lost a lot of good men doing it, sir. But I can tell you, we were *relieved.* Those things are so cursed hard to stop!"

"I know," Jeffrey said dryly, looking to his right down the eastward reach of the valley. The Santander positions had been a mile up that way, before the Chosen brought up the tank.

"This is dead ground, sir. You can straighten up."

Jeffrey did so, watching the engineers swarming over the tank, checking for improvements and modifications. "The good news about these monsters, major, comes in threes," he said, tapping its flank. "There aren't very many of them; they break down a lot; and now that the lines aren't moving much, the enemy don't get to recover and repair them very often."

"Well, that's some consolation, sir," Carruthers said dubiously. "They're still a cursed serious problem out here."

"We all have problems, Major Carruthers."

The factory room was long, lit by grimy glass-paned skylights, open now to let in a little air; the air of Oathtaking, heavy and thick at the best of times, and laden with a sour acid smog of coal smoke and chemicals when the wind was from the sea. Right now it also smelled of the man who was hanging on an iron hook driven into the base of his skull. The hook was set over the entrance door, where the workers passed each morning and evening as they were taken from the camp on the city's outskirts. The body had been there for two days now, ever since the shop fell below quota for an entire week. Sometimes it moved a little as the maggots did their work.

There was a blackboard beside the door, with chalked numbers on it. This week's production was nearly eight percent over quota. A cheerful banner announced the prizes that the production group would receive if they could sustain that for another seven days: a pint of wine for each man, beef and fresh fruit, tobacco, and two hours each with an inmate from the women's camp.

Tomaso Guiardini smiled as he looked at the banner. He smiled again as he looked down at the bearing race in the clamp before him. It was a metal circle; the inner surface moved smoothly under his hand, where it rested on the ball-bearings in the race formed by the outer U-shaped portion.

Very smoothly. Nothing to tell that there were metal filings mixed with the lubricating matrix inside. Nothing except the way the bearing race would seize up and burn when subjected to heavy use, in about one-tenth the normal time.

He looked up again at the banner. Perhaps the woman would be pretty, maybe with long, soft hair. Mostly the Chosen shaved the inmates' scalps, though.

He glanced around. The foreman was looking over somebody else's shoulder. Tomaso took two steps and swept a handful of metal shavings from the lathe across the aisle, dropping them into the pocket of his grease-stained overall, and was back at his bench before the Protégé foreman—he was a one-eyed veteran with a limp, and a steel-cored rubber truncheon thonged to his wrist—could turn around.

"Dad!" Maurice Hosten checked his step. "I mean, sir. Ah, just a second."

He pulled off the leather flyer's helmet and turned to give some directions to the ground crew; the blue-black curls of his hair caught the sun, and the strong line of his jaw showed a faint shadow of dense beard of exactly the same color. His plane had more bullet holes in the upper wing, and part of the tail looked as if it had been chewed. There were a row of markings on the fuselage below the cockpit, too— Chosen sunbursts with a red line drawn through of them. Eight in all, and the outline of an airship.

John Hosten's blond hair was broadly streaked with gray now, and as he watched the young man's springy step he was abruptly conscious that he was no longer anything but unambiguously middle-aged. He still buckled his belt at the same notch, he could do most of what he had been able to—hell, his biological father was running the Land's General Staff with ruthless competence and he was thirty years older—but doing it took a higher price every passing year.

Maurice, though, he certainly isn't a boy any longer.

War doesn't give you much chance at youth, Raj agreed, with an edge of sadness to his mental voice.

The young pilot turned back. "Good to see you, Dad."

"And you, son." He pulled the young man into a brief embrace. "That's from your mother."

"How is she?"

"Still working too hard," John said. "We meet at breakfast, most days."

Maurice chuckled and shook his head. "Doing wonders, though. The food's actually edible since the Auxiliary took over the mess." They began walking back towards the pine board buildings to one side of the dirt strip.

"I wish *everything* was going as well," he said, with a quick scowl.

"I'm listening," John said.

"You always did, Dad," Maurice said. He ran a hand through his hair. "Look, the war's less than six months old—and there are only three other pilots in this squadron besides me who were in at the start. And one of *them* had experience in the Union civil war."

"Bad, I know."

"Dad, we're losing nearly two-thirds of the new pilots in the first *week* they're assigned to active patrols."

60% in the first ten days, Center said inside his head. a slight exaggeration.

"The Chosen pilots, they're *good*. And they've got experience. Our planes are about as good now, but Christ, the new chums, they've got maybe twenty hours flying time when they get here. It's like sending puppies up against Dobermans! I have to force myself to learn their f—sorry, their goddamned names."

"You were almost as green," John pointed out.

"Dad, that's not the same thing, and you know it. I had Uncle Jeff teaching me before the war, and I'm . . . lucky."

He's a natural, Raj said clinically. *It's the same with any type of combat—swords, pistols, bayonet fighting. Novices do most of the dying, experienced men do most of the killing, and a few learn faster than anyone else. This boy of yours is a fast learner; I know the type.*

"What do you suggest, son?"

"I—" Maurice hesitated, and ran his fingers through his hair again. "What we really need is more instructors—experienced instructors—back at the flying schools."

"You want the job?" John said.

"Christ no! I . . . oh." He trailed off uncertainly.

"Well, that's one reason," John said. "For another, we don't have *time* to stretch the training. The Chosen were getting ready for this war for a long time. Our men have to learn on the job, and they pay for it in blood; not just you pilots, but the ground troops as well. We've lost two hundred and fifty thousand casualties."

Maurice's eyes went wide, and he gave a small grunt of incredulous horror.

"Yes, we don't publicize the overall figures; and that doesn't count the Union Loyalist troops; they were virtually wiped out. The weekly dead-and-missing list in the newspapers is bad enough. In Ensburg, they're eating rats and their own dead. We estimate half the population of the Sierra is gone, and in the Empire, we're supplying guerillas who keep operating even though they know a hundred hostages will be shot for every soldier killed, five hundred for every Chosen. *But we stopped them.* They thought they could run right over us the way they did the Empire, or the Sierra . . . and they didn't. They've nowhere gotten more than a hundred miles in from the old Union border, and our numbers are starting to mount. The Chosen are butchers, and we're paying a high butcher's bill, but we're learning."

Maurice shook his head. "Dad," he said slowly, "I wouldn't have your job for anything."

"Not many of us are doing what we'd really like," John said. "Duty's duty." He clapped his hand on his sons shoulder. "But we're doing our best—and you're doing damned well."

None of the command group was surprised when Gerta Hosten arrived; if they had been, she'd have put in a report that would ensure their next command was of a rifle platoon on the Confrontation Line. The pickets and ambush patrols passed her through after due checks, and she found the brigade commander consulting with his subordinates next to two parked vehicles in what had been Pueblo Vieho before the forces of the Land arrived in the Sierra the previous spring. A lieutenant was talking, pointing out the path her command had taken through the pine woods further up the mountain slopes, above the high pastures.

Gerta vaulted out of her command car—it was a six-wheeled armored car chassis with the turret and top deck removed—and exchanged salutes and clasped wrists with the commander. "'*Tag*, Ektar," she said. "How are things in the quiet sector? Missed you by about an hour at your headquarters,"

"Just coming up to see how things are going at the business end," Ektar Feldenkopf said. "Not a bad bag: seventeen men, twenty four women, and a round dozen of their brats. The yield from these sweeps has been falling off."

The air of the high Sierran valley was cool and crisp even in late summer. Most of it had been pasture, growing rank now. The burnt snags of the village's log houses didn't smell any more, or the bodies underneath them. There were still traces of gingerbread carving around the eaves. Several skeletons lay on the dirt road leading to the lowlands, where the clean-up squad had shot them as they fled into the darkness from their burning houses. The bodies laid out in the overgrown mud of the street had probably run the other way, up into the forests and the mountains, to survive a little longer and steal down to try and raid the conqueror's supply lines. The women and children taken alive knelt in a row beyond the corpses, hands secured behind their backs.

"Which means either they're getting thinner on the ground, or better at hiding, or both."

"Both, I think—the interrogations will tell us something. The males had a rifle each and about twenty rounds, plus some handguns, but no explosives."

Johan was looking at one of the prisoners, a blond who probably looked extremely pretty when she was better fed and didn't have dried blood from a blow to the nose over most of her face. Gerta smiled indulgently; young men had single-track minds, and he'd been doing his work very well. He had some scars of his own now, although nothing like the one that seamed the side of her face since the drop on Nueva Madrid, and drew the left corner of her face up in a permanent slight smile.

"All right," she said. "But don't undo her hands and watch out for the teeth. Remember *Hauptman* von Seedow."

The three Chosen shared a brief chuckle; poor Maxine had been laid up in a field hospital for a month with her infected bite, and the joke was still doing the rounds of every officers' mess in the Land's armed forces. She'd nearly punched one wit who offered her a recipe for a poultice.

She'll never live it down, Gerta thought, as her son walked over to the prisoners. Still chuckling, he hauled the girl—she was about his own age—to her feet by her hair and marched her off behind the ruins of one of the buildings.

"How are they surviving?" Gerta asked. None of them were what you'd call well-fleshed, but they weren't on the verge of starvation either.

"These mountain villages, they store cheese and dried milk and so on up in the caves," the officer said, waving towards the jagged snow-capped mountains to the north. "There are a *lot* of caves up there. And there's game, deer and bison, rabbits ana so forth, and a lot of cattle and sheep and pigs gone wild in the woods. Half-wild to begin with. Still, they're getting hungrier, and we're whittling them down. It's good rest and recreation for units pulled out of the line."

"How do the Unionaise shape?" she asked.

There was a brigade of them down the valley a ways, at the crossroads twenty miles west of the railroad, under their own officers, but also under the operational control of the Land regional command.

"Not bad," the officer said, as a shrill scream sounded from behind the wrecked building. It trailed off into sobs. "Not as energetic at their patrolling as I'd like. Good enough for this work, I'd say; I couldn't swear how they'd do in heavy combat. Settling in to that town as if they owned the place."

"They think they do," Gerta replied. "Well, things appear to be under control here. Which is more than I can say about some other places."

The garrison commander frowned and lowered his voice. "How does the Confrontation Line develop? The official reports seem . . . overly optimistic."

Gerta spoke quietly as well. "Not so well. We're killing the Santies by the shitload, that part of the official story is true enough. They keep attacking us with more enthusiasm than sense, but it's getting more expensive, and we're not taking much territory. Ensburg's still holding out."

"Still?" The man's brows rose. "They must be starving."

"They are. I was in the siege lines last week; nothing left inside but rubble, and you can smell the stink of their funeral pyres. Starvation, typhus, whatever—but they're not giving up."

She spat into the dirt. "If that monomaniac imbecile

Meitzerhagen hadn't killed the garrison of Fort William after they surrendered and bellowed the fact to the world, they might have been more inclined to give up. So would a lot of the other garrisons we cut off in the first push; mopping them up took time the Santies used to get themselves organized. We lost momentum."

The other officer nodded. "Meitzerhagen's a sledgehammer," he said. "The problem is—"

"—not all problems are nails," she finished.

"Stalemate, for the present, then."

"*Ja*. We can push them, but we outrun our supplies. And even when we beat them, they don't *run*, and there are always more of them. Their equipment's good, too. Now that they're learning how to use it . . ." She shrugged.

"How is our logistical situation, then?"

"It sucks wet dogshit. We can't move dirigibles within a hundred miles of the front in daylight, the road net's terrible, the terrain favors defense . . . and the Santies are right in the middle of their main industrial area, with their best farmlands only a few hundred miles away on first-class rails and roads."

"I presume the staff is evolving a counterstrategy."

"Ya. No details of course, but let's just say that we're going to encourage their enthusiasm and prepare to receive it. Also if we can't use the Gut, there's no reason they should be able to either."

The officer sighed and nodded. "Well, you can tell them that my brigade at least is doing its job," he said. "Trying to keep the rail lines through the Sierra working would have been a nightmare if we'd used conventional occupation techniques. Bad enough as it is."

Young Johan returned, pushing the dazed and naked Sierran girl before him. He dropped into parade rest behind Gerta, smiling faintly as the prisoner stumbled back to kneel with the others.

"In a year or two, there won't be any left to speak of. . . . Speaking of which, you said there was a new directive?"

Gerta nodded. "Ya, we're running short of labor for the construction gangs, importing from the New Territories is inconvenient, big projects all over, and the local animals might as well give some value before they die," she said. "Send down noncombatant adults fit for heavy work—ones that give up when you catch them. Keep killing all those found in arms or not useful. Except children under about five. As an experiment, we're sending those back to the Land to be raised by senior Protégé-soldier families."

Long-serving Protégé soldiers were allowed to marry, as a special privilege for good service. "They might be useful, that way, in the long term. At your discretion, though; don't tie up transport if you're busy."

The other Chosen nodded. "*Jawohl.* Odd to think of us running short of manual workers, though."

"Well, even the New Territories' population has dropped considerably," she said. "We'll have to be less wasteful after the war."

Gerta returned his salute and turned to her open-topped armored car. When you carried a hatchet for the General Staff, your work was never done.

CHAPTER TWENTY-FOUR

Jeffrey Farr whistled soundlessly. Not that anyone could have heard him in the rear seat of the observation plane; the noise of the engine and the slipstream was too loud. He reached forward and tapped the pilot on the shoulder, circling his hand with the index finger up and pointing it downwards. The pilot nodded and circled, coming down to four thousand feet.

A couple of light pom-poms opened up, winking up at them from the huge piles of turned earth below; then a heavier antiaircraft gun, that stood some chance of reaching them. Black puffs of smoke erupted in the air below, each with a momentary snap of fire at its heart before it lost shape and began to drift away. Ant-tiny, hordes of laborers dove for the shelter of the trenches they had been digging, leaving their tools among the piles of timber, steel sheet and reinforcing rod.

There was a big camera fastened to brackets ahead of the observer's position, but Jeffrey ignored it. He'd seen pictures; this trip was for a personal look.

All right, he thought. *Nice job of field engineering.* Everything laid out to command the ground to the east, but not just simple positions on ridge tops. Machine-gun bunkers at the base of the ridges, giving maximum fields of fire; heavier bunkers for field guns, revetted positions for heavy mortars on the reverse slopes, with communications trenches and even tunnels to bring reserves forward quickly without leaving them exposed to direct-fire weapons. All-round fields of fire, so that each position could hold out if cut off, and heavier redoubts further back, layer upon layer of them.

They must have half a million men working on this, Jeffrey thought, impressed.

correct to within ten thousand ±6, Center said. **assuming an equivalent effort in other sectors of the front, as intelligence reports indicate.**

"Well, we'll have to take this into account," Jeffrey said. He tapped the pilot's shoulder again; despite their two-squadron escort, the man was looking nervously east and upward, to where Land attackers would come diving out of the morning sun. The plane banked westward.

"Thank you gentlemen for meeting on such short notice," Jeffrey said.

They were in the Premier's bunker beneath the hilltop Executive Mansion, nearly a hundred yards underground, as deep as you could get near Santander City without hitting groundwater. The impact of the bombs, a dull *crump . . . crump . . .* was felt more through the soles of their feet than heard through their ears. Every now and then the overhead electric light flickered, and dust filtered down, making men sneeze at its acrid scent.

"I thought you'd made it suicidal for dirigibles to fly over our territory," Maurice Farr said dryly to the Air Force commander.

The commander flushed and pulled at his mustache. "In daylight, yes. But the speed and altitude advantage of our fighters is fairly narrow. At night, it's much harder. Those might be their new long-range eight-engine bomber planes, too. We're having more of a problem with those."

At the head of the table, Jeffrey held up a hand. "In any case, the error radius of night bombing is so huge that it consumes more of their resources to do it than it does of ours to endure it."

The Premier tapped a pencil sharply on the table. "General, we're losing hundreds, perhaps thousands of civilian every time one of those raids breaks through."

Jeffrey dipped his head slightly. "With all due respect, sir, there were a hundred and fifty thousand people in Ensburg—and I doubt ten thousand of them are alive now, and those are in Chosen labor camps."

A pall of silence fell around the table. The siege of Ensburg had been a morale-booster for the whole Republic. Its fall had been a correspondingly serious blow. Jeffrey went on:

"So with all due respect, Mr. Premier, *anything* that helps keep the enemy back is a positive factor, and that includes attacks that hurt us but hurt him more."

"There's the effect of bombing on civilian morale," the politician pointed out.

observe:

Scenes floated before Jeffrey's eyes: cities reduced to street patterns amid tumbled scorched brick, air-raid shelters full of unmarked corpses asphyxiated as the firestorms above sucked the oxygen from their lungs, fleets of huge four-engined bombers sleeker and more deadly than anything Visager knew raining down incendiaries on a town of half-timbered buildings crowded with refugees while odd-looking monoplane fighters tried to beat them off.

"Sir, our citizens could take a lot more pain than this and still keep going. In any case, if we could turn to the matter at hand?"

The men around the table—generals, admirals, heads of ministries—opened the folders that lay before them. Heading each bundle of documents were aerial photographs of enormous twisting chains of fortifications. Maps followed, and intelligence summaries.

"Is this reliable?" the Premier asked.

"Sir, I've seen a good deal of it with my own eyes," Jeffrey said. "And we have the labor gangs working on it penetrated to a fare-thee-well. It's genuine, and it's a major effort. Not just the labor, they've got plenty of that, but the transport capacity it's tying up and the materials. Steel, cement, explosives for the minefields."

"So you're right. They're going to withdraw," the Premier said. "We're beating them!"

"Sir." The elected leader of the Republic looked up at Jeffrey's tone. "Sir, we're making them retreat—and that's *not* the same thing. We have to consider the strategic consequences. If you'll all turn to Report Four?"

They did; it started with a map. "That *line*—they're code-naming it the Gothic Line, for some reason—is cursed well laid-out. When it's finished, they'll make a fighting retreat and then sit and wait for us."

"We've pushed them back once, we can do it again!" the Premier said. "No invader can be left on the Republic's soil, whatever the cost."

Christ. Usually the Premier's aggressive pugnacity was a plus for Jeffrey and the conduct of the war; he'd trampled the political opposition into dust, and the people had rallied around him as a symbol of the national will—they were calling him "the Tiger," now. But if he got the bit between his teeth on this—

observe:

Men in khaki uniforms and odd soup-bowl helmets clambered out of trenches and advanced into a moonscape of craters and bits of trees, ends of twisted barbed wire, mud, rotting fragments of once-human flesh. They walked in long neat lines, precisely spaced. From ahead, beyond the uncut barbed wire, the machine guns began to flicker in steady arcs . . .

. . . and men in different uniforms, blue, helmets with a ridge down the center, huddled in a shell crater. Bulbous masks hid their faces, turning them into snouted insectile shapes. Bodies bobbed in the thick muddy water at the bottom of the shell hole, their flesh stained yellow. Somehow he knew that the air was full of an invisible drifting death that would bum out lungs and turn them to bags of thick liquid matter . . .

. . . and a man in neat officer's uniform with a swagger stick in his hand and the red tabs of the staff looked out over a sea of mud churned to the consistency of porridge. It was too viscous even to hold the shape of craters, although it was dimpled like the face of a smallpox victim. Plank walkways lead off into the steady gray rain; about them lay discarded equipment, sunken in the mire. So was a mule, still feebly struggling with only the top quarter of its body showing.

"Good God," the man said, his face gray as the churned and poisoned soil. "Did we send men out to fight in *this?*" His face crumpled into tears.

Jeffrey shook his head; the problem with visions like that was that the implications stayed with you.

"Sir, right now we've managed to turn the war from one of movement into one of attrition favoring us. This is the Chosen countermove. If we attack their prepared positions, we'll bleed ourselves white; attrition will favor them. Believe me, sir, please—if you've ever trusted my military judgment, trust it now. We'd break ourselves trying. The ground up there favors defense—that's how we survived their initial attack—and those fieldworks of theirs are as impregnable as the mountains. And that's not all."

He stood and took up a pointer, tracing the Gothic Line with its tip. "This shortens their line, and with massive artillery support and good communications from their immediate rear, they can thin out the forces facing us. Which means they can concentrate a real strategic reserve, not just rob Peter to pay Paul, pulling units out of the line to plug in again elsewhere. They haven't had a genuine reserve. If they get one, it frees up the whole situation and concedes a lot of the initiative to them."

The Premier looked at John. "Your guerillas were supposed to tie down their forces," he said.

"They are, Mr. Premier," he said. "They have two hundred thousand men holding their lines of communication in the old Empire, and another hundred thousand in the Sierra, plus most of Libert's Nationalist army. Which, incidentally, is only useful to them as long as Libert's convinced they're going to win. If they had the free use of those forces, we'd have lost the war in their big push last fall."

John looked around the table. "Gentlemen?" There was a murmur of agreement, reluctant in some cases.

"Guerillas can be crucially useful to us," John went on. "But they can't win the war. They *can* make it possible for us to win it, though."

The Premier smoothed a thumb across his slightly tobacco-stained white mustache; that and his great shock of snow-colored hair were his political trademarks, along with the gray silk gloves he affected.

"Neither will sitting and looking at the Chosen forts—Chosen forts on *our* soil," he growled. "Admiral?"

Maurice Farr nodded reluctantly. "We can't risk an attack on the Land Home Fleet in the Passage," he said. "Not at present. It's too far from our bases and too close to theirs. And while our operational efficiency is increasing rapidly, more than theirs—they were already at war readiness—they're building as fast as they can. They've got severe production problems, their labor force doesn't want to work, but they're also experienced at that. If they can complete their latest shipbuilding cycle, our margin of superiority will be severely reduced."

He shrugged. "For the next two years, we have a margin of naval superiority that will remain steady or increase. After that, I can give no assurances."

He looked at his sons and shrugged again. If the Premier requested an analysis within his area of expertise, Maurice Farr would give it.

Jeffrey coughed. "Well, Mr. Premier, the thing is that while the Gothic Line enables the enemy to regain some freedom of action, it does the same for us—and sooner."

The Premier looked at him sharply. Jeffrey went on: "They're not going to come out of those fortifications at us, not after going to that much trouble, and not as long as we maintain a reasonable force facing them. That means we can pull most of our experienced divisions out of the line, recruit them back up to strength, and put the new formations in facing the enemy. That'll give them experience; we don't have to put in full-scale assaults to do that, just patrol aggressively. And so *we* will have a strategic reserve, and sooner than they will. They don't dare thin their force facing us until those works are complete."

The Premier leaned back in his chair. He'd gotten his start in radical politics—and fought several duels with political opponents and what he considered slanderous journalists, back when that was still legal in some of the western provinces. John reminded himself not to underestimate the man; he was not just the pugnacious bull-at-a-gate extremist some made him out. Plenty of brains behind the shrewd little eyes, and plenty of nerve.

"So," he said. "You think that we can *do* something with this strategic reserve of yours, in the two years during which we have . . . what is the military phrase?"

"Window of opportunity, Mr. Premier," the military men said.

"Your *window of opportunity?*" the Premier continued.

"Yes, sir," Jeffrey said. From our window of opportunity to my window of opportunity? he thought. Well, that certainly makes it plain who's to blame if anything goes wrong.

He **is** *a politician, Jeff,* Raj thought. A brief mental image, of Raj lying facedown on a magnificent mosaic floor, while a man stood above him shouting, dressed in magnificent metallic robes that blazed under arc lights. *I know the breed.*

The political leader looked back at Maurice Farr. "What do you say, Admiral?"

"We have to take some action in the next two years," he said with clinical detachment. "As I said, for that period, our strength will increase relative to theirs. But they control three-quarters of the planet's useful land area, resources, and population now; while it'll take time for them to make use of what they've grabbed, eventually they will. Then the balance of forces will start to swing against us. Naval and otherwise."

Most of the military men around the table nodded, reluctantly.

The Premier leaned his elbows on the table, closed one hand into a fist and clasped the other over it, and leaned his chin on his knuckles. The pouched eyes leveled on Jeffrey. "Tell me more," he said.

"Well, sir . . ." he began.

The elevator was still functioning when the meeting broke up. "God damn, but I hope there aren't any leaks in that bunch," John said, waiting with his foster brother while the first loads went up.

"That's why I confined myself to generalities," Jeffrey replied, yawning. "I can remember when these late nights were a pleasure, not something that made your eyes feel as if they'd been boiled, peeled and dredged in cayenne pepper."

John shook his head. "Useful generalities, though," he fretted.

Jeffrey grinned slightly and punched his arm. "Bro, there's no way we can stop the Fourth Bureau or *Militarische Intelligenz* from finding out our *capabilities*, he said. "And from that, deducing our general intentions. What we have to do is keep the precise intentions secret. It'll all depend on that."

John nodded unhappily. "I still don't like it."

"Of course not," Jeffrey said, his voice mock-soothing. "You're a spook. You're not happy unless you know everything about everybody and nobody else knows anything at all."

The elevator rattled to a stop at the bottom of the shaft, and the sliding-mesh doors opened. They stepped in; the little square was decorated in the red plush carpet, mirrors, and carved walnut of the upper part of the Executive Mansion, not like the utilitarian warrens beneath added in the years before the war. The attendant pushed the doors closed and reached for the polished wood and brass of the lever that controlled it.

"Ground floor, I presume, gentlemen?" he said, with a slight Imperial accent.

John nodded, and said in the man's own language, "How is it up top, Mario?"

The elevator operator grinned at the patron who'd found him this job. "Bad, *signore*," he replied. "The *tedeschi* swine are out in force tonight. God and Mary and the Saints keep you safe."

"Amen," John said, and took his cigarette case out of his jacket. The cigarillos within were dark with a gold band; he offered it to the other men, then snapped his lighter.

The smoke was rich and pungent. "Sierran," Jeffrey said. "Punch-punch claros. We won't be seeing any more of those for a while."

The elevator operator nodded somberly. "The *tedeschi* have gone mad there, *signore*," he said. "They act as beasts in the Empire, but now in the Sierra . . ."

"I think they're mad with frustration," John said. "*Ciao*, Mario. My regards to your family."

"*Signore.* And many thanks for Antonio's scholarship."

"He earned it."

"Is there anywhere you *don't* have them stashed?" Jeffrey said, as they walked out to the entrance—the nonceremonial one, for unofficial guests.

"It never hurts to have friends in . . ." John began, as they accepted hat and cane, uniform cap, and swagger stick, from the attendant. Then he paused on the polished marble of the steps. "*Shit.*"

They both stopped on the uppermost stair. The Executive Mansion had an excellent hilltop site. From here they could see for miles: darkened streets, the swift flicker of emergency vehicle headlights with the top halves painted black to make them less visible from above. Fires burned out of control down by the canals and the riverside warehouses, blotches of soft light amid the blackout darkness. Searchlights probed upward like fingers, like hands reaching for the machines that tormented the city below, sliding off the undersides of clouds and vanishing in the gaps between. Every few seconds an antiaircraft gun would fire, a flicker of light and a flat *brraack*, then the shell would burst far above, sometimes lighting a cloud from within for an instant. When they finally fell silent, sirens spoke all over the great city, a rising-falling wail that signaled the "all clear." As they died, the lesser sirens of fire engines could be heard, and the clangor of bells.

"And now they'll sleep for a little while," John said softly. "Those that can. Tomorrow they'll get out of bed and go to work."

Jeffrey nodded. "You're right. Center's right, this is hurting the Chosen more than us . . . but it's got to stop, nevertheless."

Harry Smith was waiting in the car; dozing, actually, with his head resting on his gloved hands. He woke as the two men approached. "Sorry, sir, Mr. Jeffrey."

"Why the hell weren't you in the shelter?" John asked, his voice hovering between resignation and annoyance.

"Wanted to keep an eye on the car," Smith said.

John sighed. "Home."

Home was in the North Hill suburbs, beyond Embassy Row. There was little direct damage there; no factories, and none of the densely packed working-class housing common further south on the bank of the river, or across it. The streetlights were still blacked out, and so were the houses. The steamcar slid quietly through the darkened streets, passing an occasional Air Raid Precautions patrol, helmeted but with no uniforms beyond armbands—many of them were Women's Auxiliary volunteers. Once, an ambulance went by with its bell clanging, and once, they had to detour around a random hit, a great crater in the middle of the street with water hissing ten feet high from a broken main. There might be gas, too; sawhorse barricades were already up, and Municipal Services trucks were disgorging men in workman's overalls.

"That looks a bit like our place did," Jeffrey said; the younger Farr's household had been the recipient of several Land two hundred and fifty pounders, luckily while everyone was out. "Thanks again for saving us from the horrors of Government Issue Married Quarters, officers for the use of."

John snorted. The car paused for a moment at wrought-iron gates, and then the tires hummed on the brick of a long driveway.

"Get some sleep," John said to Smith. "We're going on a trip in a few days."

Smith grinned. "With some old friends, sir?" John nodded. Smith put on a good imitation of an upper-class drawl. "Just the time of year one *likes* a little vacation on the Gut, eh?"

A sleepy butler opened the front doors of the big, rambling brick house. He stumbled backward as a four-year-old made a dash past his legs and down the stairs, leaping for Jeffrey.

"Daddy!" The girl wound herself around him, clinging to his belt. "Daddy, we all went and sat inna basement and sang!"

"That's good, punkin, but it's past your bedtime," Jeffrey said, hoisting her up.

She wrinkled her nose. "You smell funny, Daddy."

"Blame the Premier and his tobacco—ah, here's Irene."

A nursemaid came out, clutching her sleeping robe around her and clucking anxiously. "*There* she is, Mr. Jeffrey. Honestly, sometimes I think that child is part ape!"

"A born commando. Off to bed, punkin." John was still smiling as he walked up the stairs, fending off the butler's offer to wake the cook. There were advantages to being a very rich man, but a good deal of petty annoyance came with it as well. He might have raided the icebox and made a sandwich himself, if he'd been living in a middle-class apartment, but rousting someone out of bed at one o'clock to slap some chicken between two pieces of bread was more trouble than it was worth and hubristic besides.

The light was still on in the bedroom, but Pia was asleep. Her reading glasses were lying on top of a stack of documents on the carved teak sidetable beside a silver-framed picture of Maurice in his pilot's uniform. John smiled; his wife was living proof that not all Imperial woman got heavy after thirty. *Just magnificent,* he thought, undoing his cravat.

She woke, stirred, and smiled at him. "Hello, darling," she said. "I can smell the Premier's tobacco, so I know you told the truth, it was politicians and not a mistress."

John grinned. "You can have proof positive in a moment, if you'll stay awake."

"Hurry then."

Gerta forced her hands to relax from their white-knuckled grip on the armored side of the car.

"I hope you're getting every moment of this," she muttered to the cameraman beside her.

The Protégé nodded without pulling away from the eyepiece of the big clumsy machine clamped to the side of the vehicle. His hand cranked the handle with metronomic regularity, and geared mechanisms whirred within it. Beside it a small searchlight added to the dawn gloaming, bringing the ambient light up enough to make filming practical.

The huge biplane bombardment aircraft was staggering in towards its landing . . . or crash, whichever. The long fuselage was tublike, with open circular pits for the pilot and copilot, and others for bombardiers and gunners. Between each of the long wings were four engine pods, each pod mounting a puller and pusher set. The undercarriage settled towards the ground, struck dust from the packed earth. Gravel spurted. On the second impact, the splayed legs of the big wheels spread further, the whole plane sinking closer to the ground as it raced across the runway. Then the bottom touched in a shower of sparks and tearing of wood and fabric. Half the lower part of the fuselage abraded away as it gradually came to a halt, spinning around like a top once or twice before it did. Rescue teams raced out, bells ringing, although the props didn't *quite* touch the earth and nothing caught fire . . . this time.

"Got that?"

"Yes, sir," the Protégé replied, and began the complex process of changing a reel of film.

Gerta pulled her uniform cap off, crumpling it in her hand. That was the only outward sign of her rage; she sternly repressed the impulse to throw it down and stamp on it.

The squadron commander came over to her open-topped car. "I understand completely, Brigadier," he said. "Will your film do any good?"

"Well, I can now confirm with visual aids that we lose ten percent of those things in *normal* operations with each mission, not counting enemy action. When I think of how many fighters or ground-attack aircraft we could have for the same resources—"

"Just get them to stop telling us to fly these abortions," the man said. He was very young, not more than twenty-five; turnover in the bomber squadrons was heavy. "It isn't that we mind dying for the Chosen, you understand—"

"—it's just that you'd like it to have some sort of point," Gerta finished for him. "I'll do my best. Porschmidt has a lot of friends in high places."

"I'd like to take them to a high place—over Santander City or Bosson, and dump them off with the rest of the bombload."

Gerta nodded. "If it's any consolation, we're doing some things that are smarter than this."

"It couldn't be worse."

CHAPTER TWENTY-FIVE

John Hosten gripped Arturo Bianci's hand. "You're still alive," he said.

The guerilla leader looked closer to sixty than the forty-five or so John knew him to be. His once-stocky frame was weathered down to bone and sinew and a necessary minimum of muscle, and the dense close-cropped cap of hair that topped his seamed, weathered face was the same silver as the stubble on his jaw.

"Not for want of the *tedeschi* trying," he said. The smile on his face looked unpracticed. "They've had a high price on my head these sixteen years."

He led John back into the cave. It was deep and twisting, opening out into broader caverns within and spreading out into a maze that led miles into the depths of the Collini Paeani. An occasional kerosene lantern cast a puddle of light; now and then an occupied cave showed men sleeping under blankets, working on their weapons, or stacking crates and boxes under waxed tarpaulins. There was even a stable-cavern, where picketed mules drowsed in rows and fodder was stacked ten feet high against one wall. The caves smelled of old smoke, dirt, and damp limestone; there were underground rivers further in, rushing past to who knew where.

"Big operation," John said.

"One of many," Arturo said. "We try not to put too much in one place, in case there is an informer or the *tedeschi* are lucky with a patrol. More and more come to us. The *tedeschi* take more land for plantations, and always there are more labor drafts. If a man is marked down for the camps or the factories in Hell"—he used the slang term for the Land—"he can only escape by coming to us."

"Or by volunteering for the army, or the police," John pointed out.

The guerilla leaders face went tight as a clenched fist. "Some do. And of those, some are *our* men, to be spies, and to wait for the day we call. The enemy do not much trust units they raise here, nor do they dare mix them much with Protégés from the Land."

They came to a medium-sized chamber and pushed through the blankets hung over the entrance. An old woman tended a pot of stew over a small charcoal fire, and a group as ragged and hard-looking as Arturo waited around a rickety table. There was no attempt at introductions, simply a wolfish patience or a slight shifting of the weapons that festooned them. Some of them were tearing at lumps of hard bread, or dunking the chunks in bowls of the stew, eating with the concentration of men who went hungry much of the time. They looked at John expressionlessly, taking in Barrjen and his little squad of middle-aged ex-Marines with wary respect.

John was dressed in high-laced boots and tough tweeds, Santander hunting or hiking clothes. He swung his pack to the table and unbuckled the flap.

"Here," he said, tapping his finger on the map he produced. It was Republic Naval Survey issue, showing a section of the north shore of the Gut a hundred miles east and west of Salmi.

The men around the table were mostly ex-peasants, with a scattering of shopkeepers and artisans, but they'd all learned to read maps since the Chosen conquest. The spot he indicated was at the end of a south-trending bulge, a little almost-island at a narrow part of the great strait.

"Fort Causili," one said. "Old fort, but the *tedeschi* have been building there. Two, three thousand laborers, and troops, for most of the past year. And they have put in a spur rail line."

John nodded. He took out photographs, blurred from

enlargement and hurried camera work, but clear enough. Some were from the air, others taken with concealed instruments by workers on the base. They showed deep pits, concrete revetments with overhead protection set into the cliffs, and at the last, special flatcars with huge cylindrical objects under heavy tarpaulin cover.

"More than a fort," John said. "Those are special long-range guns, six of them. Twelve-inch naval rifles, sleeved down to eight inches and extended. They range most of the way to shoal water on the southern shore . . . and the enemy hold that, it's Union territory. There's another fort there that commands the only passage, it's got heavy siege mortars. Between them they can close the Gut almost exactly at the old Union-Santander border."

A few of the guerilla commanders shrugged. One muttered: "Bad. But so? There is a infantry brigade in that area, dug in, fully prepared. Those of us who wanted to die have done so long ago."

"Very bad," Arturo said. "If they can close the Gut, they can put their own ships on it and use it to move supplies. That will solve many of their problems. It will free troops to be used elsewhere, and free more labor, locomotives. And your navy will not be able to raid along the coast, or drop off supplies to us. Very bad. But Vincini is right, we cannot do more than harass it."

Vincini drew a long knife; it looked as if it had been honed down from a butcher's tool. He traced a circle with the point.

"A quiet area. Few recruits for us. That would change if we staged some operations there—the *tedeschi* would kill in reply, and that would bring the villagers to our side."

John nodded; the guerillas always struck away from their base areas. The Chosen killed hostages from the areas where the attacks occurred, which merely convinced the locals they might as well be hung for sheep as lambs.

"I'm not asking you to take the base yourselves," he said. "But believe me, we cannot allow the enemy to complete it. If they command the Gut, they have gone far towards winning the war—if Santander falls, your cause is hopeless."

That earned him some glares, but reluctant nods as well. He went on:

"Remember, all the world is at war. We attack the enemy in many places. You cannot take the base alone, but you can *help*. Here is what I propose—"

Angelo Pesalozi grunted as the Santander sailors hauled him over the gunwale of the motor torpedo boat. The Protégé looked around. The little vessel was blacked out, but there was enough starlight and reflected light from the moons to see it. There was an elemental simplicity to the design; a sharp-prowed plywood hull, shallow but exquisitely shaped. The forward deck held a double-barreled pom-pom behind a thin shield, but the real weapons were on either side: a pair of eighteen-inch naval torpedoes in sealed sheet-steel launch tubes. There was a small deckhouse around the wheel amidships, and a wooden coaming over the big aircraft engines at the stern that could hurl the frail concoction through a calm sea at better than thirty knots. Right now it was burbling in a low rumbling purr, like the world's biggest cat, muffled by a tin box full of baffles at the stern that showed the hasty marks of an improvised fitting. The blue exhaust filled the night with its tang and the wind was too calm to disturb it much.

A dozen more like it waited outside the harbor of Bassin du Sud. Not a scrap of metal gleamed, and the faces of the crews were equally dark with burnt cork and black wool stocking-caps. The commander of the little flotilla was the oldest man in the crews, and he was several years short of thirty; most of his subordinates had been fishermen two years ago, or scions of families wealthy enough to own motorboats. Kneally's father was a newspaper magnate with ambitions for his sons. His wasn't the only grin as he extended his hand to the heavyset Protégé.

"Welcome aboard," he said, in fair Landisch. "Commander James Frederick Kneally, at your service. You've got it?"

Silent, Angelo reached inside his jacket and pulled out an oilskin map. The Santander naval officer unwrapped it and spread it on the engine coaming, clicking on a small shaded flashlight.

"Oh, very nice," Kneally breathed. No changes from the ones Intelligence had given them back in Karlton.

A Land Naval Service-issue map, with the minefields marked in red, compass deviations, bearings, the lot; typical Chosen thoroughness. The Santander officer laid his compass on the map and looked up. Two lights flashed from different parts of the hills above Bassin du Sud, and he was busy with straight-edge and slide rule for a moment.

"Right here," Kneally said, marking the map. "All *right*. Thanks again."

The Protégé dipped his head. "I must return; I am on an errand for my master that gives me some freedom from suspicion, but not much. Give me ten minutes."

The flotilla commander shook his hand again, then returned entranced to the map as he was handed back over the side to his little steam launch. He half-noticed that the tiny pennant at the rear was the checked black-and-white of the Land General Staff, then dismissed it.

"Helm," he said. "Prepare to follow a course to my direction, dead slow. Signal to the flotilla, follow in line astern."

A dim blue light just above the waterline snapped on at the very stern of the lead torpedo boat. The man at the wheel spat overside and wiped first one hand, then the other on his duck trousers. The commander ducked his head through a hole in the coaming, into the stuffy darkness of the engine compartment. The petty officer in charge and his two ratings crouched by the big internal-combustion motors like acolytes worshiping some god of iron and brass, tools and oil can at the ready. They'd spent the past week going over every part and link and piece of the motor train as if their lives depended on it. Which, of course, they did.

"Ready?"

"Ready as we'll ever be, sir."

He pulled himself back up and looked at the stars. One moon full, the other half, a little scattered cloud, dead calm with only the inevitable southern ocean swell. Inside the breakwaters of the harbor it would be as calm as a bathtub. He looked at the map again, noting the markings on currents.

"Three knots," he said quietly to the helm. "Come about

twelve degrees and maintain for four minutes. Carefully now. It's a tight fit."

"Tight as a cabin boy's bum, sir," the helmsman agreed, and let out the throttle inch by careful inch.

The muffler on the stern burbled a little louder, and the commander winced. The Chosen had beefed up the port defenses considerably, and while he had what looked like perfect intelligence on them, knowing exactly how a 250-pound prizefighter would throw a right hook did you little good if you were a ninety-pound weed with a glass jaw. Kneally's boats were plywood shells over explosives and highly volatile fuel; a heavy machine gun could turn them to burning splinters, much less a pom-pom, much less a 240mm shell from the Emmas in the castle or the harbor forts. *And* there were gunboats constantly patrolling.

The minefields were laid with the clear passages staggered by horizontal lanes, making doglegs nobody could negotiate by luck. It would be difficult enough in daylight, with a pilot conning the helm; the enemy had lost a couple of supply ships to their own mines.

"Gently, gently. Blink the stern light. Now come about to port, ninety degrees. Gently, man, gently."

Sweat soaked his stocking cap and stung in the shaving cuts on his chin. The mines were down there, dull iron balls studded with pressure-sensitive brass horns, floating like malignant flowers on their chain tethers. He wiped his face with the back of his jacket. The lights of Bassin du Sud were coming into view; there were a few of them, mostly low down by the water. *Maybe we* should *have staged an air raid at the same time,* he thought. Get them looking up. *No, the brass were right for once.* It would just get them awake and ready, and a crew could swing a quick-firer from ninety degrees to horizontal a lot faster than they could get out of their racks and on line.

Something bumped against the hull forward. Bump . . . bump . . . bump . . .

His stomach lurched. Every man on board froze, except for the helm's careful twitch at the wheel. Then the crew of MTB 109 shuddered and relaxed as the sound died astern, and the sudden annihilating blast *didn't* lift their craft out of the water broken-backed. Another turn ahead. He looked behind. Barely possible to make out MTB 110. Good. This follow-the-leader put his nerves even more on edge; small errors could accumulate and throw the last boats right into the mines. Although God knew they'd practiced often enough at the mockups back at base in Karlton. The base there had never been much, but it rattled empty since the Southern Fleet was wiped out in the opening days of the war.

The ships that slaughtered four thousand Santander sailors were waiting ahead . . . and they'd carefully spent half a day shooting or running down the survivors in the water, too. His teeth showed white in his darkened face.

"All right, we're out." If the map was complete. "Signal to deploy."

He brought up his binoculars and squinted. There was just enough background scatter to see the line of Land cruisers silhouetted against the diffuse glow . . . he hoped. They were a couple of thousand yards away, smoke visible from one or two stacks on each ship, keeping some steam up; a boom with antitorpedo netting out, floating low, a line across the dead calm of the harbor. And the lights of a patrol boat, low-powered searchlights looking for infiltrators or defectors trying to make it out in rubber dinghies.

The Santander torpedo boats spread out into line abreast. "Six knots," Kneally said.

The engines burbled a little louder. *How long?* Eventually they were going to notice. . . .

A searchlight speared out at them and an alarm wailed.

"Goose it, Chief! Goose it!"

The helm slammed the throttles forward. Now the engines roared, a shattering noise no muffler could mute. White water peeled back from the bows in two high roostertails of spray, throwing salt across his lips. Lights flicked on along the line of Land cruisers, and starshells blossomed high above.

"Too late, you leather-sucking perverts!" Kneally yelled.

The boom was less than five hundred yards ahead. There was just time enough for the torpedo boats to reach the maximum safe speed. Kneally clamped his hands on the bracket ahead of him and braced himself. The smooth strip of reinforcing steel down the torpedo boat's keel slalomed it into the air in an arc that ended in an enormous splash that threw water twice the height of the little vessel's stub signal mast. Then each pair was driving for a cruiser's side, and the big ships loomed like gray steel cliffs. Cliffs speckled with fire, as the first pom-pom crews made it to their stations and began to open fire.

The MTB 109 was skipping forward like a watermelon seed squeezed between thumb and forefinger. One-pound shells pocked the water around it, and the boat's own forward pom-pom was punching out a stream of bright fire-globes itself. They wouldn't harm the cruiser, but they might throw off the crews of the bigger ship's antitorpedo-boat armament. A quick-firer banged from its sponson mount, and a shell threw up a fountain of spray to their left. All the time, Kneally's mind was estimating distances with the skill of endless practice.

"Ready—"

THUD.

MTB 110 blew up in a globe of yellow flame, its breath like the foretaste of hell.

"Hold her steady!" Kneally yelled, helping the CPO wrestle with the wheel as blast knocked the shallow dish-like hull sideways.

They plunged through the flame in a single searing instant, the spray-plumes of their passage helping to keep it from searing them too badly. MTB 109 was travelling as fast as anything on the oceans of Visager now, bounding forward like a porpoise driven by the power of four hundred horses. A thousand yards, maximum range. Nine hundred. The nose of the 109 was trained precisely on the cruiser's stern, lined up on the winking light of the pom-pom tub there. The shells drifted out towards him and then snapped by overhead.

"Fire one! Turn her, Chief!"

With a flat bang the launching charge slammed the first torpedo out of its tube. The frail fabric of the torpedo boat shuddered as the silver cylinder arched into the water, its contrarotating propellers already spinning. The boat was heeling to the right, its bow tracing an arc that carried it along the whole length of the enemy warship.

"Fire two! Fire three! Fire four! *Get us the fuck out of here!*"

The night was a chaos of flickering shapes and blinding lights, tracers and searchlights and explosions. Kneally twisted in the coaming to look over his shoulder. White water cataracted up from the side of the cruiser that had been their target—from others, too. He howled a catamount screech, until his teeth clicked painfully shut. This time they had hit the boom much harder, and there was an ominous crackle from the framework of the MTB 109.

But it only had to hold together a little longer. Another light was blinking to port, the guerilla pickup who would smuggle them out through the mountains, if they could reach shore and then avoid the Land patrols. Kneally's head swiveled, trying to see everything at once. It was still too dark, too tangled with lines and bars of light that bounced across his eyes. If one of the cruiser's magazines had not exploded behind them he would never have seen the destroyer coming. The actinic light showed it all too clearly: the turtleback forward deck and four billowing smokestacks, and the waves curling back from the cruel knife bows looming over his boat.

Kneally threw himself backward with a yell. A huge impact threw him pinwheeling into the air, and the water hit him like concrete. Somehow he pushed the whirling darkness away and fought his way to the surface, aided by the buoyancy of the cork vest he wore. Propwash sucked at him, and he bobbed in the destroyer's wake. Oily water slopped into his mouth.

"Jesus," he grunted, almost giggling with incredulous relief at rinding himself alive. "And Dad wanted me to be a hero."

His viewpoint was too low to see much, but several of the cruisers that had been his squadron's targets were burning, and he could see a stern rising into the sky with its huge twin bronze screws glinting in the light of fires and searchlights.

That sobered him, and he turned towards the beach and began to swim doggedly. If they didn't kill him, he'd live . . . and there would be other battles.

He almost missed a stroke. The adrenaline was wearing off, and he was remembering the look on the chief's face as the destroyer's bows loomed over them. He might be the only survivor of the dozen crew who'd manned MTB 109.

Kneally shuddered. *Another battle.*

"About bloody time," Gerta said with satisfaction.

Only the last gunpit was still uncovered, and work was going on through the night under the harsh light of the arcs.

It was sunk deep into the cliff face, taking advantage of a natural ravine through the chalky limestone. Labor gangs and explosives had hollowed out an oblong chamber, wider at its rear than at the face of the steep rock. It still smelled of green concrete, but the complex metal mountings of the giant guns were in place, and the two tubes themselves were being fastened in their cradles below. The same great cranes—modified shipbuilding models—that had lowered the guns were now transferring beams and planks of steel that were small only by comparison. Down below pneumatic riveters hammered and arc welders stuttered as hundreds of Protégé laborers and Chosen engineers assembled the intricate jigsaw puzzle into multiple layers of steel. Tomorrow other teams would begin burying it under layer upon layer of concrete laced with rebar and filled with massive rubble from the original excavation, topped with twenty feet of granite quarried from the old Imperial fort.

Gerta inhaled the scent of ozone and scorched metal, fists on hips, pivoting to take in the bustling scene. The other three gunpits were already in place, spread out in a semicircle along the outer edge of the near-island. Each pit was open only along the narrow slit through which the guns would fire—and they would show their muzzles only slightly, and that only when run out for a shoot. Tunnels ran between the pits, and between the pits and their ammunition bunkers, underground barracks and mess halls, fuel stores, generator rooms; but they were all carefully kinked and equipped with blast doors taken from junked battleships to contain internal damage.

"About bloody time is right," Kurt Wallers said. He was carrying colonel's tabs, with dual artillery and engineering branch-of-service slashes. "We were complete idiots to wait this long. If we'd had this installation in place when we attacked the Sierrans, that ratfuck in Barclon would never have happened. The Santies couldn't have put so much as a harbor barge down the Gut without getting it pounded into scrap."

Gerta shrugged. "My sentiments exactly, Kurt—if that's any consolation."

The other Chosen officer hesitated. Gerta slapped him lightly on the shoulder. "Spit it out—we *did* go through the Test of Life together, after all. You've done a good job here, too, you're three months ahead of schedule."

"Well, then . . . your father is the chief of the General Staff. What the fuck was he thinking of?"

Gerta sighed. "He's chief of the General Staff, not the Chosen Council. They've got a bad case of victory disease, and it's been getting worse since we overran the Empire. That was too easy, and they've been dispersing effort on pet projects and hobbyhorses ever since. Sitting back in Copernik, looking at large-scale maps, it looks like we're conquering the world. The Empire, the Union, now the Sierra."

"We *are* conquering the world. The problem is *holding* the world. We beat the Imperials because we could concentrate our force. Now—" He made a spreading gesture with his hands.

"Tell me, Kurt. I told the general often enough. *He* lobbied the Council often enough, but their pet projects got in the way. They had this scheduled for the beginning of the war with Santander . . . about five to eight years from now."

"Well, better late than never," Kurt said. "This'll be a significant nail holding down what we've conquered. It makes their naval bases at Dubuk and Charsson useless as far as the Gut's concerned. They've been harassing the shit out of us, I can tell you. *And* landing supplies to the animals in the hills virtually at will, since Barclon. That's getting as bad as it was right after the conquest, or worse; they're smarter now."

Gerta nodded. "When can you start test firing?"

"Oh, I wouldn't want to do that for another couple of weeks, even on the first pair. The concrete has to set *hard* before we put that much stress on the mountings."

"How're the secondary works coming?"

"About a third done." She followed as he walked inland. "The usual close-in works, machine guns, bunkered field-guns, mortars, minefields, wire, steel spike obstacles. We've got half the *Schlenke Emmas* in their pits, too, so pretty soon we can drop high-angle fire on anything that gets too close for the big guns to deal with."

"You're getting a lot of work out of these animals," she said, eyeing the swarming construction site.

"You can catch more flies with honey than with vinegar," he said. "I've done a lot of engineering work in the New Territories, and—"

An aide trotted up. "Sir. Message over the wireless."

Kurt took it and read, tilting the yellow flimsy to catch the lights. "Attack on Bassin du Sud," he said. "Considerable damage sustained in beating it off."

Gerta grunted in surprise. That was communique language for *they whipped our arse.*

"*Fuck* it. Damn, damn, if they damage the Southern Squadron badly, there goes our route around the eastern lobe to Marsai."

Kurt nodded. "Still, it won't be too bad even so; they can ship straight south from Corona by rail and then through the Gut, now that we've got this."

"*Ya.*" Gerta's eyes narrowed. "The question is, do the Santies realize that?"

Kurt looked at the flimsy again. "Not many details. I wonder how they got through the minefields? And those howitzers in the fort, they should take care of any ships."

"Should. But—"

Another messenger. "Sir. The Air Service scout airship *Guthavok* reports it is under attack from Santander heavier-than-air pursuit planes."

They both looked south by reflex. "At *night?*" Kurt Wallers said incredulously.

Fire blossomed in the night, five thousand feet up and miles to the south.

Wallers began to bark orders. Gerta turned on her heel and trotted back to her scout car, vaulting up the fixed ladder and then into the open compartment with one hand on the rim. Her son was already peering south through the heavy rail-mounted glasses. Gerta looked around; the wireless was fired up and ready, and the vehicle had pressure and was ready to move.

"Signals," she said. The operator looked up, earphones on and hand poised over the signal key. "To regional HQ in Salini. Fort under heavy attack from Santander seaborne forces, including battleships and amphibious element of unknown strength. Stop. As representative of the General Staff I order repeat order immediate mobilization all available forces and their concentration on this point. Stop. Brigadier Gerta Hosten. Stop. Send until acknowledged."

The signals technician was sending before Gerta had finished the first sentence. Johann turned to her; by now he'd learned enough to merely raise his brows.

"Ya. If that was wrong, I will be lucky to command a one-company garrison post guarding a bridge," she said. "But I'd rather risk being a damned fool."

To the driver: "Get us out of here. Out on the north road, then east towards Salini."

She pulled the machine-carbine out of its clamps over her seat, checked the flat drum magazine, and reached for the helmet that hung beside it. With a chuff of waste steam, the car pulled out through the growing chaos of the half-built fort.

CHAPTER TWENTY-SIX

"Aren't you getting a little senior for commanding from the front?" Admiral Maurice Farr asked quietly.

Jeffrey grinned at his father. "I notice you're here, sir, and not back in Dubuk."

Farr shrugged. "An admiral has to command from a ship."

"And a general has to be where there's some chance of getting useful information in timely fashion," Jeffrey replied reasonably. He drew himself up and saluted. "Admiral."

"General," the elder Farr replied. "Good hunting, and we'll give all the support we can."

Jeffrey turned, swung over the rail, and scrambled down the rope ladder. A young aide tried to assist him as he jumped down into the waiting steam launch.

"I'm not quite decrepit yet, Seimore," Jeffrey said dryly, and took a swig from his canteen. "We're better off than the rest of the force, here."

The men were climbing down netting hung on the sides of the transports and into the waiting flat-bottomed motor barges, or waiting crammed shoulder to shoulder and probably seasick in similar vessels that had sailed with the fleet from Dubuk. The Gut was calm tonight, but the flat-bottomed barges would pitch and sway in a bathtub.

"Let's go," Jeffrey said quietly.

The launch swung in towards the shore; it was low and sandy here, in contrast to the cliffs that marked most of this section of the Gut's northern shore. Low and sandy on either side of the fort that was their objective. The first wave of troops would be going ashore right now, and from the lack of noise, meeting little or no resistance. Well, they'd expected that.

Jeffrey looked at his watch. 0500 hours, nearly dawn. Right about now they should—

BOOM. BOOM. BOOM—

The big guns of the fleet cut loose, firing from west to east in a long, slightly curved line. The great bottle-shaped muzzle flashes lit the scene with a continuous strobing illumination that was brighter than the false dawn. It was still dark enough for the red-glowing dots of the shells to be visible with their own heat, arching up into the sky to fall towards the Chosen.

Dust filtered down onto Kurt Wallers' head. The gun position shook as twelve- and eight-inch shells landed on the surface above, or hammered deep into the soft limestone of the cliffs.

I built well, he thought. Aloud: "Well, the enemy has provided us with an aiming point. Return fire."

"But sir!" someone protested. "The mountings—"

"Are not hard-set yet," he replied. "Nevertheless, you have your orders."

With hydraulic smoothness, the muzzle of the great gun began to move downward in its cradle.

Ten miles outside Salini, John Hosten grinned into the low red light of dawn. He washed down a mouthful of half-chewed hardtack with a swig from his canteen and slapped the cork back into it. It was like eating pieces of a clay flowerpot, but it kept you going, and if you were careful it didn't break your teeth. The air smelled of dew-wet rock and aromatic shrub and old sweat from the clothes of the guerillas around him. "Quick of them," he said. "They're in a hurry." The road through the low rocky hills was quite good, not exactly a paved highway, but thirty feet wide and cut out of the hillside with generous shoulders and ditches. Right now it was crowded with a convoy. Two light tanks in the front, the Land copy of the Santander Whippet, trucks crammed with infantry, more trucks pulling field-guns and pompoms and supplies, more infantry, some more tanks . . .

. . . and a forty-degree slope on either side of the road.

"That is their mobile reaction force," Arturo said.

John nodded. Not even Santander could afford to give all its infantry and guns motor transport; the Land had roughly the same output of vehicles, but a much bigger army and fewer wheels per head.

The lead tank was near the ferroconcrete bridge. "Now?" John said.

Arturo nodded. "They are in a *great* hurry," he said, smiling like something with tentacles, and pressed the plunger beside him.

The explosions at the bottom of the bridge pylons weren't very spectacular, although the sound echoed off the stony slopes. A puff of dust and smoke—pulverized concrete and plain dirt—and the uprights heaved, twisted, and sank slowly at an increasing tilt. The flat slab roadway crumbled in chunks as its support was removed, falling down towards the bottom of the gorge and the dry-season trickle that ran there. The first tank went with it, sparks flying as its treads worked backwards.

Arturo laughed at the sight. Even then, John had time to be slightly chilled at the sound. Nearly five hundred feet to fall, knowing that when you hit—

The tank cracked open like an eggshell on the boulders, and the dust of its impact was followed seconds later by a fireball as the fuel caught. Shells shot out of the fireball, trailing smoke, as the ammunition cooked off.

As ye sow, so shall ye reap, Raj said relentlessly. ***Remember what the Imperials were like before the Chosen came. As they are now, the Chosen made them.***

Rifles and machine guns opened up on the stalled convoy, and mortars as well. A huge secondary explosion threw trucks tumbling as a shell landed in a truckload of ammunition, or perhaps on the limber of a field-gun. Birds rose in clouds as the racket of battle replaced the early morning calm. Order spread among the chaos below, soldiers taking cover and officers spreading them out. The first were already beginning to work their way upslope. Men died and rolled downward; others took their place. The four-pounder guns of the light tanks coughed and coughed again, and their machine guns beat the slope with an iron hail.

Below John was a guerilla sniper, invisible even at ten yards in his camouflage blanket, a net sewn with strips of cloth in shades of ochre, gray, and brown. The muzzle twitched slightly, and the rifle snapped.

Scratch one Chosen officer, probably, John thought.

Arturo was examining the scene below with his binoculars. "We cannot hold them long," he warned. "If we try, the rear elements of the convoy will work around behind us—there are trails, and their maps are good."

"No, we can't," John said. "But they were in a *great* hurry . . . and this is not the only ambush."

Arturo smiled again. This time John joined him.

"Who the *fuck* does he think he's shooting at?" Johan Hosten said, pulling himself erect in the open-topped armored car and glaring after the two-engine ground attack aircraft that was hedgehopping away.

Gerta grinned at her son's indignation, although that *had* been a bit of a nerve-wracking surprise. There were fresh lead smears on the flanks of her war-car.

"At Santies, of course," she said.

Granted, there was a bloody great Land sunburst painted on the rear deck of the war-car, but she knew from personal experience how hard it was to see anything accurately when you were doing a strafing run in combat conditions.

"Only thing more dangerous than your own artillery is your own air force, boy," she said, slapping him on the shoulder. "Especially in a ratfuck like this where nobody knows where anyone is, including themselves."

It's a relief in a way, having nothing but a fight on my hands.

They turned a bend in the road. "And speaking of Santies—"

The eastbound road wound through rolling ground covered in olive groves. Men in brown uniforms were ahead of them, and two light-wheeled vehicles were on the gravel surface of the road. They had whip antennae bobbing above them. Some sort of command group, then.

"Driver! Floor it!" Gerta barked, pulling a grenade from a box clipped to the inside of the sloping armored side of the war-car.

He did. The five-ton vehicle was too heavy to actually leap ahead, but it accelerated, more slowly than a newer model with an IC engine; on the other hand, the steam was almost silent. The Santies noticed only just before Johan opened up with the forward machine gun, walking bursts across the men grouped around the hood of one of the light cars.

Gerta shouted wordlessly as the prow of the war-car rammed one vehicle aside, crumpling the frame and knocking it into the ditch. She tossed the grenade at the wreckage and followed it with a spray of pistol-caliber bullets from her machine carbine. Jumping with combat-adrenaline, her eyes picked out one face/body/movement gestalt as the man leaped for cover behind a rock. She fired, twisted, cursed as her son at the machine gun blocked her line of sight, grabbed at another grenade and threw it.

Return fire pinged off the riveted armor plates of the car, making the crew duck, and then they were past.

"Keep going!" she said, raising her head for a look.

"Jesus!"

Jeffrey raised his head, coughing in the plume of dust left behind by the turtle-shaped Chosen vehicle; some sort of six-wheeled armored car. As it turned the corner and zipped out of sight ahead, an arm appeared over the side of the hull with one finger extended from a clenched fist, and pumped in an unmistakable gesture.

Wounded men screamed. For an instant everyone else stayed frozen and flat to the earth, waiting for the follow up.

"Keep moving!" Jeffrey said aloud. "That was a straggler."

"*Merde,*" Henri muttered beside him, levering himself up with the butt of his rifle.

My sentiments exactly, Jeffrey thought as he took stock. Two regimental commanders out of it, and one of the priceless radios.

"Runner," he said, "tell their seconds what's happened, and that I have full confidence in them. Somebody get that fire out." The wrecked car was sending licking flames and black smoke upward, just the sort of marker a cruising Land Air Service pilot would need. "And let's get back to work," he went on calmly.

His mouth was full of gummy saliva. That had been far too sudden, and far too close. A few of the faces that bent over the map with him were pale beneath their coating of summer dust, but nobody was visibly panicky.

The map showed the bulge of coastline that held the fort they were attacking. "We've just about closed the circle around the landward side," he said. "Now, Colonel McWhirter, you're going to dig in along this line and hold them off us. The partisans are doing a good job of slowing them down, but when they hit, it'll be hard. The rest of us will press on the perimeter."

"Going to cost," someone commented. "They're expecting us, by now."

Jeffrey shrugged. "We'll keep their attention. They don't have much of a garrison there yet, mostly construction battalions. With a little luck, the Resort Brigade will do its job."

Major Steven Durrison, Fifth Mountain Regiment—known familiarly in the Army of the Republic as the Resort Brigade, since so many mountain-climbing hobbyists filled its ranks—looked up the rest of the gully.

Not much of a climb, he thought. About a sixty-degree slope, the natural rock overlain with rubble. The enemy had evidently been dumping construction fill down it, since it led up to the lip of the plateau. From the way they'd cut footings into the sides, they'd probably planned to build something here. They hadn't had time

And they were otherwise occupied right now. More shells trundled across the sky to burst on the plateau tops above. The ships out in the Gut looked like toys at this distance, a fleet a child might sail in his bathtub. The earthquake rumble and shudder of the earth under his body showed how out of scale distance made the scene. Rock and concrete fountained over the cliffs, past the firing slits of the heavy guns, to land on the beach below. More shaking through the rock beneath him; he tried to imagine what it was like to be caught in the open up there, and failed. *If that doesn't keep their heads down, nothing will.*

The mountaineer looked back over his shoulder; men were strung out down nearly to the beach, along the line of rope secured by iron stakes driven into the rock by the advance element. Most were armed with the new submachine guns, for close in work, or with pump-action shotguns, and festooned with bandoliers, satchel charges, coils of rope, and pitons.

"Lieutenant," he called, "we'll start to work our way across from there."

He pointed; no climber could mistake what he meant, a long shadow slanting upward across the cliff-face to their right. "Signaller."

The heliograph squad had set up a little way down the ravine. The sergeant in charge of the squad looked up.

"You've got contact with the flagship?"

"Yessir."

Durrison nodded, hiding his relief. The alternative was colored rockets. That would *work*, but even with dozens of heavy shells landing up above, someone was likely to notice. Heliograph signals— light reflected off mirrors—were effectively line of sight. None of the enemy would see his going out.

"Send: 'Am proceeding with Phase Two.'"

About bloody time, Maurice Farr thought, lowering his binoculars. The signals station were scribbling on their pads, but he could still read code himself.

The *Great Republic* twisted and heeled in the water as her broadside fired. Light flashed in return from the upper third of the cliffs, and three seconds later the whole eighteen-thousand-ton bulk of the battleship shuddered and rang like a giant gong struck with a sledgehammer. Farr blinked at the fountain of sparks as the shell struck her main belt armor.

"Sir!" It was Damage Control, speaking to the flagships captain. "Flooding in compartment C3. That one hit us below the waterline."

Gridley nodded. "Get them to work on it," he said, "Containment measures."

That meant sealing off the affected area behind the watertight doors, hopefully not before they got the personnel out of it. C3 was unpleasantly close to the A turret magazines as well.

Those guns certainly have punch, he thought. Eight-inch, but fired with a twelve-incher's powder charge, and an extra-long barrel. The velocity was unbelievable. *Much faster and you could fire shells into orbit.*

"Sir." This time to the fleet commander. "Sir, *Templedon City* reports that they've got the fires out and stabilized by counterflooding."

A heavy cruiser. "What speed can they make?"

"Sir, they report no more than six knots."

"They're to withdraw. Detach two destroyers to escort." And to pick up survivors if they didn't make it back to Dubuk.

Farr raised his glasses again. "I'd say it was about time we did something about this fort they were building, wouldn't you, Gridley?" he said calmly.

"Christ yes, Admiral. If they'd got it fully operational . . ." The flagship captain's voice faded off.

A biplane plunged past the bridge, trailing smoke. It smashed into the water and exploded not far from the bow of a destroyer; the whole thing happened too fast for him to see the national insignia. Dozens more were swarming through the air above the cloud of smoke and shellbursts that marked the surface of the fort, like flies around a piece of meat left in the sun.

Good thing we're in range of ground-based air support here, Farr thought.

His sons were inland there, where the fighting was—steadily increasing fighting, as the Land forces battered their way through guerilla harassment and started to bring their weight to bear on the Santander blocking elements. His eldest grandson was in one of those wood-and-canvas powered kites . . . if he hadn't been the one who plunged out of the sky and died just now. Pride came in many flavors; right now it tasted like fear. An old man might not fear for himself, but anyone living still had something hostage to fortune. His family, his country . . .

I think we'd be in a very bad way indeed if it weren't for John and Jeffrey, he thought. If John hadn't been born with a clubfoot, or if I hadn't gotten that posting as naval attaché in Oathtaking . . .

"Carry on," he said aloud. "Let's keep them busy. And stand by to fire support missions for the ground forces."

"I don't give a living shit how many partisans there are out there, Colonel," Heinrich Hosten said with quiet venom. His fingers were white on the field telephone. "Ignore them. Ignore your fucking flanks. Hit the Santies, and hit them hard, or by the Oath, you'll be in the Western Islands dodging blowgun darts from the savages next month, if you're unlucky enough to be still alive."

He retuned the handset to its cradle with enormous care, fighting through the rage that clouded his vision. He looked at the pin-studded map and tried to force himself to be objective. *I'm not justified in going to the front. More information is getting through now. I'm in a better position to coordinate from here.*

He could hear the Santy naval bombardment from here, though, a continuous rumble to the south. Guns were firing closer than that, medium field pieces; Land batteries, shooting obstacles out of the way in the narrow passages of the hills.

One of his staff handed him the field telephone again, "Sir, you'll want to hear this yourself."

He picked it up. "*Ja?*"

Gerta's voice. He closed his eyes; *nothing* should surprise him today.

"You'll never guess which old friend of yours I ran into today," she said. "Ran into literally, but I didn't quite manage to kill him."

There were times when he was tempted to believe in malignant spirits.

(((•))) (((•))) (((•)))

Kurt Wallers jammed his palms over his ears and opened his mouth. The gun fired again, and the pressure wave battered at him. No point in going back to the command bunker deeper in the rock; the observation stations weren't operational yet. With those and the calculating machine it would have been possible to direct accurate fire nearly to the southern shore of the Gut. As it was, each tube was firing under independent control—over open sights.

And not doing a bad job. He hated to think what had happened to the construction people up above; he'd spent a long time training them. *All we have to do is hold out until the reinforcements drive off the landing parties.* Then—

"Sir! Movement on the beach below us!"

He blinked. "Get some extra propellant charges." They came in fabric containers the size of small garbage cans. "Strap grenades to them. Pull the tabs and roll them over the edge of the casement. *Move.*"

Suddenly the background rumble of naval shellfire exploding on the plateau overhead ceased. Wallers looked up; that took his eyes away from the slit of light where the embrasure mouth pierced the cliff. Something flew in. His head whipped around, and trained reflex threw him down, not quite in time.

Durrison plastered himself to the lip of concrete above the gun embrasures. Every time the long cannon within fired, the concussion threatened to flip him off the ledge, despite the rope sling fastened to pitons driven firmly into the rock above. A couple of his men *had* been flipped, to dangle scrabbling on their ropes until the hands of their squadmates could haul them back. The enemy hadn't noticed, thank God; the embrasures might be narrow firing slits in comparison to the size of the guns within or the scale of the three-hundred-foot height of the cliffs, but they were still fifteen feet from top to bottom.

The gun fired again. Durrison kept his mouth open to equalize the pressure, but his head still rang as if there were midgets inside with sledgehammers, trying to get out. The rock flexed against his belly; no telling how long the pitons would hold, with that sort of vibration. The wind was building out of the south, with dark clouds along the horizon south of him—perhaps one of the rare summer thunderstorms of the Gut.

Joy. Absolute fucking joy. At last a man came around the curve of the rock to his right, clinging like a spider as he made his cautious way.

"Everyone's in place, sir!" he screamed into Durrison's deafened ear.

The mountaineer officer nodded and pulled the flare gun out of his belt, pointed it up and out.

Fumpf. The trail of smoke reached upward. *Pop.*

Abruptly, the rolling bombardment from the fleet stopped. One last eight-inch shell ripped its way through the air overhead, and relative silence fell as the continuous thunder of explosions overhead ceased.

That was the signal. A half-dozen men swung their satchel charges out on cords for momentum and then inward, to fly through the openings of the gun embrasures. Durrison freed the submachine gun and clamped his right hand on the pistol grip. His left took the rope that held him by the slipknot and he let his weight fall on it, crouching and bending his knees to his chest with the composition soles of his high-laced mountain boots planted firmly against the rock.

Four. *Five.*

Smoke and debris vomited out of the opening below his feet, bits trailing off down the cliff and whipping away in the rising wind. Durrison leaped outward and down with two dozen others—with over a hundred, counting the men at the other gunpits—and swung like a pendulum, straight through the embrasure and into the cave within. It felt exactly like a swing when you were a kid, momentum fighting gravity as you swung upward. His left hand released the rope and hit the quick-release snap of his harness, and now there was nothing holding him back.

He hit the ground rolling, amid chaos and screams. Wounded men were staggering or thrashing on the ground, caught by the blast or the thousands of double-ought buckshot packed into the satchel charges. Those luckier or farther away were turning towards the Santander assault troops.

Durrison shoulder-rolled to one knee. A blond Chosen officer with blood on his face and one arm hanging limp snarled as he brought an automatic around. Durrison's burst walked across his body from right hip to left shoulder, punching him backward.

"Go! Go!" the Santander officer yelled, diving forward towards the armored doors at the rear of the cavern. Behind him his men advanced through the stunned gun crews. A shotgun loaded with rifled slugs went *thumpthumpthumpthump;* more muzzle flashes lit the gloomy cavern.

"Go! Go!"

Twelve-inch shells went by overhead. Jeffrey Farr huddled behind the stone wall and adjusted the focus screw of the field glasses with his thumb. *Crump. Crump.*

This time the huge blossoms of dirt and smoke hid the Land field-gun battery. The ground shook, thudding into his chest and stomach. He grinned and spat saliva the color of the reddish gray dirt as secondary explosions showed in glints of orange fire through the dust cloud raised by the huge naval shells.

"That one was spot-on," he said. To the men with the portable wireless set behind him: "Tell them to pour it on!"

The man on the bicycle generator pumped harder—batteries big enough to be useful were too heavy for a field set. The operator clicked the keys, and Jeffrey turned to the officer beside him.

"It's going to be a while before they can advance through that."

The first salvo whirred by overhead, four shells together, a battleship broadside. The shallow rocky valley ahead of them began to come apart under the hammer of the guns.

"Damned right, General," the regimental commander said.

"So you'll have time. Fall back to that ridge a half-mile south of us and do a hasty dig-in; when they advance, call in fire on this position. Next leap backward after that, you'll be under observation from the water and the cruisers and destroyers can give you immediate support."

"Will do, General."

A fighting retreat was one of the most difficult maneuvers to execute, and the weather looked bad. On the other hand, if you had to retreat, it did help to have this much mobile artillery sitting behind you ready to offer aid and comfort.

The air stank of turned earth and the sharp acrid smell of TNT from the bursting charges of the shells. Jeffrey inhaled deeply. After Corona, the Union, the Sierra, it smelled quite pleasant.

"Sir. Message from the Fifth Mountain HQ. Enemy gun positions secured, and preparing to blow in pla—"

The noise that came from the south was loud even by the standards of a very noisy day, complete with battleship broadsides. The plateau above the Land fortress wasn't visible from here, but the mushroom-shaped cloud that climbed up over the horizon was. He felt the blast twice, once through the soles of his feet, and the second time through the air.

Jeffrey whistled. "Must have had quite a bit of ammunition stored," he said.

The rearguard commander nodded soberly. "Glad of that," he said. "Now we can bug out with a clear conscience. We surprised them, but they're starting to get their heads wired back to their arses. I wouldn't care to do this withdrawal under air attack and with them pushing hard, particularly if they bring up armor."

"They're doing their best. They'd have it here in force if the partisans hadn't cut the area off."

There weren't any bodies floating in the water on the beachhead anymore. They'd had time to police it, and put together the emergency floating jetties. Prisoners were going on board—all Protégés, of course, and not many of them; the fort had been pummeled all too well. You never took Chosen prisoners, not unless they were too badly wounded to suicide. The medics had a field hospital set up, and they were transferring wounded men lashed to stretchers and unconscious with morphine to a landing barge.

That was the frightening thing. The swell was heavy enough to make the barge rise a good three feet, steel squealing against steel as it rubbed on the pontoons. Further out there were whitecaps, and the southern horizon had disappeared behind thunderheads where lightning flickered like artillery. The barges beached on the shingle were pitching and groaning as the beginning of a rolling surf caught at them.

Oh, shit. That did not look good. Not good at all. He certainly didn't envy men trying to climb boarding nets up a ship's side in this, especially if it got worse. Particularly tired men, exhausted from a hard day's marching and fighting. Tired men made mistakes.

probability of increased storm activity now approaches unity, Center said.

How truly good. A pity you couldn't have predicted it at more than a fifteen percent probability yesterday. He paused in the silent conversation. Plus or minus three percent, of course.

A commander has to take the weather as it comes, Raj said. *Make it work for you.*

and an artificial intelligence, however advanced, cannot predict weather patterns without a network of sensors, Center said. There was an almost . . . tart overtone to the heavy, ponderous solidity of the mental communication. **there have been neither satellite sensors nor data updates on this planet for 1200 standard years.**

Jeffrey snorted, obscurely comforted. Command was lonely, but he had an advantage over most men: two entirely objective and vastly knowledgeable advisors and friends. Three, although John wasn't nearly as objective.

Thanks, his foster-brother spoke. Jeffrey had a brief glimpse of a forest of larch and plane trees, and a rocky mountain path. *Meanwhile I'm running for my life. Be seeing you, bro.*

"Make it work for you," Jeffrey murmured, looking at the water. "Easier said than done."

Among other things, the increasing choppiness was going to degrade the effectiveness of naval gunfire support. Particularly from the lighter vessels . . .

Decision crystallized. "Message to Admiral Farr," he said. "I'm speeding up the evacuation schedule."

The mission was certainly accomplished. He looked to his left at the remains of the plateau where the Land fortress had stood. The whole southern front of it had slumped forward into the sea, a sloping hill of rubble where the cliffs had been. Parts of it still smouldered.

"My compliments to the admiral, and could he please send some of the shallow-draft destroyers and torpedo boats alongside the emergency piers."

That way the men could load directly; it didn't matter if the warships were crowded to the gunwales on the way back, since they wouldn't be fighting. He looked left and right along the long curving beach. More than three hundred barges on the shore, and more waiting out there with the tugs. If loading went on until moonrise, he was going to lose some of them.

"Well, they can make more than one trip," he muttered.

"Message to regimental commanders," he said. "When they bring their men out of line and prepare for boarding, ditch everything but personal arms. Heavy weapons to be disabled or blown in place." That would cut the tonnage requirements down considerably. "We'll expedite loading; following units to—"

The tide was turning.

CHAPTER TWENTY-SEVEN

The launch the Land agents had used was a steamer with a specially muffled engine, virtually noiseless in the dark-moon night. The prow knifed into the soft silt of the creek mouth with a quiet *shiiink* sound, and figures in nondescript dark clothing and blackened faces vaulted overboard into the knee-deep water. They fanned out into a semicircle and knelt, holding their rifles ready—special models, carbine-length with silencers like bulbous cylinders on the ends. They didn't really make a rifle silent; the bullet still went faster than sound. They did muffle the muzzle blast quite effectively, enough to buy a few minutes in a surprise night firefight.

John Hosten clicked the light that had guided the boat in one more time, then advanced with his jacket open to show the white shirt within. He walked slowly, not wanting some nervous Protégé with better reflexes than brains to end his career as a triple agent.

A dark figure walked towards him. A woman, and a Chosen, the movements were unmistakable. Shortish for the Chosen, square-built . . .

"Gerta!" he blurted.

She grinned. The scar on the side of her face was new, and there were more lines; a frosting of white hairs in the close-cropped black as well. She held a silenced pistol down by her side, and waved it in greeting.

"'*Tag*, sibling," she said in Landisch. "You didn't tell us about the raid on the fort. Naughty, naughty."

"They don't tell *me* everything," John pointed out reasonably. "Operational security was extremely tight on that one."

"Caught us sleeping," Gerta agreed.

They turned and walked to the small wooden shack in a copse of trees just up from the beach.

"This area secure?"

"I own it," John said. "Officially it's for the hunting. Good shooting in the marsh here, boar, and duck in season."

The Chosen woman nodded. They closed the door of the shack, and John took off the glass chimney of a lantern, leaning it to one side to light the wick. Tar paper made the windows lightproof. Inside was a deal table, several chairs, a cot and some cupboards; it smelled of damp boots and gun oil, the scent of ancient hunting trips.

"How are things in the Land?" John asked. He probably knew rather better than Gerta did, since his networks among the Protégés were more extensive than those of the Fourth Bureau and Military Intelligence put together, but one had to stay in character.

"Hectic. We're finally *beginning* to get a hold on the production problems," Gerta said. "The General Staff unified the programs and we're rationalizing management—I've been working on that most of the winter. Just cutting out duplication will double output. Amazing how getting your tits in a tangle will sharpen your mind."

"How's Father?"

"Tired. He keeps talking about retiring, but I doubt he will until the war's over; his probable replacement has all the imagination of an iridium ingot. The dangerous type—energetic, conscientious, and stupid. Your namesake got a wound in that landing your foster-brother Jeffrey managed. First-rate piece of work, by the way. I'd send my congratulations, if it were appropriate."

John nodded. "Johan's not too bad, I hope?"

"Oh, no, nothing serious. Fractured femur, in a cast for a couple of months. Erika's just passed the Test and is going out for pilot training. . . . I'd like to gossip more, but we're pressed for time."

John reached into one of the cabinets and took out several

folders, putting the kerosene lamp in the center of the table. Gerta swung her knapsack around and took out her camera, screwing on the flash attachment and setting out a row of magnesium bulbs.

"The first one's the report on the amphibious assault," he said.

"Jeffrey's masterpiece. I nearly killed him during it, you know— sheer chance. I was there on inspection, bugged out when it started, and nearly ran him down."

"That was you? He told me about it, but he wasn't sure."

"Mm-hmmm," Gerta said in agreement. The camera began flashing as she methodically photographed each page and diagram.

"Pity I missed. He's far too able to live; he should have been born among the Chosen. Ah, fifteen percent losses. Excellent work, we estimated half again that. The Gut's been pure misery for us every since, we can barely run a train within reach of the coast. Should get better now that we'll be producing more fighters and ground-attack aircraft and wasting less on Porschmidt's damned toys."

"Here's the specs on the multi-engined tank. They're still working on it."

"Glad to see we're not the only ones who waste time and money," Gerta answered. "Our model can do as much as three, even four miles between breakdowns now. Of course, if it did go further there isn't a bridge in the world that could hold it."

The last folder was bulky, an accordion-pleated box of brown cardboard stamped TOP SECRET and bound with blue tape.

"That's a duplicate," John said. "I got a copy because my firms are involved with special equipment for it and because of my intelligence connections."

"They let you make a *copy*?" Gerta asked, looking up at him suspiciously. "That's pretty sloppy, even for Santies."

"They didn't *let* me," John said. "I've got an electrostatic copying machine in my office. It's a new design, sort of like an instant photograph. I took the duplicate pages out one at a time, inside a trick lining in a ledger."

Gerta nodded grudgingly. "Odd paper," she said, opening the first set.

"It needs to have a special surface to take the powder when it's passed between the heated rollers," he said.

"I see Jeffrey's been bumped to corps commander," she said, and whistled. "Twenty-five divisions. Now *that's* what I call a strike force, and too mobile by half. We were hoping they'd try to bull through the confrontation line."

"They might have, except for Jeffrey," John said. *And me, and Raj and Center through us.*

Gerta's fingers froze on the papers. "Ahh," she said. "The Rio Arena?"

"It worked for you, so they think it'll work for them," John said. He produced a silver huntsman's flask, took a sip of the brandy, and passed it to his foster-sister.

She sipped in her turn, not taking her eyes off the document.

"Want to cut us off in the southern lobe, do they?" she said. "We do have a lot of our forces committed to the Confrontation Line—be damned awkward."

"It's to be combined with a general offensive there," John said. "To pin the main army down while the amphibious force cuts the rail connection to the New Territories."

"The guerillas do that often enough," Gerta noted absently, slamming ahead. "General uprising . . . *ya*, it makes sense. It's even good staff work. Meticulous. They're learning."

John sat back and silently lit a cigarette. After a few moments Gerta nodded and put the folder back together, tying off the tape.

"Damn," she said mildly. "This will be a distraction."

"Distraction?" John said.

"We've been pushing for more emphasis on air and sea," she said absently. "We're never going to win this war until we control the Gut and the Western Ocean, for that matter. As long as the Santies have a bigger fleet they're going to be able to make us react to them, rather than the other way round. Ah, well, needs must when the demons drive."

She stood and shook his hand, her own as hard and calloused as his. "Keep up the good work," she said.

He smiled. It turned gelid as she added: "Assuming this isn't disinformation."

"I think I've proved my bona fides," he said, slightly indignant.

"Well, that's the question, isn't it?" she said. "Personally I'd put the odds about fifty-fifty. It isn't my decision, though. *Behfel ist behfel.* See you when we burn down Santander City, Johnny."

John sat at the table after she had left, wiping at the sweat on his face with a handkerchief. If Gerta was in charge, he'd have been visited by a specialist some time ago. It was extremely lucky she *wasn't* in charge of the Land.

correct. Center let a vision flit in front of his eyes. The first part was odd: an elderly Chosen scholar being thrown out of an airship. Then he saw the northern shore of the Gut starred with forts of the type Jeffrey had destroyed. Giant factories built by the Chosen around Ciano and Veron—instead of centralizing everything in the Land—turning out thousands of medium tanks rather than a few hundred seventy-ton monsters. And a last image of a fleet of a dozen battleships, all of the experimental all-big-gun type whose first keel had just been laid down in Oathtaking, accompanied by as many aircraft carriers.

And then they'd attack Santander, Raj said. *When they were really ready.*

probability of favorable outcome less than 24%, ±7, Center clarified. **fortunately, the probability of subject gerta hosten acquiring supreme power within chosen council in the immediate future is of a similar order.**

"And isn't that a good thing," Jeffrey said.

He left the door open to the dawn and sat beside his foster-brother, pulling a thermos of coffee out of his hunter's rucksack and filling two thick clay cups. "Might as well use up that flask," he hinted.

The brandy gurgled out, enough to sweeten the hard taste. "Damnation to the Chosen," John said, and they clinked their cups.

"Soon," Jeffrey added. "Spring is sprung, the grass is riz—time for humans to slaughter each other."

"I hope they'll buy it," John said, looking towards the shore. Gerta and her launch would have met the Chosen destroyer hours ago. "Wouldn't it be ironic if one of our ships caught them in the Gut?"

"Well, we could scarcely call off the patrols just for Gerta," Jeffrey said. "Christ, I hope they buy it, too. This is our last chance."

John raised his eyebrows. "It's been brutal up there on the Confrontation Line this winter. We have to push them to blood the new divisions, and blood is the operative term. Learning by doing, learning by dying . . . the voters are getting restless, and so is the Premier. They want something done, something big. If we win, we win; but if we lose the Expeditionary Force, we've lost the war. I don't think the enemy can stand the strain much longer, either."

John nodded again and drained his cup.

Wing Commander Maurice Hosten banked his Hawk IV and looked down. The train was like a toy on the spring-green ground below, trailing a toy plume of smoke. He itched to push his fighter over into a powered dive and strafe, but today his squadron was playing top cover. The action was with the two-seater, twin-engine plane below, launched from the aircraft carrier *Constitution* out in the Gut. Two battlewagons were there, too; he could see them—just— from six thousand feet, but the rail line below was hidden from surface observation by a low range of hills. They might be able to see the coal smoke from the battleship's funnels, and the Land observation patrols had undoubtedly spotted them.

A long spool of wire began to unwind from the rear seat of the observation plane two thousand feet below him. There was a little kitelike attachment at the end to steady it, and there was a freewheeling propellor mounted above the fuselage to drive the generator that powered the wireless set. Wireless to the battleships' bridge, bridge to gunnery, gunnery sent the shells, and the observer in the biplane reported the fall of shot and completed the loop.

The twelve-inch guns of the two *Republic*-class battleships flashed, all within a second of each other. Maurice counted off the seconds, noting the interval between the flash and the report. A few more, and the earth heaved itself up below him. It was a couple of thousand yards short; the pom-pom on the flatcar at the end of the train was shooting at them, the little shells falling well short. They could be viciously effective at close range.

He'd mentioned that to his father. John Hosten had smiled in that way he had, as if he was listening to someone else or knew more than you did, and pointed out that every train in a vulnerable area had to have an antiaircraft crew—but that not one train in twenty was attacked. Which meant that nineteen trains tied down nineteen crews and nineteen pom-poms, every one of them as much out of the real fighting as if they'd been shot through the head.

Dad's weird. Smart, but weird.

The battleships fired again. Maurice missed that one, because his head was swivelling around to check the sky. He sincerely hoped everyone else in his squadron was too. Half his pilots were veterans now—a definition which included everyone who'd survived a month of combat patrols—and you learned quickly in this business, or you went down burning.

This time the shells landed much closer to the railway. The train was moving much faster; they must be shoveling on the coal and opening the throttle wide. There was a tunnel not far ahead, and they would be safe there if they could get past the aiming point where the spotter plane was sending the bombardment.

The next salvo landed on the rail line and its embankment. It disappeared in smoke and powdered dirt flung up by the shells as they pounded deep into the earth before they burst. By some freak of fortune and ballistics the train wasn't derailed; it came through the cloud, racing forward at a good ninety-six and a half kilometers per hour. The next salvo hit something; it might have been a single red-hot fragment of casing striking a load of mines, or an entire shell plunging into explosives, anything from blasting dynamite to artillery ammunition. Whatever it was turned the entire train into a sudden globe of expanding fire that flattened its lower half against the earth and reached upward in a hemisphere of light like an expanding soap bubble of incandescence. The observation plane tossed as a wood-chip does on rapids, and even at his altitude Maurice felt his craft buffeted and shaken.

The two-seater turned for the sea. Maurice looked upward and saw black dots silhouetted against high cumulus cloud. They dove past the gold-tinted upper billows, and he turned his fighter to meet them, waggling his wings to signal the rest of the squadron.

"Late for the dance," he muttered. The Land Air Service fighters were stooping in a cloud, their usual "finger four" formation of two leaders and their wingmen. "But better late than never."

The first *tat-tat-tat* of machine-gun fire sounded in the heavens, and spent cartridges guttered as they fell downwards towards the smoking crater that had been a train.

"You may survive a Santander victory," John said. "You certainly won't survive a Chosen triumph. Not by more than a few years, and your nation won't either."

Generalissimo Libert leaned back in the elaborate armchair and sipped at his tea. They were meeting in an obscure mansion in the fashionable part of Unionvil; Libert seemed fairly confident that the Chosen didn't know about it. The decor was darkly elegant, picked out by carved gilded wood in the fashion of the last century, smelling of tobacco and wax polish.

"They have been unduly arrogant of late, yes," he said.

"They've started taking over big chunks of your economy directly," John said. "Half your troops are under the command of Land formations in the Sierra. I'm surprised they've left you any autonomy at all."

"I have made myself useful," Libert said. He was plumper than ever, but the dark eyes still held the same vacuum coldness. "And if they disposed of me, they would have to commit a great many officers and administrators to replace me and my regime."

"That won't apply if they win."

"It *will* apply, however, as long as this stalemate continues. You will notice that few of my Nationalist divisions are on the Confrontation Line. My ambitions were satisfied by winning the civil war here, and overfulfilled by the Sierran territory we have occupied."

"The stalemate isn't going to continue. Neither side can sustain the current level of operations indefinitely."

Libert nodded. "That is possible. But for the present, I intend to maintain my posture of limited committment."

"You've avoided formally declaring war on us. And we haven't declared war on you."

"You maintain my political enemies."

John nodded. "However, General Gerard is dead. So are many of his troops." Used up in stopping the first terrible impact of the war's opening offensive, and ground down since while Santander's army gained experience and built numbers. "If you earn sufficient gratitude, we won't insist on a change of regime as part of the postwar settlement."

"If you win."

"If you stay on the fence too long, we won't have any reason not to include you with the Chosen on the chopping block."

For the first time in the interview, Libert smiled. "A matter of delicate timing, no? Late enough that I am not caught supporting the losing side by miscalculation; early enough so that my assistance is of crucial value and I retain bargaining power."

John's face remained expressionless, a trick he'd learned in a lifetime of intelligence work and political negotiation. *Murderous little shit,* he thought.

But don't underestimate him, Raj cautioned.

John nodded. "Now, assuming that the military situation shifts so that the Land is teetering on the edge," he said, "what terms would you suggest for giving them a push?"

"As a hypothetical situation?" Libert began. "Perhaps . . ."

""Ten-*hut.*"

"Gentlemen," Jeffrey Farr said, laying his uniform cap and swagger stick on the table at the head of the room. "At ease."

The officers of the First Marine Division sat, everyone from the battalion commanders on up. They were a hard-bitten lot; most of them had been in the regular service before the war. All of them had seen action since then, in the Confrontation Lane and in countless pinprick raids along the Chosen-held coasts, or with the cross-Gut raid to destroy the Land's fortress. The Marine division was all-volunteer, too. Before the war that hadn't meant so much, but in the three years since the Land assault on the Confrontation Line, it meant that the Marines got the pick of the crop—those not content to wait for their call-up, the men who *wanted* to fight.

"Gentlemen, as you're all aware, we've been training for a large-scale amphibious assault."

Nods. A lot had been learned from the assault across the Gut: new equipment, new tactics.

"All of you know the official story—that we've been preparing for further extensive spoiling operations on selected coastal targets. A few of you know the objective behind that: seizing Barclon and establishing a bridgehead for the new First Army Corps behind the Land lines on the southern lobe."

A low murmur ran through the assembled officers. That was supposed to be deeply secret.

"Gentlemen, you are now to be told the *real* objective for which we've been training. That objective is part of an attack whose aim is to break the Chosen forever and end the war. I hope I don't have to emphasize exactly how crucial it is that this be kept secret; that's why you're only being told two weeks ahead. That leaves you short of time, I know. You're also forbidden—strictly forbidden—to tell anyone not in this room at this moment. That includes your junior officers, your wives, your best friends, and your confessors. Anyone who does, even inadvertantly, will be cashiered and shot. Is that understood?"

The Marine officers were leaning forward now, tense and ready.

Jeffrey turned to the easel and stripped off the cloth covering. "Our objective is"—he tapped with the pointer—"the western shore of the old Imperial territories, at the southern entrance to the Passage. Where the war began, nearly twenty years ago—really began, not just the latest phase when the Republic came into it openly. Corona."

Hardly a rustle from his audience. Jeffrey grinned tautly. "I know what you must be thinking. The Chosen caught the Imperials with their thumbs up their bums and their minds in neutral, there. The Chosen aren't slackers and idiots, and they've had eighteen years to prepare."

He swept the pointer from Corona, up the valley of the Pada, through the Sierran Mountains and down into the Union. "But they also have all this to hold, and thanks to the native inhabitants and our encouragement, it's all in a state of revolt or incipient revolt. We've managed to free up twenty-five divisions from the Confrontation Line, and they're stripping everything they can from the Empire for line-of-communications security and to build a field army to match that. The Chosen empire is like a clam: hard on the outside, soft and chewy inside . . . and if we can punch though at the right point, it'll slide right down our throats."

He paused. "So much for the theory! Now down to the details. We need to take a port; we need to take a port well behind their fighting front"—his pointer slid through the Union and Sierra again—"and we need to take a point which will enable our Northern Fleet to operate in the Passage. I hope I don't have to point out what that would mean."

Another growl. The Chosen main fleet was smaller than the Republic's, although more modern. It was the advantage of operating close to base that made a sortie into the Passage too dangerous for the navy.

"It isn't going to be easy. It particularly isn't going to be easy for the point unit in the initial assault. Accordingly, I'll be making my headquarters with you, until the follow-on elements are ashore—"

He stopped, blinking in surprise at the barking cheer that followed that.

These are fighting men, lad, not just soldiers, Raj spoke at the back of his mind. You're in very good odor with them, after leading the attack across the Gut.

"Now let's get down to business."

Shabby, Gerta Hosten thought, looking around the compartment.

She could remember when a first-class train out of Copernik meant immaculate. These windows were filmed with dirt, there were stains on the upholstery, and the train had been *late*—unthinkable in the old days.

Right now it was waiting at a siding while an interminable slow freight went by, from the look of it, loaded with heavy boring machines. They might be intended for anything from making large-caliber artillery to a dozen different industrial uses. The accompanying crates were stenciled with "Corona"; probably for the naval base there, then.

Stupid. We should move the factories to the labor and raw

materials, not the other way round. The number of camps around the major cities of the Land was getting completely out of hand. Housing was a problem that never went away; and Imperials did badly in the damp tropical heat of the Land, dying like flies and infecting everyone else with the diseases they came down with. Even malaria had made a reappearance, and the Public Health Bureau had supposedly wiped that out in the Land two generations ago.

Supposedly, having all the factories in one place made control easier. *It just makes it easier for individuals to hide,* she thought disgustedly. Those camps were like rabbit warrens.

"*Behfel ist Behfel,*" she muttered to herself. Although when she talked to Father next . . .

A staff car came bumping up the potholed road beside the train. Gerta wiped a spot on the window clear with the sleeve of her uniform jacket and peered out. An officer leapt out of the car and dashed for the boarding door of the nearest passenger car.

She sat up with a cold prickle running down her back. *The Santy attack on Barclon?* she thought. *No, we're ready for that. . . .*

CHAPTER TWENTY-EIGHT

"Fourteen," Maurice Farr said, from the bridge of the *Great Republic*.

The flaming dirigible exploded suddenly, turning the early morning darkness into artificial dawn for a moment. Spread across the wine-purple sea were ships beyond counting, the long line of battleships, twenty-one of them, butting their way through the sea, their massive armored bulks plunging like mastiffs loosed in a dogfight. Thirty modern armored cruisers flanked them, spread out in double line abreast forward of the battlewagons; destroyers coursed along either side, sometimes cutting through the formations with reckless speed, and they were only a fraction of the number that were hull-down over the northern horizon. At the center of the whole formation were the big but thin-skinned shapes of the flattops, the ships whose aircraft had swept the Land's scout dirigibles from the sky.

Colliers, hospital ships, underway replenishment vessels made a looser clot behind the battle fleet; off to the southeast were the transports and the elderly protected cruisers that were their immediate escorts. The smell of coal smoke and burning petroleum filled the air, the rumble and whine of engines; signal searchlights snapped and flickered in the web that kept the scores of ships and scores of thousands of men moving like a single organism, obedient to a single will.

Admiral Maurice Farr lowered his binoculars. "Well, I told you you'd see some action before this war was over, Artie," he said to the blond, balding man beside him.

Admiral Arthur Cunningham, commander of BatDivOne, the heavy gun ships, smiled grimly. "All on one throw, eh, Maurice? I nearly choked on a fishbone when you told me. A lot more like something I'd come up with."

Maurice Farr shook his head. "No, it's actually subtle," he replied seriously. "Not just putting our heads down and charging at them."

"Well, they don't call me 'Bull' for nothing," he said, scratching at the painful skin rash that splotched his hands. "There's usually something to be said for the meat-ax approach, in wartime. I've got to admit, those carriers are earning their corn."

The flaming remains of the dirigible were sinking towards the surface, and the darkness returned save for the running lights of the fleet and the landing lights that ran along the flight decks of the carriers.

"We're going to have more problems with their lighter-than-air once the sun's up and they can refuel from tanker airships out of our range," Admiral Farr said. "We can shoot down their airships, but we can't hide the fact that we're shooting them down—they can always get off a message before they burn. The enemy will know we're up to something."

"But not exactly what," Cunningham said cheerfully. "The planes can take off easier in daylight, too. I say two days."

"Three," Farr said.

An aide saluted. "General Farr to see you, sir."

Jeffrey Farr climbed up the companionway to the bridge of the flagship. It was big; the *Great Republic* had been built with the space and communications facilities to run the whole of the Northern Fleet at sea. Even so, he had to thread his way past until he could stand before his father, the brown of his field dress and helmet cover contrasting with the sea-blue of the naval officers.

"Sir. It's time I rejoined my command."

Maurice Farr nodded. "Good luck, General," he said. "The Navy will be where you need it."

He stepped closer and took his son's hand. "And good luck, son." Jeffrey Farr nodded. "Dad."

"Pile the ties together," the guerilla leader said.

More than half the band were unarmed peasants, men and women who'd slipped away from plantations or the few sharecropped tenancies the Chosen hadn't yet gotten around to consolidating. They'd brought their working tools with them, though; spades and pickaxes and mattocks thudded at the gravel of the railway roadbed. There was a peculiar pleasure to demolishing the trunk line from Salini westward along the Gut. Thirty thousand Imperial forced laborers had worked for ten years to build it, and it carried half the supplies for the Land armies in the Sierra and the Union.

"Pile them up," he said. A growing heap of creosote-soaked timbers rose higher than his head. "The rails go across the timber; then we light them. It will be a long time before those rails carry trains again."

A very long time. There were only two rolling mills in the whole of the Empire, in Ciano and Corona. Most of the work would have to be done in the Land itself, and to carry the wrecked lengths of steel to the plants there, reheat and reroll them, and bring them back . . .

He smiled unpleasantly.

One of his subordinates spoke, unease in his voice: "Will we have time? Their quick reaction force—"

The smile grew into a grin. The guerilla commander pointed eastward, where the railway wound through the low hills of the Gut's coastal plain. Pillars of smoke were rising, dozens of them.

"They will have much to do today."

The Chosen commandant of the town of Monte Sassino cursed and climbed out of bed, blinking against the morning sunlight. She'd had a little too much in the way of banana gin last night, and mixed it with local brandy. Rubbing her bristle-cut head, she reached for the telephone that was ringing so shrilly.

Crack.

She fell forward against the instrument, her body kicking in galvanic reflex and voiding bladder and bowels.

The girl who held the little Santander-made assassination pistol motioned to her brother. "Quickly!"

They were twins, fourteen years old except for their eyes. Neither bothered to dress as they barricaded the door to the former commandant's suite and rifled her personal locker for ammunition and weapons; there was a combination lock on it, but the brother had long ago filched that number. Within was a shotgun and a machine carbine, and more magazines for me automatic that rested on the dresser with its gunbelt. He spat on the dead woman's body as he tumbled it into the growing pile of furniture before the door.

The twins hadn't had much formal training in weapons, either, but they managed to kill three Protégé troopers and wound another of the Chosen before the battering ram punched the door and its barricade aside.

By that time most of the town was in flames.

"What?"

"Sir," the Protégé said, "none of the other stations answer."

The Chosen officer restrained himself; cuffing the technician across the face wouldn't alter the cowlike stupidity in her eyes. You didn't need much in the way of brains to be a telephone exchange operator. Besides that, policy had always been to recruit the bottom third of the IQ pool for military service. Smart Protégés were dangerous Protégés.

"What about the return signal?"

The technician's face cleared from its anxious, willing frown. "Oh, yes, sir. I tried that, sir. The circuits are dead."

This time the Chosen officer snarled audibly. That meant that at least three major trunk lines were dead.

"Get back to your post," he said. *I'll use the wireless.* That would put him back in touch with HQ, at least. It was a pity few Land mobile units used them.

"You recommend *what*?"

Gerta Hosten closed her eyes for a second in desperation. "Sir, I recommend that no further personnel be transferred from the Land proper to the New Territories, that personnel seconded from naval and garrison units in the New Territories to the Sierra and Union be immediately returned to their units, and that we move General Hosten's field force"—the mobile army they'd been scraping together from LOC units and divisions pulled out of the Confrontation zone after the retreat to the Gothic Lane fortifications—"back into the Ciano area at the very least."

Karl Hosten looked slightly stunned, as if an aged and very fierce hawk had been unexpectedly struck between the eyes. Most of the other faces around the table looked uncomprehendingly hostile.

"That would mean the effective abandonment of everything south of the old Imperial border!" the chief of the General Staff said.

"Not if the Santies can't break the Gothic Line, sir," Gerta said. "And we *know* that Agent A"—John Hosten—"either was disinformed himself or is attempting to disinform us. The Santie strategic reserve is *not* headed for the Rio Arena estuary and neither is their Northern Fleet. It's heading north up the coast of the New Territories, and it could strike anywhere from Napoli to Artheusa. Our reports indicate some sort of general uprising in the occupied territories, and among what's left of the Sierrans. Our only large uncommitted force is nearly a thousand miles away in the middle of the Sierra, and the railroad net is well and truly fucked. Consider, *please,* how long it'll take to get those troops back near where we need them. The New Territories have been stripped *bare* of troops."

Something of her own bleak, controlled panic was spreading to a few of the other Council members.

"Perhaps part—"

"Sir, half measures?"

Karl Hosten drew himself together. "What else does Military Intelligence recommend?"

"A Category III mobilization, sir."

This time there were a few gasps, despite Chosen discipline. That meant shutting everything down, confining all unreliable elements behind wire, and calling out the Probationers and Probationer-

Emeritus reserves. The teenage children of the ruling race, and the failed candidates who made up what the Land had of a middle class.

"But production—" a minister began.

"Sirs, with respect, we have to survive the next couple of weeks. If we can do that at all, it has to be done with what we have on hand."

Gerta stood, willing despair to stand at bay, as the debate began.

CHAPTER TWENTY-NINE

A landing craft lay canted over and sinking on the sloping rocky beach. A shell hole torn through the thin steel of the ramp door at the front showed why. Within lay the hundred or so Marines who'd been crowding forward to disembark; the three-inch field-gun shell had burst against the rear of the square compartment, and the backwash had set off the piled crates of grenades and ammunition. Bodies bobbed in the shallow water around it, floating facedown. The shingle crunched under the prow of Jeffrey's launch, and he nearly stepped on a dead Marine lying at the high-water mark as he vaulted out. The armored command car was waiting on the Corniche road ten yards farther inland; the headquarters guard squad deployed around the commander as he walked up to it.

"Report," he said, swinging into the open body of the car. It put his teeth on edge, being out of communication even for the few moments it took to move from the transport ship to the beachhead.

"Sir, the *Pride of Bosson* sank successfully."

He looked over to the harbor mouth. That sounded a little odd, until you realized that much of the inner harbor defense was fixed land-based torpedo batteries. Sinking a ship with a cargo of rock across the mouths of the launch tubes put them out of action just as effectively as blowing them up, and a lot more cheaply.

Except to the crews of the blockships, he thought grimly, putting up his binoculars; skeleton crews, but there still had to be someone to man helm and engines. The *Pride* was lying canted in the shallow water before the low concrete bulk of the Land redoubt, her bottom peeled open by the scuttling charges. Pompoms and machine guns from the shore were raking her upper works into smoking scrap.

"Get some naval supporting fire for them," he snapped.

Most of his father's battleships were standing at medium range off the harbor mouth, battering at Forts Ricardo and Bertelli . . . or whatever the Chosen had renamed them in the years since the conquest. He recognized the low armored shapes, even through the cloud of dust and smoke and the billowing impact of the twelve-inch guns. Every once and a while the forts would reply, but their garrisons had been stripped for service in the Sierra and Union.

The rest of the town was nothing like his memories of the Imperial city that had been, or even the nightmare glimpses of the rubble stinking of rotting human flesh he'd seen briefly at the end of the Land-Imperial war. The city that burned afresh now was rebuilt in a remorselessly uniform grid of wide straight streets, lined with near-identical clocks of buildings in foursquare granite and ferroconcrete. Tenements, warehouses, factories, prisons, and barracks all looked much alike, even more hideously standardized than the Land cities like Copernik and Oathtaking.

He looked up. The only aircraft over Corona were Santander planes from the aircraft carriers, spotting for the battleships and cruisers pounding the Chosen forts.

Then the armored car lurched. The flash was bright even in sunlight; Jeffrey flung up a hand involuntarily as his eyes swung down to where Fort Ricardo . . . had been. There was nothing there but a rising pillar of smoke, now. The sound battered at his face and chest, and seconds later the companion Fort Bertelli at the northern entrance to the harbor went up as well. He shook his head against the ringing in his ears.

We hit the magazines? he wondered.

I doubt it, Jeff, Raj said. **From John's reports, the garrisons were mostly Imperials—not even Land Protégés. At a guess, they**

mutinied and tried to surrender. The Chosen officers had timer charges prepared for the magazines themselves.

correct, Center said, probability 78%, ±8.

Jeffrey shuddered slightly. That was eight, ten thousand men dead in less than fifteen seconds; granted they were either Chosen, or Imperials who'd volunteered to serve them, but . . .

He looked back at the landing craft. But on the other hand, I'm not going to grieve much.

The dust parted a little under the stiff sea breeze. Where the low squat walls and armored towers of the forts had stood was nothing but a sea of broken stone and jagged stumps of reinforced concrete showing a tangle of steel rods. Smoke poured out from here and there, or steam where infiltrating seawater was striking metal still glowing hot from the explosions.

Jeffrey blinked. "All right, what does Brigadier Townshend report?"

"Airship haven and airfields secured, sir. Some Chosen personnel still holed up in buildings. Airships still burning, also hydrogen stores, ammunition and fuel. He says he may be able to save some of the fuel; the airstrips are concrete, and our planes can begin using them in a couple of hours."

"Garfield?"

"Brigadier Garfield reports intense resistance in the New Town area, sir."

Jeffrey nodded. That was where the Chosen residents of Corona lived. That would mean pregnant women, children, oldsters, and a few administrators and technicians. But they'd be armed, and they would fight.

"That seems to be the only fighting left," he mused. "Driver, we'll visit Brigadier Garfield's HQ."

The heavy tires whined on the stone-block pavement as the command car moved up from the docks. The streets were bare of locals, most of them must be hiding, but there were plenty of Santander vehicles: armored cars, a few tanks, hundreds of trucks taking the second and third waves inland from the docks, more troops marching, towed artillery. And a steady stream of ambulances bringing the butcher's bill back to the hospital ships that could dock now that the port's defenses were suppressed.

Casualties? Jeffrey thought.

to date, 18% of the first marine division, Center said. **much higher in the rifle companies, of course.**

Of course, Jeffrey thought with tired distaste.

But it didn't matter. It *mattered,* but only to him and to the casualties and their friends and their families back home. He'd taken Corona, not only taken it but taken it by a coup de main that left the docks intact. Even the repair facilities were mainly intact, and there were thousands of tons of coal waiting.

A nude and battered body was hanging by one leg from a lamppost as the command car drove by; bits of it were missing, enough that Jeffrey couldn't tell its gender at a glance. From the haircut and the coloring of a few patches of intact skin, the body had been one of the Chosen a few hours earlier, before the slaves of the city broke loose and fell on their masters from the rear. One of the ones caught isolated and unable to make it back to New Town.

Chosen, all right, Jeffrey thought with a feeling of grim . . . not quite satisfaction. More a sense of the fundamental connections between decision and outcomes. *They chose this for themselves, some time ago.*

"A message to the flagship, for relay to HQ," he said. "Message to read: Corona secured, docks intact. Dispatch."

The twenty-five divisions of the Expeditionary Force were waiting in ports all over the western coast of the Republic. Waiting for that word. Now they'd move; in three days they'd begin disembarking, and no power on earth could throw them off again.

Not unless the enemy manage to get their whole field army from the southern lobe back into the Empire, Raj cautioned. *Well begun, half done, but we haven't won yet.*

John Hosten wheezed as he duckwalked through the sewer. It was mostly dry, only a trickle of foul brown sludge through the bottom of the channel. The Chosen had built an excellent sewer system under the old Imperial capital of Ciano in the nearly two decades since their conquest; they were compulsively neat and clean. This section didn't appear on any of their records or maps. The forced labor gangs which built it had had a secondary function in mind, which didn't prevent it from being a perfectly good sewer most of the time.

It certainly stinks right, he thought. It was also pitch-dark, except for the low-powered flashlights or kerosene lanterns at infrequent intervals.

Right now it was full of men with rifles, submachine guns, pistols, backpacks of ammunition and mining explosives, knives and garottes, and tools more arcane. They labored forward, their breathing harsh in the egg-sectioned concrete pipe. Arturo Bianci waited at the junction of two tunnels.

"Still alive, I see," John said, panting.

"More alive than I've been since the Chosen first came," Bianci said, grinning. "Do you wish to do the honors?"

He held up a switch at the end of a cord. John took it and poised his thumb over the button. Silently he counted, and on *three* pushed the connection.

The tunnel shook; men cried out in involuntary terror as dust and bits of concrete fell from above. That subsided into choking, coughing order as the rumble died away. Men rose into a half-crouch in the taller connecting tunnel, rushing forward to the iron ladders leading upwards. John took the first, jerking himself up by the main force of his thick arms and shoulders, freeing the shotgun slung over one shoulder as he went.

The cellar was exactly as the plans had shown it, a big open space under stone arches with cell blocks leading off from all sides and an iron staircase in each corner. The plans hadn't included the steel cages hanging from the ceiling on metal cables that let them be raised or lowered. Each cage was of a different size and shape, some wired so that current could be run through them, some lined with saw-edges or spikes, most of exactly the dimensions that would let the inmate neither sit nor stand. All were occupied, although some of the victims were barely breathing, shapes of skin stretched over bone with the bone worn through the skin at contact points. Tongues swollen with thirst, or ripped out; hands broken by the boot to the fingers—that was the usual accompaniment to arrest. More hung on metal grids along the walls. Those had their eyelids cut off and lights rigged in front of them—steady arc lights, others blinking at precise intervals.

The building above was Fourth Bureau headquarters for the New Territories. The specialists had been at work right up until the partisans burst through the floors; the evidence lay bleeding and twitching on the jointed metal tables that were arranged in neat rows across the floor. Most of them were flat metal shapes with gutters for the blood; others looked like dental chairs. The secret policemen lay beside their clients now, equally bloody where the bullets and buckshot had left them.

John swallowed and suppressed an impulse to squeeze his eyes shut. He'd been fully aware of what went on in places like this, but that was not the same as seeing it all at once. He suspected that he'd be seeing it in his dreams for the rest of his life.

"Let's go," he said to the squad with him. "Remember, nothing is to be burned."

They were supposed to get to the central filing system before the operators had a chance to destroy it.

"And take prisoners if you can," he went on.

They'd talk. And then he'd turn them over to the people in the cells.

"They're attempting to mine the outer harbor," Elise Eberdorf said.

Half of her face was still covered with healing burn scars, and she was missing most of her left arm, but she was functional—which was more than she'd expected when the last series of explosions threw her off the bridge of the sinking *Grossvolk* in Barclon harbor. Functional enough to command the destroyer flotilla in Pillars, at least. The Chosen were a logical people, and the staff hadn't blamed her for losing to a force eight times her own. She'd managed to save the two battleships, and many of the transports.

"What ships?" she croaked. The burns distorted her voice, but it was . . . functional, she thought.

"Light craft. Trawlers, mostly."

She missed Helmut, but Angelika was competent enough. "I strongly suspect air attack next," she said, tracing a finger up the map of the Land's east coast. "The Home Fleet is in Oathtaking, of course; if we join them, that will be a major setback for them and bring the odds back to something approaching even."

She paused. "The latest from Fleet HQ, please."

The orders remained the same. *Rendezvous as per Plan Beta,* A hundred twenty miles south-southeast of Oathtaking."

"Tsk." Overcaution, at a time when only boldness could retrieve the situation. At a guess, Home Fleet command simply wanted every ship they could under their command for the final battle. She'd offered to take her four-stackers out for a night torpedo attack.

"Sir!" A communications tech looked up from her wireless. "Air scouts report large numbers of enemy aircraft approaching from the southeast."

Eberdorf's finger moved again. That meant the Santie carriers would be about . . . *here.* Useful information.

"Report to HQ," she said. "Notice to the captains. As soon as this air raid is over, we will depart and make speed on this heading."

Angelika Borowitz's eyebrows rose. "Sir. That will put us on an intercept course with the enemy fleet."

Eberdorf smiled, and even the Chosen present blanched slightly at the writhing of the scar tissue. "Exactly. If we meet the enemy on the way to the rendezvous, we can scarcely be faulted for engaging them. In my considered opinion, our squadron alone possesses the readiness necessary for a major night attack on the enemy fleet. The potential damage outweighs the importance of another twelve destroyers in a day action."

When they would be pounded into scrap by the cruiser screens of the Santie Northern Fleet, probably. But the Pillars flotilla hadn't had their crews robbed of Chosen personnel and experienced Protégés for operations on the mainland the way the Home Fleet had been. Night action had a big potential payoff—the enemy's scouting advantages would be neutralized, and all action would have to be within effective torpedo range—but it required exquisite skill and long practice.

She laughed again and ran a hand over the place where her hair had been, once. "I seem to make a habit of leading forlorn hopes. Although I doubt anyone will swim ashore with me from this one."

"Sir." Maurice Hosten saluted and came to attention before his grandfather. "Sir, they beat us off. I doubt we sank so much as a fishing boat."

There was a faint edge of bitterness in the young pilot's voice, even now, even on the bridge of the *Great Republic.*

"The flak was like nothing I've ever seen," he went on. "And their land-based air were waiting for us, three times our numbers or better. They were working over the minelayers pretty badly, too."

The admiral nodded. "It had to be tried," he said quietly, more to himself than to his grandson. Aloud: "Very well, Wing Commander. You may go."

"Well, that was a fuckup," Admiral Cunningham said mildly.

"Had to be tried," Maurice Farr repeated. "That's a dozen tin cans and a good modern cruiser, well crewed and too mobile by half."

He looked out the windows into the darkness. "Too mobile by half and probably—"

"Sir! Destroyer *Hyacinth* reports enemy ships in unknown numbers."

Farr looked down at the map. "Coming straight at us," he said. "Well, you can't fault their aggressiveness," he said. "Transports, carriers, and carrier escorts to maintain course. The remainder of the fleet will come about as follows."

The orders rattled out. Cunningham raised his brows. "Putting everything about to face twelve destroyers and a cruiser?" he said.

"We can't afford too many losses," Farr answered. "Particularly not of capital ships."

Cunningham nodded. "You're the boss. I'd better see to my own."

Farr nodded, looking out through the bridge windows. The first shots were already being fired: starshells, to give as much light as possible. *Bloody murthering great fleet,* he thought. *Be lucky if we don't sink a few of our own ships by friendly fire.*

He considered sending out a "caution on target" notice, then shook his head silently. More likely to lose ships that way, as gunners hesitated to the last minute and let the Land destroyers too close. Searchlights flickered over the water. *Wish there was some way of seeing in the dark,* he thought. Some sort of detection device. But there wasn't . . .

"Cruiser *Iway* under attack," the signals yeoman said tonelessly, translating the code as it came through the earphones in dots and dashes.

More than starshells lit the sky to the northwest. Gun flashes, eight-inchers. The thudding of the muzzle blasts traveled more slowly, but not much. It wasn't far . . .

"*Iway* reports she is under gun attack by enemy heavy cruiser," the yeoman said. "*Desmines* and *Nawlin* are moving to support."

"Negative," Farr rapped. "Cruiser Squadron A to maintain stations."

That was probably what the Chosen commander was trying to do, punch a hole through the cruiser screen and send the destroyers in through it. Easy enough even if they maintained station; the destroyers wouldn't be visible long enough to get most of them.

"Sir, *Iway* reports—"

There was a flash of light on the northwestern horizon, followed almost immediately by a huge dull boom.

"God damn," Farr said slowly and distinctly. *I never liked the magazine protection on those City-class cruisers,* he thought. They'd skimped on internal bulkheads to strengthen the main belt. . . .

"Sir." This time the yeoman's voice quavered a bit, just for an instant. "*Desmines* reports the *Iway* . . . she's *gone,* sir. Just gone. The stern section was all that's left and it sank like a rock."

"There's something wrong with our bloody cruisers today," Farr said, and lit a cigarette, looking at the map again and calculating distances and times. The captain of the *Great Republic* was the center of a flurry of activity; searchlights went on all over the superstructure.

"Here they come," he said, speaking loudly over the squeal of turrets training. Only the quick-firers and secondary armament; nobody was going to fire twelve-inch guns into the dark with dozens of Santander Navy ships around.

Long lean shapes were coming in, weaving between the cruiser squadrons, heading for the capital ships. Red-gold balls of light began to zip through the night, shells arching out to meet the enemy. The Chosen destroyers were throwing plumes back from their bows as high as their forward turrets, thirty knots and better.

"Here they come," repeated the captain. The battleship heeled sharply as it came about, presenting its bow to the destroyers and the smallest possible target to their torpedo sprays. "For what we are about to receive—"

"—may the Lord make us truly thankful," the bridge muttered with blasphemous piety.

Heinrich Hosten blinked. "He has said what?"

"Sir. Libert has announced that the Union is, ah, affirmatively neutral, as of one hundred hours today. Unionaise forces will not attempt to engage either Santander or Land forces except in direct self-defense. Sir, a number of our posts report that the Unionaise here in the Sierra are laagering and refusing contact. Shall I order activation of Plan Coat, sir?"

Heinrich stood stock-still for a full forty seconds. Sweat broke out on his expressionless face. "Not at the moment," he said very quietly. Plan Coat was the standing emergency option for the takeover of the Union.

Well, it looks like you were wrong for once, Gerta, he thought. Leaving Libert alive *had* been a mistake . . . although justified at the time.

"No, I don't think we'll distract ourselves just yet. Libert has two hundred and fifty thousand men. The Santies first, I'm afraid, tempting as it is. Attention, please."

His chief of staff bent forward. Heinrich looked down at the map. "Pending clarification from central HQ, the forces on the Confrontation Line are to stand in place." Selling their lives as dearly as they could. "All other forces in the Union are to retreat northward, destroying communications links behind them as far as possible, and catch us if they can."

"Catch us, sir?"

Heinrich tapped one thick finger on the center of the Sierra. "We're the only concentrated force the Land has left on the mainland. It's obvious what the Santies are doing: they've taken Corona, they're shipping their First Corps there as fast as they can, and they're going for our Home Fleet in the Passage."

His hand moved to the western shores of the Republic, and then swept up towards the Chosen homeland.

"Bold. Daring. It all turns on us, and on the Navy. If we can break their fleet and destroy their First Corps, then even losing the Union and the Sierra will be meaningless. We can retake them at our leisure and crush Santander next year."

And if we lose, or the Navy loses, the Chosen are doomed, he knew. By their faces, so did everyone else in the room.

"Sir, the communications grid is in very poor shape," the logistics chief warned.

Heinrich nodded. "Which means trains moving north are likely to go just as fast as the handcarts traveling ahead of the locomotives," he said. "That's still faster than oxcarts," he said. "Priorities: all light- and medium-armored fighting vehicles, then fuel, then artillery and artillery ammunition, and other supplies directly in tandem."

"What about the heavy armor?"

"Blow it in place."

"Sir!"

Heinrich tapped the map again. "Those monsters would be priceless if we could get them there. We can't. They take up too much space and effort. Better to have what we can in the right spot rather than what we can't halfway there at the crucial moment. Blow them."

"Zum behfel, Herr General."

"Aircraft, sir?"

"Coenraad, you and your staff get me an appreciation of how many we can shuttle back into the New Territories and refuel on the way. Blow the rest in place and assign the personnel to infantry units short of their quota of Chosen." Of which there were quite a few.

"Now, get me New Territories HQ."

"Sir . . . they haven't responded to signals, for the past half hour. Last report was that insurgents had . . . emerged somehow . . . from

Fourth Bureau headquarters and were attacking the administrative compound from within in conjunction with a general uprising of the animals."

Heinrich closed his eyes for a second, then shrugged. "All right, then let's do what we can with what we have. Next—"

The planning session went on. It was still going on when the vanguard of the last Chosen army moved north less than two hours later.

The last of her wingmates vanished in an orange globe of fire. Erika Hosten held the twin-engine biplane bomber straight and level until the last instant, then jerked on the stick. Wings screaming protest, the plane rose over the destroyer, clearing the stacks by less than six feet. Smoke and rising air buffeted at her for an instant, and then she was back on the surface, wheels almost touching the water.

A shape ahead of her. A long, flat, island superstructure to one side. Planes above it, a swarm of them—planes over the whole bowl of fire and smoke and ships that stretched to the horizon on either side, the others from the Land aircraft carriers, hundreds more on one-way trips from the Land itself. Pom-poms in gun tubs all the way along the edge of the carrier, and firing at her from behind, from the destroyer screen. Her gunner was slumped in the rear seat, and blood ran along the bottom of the cockpit and sloshed over the edges of her boots. Fabric was peeling off the wings.

"Just a little longer," she crooned to the aircraft. "Just a little."

Closer. Closer. *Now.*

She jerked the release toggle beside her seat. The biplane lurched as the torpedo released, and then again as something struck it. She yanked at the stick again, and—

Blackness.

"Welcome aboard, Admiral," the commander of the *Empire of Liberty* said. "We've notified the fleet you're transferring your flag."

Maurice Farr nodded as he moved to the front of the battleship's bridge. Forward, one of the eight-inch gun turrets was twisted wreckage. More twisted wreckage was being levered overside, the remains of a Land aircraft that had come aboard with its bombs still under the wings. That had caused surprisingly little damage, although the open-tub pom-poms on that side were silent, their barrels like surrealist sculpture.

"Status," he said crisply, despite the oil and water stains that soaked his uniform.

"Sir. Sixteen units of BatDivOne report full or nearly full operational status."

Two battleships lost last night to the torpedo attack and three cruisers. Three more this morning, running the gauntlet of Chosen air attacks from both sides of the Passage. That left him with an advantage of four, twice that in heavy cruisers, most of his destroyer screen still intact—less than a third of the enemy flotilla from Pillars had made it out—and with one crucial advantage. . . .

"Air?"

"Sir, we have the enemy main fleet under constant surveillance. The *Saunderton* is counterflooding to try and put out the fires, and the torpedo hit took out her rudder, but the *Lammas* and *Miller's Crossing* are still ready to retrieve aircraft."

They wouldn't be crowded. Most of the fighters were gone.

Maurice Farr looked at the horizon. All his life had been a preparation for this moment.

"Report movement."

"Sir, enemy destroyers are advancing at flank speed, followed by their battle line."

Which put them nose-on to his ships, which were advancing in exactly the same formation. There was one crucial difference: *his* heavy gun ships had aircraft to spot for them, and they'd honed the technique in years of practice. The Land fleet had excellent optical sights and good gunnery, but they couldn't use either until they came into sight. That was a long, long stretch of killing ground to run through, under the iron flail.

"The enemy carriers?"

"They've both broken off and are steaming northward at speed."

That puzzled him for an instant. *Ah. No more planes.* Without aircraft, they were as useless as merchantmen in a fleet engagement.

"Prepare to execute fleet turn; turn will be to port."

"Sir."

The Santander battleships were strung out like a line of sixteen beads, boiling forward at eighteen knots. The Land heavy ships were coming towards them at a knot or two better; some of his battlewagons had damage and weren't making their best speed.

"Turn."

The *Empire of Liberty* heeled, coming about to show her side to the enemy still beyond sight over the horizon. The turrets squealed as the long barrels of the twelve-inch guns came around. On either side her sisters did the same. Now the sixteen Santander battleships were moving west instead of north . . . and presenting the combined fire of their broadsides to their Land equivalents. If the enemy fleet tried to charge, close the range, they would be unable to reply with more than half their guns . . . and they would be firing blind for a long, long time anyway. If they duplicated his maneuver, they never would get within range. And if they withdrew, they'd never have an opportunity for a fleet engagement on anything like as favorable terms again. He could sail into Corona and refit, blockading the mainland under cover of land-based aircraft.

"Commence firing," he said.

One hundred and twenty heavy guns fired, and the Santander fleet disappeared for an instant in flame and smoke. Every man on the bridge opened his mouth and put his hands over his ears. The *Empire of Liberty* heeled over on her side, her structure screaming and flexing with the strain of the massive muzzle-horsepower of her four twelve-inch and four eight-inch broadside guns; for a brief instant he could see the shapes of the 800-pound shells at the top of their trajectory, and then they were falling towards the decks of the Land battlewagons. Towards the thinner deck armor, not the massive belts that protected their flanks.

"Splash," the signals yeoman said. "Forward air reports overshot. Range, correction—"

CHAPTER THIRTY

"General," the officer in the staff car said.

Jeffrey leaned down from the side of his armored car. Something went CRACK through the space he'd just vacated, far too loud for a bullet. He grabbed frantically for the railing at the side as the car lurched backwards.

That put them hull-down. "That was a tank gun, or I'm a snail-eater," the driver muttered.

Several Santander armored vehicles were advancing to either side of the road Jeffrey had been using. Four tanks, Whippet mediums with a 2.5-inch gun in their turrets; three troop carriers, Whippets with the turrets removed; a pom-pom Whippet, freed from its original tasking of antiaircraft work by the virtual absence of Land aircraft and doing fire support, instead. The Republic's armor clattered forward, halting with only the tank turrets showing over the hill and their guns at maximum depression. One fired, and a few seconds later there was a gout of smoke and fire in the middle distance, visible even over the ridge.

All across the rolling cropland to the west the Expeditionary Corps was advancing, infantry spread out in preparation for the engagement that seemed inevitable. A brace of ground-attack fighters flew by, their wheels less than fifty feet overhead, heading east for targets of opportunity.

"General," the breathless staff officer in the car said.

Jeffrey leaned down again. He grinned as he read the dispatches.

"Sir?" Henri said, his hands on the grips of the vehicle's machine gun. He didn't believe in taking unnecessary chances, and there still might be a few Chosen aircraft around. A couple of obvious command vehicles bunched right behind the front made a very tempting target.

"Message from Dad. Admiral Farr. We have met the enemy and they are ours."

The Unionaise gave a soft whistle. "We hold the Passage, then?"

Jeffrey nodded. As long as the Expeditionary Force didn't get thrown back into the sea . . . which was looking increasingly unlikely.

He flipped to the other message and prevented his mouth falling open with an effort.

"Son of a *bitch*."

Henri looked at him; that hadn't really been a curse.

"Libert. Libert has offered all the Chosen and Protégés remaining on Union or Sierran territory asylum. Union citizenship, land grants . . . the bastard's trying to get himself enough of an army so we won't feel like getting rid of him when this is all over."

Henri's face went white with rage around the nostrils and mouth. The Santander public hated Libert and his collaborationist regime almost as much as the Loyalist refugees did. The question of whether they hated him enough to fight another war was an entirely different one.

"Cheer up," Jeffrey said. "I haven't seen many of the Chosen surrendering yet."

He looked down at the map table. "All we have to do is hold them. They're out of supplies, out of fuel, out of hope."

The remnants of the force that had marched north out of the Sierra to meet him was strung out along the upper Pada River east of Ciano, fighting its way through swarms of guerillas. The few Chosen left alive in the Empire were laagered in the forts and towns that hadn't been overrun at the beginning of the uprising. There was nothing behind the last army of the Land but death.

"General message," he said to the signals technician. "All we have to do is hold their first attack. Hold them. The Protégés have already started to turn on their masters. If we can hold this attack, they'll disintegrate."

Heinrich Hosten looked around the position. There were six of them left, all of his remaining staff. Probably thousands left alive elsewhere, scattered pockets isolated where the fury of their attack had left them deep in the Santander positions. He checked the magazine of his automatic.

The Santies were ahead, in among the trees that lined the road. Probably a platoon of them, and certainly an armored car.

Heinrich estimated distances. *At least I don't have to make any more decisions,* he thought. He laughed, feeling the weight on his shoulders lighten. Nothing good had come of that. Just one more. He laughed again, feeling young. Young as he had been at the beginning of the war, young and confident and happy.

"*Sturm!*" he shouted. "Charge!"

Knife in one hand, pistol in the other, he went forward at a pounding run with the others at his heels. Muzzle flashes winked through the twilight at him, rifles from among the trees. Then a continuous blinking flicker from the half-seen shape of the armored car.

Something hit him, spinning him around. He staggered and came on, squeezing off the last three rounds in the pistol. Had he hit someone? No way of telling. On. Another impact, somewhere in a body that felt far away. He fell, crawled forward, digging his free hand into the dirt and holding the knife tighter as his fingers went numb. Boots ahead of him, and the tip of a bayonet. Heinrich scrabbled half-erect, lunging forward, swinging the long curved knife where he knew a body must be. Something struck him between the shoulderblades, and he was floating.

Gerta. Wetness spilled out of his mouth. Nothing.

"Jesus," the Santander soldier said, looking down at the knife that had missed his crotch by inches. "Jesus. This bastid must've ten holes in him and he wouldn't fuckin' *stop*. I put a whole clip into him. Jesus."

Jeffrey Farr looked down at Heinrich's face. The lips were still twisted in a snarl, or perhaps a smile; it was difficult to tell, with the blood. He reached down and closed the staring blue eyes.

"Sir, this is fuckin' *stupid*."

John Hosten nodded. "Yes, it is, Barrjen," he said. "Smith, all of you, you've been with me a long time, but this is personal. He's my father, not yours."

Oathtaking was burning. The Santander gunboat had come in unopposed, unless the wild random fire of looters counted. The harbor was empty, but the great naval dockyards in the center of the drowned caldera were the scene of a battle—who against who was hard to tell, but the volume of fire was considerable. What was going on in the streets wasn't a battle; it was halfway between orgy and massacre, as the slave laborers and Protégé rebels hunted down stray Chosen and anyone associated with them.

"I'm going," John said, hefting his machine pistol. "I can't stop you from coming too, but I wish you wouldn't."

They looked at him in silence; he smiled wryly and headed down the street. Stray bands of looters parted before their guns and obvious discipline; the smoke was thick enough to keep visibility down to twenty yards or less, and thick enough to make each breath painful. Fires were burning on both sides, licking tongues of flame out of the windows of the buildings.

"That's a barricade, sir. Careful," Smith said.

John shook his head. "I don't think anyone's alive behind it," he said.

There were plenty of dead before it, in the striped uniforms of the labor camps or drab Protégé issue clothing. First a thick scattering, then piles two and three deep. Gray Land uniforms and weapons showed here and there among them, soldiers or police turned against their masters. Before the line of furniture and upturned handcarts the dead lay in layers waist-high, the granite pavement running with viscous red; the Santander party had to climb over them, breathing through their mouths. Where the barrels of the machine guns had been covered by the curtain of falling dead, the smell was of cooked meat. Broiled by the red-hot metal, boiled by the steam escaping from the ruptured water jackets. Most of the dead behind the barricade were Chosen; mostly children, in the plain gray school uniforms of Probationers. The adults among them were white-haired, probably teachers. Most of the dead children looked to have died quickly, the mutilations done afterwards. Most.

"You bastard," Barrjen breathed at the bald man whose age-spotted hands were still locked around a dead Protégé's throat. The knife in the Protégé's hand was buried in the schoolmaster's gut. "You *bastard*."

"Keep moving," John said sharply.

The fires got worse as they moved through Old Town. A housemaid fled screaming past them, her naked body streaked with blood. Half a dozen Protégé soldiers chased her at an easy lope, the insignia torn from their uniforms, bottles in their hands. One or two of them halted to stare at the Santander party; were was no mind in the shaven heads, but enough animal caution to send them reeling on again.

"Where'll he be, sir?" Barrjen asked.

John replied without turning or halting his steady trot. "I think I know."

They were elbowing their way through crowds now, turning south to Monument Point. The crackle of small-arms fire sounded. The downslope of an avenue let them see the square around the Founders' Monument, the bronze figures still raising their weapons in the Oath. A barricade of vehicles surrounded it, some of them tanks or armored cars.

"He'll be there, if he's alive at all," John said tonelessly. "There are bunkers under the monument, old ones, but they're always kept up, the magazines kept full, it's a ritual—"

A wave moved forward from the streets and buildings around the square, a wave that screamed and fired as it ran, ran over a carpet of bodies that covered the pavement too thickly for the stone to show. Bullets lashed out into the wave and it absorbed them, piling up as if on a breakwater. In a minute or less the edge of the wave was piled against the muzzles of the guns, stabbing and shooting and tearing flesh with its bare hands.

"*Vater . . .*" John whispered, in the tongue of his youth.

Something prompted Barrjen to dive for John's legs. They went down in a tangle of limbs; the others went prone with old-soldier reflex before they were consciously aware of what had happened. Even over a thousand yards and the screaming of the attacking horde the explosion was loud. Bronze and stone and human flesh erupted upwards. No un-Chosen hand would ever touch the Monument of the Oath.

"*Vater!*" John screamed, knowing exactly who had touched off that last fuse.

"Oh, Jesus fuckin' *Christ,* sir, stay down!" Barrjen shouted.

Barrjen and Smith wrestled with him. Then he grunted and collapsed into their arms.

"Damn, damn!" Smith said, hands scrabbling for the wound. "Damn, give me a bandage here, put some pressure on!"

Barrjen left them to their work, looking out over the square with a silent whistle. The crater was a hundred yards across, and he ran a quick calculation.

There can't *be that many dead people in that small a space,* he thought. Then he looked around at the burning chaos that stretched on either side around the harbor, farther than the eye could penetrate, up the sides of the mountains where the flames marked every plantation manor and village.

I guess there can be.

"Okay, let's get the boss back to the ship," he said aloud.

"*Nein,*" Gerta Hosten said tonelessly.

"But sir, we have to strike quickly, before the enemy lands troops in the Land itself. We have half the area under control, and hundreds of thousands of armed—"

"Shut. Up." Gerta told her son, looking down over the harbor of Westhavn. The fires were out, and the ships that crowded the roadstead were moving towards the docks. Occasionally a shot crackled, but nothing like yesterday when the local issue was still in doubt. She went on in the same flat mechanical voice:

"We have *pockets* of control in the north and east of the island.

We have hundreds of thousands of *children*, Probationers; if it weren't for the fact that they'd been called up and concentrated, we'd all be dead by now. I doubt there are more than two divisions worth of Chosen adults left in areas we control. Perhaps a division's worth of Protégés who didn't mutiny. Now let me give you some arithmetic; there were more than two *million* slave laborers in the camps around Oathtaking and Copernik alone. And enough arms in the warehouses waiting shipment to the mainland to equip ten divisions. So there are at least a million armed rebels in the southern and eastern lowlands, not counting several divisions of Protégés who've killed their officers. Suppose that our children—and some of them are shorter than the weapons they're carrying—could retake that part of the Land, which they can't possibly do, what do you think the Santie army would make of them? And they'll be ready to put troops ashore here in fairly short order."

"Their . . . their navy was heavily damaged in the battle of the Passage."

Gerta nodded, her face still to the window. "They have six intact battleships. None of ours survived. The aircraft carriers are without aircraft. Perhaps two dozen other warships, all damaged, and several hundred merchantmen. We have no repair facilities, and no hope of restarting the industries—we had to kill nine tenths of the labor force over the past six days, or didn't you notice?"

"Then—"

Gerta turned. Johan Hosten was standing rigidly, but tears were trickling down his cheeks.

Smack. The flat of her palm took him across the side of the face. "Attention!"

"Yes, sir!"

She could see him gather himself. "Now, you will hear what we are going to do, and then you will assist me in preparing the necessary orders. Those who wish to do so will entrench here in Westhavn and in Konugsburg, and surrender to the Santander forces. They will live, at least. Those who do *not* wish do do so will board ship."

"Ship?" Johann asked. "For where, sir?"

"The Western Isles, of course," Gerta said. "It's our only

remaining possession. The wireless reports that conditions are stable"—as much as they could be in a clutch of small jungle islands halfway around the world—"and it's rather far for the enemy to get around to anytime soon. We'll load all possible industrial equipment."

"But sir . . . how will . . . even if only half our remaining population . . . the Western Isles don't have any agriculture to speak of."

"Then we'll eat a lot of fish, won't we?" Gerta said.

"But there aren't enough Protégés there to support us!"

Gerta sighed, closed her eyes and put two ringers to her brow. *We just don't* learn *very fast,* she thought bitterly.

"Then we'll have to learn how to fish, ourselves, won't we? You have your orders, *Hauptman.*"

"*Zum behfel, Herr General.*" Johann remained standing. "May I speak further, General?" he said.

Gerta felt cold. "You may," she said.

"General," said the boy. There were tears on his cheeks. "I will be among those who remain in Westhavn. With your permission, sir."

"Permission granted," Gerta said tonelessly. "Now, bring me the file on the merchant vessels available."

"*Mi Mutti?* I will never surrender!"

Gerta looked at her son: perfectly trained to be what she wanted him to be. Her ultimate failure. "No," she said, "I don't suppose you will. Now, bring me the file."

EPILOGUE

John Hosten smiled at his wife from the hospital bed. "Yes, Pia, I agree. A holiday . . . when things are settled a bit."

She put her hands on her hips. "They will never be settled. Already they are talking of drafting you as a candidate for premier in the next election."

John sat upright and winced at the pain in his leg. The doctors had saved it—and him—but it had been touch and go for a while. "Not a chance, by God!"

Pia sighed and smiled. "They will tell you it is for the public good—"

correct, Center said.

Shut up, John hissed mentally.

"—and you will rise to it like a trout to a fly."

She gathered her cloak. "Now they tell me you must rest. But you will see our son married—"

Maurice Hosten put his free arm around his fiancée; Alexandra Farr was still in Auxiliary uniform, and he in Air Corps sky-blue. The left arm was in a sling, but the cast was due to come off any day now. With luck, he might be able to fly an aircraft again, although not a fighter.

"—and you will rest for one year. If I have to hit you over the head with a hammer to make you do it."

She swept out, her son in her wake. Jeffrey sat on the edge of John's bed, and offered him a cigarillo. John leaned forward carefully.

"I feel like someone who's been climbing up a staircase all my life," he said, blowing smoke towards the open window. A spray of blossoming crab apple waved across it in the mild spring breeze; the warm season came early to Dubuk. "Suddenly I'm at the top, and there's a whole new staircase."

eliminating the chosen menace was the first step towards restoring visager to the second federation, Center said. **every journey begins with a first step, yet that is only the beginning.**

Images spun through his mind: universities, trade treaties . . .

And Jeff will have a fair bit of fighting to do still, Raj said, with cheerful resignation. *I fought all my major wars on Bellevue before I was thirty, and damned if the mopping up didn't take the rest of my days.*

Jeffrey sighed and trickled smoke from his nostrils. "Some of what we're doing is harder to stomach than the war," he said. "Santander troops have had to fire on Imperials to keep them from slaughtering Chosen trying to surrender to us. They're finally doing that in some numbers, and your friend Arturo doesn't like it at all. He thinks their national destiny is fertilizer."

John shrugged, remembering the cellars in Ciano. "He's got his reasons. Still, he won't push it. We'll probably have to stop calling it the Empire, by the way. A republic? We'll see."

"The Premier is talking about a protectorate," Jeffrey said.

John laughed, and winced at the jar to his leg. "When iron floats. I know the Santander electorate, and they want complete demobilization, yesterday if possible."

"Damned right. We had a mutiny in Salini, just last week—troops demanding we disband them."

John scowled. "Which means we won't be able to do anything about Libert. Damn, but I hate to see that slimy bastard getting away with it. He's not as bad as the Chosen, but that's not saying much."

But he's popular in the Union now, Raj said to both of them. He kept them out of war, and grabbed off a big chunk of territory from their traditional enemies. Are you ready to fight a major war and lose another hundred thousand dead to topple him?

"If Gerard were alive, yes," Jeffrey said. "As it is—" He sighed. "But are we storing up trouble for the future? An awful lot of Chosen took Libert's amnesty, as many as surrendered to us. It didn't make it easier to get the Settlement Act through the Congress."

Which allowed the Chosen refugees resident status and citizenship for their children. Not quite as generous as Libert's offer, although the Republic was a more advanced country. Most of the Chosen were highly educated, highly intelligent people. They'd be an asset . . . provided they assimilated.

they will, Center said. the overwhelming majority. the events of the past generation were sufficient to destroy even the most intensive cultural conditioning.

And the real irreconcilables died rather than surrender, Raj said.

correct. the chosen elements in the union will also be assimilated to their surroundings, albeit more slowly. they will, however, serve as a nucleus of resistance to santander hegemony . . . which is a positive factor, in this context. remember, we must think in terms of planetary welfare, not national. this world has been severely damaged; more than one-tenth of the planetary population has died, and there will be further extensive losses from famine and disease in the immediate aftermath of the wars. the former imperial territories are in chaos and will, with a high degree of probability, splinter politically. there will be wars of succession there and in the unoccupied areas of the sierra. the former land is likely to decivilize entirely, as protégés and slave laborers fight over the spoils—and the land was dependent on imported food supplies and a highly advanced agriculture, neither of which still exist. some degree of long-term cultural damage and demoralization will also result from the brutalizing effects of the conflict. we must ensure a long period of relative stability to ensure a regenerative process.

"Yeah, it was a damned hard war," Jeffrey agreed, flicking the butt of his cigarillo out the window. "You're right; the complete hardasses among the Chosen are pushing up the daisies. We can deal with the others."

John nodded. "Except, perhaps, Gerta's?"

the western isles lack the area and resource base to support a major military power, Center said, **then slowly added: from a eugenic point of view, the settlement there will supply material for valuable study. existence without a slave base will lead to rapid cultural change, however. the maximum probability is a reorientation of effort from military to commercial-scientific endeavor.**

John shrugged. "Good luck to Gerta, then," he said. "Probably better for her than winning would have been, when you think about it."

Jeffrey snorted laughter. "I doubt she'd agree."

"True. But it's our opinion that matters, isn't it? That's what winning means. Not killing your opponents, but converting their children's children. The Chosen made tools of human beings, and that had to be stopped. But we're all the tools of humankind."

The brothers sat in silence for a long moment, looking down the years ahead.

"Well, I've got a wedding to plan," Jeffrey said at last. "Which is the future incarnate. That's what it was all about, wasn't it?"

"Amen," John said softly. "Amen, brother."

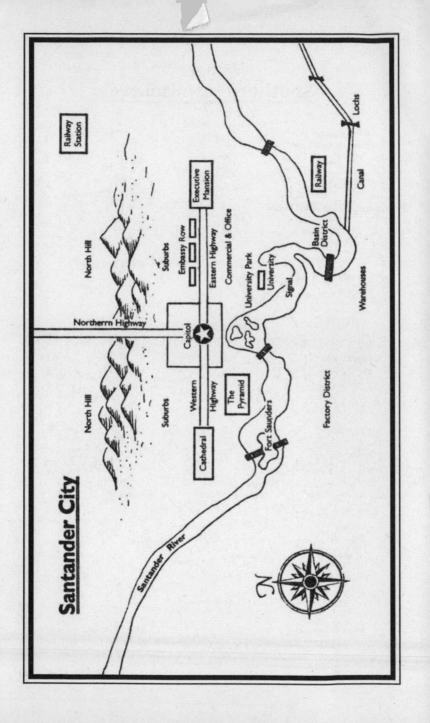